Juliet E. McKenna has been interested in fantasy stories since childhood, from *Winnie the Pooh* to the *Iliad*. An abiding fascination with other worlds and their peoples played its part in her subsequently reading Classics at St Hilda's College, Oxford. While working in recruitment and personnel, she continued to read across all genres, and started to write herself. After combining book-selling and motherhood for a couple of years, she now fits in her writing around her family and vice versa. She lives with her husband and children in West Oxfordshire.

Find out more about Juliet E. McKenna and other Orbit authors by registering for the free monthly newsletter at www.orbitbooks.co.uk.

D0028101

By Juliet E. McKenna

The Tales of Einarinn
THE THIEF'S GAMBLE
THE SWORDSMAN'S OATH
THE GAMBLER'S FORTUNE
THE WARRIOR'S BOND
THE ASSASSIN'S EDGE

The Aldabreshin Compass
SOUTHERN FIRE

SOUTHERN FIRE

Juliet E. McKenna

www.orbitbooks.co.uk

An *Orbit* Book

First published in Great Britain by Orbit, 2003

Copyright © Juliet E. McKenna 2003

The moral right of the author has been asserted.
All characters and events in this publication are fictitious and any
resemblance to real persons, living or dead, is purely coincidental.

All rights reserved.
No part of this publication may be reproduced, stored in a
retrieval system, or transmitted, in any form or by any means,
without the prior permission in writing of the publisher, nor be
otherwise circulated in any form of binding or cover other than
that in which it is published and without a similar condition,
including this condition, being imposed on the subsequent
purchaser.

A CIP catalogue record for this book is available from the British
Library.

ISBN 1 84149 166 7

Typeset in Ehrhardt by
Palimpsest Book Production Limited,
Polmont, Stirlingshire
Printed and bound in Great Britain by
Mackays of Chatham plc, Chatham, Kent

Orbit
An imprint of
Time Warner Books UK
Brettenham House
Lancaster Place
London WC2E 7EN

For my parents, without whom etc...

ACKNOWLEDGEMENTS

The first book of a new series is a daunting undertaking so I'm profoundly grateful to everyone who's offered encouragement and reassurance along the way. As ever, Steve and Sue have given the drafts invaluable attention, as has Mike, to whom also thanks for the nautical notes. My thanks to Ashok for the weather reports and the book recommendations. Thank you, Sheila, for pointing me towards some truly fascinating tomes. Thanks too to Rachel for the reportage from her travels.

I don't know where I would find the time to write and to undertake all the other multifarious tasks of the author's life, never mind being a wife and mother, without the generosity of so many people. For the continuing assistance of Ernie and Betty, mere thanks are simply inadequate. For their part in helping me keep a balanced perspective on all the domestic juggling and so much else, I am indebted to Penny, Gill and Mike, Helen, Corinne, Liz E and Liz B. On the business side, sincerest thanks go to Maggie and Camilla for all their support, and to Tim and Simon and everyone else at Orbit.

To everyone who has spurred me on with their eager interest in this book, in Dublin, Aberdeen and elsewhere, as well as over the Internet, my sincere appreciation.

CHAPTER ONE

No omens of earth or sky, just tranquillity. I couldn't ask for a better welcome home.

The sun was all but set among serene bands of golden cloud untroubled above an unruffled sea. Down in the lagoon far below, Kheda could see the little boats of his fishermen heading out for their night's work, the weather set fair. The great galley that had brought him back to this island at the heart of his domain rode calmly at anchor. Closer to shore, the first lamps were being lit above the floating frames hung with nets that gathered fingerfish for smoking above fragrant herbs. Standing high above, on the roofless platform at the top of the circular stone tower, Kheda was too far away to hear the banter of his people idling about their work on the shore.

It'll be the usual jokes and debates about whether to settle to mending nets or making gourds into new buoys. Chances are they'll opt to spend the evening with their families and friends instead. We're not so different, highest to lowest, Daish Reik always told me that.

At that recollection of his father's wisdom, Kheda yielded to the desire to greet his wives and children. He'd turned first to his duty as augur; now he was entitled to claim some time for himself. Smiling, he was about to go down the narrow winding steps of the observatory when a new thought struck him.

Those little lights to tempt curious fish look like early stars on the dusky water. What of the heaven's compass? I wouldn't

*be doing my duty if I didn't look for any new portents, even
if all the constellations are settled at their midpoints.*

Kheda turned to look inland at the sky darkening to
blue just deep enough to show the first true stars. Long
practice found the Winged Snake, rising above the dark
bulk of the island's hilly interior. The sky around the
constellation was clear of cloud, nothing else intruding
that might warn or advise. Kheda had no need to glance
down at the arcs of the compass of the earth that were
carved on the balustrade of the observatory. The Winged
Snake was in the arc where omens for marriage and all
such intense relationships would be found.

*Symbol of male and female intertwined, of courage and
the rewards of toil, of new things being revealed. Of course.
And unseen, below the horizon, the Net will underlay the arc
of the compass for birth, token of support and help, cooperation
and unity. Though the Canthira Tree, symbol of the cycle of
life and death, is in the arc of fear and retreat. Of course,
Sain will be fretting, what with it being her first baby. She'll
have all the support she needs from Janne and Rekha, that
much is quite clear, with the Vizail Blossom, symbol of
womanhood, so firmly planted in the arc of sisterhood.*

Kheda's eyes scanned the sky. What of the heavenly
jewels that drew their own courses among the stars? No,
none of them were approaching the invisible lines that
divided one arc of the heavens from the next. However
he read the compass of the skies, in triune, sextile or quartile, the distant lights drew no pattern. Only the moons
were moving between the heavenly regions in their rapid
dance around the world. The Lesser Moon, heavenly
counterpart to the pearls that were the wealth of the Daish
domain, was the merest paring of nacre, sharing the sky
with the Winged Snake. The Greater Moon by contrast
was at its full, disc patterned like the Opal that was its
earthly talisman for faithfulness and self-knowledge. It

shone, rising slowly in the sky where omens for life and self should show themselves. Kheda could see nothing beyond the pattern of stars that made up the Mirror Bird, a sign for protection and a link between past and future. The Amethyst, for calm and inspiration, was happily centred in the arc of hearth and home, and the Diamond, talisman for clarity of purpose and most particularly of warlords, was set squarely in the arc of wealth. Beyond, the Ruby, talisman of strength and longevity, rode in the arc of friendship and community.

His spirits rising, Kheda turned to quit the lofty observatory. 'Remind me to tell Sain Daish that the heavens look entirely propitious for all coming births.'

'She can only be scant days from childbed.' His sole companion sitting on the top of the stair sounded pleased. Then his stomach gurgled loudly in the evening hush.

'Well, Telouet, that's a sign that takes no skill to read,' Kheda laughed. 'It's been a long day, I know. But I had to be sure there were no portents.'

'My lady Janne has to be happy that you've discharged all your responsibilities, if we're all to sleep content on our first night back home.' Telouet grinned as he rose to his feet, adjusting the twin swords held in his wide sash as he made way for his master.

Kheda walked rapidly down the dim, familiar stairs, winding down around the tower's central core of successive rooms packed with records and interpretations and all the materials necessary to work the different divinations that he used to serve his people. Lamplight showed beneath the closed door of the lowest chamber.

'Sirket?' Kheda entered and smiled affectionate reproof at his elder son. 'Telouet's gut's growling louder than a jungle cat, so it must be time for us to eat. Join us.'

Seated at a reading slope, the youth looked up from the weighty book he'd been studying, eyes still distant in thought. There was no doubting he was the warlord's son; both had eyes as green as the newest leaves of the rainy season, unusual in these southernmost isles of the sprawling Aldabreshin Archipelago. They had other features in common: high foreheads, faces more oval than round with more sharply defined cheekbones and noses than Telouet. Telouet's nose would have been broad and flat even before the fight that had left it squashed crooked on his cheerful face. But Sirket's mother had brought him fuller lips and darker skin than his father, as well as tightly curled black hair that he kept cropped short. Kheda's hair and beard were a coarse and wiry brown, tamed only by close clipping.

'My mother Janne said we might be visiting the Ulla domain before the rains arrive.' Sirket scratched at whiskers shadowing his jaw. Not yet full grown, he was already easily the height of his father. 'I don't want to be shown up like Ritsem Zorat was last time.'

'That won't happen. I won't permit it.' Kheda crossed the room and closed the heavy tome. 'Now, go and tell your mother I will dine with the two of you, once I've seen Sain and Rekha.'

'As you command, my father.' Sirket ducked an obedient head but his smile was relieved and his step light as he ran off ahead, bare feet noiseless on the well-trodden earth. He had some years to grow before he carried his father's muscle.

'What does Ulla Safar think he will achieve by humiliating the sons of his closest neighbours?' Locking the tower door, Kheda followed more slowly. 'Ritsem Caid will surely turn down any suggestion that his son take the auguries next time they meet. Then all Ulla Safar will have is a pointless quarrel on his hands.'

'When did he ever shrink from a quarrel, however trivial?' One pace behind and to Kheda's side Telouet brushed at an intrusive frond. Night was falling with its customary rapidity and the green leathery leaves were barely distinguishable from their shadows. The bushes were musical with the songs of lyre crickets and something rustled in the darkness, a foraging animal or a startled night bird. 'Besides, Ulla Safar always wants someone to read the omens for him. He rarely bothers himself with such things and Ulla Orhan shows little aptitude for divination.'

Kheda snorted. 'That's Ulla Safar's problem and one of his own making. It's his responsibility to teach the boy. He's not doing his duty by his son or his domain.' He took a deep breath and the familiar scents of home soothed his irritation. The air was moist and heavy now they were down among close-planted plots of shrubs set in their lattice of little paths.

'Do you think we will be travelling to the Ulla domain before the rains?' Telouet asked as they walked through the scatter of houses below the fertile forested slopes, built from a miscellany of mud brick, clay-covered woven branches and close-fitted wooden planks. Thatched with palm fronds and with wide overhanging eaves to give shelter from the sun or to carry away rain depending on the season, the one-roomed dwellings thronged with activity.

'Only if Janne has some really pressing reason,' said Kheda frankly. 'We'd almost certainly get caught in the rains on the voyage back and I'd really rather not risk that. Besides, I should be here when Sain is brought to childbed.' Slatted shutters of oiled wood were not yet closed and Kheda found himself smiling at the scenes within the comfortable homes. Children were being coaxed or ordered towards their beds, or more rarely, were settling obediently among their quilts.

Will Rekha have sent the little ones to their beds or given them permission to stay up to see me tonight?

Outside, on the broad steps beneath the eaves of the

houses, men relaxed after a hard day's labour, sharing news and observations with their neighbours. All wore loose cotton trousers; some dyed bright colours, and others left unbleached white. Some men wore tunics, some relaxed bare-chested. A few wore simple bracelets of plaited palm fronds with carved wooden beads or necklaces of leather thong carrying some natural talisman such as a seedpod, shell or sea-shaped stone.

Kheda and Telouet walked through their midst, their appearance a dramatic contrast. The warlord wore trousers and tunic of indigo blue, the fine silk gathered at wrist and ankle with golden clasps. As well as chased gold chains close around his neck, Kheda wore a longer necklace of carnelian and diamonds interspersed with carved golden beads and a central trio of uncut, highly polished stones heavy on his breast, the massive diamond framed by carnelians. Bracelets of twisted gold jingled softly on his wrists and an arm ring inlaid with mother of pearl and turquoise rested just above the elbow of his sword arm. Plaques of gold filigree decorated his blue leather belt and more gold wire coiled around the dark sheath of the dagger that was his only weapon. It had the same smoothly curved blade and twisted grip as the daggers all the men of the village wore at their hip but Kheda's had a golden hilt and a single flawless pearl at the pommel. Telouet was the only man wearing swords as well as his dagger, twin blades in dark leather sheaths, their hilts plain and unadorned. He wore clothes of more sober cut in soft grey silk as befitted a faithful slave but the cloth was of as fine a quality as his master's. Like Kheda, his hair and beard were tamed with close cutting and scented oils.

The islanders taking their ease smiled warm greetings to Kheda, bowing low. Wives, deftly cooking fish or meat on cook fires placed a prudent distance from vulnerable thatch, paused to add their own heartfelt welcome. A substantial pot of pale yellow grain steamed in the embers of each hearth and greens from the burgeoning gardens behind each house seethed with fragrant spices. Kheda was pleased to see that even this late in the dry season none of his people were going hungry.

'The word is there are islands in the Ulla domain where the people are eating dry stalks and old husks, their granaries are so empty,' Telouet remarked.

'So I hear,' Kheda nodded.

A bright-eyed maiden with an inviting smile was shoved into their path by her doting mother. She held out a wooden platter lined with broad leaves each carrying a morsel of meat glistening with rich sauce. 'My lord,' she managed to say before giggles got the better of her.

Kheda nodded with approval as he ate a piece. 'Excellent. Telouet, try some.' He winked suddenly at the maiden before turning to smile at the mother. 'You must share that blend of spices with Janne Daish's cook.'

'Indeed.' Telouet's agreement was muffled by his mouthful of succulent meat.

Waving a farewell that encompassed all the islanders, Kheda walked on. Telouet was still chewing as the two of them approached the mighty walls of the compound beyond the little houses.

'Do you want to share something with the daughter? She was all but throwing herself at you.' Swallowing, he adopted a tone of spurious innocence. 'It's an even-numbered year and the wrong season besides, so my lady Rekha won't be inviting you to her bed tonight.'

'I find three wives quite sufficient without adding concubines.' Kheda laughed. 'How often do you need telling? Still, I don't want Sirket going to his wedding night all theory and no practice and the lass is certainly a fragrant blossom. You could ask her parents if she's promised herself anywhere yet. If not, she might like to join Janne's household for a season or so.'

'My lady Janne is keen to see Sirket married.' Telouet scratched his beard. 'Birut was telling me she let the wives of every domain know she was casting her net, on their way back from the Redigal islands.'

Kheda nodded. 'Which will doubtless be the topic of conversation over dinner.' He looked sideways at Telouet, the light from the lamps above the gate catching his smile. 'I still think it's rather more important to find him the right body slave just at present.'

'I've been keeping my eyes and ears open but I've yet to come across a likely prospect.' Telouet looked serious. 'Boys of that age are difficult to read and if you can't find out exactly who's owned them, that makes it harder to judge their character.' He paused to hammer on the solid black wood of the compound's doors. 'Open to your lord Daish Kheda! A slightly older slave might be a safer choice,' he continued.

'No.' Kheda shook his head firmly as the wide gates swung open. Four guards armoured in finely wrought hauberks stood on either side of the path, naked blades gleaming in the lamplight, faces hidden by the nasal bars and chainmail veils of their ornamented helms. All bowed low to their lord. Kheda inclined his head in passing and the guards fell back to bar the gate securely once more.

'He need not be too much older,' Telouet began.

'No.' Kheda's rebuke was firm though not harsh. He turned his head to look at Telouet. 'We must find him a slave whom he can trust as I have trusted you, who hears his unspoken thoughts as you hear mine, but that slave cannot be older. If Sirket defers to him once, he'll do it again and that becomes a dangerous habit. Look at Redigal Coron.' Kheda laughed mirthlessly. 'Sirket must be the master.'

'My lord.' Telouet bent his head in apparent acquiescence.

'After all, we know it's possible.' Kheda studied the thinning hair on the crown of his faithful slave's head. 'My father found you for me.'

Telouet grinned at him. 'Daish Reik's wisdom in so many things still blesses the domain.'

I wouldn't mind hearing it from his own mouth again, just occasionally.

Kheda paused to look around the compound – checking that all was well was second nature to him. Quarters for all lesser members of the vast household clung to the inside of the massive stone wall, the broad parapet above their roofs patrolled by watchful sentries. Within this protective embrace, separate pavilions stood, marble steps pale as they were brushed by the light of the Greater Moon, solid walls of grey stone dark beneath the shadows of the wide eaves. Shutters and doors of black hardwood were fitted with bronze, the roofs above of gleaming tile, patterns dazzling by day muted just at present by the half-light. Fountains playing in broad pools set in the extensive gardens around each pavilion pattered softly in the dusk.

'Shed your swords and go share a drink with Rembit.' Kheda clapped Telouet on the shoulder. 'Wait for me at Rekha's door. No, go on,' he insisted when the slave would have protested. 'You only make Sain nervous. She can do without that.'

Besides, my faithful steward will doubtless tell you a few things that he left out of his report to me on the beach.

Kheda turned his back and headed for his youngest wife's residence without waiting to see that Telouet obeyed. He soon reached the assiduously tended garden around her pavilion, the carefully selected pebbles of the path smooth and cool beneath his unshod feet, the scent of night-blooming vizail intoxicating.

Not that there is any reason for Sain to be wary of Telouet. Not that there's any reason for her to act like a nervous kitten around everyone in the compound. She's almost more at ease out among the islanders, collecting her stones and seedlings. We must make sure she gets leisure to make such trips and tend her garden after the baby is born. Perhaps she'll be less timorous after the child is born. She's very young, after all. Barely older than Sirket. Younger than you were when you found yourself ruler of the Daish islands. You found that prospect daunting enough and you had been raised to the expectation. Remember, Sain never expected to be anything more than a minor prize in marriage until her brother's ambition secured the Toc domain by right of conquest.

'My lord Daish Kheda.' A massive man rose from his seat on the broad steps in front of the door and house lizards skittered away into the darkness.

'Hanyad.' Kheda acknowledged the man with a smile, careful to hide his private amusement.

Whoever chose you as slave for timid little Sain knew what they were about, finding such a mountain of a man to stand between her and danger, real or imagined.

'How is she?'

'Weary, my lord.' Hanyad's dour warning was still coloured with whatever northern tongue he had learned at his mother's knee. As he opened the door, yellow lamplight shone on his grizzled hair and once-pale skin turned leathery from endless seasons' sun. 'My lady, your husband seeks admittance.'

Kheda waited patiently for Sain's reply. Every wife was within her rights to refuse her husband entry and one of a body slave's multifarious duties was enforcing such decisions.

'He is most welcome.' Unseen within, Sain certainly sounded tired. The big man hesitated but stepped aside to yield the threshold to Kheda.

'I shan't stay long.'

I was right to shake off Telouet. That wouldn't have gone

down well, not this late in the day and with Telouet hungry, and the last thing I need is my body slave falling out with Sain's.

Kheda entered and Hanyad closed the door behind him and sat cross-legged to bar it. 'Sain, my dear, how are you?'

'Well enough.' Wearing a loose unbelted tunic of plain golden silk, his youngest wife reclined on a bank of russet silk cushions embroidered with a riot of colourful birds. She wore no jewellery; her long straight hair was simply pulled back into a thick black plait. Slightly built and no taller than Kheda's shoulder, these last days of her pregnancy plainly weighed heavy upon her. A small girl was rubbing scented lotion into her feet and Kheda noted Sain's visibly swollen ankles.

'You look exhausted,' Kheda said frankly. Even in the muted light of the single lamp, the darkness around Sain's eyes was more than just shadow. He heard a grunt of agreement from Hanyad.

'It's just the heat.' Sain fanned herself with a delicate, copper-skinned hand.

'Which won't abate until the end of the season.' Kheda noted the increase in her gravid belly while he'd been away in contrast to face and wrists grown thinner than ever. He strove for a balance between authority and affection in his words. 'You must do nothing but take your ease until the rains or the baby, whichever comes first.' He smiled, partly at Hanyad's rumble of approval and partly to reassure Sain whose big brown eyes were wide with concern.

'My duties—'

'Tembit has already made his report on the state of the compound and the island. He tells me the fields are tilled and ready for the rains, saller grain seedlings flourish in the nurseries.' Kheda spoke with warm congratulation.

'Even all the house fowl and goats are healthy, which is rare enough this late in the dry season.'

'Naturally I strive to serve the domain.' Sain's evident pleasure brought a little animation to her face. She tried to push herself more upright but her pillows slipped beneath her, vivid colours catching the lamplight. The little slave girl barely managed to save her bowl of lotion, greasy hands fluttering in indecision.

'You've discharged your every duty to the domain. Now all we ask is you cherish yourself and this baby until you are both safely through childbed.' Kheda waved the child away.

Perhaps Sain would show a bit more spirit if her attendants weren't all such dolts.

He considered putting an arm around her shoulders once she was settled comfortably again but decided against it. Neither Rekha nor Janne had particularly welcomed close embraces so near to giving birth. He held his hand above the swell of her stomach instead. 'May I?'

'She's kicking.' Sain laid her hand on his so he could feel the baby move within her.

'Girl or boy, we'll know soon enough.' At his words, Sain tensed beneath his touch and the spark in her eyes faded.

Kheda leant over to plant an emphatic kiss on her forehead. 'Girl or boy, this child is yours to keep. And here's a gift for the babe, to prove my words.' He fished in a pocket for a small silken packet, tied securely with braided cotton.

Sain took it, long varnished nails picking apart the knot, child-like excitement brightening her tired face. 'Oh, Kheda, husband, it's beautiful.' She held up a shimmering bird made of silver chains linking opal feathers.

'Hang it for a talisman over the baby's crib,' Kheda smiled. 'For the virtue in the stones to protect our firstborn.'

'I was thinking—' Sain set the shimmering bird in her lap, her voice tremulous. 'About the baby's future. Perhaps I should visit a tower of silence. I haven't done so since I came here and the rains won't arrive for some days yet. I might dream something important there, something about the child, it is my duty as your wife—'

'You are in no condition to spend a night outside sleeping on bare earth, whatever the weather.' Kheda heard Hanyad grunt his emphatic agreement. 'Once the baby is born, once you're recovered, when we've moved north to the rainy season residence, you can think about undertaking such a ritual, with Rekha and Janne to help you with all due preparations. That will be quite soon enough to learn whatever threads from past or future this baby might hold in its hand.'

'As you command, my lord.' Sain managed a wan smile but Kheda could tell she was upset.

The last thing I want to do is play the heavy-handed warlord with you, when that's all you've ever known, but you do make it so cursed difficult.

'Go to bed, dear heart. Stay there as long as you want tomorrow morning and every day after.' Kheda rose from the floor. Hanyad was already on his feet, opening the double doors to Sain's bedchamber beyond. The little slave girl scurried past him, scrubbing oil from her hands with a scrap of cotton cloth.

Kheda helped Sain stand. She was too grateful for his support to tense as he slipped an arm around her waist. He gave her a gentle hug. 'Sleep well, my flower. Attend your mistress, Hanyad, I'll see myself out.'

Releasing her into the slave's watchful care, he went out into the humid, heady night, stifling a sigh of exasperation. Outside, in the compound, those servants and slaves whose duties were done rested and ate beside braziers set outside their quarters, faces bright in the pools of orange light.

The air was fragrant with herbs burning to deter the insidious whine of the night's biting insects and laughter rippled through the low murmur of conversation.

Telouet was waiting at the bottom of the steps. 'How is she?'

'Much as always.' Kheda shrugged.

'Not long now till the baby's here,' Telouet offered.

'And do you think it's my babe or Hanyad's?' Kheda led the way towards a much larger pavilion with a second storey in the centre and many windowed wings to either side.

'She came to your bed a virgin, my lord,' said Telouet thoughtfully. 'And I don't think she had time enough to get used to you bedding her to get curious about any alternatives.'

'True enough.'

And that had been yet another new experience for a nervous girl arriving in an unknown domain. Then you'd barely coaxed her out of her tenseness when she fell pregnant and her nausea put an end to any embraces. I really don't imagine Sain thinks she's getting anywhere near a fair share of the benefits of this marriage.

Then Kheda's mood lifted at the sound of lively voices suddenly hushed behind the pillars of his wife Rekha's pavilion. Little shadows scampered along the outer steps and Kheda ducked down, waving Telouet to do the same. They moved closer at a crouch. Kheda sprang and caught his second daughter by the waist, swinging her off her feet, growling in her ear. 'Efi Daish, what are you doing outside past dusk? Hunting house lizards again?'

'My father!' She squealed with delight, twisting in his embrace to fling her arms around his neck.

'Vida?' Kheda raised his eyebrows at his next youngest child who had managed to leap on to Telouet's back, thanks to the slave's carefully mistimed lunge for her.

'We haven't heard anyone call for us,' she asserted with spurious innocence.

'How could that be?' Kheda swept aside a lock of Efi's lustrous black hair and felt inside her ear. The child squirmed and giggled, her cotton nightshift slippery, but he held her securely, her bare feet brushing his thigh. 'No, no beeswax. Telouet, check that one for something stopping her ears. Otherwise I must mix a dose of aiho root to cure them of deafness.'

Telouet shuddered with exaggerated horror. 'But that tastes dreadful!'

Vida dropped to the floor and ran to haul open the main door just enough to slip through. 'Mother Rekha, my father is here!'

Efi was content to wait in her father's arms as Telouet knocked perfunctorily and opened the door to spill light on to the marble steps. Within, the room was bright with lamps hanging on chains reaching down from the lofty ceiling, their light striking back from walls panelled in pale wood and set with mirrors. White curtains of fine mesh covered the long windows, the cloth redolent with the sharp scent that the slaves applied to deter heat by day and biting insects by night.

'Enter and be welcome.' Andit's formal greeting sounded a little abstracted. Kheda entered and saw his second wife's burly body slave was absorbed in a game of stones with the warlord's younger son.

'Beating him again, Mesil?' Kheda enquired genially.

'Not yet.' The boy looked up and grinned broadly. 'Shall we have a wager on it, my father?'

'I've been away, what, ten days? Is that time enough for Andit to get smarter?' Kheda pretended to consider this. 'No, I don't think so.'

Mesil swiftly moved several coloured-glass roundels, his beringed fingers deft on the circular game board.

Entirely his mother's son in build and feature, his wiry brown hair nevertheless convinced Kheda he had certainly fathered this child.

'I give up.' Andit sighed. 'Third defeat this evening.'

'I believe it is the fourth.' There was amusement in Rekha's voice. Long-limbed and elegant in a many-layered dress of rainbow silk, she lay on a low couch, eyes closed. A cushion supported her neck as a kneeling slave ran a gold comb inlaid with lapis through her mistress's long black hair. 'Are you sure you're not letting Mesil win?' Rekha queried with faint reproof, her silver bracelets chinking as she settled her hands.

'Hardly. Even I can beat Andit.' Graceful in a close-fitting tunic and trews, Kheda's eldest daughter sat beside her second mother, cross-legged on a thick-piled carpet with an intricate design of canthira leaves interlaced with the flames that were both death to the tree and life to its seeds. She was holding out her hands to a young man who sat patiently applying golden varnish to her immaculately shaped finger-nails. She watched him with a smugly proprietorial air.

'Then don't play him, Dau, play Mesil,' Kheda said with a smile to soften his words. 'How else will you improve?'

'I do play Mesil.' In contrast to Rekha whose aquiline face now bore only a faint sheen of cleansing oil, cosmetics still made a bright mask of Dau's eyelids and lips. The dusting of silver on her cheekbones caught the light as she smiled at her father. Her black-rimmed eyes were the same warm brown as her mother's but other than that, she bore a striking resemblance to her full brother Sirket. 'I nearly beat him yesterday.'

'You did not!' Mesil protested, his voice cracking between its boyish tone and manhood.

'I'll bet you a day of Lemir's attendance on you that I can beat you,' challenged Dau.

'Children.' Rekha did not raise her voice but she did open her eyes and wave away her attendant slave. 'Firstly, Dau, you do not make a wager unless you are hazarding something of real value to yourself. If you wish to test your fortune against Mesil's, wager your own attendance on him or one of your talismans. Then the outcome will have some meaning.

'Secondly, I have had a long and tiring day, as has your father. Behave, and you will be treated as adults. Bicker and you'll be sent to bed along with the little ones.' She raised herself on one elbow and narrowed her eyes at Vida. 'Who are to be sent to bed a second time, I see.'

At her mistress's nod, the slave woman laid down her comb and clapped her hands at the little girls. 'Quietly now. If you wake the babies, it'll be cold saller porridge and no fruit for you at breakfast.'

Kheda set Efi down to the floor and she followed her sister obediently through an inner door opening on to a hall with a stairway beyond.

'You can play one more game, Mesil and then you go to bed.' Rekha stood up and fixed Andit with a stern eye. 'You're to tell me if he deliberately spins it out. Dau, if your hands are done, Lemir should clean your face. There's no one to see us now and your skin needs to breathe a little before bed.' She smiled gracefully at Kheda. 'Shall we take some refreshment more privately, my lord?'

'As you wish, my wife.' Kheda bowed to her.

Dress whispering on the cool marble floor, Rekha led him down a corridor to a wide empty room. The ruddy wooden wall panels were inlaid with exquisite mother of pearl and soapstone flowers and fronds. A low table of the same wood and patterning was set to one side on a luxuriant carpet bright with blood-red swirls of fern fronds.

'When did you get back?' Rekha asked as they entered.

'Just before sunset,' Kheda replied. 'So I went up to

the tower to read the sky by the last of the light.'

Telouet slid past him to light the room's lamps unob-trusively and then discreetly withdrew.

'I take it you saw all is well?' Rekha looked at him, dark eyes alert.

'The heavens are settled in auspicious aspects and there were no other portents to say different. I have a sheaf of recommendations from village spokesmen for likely swordsmen and lads with an ambition to go to sea, as well as a boatload of prentice pieces that various craftsmen have sent for your assessment.' Kheda gestured back towards the other room. 'I see your trip was successful.'

'Moni Redigal has always had a good eye for a slave,' nodded Rekha with undisguised satisfaction. 'His name is Lemir.'

'I heard. He's a little young,' Kheda said thoughtfully. 'Decorative too.'

Rekha raised one perfectly shaped eyebrow. 'You think I should have found some much-handled goods like Hanyad for our daughter?'

'Telouet tells me Hanyad was traded from one end of the Archipelago to the other before Toc Faile secured him for Sain.' Kheda shrugged. 'He can tell her a great many things that she'll find useful.'

'For a woman so inadequately raised, he's a good choice.' Rekha's voice held just the faintest hint of acid. 'Janne and I have made sure Dau does not need any such tutor. She can look for wisdom or cunning in a slave when she's of an age to decide for herself that she needs it. For now I want her adored and indulged by a lad handsome enough to be the envy of all her equals among the other domains through these last seasons of her girlhood.'

Telouet's arrival saved Kheda from having to find a reply to that. He and Rekha stood silently as the slave set a tray on the low table and poured pale fruit juice from a long-necked, fat-bellied ewer of beaten bronze into gleaming goblets.

'We'll serve ourselves.' Kheda took a long drink as Telouet served Rekha and retreated towards the door. It was lilla juice, inevitably at this season. 'Adored and indulged is all very well but does this Lemir know how to fight, and when to fight, come to that?' He turned to refill his goblet and caught Telouet's eye as the slave closed the door. Telouet nodded infinitesimally.

'He comes well recommended by Moni Redigal and her body slave both,' Rekha replied confidently.

'Very well.' *Besides, Telouet will put the lad through his paces as soon as he joins the household's other body slaves on their private practice ground.* 'So, now she has a slave of her own, will you be taking Dau to the pearl harvest after the rains?' Kheda sat, cross-legged and straight-backed, on the carpet softening the marble floor, entirely comfortable.

'I think so.' Rekha chuckled as she sank elegantly on the other side of the low table, folding her feet beneath her. She held out her goblet for more juice and wrinkled her fine nose comically. 'If nothing else, learning to keep a straight face through all that stink will be good training. If she behaves herself, I'll take her with me on my next journey north and maybe even let her do a little bargaining with some seed pearls, just for everyday wares.'

'She'll like that.' Kheda smiled. 'And what other successes did you win for the domain in your recent voyage?'

Rekha smiled with satisfaction. 'Moni Redigal will supply a shipload of brassware between now and the end of the rains in return for a full eighth share in the pearl harvest as it leaves the sea.'

'She's always a woman for a gamble.' Kheda shook his head. 'What if half her oysters come up empty?'

'That's the risk she chooses,' said Rekha without concern. 'Though I don't see her losing by it, even if she doesn't see quite the gains she dreams of. My divers speak well of the condition of the reefs. Taisia Ritsem prefers to wait, hardly a surprise. She'll see what the oysters yield and then trade finished silks for graded pearls and cleaned nacre.'

'Excellent,' Kheda approved. 'How did you fare with getting Mirrel Ulla to settle her accounts with you?'

'She claims a dearth of sandalwood makes it unexpectedly impossible for her to meet her obligations.' Rekha's disbelief was patent. 'I said I hoped she would soon regain the necessary authority over her loggers. No matter. Mirrel needs tin for her tile makers' glazes and the nearest domain that can supply that is Redigal. I can make life very difficult for Mirrel, if I call in a few debts from Taisia Redigal.'

Kheda recalled Sirket's apprehension. 'Are you or Janne thinking of making a trip to the Ulla domain before the rains?'

'We considered it.' Rekha drank before shaking her head. 'Then we decided we should both be here for Sain's first baby. Anyway, it'll be a quicker trip from the rainy-season residence, once we've moved north. It'll do no harm to let Mirrel Ulla fret over just what I might be doing in the meantime.'

'I have every confidence in your abilities to serve our domain,' chuckled Kheda.

I certainly did well by my children in finding such an intelligent wife to secure their future through her impressive aptitude for trade. And the lack of passion between us means I always know what to expect from Rekha.

'How was your trip?' Rekha observed her husband over the rim of her goblet. 'How fares our own domain as the seasons turn?'

'Satisfactory.' Kheda pursed his lips. 'Every isle had the usual pointless disputes and endless debates—'

'Inevitable just before the rains,' Rekha interjected. 'Were there any killings for you to sit in judgement over?'

'No.' Kheda didn't hide his relief. 'And it's a rare year when the heat doesn't tip someone into lethal folly, so I think we can take that as a favourable omen. Other than that, the beacons are well maintained and fuelled. Every watch post has its message birds preening happily. No village had any disease to report and the omens were set fair wherever I read them.'

'There'll be an outbreak of some pestilence or other come the rains,' Rekha commented a trifle dourly. 'It's hardly the best time for Sain to be bringing a child into the domain.'

'I've seen no evil portents,' said Kheda mildly.

It's your privilege to arrange our children's births as you see fit but I've no quarrel with Sain showing a little less rigorous design than your scheme of births in alternate years, falling in the fruitful, cooler days when the rains have just ceased.

'The children all look well,' he observed with a fond smile.

'They are thriving.' Rekha's face softened. 'Mie will be walking any day now. I'm glad you're home to see it. Noi has been running us all off our feet as usual; she lost that wooden goat Birut made for her yesterday and I swear we must have searched the whole compound three times over.'

Kheda laughed. 'Did you find it?'

'In Mie's quilts but Noi finally forgave her.' Rekha shook her head with fond exasperation.

'I'll see them first thing in the morning,' Kheda promised.

I can take half a day to relax with my little girls before addressing whatever's cropped up here in my absence. I am the warlord after all.

'Make sure you bring something with you,' warned Rekha with tart amusement. 'Efi's been telling them how any of us returning from a voyage always means presents.'

'They're both old enough to understand that?' Kheda groaned in mock distress. 'I'll be beggared by this time next year.'

'Not with me trading the fruits of the pearl harvest, you won't.' Rekha plainly relished that prospect. She rose in one fluid movement, shaking out the folds of her gown over her slim feet. 'If there's nothing else you want to discuss, my husband, I'll bid you goodnight. I'll be drawing up my ledgers tomorrow if you want to look over them.'

Which will show a handsome balance in Daish favour, I have no doubt.

'Good night.' Kheda didn't get up, pouring himself the last of the fruit juice instead. He drank it slowly, listening to the protests from the far room. Neither Dau nor Mesil were sufficiently grown not to try pleading and wheedling for some extra leisure before bed.

Telouet entered on silent feet, visibly amused. 'You'd think they'd have learned by now that Rekha never changes her mind, no matter what fuss they make.'

'Youth is all about hope.' Kheda grinned and emptied his goblet.

'You sound like a sage in his seventieth summer,' Telouet mocked.

'After sailing the length and breadth of the domain, I feel it.' Kheda groaned and held out a hand.

'A good night's sleep will put you to rights.' The slave hauled him to his feet. 'Where are you sleeping?'

'Let's go and see how Janne feels about that.' Kheda nodded to the far door of the reception hall and Telouet opened it. 'What do you make of Dau's new plaything?'

'He made a good job of her nails.' Telouet pursed his lips. 'I'll want to see him tested on the practice ground.

Still, Andit will have put him through his paces as soon as he saw my lady Rekha was considering a trade for him.'

'Let me know how he fares.' Kheda knew Telouet had a high regard for Andit's swordsmanship; the stocky warrior had been traded down through several domains from the central islands where recurrent battles always honed such skills to a fine edge.

Outside, the compound was appreciably quieter now as the warlord's household had largely retired to bed, well aware that their duties would return with the dawn and sleep would be hard to come by now the oppressive heat was building to the ceaseless trial that only the rains would relieve. Sentries patrolled the parapet on silent feet and one aged slave was slowly treading the white paths that wove through the pavilions' gardens, alert for snakes or scorpions that had no business there.

Janne Daish's pavilion didn't have an upper storey but wings had been added on either side. Kheda headed for one side door where lamplight showed and Telouet hastened to knock for him.

'Enter and be welcome.' Janne's words overrode Telouet's formal request so he simply pushed open the door. A trio of musicians rose smoothly to their feet and bowed, taking themselves and their lyres and flutes away.

Janne's personal retreat was furnished with plenty of cushions, myriad side tables laden with curios and ornaments, the walls covered with intricately woven hangings bright with patterns of frolicking animals that framed silver lamps set in crystal-lined niches to scatter a soothing light. Kheda felt the tensions of the day leave him as he relaxed in the comfortable familiarity of the room. Then his own stomach rumbled with appreciation at the spread of dishes on the low table. Mingled spicy scents rose from silver platters of vegetables sliced and sauced and carefully blended for an aesthetically pleasing mix of green leaves, blanched stems and fine sliced orange roots. Morsels of dark bird meat rested on a bed of yellow shoots dotted with shreds of brilliant red seedpods.

'Is that a chequered fowl?' Kheda took a seat on a firm cushion across from his most senior wife. Telouet went to help Birut, Janne's personal slave, who was entering with a tray laden with still more dishes.

'One of the hill men brought a brace down this morning.' Janne was already scooping finely spiced saller out of a substantial brass pot and into a gold-rimmed white ceramic bowl. She handed it to Kheda. 'Pour your father some wine, my dear, and some for yourself.'

Sirket halted as he fetched a fluted silver ewer from a side table. 'For me?' He looked at Kheda for permission.

So, Janne, your thoughts and mine chime in harmony, as so often.

'You're of an age of discretion,' Kheda said casually. 'It's time you widened your experience.'

'Better you learn the pleasures and pitfalls of liquor within our own walls than by disgracing yourself like Ulla Orhan.' Janne smiled to soften her words.

Inadequately hiding his pleased smile, Sirket poured three goblets of clear golden wine before sitting and accepting his own bowl of steamed grain.

'A little light wine, when you have met all your responsibilities, when there will be no call on your judgement, that's entirely acceptable. Distilled liquors—' Kheda pointed an emphatic finger at his son. 'Potent spirits are a whole different nest of snakes.'

'No warlord with a taste for those holds power very long,' agreed Janne. 'Or one who tolerates any drunkenness among his swordsmen.'

'There will always be eyes on you watching for weakness.' Picking up his goblet, Kheda drank. 'Learn your own limitations and you'll notice anyone trying to exploit them.'

The slaves set the last dishes down and removed themselves to sit silently in the corners of the room.

'I take it all is well around the domain?' Even for this informal meal, Janne was still dressed with all the elegance expected of a first wife. Gold and red paints on her eyes were bright against her dark skin, matching the ruby-studded chains of precious metal around her wrists and neck. Her mature figure was flattered by an inviting dress of gold-brocaded crimson silk.

'Well enough.' Kheda settled himself comfortably on a cushion and reached for the dish of fowl meat. 'I'm still not sure about that new spokesman on Shiel though. He hasn't got the village men together to clear the river margins of dry season growth.' Though it was hard to be concerned with such things in this room's welcome embrace. Kheda took a moment to smile at Janne. She smiled back, her full lips luscious with a scarlet gloss of paint.

'If the rains don't find a clear channel, they'll all be up to their knees in floodwater, won't they?' Sirket looked from one parent to the other.

'Which will give those who wouldn't respect their spokeman's authority pause for thought,' Janne said unperturbed. 'We'll see how he handles himself through the wet season.'

'Perhaps.' Kheda shrugged, non-committal, as he savoured a faint citrus tartness offsetting the sweetness of spiced honey soaked into the fowl meat. 'So, Sirket, have there been any portents around the compound while I was away?'

Chewing, the boy considered his reply. 'Two black-banded snakes were caught the night before last. They're not unusual at this season and they weren't a pair. I mean, one was by the gate and the other was in Sain's garden. They were both caught just before dawn, so that's a favourable omen, if it's anything at all. Neither had eaten anything and there were no marks or deformities in their entrails.'

Kheda leaned over the table, reversing his silver spoon and using the twin tines on its end to spear a smoked fingerfish dusted with finely ground spice. 'So their presence means what?'

'To be vigilant in our care of the domain,' said Sirket confidently.

'As always.' Kheda smiled. 'A reminder never comes amiss.'

I wouldn't wager a broken potsherd on Ulla Safar's chances of humiliating you, my son.

All three turned their attention to making a hearty meal in companionable silence.

'How is Sain this evening?' Janne asked as they paused to allow the slaves to clear away the meats and bring the fruit course to the table.

'She looks exhausted.' Kheda didn't hide his displeasure, crunching creamy nuts from a dish of poached purple berries. 'And still too thin.'

'She always ate like a bird and with the heat and the baby so heavy on her stomach, Hanyad can barely get her to take more than a mouthful.' Janne shook her head, hair braided close and dressed with heady scented dye to redden the grey among the black.

'She's what, ten days from childbed, maybe fifteen?' Kheda took a handful of crisp slivers of fried red fruit. 'That's going by the moons though. It's a big babe and she's none too sturdy to carry such a weight so it could arrive any time.'

'First babies are often late,' Janne countered.

'I shan't let it linger too long. I made fresh pella vine salve before I went away.' Kheda spoke indistinctly through another mouthful of nuts. 'And I gathered plenty of bluecasque on the trip.' He glanced at Sirket. 'Have you been busy about your grinding and decocting?'

The boy grinned. 'We're well supplied against every wet-season disease I've found listed in the pharma-copoeias.'

'And what of cleansing and healing salves?' Kheda nodded at a graze on Sirket's knuckles. 'Miss a sword pass on the practice ground, did you?'

'Birut caught me by surprise.' Sirket looked a little shamefaced.

Kheda grinned back at the boy. 'Better a slave doing that in practice than some assassin in the night.'

'Sain seems to have her heart set on visiting a tower of silence.' Janne sighed. 'Has she spoken to you about that?'

'Yes and I've told her it's entirely unnecessary until the child is safely born,' said Kheda decisively.

Janne's face softened. 'It's just that she's so fearful she'll bear a son and that will be the last she'll see of him.'

'I wish I knew why.' Kheda shook his head in frank exasperation. 'I've told her time and again that we will raise the baby, boy or girl, to serve the good of the domain and all our alliances.'

'She came from a domain still running with the blood of its children,' Janne pointed out. 'Old Toc Vais may have raised all his sons and grandsons in his own compound but they still had to fight for power among themselves when he died.'

'Which was a bloody enough affair,' allowed Kheda. 'And I don't suppose we heard the half of it outside the domain's borders.'

'I hope she does bear a boy.' Janne tilted her head on one side. 'Then she'll learn once and for all that you're a man of your word. Otherwise she'll go through all these same agonies with her next pregnancy.'

'If she decides to risk another child.' Kheda allowed himself a sour expression.

'I'm confident you'll have convinced her to invite you back into her bed,' Janne chuckled.

Sirket coughed and spoke rather louder than was necessary. 'Is it true that Ulla Safar has any sons born to his wives killed?'

'And even to his concubines.' Kheda answered with a briskness that didn't quite disguise his distaste. 'Doses them himself with frog venom, according to what he tells me.'

'Why?' Sirket frowned. 'If Orhan dies—'

'He's none so hale after that attack of breakbone fever last year,' commented Janne.

'And there's always accident or malice to fear.' Kheda's look challenged Sirket. 'What happens then?'

'Tewi Ulla inherits as next eldest child.' Sirket shook his head. 'She's afraid of her own shadow. She won't find a husband willing to stand as consort and let her rule in her own right.'

'Without younger brothers to command the domain's swordsmen, she'll be lucky to escape marriage by abduction,' commented Janne.

'So why does Ulla Safar want a quiver with only one shot?' Kheda leaned back from the table and studied his son.

What do you think, now you're discovering things that your parents know yet never discuss openly? How far are you going to take this?

Sirket hesitated. 'Because he fears younger brothers would be a threat to Orhan's hold on the Ulla domain.'

'Tule Nar was overthrown by his brothers,' Janne agreed in apparent support.

'Do you think it was as simple as that?' Kheda raised his brows at Sirket.

'Tule Nar had lost both the love and respect of his entire domain,' Sirket said slowly. 'There were endless hostile portents before his brothers took up arms against him.'

'Do you think Tule Reth holds the domain securely now?' Kheda prompted.

'Tule Dom and Tule Lek would both die for him,' Sirket nodded. 'And both have their own compound as well as permission to own slaves in their own right.'

'Duar Tule grants all their wives shares in the domain's trading rights as well,' added Janne.

'A loyal brother can be worth his weight in pearls.' For all Kheda was smiling, he pointed his spoon sharply at Sirket. 'Never give Mesil or any son that Sain may bear us any reason to think you don't value them.'

'You don't fear two might conspire against me when they're grown?' asked Sirket, emboldened.

'With you the eldest and them so widely spaced in age? Your mothers and I made sure of that much.' Kheda held his son's gaze. 'It's for you to make sure your rule is wise enough for them not to feel a need to remove you.'

'We'd be remiss in our duty if we left the domain with no alternative to a tyrant.' Janne smiled too but there was a steely glint in her dark eyes.

Sirket chewed his lower lip. 'Rekha bore a second son between Vida and Mie. What happened to him?'

If this question has finally come, perhaps it is time to think of marrying you, my son.

'I have no idea,' replied Kheda honestly. 'Rekha took him north and made her own arrangements for his care. He's now of some other domain.'

'The child will never know different to what he's raised with,' Janne commented.

Sirket's expression turned both determined and fearful. 'Am I your only son?'

'Yes. I bore another the year after Dau but he didn't live beyond the rains.' Janne smiled wistfully. 'I would have sent him to one of my sisters to raise in her own household.'

'Daughters are a boon to every domain. Sons can be

blessing or curse. Every warlord has to make his own decision about how many to raise and what to do with those
who cannot inherit his power.' Kheda looked at his son
with open challenge. 'Why do you think Ulla Safar kills
babies still wet with their birth blood?'

Sirket couldn't hide his revulsion but did his best to
consider the question with detachment. 'A life cut so short
has little chance to become embedded in the affairs of the
domain, so I suppose the death cannot harm the domain
too much. But does he look for portents? There's always
the chance the child's life would benefit the domain far
more than its death, isn't there?' He looked from father
to mother and back again.

'Of course,' Kheda agreed.

*And while every warlord must makes such decisions alone
and none may gainsay him, I'm so very glad to see your
disgust at the notion of murdering infants, my son.*

'Ulla Safar considers removing any rival to Ulla Orhan
sufficient,' shrugged Janne. 'And no, from what I've heard,
he never bothers with any augury beforehand.'

'Then the sire's as much a fool as the son,' Sirket
muttered unguardedly. He reached for a lilla fruit and began
stripping the outer husk from the pod with angry fingers.

*Is this the time for the next question? 'Did you have any
brothers, my father?' What will you make of Daish Reik's
solution to the eternal problem of his sons?*

Kheda took a drink of the light, fragrant wine. Sirket
stayed silent, intent on scooping the creamy seeds from
the dark green flesh of the lilla fruit.

Kheda glanced over at Janne. 'Where do you think
Sirket might look for his first wife?'

Sirket looked up, startled. 'You think it's time?'

'You're much the age your father was when I married
him,' Janne smiled.

'Newly widowed of Endit Cai and divorced of Rine

Itan before that.' Unexpected recollection startled Kheda into a chuckle. 'I can recommend a much-married girl as your first wife.'

Janne quelled her husband with a stern look. 'So she can share her experience of the wider Archipelago.'

Kheda was tempted to a ribald reply but forbore for Sirket's sake.

'How are you faring in your hunt for a suitable body slave?' Janne looked at Kheda. 'You wanted that arranged first, so you were saying.'

'I've still to find the right man.' Kheda grimaced at Sirket. 'Sorry.'

'Perhaps you should be looking for an adequate slave rather than the ideal.' Janne drained her goblet. 'He needs to travel and he can't do that without an attendant. Find one who will do and once Sirket's out and about, he can look for a better prospect himself.' She stroked her son's hand affectionately.

'That's something to consider, certainly.' Kheda twirled his own goblet by its faceted stem and studied the cloud-like patterns that the craftsman's skilful hammer had left on the metal.

A notion to consider and reject; my son isn't facing the manifold dangers threatening any warlord's heir without the best swords I can find protecting him, not as long as I have the final word in the matter.

'We're finished here, aren't we?' As Sirket and Kheda nodded, Janne waved a hand at Birut and Telouet. 'You may eat. Good night, Sirket.'

'Good night.' After a fond embrace for each parent, Sirket took himself off. The two slaves hungrily applied themselves to the remnants of the meal as Kheda followed Janne into her boudoir.

Rather than light the lamps, she crossed to a far window, throwing open the shutters to gaze upon the moonlit garden beyond. A pool edged with white stones shone among the dark bushes. Kheda came to stand behind her, folding his arms around her and resting his chin on her shoulder. He wasn't holding the firm slimness of the girl who'd both intoxicated him and intimidated him, nine years and more his senior but no matter. The feel of her still made his heart race, however the passage of years and the trials of childbirth had changed her body. He closed his eyes and breathed in her familiar, beloved perfume.

'It's hard to think of Sirket marrying,' Janne murmured softly. 'It's easier with Dau, I don't know why.'

'As it happens, I feel quite the opposite.' Kheda kissed Janne's ear. 'About her and all the girls.'

She smiled. 'I thought you'd be tired after such a long trip.'

'Not too tired.' Kheda kissed her again. The wide neck of Janne's dress was held together at the shoulder by fili-gree brooches. He undid one and kissed the smooth skin beneath.

Janne untied the jewel-encrusted sash that wrapped the dress around her soft midriff and let it fall to the floor. 'You haven't bathed, my lord.'

'Am I very ripe?' Kheda wrinkled his nose as he undid another brooch, letting the silk fall away to reveal the enticing swell of her bosom.

'Yes, but we can easily remedy that.' Janne turned in his embrace and kissed him long and deep as she began stripping away his jewellery. Kheda spared just enough concentration to undo the remaining brooches and ease the dress down over Janne's accommodating arms, letting it fall to the polished wooden floor.

Janne stepped out of the puddle of whispering silk and held out her hand to lead Kheda to the bathing room beyond the broad bed waiting for them with its pile of soft quilts.

CHAPTER TWO

Telouet's urgent hand shook Kheda out of a dreamless sleep. Fists clenched, he was ready to fight until the warm quilts reminded him he was safe in Janne's bed, his startled wife rousing beside him.

'Is it Sain?' He brushed Telouet's hand away, sitting up and reaching for his trousers. 'The baby?'

Janne yawned. 'What is it?'

'Beacons, my lord.' Telouet stood tense, half crouched in the shadow, one hand on a sword hilt.

'Where from?' Kheda scrubbed a hand over his beard as a surge of concern brought him fully awake. 'How many?'

'From the south. All of them.' Telouet's dark eyes were rimmed with white as he handed Kheda his tunic.

Janne threw aside the quilts, catching up a robe to cover her nakedness. 'Birut!' Her slave was already opening the far door with his shoulder, buckling a silver-studded belt around his mail hauberk. 'Wake Hanyad. He's to take Sain to Rekha's pavilion. I'll go straight to the children.' She turned to look at Kheda. 'Be careful.'

'Where's Rembit?' Kheda pulled his crumpled tunic over his head.

'With Serno.' Telouet followed Kheda out of the pavilion and down the steps to the compound. 'Wait here while I get your armour.'

Every light and brazier had been doused. The warm night was scented with smoke. Kheda saw his smooth-faced steward talking intently with Serno, commander of the compound's guards. Above their heads, armoured men lined the parapet with steel, naked swords gleaming in the moonlight. Archers held bows, black curves in the moonlight, peering out for any target careless enough to betray itself. The boy each archer had in training scurried behind his mentor, loaded with sheaves of arrows with various heads for piercing armour or ripping flesh. Serno nodded, slid the pierced faceplate of his helm down and secured it with a twist of the fastening before turning to climb a ladder to the upper walkway. Rembit went to direct slaves and servants ferrying water casks and chests, some up on to the parapet, others over to Rekha's pavilion.

All's as it should be. You saw every medicine casket had its salves and bandages before you set sail. There'll be water and food to sustain the men if this turns out to be a lengthy vigil. But what are we watching for?

'Father!' Armoured in bronze-studded, purple-dyed leather, Sirket arrived at Kheda's side, eyes uneasy beneath a brow beaded with perspiration.

Kheda glanced at his son and apprehension twisted his stomach.

You could have settled on an adequate body slave for the boy. Then he'd be raised to full manhood, armoured in chainmail rather than the coat of a thousand nails. Mesil could have that honour now.

As he thought this, Telouet reappeared, dumping his burden on the ground with a wordless exclamation. 'Let's get you armoured, my lord.' He took Kheda's hand and thrust it into the sleeve of a padded jacket.

Kheda shrugged the garment on and reached for his chainmail. Bronze links worked a lattice pattern through mail wrought of links barely bigger than baby Mie's thumbnail. Solid metal plates inset front and back to protect Kheda's vitals were chased with gold that gleamed in the moonlight. Kheda thrust his hands inside and took the weight on his arms before ducking his head to shrug the mail on. The hauberk jingled softly as it slid down his body and Kheda cursed silently as the shifting links plucked hairs from his head.

'Do we have any word from the south? Any messenger birds?' He took the broad belt that Telouet held out, buckling it tight to his hips to relieve the weight of the armour on his shoulders.

'Not yet.' Telouet knelt to secure Kheda's sword belt around his waist.

Sirket bent to pick up Kheda's helm, making sure the cotton lining was smooth before handing it over.

'Go to the bird tower,' Kheda told his son. 'Bring me any word as soon as it arrives.'

Sirket nodded mute obedience and took to his heels. Kheda thrust his gold-ornamented helmet firmly on his head and pulled the dagged chainmail veil forward around his shoulders to secure its front clasp. The pierced faceplate was still locked on its sliding bar above his forehead but, other than that, he was now armoured in steel from head to knee. In the humid heat of the night, sweat immediately started prickling between his shoulder blades.

'My lord?' Telouet proffered leather leggings with their own intricately decorated metal plates to foil blade or arrowhead.

Kheda shook his head. 'I don't need those on the battlements.'

Telouet scowled but didn't press the point, following Kheda up on to the parapet where one of Serno's men steadied the ladder.

'First things first.' That's what Daish Reik always taught you. That's the wisdom that brought him safely through two invasions of the rainy-season residence. But what peril could be coming from the south?

Kheda looked out to sea. The moons made shimmering

damask of the lagoon where the island's fishermen were taking to their boats, cutting tethers in their haste to lose themselves in the night before any disaster fell upon them. Beyond, the great galley was slowly turning along its length, oars cutting luminous trails in the water. As the broad vessel with its single row of oars hurried to abandon the sheltering reef in favour of flight to the north and safety, the longer, leaner shape of a trireme appeared, questing prow and bronze-sheathed ram turned to the south. More would soon be following, that was certain.

Beacons blazed on the closest islet, barely more than a reef itself but ideally placed to see in all directions. Kheda counted the lights. Telouet was right. Every island to the south was reporting some calamity.

What can be happening? All the flames are burning natural gold. So it's calamity but not some identifiable evil to prompt signal fires coloured to an agreed hue. That means it's not invasion, fire or flood, not sudden sickness or some infestation with vermin.

Kheda glanced up at the sky. There was no hint anywhere in the heavens, no shooting stars to scar the night, no unexpected blemish disfiguring either moon.

'Father!' Sirket scrambled awkwardly up the ladder, clutching a handful of little silver cylinders. Telouet grabbed the lad's hand and hauled him bodily up on to the parapet.

Kheda snatched one of the metal tubes and began unscrewing the end caps. 'Telouet, get some light.'

'Not up here, you don't,' the slave rebuked him robustly.

Kheda stared at him for a moment before realising what he had said. 'A dark lantern then. Hurry.' He dropped to his knees, unfurling the fine roll of paper below the shelter of the battlements, squinting to make out the crabbed writing in the moonlight.

Sirket hissed in exasperation as he studied a curling slip. 'This one's from Gelim but it's in cipher.' He reached for another.

Kheda could just make out the words on the paper he held. 'Chazen boats arrive. Men, women, children. They flee unknown disaster.' He looked for the identifier at the end of the perplexing message. It had come from the central message-bird tower on Dekul.

Whatever this cataclysm may be, its ripples are lapping at the southern and westernmost of my domain's islands.

'Father.' Sirket was peering at another message in the grudging light of the dark lantern Telouet had procured from somewhere. 'Chazen Saril has seized the Hyd Rock with five triremes.'

'Why would they do that?' Kheda frowned.

'Chazen Shas made a bid for the pearl reefs east of the Andemid shoals in Daish Reik's day,' Sirket said dubiously.

'Pearl reefs have some value. The Hyd Rock is a barren lump but for a brackish pool fringed with stunted palms. That's why Daish Reik designated it a neutral anchorage for galleys travelling between our two domains,' Kheda reminded him.

'Is it an invasion?' wondered Sirket.

'Not if the whole population is fleeing.' Kheda handed his son the message he had just read. 'There was no word from Chazen while I was away, was there? No hint of a quarrel?'

'No!' Sirket insisted. 'I'd have told you.'

'And they know we could drive their warriors back into the sea without breaking a sweat,' said Telouet robustly.

'Bring that lamp closer.' The next message was unhelpfully smudged and Kheda reached out to raise the dark lantern's smoked glass slide a little.

'Chazen is invaded from the south. They bring

wounded and beg sanctuary.' That was from one of the message towers on Nagel, the largest isle in the southern reach of the Daish domain. 'What's south of Chazen?' Kheda wondered aloud, slowly lowering the fragile paper weighted with such ominous words.

'South of Chazen?' Telouet looked at him with surprise.

Sirket shook his head, mystified. 'Nothing but ocean.'

Kheda handed him the message. 'Then what do you make of this?'

'Invaded?' Telouet was peering over the lad's shoulder. 'Then they'd be holding the Hyd Rock to stop whoever it is coming any further north.'

Kheda sorted through the rest of the messages. 'These all tell much the same tale: Chazen domain is beset from the south. We'd better break the coded one, even if all it says is the same. Sirket, get a bucket of embers from the kitchen cook fire. Bring it to the observatory tower.'

'Yes, Father.' Visibly confused, the youth nevertheless hurried off without question. Kheda followed him down the ladder.

'If we're going outside the gates, you wear your leggings.' Telouet thrust the heavy leather at him as soon as they set foot on the ground.

'Yes, master.' Kheda pulled the hateful things on with a grimace. The weight of the metal plates dragged at his feet as he followed Telouet towards the small postern gate on the landward side of the compound, his toes uncomfortably confined by the hard leather.

Look on the bright side. You don't have to worry about snakes if you're clumping along like some booted barbarian.

Unhampered by his own leggings, Telouet drew his swords and ran ahead to the knot of swordsmen poised by the postern.

'We're going to the augury tower,' Kheda said tersely. The chief of the guards drew the bolts on the gate and threw it open. His men rushed through, spreading out, ready to meet any threat. Telouet waited, standing between his lord and any unseen danger.

A noise behind turned Kheda's head and he saw Sirket running beside a kitchen servant who was carrying an iron bowl of live coals held tight between two lengths of fire-wood.

'Stay behind me.' Kheda drew his own sword.

Could this just be some ploy, to throw us all into confusion, to let some killer slip ashore unnoticed? I doubt it, but regardless, no assassin reaches Sirket while I am lord of this domain.

They ran past silent houses, shutters closed, doors swinging, a few fallen garments here and there, a scattering of broken crockery crunching under the guards' heavy-soled sandals. Relief tempered Kheda's apprehension.

Your people are safe, fled to the secret forest gullies and hidden mountain caves where everything they might need waits in sealed pots and metal chests proof against rot and insect.

The night beneath the trees was a lattice of black shadow and white moonlight. The swordsmen fanned out to either side, but met no hidden foe. Telouet scanned the path ahead, armour chinking softly as they ran. Nothing moved in the darkness beyond a few startled night birds, fluttering from swaying bushes. The solid blackness of the observatory soon loomed above them.

'Who goes there?' the tower guard challenged.

'Daish Kheda!' Several swordsmen echoed Telouet's bold declaration.

'Stand forth and be recognised.' The guard lifted a cautious half-shuttered lantern before bowing low.

Kheda sheathed his sword to unlock the door of the tower. 'Telouet, keep watch up above. Sirket, take the fire into the lower room. We are not to be disturbed.' Kheda took the guard's lantern and went in, leaving the doorway to the assembled swordsmen.

A vast circular table dominated the round room at the bottom of the tower. Sirket looked across it to his father, the glow from the embers he was holding casting mysterious shadows up on to his face. 'What do we do now?' His voice was tense, his hands steady.

Kheda smiled encouragement. 'Light the brazier.' He touched a spill to the glowing coals and went to light the lamps set in sconces around the wall. Then he took off his helm and rubbed a grateful hand through his sweaty hair.

As Sirket busied himself with a small iron fire-basket set on a slate plinth below the window, Kheda took a fine gold chain from around his neck and found the key to unlock a tall cupboard recessed into the wall. Inside, narrow boxes of ironwood with looped brass handles were packed tight. Kheda removed one and set it on the table.

Sirket looked up from tipping the live coals on to a bed of charcoal. 'Mesil was saying we should keep the keys to the ciphers inside the compound. An invader could take this tower before attacking us.'

'If invaders ever set foot on one of our residence islands, we abandon every cipher we've ever used and start with a clean sheet of paper.' Kheda unlocked the box. 'I worry about spies more than invaders in the ordinary course of things. Too many people come and go through the compound, even if they have to pass Serno and his men to do it. Up here, it's easier to see someone skulking where he's no business and only you and I hold keys to this place.'

Leafing through papers in the box, he pulled out the single sheet that hid the particular variant of the cipher agreed with the Gelim bird master woven in a cryptic riddle of its own. Kheda quickly translated the simple message. Then he did it again. He took a deep breath and studied every encoded character and its counterpart in turn. The message remained the same.

'Those of Chazen flee magic. They beg for sanctuary or a clean death as you may decree.'

'What does the Gelim message say?'

Kheda looked up from a fruitless attempt to wring a different meaning from the words to see Sirket using a small bellows at the base of the fire-basket. The lad's face was running with sweat.

What can you read in my face?

'I'm not sure.' Kheda walked round the table to throw the screw of paper on to the charcoal where it flared into ash.

Such a suspicion cannot be left for another to read, not even my son. Not till it's proved beyond doubt. That Gelim's spokesman ever wrote such a thing, even in cipher, is bad enough.

Kheda took another deep breath but could still feel the blood pulsing in his throat. 'Let's see what fire and jewels can tell us.' He returned to the cabinet and removed a small box from a top shelf.

'Father?' Faint alarm coloured Sirket's curiosity as he took a highly polished sheet of brass from a hook on the wall and laid it on top of the coals.

'Pay close attention.' Kheda smiled reassurance as he opened the little box to reveal gemstones shining softly in the lamplight. 'This is a divination only to be used on the most serious occasions.' He threw a scatter of uncut jewels on to the warming metal. They rolled and slid, irregular shapes polished to reveal their natural beauty.

'Take heed where they move in relation to the earthly compass and the arcs of the heavens,' Kheda said softly. 'Watch for any change in colour.' He pulled a sheet of paper towards him and took up a reed pen; ink ready to hand on the table.

Sirket glanced involuntarily at the window to check the stars. Kheda didn't look away from the stones. He closed his ears to the low voices outside the door, to the sounds of the night beyond, ignoring the stifling heat of the room.

As the metal grew hotter, the gems began to move. An emerald shifted furtively, edging towards the north. A yellow spinel startled them both by suddenly rolling on to its side where it knocked into an amethyst.

'What does it mean?' Sirket asked breathlessly.

Kheda kept his eyes on the stones, not looking at the notes he was making. A few blots wouldn't alter their meaning. A sapphire was sitting motionless to one side. Was it his imagination or was that blue darkening? A small topaz danced over towards the east. Kheda studied a ruby as it rocked slowly to and fro.

'Go up above and read the sky for me,' he said slowly. 'Read the cardinal square and then draw a triangle from the south.'

That's where the trouble's coming from. Let's see what you make of it.

'As you wish, my father.' Sirket set his jaw and left the room.

Kheda was still watching the gemstones.

Yes, that sapphire is definitely getting darker. That's an ill omen; some powerful man threatens them. The ruby and the emerald together like that speak plainly of evil to the south. It's an evil that spinel, gem of innocence, fears so much it seeks the shelter of the amethyst. So the Daish domain will need trusted allies. But that topaz warns of treachery. Treachery coming from Chazen or betrayal by some carrion lizard like Ulla Safar? Diamond, carnelian and moonstone are all unhelpfully still and mute.

Kheda scooped the gems back into their box with a fold of reed paper. Finding a square of soft leather in a drawer in the table, he used it to lift the brass plate from the coals and hang it back on its hook.

What now? The sky gave no hint earlier so, realistically, it's unlikely Sirket will see anything new. Reading the flight of Janne's birds is the obvious next step but that will have to wait for dawn. Almost every divination needs daylight, doesn't it? Moonlight's too chancy to use for reading omens when such a potent danger as magic is suspected. Is that significant in itself, that all other means of enquiry are barred to you? Of course it is. You must go and see what's happening for yourself.

Kheda rapidly returned everything to the cabinet and locked it securely. Catching up his helm and crossing to the door, he hailed one of the swordsmen who'd escorted him. 'Tell Serno to signal the *Scorpion* in to shore.' That was the only ship he would want carrying him south if there was even the possibility this rumour of magic was true. 'Signal them to pick up Atoun.'

As the man ran off, Kheda shouted up the stairwell. 'Telouet! Sirket!'

'My lord?' The slave's voice echoed down from the top of the tower.

'Come down here.' Kheda turned to the remaining guards. 'You three, we need a deer calf. Find a game trail and don't come back till you've got one.'

One of the men he'd designated glanced up to the dark bulk of the mountains, the chainmail fringing his helm jingling. 'The deer won't stir till first light. Will that be soon enough?'

'Bring it to the compound.' Kheda nodded as Telouet appeared on the stairs, Sirket behind him. 'My son will read the entrails.' He glanced up at Sirket and smiled at the youth's startled face. 'You've stood beside me often enough. You can do it. Was there anything new in the sky?'

'The triune reading showed nothing at all.' Sirket all but spat his frustration. 'The Canthira Tree's in the arc of fear and foe but there's nothing else there to hint at what we might be wise to fear. The Spear rides in the arc of death and passion but there's no heavenly jewel anywhere close, nothing to give any hints as to where to concentrate our own strength or what violence our enemies might be threatening us with.'

Is that absence significant in itself? All our divinations tie us to the threads of past and future, as we discern patterns in the events that have brought us to this present and chart their unseen unfolding for our better guidance. There's no force disturbs the natural order of such things so completely as the foulness of magic.

Aware that everyone was watching him closely, Kheda smiled, unhurried. 'We're done here. Get rid of the fire and lock up, Sirket. You three, escort my son to the compound when he's ready.' He turned and began walking down the path to the compound, Telouet at his side.

'Why does Sirket have to read the deer calf's entrails?' demanded Telouet.

'Because we're taking a ship to the south.' Kheda walked rapidly on feet unpleasantly moist in the muffling leather of his leggings. He could feel the clothes beneath his armour soaked in sweat.

'Is that what that message asked you to do?' Telouet asked warily.

'I read some complex omens in this.' Kheda's tone dared the slave to challenge his evasion. He halted at a fork in the path. 'I'm going straight down to the beach to wait for the *Scorpion*. Fetch me a few clothes, nothing too elaborate. Tell Janne and Rekha I'll send a message bird as soon as I have news.'

Telouet stood stubbornly still. 'My lady Janne won't

like the idea of you heading south without a clearer idea of the perils there.'

'Then you can be grateful that she's not a woman like Chay Ulla who takes a lash to any passing slave if something displeases her.' Kheda grinned at Telouet.

The slave didn't smile back. 'She'll slap your face for you when we get back, if she thinks you deserve it.'

'Not for the first time,' agreed Kheda wryly. 'Which is why I'm going to be waiting on the beach while she's securely locked in the compound.'

Telouet shut his mouth on further protest and turned on his heel. Kheda took the other path and soon reached the beach. The hurrying feet of fishermen racing for their boats had churned the fine white sand. There was no one to be seen now; even the little lamps above the hanging nets had been doused. Kheda walked slowly along the strand, looking for anything unusual cast up on the shore, any sign of unseasonal activity by the crabs or the other denizens of the lagoon.

'All that was, all that is and all that shall be are indivisible. We dwell in the present but everything we see, we see in the invisible light of what has gone before. The future can be illuminated by that radiance if we see how it is struck from the facets of nature. We must learn to see every separate sign and interpret its meaning for the whole.'

They had been standing on this very beach when his father had spoken those words. Daish Reik had heaved a large stone high above his head before hurling it into the air. All the children had cheered as it crashed into the water.

'You think that stone is gone? Not at all; you just cannot see it sunk in the sand. But you can see the sand clouding the water. You can see the ripples running across the lagoon. Look at those ripples. Those tell you that net frame over there will soon be shaken. If it's not anchored safely, it might even drift loose. If you realise that in time, you might be able to pull in

the nets, strengthen the knots, shelter it with a skiff in the water.'

'But how would we know what to do for the best?' Kheda remembered asking.

His father had tousled his hair. *'That's a lesson for another day.'*

Have you learned your lessons well, now that everyone's fate depends on how you judge these ripples spreading up from the Chazen domain? Is your father trying to tell you something through that memory? What would Daish Reik have done? That's no puzzle. He'd have gathered all the information he could and then acted more quickly than anyone was expecting.

Kheda looked out over the lagoon to see the *Scorpion*, black against the star-filled sky, her oars plashing in the water. He'd named her himself, for the way the vessel's upswept timbers rose in a half circle above the stern and for her reinforced bow beams reached outwards on either side of the ram. The anchors they held on either side of the prow looked like claws to him.

Is there an omen there? The scorpion foretells chastisement, bitter retribution for arrogance. It's certainly my duty to punish anyone who'd bring the foulness of magic into my domain.

He watched a small boat emerge from the trireme's shadow and row for the shore.

'My lord.' Telouet came running on to the beach just as the little boat grounded in the shallows. 'My lady Janne is most unhappy about this.' He let a securely tied pack slide to the ground.

'My lady Janne does not make such decisions for the domain,' said Kheda tersely.

Telouet didn't relent. 'Why can't we wait for couriers to bring clear news? Chazen Saril will surely be sending an emissary. He cannot want war with us.' He thrust a water skin at Kheda. 'Drink, my lord.'

Kheda considered his reply as he gratefully quenched his thirst. 'The Gelim headman says they're fleeing magic,' he told Telouet simply. 'I have to see for myself and quickly.'

Telouet stood silent, mouth half open, then abruptly snatched up the pack and strode to the water's edge. 'Right, you sluggards, put your backs into it! Let's get aboard.'

It won't do to vent your feelings on hapless oarsmen, however much you envy Telouet that release. Daish Reik taught you better than that.

Kheda climbed into the little rowing boat. Besides, his slave's disrespect was enough to spur the rowers to carry them to the waiting trireme with impressive speed. Once aboard, he hurried to the stern platform.

'My lord.' The shipmaster was waiting in front of the twin tillers that governed the pair of great stern oars guiding the lean ship's course.

'Jatta, set a course for Nagel,' Kheda ordered tersely.

'Nagel?' The commander of the domain's swordsmen stood beside the shipmaster, newly arrived himself from one of the heavy triremes now visible just beyond the surf-crested reef that guarded the island's anchorage.

'Later, Atoun.' Kheda interrupted the heavyset warrior with an apologetic wave. Atoun fell silent, dark eyes alert beneath thick brows still black as jet for all his wiry hair and beard were greying. His muscles were still as hard as any man's twenty years his junior. Of an age with Janne, his experience had proved invaluable to the domain time and again. His presence reassured Kheda until he wondered how the warrior would react to an assault by magic.

'Let's be about it!' The tall shipmaster in his long robe snapped his fingers at the helmsman waiting in his seat set just forward of the upswept curve of the sternposts.

He waved to the rowing master waiting down in the gangway running the length of the ship, a black gash separating the two halves of the upper deck that hid the three ranks of rowers below. At the rowing master's command, the piper sitting amidships sounded the warning note that brought every oar up and ready. At the cane flute's next sound, every blade crashed into the water and Kheda felt the vessel surge beneath him.

'My lord.' Telouet appeared at Kheda's side with a small wicker cage.

'Thank you.' Kheda took it and descended the steep stair down to the gangway, walking rapidly forward to the steps leading up to the bow platform. As he skirted the piper sitting on the wooden block where the mast could be stepped, toiling oarsmen glanced sideways as their lord passed, their eyes a curious gleam beneath the shadow of the deck.

Kheda paused to smile at the rowing master who was as always roving up and down the gangway. 'I want to reach Nagel by dawn.'

'We'll do it in one pull, won't we, boys?' The rowing master smiled encouragement at the oarsmen as the piper signalled a slightly faster rate with his flute.

The ten men of the sail crew waited calmly beneath the shelter of the bow platform, ready to rig the mast or take a turn at an oar. The bow master bowed a dutiful head to Kheda as he took the steps up to the platform narrowing to the vessel's sharp beak. Up above, the vessel's guard of ten swordsmen sat patiently on the unrailed side decks, scanning the sea in all directions. The four archers were gathered on the bow platform for a brief discussion before separating to keep watch on either side at prow and stern. Each carried a full quiver of arrows for all potential enemies and signalling besides.

Opening the little wicker cage, Kheda caught the

augury dove within with a careful hand. The little white bird blinked with confusion but rested calmly enough as he drew it out and threw it high into the air.

Where will it fly? Will it condemn this voyage before it's even started?

The dove wheeled above his head, fluttering awkwardly, bemused by the darkness. Then it dipped abruptly down and headed straight back to the cages stowed in the carpenter's domain beneath the stern platform. Kheda heard the rearmost rowers chuckling.

The rowing master came forward, looking up from the lower gangway with a broad grin. 'It wants to be let back into the cage with the rest of them.'

'No help there then,' muttered Telouet.

'A sign that we should reserve judgement,' Kheda said firmly, descending the steps and striding back down the length of the trireme.

Atoun was waiting impatiently on the stern platform. 'What's happening in Nagel that we need to make a night voyage?' He glanced out to sea where the heavy triremes with the best of the domain's warriors were waiting. The *Scorpion* was both narrower and shorter, a fast trireme designed for ramming, not for carrying or landing a fighting force.

'Chazen boats are coming ashore in some number,' Kheda explained. 'Bringing men, women and children. I want to know why.'

'It's no invasion, not at this season,' said Atoun with a decisive shake of his square-jawed head. 'Chazen Saril might be a fool but his warriors wouldn't follow him into a campaign that would bog down in the rains before it was halfway done.'

'It seems the Chazen people are fleeing some calamity,' Kheda said carefully. 'It seems to be coming from the south.'

'There must be some confusion. There's nothing to the south of Chazen.' The shipmaster Jatta moved to join them, a head taller than all three other men. 'I've heard Moni Redigal would dearly love some turtle shell trade of her own,' he added. Atoun wore his hair and beard cropped close as befitted a fighting man but Jatta favoured narrow braids for both in the manner of elder islanders and village spokesmen.

'She can go on wanting,' Telouet said robustly. 'Redigal Coron would never launch an invasion just to please her.'

'Chazen Saril doesn't have an heir of age of discretion,' Kheda remarked thoughtfully.

'Which always makes a domain vulnerable,' nodded Atoun.

'A domain that's worth having.' Jatta pursed sceptical lips. 'What's Chazen got that anyone would want so badly?'

'Turtle shell and a few paltry pearl reefs?' Telouet wondered derisively. 'Shark skins and whatever whalebone they find washed up on their beaches?'

Kheda was considering a different aspect of the puzzle. 'Even if Redigal Coron, or should I say his faithful advisers—' The other men laughed. 'If Redigal ships were attacking Chazen, they've got a straight course down from their own waters. They hold sizeable islands due north. Why would they be sailing all the way round the domain and attacking from the south?'

'They'd have to swing out so wide into the open ocean. That's insane.' Jatta shook his head decisively. 'With the rains due any time after the dark of the Greater Moon.'

'You find this as much of a puzzle as I do.' Kheda nodded briskly to Atoun and Jatta. 'Let's hope we find some answers on Nagel. Signal the heavy triremes to follow at their best speed.'

As Jatta relayed the message down to the rowing master who passed it forward to the bow master, Atoun yawned.

'I'll get some rest, with your permission, my lord.'

'Of course.'

As Atoun lumbered heavily down the steps to settle himself in the cramped stern stowage with the messenger birds and the ship's carpenter, the penetrating note of the signal horn sounded out from the prow. Kheda turned to look past the upswept stern timbers that carried the runs of close-fitted planking up into a curved wall. The heavy triremes were forming up to follow the *Scorpion*.

'Let's see if they can keep up,' grinned Jatta as he settled himself into his own chair, raised just behind the helmsman's seat. The helmsman leaned forward, gripping the twin steering oars in capable hands.

Kheda slipped past Jatta to the small area of stern deck behind the shipmaster's chair, pretty much the only place to sit on the *Scorpion*'s upper level where a man could risk sleep without the immediate danger of rolling off the side of the vessel. No fast trireme tolerated the extra weight of rails.

'You're not warning them of what you suspect?' Telouet asked quietly. Unbuckling the leather strap of his bundle, he unrolled the outermost layer. It was a blanket. 'Here, it'll get colder than you expect.'

'There's been no word that the evil Chazen's people are fleeing has arrived on our shores.' Kheda glanced at Jatta's back as the shipmaster settled himself in his seat but the man's whole attention was on the vista beyond the narrow prow of his ship. 'I don't want to raise unnecessary fears.' He set his jaw. 'This could just be hysteria fired by rumour, maybe even a deliberate falsehood spread by whoever's attacking Chazen.'

'In their determination to claim a slew of sandy rocks that only a turtle could love,' muttered Telouet sarcastically. He took a second blanket for himself and hunched, glowering, beside Kheda.

And if it's not falsehood, if there's some appalling truth in this, then we do all we can to stop whoever might be wielding magic in these reaches, in spite of every warlord's laws and judgements. If it takes every man's life to stop it spreading into the Daish domain, that's a worthwhile trade of our blood.

Kheda shivered involuntarily in the cooling breeze garnered by the speeding ship. The dark isles of his domain slid past in the silver sea. No lights showed. Every village would be as empty as the one outside his own compound. His people would be cowering in their hidden refuges, the old, the young and the women, at least. The spokesmen that every village chose would be gathering the farmers, the fishermen, the hunters from the hills, readying themselves to repel any invader, determined to hold until some detachment of the warlord's swordsmen could come to their relief. The swordsmen would be as resolute, intent on defending the islands they had been plucked from, whose labours supplied their needs.

Ahead, he saw a single fishing boat slide behind a black zigzag of rocks, laggard behind its fellows. Where the channel opened out into a wider sea, another trireme kept watch. At Jatta's command, the great horn announced the *Scorpion*'s passage south. The ship creaked and vibrated beneath Kheda, the piper's measure regulating the steady oar strokes, the splash and rush of the water a ragged counterpoint to the flute. The piper began a tune now that the rowers had their rhythm, though one with the constant beat that the oarsmen demanded. Voices floated up from below; the ceaseless murmur of encouragement and guidance from the rowing master and the regular banter of the sail crew bringing water to the thirsty rowers. An abrupt hammering told everyone that the carpenter was making some running repairs, nothing unusual in that. The rowers pulled ceaselessly on their oars. Soon the swift trireme had left the heavier vessels far behind. Lulled by the motion of the ship and the hypnotic gliding waters, Kheda dozed fitfully. Every time he jerked awake in a muffled rattle of chainmail, the moons were a little further in their course.

The next time he opened his eyes, the sky was paling and all at once it was dawn. The sun rose brighter than any beacon, throwing new light on the scatter of islands ahead. Beyond, Kheda could see the sprawling bulk of Nagel, its heights marching away into the distance. This was an island of fire mountains but the boiling craters of the live peaks were far inland. Here the tree-clad slopes ran down to pale beaches of coral sand.

Kheda threw off his blanket, scouring the drowsiness from his eyes with the back of one hand. As he stood, he saw a dolphin leap from the foam arrowing out from the trireme's bow, sparkling drops flying from its fin. It plunged back into the sea but another cut across the vessel's spreading wake, then another.

'There's an omen for us, and one of the best!' He pointed and Jatta relayed the news to the lower deck. As the rowing master and bow master spread the word, Kheda heard a muted cheer from the weary rowers. The piper moved seamlessly from the gentle tune he had been playing to a spirited dance measure and the humming of the rowers rose up from below.

They passed the outlying islets and Kheda scanned the Nagel shore. The first sign of life was a collection of huts built on low stilts along the high-water mark.

'Only to be expected, that they'd be deserted this late in the dry season,' observed Telouet bracingly. He swung his arms to ease stiff shoulders. 'I really do hate sleeping in armour,' he said with feeling.

'Everyone but the hardiest fishermen will have moved to the cool of their heights a full cycle of the Lesser Moon since,' Kheda agreed.

This really is a senseless time of year for anyone to launch an attack. But there is no sense in magic, is there? That's its wickedness, its wanton chaos, throwing all the unity of nature into disarray.

One of the archers keeping watch on the landward side of the trireme's split deck gave a sudden shout. 'Wreckage!'

At Jatta's word, the rowing master gave the order to slow and the rowers counted down their strokes in unison. Kheda moved for a clearer view. The hull of a fishing skiff lay upturned on the beach. The mast sprawled broken beside it, spars and sail tangled. Movement was just discernible on the sands; crabs were busy around bedraggled tangles of cloth. There was no one to be seen but the archers knelt braced and ready, arrows nocked. The *Scorpion*'s swordsmen rose to their feet.

Telouet looked at the upturned hull. 'What do you suppose happened there?'

'It's not breached anywhere that I can see.' Kheda shrugged. 'Anything from a freak wave to a sea serpent could have rolled it over.'

'It's the season for them,' Telouet acknowledged.

'Let's make for that,' Kheda ordered, pointing at a column of smoke rising in the distance.

Jatta's curt commands were relayed and the ship moved along the shore.

'My lord.' One of the sail crew stood on the gangway below them. He offered up wooden cups of water and a bowl of cold sticky saller grain.

'Thank you.' Kheda drank deeply, the cool water refreshing him. He scooped cold grain, nuts and shreds of cooked meat from the bowl with his fingers. The edge of his hunger blunted, he passed the bowl to Telouet still half full. 'Have you any besa?'

The slave knelt to rummage in the bundle and handed up a small silver pot. Kheda unscrewed the top as Telouet rapidly ate his share of the breakfast. As he scrubbed his teeth with a finger dipped in the tiny black grains, the pungent seeds cut through the sourness of sleep in his mouth. He handed the pot back to Telouet as the trireme passed a narrow promontory, which hid a marsh-fringed river mouth. A drift of small boats clustered on the mudflats below a tall tower whose beacon was throwing thick black smoke into the air. Figures huddled around the boats, their hanging heads and hunched shoulders wretched and defeated. A line of men with fishing spears, hoes and saller scythes stood ready to stop anyone making a break for the shelter of the broad-leaved lilla trees fringing the beach. As some watchman on the tower saw the trireme, a harsh horn sounded frantically.

'Call a boat out to us.' Kheda waited as Jatta ordered a signal from the trireme then drew a deep breath. 'Let's see what's washed up here. Get your men fed and watered as quickly as you can.'

He watched, outwardly calm, as a fishing skiff rowed out towards them. Apprehension crawled down his spine like some insidious insect. One of the sail crew came up to sling a ladder over the trireme's stern, and as Kheda turned to climb down, he caught Telouet's eye.

You're as grim-faced as I've ever seen you, my faithful slave.

Pausing on the ladder, Kheda recognised the spokesman of one of Nagel's larger villages waiting in the boat below. 'You're Gauhar, aren't you?'

'There's a woman ashore claims to be Itrac Chazen, my lord.' Stocky, with the more tightly curled hair of a hill dweller, the man looked up, consternation plain on his brown face.

Kheda smiled reassurance at the man. 'Who does she have with her?'

'Ordinary folk, a lot of them hurt.' The man shook his

head dubiously. 'They have Olkai Chazen with them but she looks close to death.'

Kheda turned back to the trireme. 'Telouet, bring the ship's remedy chest.'

Telouet passed the ebony casket down. Kheda sat as Gauhar leant into his oars and pulled for the shore. As they drew closer, Kheda could see a patterned cloth had been stretched to make a shelter between the boats lying all askew on the mud. An ominous number of figures lay prostrate beneath it. 'What manner of injuries do these people have?'

'Broken arms and ankles.' Oar strokes punctuated Gauhar's words. 'Burns.'

'Some fool could have let a fire spread, people getting trampled in the panic running riot after it?' hazarded Telouet.

'It wouldn't be the first time.' But Kheda heard the doubt in his agreement so turned to studying the hastily beached boats on the shore instead. The largest was no more than a despatch galley, rowed by a mere ten men to a side, each with a single oar.

Hardly a vessel a Chazen wife would ordinarily travel in. Doubtless prestige is a secondary consideration when fleeing for one's life.

Kheda bent to unlace his leggings as Gauhar drove the bucking boat through the turbulent water where the river fought the sea.

'My lord.' Telouet frowned with disapproval.

'We don't want them getting wet, do we?' Kheda stripped off the detested encumbrances. Gauhar pulled beyond the reach of the river and turned for shore. Mud hissing beneath the hull, the boat grounded close to those so unexpectedly cast ashore. Shallow ruffs of surf rippled around them and swept up the beach

'I don't suppose they'll want to make a fight of it but

I'm going first.' Telouet jumped over the skiff's prow into the knee-deep waters. Kheda followed, relishing the soothing coolness of the sea on his sweaty feet. Muddy sand, gritty with fragments of shell, oozed beneath his toes.

Kheda made a rapid survey of these unknown unfortunates. Most were humble islanders, in plain cotton clothes, with hands and faces hardened with toil, wind and sun. They stood, eyes dutifully downcast, salt-stained and soot-smudged. A few wore dishevelled remnants of slaves' and servants' clothes; finer cloth, silk-embroidered, less serviceable for the hardships of flight over the seas. He could see sprawling bruises on just about every exposed limb, some plainly footprints. Several islanders had torn their sleeves away to spare their touch on raw and angry burns while most of the servants held up painfully blistered hands. Two children, faces grey with pain, clutched obviously broken arms.

'We beg for sanctuary.' A woman in a torn tunic of sea-green silk embroidered with azure waves scrambled out from beneath the makeshift awning. 'I am Itrac Chazen.' Her voice was high and strained and she snapped her mouth shut with an audible click of teeth. She was tall and sparely built, much-mingled blood favouring her with a honey-coloured skin and long black hair. Kheda remembered that flowing sensuous to her waist with barely a curl in it. Now it was tangled and sandy, twisted up into a fraying knot bound with a scrap of cloth. She wore one long earring of turquoise beads but its pair had been torn from her other ear, leaving a dark stain of dried blood on her neck. The silver chains around her neck were tangled and broken and the heavily carved rings on all her fingers were black with filth.

'I recognise you,' Kheda replied with smooth courtesy. 'What brings you to my shores?'

What was it Janne told me about you? Barely older than Sain for one thing, third wife and married less than a year. Not yet a mother. Rekha said something about you managing some promising trades, even with your paltry share of Chazen's limited wealth.

The woman hesitated, then spoke hurriedly. 'I beg your care for our wounded. Olkai Chazen is near death.'

'I'll do all I can. Telouet, bring the remedy chest.' Kheda walked forward to meet Itrac.

If you've got a weapon concealed beneath those sodden, ragged clothes, I'll eat those cursed leggings. Besides, even if you have got a knife, it can't be large enough to threaten chainmail.

'There.' Itrac pointed beneath the fluttering shade of the awning.

Several women sat huddled together on the ground, heads bandaged, faces grazed. One lay on her side, arms folded tight across her belly, eyes screwed tight on fear and pain. An older man lay motionless on his back; blood crusted around his mouth and nose, a blank-faced child helplessly fanning inquisitive flies away with a dirty hand. Two bruised and salt-stained slave girls knelt either side of a woman who murmured with pain as she tried to roll from side to side. The girls restrained her with gentle hands, faces taut with concentration. A single length of the finest cotton covered their mistress so that all Kheda could see was the callused soles of her brown feet.

'Let me see.'

At Itrac's nod, the girls lifted the cloth aside and Kheda knelt on the muddy sand.

'Send Gauhar for honey, as much as he can find,' he said to Telouet. 'Have you made her drink?'

'We have been trying,' Itrac quavered. One of the slave girls nodded wordlessly towards a brass water jug with a long curved spout.

'Well done.'

For all the good it might do.

Kheda forced his face into immobility as he studied Olkai Chazen's injuries. If he hadn't known her nigh on all his life, born Olkai Ritsem less than a year after himself, he'd have struggled to recognise her. She lay naked, thanks to whoever had had the sense to strip her burning clothes from her. Her right side was largely uninjured, her right hand loosely curled, fingernails painted, garnet-studded rings gleaming silver. Her left hand was burnt to the bone, fingers clawed and blackened. Deep burns covered the left side of her body from shoulder to knee, splashed across her stomach and thighs, raw flesh weeping, framed by charred and blistered skin.

You raised that hand to fend off the fire.

Then the flames had flared upwards, to sear away her hair, leaving that side of her skull burnt to black stubble, face swollen and cracked, crusted oozing eye surely blind. Kheda winced as she moaned softly, lost in a delirium of pain.

'How did this happen?'

'We do not know.' Itrac's brittle defiance bordered on hysteria. 'It was dark. We were attacked. Everything was set alight.'

'Sticky fire?' Telouet looked down at Olkai's injuries with undisguised horror.

'Perhaps.' Kheda bent to sniff. There was no hint of sulphur or resin hanging around the wounds. He sat back on his heels.

Perhaps, if someone threw a pot of sticky fire right at her, catching her full in her belly. Who would do such a thing? You don't use sticky fire against people. You throw pots of it to set light to thatch or to scatter flames across the ground to ward people off.

'Gauhar, let these people gather firewood in the forest

and leatherspear for their burns.' Kheda turned to open the remedy chest. 'Telouet, set me some water to boil.' He found the small glass bottle he sought and turned to Itrac. 'You let the water cool and then mix this into it. One measure like this to that ewer full of water.' He unstoppered the bottle and shook fine crystals out on to his palm. 'Wash the wounds with it, as gently as you can.'

Itrac stared at him, hugging herself, shaking. 'But the pain—' She couldn't force the words out.

'I'll ease that.' Kheda opened a compartment at one end of the chest and took out a crystal vial. Finding a silver spoon, he carefully measured out drops of viscous golden fluid. 'Lift her head, carefully.'

One of the slaves, tears trickling down her face, cradled the unburned side of Olkai's head in her hands with infinite care. Kheda eased the spoon between her slack lips, pushing at the gummy spittle clogging her mouth. Bending close, he heard an ominous hoarseness in Olkai's breathing.

A strong enough dose of the dappled poppy and I could ease all your pains. Is that what I should do? Your life is surely done, for the good or ill of your domain. How can I hope to bring you through such injuries? Would you want me to, when you'll be scarred and crippled, even if you should live? A living omen of ill luck? Forgive me, Olkai, I have to try, if only to bring you to your senses long enough to tell me what you know. I have to think of my own people first.

'When you've bathed her wounds, cover them with honey, as thick as you can.' Kheda replaced the vial of golden poppy syrup and closed the chest. 'Wash it off and renew it at dawn and dusk.'

'Will she live?' Itrac asked hoarsely.

'We can but hope.' Kheda took a breath before continuing. 'Keep some honey aside. Mix a spoonful in a cup of boiled water as well as three spoonfuls of lilla juice and a pinch of salt. Tell Gauhar I said to give you everything you need. Clean out her mouth and then spoon it in. Don't stop. As soon as she's drunk one, make another cupful.' He stood and looked at Itrac. 'You've people here with broken bones. I'll set them as best I can and then do what I'm able for those who were trampled. You must tend everyone else's burns. Split the fleshiest part of the leather-spear leaves and lay the pulpy sides on to the wounds.'

'My lady Itrac.' Telouet was looking around the beach, frowning. 'Where are your body slaves?'

'I think they died to win us time to flee.' Itrac burst into sudden tears. 'It was horrible. We were attacked. Savages came out of the night to slaughter us all—'

'Walk with me. Telouet, see my orders are obeyed.' Kheda's stern command at least did something to quell the stir of consternation among his own islanders now gathered round. The Chazen islanders were raising fresh laments prompted by Itrac's words.

Telouet raised his voice to purposely drown them out. 'My lord grants them fire. We need kindling. Gauhar, fetch an ember from the tower's signal fire.'

Kheda caught Itrac by the elbow and led her some way along the beach. Too distraught to stand on her dignity, she didn't resist. When he was satisfied they wouldn't be overheard, Kheda turned, his face hard. 'Do not make your people's plight worse than it has to be, with point-less reminders of what they have suffered. Nor do I want you spreading useless alarm among my people.'

Itrac stared at him, shocked.

'I must do my duty by my domain,' Kheda warned her. 'As must you. You're the only one here to look after these people with Olkai so gravely injured. Now, before I can grant you sanctuary, I must know exactly what you flee. Tell me everything you saw, everything you heard, every-thing you suspect. For my ears only, mind you. Otherwise

I'll have my men drive you all back into the water.'

As he'd hoped, his harsh words turned Itrac's thoughts from her distress to her responsibilities.

'We were visiting Boal,' she began slowly. 'Me, Olkai and Chazen Saril. We wanted to talk to the islanders about the turtles. They'll be coming soon, with the rains. We wanted to decide which beaches would be left and where they could gather eggs. Saril wanted to see for himself.'

Kheda suppressed the desire to hurry her through such irrelevancies. He could see the same desire on Telouet's face as the slave came up to stand unobtrusively behind Itrac.

Is there any significance to an attack on Boal? It might be one of the largest of the Chazen islands but it has little to recommend it beyond some arid farmland on its northern face and the turtle beaches facing the southern ocean. It's no great prize.

'There's a nice residence we keep on Boal.' Itrac reached unconsciously for a bracelet she no longer wore. 'All the village spokesmen brought us gifts. There was to be a feast.' Her distant eyes suddenly fixed on Kheda. 'They came at sunset.

'Out of the setting sun, so we couldn't see them for what they were until it was too late. Besides, why should we expect any attack? Their boats were strange, so slight, so crude, just hollowed from a single log with the men standing and paddling. How did they do that? How did they not overturn out on the open water?'

She didn't wait for Kheda to answer. 'They were all but naked, leather loincloths, painted in wild colours, feathers and horns in their hair and around their necks. They didn't even have metal heads to their spears, just fire-hardened wood sharpened to a point. Their weapons killed all the same; men, women, children, they all died. They used clubs of studded stone as well, smashing skulls, breaking bone.' She was shaking without ceasing, hands knotted together, not feeling the rings digging painfully into her flesh.

'There were hundreds of them, howling and killing. There was so much blood. Saril called for the horns to be sounded, the beacons lit to summon all the island's men but no one could hear him and the wild men were still coming ashore, They hit out at everyone. All they wanted to do was kill. Everyone was screaming. There was so much blood.' Itrac's eyes were still fixed on Kheda but saw only her horrifying memories

'Ket, my body slave, and Stiwa, that was Olkai's, you remember? They found bows from somewhere. The hunters of the village, some of them found theirs. The arrows, they burst into flames. The arrows just burned as they flew through the air.' Her voice trailed off in disbelief.

'And then,' Kheda prompted gently.

'We ran—' Itrac stumbled over her words. 'We ran for the residence. The swordsmen barred the path as long as they could but the wild men kept on coming. They didn't care how many of their own died. There were always more of them. Then the ships started burning. Fire was falling out of the sky, out of nothing. How could that be? Everyone was screaming and the wild men were cheering. Then the fires started falling on the residence. That's when Olkai was burned.' Tears poured down Itrac's face.

'All right, that's enough, calm yourself.' Kheda reached out and gripped Itrac's hands until the tremors racking her slowed. 'Did you understand their tongue?'

The unexpected question stirred Itrac from her waking nightmare. 'No. I never heard the like. I never saw the like of such people either, nor heard tell of any, not in any domain.'

Nor had Kheda. 'What did Saril do?'

'He told Ket and Stiwa to get us to a boat.' Itrac swallowed a sob at the thought of her lost body slave. 'We had to leave. I had to look after Olkai. He said he had to get back to Sekni and the children. They were all at the dry-season residence. Oh, Daish Kheda, what will have happened to them?' Itrac stared at him, appalled.

'There's no way of knowing.' Kheda resolutely turned his mind from all he could imagine. 'Did Chazen Saril get to a trireme?'

'He got to a fishing boat, I think,' Itrac said dully. 'But there was so much fire and smoke, I can't be sure. Then Ket and Stiwa got us to the despatch galley but the wild men attacked as we were pushing off. When we got clear, we found we'd lost them both. I don't know if they're alive or dead, any of them.'

'It's possible we may yet have news of them.' Kheda released her hands. 'I've had word that Chazen triremes are holding the Hyd Rock.'

Itrac stared, mouth open. 'Chazen Saril lives?'

'It's possible, but no more than that, I cannot lie to you. As soon as I know anything for certain, I'll send you word.' Kheda looked back towards the boats. 'We had better get back to Olkai.'

Itrac hesitated, uncertain. 'What happens now?'

'You may have sanctuary here, on this shore and beneath the trees, within reason. Gauhar's people will feed you and help tend your wounded, ' Kheda said firmly. 'I will sail for the Hyd Rock and find out what I can. Whatever happens, I will summon all my warriors to fight these invaders.' He smiled at Itrac. 'Go on. Tell your people they are safe.'

'I will. Thank you, Daish Kheda. We of Chazen are in your debt.' Itrac moved slowly at first, then began walking with more purpose, her back straightening, her head lifting.

'She didn't say anything about magic,' commented Telouet quietly.

'Would you?' Kheda asked sardonically. 'If you were seeking sanctuary from people who can cross an ocean balancing on hollowed-out logs and call a rain of fire down from an empty sky. What else could it be?'

'Then why do you risk giving these people sanctuary?' Telouet grimaced. 'Attacked by magic is touched by magic and magic corrupts everything it touches.'

'Wise men have written that an innocent victim of magic should not be condemned,' Kheda said slowly. 'They'll be tainted by its touch, true enough, but it's suborning magic, deliberately calling it forth, that's the true abomination, according to many sages. Besides, we have to fight it. We cannot just run before it like storm-tossed birds. There are talismans to turn its malice aside, aren't there?'

Telouet looked unconvinced. 'What do we do now, my lord?

'I'm not going anywhere till the heavy triremes catch up with us. Then all the crews will need to be fed, watered and rested. While they're doing that, we can send a message bird to Janne and Sirket. Who knows, they might have news for us as well.' Kheda shrugged. 'I want every fisherman Gauhar can spare sent out to scout for other Chazen survivors. They can spread the word that they're to be sheltered for the present. Then we make for the Hyd Rock and see what those Chazen triremes can tell us. Hopefully we'll find out just what disaster has come up from the south and if it's likely to come any further north.'

CHAPTER THREE

'What if Chazen Saril is indeed dead?' Telouet handed Kheda a cup of water.

The warlord drank it down gratefully. Even with the breeze of their passage over the water, the sun was still punishingly hot. He was still in his armour but he'd discarded his helm before it could broil his brains. 'Then we offer however many of his ships have fetched up at the Hyd Rock the choice of flight, death at our hands or swearing allegiance to the Daish domain.'

'Offering fealty's their only sensible course,' declared Atoun.

'If Sekni Chazen is still alive, and with some of the children, they might think different.' Seated in his ship-master's chair, Jatta was leafing through a small book bound in battered scarlet leather, locks on its three clasps.

Kheda could never see Jatta consulting his book without recalling Daish Reik's pointed advice.

'Leave the business of sailing to your shipmasters and see to your own responsibilities. Do not get too curious either; a true seamaster will give up his first-born child before he'll share the secrets of his routes.'

Every shipmaster made a record of the seaways he travelled, both those open to any ship wishing to traverse a given domain and those supposedly permitted to local vessels only. Allegedly unbreakable ciphers hid notes of landmarks, warnings of every lurking reef and sandbar and peculiarities of tide and current to help or hinder. 'I hate to say it but I think it's highly unlikely Sekni Chazen still lives.' Kheda handed the cup back to Telouet. 'Even if she does, I cannot see her trying to establish a regency when there's no child anywhere near an age of discretion.'

'No ship will hold out for Sekni or Itrac, come to that, not now they're in our waters,' opined Atoun robustly.

'Not and commit themselves to returning to a domain overrun by mysterious invaders who burn everything in their path.' Telouet looked meaningfully at Kheda.

The warlord shrugged, face non-committal. 'Let's hope Chazen Saril is still alive.'

The other men looked at him in some surprise. Kheda met their stares, composed.

'If he's alive, we round up every last one of his ships and men and send them back to join him in driving off these invaders, whoever they may be. If he's dead, we either wait for these wild men to come north and attack us or we take on the burden of claiming the domain and dealing with its difficulties ourselves.'

'Neither being an inviting prospect,' Atoun acknowledged.

'And Ulla Safar, Ritsem Caid and Redigal Coron might well object if we seized Chazen lands,' Jatta observed as he returned his attention to the seas ahead of the trireme.

'Ulla Safar would flog his oarsmen to bare bones, if he thought he could claim some Chazen island,' growled Atoun. 'He'd love to see us with his forces on either hand.'

'Ritsem Caid wouldn't stand idly by while Safar did that.' Telouet shook his head.

'No, he wouldn't.' Kheda got to his feet. 'So we could find the Caid domain attacking Ulla troops to the north while we were embroiled with Safar's men down here, with the ships fleeing Chazen getting in everyone's way. That would leave these invaders digging in, quite undisturbed and doubtless making ready for their next step north to our lands.'

The silence between the four of them was surrounded by the rush of water, the piping flute and the creak and splash of the oars.

'So we're all going to be pleased to see Chazen Saril's fat face safe and sound,' Atoun grunted.

'And we'll show him appropriate respect,' said Kheda mildly. 'How soon will we be there, Jatta?'

'We're slowing a little in the currents hereabouts.' The shipmaster gestured to a line of shoals and reefs off towards the south. The dark scar stretched across the azure sea fore and aft of the *Scorpion*, foam boiling up where the furious waves forced themselves through the scant fissures between the rocks.

'The Serpents' Teeth should give these invaders pause for thought.' Atoun looked with some satisfaction at the natural ramparts. 'They've always broken Chazen ambitions.'

'Chazen Saril has always been content with his lot.' Kheda found himself hoping Saril was still alive and not just for reasons of governance. The southernmost warlord of the entire Archipelago might be inclined to indolence but there was no malice in him. Kheda let slip a wry smile.

Remember when you told your father how you envied Saril's lesser burden, with his circumscribed domain and its scant resources, goaded beyond endurance by Daish Reik's expectations? You expected a tongue lashing, if not a beating, not his booming laughter.

'You'd better be the best foreteller between the southern ocean and the unbroken northlands before you wish for another man's life. Who knows what lies beyond the next rains for any of us?'

Neither of us realised those words had the ring of portent, did we, my father? Neither of us foresaw your death before those next rains had ended, leaving me ruling the domain, barely married to Janne, not even as old as Sirket.

'They're putting up sails back there.' Telouet was looking past the sternposts to the heavier triremes following the *Scorpion*.

'They'll be pulling their canvas down soon enough.' Jatta clapped the helmsman on the shoulder. 'Cai was born and bred in these waters. He knows how contrary the winds are.'

Cai grinned as he concentrating on feeling the ship's course through the twin stern oars. Kheda noted the helmsman's own book of sailing notes tucked securely by one thigh.

I wonder how soon Jatta will be telling me he's willing to see Cai raised to command of his own ship, a despatch galley or such? Well, he'll have the pick of the domain's best mariners to replace him, for the warlord's personal trireme.

Kheda glanced back at the heavy triremes surging in their wake. Unlike the *Scorpion*, such ships drew their whole crew from the particular island whose produce supplied them, spare sons opting to serve the domain by taking up an oar instead of a plough or a hunting spear.

Jatta's head snapped round as they all heard a flurry of horns passed from one ship to another.

'They're changing course.' Telouet squinted across the brilliant sea.

'The signal is to summon help for one of our own, under attack.' Jatta's angular brows met in a scowl above his beak of a nose.

'Then we join them.' Kheda's voice was untroubled; his face a bland mask but apprehension twisted around his gut like one of Sain's flowering vines strangling a sapling.

Is it come to this already? Have these invaders come north in the night? Are we going to be sunk with fire and magic before we even reach the boundary of our own waters?

Jatta whirled round to shout orders down to the rowing master. The sweating oarsmen strove to turn the narrow ship in an impossibly tight circle. Jatta joined Cai in hauling on the twin tillers as the seas seethed around the biting blades.

With the *Scorpion* rocking, struggling back through the waters the rowers had just stirred up, Kheda saw the heavy triremes surging behind a narrow islet of white sand topped with a sprawl of dusty green brush and the darker tufts of nut palms.

'We can cut round up there.' Jatta was standing at Cai's shoulder, pointing, and his route book open in one hand. Absently, he fingered his braided beard. The scars and calluses he'd earned as a rower in his youth were vivid on honey-coloured skin bequeathed by some distant ancestor from the north where Aldabreshin territories touched the unbroken barbarian lands.

Atoun tapped an impatient foot on the close-fitted planks of the deck, oblivious to Telouet's exasperated glare. The toiling oarsmen hauled the trireme past the little island; the rowing master and bow master both pacing up and down the lower gangway, shouting exhortations.

The channel opened out ahead of them. Thanks to Jatta's short cut, the *Scorpion*'s course now lay alongside the heavy galleys as they ploughed through the strait.

'It's a Chazen merchant galley.' Jatta's contempt rose above the noises of sea and ship. 'Chasing down a low galley of ours.'

Reefs forced the *Scorpion* away to the side. As the trireme hastened towards clear water Kheda got a good view of the chase underway ahead.

The low galley was one of many such vessels linking the myriad islands within every domain. Men sat three to a bench and sweated over their oars on a single open deck.

Shipmaster and helmsman shared a meagre stern platform canopied against the sun. A square-rigged mast stood
always raised behind the first six banks of oars, twice that
number behind. At the moment, the Daish men were
dropping their sail in a confusion of cloth. The great galley
had three masts to their one, so no wind would help them
outrun this pursuit. Their only hope of escape was their
smaller ship's shallower draught as they sought to skip
across the reefs cutting through the strait, heading straight
for the *Scorpion*.

'I hope that helmsman knows his shoals,' murmured
Jatta fervently.

The low galley darted between two spiky reefs; the
roaring sea splashed right up over the Daish ship's shallow
sides, soaking her unprotected oarsmen. The great galley
couldn't follow and seeing the heavy triremes bearing
down on it, wallowed in the deeper waters in an attempt
to turn its course to the channel where the *Scorpion*
waited.

'Do they think they can pass us?' scowled Atoun derisively.

'They're not slowing,' Telouet observed.

'They're heavily laden,' said Jatta thoughtfully.

'And heavily manned.' Kheda could see archers lining
the side rails of the upper deck and the glint of sun on
chainmail armouring the men behind them. Rowers
would be sweating on the middle of the three levels below,
thirty banks of three oars to each side. Great galleys were
happy to take the weight of so many men in trade for the
muscle needed to propel their vast cargoes between
domains. Kheda took a moment to judge the Chazen
ship's speed between two usefully prominent clumps of
wind-tossed palms. Yes, the great galley was certainly
heavily laden; that was probably all that had saved the
lesser galley thus far.

*What's in your capacious holds? Trade goods, or Chazen
troops to attack helpless Daish vessels, to seize Daish land
now you've been driven out of your own?*

'I don't think they fancy their chances just now,' said
Atoun with grim satisfaction.

Belatedly, the shipmaster of the Chazen great galley
had ordered a sudden stop. The sails on the three tall
masts were being struck. The oars on one side began
backing while the others dug deep with new urgency.

'He's going to try and make a run for it.' Jatta glanced
at Kheda.

'Ram him before he can make the turn,' Kheda ordered.

The shipmaster barked the order to the rowing master
and the piper's note sounded shrill and rapid. The
Scorpion's swordsmen and archers ran for the prow, to
find a safe handhold for the collision and to be ready for
the fight that would follow.

'Signal to the heavy galleys to make ready to board.'
Kheda moved to call down to the bow master, who hurried
to the prow. As the signal horn drowned out the flute's
voice, the rowers marked their own time with a low
rhythmic growl, an ominous sound as the trireme bore
down on the enemy.

'They're a good crew,' said Jatta dispassionately. The
great galley had all but made the whole turn as the *Scorpion*
drew near.

'Aim for the stern,' Kheda told Jatta. 'Cripple their
steering.'

The shipmaster moved to take one of the *Scorpion*'s
two tillers from Cai.

Kheda recalled the conversation he'd had with Daish
Reik, the first time he'd been in a battle at sea, just a little
older than Mesil.

*I've heard tell hitting a ship at the wrong angle can rip
the ram clean off a trireme. And very silly we'd look without*

it. Which is why you'll see the helmsman match their course as soon as we hit.' Daish Reik had been smiling with vicious anticipation, teeth white in his black beard. *'Besides, the ram's built separate from the hull just in case he gets it wrong. We won't sink. Now hold on to something.'*

Kheda took a firm grip on the shipmaster's chair. The *Scorpion* surged through the sea, the white beaches and the myriad greens of the shore flashing past.

'They're yielding!' came a shout from somewhere.

Kheda shook his head at the hoarse cries of the Chazen galley's frantic signal horns. 'Too late.' The *Scorpion* was already within a ship's length of the great galley.

The trireme's brass-sheathed ram ripped into the planks right on the waterline. A shudder ran the length of the *Scorpion*. With a grunt forced out of every man aboard by the impact, it was as if the ship herself groaned. Cai and Jatta threw all their weight against the twin tillers. The crossbeams at the *Scorpion*'s bow, reinforced where they projected on either side of the ram, crashed into the galley's side, springing the weakened seams of her planking still further. The jutting timbers smashed the great galley's rearmost oars. Screams came from the galley's middle deck as rowers were clubbed by their own splintered oars sent in all directions.

'Back!' yelled Jatta.

The rowing master had already set the oarsmen to dragging the *Scorpion* back from the great galley. Water poured in through the gash in the wounded ship's side and she began listing almost immediately. The sea was suddenly full of men desperately trying to swim clear of the foundering vessel amid a confusion of broken and flailing oars.

There was a second crash and then a third as two Daish heavy triremes drove their prows into the great galley. Their rams rode higher than the *Scorpion*'s, designed more to bite and hold fast to make a bridge for swordsmen intent on boarding. The stricken vessel shuddered, already sunk to her oar ports. The warriors on the great galley threw their swords into the sea in open surrender as the deck filled with all those who'd been below decks fleeing the encroaching waters.

Kheda saw women and children struggling in the confusion of noise and panic.

They're not raiders. They've fled whatever disaster it is that's ravaging Chazen. I need to know where they've come from, what they've seen.

He took a step forward. Telouet stretched out an arm to bar his way. 'You'll go no closer to their archers than this, my lord.'

Kheda turned to Atoun who was watching the Daish swordsmen taking possession of the galley with visible frustration. He pointed to a man feverishly ripping pages from a book to let the heedless wind blow them away to oblivion. 'Bring me that shipmaster!'

Rope ladders were already slung over the *Scorpion*'s stern and Atoun disappeared at once, soon reappearing in a small boat rowing for the ruined galley.

Kheda sat in the shipmaster's chair watching the great ship sink to rest on a hidden reef, uppermost deck knee deep in water, only prow and sternposts rising clear of the sea. Every time a wave lapped at the wreck, the sound of breaking wood rippled through the air.

Close at hand, the sounds of hammering and urgent repairs reverberated through the *Scorpion*. Kheda leaned forward to call to Jatta.

'What's the damage? Are we still fit to sail for the Hyd Rock?'

Jatta came halfway up the stairs from the lower gangway. 'There're a few seams need caulking and there's the usual damage to oar loops and such. Nothing we can't bear.' He disappeared again.

'My lord.'

Kheda turned to see what Telouet was looking at.

'I don't think he was going to wait to pay his duty to you,' said the slave thoughtfully.

One of the Daish heavy triremes was escorting the lesser galley whose aid they had come to. The smaller ship was limping along with several broken oars and Kheda could see his own swordsmen on the deck. One was on the stern platform and the sun glinted on his naked blade.

'Let's see what he has to say for himself.' He looked to see if Atoun was on his way back.

The two mariners arrived at much the same time. Unhampered by the naked blade in one hand, Atoun drove a battered and hangdog man up the ladder before him, Telouet standing over him with a ready sword as soon as he set foot on the deck. The master of the lesser galley stood proud on his own stern platform as his vessel drew up smartly beside the *Scorpion*. Gaudy pennants flapped from the poles supporting the canopy fluttering just below the deck level of the *Scorpion*. The Daish mariner judged the distance to a nicety, jumping to catch hold of the rope ladder and climb lithely aboard.

'My lord.' He knelt on the deck and bowed his head to the planking.

'Your name?' Kheda stayed in the shipmaster's chair, face impassive.

'Maluk, great lord.' He looked up, eyes bright.

Kheda considered the equally bright gleam of gold in his ears and around the man's neck. He did not smile. 'And you, of Chazen?'

'Kneel before Daish Kheda!' Telouet threw the man down on to his knees. He slumped, chin sunk on his chest, hair matted and cotton tunic stained with blood from a split in his scalp that Kheda judged to be a day or so old.

'Chazen man,' Kheda said sharply. 'What is your name?'

Telouet would have reminded the man of his manners with a smack round the head but stilled at Kheda's look.

'Rawi, great lord,' he mumbled.

The warlord noted a hint of uncertainty cross Maluk's face. 'What brings you uninvited and flying no flag of mine to grant you passage through my waters?' he asked mildly.

Now Rawi looked confused. 'We were told to flee, to take all we could carry and flee.' He shivered despite the baking heat of the sun. 'My lord's soldiers came. They drove us all from our homes, threatening to club us if we tarried. They said we would die if we stayed. They said an enemy had come—' He broke off, swallowing hard, and raised horror-struck eyes.

Kheda could see the man's quandary reflected in his eyes.

If you warn me of magic, will I be grateful or just put you to death where you kneel?

With hopeless resignation, Rawi opened his mouth.

Steel in his voice, Kheda interrupted. 'Why were you pursuing my ship?'

'We were not alone. There were skiffs with us, fishing boats, anything that would float.' Rawi shot Maluk a look of pure hatred. 'He has followed us for a night and a day, picking them off. We took as many aboard as we could—'

'We sought only to protect the Daish domain,' Maluk declared robustly.

'From what, exactly?' Kheda queried sternly.

'We feared invasion, great lord,' Maluk insisted with a little too much wide-eyed innocence. 'We thought men of Chazen were come to steal our islands. The beacons were burning!'

'Men of Chazen? Come to raise battle with their

families in tow?' Kheda stood to look at the two heavy
triremes where the tally of bound and kneeling swordsmen
was at least equalled by women and children, the decks
now cluttered with hastily filled sacks and roughly tied
bundles, all sodden and wretched. 'Didn't you look for
help to tackle a ship so much stronger than your own?'

Maluk spread uncertain hands. 'We signalled to other
ships and to villages that we passed with our lanterns. I
don't know if they saw us. No one came to our aid. But
we dared not lose sight of the enemy,' he continued, a
little bolder now. 'We had to know where they might land,
my lord. Then we would have carried word to the nearest
beacon towers, to summon your warriors.'

*A claim impossible to prove or disprove. And there are
sufficient fighting men aboard Rawi's galley to justify Maluk's
assertion that he'd feared invasion. All the women and children would have been below decks, and every man driven
from his home by threats of unspecified foes would have carried
a weapon if he could. So, hoping to get away with it unseen
but confident in his excuses if not, Maluk's been raiding this
Rawi's haphazard flotilla, claiming whatever loot he could
for himself. And then, well aware his life was all but forfeit
for sailing in my waters without a pennant to authorise his
passage, the Chazen shipmaster finally turned his great galley
on his tormentor. Proving this Maluk's ill faith could doubtless be done, if I had half a season to spare. I don't have half
a day. I have to get clear of this tangle and make best speed
to the Hyd Rock.*

The *Scorpion*'s stern platform was an island of silence
in the uproar of wood and water all around, every eye on
Kheda as he considered the choices before him.

*Don't think you can hurry me. I am the warlord; my word
is law. Mine is the right of life and death over all of you.*

'Every life is woven into a myriad others throughout the
course of each passing day. Every child is born of a web of

*ancestors and grows to be half of a union giving rise to unfore-
seen lives. Never take a life without considering all the possible
consequences. Breaking a single thread can be all but invisible or utterly catastrophic.'*

We had been walking in my mother's garden just after
dawn. Daish Reik stopped by a dew-jewelled spider's web,
suiting his actions to his words. His first touch had left the
shimmering pattern unaltered. The second had destroyed it.

*How many are already dead, thanks to Maluk and Rawi
both? The pattern of life and death, past, present and future,
must already be pulled this way and that. How can I cut
through this tangle they have made between them? How can
I make it plain beyond doubt that I will not permit Chazen
ships to wander at will through my domain, any more than
I'll tolerate Daish hunters preying on the helpless? I cannot
sail south and leave undeclared warfare to strangle my
domain.*

Kheda looked at the expectant Maluk, plainly all too
ready to spring up from his knees and return to share his
loot with his crew. Beside him, Rawi hunched, staring
hopelessly at the deck planks.

Kheda looked beyond the pair of them to Atoun and
to Telouet, giving both warriors an infinitesimal nod.
Atoun stepped forward and jabbed the tip of his long
curved sword into Rawi's side, just below his ribs. Rawi
stiffened involuntarily, his back arching away from the
pain.

Telouet's similar thrust startled Maluk who had turned
to gape at Rawi's whimper. Instinct brought his head up
and back as Telouet's sword was already sweeping around
and down to behead him in one clean stroke.

Atoun's blade flashed in the sun. Rawi's body fell
forward, blood gushing from the stump of his neck in a
sprawling arc that spattered the toes of Kheda's booted
leggings. His head, sightless eyes still startled, rolled

towards Maluk's headless torso. Telouet stopped it with one foot, looking a question at Kheda.

'Throw then both into the water.' The warlord kept his face impassive. 'If all that Rawi had become in life cannot be returned to his birthplace in death, then his body can feed the fish hereabouts and share whatever goodness lay within him with the Daish domain. I do not see that he deserves burning to ash like some unregenerate evildoer. I don't feel inclined to delay to see Maluk restored to his people though. I'm not convinced they would benefit by his influence on their future. Let the sea wash away his transgressions.'

Telouet sent both heads overboard with rapid kicks and moved to catch Rawi's corpse by one flaccid hand. Atoun grabbed at Maluk and threw the dead man overboard without ceremony. The abrupt splashes brought faces round on all sides, the shock of realisation plunging everyone into a spreading circle of silence broken only by the incautious cries of a child and the murmur of sea against sand and wood against rock.

Jatta startled Kheda by throwing a bucket of seawater over his feet and the deck of his beloved ship.

Might that blood have shown some pattern of omen? You didn't think to look in time, did you?

Kheda bit back a rebuke for the shipmaster and looked out over the water, noting a plethora of little vessels as the local islanders had come to see what this commotion might portend for them.

'Jatta, tell the helmsman of Maluk's ship that he is raised to the mastery and if he wants to keep that rank, never mind his own head, he had better return whatever loot was stolen from the Chazen fleet.' Kheda's face was hard. 'Atoun, summon some of those skiffs and send word to all the local villages that they are to shelter these unfortunates until I send word that the people of Chazen are to sail once more for their homes. We of Daish will do our best to defeat whatever vileness has attacked them, not least because it's in our own interests to secure our southern borders. Telouet, tell the men and women of Chazen that my mercy will last only as long as they cause no trouble. If they cannot accept our kindness with due humility, they will be driven out to meet whatever doom awaits them. Village spokesmen are to send word to Janne Daish of any such trouble. Jatta, I want to be ready to sail for the Hyd Rock as soon as may be. The heavy triremes are to follow as soon as they can set these Chazen people ashore.'

Kheda folded his arms slowly. Everyone else sprang into action.

This news will doubtless spread faster than the light of a burning beacon. Good. Everyone will benefit from learning that Daish's warlord has absolutely no intention of letting this unforeseen catastrophe undermine his authority.

Jatta returned to stand before Kheda. 'I would like to take on some more water, while we have the chance.'

'As you see fit,' Kheda nodded. 'Then we must make best speed.'

Once Jatta was satisfied the helpful locals had supplied sufficient fresh water to replenish the *Scorpion*'s casks Kheda rose to yield the shipmaster's chair. A rapid flurry of orders set the trireme on her way. Kheda walked the length of the ship along the side deck, Telouet striding along between him and the drop to the water.

Finding some release for the tension knotting his back and neck, Kheda returned to the stern platform. 'This crew have done far more than we should usually ask of them,' he remarked to Jatta. 'We must make sure they are suitably rewarded.'

Atoun stood beside the shipmaster's chair. 'We must assess the situation at the Hyd Rock and once we know

Chazen Saril's fate, we must decide where to send our triremes.'

'I'd advise blocking the seaways to these invaders and all those fleeing before them,' said Jatta grimly. 'This haphazard fighting will spread quicker than contagion if we don't pen the Chazen boats in.'

Telouet grunted his agreement.

Kheda shrugged. 'The first thing we need to see is what is at the Hyd Rock.'

The men all fell silent, looking ahead past the narrow upcurve of the prow as the doughty rowers, still unflagging, drove the trireme westwards through the turbid, raucous waters bounded to the south by the Serpents' Teeth. The sun beat down, striking blinding light from the shimmering surface of the sea. Finally, after what seemed like half a lifetime, the rocks and reefs petered out to leave the irregular broken hulk of the Hyd Rock standing alone among the waves.

'Ships!' The cry from the watchful archers in the prow was immediately drowned out by Jatta's shout. 'Chazen vessels!'

Atoun immediately looked aft to check the position of the domain's heavy triremes. 'We don't land without a full complement of swordsmen, my lord,' he said bluntly.

'How many ships?' Kheda moved to get a clearer view of the triremes anchored in the shallow curve of the little island's northern face.

'Four,' murmured Jatta. 'Two heavy, two light.'

Kheda grimaced. 'That's no great strength.'

'They've brought more than their usual crews with them,' said Telouet dourly. 'You can barely see the sand for people.'

Not that there was much sand, just a narrow strip of storm-soiled beach with a few clusters of stunted palms sheltered by the brutal black outcrop that made the whole southern side of the islet a wall of rock.

'Let's hope there are plenty of fighting men, to carry the battle back to their enemy before we have to risk any Daish blood,' Kheda remarked.

'I wonder how many wounded they have.' Telouet scanned the shoreline cluttered with awnings and fire pits.

'Chazen Saril's pennant!' Jatta stood to point at an azure finger of silk waving on the sternpole of one of the fast triremes.

'Then he's alive!' exclaimed Telouet.

'If he isn't, I'll use it to hang whoever thinks he's some right to fly it,' Kheda promised. 'Raise my own standard.'

Atoun was already hauling up the scarlet silk scored with the sweeping black curves that proclaimed Daish authority.

'I want our heavy triremes anchored so that none of them can break out without my permission,' Kheda said abruptly.

'I'll give the signal.' Jatta pointed at a battered skiff bobbing beside one of the Chazen heavy triremes casting loose to make its way across the water towards the *Scorpion*. 'There's a boat.'

'Telouet and Atoun, I'll want your counsel.' Kheda put his helmet back on and wordlessly accepted the detested leggings from Telouet. The blunt toes made his feet cursed clumsy as he climbed carefully down the ladder slung over the *Scorpion*'s stern. Mindful of his sword, he settled himself as his slave and his commander joined him.

'Where is Chazen Saril?' Atoun demanded with a scowl.

'Ashore, honoured master, great lord,' replied the man at the oars, shrinking in an attempt at a bow, encumbered as he was.

Kheda sat upright in the stern of the boat, face calm. He didn't move when the man at the oars drove them aground, waiting for Telouet and Atoun to jump over the side. Both scowling ferociously, they splashed through the waves to scatter those waiting open-mouthed and apprehensive on the sand with the threat of their drawn swords.

'Remember you are always on show, my son. Someone is always watching you, be it in awe of your power or because they're wondering if they might find a way to fill you full of arrows.'

'My lord,' Telouet turned and bowed, 'you may come ashore.'

And it won't do to trip and fall flat on my face in the surf. Kheda stepped carefully over the side of the boat. At least the sea water seeping into his leggings cured the sweaty itch plaguing his feet.

Chazen Saril came hurrying through the crowd, hands outstretched. 'Daish Kheda, I am relieved beyond measure to see you here.'

'And I you.' Kheda clasped the southernmost warlord's hands as custom dictated. He felt an entirely unceremonial tremor in Saril's fervent grip.

A drowning man couldn't hold on tighter. All of you look worse than people who've suffered a whirlwind breaking their huts into kindling and bringing the seas to surge over their crops and pens.

Chazen Saril's plump face was drawn with weariness, dark shadows smudging the coppery skin below eyes so dark brown as to look black. Blood and char stained his once elegant white silk tunic, the gossamer fabric of a sleeveless overmantle rich with golden embroidery torn and snagged in numerous places. The diamond rings on his fingers and the braided chains of pearls and gold around his neck only served to emphasise his dishevelment.

Mighty warlord of the Chazen domain, you look as shaken and confused as little Efi woken from a nightmare and not yet realising a father's arms are around her.

'You bring a great many men to this resting place for rowers.' Kheda smiled to soften his rebuke. Reminding Saril of established agreements might be necessary but this was no time to start a fight over something so trivial.

Saril had no time for any such niceties. 'This is the only place for us to make a stand. We are invaded—'

'I know.' Kheda cut him short. 'I have spoken with Itrac.'

'She lives?' Saril gaped at him. 'And Olkai?'

'Itrac does well enough. I have granted her and her people sanctuary for the present.' Kheda held Saril's gaze and allowed his pity to show in his eyes. 'Olkai is burned, very badly, very deeply, over much of her body.'

Daish Reik had never thought much of Saril's skills as a healer but Kheda saw the man knew what he was being told. His mouth quivered and a tear he could not restrain spilled from one eye. 'Have you news of Sekni?'

'No, I'm sorry,' Kheda said with genuine regret. 'We've heard nothing.'

Saril turned his head aside, grimacing as he struggled not to weep openly.

So much for envying Saril the freedom to marry as his fancy prompted, himself a sufficiently meagre catch to be allowed romantic liaisons with lesser daughters.

'You're weary and overburdened, that's only to be expected.' Kheda looked at Telouet. 'Where can we sit at our ease, while we discuss what must be done now, for the sake of both our peoples?'

Saril looked at him with desperate belligerence. 'You must give me and mine sanctuary.'

The man's mood is veering as wildly as a pennant in a rainy squall.

Kheda hardened his heart. 'You must drive these invaders from your domain. I will give you and yours what shelter and food we can spare in the meantime, for suitable recompense in due course.'

A sigh of disappointment swirled through the crowd like the rustle of the wind-tossed palms at the edge of the beach.

Saril's expression settled in a guarded neutrality. 'Naturally.'

'And we of Daish will back your fight, on account of the long friendship between us,' Kheda continued. 'Once I know just what it is I am committing my people to.'

Saril raised his head, squaring his shoulders. 'Shall we sit?' He gestured towards a stand of three unimpressive palms where cushions had been piled. The sparse growth of the current season was dull and dry, more brown than green, older fronds from earlier years hanging down around the gnarled and swollen trunks in tattered curtains.

'Thank you.' Kheda followed Saril with slow deliberation, flanked by Telouet and Atoun.

The Chazen warlord stumbled in the soft sand, heedless of the anxious eyes fixed on him.

'Barle must be dead,' Telouet whispered to Kheda. 'He'd never let him wander about without so much as a thickness of leather between him and a blade.' If Telouet had never had much time for Saril, he'd at least approved of the warlord's personal attendant.

Kheda silenced his slave with a curt gesture as Saril turned by the scatter of cushions. 'I can offer you no refreshment beyond water.' His wave was no more than a sad shadow of his former exuberant hospitality.

'That suffices with your domain at war.' Kheda settled himself, legs crossed. The leggings dug into the backs of his knees and his shoulders protested at the unceasing burden of his mail coat. He resolutely ignored the discomfort as Telouet and Atoun stood on either side, between the two warlords, faces to the crowd, drawn swords levelled.

'There'll be more than my domain at war with these

wild invaders,' Saril retorted with some spirit. 'If we do not deny them Daish waters, they'll sweep up to Ritsem, Ulla, Endit and beyond. They may even now be burning Redigal lands.'

'I don't believe so, not yet,' Kheda countered. 'And if we fight together to deny them now, you can rally your people and strike back before they take a firm grip of your lands.'

An imperceptible hope crept into the closest faces on the edge of Kheda's vision.

On the other hand, Saril's expression hovered on the brink of outright despair. 'Perhaps we might claw back something, after the rains.'

'No.' Kheda shook his head emphatically. 'We strike now.'

Saril looked at him, uncertain. 'If we can rally my people, gather them on some lesser island.'

'Daish does not cede lands to Chazen.' Telouet glowered at the harassed warlord.

'Chazen slaves with such impertinent tongues can expect to be flogged,' Saril shot back in reply.

'I beg forgiveness, great lord,' said Telouet, his expression far from contrite.

'We will shelter your people but only until they can return to their own.' Kheda smiled to sweeten his unpalatable words. 'Better those of Chazen return home to plant their crops than labour in my domain without reaping any reward. You won't still be here at harvest, come what may.'

That much I must make sure of, or we'll never be rid of you.

'We always carry the fight to an enemy. It is for us to act and our foes to react. Daish Reik taught me that and I doubt Chazen Shas ever said different,' he said with a hint of challenge.

'That's all very well when your foes are familiar, their strengths apparent and weaknesses known. Neither my father nor yours ever had to face—' Stubborn, Saril shook his head. 'We cannot hope to carry the battle back south during the rains. I must find my people a home until then. I could look to Ulla Safar or Redigal Coron.' His hoarse voice betrayed his desperation. 'They will not spurn alliance with my domain. I have daughters nigh of an age to marry. Are you willing to see me make such an alliance? Sirket must be seeking a wife by now?'

And the honoured Janne Daish will threaten her esteemed husband with castration, never mind a slap in the face, if he agreed to such a paltry bride for their son. As for Ulla Safar or Redigal Coron, they'd not only spurn your daughters, they'd laugh in your face for suggesting such a notion.

Kheda swallowed the impulse to tell the man so. 'I have already said we will shelter you for the present. Rekha Daish will negotiate suitable recompense with Itrac Chazen once we see you safely restored to your own. As for Ulla Safar and Redigal Coron, I believe they would baulk at helping you, if magic has assaulted your domain.'

Saril hung his head, fragile defiance collapsing. 'You've heard about that.'

'Is all that Itrac tells me fact?' The miserable acquiescence on the faces Kheda could see at the corner of his eye left Saril with no room to lie. 'I charge you on the honour of your domain to tell me the truth.' Kheda spared a glance for Atoun and Telouet and saw both men frozen, appalled at what they were hearing.

The time for secrecy is past. Daish crews and warriors coming ashore to eat and drink, to make good the ravages of such a forced voyage on the ships, they'll be hearing what transpired in Chazen. I need to meet that news with a plan ready for us all to implement, to give everyone something to think about besides the abhorrence of magic.

Kheda set his jaw. 'Did you see magic used in plain sight? What did you see?'

Saril hesitated before finally answering. 'They had no ships, yet they came out of empty ocean, riding in no more than hollowed logs. They had no swords, no knives, just wooden spears and stone clubs, yet they had no fear of our blades. Why should they fear us?' He laughed mirthlessly. 'They could call fire out of the empty air, fire and lightning. They could call up waves to drown our people. And there were more of them than a swarm of bloodflies. Our arrows could not harm them. They bounced off their naked skins like sticks tossed at boiled leather.'

'My lord, if these people truly bring magic—' Already swarthy, even before a lifetime weathered by the unforgiving sun, Atoun still visibly paled behind his beard. 'What shall we do against them?'

'We kill them all.' Kheda hid his own misgivings. 'As fast and as completely as we may. If we cannot fight them in open battle, we'll burn them wherever they may be hiding, burn this foulness from any land it touches. Fire cleanses all.'

'All the more reason to attack before the rains come,' said Telouet stoutly.

'But of course, it was night and we were in no sense prepared for attack.' Saril's voice rose in sudden challenge. 'How do we know it was truly magic? Who among us has ever even seen the fakery of some barbarian wizard of the north? Perhaps it is all some cunning counterfeit to play on our fears.'

From the dubious murmurs all around, it was clear the other men and women of Chazen were convinced of what they had seen.

Kheda took a moment to be sure his voice was calm and level. 'We cannot decide how best to fight until we know just where these wild men are gathered in strength. Atoun, ask all of Chazen's shipmasters exactly where they have seen these invaders. Find out just where anyone put to flight has come from. I want to know where the closest nest of these savages may be. We can take three ships at first light tomorrow and launch a quick raid to take their measure.'

'You think we broke and fled?' Bitterness twisted Saril's face. 'That all this talk of magic is just some excuse for our cowardice?'

Well, if they were facing magic, I'd certainly back the quality of Daish warriors over Chazen's.

'I don't know what to think. Up, Chazen Saril,' Kheda commanded briskly, getting to his feet. 'It's time we looked to our own responsibilities.'

There was little change in Saril's despondent expression. 'All my responsibilities lie ravaged or scattered to the far horizon.'

Kheda kicked his knee, just hard enough to startle a look of outrage from the plump man. 'We must read the auguries, Chazen Saril, the two of us together and the sooner the better.'

Saril caught his breath. 'I had not thought to even look where the birds flew at dawn.'

'Stars above, man, that's hardly surprising.' Kheda allowed himself to show a little compassion. He held out a hand. 'You're attacked with fire above all else, so we should read ashes, agreed?'

Saril scrambled gracelessly up before looking around the meagre island, new purpose in his face. 'We need as many different woods as possible. The more widely the fuel for the fire is rooted in past and present, the clearer the guidance the ashes will offer.'

A shiver of anticipation ran through the crowd.

'Let's see what the sea has brought us,' Kheda suggested.

'Cut some palm fronds as well,' Saril ordered a hovering skein of Chazen mariners as he brushed sand from his stained orange trousers.

'These fires will have stripped all the driftwood from the beach,' said Telouet, looking at the huddled masses with disfavour.

'Then let's see what's caught around the rocks.' Kheda restrained an impulse to strip off his damp leggings and feel the sand beneath his feet. At least he could climb over the razor-edged rocks in safety if he wore them.

The great black outcrop broke into ridges and rubble at the far end of the beach. Kheda moved cautiously over the slanting slippery facets, Telouet hovering at his side. The currents that wrecked the incautious on the ominous rock had carried plenty of debris up with the tides. Bleached drifts of shells and broken crab claws were piled in the hollows and crannies.

Will those invaders come to grief here? Do they have magic to carry them over the sea's capriciousness? No, you have to turn your mind from such distractions, from the unhappy people on the beach, from the insidious doubts that you did right by Olkai, from the fear that this disaster overtaking Chazen lurks just below the horizon to come sweeping up to crash down on the Daish domain. Remember Daish Reik's words.

'You must not merely see or hear the omens; you must feel every thread that ties you to every other living being. You must breathe the air that all passed from sight have shared, that all to come will taste in turn. You must know your place in the great scheme of things and see everything from that vantage point.'

Kheda stood still to draw the salt-scented air deep into his lungs. The noises around him faded as he closed his eyes and concentrated a steady exhalation to the exclusion of all else. Opening his eyes, a sea-stained tree root immediately caught his eye. Stooping, he picked it up and as he did so, he saw a worm-eaten fragment of a nut palm's trunk cast up beneath an overhang.

'My lord.' Telouet offered him a length of rope, snapped and frayed.

'Good enough,' Kheda nodded. 'It'll all burn.'

'Daish Kheda!'

Surprised by Saril's vigorous hail, Kheda nearly lost his footing on the hostile stone. 'What do you have there?'

The Chazen warlord was hurrying up the beach weighed down with an armful of splintered spars and shattered oar blades, even a few lengths of broken planking, one tarred length blistered and burnt. 'All this should carry some memory of whatever malice propels these invaders,' he said grimly, throwing his burden to the ground with a resounding clatter.

'Telouet, pass me those palm fronds.' Most definitely not wanting to complicate matters by spilling his own blood into the fuel for this fire, Kheda carefully used his dagger to strip back the tough brown stem and tease apart the clustered fibres of the yellow core.

Chazen Saril knelt over a scrap of wood where he'd gouged a shallow hole, a notch cut in one side. He carefully placed a sharpened stick in it, the looped string of a fire bow drawn tight around it. Drawing his hand back and forth slowly at first, he rapidly increased the pace and black dust gathered around the spinning point.

'Now.' Saril kept the stick whirling ceaselessly.

Kheda piled his tinder by the notch in the scrap of wood; it showed the faintest breath of white. As Saril pulled the fire bow away, brushing sweat from his forehead with a shaking hand, Kheda gathered up the scrap of wood, blowing gently into the frayed palm fibres, just enough to coax the nascent flame, not so much as to damp it with the moisture of his breath. A gleam of gold blinked among the pale smoke. Kheda cupped his hands to shelter the tiny fire from inquisitive breezes that could stifle it at birth.

No one needs that kind of omen.

'Here.'

Saril had built a nest of sticks and Kheda tucked the little flame safely inside it. Chazen Saril fed it with powdery scraps crumbled from a rotting branch and then sat back, watching greedy golden tongues licking at the sturdier wood he had brought from the wreckage of his ships.

Kheda saw the Chazen warlord's eyes grow distant, the energy born of having a task to accomplish deserting him.

'We're not here to read the flames,' Kheda told him sharply as he stacked the rest of the fuel around the burning heart of the fire. 'It's the ashes we need.'

Saril looked up with a sudden grin that caught Kheda by surprise. 'Did you ever make the mistake of suggesting dousing an augury fire with water, just to hurry things up?'

'I did,' Kheda laughed. 'But only the once.'

'My father slapped me so hard he knocked me clean off my feet.' Saril sounded perversely amused at the recollection.

Daish Reik wasn't given to beating any of his children, always more inclined to teach through laughter, even when there was only me left to learn such vital lessons for the good governance of the domain.

'This should burn down quickly enough.' Kheda stood and looked back down the shore, pleased to see the Daish ships had organised regular ranks of cook fires, rowers taking a well-earned rest as swordsmen shared the tasks of preparing a meal and ensuring armour and weapons were ready for any battle that might offer itself. Others were spread around the island, silhouetted vigilant against the sky as they perched on the heights of the rock, eyes turned to the south.

There's no real purpose among the Chazen men, even those that aren't injured. Is that just the shock consuming them or some insidious taint from magic?

Kheda looked at Telouet and saw his own thoughts reflected in the slave's dark eyes.

Unharmed and walking wounded, they will be going ahead of Daish men, to face whatever peril lies to the south.

He glanced at the fire but it was still blazing merrily, oblivious of his burning desire to read what counsel might emerge from its ashes.

Atoun's burly figure caught Kheda's eye. The warrior was standing with Jatta and a Chazen shipmaster from one of the heavy triremes, scratching something in the sand with a stick.

Telouet came to stand beside him. 'There's a man with the sense to see this danger weighs heavier in the scales than any concerns about keeping the secrets of his domain's seaways.'

'As soon as we're done here, we need to meet with Jatta and Atoun, and whoever Chazen Saril deems worthy among his shipmasters. We'll take four ships south. We need to decide where best to set the rest, to be sure of the earliest possible warning of any move north by these foes.'

'And to discourage any fleeing Chazen who think they might escape notice long enough to dig themselves into a new home,' scowled Telouet.

'We dare not spread our resources too thinly,' Kheda reminded his faithful slave. 'If we're to drive these people out, we'll need to take a substantial force when we make our main attack.'

So as to have enough men to finish the task, if magic rips the rest to rags of sodden flesh or burns them to charred bones.

'It'll be no easy task feeding a domain's full force gathered so late in the dry season,' Telouet muttered. 'Where will you muster them? The rains are due any time after the Greater Moon shows itself; we can't risk losing half our ships if a squall hits them on a bad shore.

Will allying myself with Chazen be the right course to protecting my people or am I letting myself be carried off by a current I should have steered well clear of, to be wrecked on an unseen reef? Was Chazen attacked merely on account of lying southernmost in the Archipelago or is there some darker reason for this disaster befalling Saril?

'That's burned enough, isn't it?' The other warlord's voice startled Kheda from his thoughts.

He was surprised to see how quickly the fire had died.

'If we use gloves,' he said cautiously.

Telouet handed him a pair pulled from his belt, heavy leather reinforced with metal plates to foil a slashing sword.

'I don't have any.' Saril looked down at his hands before gazing around as if expecting his lost slave to appear with such things.

'I'll go first.' Kheda wasn't sorry to seize that opportunity. 'You can borrow these.'

Drawing on the thick gloves, he scooped a double handful of charred wood and feathery ash from the edge of the still-smouldering fire, taking a moment to judge the wind before flinging the ashes in a wide arc. In the corner of his eye, he saw all activity down the beach had stopped.

Chazen Saril backed away. Kheda stripped off the gloves and thrust them at him. 'You must throw before we look for signs.'

The Chazen warlord drew them on reluctantly. 'We're both in this together, I suppose.'

Kheda fixed him with a hard look. 'That remains to be

seen, as much as anything else, don't you think?'

Saril gathered dying embers between his hands. Heaving a sigh, he tossed the blackened fragments out across the white sand, face tense with apprehension. 'Well? What do you see?'

Kheda walked slowly round the scatter of ash and cinder, searching for some familiar outline, some shape or shadow. 'Is that a sword?'

'More like wishful thinking,' Saril replied dubiously. 'Could that be the arc of a bow?'

'No, not with so many breaks in the line,' Kheda said with regret.

Saril began a slow circuit of the soiled sand, bending to peer more closely from time to time. Coming back to Kheda, he shook his head, bemused and defensive at one and the same time. 'I cannot read anything clearly. I must be too tired, too dazed by all that's happened to be properly attuned to the portents.'

Kheda was still intent on studying the ashes. 'Can that be a snake or a sea serpent?' He squatted down to draw a finger around the shape he was seeing.

Saril gave it a perfunctory glance. 'Not crooked at that angle.'

'There must be something to see.' Kheda looked up at him exasperated. 'Some representations of the heavenly bodies, the symbols of season and reason, the arcane forms of the various domains. Tell me what you see,' he demanded.

'Confusion,' Saril answered slowly.

'Where?' Kheda looked down at the scatter of ash and sand. 'For all of us? Or just for Chazen?'

'I don't mean a portent of confusion.' Saril stared down at the sand, face slack with fear. 'All I see is confusion. I can't trace any patterns, read any guidance. This is just,' he struggled for words, 'meaningless.'

'No.' Kheda set his jaw. 'There will be a meaning in this, if only we can read it.'

'What is a portent?' Saril asked suddenly.

'A sign arising from all that is and has been, that may guide us for the future.' Kheda couldn't keep a weary sarcasm out of his voice.

'Chazen Shas taught me to think of a forest tree, that can be fallen, the whole decaying yet the broken branches taking root, nourishing new shoots. He said all portents are rooted in the past, coming to bloom in our hands, that we may see the seeds of the future.' Saril looked at Kheda, face haunted. 'But there has never been magic used here, not within the whole memory of my domain. The records of our observatory towers reach back past a hundred cycles of the most distant jewels through the heavens, those that take years to pass between one arc of the heavens and the next. How can the past show us the future when we're faced with something that has never been part of our past, left no trace?' Just as Kheda thought hysteria was going to overwhelm the southern warlord, Saril broke off and stared at him, aghast. 'I believe there's something else working its ill influence here. Didn't your father warn you how thoroughly magic corrupts the natural order? I am very much afraid that the miasma already clouds our auguries. That's why there's nothing to see here!'

'Then how are we to know what to do for the best?' cried Kheda before he could stop himself. He took a long slow breath. 'No matter. We'll just have to go south, as I said before. We'll have to see what we're facing with our own eyes.'

CHAPTER FOUR

The colour of this water's more like a river than the sea. It doesn't even have waves, it's so confined in this maze of mud and rock and oh, what I wouldn't give for some clean salt air, instead of this stifling stink.

Kheda hastily suppressed that thought before he inadvertently made any kind of wager with the future. 'Is this a course Cai's ever sailed before?'

'We've neither of us been in these waters.' Jatta shook his head, keeping his eyes fixed on the gap between two dusty islands lying half south ahead. 'We're well off the usual trade channels.' The shipmaster had his red route book absently clutched in one hand.

Kheda looked past the *Scorpion*'s prow to the stern of Saril's fast trireme, the *Horned Fish*, a precise two ship's lengths ahead, thanks to Jatta's expert guidance. 'Is it evidence of his good faith, to show us these byways?'

'He has little enough to lose.' Jatta sounded noncommittal. 'I'll warrant heavy triremes will be ready to stare us down, if we try coming this way once he's back in his compound again.'

'You'll be making your notes on these seaways though?' enquired Kheda innocently.

'I'd be remiss in my duty to the Daish domain if I didn't.' Jatta's wicked smile belied his lofty tone. 'And a little skiff on a moonlit night can generally find a quiet channel to slip past a heavy trireme.'

'Which might be useful under some different turn of the heavens,' allowed Kheda.

If not for us, maybe for Sirket in some unforeseen future. Remember what Daish Reik told you at much the same age as he is now. 'Never assume that any situation will remain as it is, no matter how long it has resisted the twists of fate.' Are we truly going to find ourselves facing magic here, in the face of all expectation?

Jatta turned a serious face to Kheda. 'Have we left our own ships ready to chase off any Chazen ships using this panic as excuse to spy out our seaways?'

'I had the signals sent before we left the Hyd Rock, and explicit orders to Janne Daish.' Kheda glanced back past the *Scorpion*'s sternpost to Atoun's heavy triremes, Saril's two vessels leading them on. 'Besides, if we can win Chazen at least a foothold back in his own domain with a rapid strike, his people will have no choice but to retreat to their own waters.'

'Do we know how many of these invaders hold this place?' Jatta was studying an island just coming into view. It was no great size but boasted the conical peak of a fire mountain rising stark and grey above thickly forested slopes. Knot trees reached down to the water and beyond, the solid ground fringed by swamps of tangled grey roots lapped by sluggish seas.

'According to everything Atoun can determine, only a small force came this far east. Chazen Saril says they will surely be keeping to this one island. It's the only land in this reach with year-round springs of water.'

I sincerely hope the assurances of the Chazen men are trustworthy. Most particularly in reporting no suspicion of magic hereabouts.

'Chazen Saril's helmsman had better know where he's taking us.' Jatta looked at a confused cluster of little islets with disfavour. 'Some of these channels are so narrow and shallow a shoal of real horned fishes would be swimming in single file.'

'There'll be scant landing, from what I hear.' Cai adjusted the *Scorpion*'s course as signal flags fluttered from the *Horned Fish*'s stern platform.

'So once we've killed these invaders, we have only the one beach to guard against any more of them,' Kheda said bracingly.

'That's Atoun's task, killing and guarding.' Seeing the *Horned Fish* slow, Jatta looked down the gangway and waved to the rowing master. The piper drew out his note and the *Scorpion* obediently loitered in the strait. Baffled by the tree-smothered islands in all directions, the currents made little headway against the rowers' determination.

Kheda raised a hand in salute as the first of the heavy triremes passed the *Scorpion*. Atoun, unmistakable on the stern platform, raised his naked sword in salute. One of the Chazen ships passed on their other flank, the shipmaster rising from his seat to sweep a low bow to Kheda. As Kheda inclined his head in recognition, he saw Saril at the stern of the *Horned Fish*, naked blade in his hand, directing the heavy triremes with urgent gestures as they surged past.

'He's going ashore?' Jatta was astonished.

'It's his domain that's been invaded,' shrugged Kheda, impassive.

'It's not the place of warlords to get themselves killed in skirmishes like common swordsmen,' Telouet growled. 'Hasn't he heard enough poets' laments to know that?'

'I don't suppose many decent poets bother coming this far south,' commented Jatta with faint derision.

'I doubt he'll go ashore. He's got no armour for one thing.' Kheda saluted Chazen Saril who was still wearing the remnants of his bedraggled finery.

The heavy triremes laden with swordsmen passed both the *Horned Fish* and the *Scorpion*, leaving the two fast ships blocking the seaway, ready to foil any escape by the unknown invaders.

'You'd have had the sense to find yourself a hauberk, even if I wasn't there to lead you by the hand,' Telouet snorted.

'Keep such thoughts to yourself when Chazen Saril's within earshot,' Kheda remarked mildly. 'Or he really will demand I have you flogged.'

'And refusal would cause such unwelcome offence.' Jatta spared Telouet an irreverent grin.

'There's the landing.' Cai pointed to a stretch of dank grey sand barely visible between the bigger ships.

The *Scorpion*'s archers and swordsmen stood on the bow platform and side decks, alert to any danger from the lesser islets that all but enclosed this anchorage. Here and there a sheer cliff of black rock rose from the shadowed seas but, for the most part, dark green knot trees with their stubby, fleshy leaves came right to the water's edge. There was no sign of movement among the twisted grey branches, and scant breeze cooled the sweat on Kheda's forehead. A scent of decay hung heavy in the air, which hummed with the chirrups of countless, nameless insects.

With rapid strokes, the heavy triremes were turning stern on to the beach, steering oars raised out of harm's way.

'Invaders,' hissed Jatta as they all saw some movement on the sand

With a rush that drowned out his words, the heavy triremes drove for the shore. They grounded hard, barely still before armoured men poured down the stern ladders, plunging through the waist-deep water, swords drawn. Dark-skinned men erupted from the tree line, howling wordless, meaningless cries.

The hair on Kheda's neck rose. 'They sound like beasts.'

'Let them die like beasts,' said Telouet fervently.

'Indeed.' Kheda heard the savage howling broken by screeches of pain with vengeful satisfaction.

'Are they breaking?' Jatta was watching the greater contingent of archers that had been gathered on the *Horned Fish*. They were sending a storm of arrows across the beach, heavier than a rainy-season squall.

'I can't see.' Kheda ran lightly along the *Scorpion*'s landward-side deck to the bow platform, Telouet at his heels. Kheda's spirits rose at the better view of the carnage ashore. 'It's true,' he marvelled. 'They're only using wooden clubs and spears.'

He pointed as Chazen and Daish blades flashed in the sunlight, cutting down the shrieking savages.

'Which can still crack a skull or skewer a man like a roasting fowl.' Telouet scanned the shore, keeping himself between Kheda and any unseen, unanticipated threat. 'And we don't know they've no slings or arrows of their own. Get behind the bowpost, my lord.'

'They're the ones being skewered.' Doing as Telouet bade him, Kheda nevertheless saw invader after invader fall to ruthless sword blows. The Daish warriors weren't even having to call on the skills honed by years of training, with no armour to foil, no razor-edged blades opposing them, ready to punish any errors of timing. A second wave of yelling men came charging out of the trees but arrows felled half before they joined battle with the steel-clad line of swordsmen now advancing up the beach.

'Let's hope we take back every island as easily as this one,' said Telouet with satisfaction.

'It's not won yet.' Apprehension kept a tight grip on Kheda's guts. 'Let's hope we don't suddenly find ourselves facing magic.'

'What's that?' Telouet started at some commotion on the *Horned Fish*'s stern platform, everyone pointing to the shore and shouting.

Kheda's heart missed a beat when he saw what was happening. 'It's Chazen's own islanders!'

'Come out from their sanctuaries,' approved Telouet with a spreading grin. 'They'll want to play their part in taking back their homes from these despoilers.'

'They've got them caught between a storm and a wind-ward shore now.' Kheda shook his head slowly. 'This is a slaughter.'

'Good,' said Telouet robustly.

Fisherman slashed at the savages with boathooks and fishing poles. Those used to tilling the soil swung hoes and rakes. Hunters carried the broad curved blades that they used for hacking through underbrush and tore into the naked backs and legs of these unforeseen foemen. Chazen islanders who'd arrived empty-handed picked up wooden spears fallen from nerveless fingers and thrust them to deadly effect. The clamour on the beach rose to a new pitch of ferocity until Atoun blew a throbbing blast on his horn. A tense hush fell pierced only by groans of agony.

Kheda saw Chazen Saril already beckoning to a row-boat creeping cautiously out from beneath a fringe of swamp trees. 'Telouet, we're going ashore.'

'My lord.' The slave didn't bother trying to argue the point, following his master back to the stern platform.

Chazen Saril waved up at Kheda from the little boat. 'My lord Daish! Let us visit our victory together!'

'Nice of him to share the credit,' muttered Telouet. 'When we brought five times his warriors to the party.'

'Rekha Daish will make him pay what he owes us.' Kheda followed Telouet deftly down the *Scorpion*'s stern ladder to join Chazen Saril in the rowboat.

As they approached the shore, the little vessel nudged

aside bodies bobbing in the sluggish wavelets, blood
vanishing in the silty water. They looked as if they'd been
savaged by wild dogs; arms and bellies ripped open, gashes
gaping in ruined faces.

*Train your men as the most ferocious swordsmen and your
domain will be protected. It will also be more at risk, because
all such men want to do is fight, while you doing your duty
as their warlord means they seldom get the chance. A ruler's
life is full of paradoxes.*

Telouet was marvelling at the corpses' scant loincloths
and few paltry ornaments of feathers and paint. 'What
kind of fool goes into battle naked as a newborn pup?'

Kheda shot him a hard look. 'A man who believes he
has something more powerful to rely on than leather and
steel.'

'But there was no fire.' Chazen Saril was looking
confused. 'There was so much fire, before.'

Eager hands reached out to draw the rowboat high on
to the shore so that both warlords could step out on to
dry land. Chazen and Daish warriors pressed close, swords
still drawn.

'Go, speak to your people.' Kheda caught Saril by the
elbow and turned him towards a slightly built man who
stood wringing his hands anxiously. 'Find out just what
else we might be facing. Telouet, let's see what the
wounded have to tell us.'

With his slave close by, Kheda hurried along the shore
where the Chazen islanders and those who'd come to
rescue them were dispatching fallen wild men with ruthless efficiency.

'Wait,' Kheda commanded curtly as he saw a Daish
sword raised above an invader felled by a blow that had
left his knees a ruin of white bone in a mess of torn flesh
now blackened with flies, his lifeblood soaking into the
dry ground.

'It's all very well remembering your training,' Telouet commented to the Daish swordsman. 'But when a man's not wearing a hauberk, why not just run him through?'

'True enough.' The Daish warrior smiled ruefully.

The dying savage thrashed from side to side, scrabbling for some weapon. He tried to throw sand into the Daish men's faces but his strength failed him and his arm fell back. Telouet scowled and planted a heavy foot on the savage's wrist, nodding to the swordsman to do the same.

'Who are you? Do you understand me? Do you know who I am?' Kheda crouched down beside the invader.

'He doesn't look barbarian,' said Telouet, puzzled.

'Not like any northerner, certainly,' agreed Kheda. Though, similar as his features might be to any Chazen or Daish man on the shore, this wild man was taller than most Aldabreshi by half a head, even the coastal people of the largest islands who tended to top hill dwellers by much the same measure. On the other hand, he was darker-skinned than even the people of the remotest heights.

'What's that in his hair?' Telouet prodded cautiously at the man's head with the tip of his sword. Even with his strength visibly failing the man tried to twist away, spitting at the blade.

'Paint of some kind?' Kheda couldn't tell if the savage's hair was inclined to curl like a hill dweller's or fall straighter, more like those with coastal blood, since it was caked solid with some thick red substance. 'Or just mud?'

The man writhed weakly, muttering something with harsh defiance.

'Does that sound like any tongue you've ever heard, any dialect from some distant reach of the Archipelago?' Kheda looked up at Telouet and the Daish swordsman.

'No, my lord.' Both men shook baffled heads.

'I've never heard the like,' Kheda admitted. 'Nor seen the like.' He stood and looked down at the dying man struggling for breath. His ribs rose and fell beneath a crudely daubed pattern of red and white discoloured with stains and sprays of drying blood. 'All right. Put him out of his misery.'

As Telouet's sword thrust ended the wild man's torment, Kheda looked around the beach. Beneath their raucous paints, the next corpse and a wounded man just beyond looked remarkably similar to the body at his feet. 'Wherever these people come from, they don't get much new blood, do they? They look close as brothers.' Kheda turned from the sight of a ruthless islander smashing the wounded man's skull with an oar shaft. 'What exactly were they using for weapons?'

Telouet bent to strip the body between them. 'That spear's no more than a fire-hardened spike of wood. This took a bit more making though.' He picked up a heavy club of coarse-grained hardwood with sharpened flakes of black stone embedded in it, blood and hair caught among them.

'Do you recognise the wood?' Kheda took the club and turned it this way and that, mystified.

'I can't tell lilla wood from nut palm, my lord. And this must have been what he called a knife.' Telouet pulled a blade of sharpened black stone from a crudely stitched leather scabbard tied to the dead man's brief leather loin-cloth.

'So how have these people put nigh on an entire domain to flight?' Kheda gave the black stone knife a cursory glance and tossed it down on the sand. 'Atoun!'

'My lord.' The heavyset warrior came running at the summons. Sweat ran in fat drops down his face to disappear into his grizzled beard. There was gore on his leggings and splashed across his sword arm and flies hovered greedily around his bloodied sword.

'What injuries have we suffered?' demanded Kheda.

'Our men took no worse than a few cuts and bruises. A few of Chazen's were caught by surprise, but they're weary and nervous besides,' Atoun allowed grudgingly. 'A couple of the islanders had their skulls split, a few won broken arms for their pains.'

'How did these wild men fight?' Kheda moved to allow two grim-faced islanders to drag the corpse from between them, the body thrown on to an untidy pile of slack limbs and lolling heads.

'Like madmen.' Atoun's grimace mixed bemusement with a degree of unease. 'No armour, weapons no better than a child's plaything and they came at us howling like heat-crazed hounds. Couldn't they see we'd cut them down like saller stalks?'

'Naked or not, they could still overwhelm us, if they have as many men as stalks in a saller field.' Kheda walked over to the heap of hated dead and frowned at a corpse with bloody froth gathered around his mouth. 'Gloves please, Telouet.' Pulling them on, he drew his dagger and used it to prise open the dead man's mouth, hooking out a chewed wad of fibrous pulp.

'What's that?' wondered Telouet.

Kheda raised the tip of his knife and sniffed cautiously. 'I don't recognise it but it smells pretty potent. Something to enrage, to dull pain? To drive men to a madness that carries them beyond fear of death?'

'Northern barbarians use drink and intoxicants to raise themselves to bloodlust,' commented Telouet.

'Then perhaps there is no magic, my lord,' said Atoun slowly. 'These apparitions come shrieking out of the night to attack the Chazen islanders, breaking heads and clubbing down anything in their path, throwing firebrands and maybe something like dreamsmokes to muddle their victims. Couldn't this talk of magic just be fear and fancy?'

Kheda shot him a stern glance. 'It wasn't some over-active imagination burned Olkai Chazen nigh to death.'

'But that could have been sticky fire,' said Telouet with cautious hope.

'Find me any scorched potsherd or scrap of naphtha cloth,' Kheda challenged. 'Find me anything needful for making such a weapon. In the meantime, let's see what tale Chazen Saril's people have to tell.'

He crossed the shore in rapid strides to join the other warlord, who was still talking to the village spokesman. 'Chazen Saril, what happened to your people here?'

'Much as befell the rest of us,' replied Saril grimly. 'These wild men came in the middle of the night, with fire bursting out of the empty air to burn the huts and storehouses while dust storms smothered any man of the village who tried to fight back. My people feared magic and fled.'

'We've seen no magic today.' Kheda said carefully. 'How is that?'

'The leader of the savages sailed west the day after their attack here.' Saril gestured vaguely towards the heart of his domain. 'He took most of his forces with him as well. He must have been the wizard.'

Perhaps, but what is it that you are not telling me? What is the secret hiding behind your eyes, Chazen Saril?

Kheda nodded slowly. 'Then we may hope, even if they have magic, there are none too many wizards to spread it around.'

Chazen Saril seized eagerly at this notion. 'Even the northern barbarians of the unbroken lands aren't overrun by their spell casters.'

'So we've taken the first step in reclaiming your domain, honoured lord,' Kheda congratulated Saril with a wide smile. 'You had better see if this island can offer any kind of accommodation appropriate to your dignity.'

'You think I'm staying?' Startled, Saril gaped. 'I didn't intend—'

'You there!' Telouet snapped his fingers at the wide-eyed village spokesman. 'Your lord requires a bath and a change of clothes. See to it!'

'It's time to take some care for appearances,' Kheda said in a low voice as the man scuttled away. 'You want to instil as much confidence in your people as possible when they start gathering here.'

'We will send signals north as soon as possible,' Atoun broke in. 'Make sure all your people know where to come.'

'You need armour,' Telouet added. 'And a personal attendant, my lord.'

'Indeed,' Kheda agreed. 'There must be someone among your swordsmen who can serve for the moment. As and when they arrive, you can choose a new body slave from those of your household who survived.'

'You are abandoning me and mine, Daish Kheda?' Chazen Saril stared belligerently at him. 'After this one paltry fight?'

'Not at all.' Kheda folded his arms and faced the plump man down. 'I am seeing you consolidate this first step to restoring you to your own.'

Saril's expression turned petulant. 'These mud islands scarcely sustain the people who live here. How are they to support the whole population of the domain?'

'I suggest, my lord, that we look to reclaim some more of your territory, to give everyone room to breathe,' Kheda retorted.

'How far is the next sizeable island? Might that make a more defensible position, offer a more fitting residence?' Even with Atoun's tone entirely respectful, there was no getting away from the impoliteness of that question.

So why aren't you indignant and demanding I chastise my

impertinent underling? Why are you just chewing your lip and looking shifty, my lord of Chazen?

'Leave us.' Kheda waved Atoun and Telouet away with a curt hand and both men reluctantly retreated a short distance. 'Whatever you tell us of your domain's resources, whatever we learn of your seaways, Chazen Saril, I swear to you that I will not look to take undue advantage in our future dealings. Take whatever augury you like, to see my good faith on this.'

'With the miasma of magic all around us? What divination do you imagine will hold true? Oh I trust you; that's not my concern. The thing is, the next island we'd need to take, to be sure of holding this one—' Saril tugged at his tangled beard, not meeting Kheda's eyes.

'It holds some secret?' Kheda tried to be patient with the man.

'It holds my brothers,' snapped Saril abruptly.

'Oh.' Kheda kept his voice carefully neutral. 'And it's vital that we hold it? If we're to keep the invaders at bay in this reach of the domain?'

'Yes.' With another of his quicksilver changes of mood, Saril heaved a defeated sigh and caught up a broken spear shaft. He sketched a rough map in the sand. 'See how the currents run? If we hold that island, we can deny these invaders the rest of this reach.'

As long as they don't have magic to carry them over the waters heedless of such things.

Kheda nodded slowly. 'Do you know if the invaders have taken it?'

Saril flung the broken spear shaft away into the trees. 'It's all but certain.'

'Perhaps these invaders merely see the island's strategic value.' Kheda hesitated before continuing. 'Or is it possible that they have some deeper purpose in taking it? Could they know what they would find there?'

'Much good it will do them, even if this is all some insane pretence to cover up an attempt to cast me from my domain.' Chazen Saril's voice was hard and bitter. 'My father may have held back from killing my brothers outright but he decreed they should be gelded and blinded, their tongues slit. There were four. One killed himself soon after. Another died when an attack of break-bone fever turned to bleeding sickness in the rains three years since. Two remain.' Saril's eyes bored into Kheda's, searching for any reaction. 'Nameless.'

'Are these nameless housed separately or together?' Kheda asked dispassionately.

'They're held together, in a compound in the centre of the island.' Saril knelt to find a seashell. His hand hovered over the map scrawled in the sand before stabbing it with the white spiral. 'I believe you owe me a secret in turn. What does the Daish domain do with its surplus sons?'

'I will only speak for my father.' Kheda wasn't about to give away anything more than he had learned. 'Daish Reik's final decree offered my younger brothers the choice of death, or of castration and passing into my hands as zamorin slaves.'

'What did they choose?' demanded Saril.

'That is none of your concern.' It might be an open secret among Kheda's household that Rembit had been born of Daish Reik and his second wife Inril but everyone knew to keep their mouths shut. 'Your concern is retaking your domain from whoever these people are, spell casters from some unknown land or mere counterfeits, intent on setting up one of your crippled brothers as figurehead in your place.'

'I must consider what to do for the best before we make any more voyages.' Saril shook his head stubbornly. 'We must see to the dead here first. Their crimes warrant burning but that would make this beach a place of ill omen and this island has no other landing.'

And you could spin out such debates with yourself and your people to lose us any benefit accrued from the battle we've just won.

'Atoun!' Kheda snapped impatient fingers to summon his commander. Telouet came too. 'This is the next island we must take.' Kheda pointed at the map drawn in the sand. 'Ask the Chazen shipmasters for only such waymarks and warnings of currents as we will need to reach it safely.'

'Do we know what forces to expect?' Atoun studied the map and pointed at the bleached white shell. 'Is that some stronghold?'

'A retreat for some afflicted unfortunates of the warlord's family,' Kheda said blandly. 'They do not suffer from anything contagious.'

Just the hereditary affliction of being born a son to a ruling lord.

'My lord Chazen Saril—'

Kheda turned ready to quell any ill-timed curiosity from Telouet but the slave was thinking about something else. 'We should be on our way to this next island before any burning of the dead. We don't want to raise an alarm for whoever awaits us with a column of smoke.'

'I don't know where we can burn them,' said Chazen Saril obstinately. 'Not so late in the dry season. We could set the whole island alight. I shall have to take time to consider this carefully.'

Kheda looked at the bodies piled up in ungainly heaps 'Have them taken to the mountaintop and thrown into the crater. They burn and your island is purified at one and the same time.'

Chazen Saril opened his mouth to protest but Telouet forestalled him.

'As you command, my lord.' The slave bowed low and turned to shout orders at the village spokesman.

'I'll be sure the ships are ready to depart.' Atoun's bow was more perfunctory, his mind already on the next assault.

'You lay a heavy burden on my people, Daish Kheda,' cried Saril angrily, jowls quivering. 'Hauling this many dead all the way up to the peak. You don't think this risks binding these invaders to this island? You don't fear the malice that brought these people here will now pour molten rock down on these defenceless forests? But now you've given your orders,' he concluded with grim satisfaction, 'I will not humiliate you by countermanding them. We will just have to wait, and for my own requirements to be met. I was about to set these people to setting up watch posts and fuelling beacons, so we might at least know if our retreat is cut off, when we set about this next conquest of yours.'

'I must consult with Jatta.' Kheda bit his tongue and walked away without ceremony.

Actually, Chazen Saril has a point there. It wasn't the most sensible thing to suggest, that the dead be thrown into the fire crater. 'Never make decisions in the heat of anger or the chill of shock.' Daish Reik is proved wiser than you yet again. Are you wise enough to meet this challenge? You may be wiser than Chazen Saril but that's not saying a great deal. Do you remember him being so prone to switching between fear and folly? What are you risking, for the Daish domain, fighting alongside a man ill prepared to meet the demands upon him?

As he crossed the beach, Telouet caught up with him. 'What now?'

Kheda's pace didn't slacken. 'We drive these savages from this next island. The sooner we hand Chazen Saril a territory he has some chance of holding, the sooner we return home and ensure all his people go back to demand his protection. Summon a boat.'

Kheda stood aloof as Telouet hailed a skiff. Once aboard

the *Scorpion*, Kheda claimed the shipmaster's seat to take the weight of the armour off his weary feet. Closing his eyes, he strove to calm himself, recalling the subtle exercises to relax his shoulders and back, arms and legs that Daish Reik's ever-faithful body slave Gaffin had taught him.

What was it he told you? 'Not as good as sleep, but good enough when there's no chance of sleep.' What else would he be telling you, him or Daish Reik? That you being irritated with Saril will only benefit your foes? Let the Chazen warlord see to his domain's concerns. You address your own.

Some indeterminate time later, Kheda heard the shipmaster's step on the deck. He spoke without opening his eyes. 'Jatta, have we been given all the water we need? Are the men fed? We don't want to go into a fight and find half of them disabled by cramps.'

'It's all in hand, my lord,' Jatta assured him. 'And something's put a goad into Chazen Saril,' he added with some surprise.

Kheda opened his eyes at that.

'He's probably afraid we'll leave without him,' Telouet mocked. He handed Kheda a cup of water, sweet with a hint of purple berries. 'At least someone's found him some armour.'

Kheda saw Saril now wore a chainmail shirt and helm. The silver-chased helm didn't match the copper-ornamented plates of the hauberk but at least he looked a little more like a warlord. 'Where's Atoun? How soon will we be ready to sail?'

'The more delay, the more we lose any element of surprise,' agreed Telouet.

'We shouldn't be too much longer,' Jatta said comfortably.

The shipmaster's confidence was justified. The sun hadn't traversed much more of the heavenly compass by the time the modest fleet set their oars in the water with a determined crash. Kheda was still pacing the *Scorpion*'s side decks through sheer impatience though.

'Come back to the stern, my lord.' Telouet spoke over the urgent note of the piper. 'We won't get there any faster if we have to stop and fish you out of the sea.'

The *Scorpion*'s swordsmen and archers keeping watch on the trireme's upper level studiously avoided Kheda's eye.

'True enough.' Kheda walked carefully back down the length of the speeding ship, curbing a desire to signal the rowing master to order an ever-faster stroke.

If they spend the last of their strength now, they'll have nothing left to get you back to Daish waters, when the time comes to leave Chazen Saril to face whatever it is that's plaguing his domain. When the time comes to make sure the Daish islands are prepared to fight any such assault, be it magic or just drug-addled wild men.

The waters opened out into a major channel and the close-gathered fleet broke free of the islands tangled in their matted swamps and knot trees. The next islands were little more than scrub-covered hummocks in the distance, fringed with white sand behind crooked walls of coral. A fresh breeze blew away the last of the muddy smell that hung around the *Scorpion*.

Kheda and Telouet sat in the shelter of the sternposts, silent as the shipmaster and helmsman guided the long, lithe ship away from the vicious teeth of the reefs, the *Horned Fish* barely staying ahead of them. They soon passed the chain of barren islets and a larger stretch of land appeared ahead of them.

'That's it.' Kheda rose to his feet.

Telouet raised a signal flag on the sternpost and the heavy triremes fanned out either side of the lighter vessels carrying the two warlords. The rowing master walked the length of the gangway, lavish with his praise for the rowers. The bow master and the sail crew waited in the prow, ready to back the *Scorpion*'s swordsmen and archers, alert for any enemy that might appear.

The *Scorpion* rounded a blunt-nosed headland to find a shallow cove protected by a sizeable reef breaking the sea into white foam. Pale sand gave way to short dusty grass dotted with tall nut palms. Their grey trunks rose in graceful sweeps, fringed fronds bleached yellow by the season waving in the breeze, their rustling echoing the susurration of the sea. Well spaced and with no brush to speak of beneath them, the trees offered nothing by way of cover to any lurking enemy.

'This is the landing the *Horned Fish*'s shipmaster told me to make for,' Jatta told Kheda.

'Let's hope this is as easy a fight as the last one,' Telouet murmured fervently, one hand on a sword hilt.

'Can you see any movement?' Kheda took an unconscious pace forward.

'Nothing.' Telouet shook his head as he reached out to restrain his master with an arm across his chest.

'Perhaps the invaders never came here?' said Jatta dubiously.

Kheda shot him a sceptical glance. 'You'd pass up a clean, open island like this in favour of those stinking mires?'

'All depends what you're used to.' Jatta shrugged.

'What are these wild men used to?' Kheda wondered aloud. 'How will we ever know, if we cannot question any captives?

'Who needs to know?' Telouet was still watching the shore, trying to see beyond the palm trees into the darker green forest behind. 'All they need to know is they're not welcome here and we can tell them that plain enough without words.'

Cai and the heavy trireme helmsmen were making a cautious approach to avoid the merciless reef. Atoun and all the warriors waited impatiently, sliding down the stern ladders as soon as the ships reached the sheltered shallows, splashing through crystal-clear waters on to the brilliant sand, staying close together, swords at the ready. Archers on the side decks of the triremes stood alert to return a killing storm of barbed arrows for so much as a thrown stone.

No missiles appeared. No enemy appeared. The only sounds to rise above the crashing of the surf were the cheerful squawks of crookbeaks foraging among the palms. Atoun signalled this way and that. The warriors broke from their defensive knots and spread out. As they approached the gently curving trees, Kheda was irresistibly reminded of beaters on the hunt, flushing out forest deer and ground fowl that he and Sirket might down with swift arrows, while Rekha and Janne flew their proud hawks at lesser birds fleeing on the wing.

'Doesn't look as if there'll be much sport today,' he remarked to Telouet as Atoun raised a sheathed sword to indicate there was no more foe to be fought.

'Chazen Saril's keen to go ashore again.' Telouet pointed to the *Horned Fish*, which was approaching the shallows, Saril standing in the prow.

Keen to learn the fate of those who'd once been his brothers? Or looking to remove them once and for all from the domain's accounts?

Kheda considered his options. 'Let's join him. This domain has no great tradition of warfare so I'm not confident he's capable of meeting an unexpected enemy.'

Jatta had already given the rowing master the word and the rowers began turning the *Scorpion* stern on to the shore.

'My lord.' Telouet went down the ladder first to hold it firm for his master. Kheda hurried down the rope rungs and they waded ashore. Kheda saw his own well-hidden curiosity openly reflected in Telouet's expression.

'You are welcome to my shores.' Saril greeted him on the beach with an incredulous grin at odds with his formal words.

'I thank you for that grace.' Kheda was looking around as he gave the customary reply 'Atoun, is there no sign of these savages?'

'None.' The warrior shook his head.

'Perhaps they never came here after all,' suggested Saril with sudden hope.

'Perhaps they've come, got what they wanted and left.' Kheda fixed Saril with a meaningful look. 'We should visit this residence you keep here.'

'Very well.' Saril chewed his lower lip reluctantly. 'With just a small escort though.'

'Atoun, pick me a few good men to go looking inland,' Kheda ordered his commander. 'In the meantime, leave a solid guard for the ships and have the rest search the shoreline in both directions. Anyone who finds so much as a wild man's footprint is to raise a horn call.'

'If we're going inland, I'll scout out the path myself,' Atoun told him robustly. 'You wait here with Telouet and follow on when I tell you, my lord.'

'As you wish,' said Kheda mildly.

'You allow your people a great deal of latitude,' observed Chazen Saril, looking with disfavour at Atoun's back.

'As long as they earn it by doing their duty in exemplary fashion.' Kheda waited patiently as Atoun allotted tasks to his warriors to his satisfaction and then gathered a small detachment around himself, running along a path no more than a dry score in the turf beneath the nut palms, disappearing over a rise some little way inland.

Handpicked swordsmen came to ring Kheda and Saril, looking to Telouet for their orders.

'When we get the signal, lads,' he told them easily.

As he spoke, Atoun's familiar whistle floated up on the breeze and Kheda looked at Telouet. 'Well?'

'Everyone keep your eyes skinned or I'll peel your eyelids back with my belt knife.' With the other swordsmen on all sides, Telouet walked a few paces ahead of the two warlords, swords drawn, his face hard and dangerous.

'I haven't seen my brothers, not since—' Saril broke off, drawing the sword he'd got from somewhere. Sunlight wavered on the blade.

'You cannot blame yourself for being eldest born.' Kheda hefted his own weapon, settling it in his hand. 'And if your brothers suspected what Chazen Shas had planned, they could have fled when he lay on his deathbed.'

'They all suspected the old snake had other plans for me.' Saril surprised him with a sour bark of laughter. 'Oldest living child of the name inherits but my grandfather made sure Chazen Shas took up his sword with a deathbed decree that his body slave execute the old snake's elder brother and sisters.'

'You thought your father might do the same?' Kheda asked with a qualm.

So much for envying Saril his undemanding life.

'I've no idea,' said Saril grimly. 'As soon as I knew for certain that the old snake was truly dying, I poisoned his slave's next meal and forbade anyone else to attend him.'

And then did you hasten the end of a man whose stars were already marked for death?

Kheda couldn't ask that so concentrated on the path ahead. Beyond the rise, the brush began to thicken, palms left behind on the shore, the path curling between stands of tandra trees. The litter of last season's seedpods lay undisturbed in silky drifts of white fibres, the only footprints those of the hook-toothed hogs who had torn the pods apart in search of the dark oily seeds. Away from the shore's breezes, the air was hot and stifling with the scent of the forest. Kheda wiped sweat from his face. 'It doesn't look as if anyone's been through here recently.'

'Unless they were careful not to leave a trace, looking to surprise us.' At Telouet's nod, the warriors on either side began cutting down the undergrowth, startling beetles and crickets into whirring flight from the berry bushes. Birds overhead shrieked their indignation and bounced from fig trees and ironwood saplings whose buttress roots already promised the might of their full growth. A few broken stumps showed where such giants had fallen, letting bright sunlight into the dappled shadows to the delight of dancing sapphire butterflies.

No one comes here, not even to harvest such valuable timber? Surely someone would be making sure these despoiled and discarded men were still secure, or better yet, safely dead of natural causes that would not threaten the peace of the domain.

'Whip lizard!' A startled shout came from one of Atoun's men up ahead and everyone stopped. The swordsmen who'd been cutting down the undergrowth on either side quickly drew back to surround Kheda and Chazen Saril.

'Remember,' warned Telouet, dropping the point of his blade to foil anything rushing in at knee level. 'Even a half-grown whip lizard can knock your clean off your feet.

'And their bite festers worse than any other.' Kheda looked from side to side as they advanced, more slowly this time.

'There!' Saril's sword shot out to point at a grey scaly back brushing feathery leaves aside, stirring the heady scent of perfume bark. 'But there were no whip lizards here,' he said, puzzled.

'They can swim, you know.' Kheda took a firm grip on

his own weapon. 'There, by that red cane!'

This time the lizard was plain for all to see, standing arrogantly on the path. Body as long as a man's, it squatted low on four stumpy legs, loose belly skin rumpled like a dirty sack. Plate-like scales on its back met in ridges that ran from the blunt snout over its head and all the way to the end of a heavy tail almost as long again as its body. It hissed at them, forked tongue flickering over teeth like stained knives, yellow and pink skin inside its mouth startling against the mottled brown of its leathery hide.

''Ware behind!' Telouet shouted.

Kheda turned to see another scaly beast scurry across the path. When he looked back to the front, the one by the red cane had disappeared. 'We go on,' he nodded to Telouet. 'All of you, be ready to get out of the way if one of them tries rushing us.'

'They're wary of swords for the most part but they'll mob a downed man,' Telouet confirmed grimly.

'We could just go back to the beach.' Saril was trying to see where the one to their rear had gone.

Kheda turned him with a rough hand. 'Don't you want to know if you're going to be facing some rival for your sword this time next year?'

It wouldn't be the first time conspirators within a warlord's own compound encompassed his death and then handily produced a child allegedly born to some hapless brother who'd been literally cut out of the succession by being made zamorin.

'Lizard!' Telouet hacked at a massive beast charging across in front of him. Honed sharp enough to slice through falling silk, his sword bit deep into the lizard's back.

Ahead, a frantic horn call sounded from Atoun's scouts. Brassy blasts from the troops who'd gone to search the shore answered but to his horror Kheda realised these weren't promises of hurrying aid but new alarms being raised. Atoun's men came running back down the path, crashing through the undergrowth. They had nearly joined Kheda's men when whip lizards appeared on all sides, blocking the path, hissing and rearing up on their short rear legs.

'I didn't know they could do that,' gaped Saril.

'They can't,' protested Kheda.

Then he realised the animal's legs were lengthening, straightening, the tail behind narrowing. The beast was now standing like a man. The lizard's forelegs grew and twisted, thick black claws curved like a hawk's beak spread out into a lethal fan. Its head rolled on its shoulders as some convulsion racked the beast.

When it straightened up, Kheda saw a deadly intelligence in the inky eyes. 'Atoun!'

Too late. As the astounded warrior stared at the apparition before him, the lizard slashed at his face, claws ripping away half his cheek. Atoun screamed and Kheda ran forward, sword raised. The lizard seized Atoun by the shoulders, savaging him, foul maw closed on his face, muffling his agonised cries, growling deep in its bestial throat. Sword forgotten, Atoun's gloved hands raked ineffectually at its harsh hide.

More of the hideously changed lizards erupted from the undergrowth, knocking down Chazen and Daish swordsmen alike, brutally savaging the fallen. Kheda hacked at the one crushing Atoun's skull; the warrior's struggles in the monster's repugnant embrace growing feeble. His sword glanced off the animal. Cursing, he swung again but though his eyes told him the blow was true, the blade hit nothing but empty air. Both hands on his sword hilt, Kheda put all his strength into a stroke that should have sliced the monster in half. The weapon skidded away from the beast's shoulder like a blunted blade glancing off armour. Then Kheda saw a shimmer around the animal, like heat haze rising from sun-scorched sand.

'My lord!' Telouet sprang forward to intercept a lesser lizard intent on seizing Kheda from the side. The beast backed away from Telouet's twin blades, hissing all the while, circling for any chance to attack.

The lizard that had killed Atoun whirled around, tossing back its head and gulping down the ragged mouthful it had torn from his face.

'Back to the beach, my lord!' As the monstrous beast threw Atoun's limp body full at Kheda in a spray of blood and grey matter, Telouet stepped forward to sweep the corpse aside with his swords. The lizard came on, clawed feet digging into the blood-soaked leaves, vicious talons questing forward.

'Quick as we can.' Kheda retreated. 'Stay together, back to back.'

A scream behind him scored his nerves like the scrape of metal on marble.

'They're between us and the shore!' Saril's voice cracked with consternation and Kheda smelt the acrid heat of piss as fear got the better of someone's bladder.

'Telouet?' He was still watching the lizard smeared with Atoun's lifeblood, slowly advancing towards him, blunt head swinging this way and that. 'Has anyone drawn blood from these nightmares?'

'Before they changed. Not now they're walking,' Telouet snarled with frustration.

Kheda threatened the lizard stalking him with his sword. It recoiled a little, swaying head wary. 'They don't seem to have realised that and they look none too keen to have their precious hides sliced up. I think, if we all keep our heads, we'll get to the beach.' Behind him someone was weeping ragged tears of sheer terror. 'We don't turn our backs, we don't run or they'll be on us in a heartbeat. Shoulder to shoulder, keep your swords ready. If they get in among us we're all dead.'

Everyone began moving, huddling close.

'That's right,' Kheda approved. 'A steady pace will get us there soon enough.'

'No!' One of the Chazen men suddenly broke; shoving those either side of him away, stride lengthening as he ran for the shore.

Two lizards sprang on him, then a third, crushing him beneath their weight with an audible crack of ribs. One monster bent over the struggling swordsman, forefeet planted on his chest, snarling defiance at the other lizards. One retreated but only far enough to seize a booted foot in its vicious jaws, teeth slicing through the leather, blood oozing through the holes. The other used clumsy claws to lift the screaming man's hand to its gaping mouth, fastening on his forearm, heedless of his armoured vambraces. The first lizard hissed its outrage but both ignored it, biting down and backing away, heads twisting and pulling until the swordsman's shoulder and hip joints gave way with a crack even louder than his unbearable, inhuman shrieking. Kheda's stomach heaved.

'Faster. Let's get past them while they're distracted.'

The three lizards pulled the Chazen man out of his armour in broken bits, tearing him into gobbets of flesh and bone, feasting with repellent crunching noises.

Kheda glanced back to see the lizard that had killed Atoun still following them, eyes flickering from the men to the bright swords that the animal it had once been had feared.

How long before you decide you're not that animal any more?

'We're nearly at the shore.'

As Telouet spoke, Kheda realised the dense canopy of the forest was giving way to the lighter airiness of the palm groves. He didn't dare look away from the predatory lizard relentlessly pursuing him. 'Saril! What's happening on the beach? Have the boats been attacked here? Is there any sign of the other scouting parties?'

'There's a lot of wounded,' yelled Saril. 'But I don't think the boats have taken any damage. I can't see any fighting.'

'Mind your step,' Telouet warned.

Kheda glanced down to see white sands encroaching on the turf. He looked up again instantly to see where the horrible lizard might be. To his astonished relief, he saw the monster halt, the other hideous lizards spreading out along the fringes of the underbrush. 'Telouet,' he said warily. 'I don't think they're going to leave the trees.'

'Let's not die on account of a wrong guess, my lord.' Telouet and the Daish swordsmen stayed close around him.

Saril couldn't resist the lure of the *Horned Fish*'s promise of sanctuary. 'Chazen, with me!' He ran towards the trireme, loose chainmail jingling, and ill-fitting helm tumbling to the sand.

'Scum-sucking fool!' spat Telouet.

'Let's look to our own skins.' Kheda tensed but the lizards did not pursue the fleeing men, melting away into the shadowy depths of the forest instead.

'My lord Daish!' Confused cries of welcome and appeal broke out behind Kheda.

'Telouet, keep an eye out for those creatures.' He turned to see the other swordsmen who'd been sent to reconnoitre the shore gathered around the beached triremes. Many were wounded, some were almost certainly dead, lying still where their frantic comrades had laid them down only to find their efforts had gone for naught.

Chazen men clustered around their warlord. Saril slowed to a reluctant halt.

'What happened?' Kheda demanded of one of Atoun's trusted seconds.

Breathless, the man was standing half bent, hands on his thighs. 'It was birds, only not birds,' he gasped, muddy grey with shock. 'Birds as big as men, walking like men—'

'Yora hawks?' Kheda shook his head in disbelief.

The only place any man living sees a Yora hawk is in the constellation that bears its name! But why not? If magic has come to these islands, why not massive birds not seen for count-less generations? Can wizards piece them back together from their scattered bones, put meat back into the great broken eggs that children amuse themselves finding?

'No, my lord.' The swordsman got a grip on himself. 'Cinnamon cranes but grown huge, big enough to kick a man down and then rip out his eyes with their beaks.'

'It was raider crabs down there.' Another warrior pointed down the beach with a shaking, bloodied hand. His voice rose perilously close to panic. 'Big as hounds, breaking swords in their claws, cutting off feet clean through leather.'

'It's magic, plain enough.' Telouet looked shaken.

'Well, we all know what to do about that, don't we?' Kheda's pronouncement won him a moment of stunned silence. He continued before anyone else could speak. 'We burn this island. We set fires all along the shore and ring this foulness in flames. Back to the boats!'

As the grateful men splashed their way to safety, Saril blocked Kheda's path. 'What do you think you are doing, giving such an order!'

'Chazen Saril, your domain is afflicted with sorcery!' Kheda stared at him. 'We will burn this place together or I will leave you to your fate!'

'You have to give me sanctuary, me and mine.' Saril was wringing his hands helplessly. 'My domain is lost!'

Kheda barely restrained himself from slapping the man's fat face. 'It is not lost till you give in and I will not let you do that, you spineless worm, not for Olkai's sake, not for the sake of all who look to you, and all who look to me to keep some bulwark between Daish and this evil. I will see you safely back to those swamp islands and you can hold them or die at the hands of my swordsmen if you flee north.'

'We cannot fight these sorceries,' wailed Saril.

'Don't fight, just endure.' Kheda seized his shoulders in merciless hands and shook him bodily. 'Dig yourself a hole in the hills and hide in it if you must. I will rally the domains of the whole southern Archipelago; we are all threatened by this evil. We will bring you aid and see these invaders driven out, whatever their magics. You must do your part. Rally your people; find out exactly where these invaders have landed, where they are gathered in strength, most of all where their wizards may be. Send word as soon and as often as you have it!' Shoving the other warlord aside, he splashed through the shallows to the *Scorpion*'s ladders.

Jatta peered down from the stern platform, face twisted with bemused concern. 'Where's Atoun?'

Kheda hauled himself aboard. 'Dead. Get us a little way off shore and then signal our ships to break out their sticky fire. This place is rotten with magic and I want it well alight before Chazen Saril can argue the point. We circle this island and set fires wherever we can—'

He broke off as a blazing sphere arced through the air, bright even in the full light of day. Someone aboard one of the heavy triremes hadn't waited for orders. The urn of burning, clinging paste shattered against the base of a palm tree, flames spattering in all directions, setting the dry and dusty fronds of neighbouring trees alight in an instant. Cheers rose from all the ships, even the *Horned Fish* where Saril was gesturing at Kheda in fruitless objection. As the *Scorpion*'s sail crew and her contingent of swordsmen worked to rig their own catapult on the bow platform, a second blistering missile went hurtling ashore from the heavy trireme, followed by another and another.

Jatta studied the incipient inferno. 'The winds should work in our favour.'

'Let's call that a good omen, then,' said Kheda grimly.

'Let's just hope the rains hold off.' Telouet looked to the south and east. The strain in his face lessened a little as he saw the blue horizon was still clear of the dark lines of rainy-season clouds.

Kheda watched the fire spreading deeper into the island and consuming the brush and trees parched to tinder by the long dry season with startling alacrity.

Let those unnatural monsters choke on the smoke. Let them burn alive and suffer ten times the agonies they inflicted on Atoun and the others.

Despite the intense heat, shivers racked him, sweat chill on his body, taking him quite by surprise.

'My lord.' Telouet was at his side, a bottle in one hand. 'Drink something.'

Kheda gulped the sweet juice gratefully and the moment passed.

'Was that magic, my lord?' asked Jatta warily. 'What the men were saying?'

'What else could it be?' Kheda shook his head.

'What do we do now?' Jatta's voice was tight with urgent apprehension.

'We see Chazen Saril back safe to that island with the fire mountain where we proved these invaders can die like every other man,' Kheda replied firmly. He managed a curt laugh. 'Or die more easily than most, certainly quicker than anyone with the wit to put a mail shirt over his guts. It is for Chazen Saril to hold that and we'll send every Chazen man back to join their lord or they'll die at Daish hands. I mean it. That should slow the advance of these invaders. ' He hesitated for a moment before continuing. 'We'll offer their women and children some limited sanctuary though; we can't send them to face such abominations. Then we send out messenger birds.' He lifted his voice, so that everyone close by could hear him, rowing master, ship's swordsmen and archers. 'We send courier ships, beacons, curse it, signal arrows if we have to. We raise the alarm right across the Archipelago. Once Ritsem, Ulla and Redigal know what's happening down here, they will fight with us. No matter how many men these savages can summon, no matter what their wizards' magics, they cannot withstand such might brought to bear against them.'

'As you command, my lord!' Telouet's roar prompted a muted cheer of agreement.

Kheda smiled confidently to hide his own reservations.

And just how are you going to get the domains to fight side by side, when such an alliance has never so much been mooted, never mind sealed? Even if you can do such a thing, just what are you going to do against magic that can make monsters out of the very birds and beasts around you?

CHAPTER FIVE

'So what are you going to do? I haven't got all day.' The speaker was a short man, clean-chinned and bald as an egg. His skin was tanned like fine leather and years of sun had carved deep creases around his dark and calculating eyes. He fixed the young man studying the metal wares he had on offer with a gimlet stare.

The youth picked up a small ewer and ran a curious finger over flowers and leaves bright silver against a black ground. 'What metal is this, the body of it, I mean?'

The trader paused in his open assessment of the youth's neat blue tunic, new cotton trousers and the modest silver chains around his neck and wrists. 'No one knows.' He shrugged, tunic of faded russet riding up on his muscular shoulders, black trousers dusty beneath. The belt that circled his firm waist was none so poor, a fine strap of scarlet leather set with gold Yora hawks' heads, rubies for their eyes. 'That's Jahal ware, traded up from the south-east. They keep their craft secrets closer than a clam's lips in that domain and few enough pieces float along to the likes of us.' He cracked a smile more predatory than friendly. 'Give me something worth my while and you can impress all your friends with it.'

Plainly tempted, the youth nevertheless set the little ewer down. 'I have nothing to offer that would be worth such a piece.'

The short man's face turned ugly. 'Then don't waste my time with your crab shit.'

The youth backed away, affronted, striding straight past the next trader who sat chuckling, shaded from the sun by the nut palms fringing the golden sand of the beach.

'Dev, it never ceases to amaze me how you make a living when you're so appallingly rude to everyone.'

'It keeps them keen.' The short man grinned, unrepentant, bending over the neatly trimmed square of hide that displayed his wares. He moved the ewer to a more prominent place among some small copper boxes beaten to a mottled shine. 'See anything you fancy, Bidric?' He paused to rub a finger mark from a silver incense burner shaped like a jungle fowl with the hem of his shabby tunic.

The other trader shrugged with elaborate unconcern. He was dressed with far more care than Dev, prosperous in green trews and tunic and, despite the heat, wearing a fine sleeveless overmantle of cream cotton decorated with silken vines 'Maybe later. I want to see what I can do with these first.' He spread a plump hand over his neatly folded shawls. Some were little more than gossamer, a whisper of silk painted with sprays of delicate flowers in subtle colours; vizail blossoms, jessamine, fiola. Others offered more practical protection against a chilly night, thicker cotton cheerful with bright patterns drawn in bold needle strokes; logen vines, climbing roses, iris spears.

'It's a surprise to find you sharing the beach with we lesser traders. A pleasure, of course, but unexpected all the same,' Dev remarked with studied casualness. 'I'd have thought you'd be making your bows to Rivlin Mahaf, drinking chilled lilla juice in the shade of her audience chamber.' He gestured towards a vivid ochre wrap brilliant with little pieces of coloured glass worked into the bold design of a soaring bird. 'That Mirror Bird's just the kind of thing she likes, isn't it? Aren't the ladies of the domain here? Everyone else in these reaches has come for the last trading before the rains.'

Dev's expansive gesture took in the sizeable numbers walking up and down the beach. The men showed a wide variety of fealty in the differing styles of their daggers just as the women boasted dazzling variations in dressing their hair and tying their wraps.

'They're here, and we had every expectation of trading with them, same as always.' Bidric smiled invitingly at a woman in a plain white shawl who paused to look at his wares. She waved an apologetic hand before moving on to a herbalist loudly proclaiming the efficacy of his nostrums as he sat on the twisted root of a spinefruit tree, a substantial casket resting on his knees.

'Is one of the ladies of the domain unwell?' Dev persisted. 'Or the children?'

'There's no hint of what's going on.' Once the woman's back was to him, Bidric scowled. 'We arrive and find Mahaf Coru's gates shut tighter than a swimming rat's arsehole. I went all the way west to the Galcan domain for that Mirror Bird shawl and better pieces besides, his wives were so keen on the ones I brought them last time. But all the guard captain will say is no traders are welcome at present.'

'Did you see anyone else getting a welcome while you were kept waiting? ' Dev wondered. He looked out to the anchorage thronged with galleys and sailing ships of all sizes. 'I might find someone who'd value that kind of information.'

'That's for me and mine to know.' Bidric grinned despite himself, his eyes sliding to a middling-sized ship with a striped blue sail. 'And my boys know to keep their mouths shut.'

'Children are indeed a blessing.' Momentary serious-ness flickered over Dev's beardless face.

'Indeed.' Bidric looked a trifle discomforted, uncon-sciously running a hand over a black beard smoothed to a dapper point with scented oil. 'Well, Dev, messengers from several of those visiting triremes went straight to Mahaf Coru, going by what the guard captain was shouting. Whatever the news was, it set a good few slaves running in and out like quail caught in a dust storm.'

'Do you happen to know which triremes warranted a welcome, when others didn't?' Dev grinned broadly. 'That would be worth a choice piece of this Jahal ware.'

'The gate opened to messengers from Nor, Yava and Kithir and no one else. Then a whole flock of message birds took flight, heading in all directions. I'll take one of those scent burners in exchange for that bit of news.' Bidric narrowed his eyes at Dev. 'There's something else you should know. I heard last night that Yava Aud is as nervy as a hawk on hot sand about something. He hanged three of his warriors for being caught part-drunk at the last full of the Lesser Moon.'

'A wise warlord keeps his swordsmen alert,' Dev nodded, non-committal.

Bidric snorted. 'Stick to trading your metal wares, Dev, if you're sitting anywhere near me. I don't want to be swept up along with you if Mahaf Coru decides to clear his anchorage of vice peddlers. You'll—'

The sudden arrival of shallow boats poled ashore from one of the bigger galleys interrupted him.

'Looks like you're not the only merchant Rivlin Mahaf's too busy to see,' said Dev with malicious amusement. 'When do you suppose the *Cinnamon Crane*'s boys last had to set up their stalls on the beach?'

Gangs of youths jumped out of the flat ferryboats, pulling them high on to the dry sand. Some lads jammed poles deep into the beach before stringing gaily coloured awnings between them. Others busied themselves opening caskets packed with small bottles of glass bright in nests of tandra pod fibres. The rest were setting out sets of copper and silver bowls, unwrapping bolts of cloth, plain and patterned, mostly cotton but a few of shimmering silk. The boys soon turned their boats into enticing stalls laden with luxuries that made Dev and Bidric's offerings look very paltry. The crowds who'd been sauntering idly along the beach began heading for this new attraction, faces eager.

'Time to pack up,' said Bidric philosophically.

'I don't see why.' Dev's jaw jutted belligerently.

'Because they'll have ten times the goods to offer.' Bidric began carefully piling up his shawls and wraps. 'And will accept trades that you and I can't afford to consider.'

The youths were spreading out now, welcoming all comers with open arms. A stately rowing boat drew up at the water's edge and three burly men in fine silks, gold rings on every finger, stepped into the dutifully retreating wavelets. The boys ushered them respectfully to well-cushioned stools beneath shady awnings.

'I trade on quality, not quantity.' Dev cracked his knuckles, defiant.

'You certainly have plenty of fire, for a man—' Bidric coughed apologetically. 'You stay if you want to. I'm going to sleep through the worst of the heat.' He glanced up at the sun now at the top of its arc. 'I'll come back when that lot have offloaded their dross on the fools who don't know better. I'll wager they'll be keeping back the better stuff in hopes of an audience with the warlord's ladies.' Bidric stood and waved a signal to the stripy-sailed ship, which dipped a pennant in prompt answer.

Dev sat cross-legged for a moment and then began stacking his wares carefully together in the middle of the hide sheet. 'I'm hungry. Those fools can boil their brains in the midday sun while I find something to eat.' He folded the hide deftly, producing a leather thong from a pocket to secure it.

'I could take that back with me, if you want.' A little self-conscious, Bidric paused in his own packing. 'Firan can bring it back to your boat once the heat's off the day.'

'Firan?' Dev raised a quizzical eyebrow.

'I'm thinking he'd be wanting to stay awhile.' Bidric ran a hand over his beard. 'And one of your girls will be wanting a nice shawl?'

'Ready to try a dip in the secret sea, is he?' Dev smiled that predatory smile. 'Send him over at dusk. I'll be back to the *Amigal* by then.'

'I don't want him tasting any other of your wares, mind,' warned Bidric in a low tone. 'If I smell cane liquor on him, I'll take a whip to his arse and then to yours.'

'Not even a little sweetsap to stiffen his resolve?' Dev shook his head, mock chiding. 'Many a lad needs a dose of white brandy before he can put the first notch on his tally stick.'

'Those barbarian tastes will be the death of you.' Bidric wasn't amused. 'One way or the other. I'm telling you, Dev, I don't want my sons picking up your bad habits.'

'Blame the father who bequeathed me the northern blood,' said Dev perfunctorily. 'All right, I'll send your lad back sated and sober, never fear.' He tied the thong tight and stood brushing sand from the bagged knees of his loose trousers.

Strolling down to cast an eye over the big galley's array of trade goods he curled his lip in a sneer. One of the burly men from the galley watched him with undisguised disdain. 'We've no use for anything you're trading, Dev. Move aside for those with clean hands.'

Dev didn't so much as glance at the man as he took a small leather pouch from inside the breast of his tunic. Untying its neck, he shook out a few small but flawless sapphires into one leathery palm. The *Cinnamon Crane*'s man stiffened. Dev studied the gems before pouring them back into the pouch with sudden decision. As he strode away, several of the people examining the galley's offerings watched him with uncertain expressions.

'Good lady, I see you're interested in this wall hanging,' invited the galley merchant hastily. 'What have you got to offer me in return? We're most interested in this domain's coral beads.'

Dev allowed himself a discreet smile. Even such trivial amusements made the game worth playing. As he moved away from the beach, broad-leaved spinefruit trees clustered in shady groves and the pale sand gave way to darker earth littered with dusty scraps of bark and leaves discarded as the trees suffered beneath the merciless sun at the end of the dry season. Even the incessant insects seemed to have fled. Visitors were shunning the baking heat in the expanses between the trees, gathering instead beneath the welcoming branches where the men and women of the island were offering meat and fruit, and cloud bread baked from ground saller grain. Islanders and traders alike paused to witness promised goods bartered against full bellies and quenched thirsts.

So Mahaf Coru was getting news from the south that had him shutting up his gates. What news might that be? Perhaps a likely rumour would be drifting around some resident's cook fire. Dev headed for an old woman tending a battered cauldron resting on a bed of charcoal prudently ringed with stones in a clean-swept stretch of earth. 'What's that, mother?'

'Reed squabs cooked in pepper juice.' She squinted up, her face a web of wrinkles. 'Took them from their nests myself, still with the dew on the leaves.'

Dev looked disappointed. 'Not had time to hang them then.'

The old woman laughed as she drew a faded pink shawl

back from her grizzled hair. 'You'll have to do better than that, youngster.'

'I'm surprised your eyes are sharp enough to tell squabs from reed heads, if you think I'm a youth.' Dev sat down on a convenient tree root.

'My eyes are sharp enough, though not so sharp as your tongue.' The old woman dipped her ladle into the cauldron and stirred. 'What have you to offer in exchange for the tenderest meat you'll find on this side of the island?' She picked up a battered wooden bowl but made no move to fill it.

Dev bent forward to sniff the savoury steam appreciatively. 'I trade all sorts of things, mother.'

'I doubt your mother even knows where you are.' She narrowed watery eyes at him, not displeased. 'I've seen you on the shore. You're a metal trader, aren't you? Bracelets, necklaces, earrings, that's what I'm wanting,' she continued briskly. 'My granddaughter looks to wed as soon as Mahaf Coru gives his nod.'

Dev pretended to think for a moment and then reached inside his tunic. He took out a different leather bag to the one he'd taunted the galley merchants with and drew out a delicately wrought silver wrist chain. 'I'll be here a few days, mother. Feed me till I leave and I'll make your granddaughter the envy of her friends.'

The old woman filled the bowl and, handing it over, accepted the chain. 'Soft metal,' she sniffed.

'But pure,' countered Dev, his mouth already full. 'Not smelted from half a crucible of northern barbarian scrap.'

The old woman gave a contemptuous snort. 'I wouldn't put their trash on a body for burying.'

'Didn't I hear word of some of them in these waters?' Dev wolfed down sweet shreds of pale meat and red slivers of pepper fruits. 'Seeing what they can buy or steal before some warlord burns their boats to the waterline?'

'Barbarians? No, someone's steering you astray.' The old woman stowed the chain securely deep within the breast of her many-layered dusty grey dress. 'They never come this late in the dry season. They burn redder than boiled crabs in the sun, die of it even.'

So whatever was stirring up the local domains, it wasn't opportunists from the north. Dev tried again. 'I heard Mahaf Coru's keeping a weather eye out for some kind of trouble.' He nodded in the general direction of the warlord's compound.

'He always does that.' The old woman busied herself peeling fleshy white roots to add to her cauldron.

Dev handed back the bowl and stood up. 'I'll see you again, mother.' The old woman cooked a savoury stew, even if she had precious little information to season it.

The next clump of trees sheltered a poet resolutely declaiming a florid description of setting out to sea. Dev recognised an epic he'd heard many times before.

'Perhaps I will float on the sea of love. The surging wave will lift me up, as the sinking waters will pull me down. Now rising, now falling, the deep will take me to that ocean without a shore.'

Unimpressed, the audience was struggling not to sink into sleep beneath the combined weights of food and the oppressive, humid heat. A hook-nosed man snored abruptly, interrupting the poet's speculations as to where the currents might take him and his travelling companions.

Dev shook his head. The entire audience would be asleep before this inept bard with his monotonous mumble told how a failed romance had driven him to voyaging, lamenting his beloved's loss along with the fatigue of travel. And the poet would be going hungry. No one would offer him a noon meal in return for such a lacklustre performance

Amused, Dev savoured the lingering taste of pepper in his own mouth and moved on. The better poets would appear with the dusk, courted with the finest food the locals could offer. True artists would work new variations on the time-honoured themes of the travel epic, favourite metaphor for life's journey. Some would have musicians and dancers to accompany them. Others would have apprentices displaying scrolls of exquisite illustrations to the awestruck crowds.

They were welcome to such turgid entertainments. Dev preferred those performed away from the main throng, in the shadows of a small fire coloured with handfuls of dramatic powders, their verses enhanced by one or two scantily clad dancers, a well-muscled assistant ready to slap down anyone getting too close. Dev looked around. There'd been a one-handed poet, last time he'd visited this trading beach, a remarkably inventive lad for lasciv-ious stanzas detailing the consolations a traveller might find to replace the woman he'd left behind.

Dev nodded slowly to himself. The one-handed poet had been summoned to entertain Mahaf Coru's guards every night, him and his accommodating dancing girls. Mahaf Coru and his wives might not be admitting any traders but a poet entertaining their guards might pick up some useful gossip.

Who might know if the boy was still hereabouts? Ifal, that's who. Come to that, Ifal always had the latest news. Dev paused and looked towards the sea shimmering in the sun. He shaded his eyes with a leathery hand and tried to distinguish between the distant pennants hanging limply at the mastheads of the lazily bobbing boats.

A lively bustle at his back startled him and he whirled around. One hand went to the Yava-styled dagger at his belt but no one was coming for him. The commotion was some way inland, where the spinefruit trees gave way to a grassy bowl ringed with the sprawling, flat-roofed houses that the Mahaf islanders favoured. The domain's elders, village spokesmen and the like would be waiting beneath the shade of their wide eaves, welcoming those traders who solicited their interest with cool fruit juices and hard bargaining. Curious, Dev hurried forward, easing past people obsequiously bowing and retreating; islanders and visitors here to trade mingling with travelling entertainers clutching their scrolls or juggling balls.

The crowd was melting away in front of a tall, armoured man. The sun shone so brightly on his chainmail, Dev winced to look at him. Rock crystal glittered on the brow band of his helm and the gold mounts on the scabbards of his twin swords flashed diamond fire. An arresting woman strode along the path her body slave was clearing. Lean and as tall as her attendant, she wore a brocaded white tunic over gauzy trousers. Her tightly plaited hair was covered with an iridescent scarf worked in silver and gold thread, gleaming like a butterfly's wing. She swept the trailing end back over her shoulder with one hand laden with silver rings, bracelets studded with chrysolite sliding down her smoothly oiled forearm. A rope of crystal drops was wound in tight coils around the base of her slender throat.

'Tarita Mahaf.' Some woman identified the noble lady to an ignorant visitor. 'Mahaf Coru's third and most recent wife.'

'Born sister to Yava Dirha,' added another of the gaggle of women, eyes wide. 'She was wife to Kithir Arcis before divorcing him.'

'Why did she do that?' wondered a fresh-faced girl.

'That's no one's business but her own,' a woman who could only be her mother said repressively.

Dev stood behind the women so he looked as if he belonged with them, and stared at Tarita Mahaf with the same eagerness as the rest. She had a wide reputation as a woman not to cross as well as an enviable network of alliances in her own right. At the moment, she had the air of a woman with a purpose. That had to have some bearing on Mahaf Coru's concerns. This day just got more and more interesting.

The noble woman's slave called out to a pale-skinned, clean-shaven man who bowed low with an engaging smile. A darker, heavyset man behind him set an iron-bound chest of black wood down on the bare earth. The smaller man promptly unrolled the gaily patterned rug he'd been carrying and laid it over the chest, sitting comfortably down. His companion took a step backwards, a club of dark wood with more iron studding than the chest sloped casually over one shoulder. Tarita's Mahaf's swordsman walked around the seated trader in a slow circle, his forbidding scowl deterring anyone from coming closer. The dutiful crowd retreated a few more paces.

Ignoring them all, Tarita Mahaf spoke briefly to the man sitting on the chest. The smaller man's smile widened. He stood up, snapping his fingers to his club-wielding companion as he did so. The big man caught up the chest once again and the pair of them followed as the warlord's lady turned to stride back towards the unseen compound and its closely guarded secrets.

'What does Tarita Mahaf want with him?' wondered the pretty girl.

'That's Ifal, the gem trader,' said her mother thoughtfully. 'There's been talk of marriage negotiations with Nor Zauri. Perhaps one of the girls needs bridal jewels.'

Dev doubted it. That wasn't the kind of thing Ifal traded in. He allowed the speculating throng to carry him along to the shade of some spinefruit trees. Casually disengaging himself from the chattering women, he yawned ostentatiously and lay down in a dry hollow between two gnarled roots. The bustle of excitement was dying back all around as people returned to their previous indolence beneath the burden of the day's heat.

Noting a spot of grease from the old woman's stew on his tunic, Dev rubbed his thumbnail across it. Lying back, he draped his arm over his face, for all the world like a weary traveller shading his eyes from the sun. Unseen, he focused all his attention on the oily smear gleaming on his thumbnail.

These Aldabreshi, with their hysterical hatred of magic. Dev smiled discreetly as an enchanted emerald sheen brightened on his nail. He worked wizardry all around them, day after day, and they never so much as noticed. All those who said the Archipelago was a death trap for mages were just cowards and fools. He suppressed the not-infrequent urge to show these people just what magic could do. He could summon illusions to accompany a poet's verses, living, vibrant echoes of the musical words. The women of the domain could take their ease as he coaxed fire from the bare earth to heat their pots and then washed them clean afterwards with water wrung from the very air. He could wrap the island in a storm that would drive the waters clean out of the harbour to leave every ship beached high and dry.

But for now, his life depended on his magic's discretion. The brilliant green on his thumbnail faded away to leave a tiny, perfect image reflected in the shining grease. That must be somewhere in the residence the Mahaf wives used when visiting this isle, unseen beyond the first rise of the rolling island. Ifal was offering plaited strands of turquoise beads to a pleasantly plump, grey-haired woman whose peacock-patterned shawl was as fine as anything Bidric had to offer. Dev recognised her at once. Vidail Mahaf, senior wife, with Tarita stood at her shoulder.

Vidail waved away the turquoise, saying something that

left Ifal frozen with surprise, strings of lapis hanging limp from his fingers.

Dev moistened dry lips with his tongue and glanced up at a fitful breeze toying with the spinefruit tree's broad leaves. With infinite care, he teased a breath of air away from the tree and began guiding it gently towards the distant residence. Tension pressed down on him as he looked back to the miniature scrying on his thumbnail but the women were still deep in discussion with Ifal. Satisfaction warmed Dev in a way the sun never could. Those fools who said these spells couldn't be worked together, they should try working enchantments with the finesse he needed to keep his skin whole sailing these perilous waters. He had learned more in his first season than he had in five wearisome years in Hadrumal's dusty libraries.

Then he stiffened, seeing the gem trader digging deep in his coffer, unwrapping soft leather bundles to reveal inky blackness within.

Dev turned all his attention to threading the enchanted breeze swiftly through the air, sorting hastily through the whispers it was bringing to him. There, that was Ifal's voice, distinctive with the rasp of the eastern reaches.

'Of course, efficacy all depends on the history of the talisman.'

Dev stiffened.

'I might be better able to help if I knew just what magical malice you seek to protect your children from.'

'It's sufficient to ward them with jet, for the present.' Vidail reached for the beads, tightness in her voice. 'We will take all you have. Are there any other pieces, bracelets, rings?'

Dev swallowed, his mouth suddenly dry.

'I have a butterfly comb inlaid with satinstone.' Ifal rummaged in his coffer. 'Both stone and symbol powerful talismans against wizardry, regardless of the piece's history,' he remarked casually.

'It is indeed,' said Vidail slowly. 'You are astute, as always.'

'Astute enough,' there was a menacing edge to Tarita's voice, 'to let it be known we were interested in your sunstones and tourmalines and nothing else besides.'

'Sunstone to warm the heart and lift the spirits.' Ifal smiled peaceably. 'I'll be the model of discretion, but perhaps I'll let slip my guess that you may seek some clarity in your dreaming, my ladies? Sunstone so often conveys that virtue. It would hardly be a surprise, if one of you were planning on a night at some tower of silence, with your daughters of an age to be married.' He ran a hand over dark brown wiry hair. 'Which naturally explains your interest in my finest tourmalines. I believe I will be replenishing my stocks of pink and white cabochons, such useful stones for balancing passion and compassion in the young.'

'You have a glib tongue, trader. Be sure you know when to hold it, or someone will cut it out.' Vidail took the butterfly hair ornament and exchanged a wary nod with Tarita. 'Present yourself at our gates again, when you have replenished your stocks of jet.'

Tarita clapped her hands sharply together and her body slave opened a door. 'Our wife Rivlin has some of her craftspeople's ash-glazed pottery in payment for your jet, and for your discretion.'

'Discretion comes as part of every trade I make, great lady,' Ifal promised before following the slave out of the room with a distinct spring in his step.

As well there might be, thought Dev. The ash-glazed pottery of the Mahaf domain was highly prized. The random dribbles that the secret firing process produced in the greenish glaze were closely scrutinised for prognostic significance by the gullible fools hereabouts.

Dev let his stealthy spell-casting dissolve into the untrammelled air and sat up. There was no point in trying to get anything out of Ifal now. He'd be intent on planning how profitably to trade those valuable pots and whatever other gems he could offer the local rulers to guard them against wizardry. There was no temptation of the flesh Dev could offer to cozen a man so notoriously faithful to his partner, bodyguard and lover, and neither of them drank anything stronger than the piss-poor officially sanctioned wine of these islands.

Ifal would doubtless be trying to read some answers to this puzzle in those pots, superstitious as every Aldabreshi. Dev rose to his feet and headed back towards the beach. Time to pay a visit to those charlatans who leeched a living telling fortunes for the credulous Archipelagans. He walked along the water's edge, relishing the cool flurries around his feet, not even sparing a glance for the awnings. Blood pounded beneath his breastbone.

Beyond the traders, a blunt ridge of rock ran out of the trees, only halting at the water's edge where the seas lapped at it with lazy waves. It was a reddish stone, veined with white and broken into a series of ledges like haphazard steps. Higher up, opportune grasses and flowers clung to nooks of wind-blown soil. Down by the water's edge, a filthy old man dressed in rags crouched at the base of the rock, eyes bright with madness as he hunted in the sand for shells, which he dropped in a gourd. Close by, cross-legged on the very lowest ledge and composed in clean white cotton, a youth sat with a bundle of many-coloured reeds resting across his lap.

Dev wasn't interested in lunatics and shirkers out to avoid an honest day's work. He looked at the men who had claimed various vantage points on the rock. Head prudently shaded with a fold of cloth, a grizzled man sat chatting with another of a similar age. Both boasted a small brass urn close at hand as well as a miscellany of wooden boxes, some dull, some brightly coloured. The man lower down also had a couple of small wicker cages, augury doves cooing contentedly inside. On the flat top of the ridge sat an old man, white hair and beard reaching to his waist. Beneath his little awning, brass and copper urns ringed him and an attentive youth offered him refreshment from a silver cup. People eager to seek his guidance perched on the steps and ledges below. Some clutched offerings of fish or meat wrapped in fresh leaves, others carried easily traded trinkets. The old man beckoned to the first one, bending forward to answer the suppliant's question with a query of his own. There were always the questions, seeming so innocent yet betraying the very answers these credulous fools sought, hints garnered by the soothsayer's skilful reading of a suppliant's stance, the angle of their head, the anxiety in their face.

Dev looked instead at the soothsayer with the doves. He'd seen that man being escorted to and fro by Rivlin Mahaf's body slave on several previous visits to this island. Every sage had a network of contacts and informants feeding him information, otherwise they'd never maintain their deceits, but a soothsayer that the warlord's wives favoured would surely have inside knowledge to weight his predictions towards the success that would enhance his reputation.

The madman sidled across the sands towards Dev, rattling his split and battered gourd and bringing a rank stench that a full season's rains wouldn't diminish.

'Get lost, lizard eater,' Dev growled. The madman had enough sense to scurry away. Then Dev's expression turned to an eager hopefulness that would have astounded Bidric. The youth with the reeds raised them in a ceremonious gesture and rustled the dried seed heads, smiling with contented anticipation. Dev ignored him, scrambling up a steep face of the ridge to outstrip a couple of girls picking a more cautious route upwards.

'You show initiative,' remarked the soothsayer peaceably as Dev appeared before him. 'Always a good thing in a seeker after truth.' He was well into his middle years, grey touching his temples and the black beard that flowed uncut down his broad chest. Other than that, he could have passed for any merchant on the beach below, in his sleeveless mantle of striped cotton over sandy trews and tunic. He rested a hand with a single heavy gold ring on a little cage where two doves cooed and preened. 'But a bold man may fall, if he makes a false step on a rock face.'

'What omens might you see for a bold man voyaging to the south?' challenged Dev.

'What would you offer in return for such guidance, my intrepid friend?' the soothsayer asked silkily.

Dev reached for one of the soft leather pouches hidden inside his tunic and handed it over. 'If your word proves true, I'll bring you twice that the next time we meet. If not, I'll find you and let everyone know why I'm claiming my jewels back.'

The soothsayer looked inside and his head snapped up. 'You certainly value guidance.' He stared at Dev.

'My father may have been a mere barbarian from the unbroken lands, but my mother taught me the value of those currents that run from past to present,' Dev said calmly.

'All the more valuable, for those without firm ties to any domain.' The soothsayer twisted the heavy gold ring around his finger as his eyes flickered to Dev's dagger, narrowing slightly as he identified the style of the Yava islands. 'I've seen you before, haven't I? You sail beneath a fine array of passage pennants.'

'I have that good fortune,' said Dev smoothly. 'I trade through here as far south as the Kithir isles and north to the domain of Sazac Joa, by the grace of all those lords who grant me leave to sail their seaways. I can spread your reputation along all those routes, if I find it well deserved.'

The soothsayer's dark eyes were shrewd as he secured Dev's pouch in a leather purse tied to his belt. 'What would you have me read for you?'

Dev gestured at the doves. 'Let them fly.'

The birds waited patiently as the soothsayer lifted them out of the little cage with careful hands. He flung the white doves upwards. They fluttered uncertainly at first, wheeling around each other, wings twisting and backing in the air. Then one made a sudden decision and swooped low, heading straight for the trees at the heart of the island. The second followed almost instantly, both disappearing into the dense green.

'Well?' Dev had barely bothered watching the birds' flight, intent instead on the soothsayer's face.

The man took a moment before replying. 'You can claim friends in the north, so make that your course. Misfortune stirs to the south. Your only defence is to fly before it and seek shelter.' He halted as one of the doves returned in a flash of white and shepherded it gently back into its cage.

'You mean the rains?' Dev asked with deliberate stupidity. 'There are going to be whirlwinds?'

'I speak of adversity that moves unseen, to corrupt and destroy.' The soothsayer raised a hand for the second dove to perch upon.

'You mean a pestilence?' Dev was wide-eyed with feigned incomprehension. 'Breakbone fever returning with the rains?'

'Just take heed of my advice.' The soothsayer shot Dev

a warning look, unsmiling as he put the second dove safely back in the cage. 'That's all I have to say to you. You'll find my word more than earns your payment. Now go. Others are waiting for my counsel.' He looked past Dev to smile a welcome at the two girls waiting impatiently to approach him.

'Thank you.' Jumping lithely down to the sand, Dev brushed dust from his clothes. The line of people still waited patiently for the chance to consult the topmost soothsayer. The youth was doing his best to attract them with flourishing casts of his coloured reeds, studying the patterns with a brow wrinkled in ostentatious concentration. He was getting no takers.

Dev smiled with malicious speculation. Should he seek a reading from the self-obsessed youth? It would be easy enough to decry that lad's doubtless vague foretellings as nonsense, especially if something prompted comparison with the cannier soothsayers' more ominous warnings. It was always amusing to see a would-be oracle denounced as a fraud by some irate islanders, stripped of his mystical trappings, often his clothing as well, left with only bruises to cover his nakedness.

'Let me guide your path. I am master of the seen and unseen.' It was the madman, talking to no one in particular but prancing round and round in an ever-decreasing circle, rattling his gourd. Overcome with dizziness, he fell, motionless for a moment before springing up and peering at the marks he'd made in the sand. 'There, the Yora Hawk! The Winged Serpent consumes the Vizail that blooms in the night. Strange days are coming, my friend, strange and fearful days!'

Even the insane were sensing this undercurrent of unease lapping at the islands. No, Dev decided, cracking his knuckles absently. The fool of a boy could rest easy. He had no time to spare on entertainments. There was something going on to the south and he wanted to find out exactly what.

What news from the south had Mahaf Coru slamming the gates of his compound and sending his own messages to all and sundry? News so significant that it took precedence over the last major trading opportunity before the rains arrived. News that prompted the Mahaf wives to buy jet talismans and Ifal's silence besides with their finest wares. It wasn't some fear over the forthcoming rains. However severe the storms might be, they were all part of the natural cycle and endured as such. Nor was it some outbreak of one of the Archipelago's virulent diseases. If that was in the wind, the Mahaf wives and Coru himself would be busy securing medicinal herbs and astringent plant extracts, not messing about with shiny baubles.

The Mahaf wives wanted talismans against magic. For a few unfeasibly pale emeralds and the promise of Dev spreading his reputation, the soothsayer had warned him off sailing south, where some danger threatened a man of visibly barbarian blood and no family to vouch for him nor ties to a domain to protect him. The one thing that came from the barbarian north that the Aldabreshi feared was wizardry. The soothsayer had gone as close as he dared to mentioning magic without actually putting it into words.

So there were reports of magic stirring to the south? Probably a long way south, if the word was only being shared among the warlords with their swift message birds and rapid chains of signal beacons and couriers. It would be a while before word would trickle down to the lesser folk. Perhaps he should lay in a stock of jet before the rumour became common knowledge.

Dev shook his head with a contemptuous smile. What convinced these people that a string of polished black beads or a shiny jet brooch could turn aside magic? And what was so special about butterflies? Dev racked his brains for the scraps of lore he'd picked up on his travels up and down the Archipelago. Weren't butterflies a symbol of the Aldabreshi conviction that past, present and future were all interlinked, as the creature changed from caterpillar to chrysalis to butterfly yet remained the same individual?

Discarding that irrelevance, Dev considered the next crucial question. Could there be something in this beyond dry-season hysteria? If there was, who could be so idiotic as to flaunt their magebirth before such a hostile audience? Was it some mainland wizard with a death wish? If it was, Dev decided, let the fool learn his lesson the hard and painful way. Anyone that stupid wasn't worth risking his own exposure for.

But that was unlikely. Could it be some untutored affinity for an element, air, earth, fire or water, erupting in some hapless Aldabreshin family? The wizards of Hadrumal refused to believe the Aldabreshi, alone of all the peoples of the world, had no wizards born among them. Not that he'd managed to find a single one thus far, Dev scowled. Not in time anyway, not before their untamed abilities led them to disaster, either consumed by their own feral magic, ripped limb from limb by a terrified mob or skinned alive by some warlord's executioner. And these people called the races of the northern lands barbarians. At least the humble villages of Lescar just threw their mageborn out on to the road to Hadrumal, rather than ritually slaughtering them, even the misbegotten offspring of the local whore.

Better find out one way or the other before sending any message to Planir, Dev decided. The Archmage of Hadrumal wasn't going to appreciate unsubstantiated guesses. Nor would magic show him the truth of whatever was prompting these suspicions. He could only scry for a limited distance without being able to focus on a place or a person well known to him. So he had better sail south and find out what was going on. If the fearful Aldabreshi turned on him, he would be gone before they laid hands on him, magic carrying him back to the safety of Hadrumal, the hidden isle where the northern wizards had their city of lore and learning. Hadrumal, hard-won sanctuary for mageborn gathered from all across the mainland, where they could learn to control their inborn affinity with the elements that suffused the world, where generations of study had filled libraries with wisdom that every master mage strove to add to. Hadrumal; quite the most boring place Dev had ever lived, its only recommendation the lack of the kicks and bruises that had been his lot before he arrived there.

Dev shuddered. Sailing south into the teeth of the oncoming rainy season would be no pleasure jaunt. Still, at least he could work a few enchanted winds to help with that. Halting on the beach opposite his own safely anchored ship, he looked around the busy harbour and raised fingers to his mouth for a piercing whistle. 'Ferry!'

A man poling a shallow-sided, flat-bottomed boat through the shallows hailed him. 'Back to the *Amigal*, is it?'

Dev splashed through the wavelets to step aboard. 'I want to call on the *Silken Vine* first.'

'Bit early in the day, isn't it?' chuckled the ferryman with a hint of envy.

Dev grinned. 'I thought I'd get in before the rush starts.'

The ferryman glanced at Dev's beardless chin and drew an obvious conclusion. 'You won't get much competition round here, not for the lads' favours. It's the girls will be rushed off their feet, if you get my meaning. Well, when the sun's off the zenith. There's more than flowers wilt in this kind of heat.'

Dev shrugged. 'I don't like to follow in another man's wake.'

The ferryman leaned on his pole and drove them deftly through a cluster of fishing boats. He let the pole drift up and pushed on it to turn their course towards a wide-bellied galley resting in a prime anchorage. Her oars were shipped inboard and only a few of her crew were idling about their last tasks. A rope running from the main mast to the ornate prow was crowded with white-bordered tongues of silk proclaiming right of passage through a myriad domains.

Dev stood, balancing easily in the shallow ferryboat. 'You there! Tell Tabraze that Dev's here to see her.'

The ferryman watched the lad scurry off. 'You're known here?'

'Very much so.' Dev grinned. 'I'll trade you an introduction for the ride.'

The ferryman laughed but shook his head. 'My wife would read me my future in my own entrails.'

'I'll give you something to put a smile on her face.' Dev reached for the rope ladder uncoiling from the *Silken Vine*'s stern rail. 'If you keep an eye out this way and fetch me back to the *Amigal* when I'm done.'

'Gladly.' The ferryman pushed off from the galley's side as Dev climbed up.

'Over here.' An elegant woman with a placid smile beckoned from beneath a tasselled canopy rigged just before the ship's little aft mast. The three shallow steps of the stern platform made a natural dais where she reclined on a heap of satin cushions. She was sipping from a golden cup, her gauzy white gown all but transparent, wrists and ankles laden with chains of silver moonstones. Her oiled skin shone glossy as ebony.

'Tabraze.' Dev sauntered over, grinning with broad appreciation. 'You look well.'

She narrowed silver-painted eyes at him. 'Then come

here and give me more than flattery. Isn't it time I found out just what secrets you're hiding?' Her speculative gaze lingered on Dev's trousers.

'Not today.' He took a cushion under the shade of the silken awning and helped himself to a golden goblet from the tray at Tabraze's elbow. 'Can you take two girls off my hands?'

'I'm not sure, Dev.' Tabraze brushed a hand over the arc of silver combs that held her waist-length black hair back from her face. The artless gesture made it plain there was nothing beneath her gown but her generous breasts. 'If they're anything like the last one you tried to foist on me.' Distaste twisted her tempting mouth into a stern pout.

'Repi was a mess before I picked her up.' Dev waved a perfunctory hand. 'Anyway, she's dead. These two—'

'But you didn't keep Repi out of your little jars and boxes, did you?' Tabraze interrupted him with uncompromising reproof. 'I'll keep no girls who have to be witless on dreamsmoke before they'll lie down for a man. This ship's never getting that reputation.'

'These two both enjoy trading favours for fancies,' Dev assured her. 'And neither takes so much as chewing leaf.'

'So why are you looking to be rid of them?' Tabraze still looked suspicious. 'Or are they looking to leave you? Are you looking to touch me for a price I needn't actually pay?'

Dev leant forward to run a hand down Tabraze's gossamer-draped thigh. 'I'll pay the proper price to touch you, one of these days.'

A crewman coiling a rope down on deck paused, surprised to see the gesture.

'What do you want?' Dev challenged and the galley man moved away hastily.

'Tease.' Tabraze dismissed his words with a wave of her cup. 'So what's the deal?'

'They only sought passage to somewhere with more opportunities than the rock they were born on. I've got wind of something I want to pursue without encumbrances.' Dev shrugged. 'I thought coming to terms with you would do everyone some good. Of course, I could just slip them some thassin and get their bodyweight in liquor from the first meat trader I run into.'

'I never know what to make of you, Dev.' Tabraze gazed at him levelly. 'I don't even know if you're woman's man, man's man or zamorin.'

The crewman looked up again, startled at his mistress's frank admission of such uncouth curiosity.

Dev was unperturbed. 'You keep your secrets and I'll keep mine.'

Tabraze waved her cup again, diaphanous silk tightening across her bosom. 'I have nothing to hide.'

'Not in that dress,' agreed Dev appreciatively.

'It's too hot to play games.' Tabraze sat up. 'All right. What are you looking for from me? As long as they're healthy and willing, mark you.'

'Mahaf Coru's household warriors brought a goodly weight of supplies to pay for their pleasures last night.' Dev gestured down the broad deck of the galley to the cookhouse standing on the starboard side. 'I'll settle for a sack of saller grain and as much dried fruit as you can spare.'

'You really are in a hurry to get rid of them.' Tabraze tilted her head on one side, pink tongue delicately licking her painted lips. 'If it's not because they're too fuddled to stand upright, you must be on the scent of something good.'

'As you say, it's too hot to play games.' Dev drained his goblet and set it back on the tray with a sharp clink. 'Do I send these girls to you or just dump them on the beach and let them take their chances?'

'I'll take them.' Irritation carved a momentary crease between Tabraze's immaculately plucked brows. 'But next time I see you, Dev, I want a sniff of whatever you're chasing.' She smiled winsomely at him. 'Just a rose will suffice. I'm not asking for the whole flower garden.'

'You're the one who'll be owing me. They're good girls, you'll see. You can send that deckhand with the flapping ears over with my supplies as soon as may be. I want to catch the next tide.' Dev left Tabraze both curious and frustrated as he moved to the rail of the great galley and waved to the ferryman who'd brought him to the *Silken Vine*.

Poling back with alacrity, he grinned up at Dev. 'That was quick.'

'I've never been one to waste time.' Dev paused to make an ostentatious adjustment to his groin before swinging his leg over the stern rail.

'Back to the *Amigal*?' The ferryman pushed off.

Dev nodded. As they approached his ship, small enough to sail single-handed, large enough to carry a cargo to justify his travels, he shouted up to the deck. 'Ekkai! Taryu!' Two girls appeared over the rail, each in a simple dress of silk draped over one shoulder, one scarlet, and one blue. 'Throw me a line, you silly poults.'

One of the girls hastily flung a rope and Dev caught it deftly. 'Wait here,' he told the ferryman. 'These two are taking passage with the *Silken Vine*.'

'We are?' The elder girl's surprise reflected that on the ferryman's face.

'You are.' Dev hauled himself aboard and the two girls quickly retreated. Neither wore much by way of gold or jewels but fresh logen vine flowers in their tight-curled hair decorated an undemanding prettiness. They stood close together, round faces wary.

'Well?' challenged Dev. 'You've made it plain you're not interested in my kind of business.'

'It's—' began the younger girl hotly.

'Hush, Ekkai.' The elder gripped her sister's arm tightly enough to drive the blood from her fingernails. 'Get your things. It has to be better than sailing with him.'

'The *Silken Vine* has an honest reputation,' the ferryman called up. 'It sails under Mahaf Coru's protection.'

'That's something, I suppose.' Taryu looked at Dev with undisguised dislike. 'We'll get our things.'

Dev raised a warning hand. 'You can gather your rags and tatters, Ekkai. Taryu, you stay with me.' He stepped forward and caught her by the wrist, forcing her to the far side of the deck and out of the ferryman's earshot. 'You do right by Tabraze or when I catch up with you, I'll take the price of her disappointment out of your hide. I want her so grateful for such wonderful girls, she'll open her private jewel case and let me take my pick. Don't forget you still owe me, come to that. Keep your ears open as well as your thighs and make sure you've got solid information to balance our ledgers. Don't think this is the last you'll see of me, girl.' Satisfied to feel Taryu shaking, he let go of her hand.

'Don't think we won't find someone to protect us from your kind.' She rubbed at her wrist, defiance imperfectly masking her fear.

Dev smiled. 'I love you too, sweetness. When you get to the *Silken Vine*, tell Tabraze you owe Bidric the shawl merchant a good time for his youngest son. The lad's called Firan and it'll be his first time. You treat him gently.'

Ekkai scrambled up out of the stern hatch, clutching an armful of flimsy scarves, a few choice dresses in painted and embroidered silks and some workaday tunics in much-washed cotton. Taryu wriggled past Dev and hurried to help her roll them into a haphazard bundle.

'Not taking anything that you're not owed?' Dev turned

suddenly just as Taryu and Ekkai thought they had made their way to the ship's rail unchallenged. He grinned. 'No, you wouldn't dare, would you?'

Not troubling himself to help the girls climb down, Dev addressed the ferryman. 'When you've offloaded this pair, take a message to Bidric the shawl merchant for me. Tell him I had to catch the tide, unexpected news. He can hang on to my metal wares or trade them if he gets a good enough offer. I'll catch up with him soon enough and we can settle up then. Take a piece out of what he's holding for me for yourself, or you can take what you're owed from one of those two.' Dev nodded at the girls with a sly wink. 'Tell him they're holding what I owe him for Firan.'

The ferryman cleared his throat. 'I'll settle for a present for my wife, thanks all the same.'

Dev turned to check the *Amigal*'s rigging as the ferryman poled away. That was one less complication, or rather two. It never hurt to have some willing warmth to offer a man who couldn't be bribed with liquor or leaf but Ekkai and Taryu were far too quick-witted to take south on this particular quest. Repi had had her advantages even if she'd preferred to live in her smoke-filled dreams. It never mattered what she saw or heard; no one took her word for the phase of the moons without looking up to check.

Was there anything else he needed to dispose of before he quit this anchorage? Not that he could think of. Bidric would doubtless get the better end of the deal whenever they came to settle up over Dev's metal goods but the shawl trader was honest enough to feel himself under no slight obligation as a consequence. That was no bad thing. Dev looked up to check the sun's progress across the sky, calculating how soon he could sail.

'*Amigal*, ho!' Tabraze's crewman shouted up from a dumpy rowing boat.

'Ho yourself.' Dev threw a rope down. 'Tie the goods on to that.' Testing the weight, he began hauling the heavy sack of saller grain upwards. He grinned as he grunted with the effort, spirits rising at the thought of the challenge ahead. Trading had been getting boring. Besides, where was the profit for a mage in knowing more than anyone else about the quarrels and rivalries of the various domains? Planir never appreciated what cunning it took to learn such things. Tracing these rumours of magic to their source, that was a fitting undertaking for a mage of his talents. He was more than ready for something new. If it proved to be dangerous, that was no more than a spice to be savoured, like the pepper pods in the old woman's squab stew.

CHAPTER SIX

'Watch your every word, your every step.' Janne waved gaily to the curious crowd thronging the river bank but her voice was deathly serious as she spoke to Itrac. Standing together at the great galley's rail, both women were swathed in light wraps of nubby silk that covered them from head to toe.

'Never let Ulla Safar get you on your own.' Kheda's stern warning was just as much at odds with his beaming face. 'He's far too fond of offering junior wives some virile Ulla seed to quicken their next child.'

'If they demur, he's happy to outline the appalling consequences for their domain and its trade, if he sets his face and his wives against them.' Janne clapped her hands with delight as flowers rained down on the galley's deck and pattered on to the many-coloured silken canopy erected to shade the warlord and the women from the punishing sun. Her full lips pouted enticingly beneath immaculately applied colour but there was no hint of softness in her eyes outlined in black and red and dusted with a sweep of gold that glistened on her cheekbones before disappearing into her hairline.

Moving cautiously against the sluggish flow of the twisting, muddy river, the galley was passing between two immense watchtowers. The sprawling battlements were crowded with people welcoming such noble guests to the heart of the Ulla domain in time-honoured tradition. The scarves and banners they brandished echoed the brightly patterned sails now furled up above on the great galley's masts.

I don't know what possessed Rekha to call this ship the Rainbow Moth. *Colourful sails are all very well but nothing's going to make this massive hull remind anyone of a dainty insect.*

Kheda shifted his shoulders within his own enveloping cloak of undyed silk. 'Telouet, when you get a moment, ask around the servants. Find out if these locals came out of their own accord or were driven down to the river by the spears of Ulla Safar's warriors.'

Once we have that answer, we can discuss what it might mean with Janne.

Helms swathed in cotton to mitigate the intense heat, Telouet and Birut stood fully armoured on either side of the canopy's poles, which looked incongruously sturdy for such a frivolous burden. Both slaves were watching the rain of flowers intently for any sign of more hostile missiles.

Does anyone ashore realise this awning is lined with a sheet of fine chainmail? Does knowing, or not knowing, make any difference to what the Ulla people throw?

The notion might have been amusing, if Kheda didn't feel the chances of some kind of assault were all too high.

With the rains due any day, the heat's appalling, no relief day or night. If anyone attacks us, Ulla Safar will just claim ignorance and accept a plea of seasonal madness in mitigation.

Now the *Rainbow Moth* was passing the inner faces of the watchtowers. Itrac Chazen struggled to maintain her carefree expression as she gazed over the turbid water to the end of a massive chain, links as long as a man's leg, secured to the mighty fortification. 'That runs all the way across the river bed?'

'Right to the other watchtower.' Kheda gave Janne a significant look as the great galley passed over the invisible boundary. 'There are huge windlasses each with a gang of slaves just waiting for Ulla Safar's order to haul it up and block any ship's passage upstream or down.

Now we are within Ulla Safar's grasp. What choice did we have, with Safar refusing any of the more neutral meeting places Redigal Coron or Ritsem Caid suggested and offering his dubious hospitality instead? Well, we've taken all reasonable precautions.

Kheda felt a little better as Janne smiled reassurance at him.

'How far away are the triremes?' The concern in Itrac's dark eyes belied her apparently light-hearted smiles. She scanned the river banks where scores of little boats were drawn up on the mud, flat-roofed houses close packed above the high-water line, a patchwork of saller fields, berry bushes and vegetable plots sprawling beyond them. The many-layered greens of untouched forest couldn't be seen till the first hills began to rise in the far distance. The wide river valley was home to a multitude of Ulla Safar's people.

'They're close enough,' Kheda assured her.

Close enough to come and rescue us, if we have to take the little skiff concealed in this great galley's holds, handpicked crew hidden among the unassuming oarsmen. You may think you have the Daish rulers held close, Ulla Safar, but did your father never teach you how a palm finch can slip through the bars of a cage built to hold a mountain hawk?

Telouet was watching Itrac thoughtfully. 'Until you have a body slave of your own again, you don't go anywhere without me or Birut, my lady of Chazen.' He added the courtesy of her title a little belatedly.

Birut grunted his agreement. 'Ulla Safar's concubines say he won't take no for an answer with them. With you on your own and Chazen Saril so far away, he might just think he could get away with rape and his word that you yielded against yours that you didn't.'

'I wish Saril was here.' Itrac's wretchedness showed through the mask of pleasure Birut had painted on her face.

Kheda was hard put not to let his exasperation with the two faithful body slaves show. 'One of our first concerns will be to make it clear beyond possibility of confusion that you are travelling under Daish protection.'

Use your brain, Telouet, and keep your mouth shut as well as your eyes open. I know it's your duty to worry over everyone's safety but Itrac fretting herself into a decline is just what we don't need. This visit is going to be difficult and dangerous enough as it is.

'Daish Kheda's word will curb Safar's enthusiasms,' Janne assured Itrac. 'I also intend making sure you're suited with a new body slave as soon as possible.'

Still waving and smiling all the while, Kheda looked at her. 'I wouldn't take anyone Mirrel Ulla offers you.'

'Naturally not.' Janne's smile took on a secretive, self-satisfied quality. 'Trust me, my husband. It's all in hand.'

Itrac opened her mouth to ask something more but forgot her question as the great galley rounded a bend in the river. Her jaw dropped in amazement.

'I take it you've never visited Derasulla before,' Janne remarked, amused.

All Itrac could do was shake her head, dumbfounded. Daish Reik had told Kheda there had once been an island in the river's embrace but nothing of it remained visible now. A mighty wall of close-fitted red stone rose straight from the water, rising sheer to battlements and watchtowers jutting out over the void to give an unimpeded view in every direction. Behind this first defence, a second wall was visible, belligerent turrets marking its length as it marched away to the rear. A third wall rose beyond it and varied roofs and towers could be made out behind that, all tall enough to give vantage over the outer defences, not so much as a paving slab left where an invading enemy could stand without a rain of arrows puncturing his pretensions. Arrogance was plainly Ulla Safar's prerogative hereabouts, proclaimed by the yellow pennants flying from every coign and turret top. Any invasion would have to come in staggering strength if they were to try assault or siege; the fort was broad enough to hold an army within its innermost ring and its cellars deep enough to supply them for years.

The wind shifted and Itrac coughed, her expression turning to one of distaste. 'What is that stink?'

'Ulla Safar wallowing in his own filth like some swamp hog.' Contempt curled Janne's unceasing smile. 'His pride won't let him ever abandon his wonderful fort.'

'He keeps his household here year round,' Birut amplified. 'Though he must be scouring every dawn for some sign that the rains are coming by now.'

'I'll join him in that and gladly.' Even with the benefit of the scented oil Telouet had insisted on using on his hair and beard, Kheda did his best to take shallow breaths as the galley manoeuvred carefully between the sandbanks plainly visible in the shallow river. At this season, even the mighty flow from the folded hills and distant snow-capped mountains of this enormous island grew more meagre every day. There was nothing to wash away the ordure oozing from drains plainly visible well above the water level.

It sums up Safar and his notions of power quite neatly, this fortress of his. All magnificence on the surface but foulness beneath.

'There's the Ritsem ship.' There was relief in Telouet's voice and Kheda permitted himself a glance at Janne, to see the agreement in her eyes.

'Will Ritsem Caid want to talk to me about Olkai?'

Beneath her bright cosmetics, Itrac's face creased with misery.

'Only when you feel able. Now smile and wave,' Janne chided gently. 'We're delighted to be here, remember.'

'The Ritsem ship's moving off.' Birut nodded to Telouet. 'Let's show these mud skippers what we're made of.'

'This way.' Janne ushered Itrac back towards the steep stair leading down to the broad and luxuriously appointed cabins on the uppermost of the *Rainbow Moth*'s three levels.

'We'll stay on deck.' Kheda's glance halted Telouet and the slave returned to his master's side. Kheda grimaced. 'It may stink up here but it's stifling below.'

Telouet didn't demur. 'Let's hope the rains come soon.' He spared an involuntary glance back down river. 'Do you think the dry season's broken back home?'

'Rekha will let us know when it does.' Kheda directed the slave's attention to the landing stage that was the single breach in the Derasulla fort's outermost defences. 'Now let's see exactly what Safar's thinking of us just at present.'

'Doesn't look as if Ritsem Caid thinks too much of him.' Telouet nodded at the Ritsem domain's ship. It was a heavy trireme, fitted out with frilled canopies and silken tassels decorating sails and ropes but still unmistakably a fighting vessel and manned with experienced rowers, judging by the speed and neatness of its turn as it pulled away from the dock.

'Not quite an insult but not exactly courtesy either.' Kheda knitted thoughtful brows.

'I don't think Safar's taking offence. That's a sizeable honour guard.' Telouet nodded to the array of armoured warriors lining the landing stage. Their armour shone brilliant in the unforgiving sun, various men carrying yet more pennants proclaiming the Ulla domain's magnificence. 'Let's hope none of them faint and fall in the water.' His tone belied his words.

'So Caid's got the upper hand on something. Now what is Safar trying to tell us with this little display?' Kheda wondered aloud. As the Ritsem trireme quit the dock for a secure anchorage midstream, a significant proportion of the swordsmen were disappearing back into the labyrinth of the fort.

'That he's a discourteous boor,' growled Telouet.

Do I let them see me scowling? Will that give Ulla Safar pause for thought or just amuse him?

Kheda kept his expression tranquil. 'Let him play his games. The business bringing us here is far too serious to waste time on such stupidity.'

'Of course, my lord.' Telouet visibly set his anger aside at Kheda's sober reminder.

'Make ready!' The *Rainbow Moth*'s shipmaster shouted his warning from the stern platform. Crewmen stood alert with boathooks and fenders newly stuffed with the fibres from tandra seedpods. Kheda unobtrusively spread his feet a little.

Let's not gift Safar with any appearance of lack of confidence in my mariners by holding on to something. Besides, Telouet's always within arm's reach. He won't let me or the Daish domain suffer the embarrassment of a fall.

Two decks below, the oarsmen deftly wielded their blades to bring the massive ship edging slowly up to the landing with its stone stages like the wide-set teeth of a comb jutting forward. The high stern platform of the galley eased into a gap. Daish sailors flung ropes down with the sharp whistles common to all mariners no matter what their domain. Ulla men secured the heavy lengths of hemp to sturdy bollards, pulling the galley ever closer until the wooden stair fixed in the angle between stern platform and steering oars hung over the dock rather than the water.

Kheda turned to Telouet with a dangerous smile as he unclasped his light cloak and let it fall to the planking. 'Let's step ashore.'

As he spoke, Birut emerged from the accommodation deck, a sword on each hip, helm covering gone, and bronze adornments brilliant against the silver steel of his armour. He did not have the nasal of his helm lowered but his unsmiling face below the ruby-studded brow band was warning enough that he was ready to fight.

Janne followed him, one hand carefully lifting the flowing skirts of a scarlet gown. She paused for a moment to smooth the silk and to allow Birut to adjust the gold-embroidered gossamer draped from the points of a pearl-encrusted coronet resting among the haze of soft smoky curls that framed her face. More ropes of pearls were woven into the single thick braid that hung down her back. A triple belt of golden chains girdled her waist, the strands joined by ornate canthira leaves bright with crimson enamel. More chains were cross-tied over the gown's gold-embroidered bodice to accentuate the charms of Janne's full bosom. Gem-studded rings flashed in the sun and countless bracelets of braided and twisted gold wire jingled softly as she adjusted the splendid filigree work dotted with rubies that nestled in her cleavage. The bright varnish on her perfectly manicured nails was an exact match.

'I've seen less determination on men about to go into battle for the domain,' observed Telouet discreetly, discarding his own helm covering.

'We all fight, just on different fields.' Kheda smiled with patent admiration as Itrac emerged, pausing to settle her own skirts. He was heartened to see a new courage rise in the Chazen lady's copper-painted eyes. 'Is that your work or Birut's?'

Itrac set her jaw, lips rimmed in that same lustrous copper. Raising beringed hands, she pushed back the gold circlet set with brindled turtle shell that held her unbound, unadorned hair off her face. Reaching almost to her waist, her glossy black locks were stunning. White embroidery on a white gown with a decorous neckline did its best to flatter her modest charms while setting off the ropes of amber beads she wore around her neck. A wide belt of pale turtle shell and gold clasped her slim waist and hip-high slits at either side of the close-cut skirt revealed her slim and elegant legs with every step. Kheda caught a gleam of gold dust in the oil that protected her honey-coloured skin from the sun. Darker turtle shell ringed her wrists and ankles, gold-mounted and brilliantly polished.

'Her hair looks good. I knew that sardberry wash would bring up the shine.' Telouet studied Itrac critically. 'I wonder if we shouldn't have sewn up the sides of that gown though. Does Safar's taste run to leggy sprigs or just full-blown blooms?'

'The man has no taste, just unbridled appetites.' Kheda shifted his feet and the silver ornaments on his anklets jingled slightly. He looked down at his loose blue trousers and indigo overtunic, every seam decorated with sapphires set in silver. Silver thread coiled all around his shoulders and chest, the embroidery just hinting at the pattern of mail and plates that made up a hauberk. 'You don't think the white would have been better? That wouldn't show the sweat so much.'

Telouet reached up to untangle the chains on the earrings that were already making Kheda's ears itch. 'That indigo's dark enough to hide the marks and, anyway, everyone will be sweating like pigs in this pestilential hole. The white would show every smudge and I'd bet my sword that Safar would find a chance to spill something on you.'

'True enough.' Kheda resisted the temptation to run his fingers through his hair.

The last thing I need is canthira oil all over my hands.

He raised his voice loud enough to be heard on the dockside. 'Shall we go, my wife? Will you join us, honoured wife to my ally?'

He watched the men on the landing stage from the corner of his eye for any obvious response to his words.

No reaction? No matter. Once we're safely inside the fort, one of you blank-faced lackeys can carry my words to some underling retained to inform Safar of every whisper uttered within Derasulla's walls. The sooner the better. Let Safar chew on the fact that Daish Kheda has openly acknowledged Chazen Saril as an ally.

He offered his arm to Janne, who laid her own hand lightly upon it. Smiling as if neither had a care in the world, they walked easily down the galley's steep gangway on to the dock. Telouet followed, with an emphatic jingle of armour as he alighted heavily on the massive stones of Derasulla. Itrac came next, Birut half a pace behind her.

'This way, my lord.' An Ulla servant bowed low before them, indicating a canopied rowing boat waiting on the water-filled channel that ran all the way round between the first and second walls of the fort, yet another obstacle to any would-be invader. The only other way off the landing stage was through narrow doors set into the inner wall, leading to a room designed for the efficient killing of uninvited arrivals.

Not that there will be any bloodshed today. Not unless someone drops one of Janne's innumerable chests on his foot. Mirrel Ulla won't find my wife lacking in choice of elegance.

The sizeable Daish retinue was already disembarking from the gangway on the other side of the galley's stern. The *Rainbow Moth*'s crew were unloading the multitude of chests and coffers that a visit such as this demanded. Janne's personal musicians moved to stand aside, carrying no more than their instruments and small bags of personal belongings. Maidservants fluttered around, anxiously instructing the four blank-faced porters chosen for their broad shoulders and safe hands.

And for those far more useful attributes, names and faces unknown to the Ulla troops as practised swordsmen.

Confident all his people were about their allotted tasks, Kheda followed the fawning servant, Telouet stalking grim-faced behind him. Janne swept along serene and beautiful, Itrac doing her best to do the same beside her. Birut brought up the rear a pace behind, the challenge in his stare making it plain to anyone curious that both women were under his protection. The lackey handed them into the rowing boat and they left the landing stage. The rowers bent over their oars and pulled.

'Ulla Safar will receive you in the rose garden,' the lackey announced with the air of a man conveying wonderful news.

Kheda merely inclined his head by way of reply. He was managing to keep his face impassive but the stench of the stagnant water all around was making his stomach roil. Clouds of black flies rose and fell in the still air between the walls.

'How delightful.' Janne was made of sterner stuff.

Kheda turned to look at her and saw she'd prudently provided herself with a small pomander that had been hidden among the folds of her skirts. Itrac produced a fan of white feathers from somewhere and, as she plied it, Kheda detected it had been doused in perfume. He turned back to the front, hiding a smile.

Ulla Safar's women are no match for my Janne and it looks like Itrac Chazen is a willing pupil.

Kheda glanced apparently idly from side to side, noting the numbers of men walking the high ramparts on either side.

Will the swordsmen waiting on Daish triremes keeping

station just far enough away not to provoke Safar be a match for Ulla men? There are more warriors on this one watch than the Daish domain could summon with a full muster. Is this just some show by Safar, designed to intimidate me? It would be nice to think so. Unfortunately, this strength in arms is probably the only thing about this fort that's all it seems.

That unpalatable fact was enough to make his stomach churn even without the foulness they were travelling through.

'Derasulla is quite the largest island in the whole southern compass of the Archipelago,' Janne was telling Itrac with apparent admiration. 'With iron ore of his own to mine, every Ulla warlord can pluck as many men as he likes from their villages and arm them all, and of course, with so much land, there are plentiful resources to feed them.'

Surely we can overwhelm these savages and even their wild magic with greater numbers? Surely Ulla Safar will see it's vital for his own domain's security that he join us in fighting them?

The rowing boat passed beneath a narrow bridge giving the guards passage between the inner wall and the outer. A drain was built into the brick span, to carry the fortress's slops out to the river. Several bricks had fallen away where the curve met the outer wall and a dark stain marred the sun-baked red surface. Fortunately the rowing boat soon stopped at a water gate in the inner wall. Kheda took the steps two at a time, eager to get away from the stinking water and out of the searing sun. The cool inside the thick stone walls was almost as welcome as a draught of ice water.

'This way.' Bowing low with fluttering hands, the smooth-faced lackey led them through a maze of passages and stairways. Kheda blinked as his eyes took a moment to adjust to the dim light filtering through small windows

high in the lofty walls. Whoever had built the fort had
opted to trade light for shade. After climbing through the
outer, humbler circles of the fortress, they found themselves walking through marble halls with floors of painted
tiles. Gullies were built into the angle of wall and floor,
intended to flow with cooling water. Basins for fountains
sat beneath skylights where corridors met in vivid circles
of interlacing patterns. For the present, all the gullies and
fountains were dry, doing nothing to mitigate the heat
within the fortress. The cisterns waiting for the rain's
bounty had been dry and dusty refuges for house lizards
hunting spiders long since. Finally, they reached an
archway opening on to the merciless brilliance of the
sunlight. The lackey halted and bowed low once again, a
sweep of his arm inviting the warlord to proceed.

Kheda strode through the arch without pausing,
narrowing his eyes against the glare as discreetly as he
could. They were high in the citadel at the heart of the
fort where a courtyard had been turned into a sumptuous
physic garden.

*And the rare and exotic plants brought to the Ulla warlords
by hopeful suppliants and grateful subjects are uniformly drab
and dusty, I see. The most valuable medicinal herbs all but
dead for lack of water. Well, they'd be wasted on Safar. The
man can barely dress a cut finger.*

At the moment, Kheda saw, the Ulla warlord was taking
his ease in a sumptuous summerhouse in the middle of
the courtyard. Anyone wanting to speak to him would have
to cross the garden, sun beating down on their unshaded
heads. Ulla Safar didn't seem to have noticed their arrival.
He was cleaning his nails with the tip of a broad dagger,
one of those that characterised this domain, with the
curious handle designed for a punching blow, twin bars
to frame the forearm and a crosspiece for the palm.

'I imagine you have covered walkways in this kind of

heat, don't you? We always do,' Janne remarked artlessly
to Itrac as they strolled behind him. 'I shall have to suggest
it to Mirrel. I'm surprised she hasn't thought of it, but
then, she's in such a muddle over her sandalwood at the
moment. I don't suppose she's had time to pay attention
to much else.'

Kheda kept his face impassive.

*'Women's discussions are no business of a warlord's.' Daish
Reik told you that often enough. In any case, no one plays
these silken games better than Janne and Rekha. If Itrac gets
nothing else out of this trip, she'll get an education to leave
Chazen Saril deep in Daish's debt.*

He greeted Ulla Safar with every appearance of
contentment. 'My lord, it is always a pleasure to visit your
home.'

'You are welcome at any and every season, Daish
Kheda.' The warlord was reclining on a daybed claiming
most of the shade within the octagonal summerhouse. It
was built of the sandalwood that was one of the Ulla
domain's valued trade commodities, with walls of fretwork panels that could be drawn back to accommodate a
breeze from any direction. At the moment there was no
wind at all, even at this highest point in the citadel, but
at least the scent from the overblown rose bushes on all
sides mitigated the stink from the river far below.

'Janne Daish, a delight to see you once again. Do introduce me to your charming companion.' Ulla Safar raised
himself on one elbow with a jingle of agate necklaces and
smiled something perilously close to a leer at Itrac. A
grossly fat man, nevertheless his bracelet-laden forearms
still showed the muscle that had maintained his position
as eldest son before self-indulgence had let him run to
seed as warlord. His huge belly strained the seams of his
saffron-yellow tunic and his gold rings bit deep into puffy
fingers. A full black beard disguised his jowls somewhat,

laced through with golden chains that were looped back around his long hair to pull it off his face. His eyes were unusually pale for a man of such dark complexion.

Eyes like a jungle cat, Safar, you and your son Orhan both.

Kheda was about to introduce Itrac when Janne forestalled him.

'You know Itrac Chazen,' she chided Safar playfully. 'Chazen Saril introduced her to us all at Redigal Coron's New Year celebrations.'

'Of course,' Safar replied, his frank gaze examining Itrac with a lasciviousness that prompted identical scowls from Telouet and Birut. 'Forgive me,' he purred.

'We all forget the most obvious things,' Janne went on soothingly. 'With the heat so late in the dry season such a sore trial.'

Even with that none so subtle hint, no invitation to sit was forthcoming. Kheda turned to an arbour of climbing roses falling in a shower of blood-red blooms. 'Janne, do smell these. They are wonderful.'

Janne joined him and sniffed, her expression delighted. 'Indeed. Their attar must be something quite special.' She lifted a velvety bloom with a careful hand and as it hid her mouth, spoke for Kheda's ears alone. 'Surely Safar won't be so discourteous as to keep us standing much longer?'

'He does seem keen to show us our place from the outset.'

Just what is that place, I wonder and do we need to work out an early escape route?

As Kheda wondered, he heard voices echoing in the passage leading to this scented sanctuary. This time the lackey escorted the guests into the garden. 'Rits—'

'I see we're not standing on ceremony, good.' Ritsem Caid spoke over the servant with broad good humour but Kheda saw the calculation in his eyes.

What makes you so bold, that you're not about to let Safar make such distinctions between his guests?

'Great lord.' Kheda held out both hands and Caid grasped them firmly. The two men were much of a height and similarly built, years of swordplay building adequate muscle over long bones. Caid wore his curly hair long and braided close to his scalp, his exuberant beard tamed in a single plait. His hazel eyes met Kheda's green ones for a moment and the silent pledge of alliance there warmed Kheda's heart.

Dropping Kheda's hands, the Ritsem warlord turned to Janne and bowed low. 'My lady of Daish, beautiful as always.'

Janne smiled sunnily at him and stretched a hand out to Itrac.

'We need no introduction, do we, my lady of Chazen.' Ritsem Caid bowed almost as low as he had to Janne. 'I only wish we were meeting again under better stars. I offer my condolences and those of all of my wives.'

Belatedly, Kheda realised that Caid had only his personal slave and a few servants in attendance. 'Are we not to have the pleasure of their company?'

'Taisia is with me,' Caid answered easily, 'but the others felt it their duty to stay close to home in such uncertain times.' He smiled at Itrac before snapping his fingers to summon an armoured man from the knot of Ritsem retainers. 'Trya and Ri have sent you a gift though, in remembrance of Olkai who was their sister before she became yours. This is Jevin. Ganil speaks well of him.'

The Ritsem warlord's personal slave smiled broadly. 'I'd let him serve any lady of our domain.'

Itrac was struggling to find a suitable response so Janne spoke up brightly. 'How kind. Ulla Safar, since we're not standing on ceremony, I'll beg your indulgence and we'll go and thank Taisia.' She snapped her fingers at one of the sweating Ulla servants hovering by the summerhouse.

'Tell your mistress Mirrel that we'll attend her just as soon as she sends word she's ready to receive us.' Skirts fluttering about her gold-ringed ankles, Janne swept Itrac out of the garden, Birut and the newcomer Jevin following shoulder to shoulder and in emphatic step.

Janne, my love, you had a hand in that or I am a roof lizard.

Kheda watched them go with a neutral expression to balance Caid's wide grin and Safar's unconcealed glower.

'I do hope the rains come soon. This heat's getting unbearable.' Caid moved into the shade of the summer-house and unbidden sat on a cushion. 'I'm not surprised your guard couldn't tolerate it long enough to do full honour to the Daish domain. You'll forgive them, won't you, Kheda?'

'I assumed they were being ordered to their barracks once their commanders realised just how hot the day was.'

Do I wait for an invitation to sit? No, that's just playing into your fat hands.

Kheda sat opposite Caid; the two of them now flanking Safar on his ochre-brocaded daybed. 'We need every fighting man we can muster, so we don't want half of Ulla's forces prostrate with sunstroke.'

'We have a serious matter before us,' Caid began. He was wearing a blue tunic patterned with hummingbirds, the green of their wings mimicking the emeralds set in his profusion of gold rings and bracelets.

A good omen, that we're both wearing blue.

Kheda took a breath, about to speak, but Safar fore-stalled him.

'Serious or not, it will have to wait. Redigal Coron has yet to join us.' He didn't sound concerned.

'That surprises me. When he has the least journey of any of us?' Kheda queried mildly.

The mud worm's delaying at Safar's orders of course.

'When is he expected?' Caid didn't hide his displeasure.

'This evening, tomorrow morning perhaps.' Safar waved a casual hand.

'What shall we do in the meantime?' Kheda enquired with studied calm.

Besides finding a quiet moment to hint that you baiting Safar is exactly what I don't need, Caid.

'Improve our acquaintance with each other,' replied Safar with a jovial laugh.

'As you wish.' Caid sounded sceptical. He looked around the summerhouse and the garden. 'Will Orhan be joining us?'

'Orhan?' Safar was surprised. 'Why should he?'

'The education of your heir is your concern, my lord of Ulla.' Caid looked over at Kheda. 'I take it Sirket commands in your absence?'

'With Rekha Daish to guide him,' Kheda confirmed. 'They will relay any word from Chazen Saril. The sooner we know where our enemies lie, the sooner we can plan their destruction.'

'It's a blessing to have a son one can rely on.' The Ritsem warlord seemed intent on other concerns. 'Zorat will be receiving guests from the Endit domain in my stead. Your summons was so urgent I didn't have time to rearrange their visit.'

'It's too hot out here.' Safar snapped his fingers at his body slave, who stepped up to haul the warlord gracelessly to his feet. 'We'll discuss this uneasiness of yours when Redigal Coron arrives.' He lumbered away and out of the garden, sparing a casual blow for a slave who was a little too slow getting out of his path.

Kheda looked at Caid. 'Don't twist his ears too much. We need him and his men if we're to meet this menace from the south.'

'Maybe, maybe not.' Caid grinned, unrepentant. 'The

Ritsem domain can summon doughty warriors.'

'That I don't doubt, but not in the numbers we need, not when all your islands could fit inside this one. Besides, swordsmen need swords, so we need Ulla steel. You've no ironstone.' Then Kheda caught the glint in Caid's eye.

'But we have, my friend.' Caid's grin grew still broader, his even teeth white in the shade.

'Since when?' gaped Kheda.

'Since an enterprising lad went exploring caves in an otherwise useless lump of an island.' Caid turned his head to stare at a humble gardener tending a pink-kissed spray of yellow roses. 'Shall we go and look for some refreshment, given our host is being so unusually remiss in his attentions to us?'

And that spying servant will dutifully carry back that insult. So what else would we like Ulla Safar to chew over?

'Come and take your ease with me and Janne,' Kheda suggested. 'She'll be delighted to see you.'

'Gladly.' Caid sprang to his feet. 'I'd like to talk to her about Endit Fel.'

'I don't know that she'll tell you much you don't already know.' Kheda rose and smoothed his tunic. 'She'd only been wed half a year when Endit Cai died and she was his fifth wife at that.'

'I'll still be interested in anything she recalls about Fel's likes or dislikes,' Caid assured him.

'You've got Ulla islands all too close to the sea-lane between you and the Endit domain,' Kheda reminded Caid discreetly once they were out of earshot of the gardener. 'Provoke our fat friend too much and he might just decide to squat in your path.'

'And offend Endit Fel like that, now he'll have a choice of where to trade for iron?' countered Caid gleefully. 'Oh, I am looking forward to sticking a few pins in Safar's fat arse.'

And obviously to a new accommodation between the Ritsem domain and Endit Fel. What are you hoping to get out of that? When am I going to find a chance to ask? Not walking Derasulla's corridors, not when any number of listening ears could be hiding in these honeycombed walls.

As Kheda thought this, the ingratiating servant appeared from nowhere, bowing and dry-washing his hands. 'My lords, may I escort you to your quarters.'

'Take us to my lady Janne.'

The two warlords walked in silence as the beardless servant bobbed and bowed before them, his meaningless compliments for themselves as ceaseless as his praise for his master. Kheda heard Caid's man Ganil matching Telouet step for step, chainmail jingling softly.

'How much lower in the citadel are we going?' Ritsem Caid asked sharply as their walk continued.

'Here we are.' The slave led them around a corner and gestured at a door. 'My lady Janne Daish's apartments. Your accommodations are just along the corridor, great lord.' The slave struggled to bow and point at the same time.

'I will see that everything is as we require.' Telouet headed for the door, face promising comprehensive retaliation if everything was not exactly to the standard befitting his master.

'You may go.' Kheda dismissed the fawning slave and knocked on Janne's door.

Birut opened it a hand's width with a forbidding scowl. 'My lord.' Face clearing, he flung the door open. 'And my lord Ritsem Caid, my ladies.'

Janne was seated with Itrac on a midnight-blue carpet patterned with stars and ringed with a bank of luxuriantly stuffed cushions. Intricately carved sandalwood side tables bore silver incense burners in the form of questing hounds and shallow bowls of cobalt ceramic were piled high with yellow rose petals. Half sunk into the earth of the original river island, the room was broad with an airy feel thanks to the white marble lining its walls where tall vases of alabaster stood full of fresh vizail sprays filling the room with their heady scent. By contrast, the floor was brilliant with tiles making an intricate interlace of green and blue. The windows high in the north-facing wall were shaded with awnings as was the flight of steps leading up and out into a private garden where Kheda could hear the soothing plash of a fountain and smell the shady promise of perfume trees.

'Do these rooms suffice, my wife?' Kheda asked with a faint note of displeasure. 'They are rather small.'

'They are adequate, my husband, and cooler than any suite on the heights. Doubtless Mirrel Ulla had the sense to realise we'd be more concerned with our comfort than our consequence at such a time of trial. Birut, drinks for our lord and our honoured guest.' Janne nodded to the slave, who picked up a splendid set of ewer and goblets in gleaming Jahal ware from a side table.

Kheda took the cup Birut offered and sniffed it cautiously.

'Lilla juice and spring water.' Janne nodded to the Daish musician sat in one corner of the room with more modest rug and cushions. He had been plucking a soothing lilt from his circular lyre. Picking up his bow, he started a livelier tune with a loud flourish.

'At least he's not trying to poison us with river water.' Kheda shrugged and drank.

'It will be nice to have a change from lilla fruit, when the rains come,' Itrac ventured unexpectedly.

Ritsem Caid had emptied his goblet and was holding it out for a refill. 'Where are you housed, Itrac Chazen?'

'She's sharing these apartments with me,' Janne answered for her, a glint in her eye.

'Mirrel Ulla offered me a room among her own household,' said Itrac uncertainly. 'Since I am here with no retinue of my own.'

Caid snorted. 'You're here with Janne Daish, celebrated first wife and her husband an honoured guest. She just wanted you locked up with the rest of Safar's women, so we could all get used to the notion.'

'That's what I suspected,' agreed Janne.

'I take it you're ready to marry without delay?' Caid looked sharply at Kheda and then to Itrac. 'If you hear the worst from Chazen.'

So you spared some thought for the complications of the Chazen situation, in between gloating over your new opportunities and making plans to ally with Endit Fel. That's a relief.

'I was thinking it might be less of a slap in the face for Safar if she married Sirket.' Kheda smiled reassuringly at Itrac. 'But let's hope it doesn't come to that.'

'What do you mean?' Itrac stared at the two warlords, plainly confused.

'I hadn't thought it appropriate to discuss the delicate issue of her status with Itrac.' Janne rebuked both men with a minatory look. 'Not while she still mourns Olkai Chazen's death.'

'If Saril is killed,' Itrac said, eyes dark with pain, 'I'll just go to the Thelus domain. My father would welcome me back.'

'Your father is far from here.' Janne forbore to rebuke such naivety with some effort. 'With Olkai dead and Sekni's fate unknown, you are senior wife to the Chazen domain and as such, you would hold considerable power, should we hear that Chazen Saril is dead.'

Itrac hid her face in shaking hands, the jaunty music of the lyre at cruel odds with her distress. A piper joined the tune, in an attempt to cover the rising voices in the room.

Janne gathered her close in comforting arms but her voice was gently implacable. 'There is no Chazen child yet of an age of reason. Even if there were, the domain would still be vulnerable without a strong regent. That would be Olkai's duty but with her dead, you must take up the challenge.'

'It's your duty to the domain to wed a man strong enough to rule as warlord until one of Saril's children is of the age of discretion,' Caid agreed soberly.

'Which is why I thought of Sirket,' explained Kheda. 'With his own inheritance waiting, he wouldn't disinherit Saril's children in favour of his own.'

Not while I'm alive to tan his hide for trying, anyway.

'Safar won't back down for anyone less than another warlord.' Caid shook his head emphatically. 'Anyway, Sirket's not here. You must be wed inside the day some message bird brings word of Saril's death, Itrac, if you're to safeguard your domain. You should have brought Sirket with you if that was your plan, Kheda.'

'I wasn't prepared to bring him into this kind of danger, any more than you were about to risk Zorat,' Kheda retorted.

'Zorat is needed in the Ritsem isles,' declared Caid.

'If either of them was here, Safar would just be taunting them to provoke some rudeness or argument to give him an excuse to ignore the real concerns before us,' Janne said curtly. 'We cannot afford to indulge his nonsense when all our safety is at stake. If we do not stand together against magic, we'll all be lost!'

The mention of magic silenced everyone, even the sweeping lyre and piping flutes of the musicians. Janne snapped furious fingers at them and they hastily resumed their tune.

The music barely covered Itrac's sudden sobs. 'Why are we talking like this? You're talking as if Saril's already dead. Maybe he is. How will we ever know? Who's ever going to hold the Chazen islands anyway, plagued with magic and monsters, and anyway, everyone's going to be dead, Saril and Sekni and all the children, just like poor Olkai, burning in agonies and—'

'Birut, the door,' Janne snapped, gesturing at the entrance to the sleeping quarters. 'Get her up.' Finding the hysterical girl unable to stand, Jevin deftly swung her up into his arms. 'Kheda, get something to soothe these vapours or she'll be in no fit state to deal with Mirrel whenever that bitch deigns to receive us.'

'Of course.' Kheda turned and hurried to his own apartments, Caid at his elbow. 'Telouet, my small physic chest.' He reached beneath his tunic for the key chain around his waist as Telouet held out a small coffer of silver-bound satinwood.

'I'm sorry, I assumed you'd all discussed her future.' Caid fell silent

'No,' Kheda said shortly. He sorted through tightly sealed glass jars until he found the one he wanted. 'She's barely over the shock of everything that's happened. Telouet, get a mouthful of water, no juice.'

'Silvernet?' Caid watched Kheda shake a greyish-white pulp into the cup the slave handed him. 'You don't think she'll need something stronger?'

'It'll calm her without dulling her wits.' Kheda swirled the water around, watching it grow cloudy. 'We all need our wits about us here.'

'I was sure you'd have talked the options through with her,' Caid apologised again.

'Give this to Janne.' Kheda handed Telouet the cup and waved him away. For the first time he noticed the room. As plushly appointed as the apartments Janne had been given, it had the same white marble walls and a cream- and red-tiled floor.

'Did you let Olkai die in agony?' Caid asked abruptly.

'What?' Kheda looked at the Ritsem warlord, appalled. 'How can you ask such a thing?'

'Your messages weren't exactly clear.' Caid shrugged awkwardly. 'Had Saril tended her, before you found her?'

You want someone to blame, don't you?

'I nursed her myself until she died.' Kheda closed the physic chest with slow deliberation. 'Her women had done all they could; I can't fault their care of her. Then I used every skill my father taught me for her burns but it was plain from the outset she was doomed. I'm sorry. All I could do was ease her pain and believe me I did so. Not that it makes her death any easier to bear, I know.'

'She was the best of all of us, everyone's favourite. That's why my father let her marry for love of that feckless beachcomber Saril.' Grief twisted Caid's face. 'He said the omens were good. The old fool must have missed something. Saril must have missed every portent this past year, not to have foreseen this disaster.'

'Magic makes a mockery of every omen,' Kheda reminded him gently. 'You cannot blame Saril for that. I couldn't read any clear portents south of the Serpents' Teeth. At least the miasma doesn't seem to have reached north of there, though. I could read the portents plainly enough once I was back in my own waters.'

And you cannot imagine what a relief that was, my friend.

Caid pressed the back of one hand to his closed eyes before speaking with low contempt. 'What is our esteemed ally Chazen Saril doing now?'

'Fighting to maintain a presence in his domain, so his people may rally to him.' Kheda chose his words carefully for the benefit of any curious ears. 'Sending out scouts and searching out news so that we might have some idea of just what islands these invaders hold and where their magicians might be lurking. We will need to know all we can when we go to drive them back into the southern ocean.'

Caid's thoughts were still with Olkai and her future. 'She's been taken to a Daish tower of silence? I know I have no rights in the matter but I'd rather see her virtues adorn your domain than go back to Chazen.'

'It seemed the best thing to do,' Kheda said a little awkwardly. 'With magic rampant in the south, I didn't want all that she was corrupted by it.'

Caid would have said something but for a rap on the door. Ganil, waiting in silent attendance, opened it to reveal the beardless slave.

'My lords,' he simpered ingratiatingly. 'Redigal Coron has arrived unexpectedly early. Since you feel your business is so urgent, Ulla Safar invites you to join them both in his audience chamber.'

'All in good time.' Kheda gestured and Ganil slammed the door in the servant's face.

'He's playing games with us,' growled Caid.

'Of course.' Kheda smiled without humour. 'Off balance and hungry, that's how he wants us.'

As he spoke the door opened again. Ganil's scowl cleared when he saw Telouet carrying a broad platter of freshly prepared fruits and roughly torn bread piled in a basket.

'We'll keep Safar waiting just long enough to make the point that we're not at his beck and call.' Kheda helped himself. 'And make sure it's not our bellies rumbling that give him an excuse to cut the discussions short.'

'You talk about me twisting Safar's ears.' Caid chewed the speckled bread with a frown. 'How many insults are you going to swallow from him? This is far too coarse to give to guests.'

'It wasn't given, it was taken.' Kheda grinned

Telouet spoke up at his master's nod. 'The bread's from

baskets in the northern servants' kitchen. The fruit's from the anteroom serving the audience chambers of Mirrel Ulla and Shay Ulla. I peeled and chopped it myself.'

'There's no way you had time to go all that way.' Curiosity lit Caid's eyes as he took a slice of melon, careful not to let the juice stain his sumptuous tunic. 'Who—?'

'Let's go and see if the ladies are ready, shall we?' Kheda took a damp cloth that Telouet was offering and wiped starfruit juice from his fingers.

'Do we want them in the audience chamber?' Caid stood patiently as Ganil brushed crumbs, real and imagined, from his chest. 'The more people there are, the more confusion Safar will try to sow.'

'Quite,' Kheda agreed. 'Which is why Janne will be keeping Mirrel and Shay both well away from the four of us. Shall we go?'

'As you wish, Daish Kheda. Let's show Ulla Safar that it's time to take our business here seriously,' said Caid pugnaciously.

'Do you remember the way?' Kheda asked out of the side of his mouth.

'I think so.' But Caid didn't sound entirely sure as they went out into the corridor, slaves dutifully at their heels. At the end of the passage, they climbed the first set of stairs leading to the upper levels of the citadel.

'East here,' prompted Ganil under his breath when Caid slowed at a junction of identical corridors on the next floor.

'And north at the next stair after this,' murmured Telouet.

Kheda and Caid shared a grin but by the time they had negotiated the maze of the citadel and turned into a short passage ending in heavy wooden doors of bluntly carved black wood, both their faces were deadly serious.

CHAPTER SEVEN

'Announce us, Telouet.' Kheda halted and gave the armoured guards flanking the entrance his most intimidating stare.

We'll come before Ulla Safar and Redigal Coron with full ceremony or not at all.

Telouet slid past the warlords to stand menacingly before the door wards. Ganil moved slightly to guard them both from the rear.

'Open to Daish Kheda, son of Daish Reik, reader of portents, giver of laws, healer and protector of all his domain encompasses,' Telouet challenged, hands on both swords. 'Open to Ritsem Caid, son of Ritsem Serno, ruler, scholar, augur and defender that all his domain may call on.'

The guards bowed acceptably low and pushed the heavy doors open. Ulla Safar's personal slave was waiting just inside, a naked sword in either hand.

'Enter and be welcome to bring tidings, share counsel and accept the wisdom of Ulla Safar who is guardian of our health, wealth and justice.' He thrust his swords back into their scabbards with a rushing rattle and stepped back. Telouet held his hands away from his own weapons and moved the two warlords into the room.

So Safar has a new secretary writing his boasts and one with a taste for the ostentatiously poetic rather than the accurate. Our wives protect the domain's wealth. Let's see if Safar's man has concocted some similar new flourish for Redigal Coron's body slave to declaim.

The fourth warlord was already seated close by Safar with his back to the long windows shedding the bright sunlight into the wide and lofty room. If need be, it would doubtless accommodate every spokesman from every village even of this vast island. The roof reaching up through two storeys of the citadel above them was held up by pillars of ironwood covered with vines of burnished gold leaf, the hammer beams high above carved into fanciful beasts brilliantly painted: jungle cats, hook-toothed hogs, water oxen and the chattering loals that fanciful children called guardians of the forest.

One of the gaggle of old attendants that trailed every-where after Coron had usurped the bodyguard's place just behind the warlord, a white-haired, clean-shaven slave who knelt there submissively. The swordsman was sitting some way further back, a heavily built youth with a bull neck and a hint of arrogance in his boredom. Kheda didn't recognise him but then he rarely saw Coron with the same body slave twice. Redigal Coron looked apprehensive.

As if we needed to see your expression, Coron, to know you'll be trying to balance toadying to Safar with whatever advice your so faithful adviser whispers in your ear.

The Redigal warlord was sturdily built with long legs, a good head taller than all the other warlords. Eldest of the four, touches of grey were beginning to show in his hair and beard but he was in no sense past his prime. Well muscled, his dark skin gleamed with health beneath a profusion of topaz and silver jewellery that proclaimed the prosperity of his fertile and peaceful domain. A lively pattern of prancing golden deer decorated his purple satin tunic, the archers pursuing them embroidered on his sleeveless overmantle.

What a mystery it is, that such a well-favoured man should be so spineless. Would I have some answers, if I'd known Redigal Adun? You never told me, Daish Reik, why you

*disliked him so much. Is he the key to the puzzle of his son's
failings? Or is it your faithful companions, Coron, these white-
haired zamorin, always at your elbow since before your accession to your father's dignities? Those of us who thought this
a passing irritation have certainly been proved wrong; as
adopted sons and nephews join the coterie when older retainers
withdraw to their extremely comfortable retirement.*

'Are we expecting anyone else?' Caid stood, arms
folded, looking down at Safar who reclined among a profusion of cushions at the northern end of the luxurious
carpet that filled the enormous room.

Kheda noted everyone else got a single cushion with a
gaudy pattern of pomegranates. 'Shall we sit?'

'Of course,' Safar said easily. 'Now, let's see if we can't
make sense of this panic. You were wise to look for my
counsel before letting rumour spread unnecessary alarm
throughout the entire southern Archipelago.'

Kheda took his time settling himself facing their host.
Caid completed the compass square and subjected Coron
to a searching stare. Coron's slave frowned and leaned
forward to whisper into his master's ear. Kheda heard a
clink as Telouet knelt behind him in the formal pose of a
slave ready to draw his sword and die for his master.

Let's be sure nothing like that becomes necessary.

'We didn't expect you until tonight at the earliest.' Caid
addressed Coron with a hint of sarcasm. 'I'm pleased to
see you chose to make haste, when we must decide how
to deal with such obnoxious dangers.'

'You are the one being too hasty,' interrupted Safar
with an unpleasant smile. 'We should read the portents
for this council.'

'I have read the skies every night as we travelled here,'
Caid said with barely concealed contempt.

'As have I.' Kheda spoke loudly to forestall Safar's
retort. 'The Horned Fish rises, clear sign that we should

not ignore the stars' guidance. The heavenly Ruby counsels courage and unity as it moves from the arc of friendship into the realm of our foes.'

'It lies in a clear line with the Topaz that marks the year,' added Caid. 'It is plain that these events are truly momentous.'

'Both those jewels are set in the compass directly opposite the Amethyst, talisman against anger and gem to stimulate new ideas,' Kheda continued, hiding his irritation at Caid's interruption. 'The Amethyst rides with the Pearl of the Lesser Moon, in the sky where we look for signs to our children's fates. The need for our cooperation to safeguard their futures could not be plainer.'

'Amethyst and Pearl both ride among the stars of the Sea Serpent,' said Coron unexpectedly. 'That is a complex sign where portents can hint at hidden foes and unexpected dangers, for children most of all. We must be careful in our deliberations, you in particular, Daish Kheda, with the Pearl such a potent symbol for your domain.'

'The Diamond for leadership lies in the arc of brotherhood, cradled within the stars of the Bowl that counsels sharing between friends and allies.' Kheda kept his eyes on Ulla Safar.

'But the Greater Moon, the Opal, it sits in the arc of self, so we must look to our own instincts to guide us above all else. It shines through the branches of the Canthira Tree that reminds us of the whole cycle of life, death and renewal.' Ulla Safar's pale, animal eyes were all but hidden in folds of fat. 'How else can canthira seeds sprout, if they have not first been scorched by fire? It is my duty to make sure we seek every guidance, as lord of this domain.' Safar half clapped his hands briskly with a rattle of his agate bracelets.

This is a first, my lord Safar. Your attitude to your divinatory duties is haphazard at best, unless there's a chance you can humiliate my son or Caid's on the pretext of granting them an honour and then querying every interpretation they make of the plainest portents.

A dutiful servant scurried into the room carrying a shallow brass-bound cage of white wood. He knelt before Safar, placing the cage on the ground and shuffling backwards, bowing so low he banged his forehead on the ground with an audible thud. Scrambling to his feet, he fled for the doorway.

Safar leant forward with a grunt, his gargantuan belly impeding his efforts to reach the cage. Opening it, he thrust a fat hand inside and drew out a small green lizard, a fan of black scales crowning its pointed head and a black line running the length of its back down to the tip of its bony tail. 'Are we ready?'

Without waiting for any reply, the Ulla warlord half dropped, half threw the squirming reptile on to the carpet between them. It landed with a soft thud and crouched down, long toes splayed on the unfamiliar surface, head weaving and cautious tongue tasting the air. It took a few wary steps in Coron's direction before freezing, the scales on its head rising to a startled crest. Wheeling round, it scurried noiselessly towards Safar and disappeared in the cushions plumped at the fat man's back.

'It would seem the responsibility for guiding our counsels rests with me,' remarked Safar with bland complacency as his body slave began a furtive search among the cushions for the lizard.

'Though, when dealing with such grave concerns, we should read every augury,' Caid countered with commendable restraint.

'Let's study the skies at sunset, the clouds and the flight of the river birds,' Kheda suggested.

You can't have trained those to follow whatever secret scent duped that lizard.

'Very well.' Safar pretended surprise and made as if to stand up. 'We can gather again in the morning.'

'You misunderstand me,' said Kheda sharply.

'We will discuss these threats now,' Caid insisted at the same time.

'We can consult all available portents to divine our best course before we act,' agreed Redigal Coron cautiously. Behind his shoulder, the white-haired slave was watchful.

'As you wish.' Safar shrugged his massive shoulders and settled himself once more on his cushions. 'Now, Daish Kheda, just what do you think you saw on some scrubby Chazen beach?'

Safar's slave had caught the lizard and was making a clumsy attempt to return it to its cage. Kheda looked down and counted four white trumpet flowers and five blue logen blooms woven into the carpet before the creature was caged and removed. He looked up.

'I don't think I saw anything. I know I saw monsters wrought of foul enchantment leaving my people and Chazen Saril's dead and injured. But that was not the start of it, nor the worst.'

It seems almost unreal, like some poet's recital of imagined horrors, yet it is so very real, so brutally true. You have to believe me.

He took a breath and detailed the first alarms rousing the Daish compound before continuing through every aspect of the punishing voyage south and the grief of discovering Olkai Chazen's suffering. Seeing Safar about to interrupt, Kheda gave him no chance, pressing on to explain their unexpected initial successes in the south so rapidly followed by the horrifying setback of the monstrous whip lizards' attack. Telling of Atoun's death prompted a grating shift from Telouet behind him and Kheda saw the Redigal zamorin watching the slave thoughtfully. Clearing his throat, he concluded his stark recital of the events that had sent terror rippling through the southern reaches.

'For now, Chazen Saril holds a small group of swampy islands on the easternmost fringe of his domain. He is seeking to learn exactly where these invaders are gathered and in what strengths, as well as how many wizards they have to call on. I am keeping him supplied with message birds so he can send word of every new discovery to Rekha Daish. Sirket will alert us to any significant developments while we are here.'

'You trust the boy to judge what's significant?' Safar's amusement was just short of disbelief.

'I do, and he has Rekha Daish to advise him.' Kheda replied with determined calm.

Try casting aspersions on my second wife's wisdom, Safar, when everyone here knows how emphatically your own women always find themselves on the wrong side of the balance in their dealings with her.

'Now you've heard with your own ears what Kheda sent us in sealed and ciphered messages days ago,' said Caid tersely, 'let's not waste any more time going over old ground. We must act!'

'I see no need for me to act.' Safar smiled with genial unconcern. 'This is no concern of mine. The Chazen domain is many days' passage away even by the fastest trireme.'

'It'll be your concern all too soon if these magicians come north,' retorted Caid.

'Unless I mistake Daish Kheda, they show no signs of coming north?' Safar looked at him with polite query. 'They don't even seem to have attacked Chazen Saril again?'

'Not as yet,' said Kheda tersely. 'I imagine that they realise that the imminent storms will make any voyaging too hazardous. I have every expectation that they will come north in strength as soon as the rains have passed, maybe even as soon as the first break in the squalls.'

Unless they can master water as well as fire and simply ignore the weather. In which case we're all in more trouble than we can imagine. But you can't imagine, can you, any of you? You haven't seen what I have seen.

Redigal Coron's slave whispered something to him. Coron cleared his throat. 'It would be as well to decide what we might do, should they come north once the rains have passed.'

'Since your domain and mine will be the first to be invaded,' Kheda agreed with uncompromising harshness.

'That would certainly give me cause for concern,' Safar assured Coron. The Redigal warlord didn't look convinced.

More importantly neither does that slave of his.

'It'll be a little late to be concerned when they're landing on our beaches,' said Caid with biting precision. 'Let's stop them now, before they even think of attacking the Daish or Redigal domains.'

'But who are they?' pleaded Coron. 'What do they want?'

'They must want something, whoever they are.' Safar looked more alert. 'What are they seeking from Chazen?'

'I have no idea.' Kheda didn't mind letting the others see his frustration.

'I don't see we need to know that, not to fight them,' said Caid robustly.

'While they fight us with magic,' retorted Safar. 'How do we fight that?'

Anxious, Coron nodded. 'We don't have enough talismans to turn magic aside from one in ten of our warriors. If we look to other domains to trade for the relevant gems, they'll simply strip us of everything we could offer.'

Those are Ulla Safar's words in your mouth, aren't they?

'I doubt it.' Kheda set his jaw. 'Not when we're stopping this flood of malice before it reaches their shores.'

'You think they'll credit our claims of magic blowing up from the southern ocean like some whirlwind out of season?' Safar shook his head. 'Do you want to try convincing Tule Nar, Viselis Ils, even Endit Fels? There's no record of magic in any of our islands within time of memory.'

'It's the northernmost domains are plagued by wizards, not us.' Coron glanced back over his shoulder to seek his slave's confirmation.

'I still find it hard to believe myself.' Safar's tone turned sceptical. 'Are you sure this wasn't some delusion, some drug in your drinking water, some dreamsmoke blown across your sleeping ships?'

'Believe it,' Kheda said coldly. 'Before the roofs of your own fortress run with sorcerous fire.'

'Are you sure this isn't all some deception, some trickery?' Coron pleaded.

Kheda looked straight at him, unblinking. 'No delusion ripped Atoun's face off and showered me in his life's blood. No smoke burned Olkai's hand to a charred claw and left her dying through days of unconscionable suffering. We can summon Chazen Itrac to tell us of her experiences if you choose not to believe me, though I should warn you, Janne Daish will not be pleased to see her put through such an ordeal.'

He turned his gaze on Safar. 'Who would make such a pretence, that his domain was being invaded and polluted by magic? Chazen Saril? What could he possibly hope to gain?'

'Who knows, indeed?' Safar stared back at him with level indifference. 'I suggest you go back to your islands and prepare to meet this threat. I shall make ready to deal with it as and when it touches my domain. It may be that they find whatever they seek among the people of Chazen and don't even bother us.'

'But how do we deal with magic if they do come north?' Coron was definitely agitated on that score, even ignoring his attendant slave, who plainly wanted to whisper something.

'I don't imagine a magician is any more proof against an arrow through the eye or a sword in the throat than any other man.' Safar shrugged. 'How many could he kill before one of ours got through and ended his evil? I have plenty of men to throw at him.'

'I'm glad to hear it,' said Kheda. 'They will all be needed in the south.'

'How do you know these magic wielders are not proof against swords and arrows?' Redigal Coron looked nauseated. 'Ancient lore tells of magic making men impervious to iron and slingshot, fire and drowning.'

'Then let us search that same lore for any clue as to how such magic was defeated,' Caid suggested forcefully.

'It is the question of magic's taint that worries me,' said Safar silkily. 'I owe my people a duty of care to keep them safe from any such contamination.'

'I have always believed in the innocence of those unwillingly touched by magic,' Kheda said firmly.

'As have I,' nodded Caid.

'Whereas so many of my books argue otherwise.' Safar shook his head with a fine show of regret. 'Purification is a chancy business at best. Those who go to fight may well find themselves exiled from their own islands.'

'It's a debate with cogent argument on either side.' As Redigal Coron spoke, his slave leant forward with some whispered contribution.

'All the more reason not to run the risk, until my own waters are threatened,' sighed Safar.

'You think your people will thank you for dallying with philosophical questions until they wake up with magic besieging them?' retorted Caid.

You think I'll believe you'll be studying your annals and all those fine tomes of argument and observation, when you're all but illiterate and, worse yet, you see no shame in it, you greasy, sweating hog, no disgrace in substituting brutality for wisdom in order to rule this vast domain?

Kheda studied Safar's cunning face. Beneath the bearded jowls, he saw the other man's jaw was resolute, dislike of Kheda shining in his pale eyes.

I could sit here and talk until the sun has set and both moons come and gone and you will never agree to fight these unknown invaders. I could bring Itrac here and make her relive every terrified breath of her ordeal and all that would do would titillate your taste for women in distress. Telouet's told me how you like bruises on your concubines. You'll lurk here in this great fortress like some toad beneath a rock and watch every domain to your south fall to these foul magicians; happy to see your rivals fall even to such a foe. You'll only fight when magic threatens the Ulla domain, you fool.

Then a horrible suspicion chilled Kheda's spine.

Or will you fight? Or if you find out whatever it is these evil invaders seek, will you look to trade it for peace across your domain? You won't care if every other island in the southern seas is corrupted with magic, as long as your own fiefdom stays untouched to pander to your repellent whims.

Kheda studied the myriad sprawling tendrils of green vines and darker leaves that coiled across the ruddy silk nap of the carpet, blue logen blooms dotted seemingly haphazardly with white trumpet flowers and tangles of yellow firecreeper.

A carpet can look like nothing more than a muddle of motifs that caught the weaver's fancy as he worked his way up the loom. You never see a weaver copying a pattern, after all, and you can't see any decoration used the same way twice within arm's reach of where you're sitting, can you? Stand back, my son, and separate the essentials, follow each

*different element. Then you'll see the patterns hidden from
the untutored eye by those that overlay them.'*

Kheda looked away down the fine lattice of dark vines
worked aslant over the whole carpet, trumpet flowers and
firecreeper weaving their own design through empty
spaces.

He looked at Safar and then Redigal Coron. 'There is
another course of action we could consider.'

'Let's hear it!' Ritsem Caid's desperation betrayed his
own realisation that Ulla Safar wasn't going to shift his
ground.

'Even after seeing these monsters, we know nothing of
magic beyond the evil it brings in its train.' Kheda swallowed on a dry mouth. 'As you say, we have seen no wizards
in these reaches for time out of mind. There are domains
in the northern islands that have not been so fortunate.
We've all heard of barbarian raids to steal spice bushes and
slaves, to plunder merchant galleys plying between domains.'

'That's nothing to us.' Safar made to rise but his own
gross weight and the treacherous silk of the cushions
betrayed him. Unwilling to lose his dignity in further
struggle, he subsided, cruel eyes all but disappearing in a
scowl.

'My father told me that, in days gone by, the wizard-
plagued domains closest to the unbroken lands would
pander to barbarian lusts for gem stones, paying for peace
instead of shedding Archipelagan blood, until they could
drive off those invaders made bold by magic.' Kheda was
heartened to see Caid caught by this unexpected notion.
The slave behind Coron was watching him intently too.
'Could we not ask those northern warlords to share what
they learned of driving off wizardry, of forestalling the
stain of magic on their lands?'

'That would truly be a desperate step,' said Caid with
distaste.

'Aren't these desperate times?' countered Kheda.

Redigal Coron nodded slowly, face sombre, as the white-haired slave knelt forward with some whispered comment. 'Might we not find ourselves caught between fire and flood, though, if these northern warlords thought lending such aid gave them a claim on our lands?'

'I would never consider such a course. Their spies would search out every seaway, every island's wealth and resources. You might as well cut your son's throat and offer up your daughter, her ankles tied wide to her bedposts!' Safar's outrage echoed loud in the great hall but none of the other warlords were looking at him.

'How would any lord from the furthest north launch an attack, with the whole Archipelago between us?' Kheda looked at Coron. 'Besides, I believe they would settle for us halting this tide of evil. Under constant threat of wizards from the unbroken lands, I doubt they'd relish some magical assault from the south.'

'My father told me that the northern lords drove out the barbarian wizards by hiring sorcerers of their own,' hissed Safar venomously.

'I have read that they managed to set the wizards fighting among themselves,' Coron said unexpectedly.

'Fighting fire with fire?' Kheda mused. 'We've all done that.'

'Which would make the Chazen domain our firebreak,' said Caid grimly.

'The land is already tainted with magic,' Coron acknowledged.

'Then go and raise a real fire,' snapped Safar. 'Burn every island and reef to bare earth and blackened stumps and leave the invaders' bones lying splintered among them.'

'You don't suppose these wild men and their wizards might oppose such an attack?' Caid's sarcasm was withering.

'What do you suppose the northern lords would ask from us in return for their lore?' Coron looked uncertainly from Kheda to Caid.

'Steel, most certainly.' Safar shot a pointed look at Ritsem Caid. 'All that we could spare and more besides, I don't doubt.'

'Let us—' A resounding knock interrupted Kheda.

He narrowed his eyes at Safar, who didn't bother to hide his smugness. 'Enter.'

It was the fawning, smooth-faced lackey. 'My lady Mirrel sends her compliments and asks that you grace her reception with your presence.'

What signal summoned you, seen through some hidden spy hole, as soon as Safar saw control of this debate slipping out of his grasp?

Kheda risked a knowing glance at Caid but the Ritsem warlord didn't notice, face stony, eyes inward-looking. Redigal Coron was seizing the opportunity to confer hurriedly with his attendant slave. Ulla Safar's body slave had the unenviable task of hauling his master to his feet.

'We will not disappoint my lady Mirrel.' The fat man heaved a sigh and wiped sweat from his forehead. 'We would all do better to think on these matters before we talk again.' He strode from the room, scowling ferociously.

'My lord.' On his feet the instant etiquette allowed, Telouet stood before Kheda and offered a hand.

Kheda waved his help away, raising an enquiring eyebrow. With the minimum of expression, Telouet managed to convey the equivalent of a shrug.

So you have no more idea than me how much progress we may have made.

Ritsem Caid's expression gave nothing away and his slave Ganil's face might have been carved out of the same ironwood as the pillars as the two of them stalked out. Redigal Coron was still talking to his softly spoken zamorin, bodyguard hovering uncertainly. Kheda saw the door wards listening with blatant curiosity.

Telouet followed his gaze. 'It seems liberal use of the lash is no guarantee of a well-mannered household, my lord.' His comment was just loud enough to reach the door wards.

'It is not your place to comment on another domain's practices.' Kheda's rebuke was perfunctory at best. 'Let's pay our respects to Mirrel Ulla and see if she at least will show us proper courtesy.'

'Do you want to change your clothes?' Telouet asked as they passed the door wards.

'It's not as if I've worked up much of a sweat.' Kheda shook his head. 'If we delay, we'll be hearing barbed comments about tardiness from Mirrel until we leave for home.'

Let one of the spies infesting this ant heap carry that kernel of gossip to her.

Telouet nodded discreetly to indicate the stairway they should take. 'Ritsem Caid and Redigal Coron show every sign of seeking help from the north.' He spoke just low enough to suggest a confidence but loud enough for listening ears.

'Not that they would want to, any more than we of Daish,' Kheda sighed. 'Let's hope we find some better alternatives tomorrow.'

Surely Safar will back down and form an alliance so we can drive out these invaders ourselves? He cannot risk losing his influence to unknown warlords who might well covet the riches of his domain, once they're invited into these reaches.

'East here, my lord.'

As Telouet muttered directions through the maze of corridors, Kheda found himself speculating what might happen if Ulla Safar did remain obdurate.

Janne warned you the fat toad would call your bluff, so

she's won that wager. But what if it wasn't a bluff? Could there possibly be some honourable northern warlord who could tell us how to drive out this threat of magic. Could we find an ally strong enough to overthrow Ulla Safar when this is all over? Maybe you and Caid should investigate the possibility. You could trust each other in such an alliance, limited to a single objective, division of the spoils agreed in advance? But who would get this island and the massive strength of Derasulla? Do you hate Safar enough to see the Ritsem domain add such power to its own? A difficult question. Caid would certainly never let it pass to Daish, that's easy enough to see.

Such musings carried Kheda through the long corridors and up several flights of stairs. The Ulla wives all had apartments facing up river and, as first wife, Mirrel Ulla commanded an imposing suite on the very highest level where the air was freshened with the scents of the distant hills. Women slaves in lewdly diaphanous gowns and gaudy enamels simpered a welcome at the door.

'I see Safar has a new set of concubines to flaunt,' Kheda remarked to Telouet as they approached.

'I wonder where the old ones washed up downstream,' the slave murmured grimly.

They entered the room and Mirrel Ulla turned from windows that reached from floor to ceiling, opening on to a broad terrace shaded by diligently tended nut palms and perfume trees in ornate pots. Kheda stood where he might catch a breeze but the air was hotter than ever.

'My lord Daish, you grace our humble home with your presence.' A woman of moderate height and slender build, Mirrel advanced, arms outstretched, wrists laden with golden bracelets.

'No room could be called humble with you to adorn it.' Kheda took her hands and bent to brush them with his lips, careful not to catch any of her ornate rings in his beard.

Mirrel laughed prettily, laying an ebony hand across the breast of a black silk gown covered with tiny glass beads sewn into the patterns of feathers, as if some fabulous bird, every silver feather edged with gold, had been trapped and plucked. The bodice slid from silver to gilt with every breath she took, low-cut and close-fitted to display arms and bosom with calculated seduction, though the swell of her breasts was all but invisible beneath a convoluted necklace studded with sizeable diamonds. The skirt shimmered, made from separate lengths of cloth worked into individual gleaming plumes, all the better to display her elegant legs.

Your spies obviously told you Janne arrived displaying all the wealth and power of the Daish domain.

Mirrel's eyes looked beyond him, their hardness making a nonsense of the soft appeal of her artfully painted lips. 'Ritsem Caid! You are welcome, so very welcome, and Taisia!'

Kheda bowed and stepped away, releasing Mirrel to advance on Caid. Redigal Coron and his senior wife followed soon after and she quickly gathered him into their circle. Moni Redigal with her sizeable retinue headed for the junior Ulla wives who were gathered in a watchful knot, their own gowns similar in cut to Mirrel's but bare of beads, merely brocaded in feather patterns. The noise in the room rose as attendant body slaves allowed their masters and mistresses a little leeway, drawing aside to share their own news with each other, tolerating the intrusion of Derasulla's senior slaves as necessary.

Kheda glanced appreciatively around in order not to catch anyone's gaze and oblige himself to conversation before Janne arrived. The audience room was certainly worth admiring. Sandalwood shutters on the windows were the finest the island's carvers could supply and the cinnamon-coloured floorboards were waxed to glossy

perfection underfoot. The walls were tiled; all the better
to display the domain's other highly prized craft to visitors.

Mirrel's rooms boasted the lustre tiles that were so
sought after in trade. Guests entered through a wall where
golden tiles shaded imperceptibly to a sunset hue on one
side and a fertile green on the other. As Kheda turned
slowly towards the windows, he saw green sliding towards
an airy blue on the one hand, orange blushing to soft red
on the other. In the spaces between the tall windows, the
advancing colours blurred into a dusky violet. With the
delicacy of the pigments used, the effect was both subtle
and eye-catching.

*It's like being wrapped in a rainbow, a fine symbol for
Mirrel, with its contradictions between blessing and caprice.*

'My lord.' Telouet appeared with a crystal goblet.

'I notice neither our rooms nor Janne's have any of
these lustre tiles,' Kheda remarked in an undertone. 'Do
you suppose that's some insult? Should we seem oblivious or devise some retaliation?'

'Ask my lady Janne,' Telouet suggested.

'Kheda.' Moni Redigal appeared at his elbow, smiling
cheerfully. 'How does that slave suit Dau? I do hope Rekha
is pleased with him. How is she? How are the little ones?'
Moni Redigal's appearance was nicely calculated not to
outstrip her hostess but at the same time to make the room's
decoration a backdrop to her own. She made a fine display
of a warlord's wife, in gold silk shot with silver and wearing
a rainbow array of gem-studded necklaces and bracelets.

*Do I thank you for supplying a pair of competent hands
to raise swords between my family and any invaders while I
play Ulla Safar's pointless games?*

'He seems entirely suitable, thank you. Rekha is well
and all the children.' Kheda smiled back.

'I must write to Rekha.' Moni sipped before looking a
little puzzled at her goblet. 'One of my sisters has married

into the Kithir domain. I am to visit her soon and she may well be interested in trading Kithir carpets for pearls.' Born quite some distance to the north where crossing trade routes mingled many bloodlines, Moni was paler-skinned than all but the barbarian slaves in the room, her tight curled hair a distinctive russet.

'How far north do your trading contacts reach nowadays?' Kheda asked idly.

'Well into the islands of the central compass.' Moni laughed with high good humour.

Coron's ever-present guardians chose well, when looking for a woman with the talents to be senior wife of a complex domain as well as possessing a keen understanding that the warlord's duties were absolutely none of her concern and her opinion would never be sought or appreciated.

Kheda sipped at his own wine and the cold bite of alcohol surprised him into an unguarded comment. 'I'm surprised to find Mirrel serving us something this intoxicating at such a tense time.'

As he spoke, Mirrel appeared but it wasn't his words agitating the headdress of trembling gold and silver bird wings that all but obscured her dense midnight curls. 'Moni, my dearest, come and talk to Chay. She wants to discuss sending some of her tinsmiths to your domain for a season or so, for a trade of skills.'

Clumsy, Mirrel, clumsy. That arrival's rather too precipitate and your voice is certainly too urgent for such a trivial request. Who ordered you to make sure I didn't get a chance to count the links in Moni Redigal's chain of connections to the wizard-plagued north? As if I needed to ask.

'Don't let me stand in the way of your duties, my ladies.' Kheda smiled and bowed to relinquish his claim on Moni before handing his crystal goblet back to Telouet. 'Find me some fruit juice.'

Kheda watched several of the Ulla slaves sliding

speculative glances at Telouet as his body slave crossed the room to the broad array of gold and silver ewers standing in trays of crushed ice melting so fast the harried servants were constantly replenishing it.

'Lilla juice, I'm afraid.' On his return, Telouet handed Kheda a goblet with a rueful grin. 'That's all there is apart from wines.'

'What's Safar thinking of?' Kheda shook his head as he took it. 'Ah well, maybe he'll miscalculate his own drinking and drop dead in tomorrow's heat. Do you want to circulate a little, Telouet? See what you can learn for us? Some of those girls look as if they might trade some useful information for the pleasure of your presence in their bed.'

And they'll certainly learn nothing from Telouet, who assuredly knows idle chatter isn't among the proper uses for his tongue in the throes of passion.

'I'd rather not, if it's all the same to you, my lord,' Telouet said, though not without regret. 'I was talking to Ganil and he says the women slaves are desperate to get with child by some outsider, to get some claim on another domain and the chance of escape from this pesthole.'

'That's a new development.' Kheda frowned as he drank. 'Have their lives really become so insupportable here? Or is Safar prompting them? I wouldn't put it past him to come up with some spurious objection if one of his slaves insisted on her rights to demand support from the father of her child. He could easily finesse an argument over that into a wider conflict.'

'Or look to plant a spy on us.' Telouet's gaze slid to a pretty slave girl demure in a gown of silk gauze that left little to the imagination. 'Do you want me to try and find out?'

'Only if you find the ground bitterspine leaves in honey paste in the bottom of my physic chest first,' Kheda advised. 'Tip your sword with that before you sheathe it.'

'Dear me, you look very serious.' Kheda turned to find Taisia Ritsem at his elbow. 'But then this is rather a dull gathering. Isn't Janne with you?'

Kheda smiled with genuine pleasure. 'My lady Taisia, a delight to see you, as always.'

'Save your flattery for Mirrel,' she recommended with a fond twinkle as her body slave retreated to a discreet distance along with Telouet. No great beauty, Taisia wore a solitary comb to tame her dark, wiry hair, an elegant piece of silver filigree. The vivid blue of her draperies flattered her warm brown skin, a plain dress caught at each shoulder with a brooch of knotted silver strands worn beneath a wrap painted with a brilliant shoal of coral fishes. She wore a single necklace, a heavy chain with an uncut sapphire pendant nestling at the base of her throat.

'Then I'll say you're looking tired and apprehensive, shall I?' Kheda could well see what her body slave had sought to conceal beneath her cosmetics. 'And mourning Olkai.'

The barest suggestion of tears came and went in Taisia's dark eyes. 'Much to Mirrel's surprise, with her so long departed from our domain.' Her tone was acid.

'Rekha always says Mirrel's worst flaw is assuming everyone else thinks as she does. Janne should be here soon. Perhaps she's having trouble convincing Itrac to face everyone.' Kheda looked towards a stir by the door but it was only Safar arriving, all expansive gestures and jovial smiles.

Where did you go, when you left our council, rather than coming straight here as you implied? You haven't changed that yellow tunic, and is it just the heat prompting all that sweat darkening the armpits or have you been about something more exerting?

An instant later Janne's appearance drove any such

considerations out of Kheda's head. Within a couple of breaths, all heads were turned to the door, captivated by the sight.

Janne wore a simple dress of dove-grey silk, two lengths of cloth sewn at shoulder and sides, shaped only with a sash of the same material. Her hair was drawn back in a single plait, oiled to sleekness with no jewel to relieve the smoky darkness, and the merest hint of silver highlighted her eyes and lips. Janne's sole adornment was a single string of pearls that reached to her waist. A single string, but pearls that would take a lifetime to match, even with access to every harvest that reefs could offer the length and breadth of the Archipelago. The black pearls at the centre must have been years in the making at the bottom of the ocean, layer upon layer of radiance building a handful of perfect spheres broader than Kheda's thumbnail. Lesser in size but no less flawless, the pearls on either side faded through charcoal darkness to a grey of vanishing smoke then brightened to the clear pallor of a dawn cloud. Then the colour of each successive bead grew richer, more noticeable until the pearls that disappeared beneath Janne's hair were a sunrise gold.

'Janne, my dear.' Mirrel's brittle cry broke through the silence that had fallen.

She moved to embrace Janne who smiled warmly and hugged her close. 'Mirrel, so good to see you.'

Birut was standing at Janne's shoulder. The slave's burnished mail was patterned with brass rings polished to a golden shine. He wore a heavy collar of gold set with crystals and the gilded brow band of his helm bore more of the same. Kheda hid his smile in his glass.

Dear me, Mirrel, with Janne stood between you, your fabulous dress looks no better than this mere swordsman's cheap simulacrum of wealth.

Just as everyone in the room was coming to that conclusion, Janne beckon to Itrac, who had been waiting on the threshold. 'Mirrel, you remember Itrac Chazen? Of course you do. She's staying with us until she can return to her own domain under favourable portents.'

'Indeed.' There was just a hint of disbelief in Mirrel's smile.

'You don't think Chazen Saril will object, when he hears she's being dressed like one of your junior wives?' Taisia murmured to Kheda, raising an eyebrow.

'I'm sure Janne knows what she's doing.' Though Kheda was as nonplussed as everyone else to see Itrac wearing a triple-stranded collar of the pink pearls that were one of Daish's most coveted treasures. Her white silk tunic was belted with another three rows, her wrists bore identical bracelets, and anklets in the same style gathered the fullness of her loose white trousers. Her long plait was all but identical to Janne's.

'Those look fine enough to be talisman pearls,' speculated Taisia. 'Itrac's, I mean, as well as Janne's.'

'You don't think she looks more like a daughter than a wife?' Kheda cocked his head at Taisia as Safar advanced on Itrac with expansive gestures and a smile that didn't entirely disguise the cunning in his eyes touched with more than a hint of lust. The contrast between his predatory bulk and her vulnerable slenderness was striking.

'She does rather, doesn't she?' Taisia allowed. 'And one barely of an age to be wed.'

Janne said something to Safar before bowing prettily away and gliding across the room to join the two of them. 'Taisia, my dear.'

'Janne Daish.' Taisia's greeting was formal but her embrace was fond.

'You're leaving Itrac to their tender mercies?' Kheda watched Mirrel and Safar flank the girl, Mirrel laying a proprietorial hand on her arm.

'Just long enough for them to look like insensitive pigs

harrying her in her time of grief.' Janne did not need to turn round to see this happening. 'Taisia will rescue her in good time.'

'I do have much to discuss with her.' Taisia nodded.

'I wouldn't leave it too long, if you don't want outright tears,' Kheda advised. 'Or a fight. That new body slave of hers is giving Mirrel's man and Safar's a very hard look.' He shifted his head to catch Telouet's eye and his slave idly separated himself from a fawning gaggle of slave women to drift into Safar's slave's line of sight.

Let's just make it plain Itrac's new body slave won't be without allies if some Ulla men feel inclined to hunt him through this warren of a fortress should they get the chance.

'I'll speak with you later, Janne.' Taisia left them to deftly sweep Itrac away from Safar with a plea for news of Olkai's last days that could not be denied.

Kheda kissed Janne's satin cheek. 'You look exquisite tonight, my wife.'

She smiled confidently. 'I'm glad you approve, my husband.'

Kheda glanced at Itrac, now safely in conversation with Taisia and Ritsem Caid. 'You've dressed her like one of our own, I see.'

'Just to keep the Ulla and Redigal women guessing.' Janne fixed Kheda with a steely look. 'She will not be marrying into the Daish domain. You had better tell Ritsem Caid you're having second thoughts on that score.'

'Why?' Kheda felt unexpectedly wrong-footed.

'I will not countenance anyone so grievously afflicted by magic coming within our family circle.' Janne's smile was serene but her words were bitingly precise. 'Marry her and I will divorce you as will Rekha and we'll take little Sain with us. Then we'd seek aid from all our brothers to help us set you aside in favour of the children.'

Kheda was stunned into silence by the effort not to let his shock show in his face.

'As for Sirket, I'll make him zamorin with my own hands before I let him make such an accursed marriage.' Janne stood on tiptoe to brush a kiss on Kheda's cheek.

He found his voice from somewhere. 'You don't think we should discuss this further? If she ends up the key to securing the Chazen domain, will you see her married to Ulla Safar?'

'There are ways of ensuring the question of Itrac's future won't arise for a while yet.' Janne shrugged, adjusting her fabulous pearls. 'I must go and discuss a few things with Moni Redigal.'

She kissed Kheda again and walked gracefully away. As she did so, Chay Ulla stepped up with a smile that was more of a smirk. 'Daish Kheda, I've been waiting an age to speak to you.'

'And now you have my whole attention.' Kheda inclined his head first to Chay and then to the pretty girl with her.

Chay was a tall woman with skin a shade lighter than her dark brown eyes, handsome rather than beautiful though her strong bones were unexpectedly flattered by the style of dress Mirrel had dictated for the Ulla wives. *She seemed an unlikely choice for Ulla Safar, who demanded beauty as a prerequisite in his wives, even more so given Chay had brought no particularly valuable alliances to their marriage bed.*

She whirled round to draw the girl closer with an impulsive hand. 'Daish Kheda, this is Laisa Viselis, well, for the moment,' Chay simpered.

'I am honoured to meet you.' Kheda bowed.

And why would Viselis Ils be trusting one of his younger daughters to this bitch? You can smile all you want, Chay; I've seen the cruelty in your eyes is a perfect match for your lord and husband's malice.

'My lord of Daish.' The girl, demure in tunic and trews not unlike Itrac's, bobbed an answering courtesy.

Chay favoured him with an insincere smile. 'Laisa has heard some most peculiar rumours about your father's death.' Her words were just loud enough to be sure everyone at hand could hear.

The girl's hazel eyes widened, startled. 'I didn't—'

Chay's hand tightened mercilessly on Laisa's. 'I thought it best she heard the truth from your own lips.'

Do you know that one of your maidservants told Telouet how you send your body slave to catch mice for your house cat to torment while you watch?

Kheda smiled reassurance at the girl. 'It's a simple enough story.'

Never fear, Chay, I've had more than enough practice making the telling of it entirely unremarkable.

'Daish Reik, my father, had climbed to the top of his observatory tower, where he kept certain birds he favoured for augury. It was his custom to let them fly at dawn, so he might read their movements in conjunction with the early skies.'

And now I understand why he valued such moments of solitude and reflection and guarded them so jealously.

'That morning,' Kheda shrugged, 'the parapet gave way and he fell to his death.'

'Entirely unforeseen.' Chay shook her head in false wonderment.

'How shocking for you,' Laisa stammered. 'To suffer such a bereavement.'

'It was a long time ago.' Kheda nodded with calm resignation. 'One learns to live with such things.'

'If only there had been someone to read the omens as the birds flew.' Chay pretended concern. 'Daish Reik had just released them,' she explained to Laisa before turning to Kheda with a glint in her eye. 'Do you suppose he saw something in their flight as he fell? That he died without being able to share?'

Are you just looking for your usual amusement in someone else's pain, Chay, or does Ulla Safar want to stir up all that old speculation, that Daish Reik had seen some appalling catastrophe predicted for the domain, so unspeakable that he had thrown himself to his death? Does he think that will distract us all from this invasion of Chazen?

'The rains had been unusually heavy that season, the stonework was old, the mortar crumbling.' Kheda addressed himself to Laisa, voice untroubled. 'My father's death taught me that no one, no matter how potent, how exalted, is proof against a sudden fall.'

Chew on that, Chay, and may it choke you.

'How he could have let his own observatory fall into such disrepair.' Chay shook her head again. 'You had to demolish the whole of the tower, didn't you?'

'It was sound enough but I chose to rebuild, out of respect for Daish Reik's memory.' Kheda continued to look steadily at Laisa.

After taking the tower apart, stone by stone, down to its very foundations in a search for some answer.

'My father had been busy seeing to the needs of our people after some devastating storms. Perhaps he waited too long before seeing what damage had been done to his own compound,' Kheda continued evenly. 'I read in his death the ultimate confirmation of his words to me in life, that a warlord should pay attention to every detail, see that every thing, every person, no matter how humble, plays its part in supporting the power of a domain and its lord.'

And I considered every other possible interpretation, as well as searching the crumbled parapet for any sign of evil intent behind the calamity. Janne and I scoured every book of lore for some hint as to how to read such a startling portent.

'My father has always told me it is for my brother to

speculate on such matters,' the girl said uncertainly.

'Your father is a wise man,' Kheda assured her. 'It is a warlord's highest duty to read and interpret the auguries and omens that guide his domain and its people, just as it is a wife's highest duty to ensure their continued prosperity.' He didn't need to look to see Chay scowling at the implied rebuke.

'Of course Daish Reik's death deprived you of his wives as well,' she said nastily. 'And all the guidance they might have given you.'

'I was newly married to Janne Daish.' Kheda paused to smile affectionately at his wife. 'My mother and her sister wives had every confidence in her as new first wife of the domain and certainly no wish to challenge her by staying.'

So they were scattered, each to take their grief to the domain they had been born to and leaving me to my own sorrow. And you'll never know what heartache that cost me, Chay.

'If you'll excuse me, I must speak with Redigal Coron.' Smiling at Laisa who was looking sorely uncomfortable, Kheda bowed and moved away.

Let's see if Coron can let slip why our domain's rawest sore is being prodded again. I'd better warn Janne as well and I think Telouet had better resign himself to a night of raising some slave girl's hopes, for the sake of whatever we might learn that way.

Anyway, Daish Reik's death cannot have been a long-distant omen of this calamity. We'd have seen something else, some recent portent to turn our thoughts to that death as precursor. If I'd missed it, Sirket would have caught it. I've shared all my speculations on Daish Reik's fate with him. He watches as anxiously as me for any sign that might confirm or deny a particular theory.

'My lord.' Telouet approached with a pitcher of that same cursed lilla juice.

Kheda held out his goblet and the lip of the jug trembled on the rim. 'Are you all right?' He looked more closely at his faithful slave.

'I'm not sure.' Telouet's mouth was pinched, his skin greying.

'What's wrong?' Kheda noted more beads of sweat on the other man's forehead than the heat could account for.

'Stomach cramps,' the slave replied tersely.

'When did that start?' Kheda frowned.

'Forgive me, my lord, I'm going to be sick,' Telouet said through clenched teeth, a muscle pulsing in his jaw.

'Outside.' Kheda handed the jug and goblet to the nearest maidservant, driving Telouet towards the door. In the corridor, Telouet barely reached the stairwell before he doubled up, falling to his knees retching. Kheda took off the slave's helmet and held his shoulders as spasms racked him. Telouet groaned and tried to stand up, wiping cold sweat from his face with a trembling arm, but another paroxysm seized him. Kheda took a shallow breath, swallowing his own nausea at the sickening smell.

'My lord?' It was Birut, face anxious.

'Find some servant to clear this up,' Kheda ordered. 'I'm taking him back to our quarters.'

'My lord—' Birut sounded uncertain.

Kheda looked at him with some exasperation. 'I can hardly go back in there.' He gestured to his vomit-spattered clothes. 'Tell Janne I'll dose Telouet and rejoin her when I'm satisfied he's settled.'

Birut nodded, no choice but to obey. He turned to go.

'Wait.' Kheda managed to get Telouet upright, one shoulder underneath his arm. 'Which way to the main corridors from here?'

Birut grimaced, seeing Kheda so burdened. 'I'd better come with you.'

'I can guide us back,' Telouet said hoarsely.

'You can't leave that new lad responsible for Itrac and Janne both, Birut, not here,' Kheda said bluntly. 'We'll collar a servant if needs be.'

Where's that oily zamorin lackey, when he might be useful?

'Take the far stair.' Birut pointed. 'Go down two floors then bear east along the passage. That'll bring you to the central traverse.'

Telouet tried to bear the weight of his armour but nausea racked him again and again. He was leaning heavily on Kheda before they had reached the main arcade that ran the length of the fort's inner citadel.

'Come on; let's get you to a bed. Some river clay and poppy juice and you'll be fresh as the rains come the morning.' Sweat trickled down Kheda's back as he helped Telouet negotiate a crowded corridor, every Ulla face curious.

What are you wondering at? That we've brought some rainy-season contagion with us? More likely some foulness from your filthy river has worked its way into the fort.

Kheda waved away a hovering maid, plainly anxious to help as Telouet emptied his stomach again, this time of no more than bile and slime.

No blood, that's some relief. No scent of any poison that I know either. Anyway, what would poisoning Telouet achieve? Janne will be there to see any discussions between Safar, Caid and Coron happening without me.

'I'm sorry, my lord,' Telouet whispered as they paused on a landing halfway down an awkward flight of stairs to the citadel's lower levels.

'For what? For getting me out of one of Safar's tedious banquets? I don't think I'll be punishing you for that.' Despite his light words, Kheda scowled as the swordsman stumbled on numb feet.

'You should go back.' Telouet tried and failed to

disengage himself from Kheda's arm. 'I can get to the apartments from here.'

'If I go back now, I'll have Mirrel pretending surprise that I feel it necessary to see personally to the ailments of my slaves while Safar congratulates me for my detachment in leaving you to your own devices. I don't particularly feel inclined to let them set everyone a choice between condemning me as overindulgent or heartless.'

Telouet didn't hear him, his knees finally giving way. Kheda couldn't hold him any longer. At least they were at the turn to the corridor where they were lodged.

Kheda propped Telouet against the wall and shouted. 'Daish! You are wanted!'

'My lord?' One of Janne's women opened the door to the women's apartments, startled.

'Get him into my rooms.' As more servants appeared, Kheda let the four porters take Telouet between them. 'On the bed.'

'I'll get some clean quilts.' As the woman hurried away, one of the porters produced a knife to cut the leather thongs that secured Telouet's chainmail. 'We'd better get him out of this.'

'You can curse us for wrecking the fit of it later,' Kheda told the slave. Telouet barely groaned as they slid the armour off him with no little difficulty. Kheda tore off the padded arming jacket and found it sodden with rank sweat.

The woman returned with an armful of clean cottons and a maid following her with a bundle of quilts. 'Get me water and my physic chest, the silver-bound, satinwood one. Come on, Telouet, I need you awake.' Kheda slapped his slave's face with calculated severity. 'Open your eyes.'

No need to give an emetic, even if this is poisoning. There's nothing left in him to bring up. Should I dose him with charcoal all the same? At very least we must get some water into him but how can we be sure the water's clean in this cesspit of a fortress?

He turned to the porter who was standing, grim-faced, at the foot of the bed. 'Get a charcoal brazier brought in here, at once. From now on, we boil every drop of water any of us drink and Ulla Safar can chase his own tail, if he thinks we're insulting him.'

CHAPTER EIGHT

Kheda heard a patter on the fringed leaves of the perfume trees in the garden beyond the window, briefly drowning out the grating crickets and other insects. The rain was just enough to stir the heady fragrance before the false promise of the shower passed away, leaving the humidity even more oppressive than it had been before. The pale light of the Lesser Moon shone through the slats of the shutters and Kheda looked at it, riding unchallenged in the night sky now the Greater Moon had retired to days of seclusion.

The Pearl, whole and brilliant, clouds passing swiftly without obscuring it, that has to be a good omen for Daish. Heavens send the true rains soon though. Even the night gives no relief from this heat now.

Kheda wiped Telouet's forehead with a damp cloth, the insensible slave now stripped naked beneath a light coverlet on the bed, his breathing harsh and slow. Hearing soft footfalls in the corridor, Kheda straightened up, putting the cloth in a bowl of besa-scented water, the astringent oil counterfeiting coolness on his hands. A brisk double rap on the door sounded loud in the silence and startled a tiny green house lizard across the ceiling. Outside, whoever had knocked was rebuked with a vicious hiss.

Kheda smiled a little. 'Enter.'

'Ulla Orhan, beloved son—'

'Shut up, Vaino.' The heir to the Ulla domain pushed past his body slave and bowed deep to Kheda.

'You are welcome.' Kheda stood in the pool of light cast by the single oil lamp he had lit against the deepening shadows outside. Arms folded, head tilted, he looked at the boy.

I haven't heard that note of authority in your voice before, my lad. Do you know how much it makes you sound like your father?

'How's your slave faring?' Orhan looked down at the oblivious Telouet. Ulla Safar's only living son bore a disconcerting resemblance to his sire, although, as yet, he was nowhere near as fat. Only his jaw and mouth differed, sole inheritance from his long-dead mother.

'Well enough,' Kheda said calmly.

'It seems we have something of an outbreak of this contagion.' Orhan's open sarcasm startled the Daish warlord. His sharp eyes took in the cup that had held the charcoal draught. 'I am on my way to see what can be done. Do you need any herbs or tinctures that you do not carry with you? Do you have tasselberry root? Sawheart? Enough for any of your other people who might be struck down?'

Both sensible choices for someone suffering a waterborne vomiting illness though, of course, also the two herbs most specifically recommended when poisoning is suspected.

'Yes, thank you, I have all I need.' Kheda saw Orhan's body slave was looking apprehensively at his master. Kheda didn't recognise the man.

Not that there's any point remembering your face, when Orhan's seldom permitted to keep the same slave for more than a season or so.

'No, there's something you can send me, some ice, if there's any left in your cellars.'

Orhan nodded as if some unspoken question had been answered. 'At once, Daish Kheda. I'll bid you good night then, but don't hesitate to send word if you need anything, to my own quarters.' He paused on the threshold. 'I was sorry not to see Daish Sirket with you. Do give him my regards on your return to your own domain.'

'Of course.' Kheda bowed briefly as the slave shut the door and hurried after his master as Orhan's determined stride faded into the distance.

If you show no aptitude for divination, my lad, you've certainly been paying attention to your herbal studies. I wonder if you are so very inept at divination? Are you playing some deeper game? Maybe you suspect the water sickness that carried off your mother was no such thing. You wouldn't be the only one to wonder. If you are trying to deceive Ulla Safar as to your true nature, I wonder how long you'll manage without losing your life for it, sole son or not?

Kheda sat in the silent gloom and considered his recent dealings with Orhan in the light of this new notion. Some while later, more footsteps in the corridor diverted him from such speculations. This time, it was an anxious trio of servants led by an old man carrying a bowl of ice chipped from the blocks carried down from the freezing mountain heights and packed beneath straw in the citadel's deepest cellars. Behind him, two girls struggled with a tray laden with covered dishes.

'My lord, my lady Mirrel bids you eat, even if you cannot join the company in the dining hall,' one said with an anxious smile. 'She hopes your slave is recovering.'

'Set that down there.' Kheda nodded at a sandalwood side table and the girls hurried to obey.

The male servant smiled ingratiatingly as he put the bowl of ice on the floor. 'Let me serve you, great lord.' He lifted a cover from a bowl of steamed saller grain dotted with dried sardberries and dusted with shredded pepper pods. Appetite twisted Kheda's stomach.

'I'll serve myself. Leave before you wake my slave.' The edge in his command sent all three scurrying away.

Kheda sighed as he stifled the tempting scent rising from the yellow and white dish with the lid and scooped up some ice, dropping it into the water he had been using to bathe Telouet's forehead.

I beg your pardon, Mirrel Ulla, but there's no chance I'll be eating any of this. How to get rid of it, though, so untouched food won't be an insult? Nosy Ulla servants will doubtless report anything unexpected in the chamber pots. What would Safar make of word that I've been seen burying cane shoots and spiced duck in the garden?

Kheda grinned at the absurdity of that notion and reassuring himself that Telouet was still sleeping peacefully, he picked a book out of the open physic chest and sat down on a cushion, leaning his back against the bed.

He had read through all Daish Reik's specifics for treating sicknesses of the gut, and just for good measure, those against poisons, when he heard the others returning from the banquet; Janne and Itrac's voices bright with inconsequential chatter until they might reach the dubious sanctuary of their apartments. Kheda paused, laying the book down on his lap as the door along the corridor opened and closed. With all the shutters open in a vain attempt to find some cool in the night, the conversation on the other side of the wall floated out to the garden and back in through his own windows. He heard the brisk notes of orders given and obeyed punctuated by the sharp sounds of coffers and chests opened and shut and the muffled flop of quilts and cushions fashioning beds for the servants and musicians to soften the hard tiles of the floor. Gradually the bustle slowed and finally stilled. Soon after, a soft single knock came at his door.

'Enter.' Kheda got to his feet and stretched stiff shoulders.

Birut opened the door to admit Janne, the slave's face showing open concern.

'A shame you did not join us, you missed a splendid banquet.' Janne's voice was sweet with sarcasm. 'An entire table of river-fish dishes and a separate one for coral crabs and sea fish. Every platter of duck and jungle fowl was decorated with their tail feathers and the sweetmeats were garnished with gold leaf.'

'I saw no point in leaving Telouet just to have Safar and the Ulla women draw me into endless speculation about his illness.' Kheda placed a strip of tooled leather in his book and closed it carefully. 'They'd doubtless have tried to make out I was accusing them of poisoning him.'

'As if you would suspect such a thing.' Janne sounded shocked for the benefit of any hidden ears but raised her eyebrows at Kheda in silent question.

He shrugged to convey his inability to answer that. 'Besides, I thought Ritsem Caid might prefer to discuss our current predicament with Coron without such distractions.' Now he was the one looking at Janne for an answer.

'Redigal Coron seemed more concerned to discuss Chay's news of a spate of vomiting servants in the lower levels,' Janne told him sourly.

'Charming conversation for dining over,' grimaced Kheda.

'As Moni told Coron in no uncertain terms.' Amused recollection momentarily brightened Janne's weary face.

'Do you think she was telling the truth? Chay, I mean,' Kheda wondered incautiously.

Oh, surely Safar's spies have finally gone to bed along with everyone else.

Janne nodded reluctantly. 'Some of Moni Redigal's maids have fallen victim and one of Taisia's musicians. I believe Ulla Orhan has been sent to tend them, though much good it will do Safar if his only son drops with the same sickness.'

'Orhan stopped by to see if I needed anything for

Telouet.' Kheda gave Janne a significant look. 'I believe he has grown commendably mindful of his duties this past season.'

Janne froze for a moment before she raised an eyebrow at Kheda. 'It is a shame he had to leave the banquet. He might have learned a great deal from observing his father's conversations with Redigal Coron and Ritsem Caid.'

Would Safar poison a whole slew of people, just to get his son out of that banquet? Is he starting to fear Orhan might challenge his supremacy, even after so many years of belittling the boy and undermining his confidence at every turn? Is poisoning his every other son Safar's way not so much to deprive Orhan of competitors as to deprive him of potential allies? Or are hunger and tiredness running away with your imagination, Daish Kheda?

'What did Orhan miss?' he asked bluntly.

Janne yawned inelegantly. 'Not a great deal, even when we managed to stop talking about vomit. Ulla Safar maintains this threat of magic isn't sufficiently proved to require his intervention. Redigal Coron is inclined to follow his lead, though I suspect he's less convinced by Safar's arguments than those pestilential zamorin of his. Ritsem Caid disagrees but—' Janne yawned again. 'He's hardly in a position to act, if Safar and Coron won't.'

Kheda wasn't convinced about that. 'What did you and the other wives discuss?'

'The usual dealings in materials, finished goods and our artisans' skills. Taisia Ritsem is at least as concerned with establishing her domain's new trade in iron and steel as she is with wizards to the south,' Janne replied waspishly. 'Chay and Mirrel were happy to advise her. Neither see any reason why life shouldn't go on as normal.'

'Did Itrac agree?' asked Kheda curtly.

'No, she became increasingly distressed at such heartlessness.' Janne glanced involuntarily over her shoulder.

'I'd better not leave her long. We're all too weary to be dealing with hysterics half the night.'

'There's silvernet by your bed.' Kheda took a step towards her then thought better of it. 'I don't suppose this is a contagion but better not risk it.'

Janne looked around the room. 'You're not having anyone else sleep in here tonight?'

'There's no point in anyone risking sickness who doesn't have to.'

'At least let Birut help you settle for the night.' Janne shot Kheda a meaningful look, then, without waiting for a response, walked noiselessly back down the dark corridor to her own quarters.

Kheda scrubbed a hand over his beard. 'You can take those for the midden.' He pointed at the heap of stained clothing he and Telouet had been wearing earlier.

'Let me pour you some water to refresh yourself.' Birut beckoned Kheda to the washstand and moved to whisper in the warlord's ear as he lifted the ewer high to make as much noise as he could. 'We should watch the Redigal retainers,' he hissed urgently. 'Telouet said he'd heard rumour that one of those zamorin is no such thing, that he has his stones and a son besides, and the gang of them are planning to set up their own dynasty.' Birut set the brass ewer down with a clang and looked at Telouet. 'He is going to be all right, isn't he?'

'All the omens are favourable,' nodded Kheda. 'Now, go tend to your mistress.'

Birut caught up the soiled clothing and departed. Kheda dumped a handful of already slushy ice in the bowl and shivered as he rubbed cold water around the back of his neck and his face. As he stood, cool trickles soaked the clean buff silk tunic and trousers he'd pulled haphazard from one of the many clothes chests. It didn't do much to clear his mind.

*There's another puzzle and one we've no hope of resolving
as long as Telouet's insensible. It'll just have to wait for the
morning. If we're to get the better of Safar, to rouse the allies
we need against this accursed magic, I'll need all my wits
about me, not be half dead with tiredness in the morning.*

Kheda looked at the ostentatious bed where the slave lay.

*Big enough for Safar and however many women it takes
to slake his lusts but better not share it with Telouet, just in
case this sickness is catching. Better be ready to help Telouet,
in case some crisis comes on him in the night.*

Pulling the tunic off over his head, he dropped it on
the end of the bed before drawing the oil lamp's wick
down to a dim glow. Laying one of the smothering silken
quilts down on the floor, he pulled up a cushion to pillow
his head and tried to compose himself for sleep, despite
the questions that plagued him and the relentless, stifling
heat.

*Might there be a coup in the Redigal domain? Is that
possible? How would Ulla Safar and Ritsem Caid react? What
of the domains to the north?*

Then he realised he was wide awake. Close on the heels
of that insight came the bemused understanding that he
had indeed drifted off to sleep. Kheda sat bolt upright.

*What's that smell? Burning? The brazier? Surely not; I
let it die back once I'd boiled enough water for Telouet's immediate needs and put it in the corridor. What's happened to the
lamp?*

The room was in absolute darkness but for splinters of
moonlight cast through the slatted shutters. Kheda
coughed and tasted a rank sweetness at the back of his
throat. He coughed again and a lurking headache tightened a vicelike grip around his temples. Cursing under
his breath, he felt his way through the room to the side
table with the lamp, cursing again when he touched the
hot glass that had sheltered the flame.

Someone's turned this out and none too long ago. Birut being overcautious again? But there's nothing here for it to burn. Where is that smell coming from? Has some fool dumped something on that brazier outside?

He took a moment to check on Telouet. The slave was still sleeping but his forehead was cooler to the touch. Kheda allowed himself an instant of relief before realising the scent of sullen smouldering was growing increasingly strong. Feeling his way to the door Kheda pulled it open, drawing breath to summon some attendant. Instead, rank smoke filling the corridor caught in his throat and provoked a fit of coughing to whip his headache into a raging fury. Kheda shut the door, leaning against it until the paroxysm passed, leaving him shaking and breathless.

A fire and no alarm raised? How could that be in a residence this size? We have to get out of here before we're all smothered in our sleep!

Kheda took as deep a breath as he could without coughing again and opened the door a crack to slip into the corridor. He walked slowly towards Janne's room, one hand tracing the cool marble wall, the nagging impulse to cough almost choking him, eyes stinging as the smoke swirled around him like tangible malice. He found the door to Janne's apartment ajar.

When did Birut last go to sleep without securing his mistress's safety?

Kheda opened his mouth to call for the slave but the acrid smoke tore into his throat again and he coughed convulsively, chest heaving. No one inside so much as stirred, not the musicians, the maidservants nor the porters. This room was darker than his own; someone had let down the awnings outside and tied them tight across the shutters to block out both light and air. Kheda stumbled across sleeping bodies heedless on feather-filled pallets as he struggled to find the door to Janne's sleeping chamber in the cloying darkness. Flinging it open, he fumbled his way to the bed, barking his shins painfully on some dress chest. Thrown off balance, his next step found Birut, asleep on his pallet at the foot of the bed.

'Wake up!' Kheda seized the man's naked shoulder, shaking him roughly.

The man rolled unresisting beneath the assault with a faintly resentful murmur. Kheda dropped to his knees, bending close to feel Birut's laboured breath slow against his cheek. Moving with new urgency, Kheda reached for Janne, finding her curled up beside Itrac in the wide bed, both women lost in sleep too deep to be natural.

'Janne, dear heart.' Feeling for the beat of her blood, Kheda found it suspiciously sluggish. He stroked the hair from her forehead before slapping her cheek, lightly at first then with more force. 'Janne! You have to wake up!' Dread as well as the heat of the night sent cold sweat trickling down Kheda's spine.

So how do I wake everyone before this smoke stifles them in their sleep? Well, let's see if we can't get rid of some of this smoke first. In fact, let's see what's going on, rather than flailing around in the dark.

Dropping to one knee, he found Birut's tunic and rummaged in the slave's pockets for a spark maker. Finding an oil lamp on the table beside Janne, he lit it with careful hands. The women and the slave slept on, undisturbed by the light. Kheda was not sanguine, seeing thick coils of smoke drifting through the shadows of the room. Taking the lamp out into the corridor he saw the double doors dividing these apartments off from stairs at either end of the corridor were closed. Dark smoke was sliding through the cracks around the set to the north. Kheda hurried to the southern doors and shoved them hard. They wouldn't shift. He set down the lamp and put his shoulder to them. Nothing gave. They were locked.

'Lizard eaters,' Kheda muttered furiously before picking up the lamp again and cautiously approaching the doors at the other end of the corridor. He didn't have to touch the polished wood to feel the heat coming off them. He could hear the hungry crackle of fire digging into the wood on the other side, getting a firm grip. That same strange taint he'd tasted on waking caught at the back of his throat.

These corridors are lined with marble, floor to ceiling. What is any fire going to burn, to get from room to room, from door to door? This fire's been set deliberately and as soon as those doors burn through, we'll be blinded by smoke and burnt like Olkai in the flames.

Something's riding on this smoke, an intoxicant of some kind. We always suspected Ulla Safar knows his poisons, even if he pays scant attention to curative lore. Is this his final touch on some murderous plot, a smoke to send us into a stupor we'll never wake from? Was there something in the food at the banquet as well? Something to keep the Ritsem and Redigal contingents sleeping through any uproar while we of Daish get a second dose in the smoke, just to be sure we sleep while the fire does its work?

Though fires are always a peril at this season, with everything so dry and everyone on edge and distracted because of the heat. You'll be so distraught, won't you, Safar, that such a thing should happen in your very residence. You may even be burning a few of your own slaves, to quell Ritsem Caid's suspicions. Well, forgive me, Safar, if I make sure all your efforts are wasted.

Kheda left the doors well alone and returned to Janne. He caught up a water flagon from the washstand, kicking Birut and Itrac's new slave Jevin mercilessly, both men still sound asleep by the bed. Exasperation rising to rival his anxiety, Kheda dashed the water he'd so painstakingly boiled earlier all over Janne and Itrac. Banging the metal vessel on the marble wall, he raised a deafening clangour.

'What—' Birut looked up in blurred confusion.

'There's a fire!' yelled Kheda.

Fierce, instinctive loyalty drove Birut to his knees. He grabbed at the carved foot of the wide bed. 'What?'

'Fire!' Kheda was shaking Janne with ungentle hands. 'Get everyone moving!'

Janne stirred but only to push Kheda away with a murmured apology. Biting down on another cough, he rolled her over to administer a stinging smack to her silken buttock. The unexpected shock finally penetrated Janne's stupor. She reared up, one arm flailing to fend off her attacker.

Kheda grabbed her hand and held it painfully tight. 'Janne, wake up. There's a fire.'

'What?' Janne looked at him, uncomprehending.

Birut was stumbling towards the door to the audience room. 'Everyone's asleep.' He looked foggily surprised as a coughing fit seized him.

'We have to get out of here.' Kheda reached across Janne to drag Itrac over and slap her rump as well. 'Birut, we have to get out into the garden.'

'Itrac!' Janne seized the girl and began shaking her. When he was satisfied both slaves and women were sufficiently awake to realise their predicament, Kheda hurried back into the audience room, banging on walls and tables with the dented brass ewer as he went. At his shouts and kicks, servants and musicians began to stir, looking groggily to Kheda for instruction.

'The fire's that way.' Kheda pointed and everyone heard the menacing susurration of the growing blaze. 'The other doors are blocked. We have to get out into the garden.'

Partly stupefied or not, those closest to the outer doors immediately began pushing, heedless of the sharp carvings digging into their hands and shoulders.

'It won't open!' Kheda heard panic in the flute

player's words. 'It's jammed on the other side.'

'Someone get out through the windows.' Kheda looked up at the dark shutters too high for a solitary man or woman to reach.

'Where are the poles for the shutters?' wondered one bemused maid.

'Someone help me get up there.' Jevin, Itrac's new slave, appeared, a scrap of torn silk masking his face.

'Here, on my back.' One of the supposed porters turned to face the wall, arms outstretched, legs bent to brace himself. Jevin clambered up on to his shoulders, flattening himself against the smooth marble as he reached up with one desperate hand. He just managed to catch hold of the lower sill, swinging his other hand up to heave the shutter back.

'Up you go, lad.' Another of the porters was ready. He seized Jevin's foot, propelling him upwards.

The slave hauled himself up, teetering on his stomach before he managed to swing a foot round to pull himself astride the opening. 'What do I do now?'

Kheda took a pace forward. 'Open the garden door!'

Jevin swung himself over the sill, lowering to the full extent of his arms for the drop to the garden. As he disappeared, Birut emerged from the sleeping chamber supporting Janne and Itrac on each arm.

'Forget everything but the jewels,' Janne snapped, her brow creased in a scowl of pain. 'You, and you, fetch your lord's personal coffers and his physic chest.' She stabbed a finger at two whimpering maidservants. At the sound of her voice, other girls began frantically cramming silken draperies into chests.

Banging came from the other side of the door. Jevin was shouting, and at some command from the unseen slave, all four porters shoved on the door. With a vicious splintering, the doors yielded.

'Wedged, my lord.' Jevin held up a split and dented block of wood.

Night air flowed in, almost cool after the fug in the apartment. Everyone in the room stopped still for a moment, in the relief of a clean breath and of seeing their way out. That solace was short-lived. The crackle of the fire beyond the doors in the corridor audibly quickened, deepening to a hungry snarl. With the door to the garden open, the room and the corridor drew air through the fire like a chimney.

'I'll fetch Telouet,' Kheda shouted to Birut. 'Get everyone outside.'

Birut didn't need telling twice and half carried Itrac and Janne to the door, the women and musicians pressing behind them, Jevin and the porters dragging those worst affected by the smoke.

Kheda grabbed the lamp, unable to stop himself coughing as he went out into the corridor. Smoke swirled thicker than ever in the darkness, motes dancing in the halo of light. In his own sleeping chamber, Kheda hurried to lift Telouet from the bed, slinging one of the slave's brawny arms over his shoulder and seizing him around the chest.

'Come on, it seems we must decline Ulla Safar's hospitality.' Telouet was still too deeply asleep to be more than a dead weight in Kheda's arms. Catching up his lamp and dragging the slave out into the corridor, Kheda saw flames. The far doors had yielded to the fire and were now burning fiercely.

As that realisation struck Kheda, so did a solid blow. If Telouet's arm hadn't broken the force of it, Kheda would have been knocked senseless. As it was, he staggered forward, letting Telouet fall heavily. He whirled round, trying to dodge any second blow and to see who could be attacking him.

A burly figure masked against the thickening smoke loomed out of the darkness. He swung a studded club in a two-handed grip, aiming for Kheda's knees. The warlord sprang aside, his agility surprising the would-be assassin. Realising his victim was neither stunned nor doped for an easy kill, the man's next blow connected with Kheda's thigh, knocking him sideways. He fell to his knees. The assassin raised his club to smash the side of Kheda's head. The warlord threw the lamp full in the man's chest, glass shattering and burning oil splashing him. The man reared backwards then froze, mouth open on a cry of angry pain, before collapsing forwards.

The fawning zamorin servant pulled a broad-bladed dagger out of the assassin's throat and held out a hand to help Kheda to his feet.

'If he'd had a sword, he'd have had me,' Kheda gasped, shaken.

The zamorin shook his head as he replaced the dagger in the would-be killer's own sheath. 'Too hard to explain how you came by stab wounds, when your body's found beneath some beam or fallen doorjamb.'

Between them, the two men got Telouet up from the floor. Kheda reached out to grasp the lackey's shoulder. 'Thank you.'

The lackey nodded to Janne's room and the garden beyond. 'Raise as much noise as you can. He can't pretend ignorance if you rouse the whole fortress.'

Kheda halted. 'You won't be suspected, will you?'

'No.' He stopped by the doors, now unlocked. 'This was my task, opening these, so we could all lament how you failed to find such an easy way out, disoriented in the smoke. I'll just say I found him dead.'

Resting Telouet's weight against the wall, Kheda smiled. 'I was always proud to call you my brother, you know that.'

'And I you.' Kheda heard rather than saw the zamorin's grin before the man fled on noiseless feet.

As he hauled Telouet bodily into Janne's apartments, two of the so-called porters rushed to Kheda's aid. 'My lord!'

'Are you hurt?' asked one, alarmed at the blood on Kheda's bare chest and shoulder.

'What?' Kheda looked and realised it was the assassin's blood. 'No, I'm fine.' Though as he spoke, he realised Telouet's arm was deeply scored where the assassin's club had struck him.

They fled for the garden together. The first breath of cool night air made Kheda's head throb unbearably. A shudder ran though him and he coughed convulsively. When he finally managed to stop, his head was swimming as if he'd been guzzling some distilled barbarian liquor.

'What do we do now?' Janne clutched at his arm, her legs bare beneath a tunic not her own, hair half pulled from its night plait, naked face showing every year of her age. Beyond her, Itrac sat huddled on a chest, face hidden in her hands, shoulders heaving. Jevin knelt before her, his gestures eloquent of uncertain attempts at reassurance.

'Raise an alarm,' rasped Kheda. He looked up with abrupt fury at the blind shutters of the inner citadel's higher levels. 'Find something to throw at those. Shout as loud as you can.'

The maidservants needed little encouragement to lift their voices in frantic cries for assistance. After a moment's thought, one of the porters gleefully shoved a substantial glazed urn from its plinth, the others catching up the bigger shards of rim and base to hurl at the upper windows. Lights soon began showing up above, to Kheda's grim satisfaction.

Let Ulla Safar's people try to ignore this commotion.

He took a careful breath of clean air so he could speak

without coughing. 'Listen to me, everyone. We're going back to the galley. If Ulla Safar's servants can't show a modicum of care with night-time candles, we will be safer there.'

'We certainly can't use these rooms until they're restored to some order.' Janne rallied her wits. 'If we return to the *Rainbow Moth*, we won't discommode Mirrel Ulla by requiring alternative accommodations.'

Shouts were coming from inside the fortress now, genuine consternation beyond the smoke-filled rooms that the Daish contingent had fled. Some of the instructions were clearly audible, calling for buckets of earth and palm flails to beat down the flames. Musicians, maidservants and porters alike looked at their master and mistress, alert for unspoken instructions as to the attitude they should adopt.

'Let's get to our ship as soon as possible. Itrac is plainly most distressed. This unfortunate accident has doubtless redoubled her memories of those fires that have ravaged the Chazen domain.' Kheda caught Janne's eye and she nodded her understanding.

Let Mirrel open up the most lavish suites this fortress has to offer. Once we're back aboard, Janne won't shift from polite refusal to subject Itrac to any more upheaval. So that'll be them safe at least.

Kheda sat on a convenient bench of pierced wood. 'Birut, did you get Telouet's swords?'

'Of course, my lord.' Birut came over. 'And my own.'

Kheda realised with weary amusement that was the only reason the slave had bothered with a breechclout, to give himself something to thrust his scabbarded swords through in lieu of his proper belt.

'Bring them to me.' Kheda took the weapons and weighed them in his hands before handing one to the porter who'd been watching anxiously over Telouet. He jerked his head towards the other burly men. 'Birut, give one of them your second sword and get Jevin's off him. Draw lots for whoever has to end up with a stick.'

As the man departed, Kheda knelt to look at Telouet's new injuries. Lifting the slave's bloodied forearm, he carefully tested the bone and cursed under his breath as he felt the distinctive grate of a break. Worse, a foetid smell wrinkled his nostrils. Their murderous attacker had smeared excrement on the studs of his club.

'Janne!' Kheda looked over to see her making a sharp-eyed inventory of everything the maids had managed to salvage, despite their orders to leave with nothing but the essentials. 'Do you have my physic chest? You, Jevin, get me some bits of wood.'

One of the girls brought it clutched in white-knuckled hands. Kheda rummaged inside for the salve to curb the foulness that could leave Telouet's arm festering. Smearing pungent yellow on a length of cotton, he bound it tightly over the deep scores before carefully splinting the broken bone. New purpose burned through Kheda's weariness, even mitigating his headache a little.

My most faithful slave isn't going to lose a limb to Ulla filth, not if I can help it.

'My lord, are we waiting to send word to the ship by one of Ulla Safar's servants?' The porter was back, Jevin's second sword held purposefully in one meaty fist. One of his companions stood at his shoulder, holding Birut's other blade. Both looked incongruously happy to have weapons in their hands. 'Or shall we take a message to the landing stage, make sure they summon the galley at once?'

'It's Gal, isn't it? And Durai?' Both were faces from the rearmost ranks of the Daish swordsmen and Kheda had barely looked at either of them on this trip, not wishing to draw any attention to them.

'Dyal, my lord,' said the second.

Kheda looked around the garden. There were windows to rooms on three sides but all those corridors would lead back towards the fire, which was still blazing unrestrained. There would no getting back inside the fortress until that was under control. He turned to look at the tall wall behind them that reached up to a parapet with low towers watchful on either side, though, curiously, no sentry had appeared to see what all the commotion was about.

'I don't feel inclined to wait for Ulla Safar's minions to sort out their mess before coming to our assistance. We'll get up to the walkway.' He pointed. 'Then we can follow the rampart round to the other side of the fortress and signal the *Rainbow Moth* ourselves.'

I should have suspected a scorpion under the bed, shouldn't I, when Ulla Safar put us so far away, quite out of sight of our galley. How could I have missed some hint of this in all the auguries I took before we sailed?

As Kheda thought this, a streak of light high above caught his eye. A shooting star or firedrake seared its brief path across the night sky. He stared, open-mouthed.

That's out of season, or at least early, with the rains not yet come.

'What have we got for a rope?' Dyal was already catching up lengths of discarded cloth trailing from the garden's battered perfume trees.

Gal darted back down the steps and vanished into the smoke-filled audience room, appearing moments later with arms full of silken coverlets, face congested with the effort of not breathing. 'Who's got a knife?' he gasped.

It turned out some instinct had prompted every man to catch up his dagger. Kheda drew his own and sliced the fine weave with as much relish as if it had been Ulla Safar's throat. 'How do you suggest we get the first man up to the parapet?'

Dyal was already plaiting strips into a sturdy cable. 'Leave that to us, my lord.'

When the silken rope looked barely long enough to Kheda, three of the erstwhile porters formed a practised ladder against the battlement wall and Dyal climbed deftly up their backs and shoulders. Once aloft, he threw a loop around a sturdy merlon and dropped the rope to Gal waiting eagerly below.

'You two stay here, back up Birut and Jevin,' Kheda said to the other porters. He climbed up after Gal, Telouet's sword awkwardly thrust through his belt. As he reached the parapet, the first concerned shouts from Ulla servants sounded in the garden below. 'Daish Kheda! Great lord!'

'Ignore them.' As he ran along the wall walk, Dyal ahead and Gal bringing up the rear, he heard Janne's furious censure intercepting whoever had so conveniently managed to make a way through to the garden as soon as it seemed Daish Kheda was escaping the trap.

The watchtower barred their way, the only route to the parapet beyond, the inward-looking window unaccountably shuttered. Dyal hammered wrathfully on the door. 'Open to Daish Kheda! Are you deaf as well as blind?'

Kheda heard muffled movement inside hastily stilled. He stepped forward and bent close to the crack of the door, speaking with cold precision. 'I am Daish Kheda. Open to me now or I'll demand your heads for your insolence.'

The bolts were immediately withdrawn and the door opened to reveal two youths barely old enough to shave, never mind serve in a warlord's personal guard. Neither spoke, terror plain in their white-rimmed eyes.

'Treacherous scum.' Dyal stepped forward, sword half unsheathed.

The doorway beyond stood open and Kheda saw a figure running along the wall walk. 'They're not worth the waste of our time.' He shoved Dyal towards the far door. They ran on, all three with swords now drawn, bare blades shining like parings from the Lesser Moon bright above. Lights began showing all along the citadel's upper levels. Kheda ignored them.

Young lads on watch and barely trained. Ulla Safar would be distraught as he excused himself to Ritsem Caid and Redigal Coron, bemoaning his guard captain's folly in trusting to youths who had concentrated all their energies on looking outwards, rather than into the fortress. Of course, with the tales of magical foes coming up from the south, that was to be expected, if not excused. The boys would naturally be sentenced to impaling, the captain to a flogging to leave him scarred for life. But I would still be dead, along with my most influential wife, the inconvenient Itrac Chazen and as many as possible of our retinue who might be able to shed some light on these dark dealings.

The next watchtower was empty, doors wide open. The one beyond was barred. Dyal raised his sword hilt to hammer on the stubborn wood. Before his blow landed, the door opened and an armoured Ulla warrior rushed out. He charged into Dyal, knocking him off balance, the Daish man's blade scraping ineffectually over his mailed shoulder. Falling, Dyal grabbed at his assailant, wrapping his arms around his neck, tangling his legs with his own. The pair fell from the parapet, landing with a sickening crunch of bone and an agonised scream in the stone-paved courtyard below.

Kheda's sword met the shining blade thrust forward by the next man out of the watchtower, anonymous as the first behind face guard and the fine chain veil of his helmet. The warlord backed away, parrying a second stroke sweeping in at waist height. There was no way he could attack, not bare-chested against an armoured man.

'Let me past, my lord!' Gal pressed close behind him.

'There's no room.' Kheda twisted his wrist to foil another lethal thrust at his belly.

'My lord!' Alarm sharpening Gal's voice alerted Kheda to running feet at their rear.

'Sheathe your swords!'

When he heard Ulla Orhan's voice behind him, Kheda's surprise nearly gave his opponent an easy kill.

'Put up your blades.' The youth's furious words rang with an ominous echo of his father's ruthlessness.

The man facing Kheda took a step back, sword lowered warily. 'We were told of invaders on the walls.'

'In the inner citadel?' Orhan's voice was cold with disbelief. 'With no breach of the outer defences?'

'There's word of magic attacking in the south.' The warrior still didn't sheathe his blade. 'Who knows where wizards might appear?'

You're very bold in defying the domain's heir apparent. You've had your orders from someone close enough to Safar to be the warlord's mouthpiece.

All the same, Kheda risked a glance backwards and saw Orhan was in armour of his own, a troop of mailed men at his back. The boy had come prepared to fight.

'Ulla Orhan, I am going to the landing stage, to signal to my galley to take us back on board,' Kheda told him forcefully. 'I am not risking my people's safety any further in a night of such confusion.'

'I will not gainsay you,' said Orhan tightly. 'Much as it grieves me to see my father's fortress embarrassed by such inadequacy.'

'Back off,' Gal snarled at the swordsmen blocking their path.

The warrior took a pace backwards. Kheda took one forwards, Gal at his shoulder, his breathing harsh in the tense silence. Behind, he heard Orhan giving some low-voiced order and the rattle of mail as one of his men ran off, doubtless to carry a message to some ally. To their fore, the armoured man gestured to those behind him and they melted away, leaving the parapet clear.

'I shall not forget this.' Kheda's tone was neutral as he wiped sweat from his forehead. 'Any of this.'

'Nor shall I.' Orhan blinked slowly. Then noises below prompted a new concern into his eyes. 'Did someone fall?'

'Dyal, one of my men. Tend him well because I'll be holding you to account for him.' Kheda turned to continue his race along the parapet.

Let Orhan prove his good faith with decent care for Dyal, if he's not already dead.

Whatever word had gone out, it saved Kheda and Gal from further challenge, each watchtower opening almost before they reached it, sentries standing aside with their faces an eloquent mix of shame and apprehension. Kheda counted off the turrets as he and Gal passed through them, chest heaving when he finally reached one that would give him a suitable vantage point over the river, the toothed expanse of the landing stage far below. 'Signal lantern,' he snapped at the cowering guard.

Snatching it from the man, Gal climbed the ladder to the trap door opening on to the roof of the tower. Kheda hurried after him, three steps to one stride. Gal set the heavy lantern in its high seat, the brilliance painful to their eyes. Kheda pulled the lever that closed the shutters set into the lantern's sides. Counting the beats of his heart, he snapped the light open again, closed and then open, in the sequence that the *Rainbow Moth*'s captain should recognise. He peered through treacherous darkness, a few scant lights marking out the profusion of huts and shelters on the bank beyond the anchorages. His own vision was a confusion of false glimmers prompted by the lantern's dazzle. 'Gal, can you see anything?'

'Not yet, my lord.'

They waited.

'Yes, there!'

Kheda found the answering gleam where Gal was pointing. Breath caught in his throat, he counted off the pattern of light and dark.

And that's the true signal, not some random pretence, nor yet covert warning that the ship's been seized, shipmaster under duress, crew quaking for fear of their lives.

'We go down to the dock,' he told Gal decisively. 'As soon as the galley's here, you go and fetch my lady Janne and the others. If Ulla Safar's going to make another attempt on my life, he can make it in full view of too many witnesses even for him to kill. I'm not risking myself in any dark corridors, so Safar can wring his hands over some panicked underling's tragic mistake, and I'm certainly not having Janne caught up in some skirmish.'

'This way, my lord.' Gal led Kheda unerringly down the stair curling below the watchtower in the thickness of the wall and then through corridors busy with startled underlings. Lamps were being lit, doors opening and closing, servants and slaves alike shying away from the two men's drawn swords and dangerous expressions.

A final turn and a flight of steps brought them to the door leading to the room behind the dock in the fortress's outer wall. Gal hammered on it.

'Open to Daish Kheda!'

The heavy iron-bound wood swung open so fast, someone had to have been waiting behind it. Kheda followed Gal through it to find they were in a lofty hall with torches burning in brackets high on the walls and another door opposite. Arrow slits piercing the walls all around and holes in the ceiling for the better delivery of boiling oil, scalding water or just skull-crushing rocks would make sure no one uninvited would get a chance to use either entrance to the fortress. A sizeable contingent of Ulla swordsmen stood in the centre of the floor, between Kheda and departure.

'Open the outer doors, if you please.' Kheda addressed himself to the captain whose brass-decorated helm denoted his rank. 'My galley will be arriving in a moment.' He kept his voice mild.

Gal's scowl and the menace in every line of his body should make it plain we're not to be trifled with. That and our naked swords. Do you have the stones to ask us to put them up, I wonder?

'As you command, great lord.' The sentry captain bowed low and jerked his head to send a couple of his men unbarring the heavy double doors. Kheda walked forward, not looking at any of the Ulla guards. As he walked out on to the landing stage, he saw the Daish galley looming out of the night, moonlight catching the white foam stirred up from the river as the oarsmen turned the mighty ship around. The Ulla men followed him out, drawing up in solid rank along the edge of the dock.

'Get those chains clear!' Kheda looked up to see an armoured man shouting from the stern platform, the ship's contingent led by one of Serno's most trusted subordinates. More men crowded the deck, looking every measure warriors even in the cotton trews and open-necked sleeveless tunics of a galley crew. The captain of the dock sentries jerked his head to send his men to unhook the heavy chains rigged across to prevent any unbidden ship sliding into the welcoming embrace of the landing stage.

'Go and tell Janne Daish we are returning to the shelter of our own galley.' Kheda nodded to Gal who immediately disappeared back into the labyrinth of the fortress. Kheda stood, arms folded, forbidding arrogance challenging the sentries to notice his bare chest, torn and dirty trousers, the absence of everything that should have proclaimed his status as warlord.

The galley docked behind him in a flurry of rushing water. Rapid feet on the stern ladder announced the swordsmen jumping ashore, drawing up around their lord to join in staring down the Ulla sentries. Kheda looked discreetly from side to side, caught Serno's man's attention and narrowed his eyes in mute warning.

The last thing we want is belligerence and mistrust on both sides turning this confrontation into a dockside battle. How to put a stop to that?

Kheda lifted his eyes casually to the sky, studying the heavens. No swordsman would make a move while a warlord was looking for portents. More than one battle had never been joined because an omen had decided the outcome in advance.

As he looked up, more than half his attention on the tense situation all around him, Kheda saw two more white streaks of light in the night sky. More shooting stars, crossing the north of the compass, to vanish in the arc of travel and learning.

It seemed as though half the night had passed before Kheda heard Birut's familiar bellow clearing the way for Janne Daish, first wife and beloved mother, cherished by all her domain. The porters threw open the double doors to the entrance hall and the entire Daish retinue poured out on to the landing stage, maids and musicians alike burdened with an amount of salvaged property that astonished Kheda. His wife's appearance came as less of a surprise.

'My husband.' Janne strode forward, Birut glowering at her shoulder. Somehow, she had managed to find time to dress in a simple yet brightly embroidered gown of blue logen vines on white silk and even had sapphires gleaming around her throat and in her tightly rebraided hair. Jevin hadn't managed to find jewellery for Itrac but she too was at least dressed in something approaching respectable ostentation, in a flowing dress of silk brindled like turtle shell and enough bangles of the real thing to remind everyone whose wife she still was.

'My lady wife.' Kheda waved away Birut who was advancing with a suitably lordly tunic over one arm, intent on improving his master's appearance. 'I suggest we depart and allow Ulla Safar to restore some order to his residence after all these most unfortunate accidents.'

'Indeed.' Janne looked around the Ulla sentries with searing contempt. 'I will not lie to you though, my husband. This has been a most disagreeable visit thus far.'

Kheda nodded to the attendant maids clutching jewel coffers tight with frightened hands. 'Get aboard.' He drew Janne aside, with a sharp gesture to dissuade Birut from approaching.

'Ulla Safar has made every attempt to kill me tonight, short of stabbing me in the back himself. If he doesn't know where I am, he can't try again.' He spoke low and urgently. 'I'm not going to play these games on his terms any longer. We cannot afford to and I need time to think. Tomorrow morning, you will be wanting to make your meditations at the tower of silence by the waterfall upstream, where the brook from the black rock joins the river. Do you hear me?'

Janne nodded, eyes wide with a myriad questions. 'But Kheda—'

He silenced her with a kiss, catching her around the waist and pulling her close. Breaking free of her lips was one of the hardest things he had ever done. 'We're going. Get Itrac below and stay there.' Abandoning Janne he ran lightly up the *Rainbow Moth*'s stern ladder, making his way through the crowded deck to the high stern platform, to stand behind the helmsman watchful by the long tiller that governed the mighty rudder below.

Apprehension twisted Kheda's innards as he waited for everyone to get aboard, the galley's crew shoving off as none of the Ulla men moved to lend a hand. The rowers bent to the oars and the galley soon hauled itself out into the broad main channel. Inadequate as the earlier showers had been, they had still brought a little more water to speed the river's flow. Kheda waited, judging their progress till they were beyond the light shed by the fortress's lanterns, not yet winning close to the random glimmers from the shore.

'What's that?' Kheda pointed into the darkness of the waters, voice sharp with alarm. 'There, did you see it?'

'My lord?' Startled, the helmsman and shipmaster both followed his gesture.

'What is it?' Kheda stared into the night, astonishment in his voice.

After the chaos of the night, that was all it took to set a ripple of panic running through the vessel. The shipmaster hurried to the forward rail of the stern platform, helmsman half standing, face questing. Stealthily, Kheda began taking deeper and deeper breaths.

'Bow watch, what can you see?'

As confused shouts echoed along the deck, Kheda moved backwards, unseen, to the very edge of the stern platform where it hung out over the water, nothing but empty air beneath. He toppled backwards, hitting the water with an inelegant splash. Shouts of alarm just reached his ears before the heavy, turbid water wrapped him in silence.

Keep your mouth shut. Let's not swallow any more of Ulla Safar's shit tonight, and let's get as far away as possible before broaching the surface. This isn't going to work if they drag you out of the river like a half-drowned pup.

He struck out strongly beneath the concealing water,

driving his arms and legs on until his chest burned and his limbs trembled. Finally forced to the surface, he rolled on to his back, barely letting his face rise clear of the pungent water. He floated for a few agonising, stealthy breaths, alert for lights that might betray him, just lifting his head enough to hear the shouts and commotion downstream, the galley wallowing in dismay as everyone searched the black water around the vessel for any sign of him.

And when they can't find me, they'll look downstream, hopefully. That can stand for a test of all this. If I'm following the right course, they will take the wrong one.

Rolling around, Kheda began to swim upstream, sliding his overarm stroke smoothly into the water to avoid any sound of splashing. Leaving the few lights of the bank behind, he risked a little more speed.

Get clear of these houses and out of the river before dawn brings fishermen and bird hunters out on to the water. Then move fast through the forest; Ulla Safar will be sending out search parties at the first hint of light. More than that, Janne will be wanting to know what under all the stars I'm thinking of, so I'd better be at the tower of silence by the waterfall before she is. I'd better have worked out just why it is those shooting stars are turning me to the north.

CHAPTER NINE

'*If you're going to take your omens at dawn, you have to decide when that is. Some say it's when you can first tell a black thread from a white laid across your palm. Others say it's not till the sun is fully clear of the horizon. That's a goodly difference in time, when it comes to reading portents, my lad. I take it as the moment when the light of the coming day turns from grey to yellow.'*

I never shared your confidence in judging such a subtle shift, my father, so decided to making sure I always have a view of the sea when taking such omens and watching for the first brilliant edge of the rising sun. Which does me little good, when all I can see is trees and bushes. Still, unless someone turns up with a handful of black and white threads to say otherwise, it must surely still be before dawn.

Kheda paused to catch his breath in the dim half-light that was just beginning to outline the crudely plundered scrub that bordered the Ulla islanders' vegetable plots and stands of carefully tended fruit trees. He looked up but there were no more shooting stars to be seen. Rubbing a hand over eyes sore with weariness and whatever filth had been in the river, he pushed on through the brittle vegetation. Everything was parched and desperate for the rains, even in this well-watered island of mountains and rivers. Moving off once more, his feet found a bare line of earth marked with the dainty slots that betokened forest deer, overlaid at one point by the thicker, deeper prints of a foraging hog. A game trail.

Follow it for a little while, for the sake of moving fast and quiet, just as long as you're off it before any trappers come up from the farmland looking for forest meat. Remember to look for their snares while you're at it. You still can't risk discovery.

As he ran, he kept a wary eye on the strengthening light above the treetops as well as staying alert for any sound of voices or dogs. He had come far enough to be confident no search sent out from the fortress would find him, but encountering some hunting party returning from a night expedition would be just as bad. Apprehension lent new vigour to limbs aching from ceaseless effort. When the light brought a measure of true colour back to the scrub around him, Kheda reluctantly abandoned the track, climbing a little higher up the side of the broad valley for the thicker cover offered by the margins of the true forest. The denser growth forced him to slow but walking rather than running didn't come as much of a relief. The temptation to stop altogether grew stronger and more insidious.

Just a few moments wouldn't make any difference, not just a little rest to rub your exhausted muscles. Shouldn't you be stopping to look for a stream? You're so very thirsty. No? No. Don't be such a fool. Keep going and think about something else.

The smell of smoke distracted him from the wearisome repetition of such thoughts. After the first rush of alarm froze him among the dusty saplings like a startled deer, Kheda realised the pungent scent was no more than a taste on the breeze, carried up from the distant huts among the saller plots that lay beyond the scrubby brush and the haphazard band of cultivation. Pounding heart slowing, Kheda moved on, smoke-prompted memory uncoiling before him.

'Of course this is a hunting trip. We'll be calling for men

from the villages to carry the meat down for smoking on the shore every second day.' Daish Reik had smiled down, green eyes bright, black beard curling exuberantly now it was freed from the dictates of oil and comb. 'We'll eat well right through the dry season, us and all the islanders who lend a hand.'

'But that's not all this trip is.' Kheda could see several of his brothers had been thinking the same.

'Isn't it?' Daish Reik had cocked his head to one side, face alight with challenge. 'What is it then?'

All his brothers had been watching him, silently urging him on, encouragement in their half smiles, relief in their eyes that he was the one taking the risk.

'You're looking to—' Kheda had searched for the right words. 'You're looking to be sure of the well-being of the domain,' he declared abruptly.

'This is no progress with wives and servants, slaves to do my bidding.' Daish Reik had shaken his head, his gaze intent. 'I make those visits to each island at the start of the dry season, to hear pleas, give judgement and read the omens for each village. You know that.'

'When they know you're coming.' Kheda had stood straighter, head on a level with Daish Reik's shoulder. 'When any misfortune can be tidied away and everything set fair for the most propitious omens.'

'We're not staying in any of the villages.' Daish Reik had spread his broad, thick-fingered hands in apparent puzzlement. 'We're scarcely visiting them.'

'You're talking to everyone we meet on the tracks between them,' Kheda had countered, folding his slender arms across his slightly muscled chest. 'When they're not all tense and anxious that their village shows itself to best advantage, when all the women aren't fussing that the food they have to offer is as good as the next village's, better if possible, and the men are worrying if such generosity is going to leave them hungry by the end of the dry season.' He had looked around the half

*circle of his brothers, reassured by their nods of agreement.
'This way you're not talking to people shoved forward by the
spokesman, to tell you how wonderfully he's leading the
village, how the young men organise the work between them
with never a cross word.'*

*Then he had stopped, unsure, seeing amusement twisting
Daish Reik's full mouth.*

*'Very astute, my son,' Daish Reik had said cordially. 'I
don't imagine these tracks see half this quantity of feet when
we're not in the area with a hunting party.' Then he had
dropped into a crouch, holding Kheda's eyes with his own.
'But you are failing to see I have one more essential objective in these trips.'*

*Kheda had managed not to flinch, aware that all his
brothers were watching, cudgelling his brains for something
else. 'We share our meat with the villages, rather than eating
up their stores. I imagine that leaves them better disposed to
our presence.'*

*'Very true,' Daish Reik had agreed. 'But there's more
besides that.'*

*Kheda hadn't been able to see it so he'd squared his shoul-
ders, lifting his chin. 'What might that be, my father?'*

*In one swift movement, Daish Reik had scooped up a
handful of leaf litter and thrown it at Kheda. 'Having some
fun and getting filthy without your mothers scolding us all
into baths and clean clothes!' Springing up, he'd flung more
handfuls at the other boys. 'The first one of you to get leaves
down my tunic can help me make the fires tonight.'*

*It had been Ajil, brother now lost, zamorin and assiduous
in his duties as one of the lowest ranked of Redigal Coron's
retinue, who had won that much prized duty.*

Kheda paused as he found himself beside a little spring
carving a runnel through the clutter of the forest floor.
Kneeling, he cupped water from the leaf-stained trickle
in his hand and drank, throat aching as he swallowed.

Running a dripping hand over his beard, he forced himself to his feet once again. He ached, all over, from head still suffering from the lingering remnants of Ulla Safar's smothering smoke to feet scored and bruised by missteps in the darkness.

Redigal Coron. What about this plot that Telouet has got wind of? Could you have used that knowledge to bring Coron into an alliance with the Daish and Ritsem domains, instead of opting for this insane course? But would Coron have believed you? How long would it take to unravel the threads of such a conspiracy? No, it would all take too long and you cannot afford to take your eyes off the Chazen threat.

With a groan, he pushed himself on, tendrils from untamed berry bushes catching at his ragged trousers now dried to stiff creases with the silt of the river chafing at his skin. Away from the thinner brush where the Ulla islanders gathered their firewood, the forest closed around him, hostile, unyielding. Kheda drew Telouet's sword and began reluctantly cutting himself a path, doing his best to leave as little of a trail as he could.

Forgive me, Telouet, I know full well this is a task beneath your blade's dignity but it's all I have to hand.

Not that this is the first time I've been out in forest like this with a blade in my hand. That was another of Daish Reik's purposes, on those hunting trips. Was that something else that counted in my favour, that I realised it?

'Why do we have to learn all this?' His brother Kadi hadn't been complaining, just curious, as he had paused in the pattern of sword strokes Daish Reik's slave Agas had been drilling them all in.

'Since we've left everyone but Agas and a few guards behind to look after your mothers, it's as well you learn to defend yourselves.' Daish Reik had been shaving a length of hard, aromatic lilla wood into a feathery tinderstick with rapid strokes of his dagger.

'With these?'

The boys hadn't been given swords, just the long blunt-ended blades that hill men and hunters carried for carving a path through the undergrowth.

'Learn the moves with something as clumsy as that and they'll come all the easier when you deserve a real sword.' Daish Reik's knife had resumed its regular rasp.

Kheda had done his sword practice earlier. He had been sitting nearby, checking his bow and his arrows. Archery was another skill that those hunting trips had taught him. 'What must we do to deserve that?'

'Earn the respect of those swordsmen you expect to go before you into battle, by showing them you can do yourself everything with sword or arrow that you are asking of them.' Daish Reik had pointed the curved blade of his dagger straight at him, emerald eyes hard. 'Deserve their loyalty by showing you value the work that goes into supplying all your wants and more, that you value those who provide for you, whether it be the essentials of fire, water and food, or the luxuries of soft clothes, pretty trinkets and comfortable living.'

'Is that why you said we'd go hungry, if we couldn't catch our own meat on this trip?' Kheda had ventured, mindful of the chequered fowl he'd failed to bring down earlier.

'If you do not know what it is to lack such necessities, you won't see your people's anxiety if a spring fails in the dry season or a rainy-season storm leaves a village's saller rotting in the granary and all the firewood so sodden, a flame to dry it simply cannot be sustained.' Daish Reik's smile had been more challenge than reassurance. 'If you do not see such obvious things, how can you see the greater subtleties of portents? Share the concerns of the domain and its people and they will drive you to puzzle out the meaning of omens. Value the stuff of life, those that bring it to you and the domain that provides it, and people and domain both value you.'

I do value my domain and its people both and I'll risk the

taint of magic by defying these wizards with a sword in my hand myself, before I let them stain and despoil the Daish islands. Redigal Coron can look to his own problems. I must find some way of defending the Daish domain.

Kheda cut down a half-dead tandra sapling rising from a stained tangle of last year's fibrous pods and suddenly found himself face to face with a startled hook-toothed hog. The beast grunted and shied away but it didn't flee. With the bristling crest running along its arched spine on a level with Kheda's midriff, it didn't need to. Planting its hooves in the remains of the rotting log where it had been foraging, it turned red-rimmed black eyes on Kheda with a belligerent snort. Its lips, slimy with spittle and dirt, drew back from the downward curve of its lower tusks, fangs the length of Kheda's dagger, yellow and spotted with leaf mould where it had been digging for grubs and beetles in the log. Its upper tusks curved the other way, coiling round to meet over the long flexible snout twitching at this new, intrusive scent. Kheda took a careful step backwards.

'Not fast enough to provoke it into a charge, nor yet slow enough for it to decide you're a threat and it may as well get its attack in first. If it does run at you, get out of its way, up a tree if you can. Those tusks can disembowel a man and leave him bleeding his life out on the forest floor. And remember, if it does kill you and no one finds your corpse, it'll come back when you're rotten meat and eat you itself.'

That's something else we learned on those hunting trips, isn't it, Daish Reik, that there are more ways than one of killing or catching every kind of prey and stealth a part of most of them. Challenging these wizards face to face would be a quick way of getting myself killed. I have to find some more subtle weapon. Show me I am on the right path here, hog.

Kheda halted and waited. The hook-toothed hog looked

at him, almost comical as it peered past the twisted tusks in front of its eyes. With another snort and a shake of its mottled brown and black hide, it turned tail and disappeared into the all-enveloping leaves of a sardberry thicket, the forest soon muffling the sound of its retreat.

A flock of little scarlet-headed waxbeaks swooped down to land on the ravaged log, trilling with excitement as they pecked at insects disturbed by the foraging hog. Kheda realised the trees and bushes all around were bustling with birds of all sizes and colours stirring to greet the new day. He hurried on through the trees, moving back down the long shallow slope of the river valley. Cautious, he looked out across the patchwork of vegetable fields and saller plots and to intermittent huts of Ulla Safar's people marking out the line of the distant river, narrower here but still wider than any in the Daish domain. Mists still hung in swathes across the low-lying land, drifting into rags and tatters where breezes tugged at them.

There it was. Indistinct yet unmistakable, a raw outcrop of black rock broke through the valley side, stark intrusion shocking against the soft green, irresistibly drawing the eye to its brutal shape. Sheer sides rose up as clean and glistening as meat fresh cut with a fine-honed blade. No plants had managed a foothold on that slick surface. On the foremost crest, a few scrubby bushes had sprouted, only to be crushed beneath the sprawling weight of an enormous nest, built by the silver eagles who had claimed the crag for their own. The ground below the crag was untouched. None would dare till it and risk being touched by the great birds' shadows, wide as the span of a grown man's arms, as they wove their portents in the skies. Only in the thirstiest season would they approach to draw water from the pool beneath the unfailing waterfall tumbling in gouts of brilliant white down the midnight face of the rock. No matter what the season, no one would approach the ornately carved gate in the high wall that surrounded the topless tower standing just to the south of the crag. No one except a warlord or his acknowledged wife.

Kheda began making his way towards it, finding a path winding through the remnants of the much-harvested brushwood. Soon stands of berry bushes and little lilla trees marked the edge of proper cultivation. There was no fruit to be had though, no matter how fiercely Kheda's belly griped with hunger. Then a few black-veined ruddy leaves wilting beneath a lilla sapling caught his eye. Hira beets. Dropping to his knees, Kheda dug with his dagger until he uncovered the roots. Hands clumsy, he peeled them, the dark juice staining fingers and dagger alike. Wizened and leathery at this season, they still had some sweetness as he chewed them resolutely.

Let that chance find be a good omen, like the hog, that I'm on the right path.

Meagre as it was, this food put new heart in him. Kheda hurried on, seeing the great black crag grow brighter with every touch of the strengthening daylight. The mists shifted and drifted around it, shapes half seen tempting his eyes and memory but disappearing before he could decide just what they were. Following the lie of the land, slipping gradually downhill, the path took him more than half the way to the great black crag before it swerved in a prudent detour back towards the huddles of close-shuttered houses. Kheda looked warily over towards the river. He could see a few figures now, tiny and indistinct in the mists, stooped over nursery beds where the saller seedlings were being cherished, waiting for the longed-for rains to soak deep into the earth-banked fields lying hoed and ready.

There's a time for stealth and this isn't it. This is no time to be seen and hailed, asked who you are and what you're doing, half naked and filthy and yet carrying a sword twice the value of any of those houses and everything in it. Not that any of them would recognise you in this state, not as the mighty lord of the Daish domain, reader of portents, giver of laws, healer and protector of all his islands.

Leaving the track, Kheda cut a straight path towards the white stone wall surrounding the tower of silence. A perfect circle, it was topped with sharp peaks of opaque white crystal and broken only by a single gate of ebony stained with the verdigris that had long since dulled the bronze fittings to a murky green. Kheda laid a scratched and dirty hand on the latch and, pushing the gate open, slid inside the compound. His breathing sounded harsh and ragged in his ears as he leaned against the wall, relief suddenly robbing him of any strength for an endless instant.

The solid pillar of the tower rose above him. Broad, shallow steps wound up the outside in a slow spiral for those who would bring the honoured dead of the domain here, to lay them down on the empty, open platform at the top, its four pillars set in a cardinal square. There were no rails or barriers. For anyone engaged in such hallowed duties to complete them in safety or, by contrast, to fall to injury or death was a potent omen either way. Kheda walked slowly across the dusty space, intent on putting the tower between himself and the gate. Out of long habit, he noted the few plants that had seeded themselves inside the enclosure.

Saller stalks rattling dry kernels cloaked in rough husks; a good omen that, for the fertile land all around supplying the vital harvest to come. That tiny sapling already has the distinctive leaves of the bloodfever tree, though it's a fragile promise of health for the people hereabouts. I wouldn't be any too sanguine for local villages, not with the size of that serpent bush thriving next to it.

That was one of your other purposes on our forest hunting

trips, wasn't it, my father, teaching us to recognise our healing plants.

'See these upthrust ridged fingers hidden among the sard-berry leaves? This is a serpent bush and it's as vicious as any snake, its sap just as venomous. Never touch it; these spines will break off in your fingers and fester. Don't cut it; the juice will blister your skin. Make sure you never gather any in with dead wood for your fire. Meat cooked over it will kill you.'

'Then what purpose does it serve?' Kheda had stammered. He'd not long begun his herbal studies but the one thing he had already learned was every plant was supposed to have a function.

Daish Reik had looked at him for a long moment of silence. 'It serves as a warning. Let that be sufficient for now.'

It was only later, when I was left your sole son, searching the tomes of herb lore in the tower for all the teaching your untimely death had denied me, that I learned its full potential among the subtler means of attacking one's enemies, of inflicting timely indispositions and discreet wasting sicknesses. Is this one of the malevolent plants that Ulla Safar uses to clear inconveniences like Orhan's mother from his path?

Is this where Ulla Safar brings those pathetic little corpses he writes out of this domain's records barely before they've drawn breath? Does he deem them important enough to be raised to the silent heights, that the birds and the insects might disperse their essence as widely as possible over the domain? What influence could they have, such tiny children, for good or ill on the domain? Perhaps he simply buries them, like humble islanders with no greater ambition than returning all that they have become to the place where they lived out their lives. Or does he deny them even that grace, since he doesn't deem them worthy of even the chance of life, something even the scrawniest offspring of the lowest dirt farmer can claim in the Daish islands. Does he burn the tiny bodies or throw them to the tides to be washed far from the Archipelago? I wouldn't put it past him. Still, at least it doesn't smell as if he's murdered anyone with a blood claim on the domain of late.

Kheda sat with his back to the tower and looked up at the steps rising above his head. The still air was fresh with the transient cool of dawn, no carrion stench drifting down from the tower. There were a few scraps of cloth on the ground, sun-bleached and rain-faded, some dull white rounded pieces that could only be bone. The greatest concentration of both was clustered around the base of the serpent bush.

'It serves as a warning. Let that be sufficient for now.'

Kheda stared unseeing at the blank stone wall in front of him. There was no sound but the steady thrumming rush of the ceaseless waterfall hidden from view by the enclosure wall. The sound made Kheda thirsty again, his mouth as dry as sun-bleached cotton. Resolutely ignoring it, he marshalled the arguments he would need honed and ready, if he was going to keep the upper hand in the inevitable argument with Janne, to convince her of the truth that had come to him in the darkness of the night, alone on the silent river bank. Despite his determination, he still didn't feel ready by the time he heard Janne's sharp voice rising above reluctant steps drawing close to the gate in the wall. He sat, motionless, forcing himself to breathe slow and careful, trying to still the pounding of his heart.

'Wait at the bottom of the rise.' Janne's voice outside the gate was harsh with weariness. She rounded on some low rumble of protest from Birut. 'Because I do not want any distractions.'

Tense, Kheda waited as she lifted the latch, entered and closed the gate firmly behind her. He heard her heave a tired sigh before her soft tread approached the tower. 'Kheda?'

He stood and looked cautiously around the curve of

the stone. 'I'm here. Who's with you?' he asked in the same low tone.

Janne took an impulsive step forward, hands outstretched, before she halted, hugging herself instead. 'Birut, a detachment of our own swordsmen and some of Ulla's men who insisted we could not make such a journey without fitting escort. Don't worry; I've left them well out of earshot and Birut will make sure no one trespasses on my grief.' Her face showed all the strain of the long and troubled night but she was immaculately dressed regardless, a white shawl of silky goat's hair wrapped around the shoulders of a grass-green dress with a pattern of dancing herons. Braided close, her hair was adorned with chains of emeralds mounted in silver.

'How's Telouet?' That abrupt concern overrode what Kheda had intended to say.

'His arm is broken and the wound looks dangerously inflamed but he's awake and says his sickness is past.' Janne paused, anger and hurt naked in her tired eyes behind their mask of cosmetics. 'Frantic about you, I might add. What am I to tell him?'

'What did you tell Ulla Safar?' Kheda had questions of his own before he'd be giving any answers.

'That every portent must be sought, every omen consulted as to where the river might have carried you.' Janne settled her shawl lower on her arms, speaking with something of her customary self-possession. 'Since visiting a tower of silence is the sole divination that's a wife's province, I said I would come here and seek some dream to give us a hint as to your fate. As I have not slept, the chances of some guidance must be all the greater.' She looked at him meaningfully.

Kheda looked past her to the gate, face thoughtful. 'What signs has Safar pointed at, in his interpretation of events?'

'He has yet to devote himself to such considerations,' Janne said with asperity 'He feels the first priority is organising search parties to scour the banks downstream for your corpse. He wished me peace in my meditations and, of course, to let him know at once whatever image was in my mind on waking. He said I could have Orhan to assist me in divining its meaning.'

'How generous,' said Kheda dryly. 'You should keep an eye on Orhan though. He may be looking to the Daish domain for an ally. He certainly saved me from death at least once last night.'

'Could that be why Safar tried to have you killed?' Hope rose in Janne's voice. 'Could the Chazen troubles have nothing to do with the night's calamities?'

'I don't know and I don't really think I care,' Kheda said brusquely.

Janne was taken aback. 'We have to know what lies behind all this. This is our first chance in years to get the upper hand over Safar. We have to decide the best time for your return, to our best advantage. Redigal Coron is all but shoulder-to-shoulder with Ritsem Caid now. Safar was summoning his people to mourn your death when Coron stepped in and forbade it, insisting there's every chance you're still alive.'

'But what if I am not?' Kheda asked softly.

Janne looked puzzled. 'What do you mean?'

'What if I am dead?' he persisted.

Janne stared at him, still uncomprehending. 'Don't say such a thing, not below a tower of silence. You tempt the future, my husband.'

'What if I am dead, my first wife?' repeated Kheda, steel in his voice.

Janne cupped her face in her hands, closing her eyes. 'Then Sirket inherits, if we can get word to him to make sure he declares your death and his accession before anyone else can do it.' Her eyes opened with a snap. 'Which is why Safar is searching so diligently for your corpse. If he can prove your death before Sirket has a chance to declare himself, the domain is masterless, the chain of succession broken.'

'To be seized by whoever may prove strongest.' A humourless smile twisted Kheda's mouth. 'Safar must be all but spilling his seed at the prospect.'

'Caid would never stand for it.' Janne looked appalled. 'It would be war between Ulla and Ritsem.'

'It's a good thing there's no corpse to be found then.' Kheda shrugged with sour satisfaction. 'Sirket must declare himself as soon as possible. If Telouet's fit to travel, send him. Everyone will suspect what that signifies but no one can challenge you, not as long as you stay here and encourage Safar in his search parties and dragging the river bed.'

'What are you saying?' A sharp frown creased Janne's brow. 'You want Sirket to take on the domain, an untried boy between Ulla Safar's malevolence to the north and reeking savages wielding magic to the south? What are you thinking?' Barely catching herself before her voice rose to a shout, her words rang with suppressed anger.

'As long as there is no body to display, for weeping and lamentations over such a tragic accident, Safar cannot move against Sirket.' Kheda kept his words calm. 'Doing so would be as good as saying he knows I am dead because he killed me himself. Caid will never stand for it and I don't imagine Coron will either. His retinue won't let him for one thing. That reminds me, you must talk to Telouet as soon as he's got his wits about him. He's heard word those Redigal zamorin are planning their own change of dynasty. They won't want Safar starting a new trend for seizing disputed domains by force of arms.' Kheda ticked off his next argument on his fingers. 'If Sirket is warlord, facing this threat of magic, Caid and Coron will back him, out of self-interest as much as compassion. They might have left me to make shift against unknown invaders as best I could but they won't see Sirket as anything like a strong enough bulwark between them and that danger.'

'And you do?' snapped Janne, incredulous. 'He's barely grown!'

'I have considerable confidence in him,' Kheda replied firmly. 'Still more since he'll have you and Rekha to support and advise him. He's not yet married, so no one will be expecting either of you to quit the domain. He'd better not wed,' he added sharply. 'I know it'll be expected but let him adopt Mesil as a son, if you feel it necessary to demonstrate the succession is secure.'

Janne just stared at him. 'And what of Sain?'

Kheda was thrown off his stride. 'What of her?'

'You'll let her think you're dead, that her babe is to be fatherless? You'd condemn the child to birth under such ill omen, all the while knowing it to be falsehood?'

'If it is no true portent, the child cannot be harmed by it.' Shaken, Kheda tried not to show it.

'You expect Sain to conceal such a truth?' Janne shook her head, disbelieving.

'No,' said Kheda gruffly. 'She must not know the truth, nor must Rekha. You must not breathe a word of this to anyone, not even Sirket, or Telouet.' He swallowed a sudden tightness in his throat. 'Telouet must become Sirket's body slave. There is no one I would rather trust either of them to.'

'Kheda, the children will be devastated! Rekha will grieve as you cannot imagine. It's a good thing Sain's all but reached her time; otherwise such news would likely make her lose the babe. But you're not dead. Why are we talking like this?' Janne ran silver-ringed hands into her thick hair, gripping painfully tight, before staring into her husband's eyes. 'Disappearing for a night, even a few days, if only to save yourself and to disconcert Safar, yes, I can see that, but what can we possibly gain from persisting in this folly?'

'We came here looking for help against the magic that's afflicting the Chazen domain.' Kheda reached forward to disentangle Janne's hands from her hair, holding them close between his own. 'We find everyone playing the same old games of suspicion and intrigue, nursing festering grudges and seeing every augury through the twisted prism of their own hatreds. We cannot afford to get caught up in this tangle of squabbles and intrigue when unknown savages are wielding brutal magic no more than a few days' sail to our south.'

'So you propose to play dead?' Shrillness in Janne's words cut the stillness like a knife.

'Safar cannot distract us with any more attempts on my life if I do, or worse, actually succeed. We talked of sending word to the north, remember?' Kheda held her hands tight between his own. 'To ask if any domains would share their tactics for dealing with barbarian wizards from the unbroken lands?'

'We agreed you would suggest it, simply as a ploy.' Janne narrowed her eyes at him. 'To make Safar and the others believe aiding the Daish domain themselves was lesser evil than inviting strangers into these reaches.'

'I saw firedrakes in the sky last night, Janne, burning a path to the north. What if I follow them, go looking for such lore, in all truthfulness?' Kheda swallowed hard a second time. 'You said yourself, the price we'll have to pay for aid from Ulla Safar and Redigal Coron will beggar our domain for ten years or more. What if I could find some other means, some arcane knowledge that would enable us to drive this vileness out of Chazen and into the southern ocean?'

'We can hold them off, with Ritsem Caid at our back,

and Redigal Coron,' Janne protested. 'If you are there to lead the Daish domain, that is.'

Kheda shook his head resolutely. 'The best we could hope for is holding them to the Chazen isles. How long can we do that, especially once the rains have passed? Simply stopping their advance is no answer, not beyond a season or so. We need to drive them out of Chazen isles and Daish alike, clear down to the southern ocean. I truly believe the only way we'll find the means to do that is if I seek it in the northern domains. I can travel through the rains and be back before the dry season reopens the seaways.'

'And what becomes of Sirket when you return to us?' Janne burst out, pulling her hands free of Kheda's, heedless of her shawl falling to the ground. 'If he declares himself warlord, you have to fight him to regain your place. How's that to be resolved without one of you killing the other?' Fury all but choked her.

'Sirket is in no danger from me.' But Janne had thought he might be, if only for a moment, even after all they had shared together. Kheda felt cold despite the heat of the sun now rising above the tree-crowned crest of the valley side. 'He can step aside; the Daish domain answers to no one else, as to how we manage our affairs. And having proved his quality in this trial, his eventual succession will be that much more secure.'

'And what if you don't come back?' Janne's eyes were brimming with tears. 'Don't go! Don't risk yourself like this—' Words failed her.

'I have to.' Kheda drew a deep breath as he bent to pick up Janne's fallen wrap. 'I have to find some way of countering this magic and it's plain I'll not find it here or in any of our neighbours' domains. None of them sees the peril that lies over the southern horizon for the danger it is. There's more, besides. I couldn't read the portents on the Chazen beach, did I tell you that? I'm beginning to wonder if the taint of this magic is spreading ahead of these wizards, corrupting the omens that should be convincing Caid and Coron.'

'What?' Janne stared, disbelieving, ignoring the proffered shawl.

'I saw none of this.' Angry, Kheda waved the white wrap in an arc encompassing the tower, the crag and the whole Ulla domain. 'I worked every divination I thought appropriate before we set sail, you know that, and a few that I give precious little credence, just in case. I sought every possible guidance, alert for any potential warning. I saw none of this,' he repeated bitterly. 'I had no notion that Safar's hostility could reach such a pitch as to have me killed. I saw no augury of sickness, real or induced, nor any sign of a fire to threaten us.' He was twisting the fine silky wool until it cut painfully into his palms. 'The only sign I have seen that can have any meaning is last night's shooting stars. At the very least I have to travel north until I'm free of this miasma and can see our path clear again. I cannot lead the domain in a fight against wizards if the touch of that magic is cutting me off from every sign that should guide me. I would only lead the domain into darkness and death.'

'And how is Sirket to do better?' Janne waved frantic hands, bracelets jingling.

'Sirket did do better,' Kheda said ruefully. 'He did see peril waiting here for me, when he consulted the triune candles, even if it was unclear. I don't think the same confusion is afflicting him. Maybe it's because I went south, actually faced these wizards' monsters.'

'Caid and Coron haven't. Why should they be afflicted?' Janne's anger was rising above her distress. 'Besides, you assured Itrac that to be an unwilling victim of magic is to remain innocent.'

'And half the books in the tower library argue different.' Kheda threw up his hands. 'I don't know. All I do know is we're finding no help here and we need help, Janne, we need it. It's my duty to find it and the only path I can see offering any hope leads north.'

Janne snatched back her shawl and wrapped it close around her shoulders. 'And what are we to do, my lord and husband, while you are following this path?' Her voice was cold but a single tear traced a shining line down her cheek.

Kheda cleared his throat. 'Make sure anyone fleeing north from Chazen is kept in our southernmost islands. They can fish from the shore but not from boats. Don't let Sirket get lured into an advance if the invaders do come north,' he said with more urgency. 'He must fight where he can, kill where he can but don't let him go on the attack, not until I have brought some means to counter the sorcery. If the savages should attack in the rains, our people should fall back, hide in the forests, keep themselves safe until we can carry the attack to these wizards with real hope of success.'

Janne closed her eyes on more tears, shoulders trembling. 'Until you return?'

Kheda embraced her, holding her tight. 'Until I bring whatever lore the northern warlords use to keep magic's evil from invading their domains, to defend our children and their future.'

Janne nodded mutely, stiff within the circle of his arms. 'Tell me, how do your propose to travel north, all but bare-arsed and with no status to call on?'

'I'll cross the central heights and make for the trading beaches on the north side of the island. I will take an oar in a merchant galley in return for passage north.' Kheda shrugged. 'I'll find some clothing on my way. I believe the Ulla domain owes me that much at least. I can feed myself from the forest.'

Janne broke free of his hug and wiped away her tears with the fringe of her shawl, careful not to smudge the green and silver paint around her eyes. 'The Ulla domain owes the Daish a great deal more than tunic and trews for the loss of its lord under Ulla Safar's hospitality.' Her mouth set with new purpose.

'Then you and Rekha can make sure they pay, in arms and men to hold back these wizards until I get back,' Kheda said vehemently.

'How will I know when you have found this lore to drive out magic, that you're on your way home?' Janne looked at him. 'You'll have no message birds, no couriers.'

Kheda scratched at an itch in his beard. 'We'd better keep it secret, that I am still alive, until I am safely back in Daish waters or, better yet, carrying the fight to these invaders in the Chazen isles. I don't want to give Safar a chance to finish last night's work or to get caught up in explaining myself to any other domain. They can find out what I've been doing once I've driven these wizards out. That should put paid to most of their questions of itself.' He paused, thinking. 'There's a tower of silence on the thousand-oyster isle, do you know the one I mean?'

'Where your great grandsire and his elder sons were dashed to death on the reefs.' Janne nodded, visibly determined to get a grip on her unruly emotions.

'No one will be going there until the pearl harvest.' Kheda nodded. 'That's where I'll head for. You can meet me there and tell me how things stand in my absence. Then we can decide how best to go forward.'

'I'll send a trusted slave to keep vigil there,' Janne said slowly. 'Because the sea has yet to give up your body.'

'I will be back as soon as I can,' Kheda promised.

Janne looked straight at him. 'While you're looking for lore to drive out magic, search out as many rites of purification as you can. We have to rid ourselves of every stain these wizards leave.' She shook herself, her white shawl fluttering like the wings of a bird. 'I don't think we have anything else to discuss. I'll return to Derasulla.'

'So soon?' Kheda was surprised. 'Ulla Safar will be expecting you to look for some guidance in a dream here.'

'I've changed my mind,' Janne said with steely precision. 'That is ever a wife's prerogative. If he presses me, I shall simply become distraught with grief.' Her face was cold and calm.

Kheda drew a deep breath. 'So this is farewell, my wife, until the thousand-oyster isle, that is.'

'Farewell, my husband.' Janne turned abruptly towards the gate, lifting the latch and sliding through it. Birut's voice approached, concern lost in the solid clunk of ebony on stone and the rattle of the handle.

Kheda slid down to sit at the base of the lofty tower, struggling not to yield to the doubts suddenly clustering round him.

How long to leave it before escaping the confines of the enclosure? Long enough to avoid being seen by Janne's departing escort but not so late that some labourer in the saller fields or some child sent to gather firewood raises a hue and cry after this unknown man profaning the sanctity of the tower of silence. Then it's into the forest and head for the heights, for the passes that will take you over to the northern side of the island, to the trading beaches and passage north. How am I to secure that?

'How am I to do this?' The knife in his hand had been as long as his forearm but had still looked entirely inadequate to Kheda, faced with the thick brindled belly hide of the dead water ox.

'Think it through,' Daish Reik had said firmly. 'Decide what you must do first. Do that and then you'll see the next step.'

Hunting for dappled deer, they had surprised the water ox

*drowsing where a stream formed a pool around a stubborn
rock in its path. Daish Reik would never have chosen such a
quarry with the children in the party but now it was roused,
the beast was far too dangerous to leave. He had shouted at
Kheda to get all the boys into the trees, Agas already throwing
hunting spears to the other swordsmen. The warriors had
fanned out into a half circle, the broad leaf-shaped spearheads
held low, as the ox lumbered out of the water brandishing its
vicious, down-curved horns, incongruously draped with a
tendril of the waterpepper weed it had been browsing on.*

*Two men and Agas had challenged the beast with shouts
and taunts. It had charged them, the force somewhat dissi-
pated by its inability to chose a target, but it had still sent
one of the men flying with a great buffet of its brutal head.
His valour had served its purpose when Daish Reik had driven
his spear into its back, in between the animal's angular
shoulder blades, deep into its vitals. Its knees had buckled,
bowels voiding, collapsing even as it still sought to gore the
fallen swordsman.*

*'Kheda, deal with it.' Daish Reik had abandoned the ox
as soon as he was sure it was dead, turning to salve the horrifying bruises on the man's chest, tearing up his own tunic to
wrap his broken ribs. 'That's too much meat to leave for the
jungle cats.'*

*Which was why Kheda had stood before the massive,
stinking, steaming carcass.*

'How am I to do this?'

*How was he to get the leathery hide off without ruining
it? How was he to gut it without puncturing the endless loops
and pouches of its entrails? How was he to read any signs in
the heavy, slippery liver before the sheen that reflected the
unseen future dried in the heat? How was he supposed to direct
the other boys in butchering something that weighed as much
as all of them put together? Where were they going to find
the perfume leaves to smoke this much meat?*

*'Decide what you must do first. Do that and then you'll
see the next step.'*

Tense, waiting until the sounds of Janne's departure
had subsided, Kheda lifted the latch of the gate and
slipped out of the silent tower's precinct.

*First things first. Which means you want a tunic and a
belt to hang Telouet's sword on, since the one Daish Reik
made for you from the water ox's hide is back in Derasulla.*

CHAPTER TEN

Was he going to find what he was looking for here? Or was he going to end up chasing his tail again like some serpent maddened by the heat? After so many frustrations, it was almost enough to make Dev spare a prayer to the gods of his childhood. Not quite enough. After all, they'd never answered him.

Dev hauled on the rope to spill wind from the *Amigal*'s triangular sail, pushing the tiller away as he did so. The lithe little ship turned through a narrow channel cut between two gaunt islets of bare, crumbling stone. Rocky hummocks of veined and fluted coral rose to within a finger's width of the sea's surface, the frothing gullies between them thick with vicious prongs of jagged sea thorn.

'Can you lend us a hand?' A light galley slightly bigger than the *Amigal* was wedged firmly on a reef. Her embarrassed master shouted over the noise of the breaking waves, his exasperated rowers slumped idle over their oars.

'I told you it was too late in the day to make the passage with this much cargo weighing us down,' the helmsman said with unnecessary recrimination.

'High tide will float you off before morning.' Dev held to his course. If they'd lost the best of the market for whatever they were carrying, that wasn't his problem.

He grinned as the deft *Amigal* sped through the narrow passage to waters suddenly crystal clear over white sand spangled with bright blue seastars and giant clams gaping

up at him, sinister green lips crinkled in the deep. Scanning
the broad bay girt by fawn-flanked peaks, he looked for any
ships he recognised among those who'd thought it worth
their while to negotiate the tortuous maze of stony spikes
and fans of corals to claim Taer Badul's protection. Besides,
Taer Badul's swift triremes would be about their usual business of forcibly discouraging any traders seeking alternatives to the few anchorages the warlord permitted.

There were certainly more ships than expected, when
anyone with any sense should be heading for home or a
friendly landing and shelter from the imminent rains. Dev
studied the beach, a slim curve of white above the aquamarine waters with the Taer settlement no more than a
line of sturdy huts built high on stilts against storm surges.
Beyond, a narrow tangle of nut palms and perfume bushes
soon yielded to the naked screes of the mountains, which
the setting sun was gilding with a spurious beauty. Taer
Badul's designated trading beach offered precious little
welcome to anyone thinking of jumping ship to find a
foothold in a new domain. Which made it all the more
surprising that the sand was crowded with men, women
and children, gathered around cook fires or huddled
beneath rough shelters of ragged cloth and green wood
in some vain attempt to escape the heavy heat.

Satisfaction warmed Dev. Someone here should be able
to tell him more than vague rumours of ill-defined misfortune stalking the southern reaches. People didn't uproot
their entire lives lightly, not in the Archipelago. Better yet,
the *Amigal* had a hold full of things to loosen tongues. He
spared a moment of regret for the loss of Taryu and Ekkai.
There were always those who preferred willing flesh to
warming liquor. Well, that was past praying for, so he'd
just have to do the best he could with what he had.

He coaxed the *Amigal* past the tall sterns of substantial galleys swinging lazily at their anchors, carefully

summoning an invisible touch of wind to give him just a little more steerage now that the calm of dusk approached. Pennants fluttered on the sternposts, permission to travel Taer Badul's waters prominently displayed and many others besides. Dev carefully studied the galleys. There had to be one he'd done business with somewhere. After a handful of strangers, he recognised a bold design on a part-furled mainsail. Not the one he was looking for but good enough to make a start. Good enough to be one of those random coincidences the Aldabreshi seized on as proof that they were reading their omens right, living cleanly or whatever else they wanted to know.

'Hello the *Spotted Loal*,' he called out boldly.

'Hello yourself.' A rower leaned over the fat-bellied galley's rail. 'Do I know you?'

'Lots of people know me and the *Amigal*, pal.' Dev favoured him with a cheery grin. 'Ask your shipmaster if he remembers Dev.' More importantly, with any luck, he'd also remember the deceptively smooth Caladhrian red wine the *Amigal* carried, so effective for encouraging tipsy confidences. Dev maintained his smile with some effort. It was about time he won some useful information about these rumours of magic, in return for all the precious liquor he'd squandered up till now.

'Where are you come from?' The crewman hefted a pole; ready to fend off, as Dev drifted close to the galley's steering oars.

'Barbak, looking to swing north to Galcan waters if I can make it before the rains.' Dev patted his belt where he now wore a dagger with the straight and narrow double-edged blade and ornamented thumb ring that Barbak weaponsmiths favoured. That was a plausible voyage to excuse any ignorance of local concerns. He slid the *Amigal* skilfully under the galley's stern. 'How about yourselves?'

'Up from the Tule domain,' the crewman said rather more tersely. 'And heading north as soon as we're rested and fully watered.'

'I'd like to make myself known to your shipmaster again,' Dev remarked genially. 'Is he aboard?' There was just enough space between the *Spotted Loal* and the huge galley anchored beside it for the *Amigal* to slide through.

Dev leaned into the tiller and turned the boat's prow out to the bay. The sail caught the fading breeze and pushed the *Amigal* back towards the steeply sloping beach. Dev slipped a rope loop around the tiller to hold it steady and ran to the prow to drop an anchor. It dragged through the sand and corals, slowing the boat. As soon as Dev felt the stern brush the beach, he tied the rope off. Hastily lowering the sail as he passed, he hurried back to the stern to jump ashore with a second anchor. Not daring to use any hint of magic under the galley men's inquisitive gaze, he muttered an obscenity under his breath. Landings like this had been a cursed sight easier with Ekkai and Taryu to set struggling with the heavy anchors.

'He's ashore, the shipmaster.' The galley man watched as Dev pounded his anchor's spear-like flukes deep into the sand. Another man joined him and they exchanged a few words. Diving smoothly from the galley's stern, the rower swam ashore, wiping water from his eyes as he approached Dev.

'Our rowing master reckons he knows your ship. He says you can share our fire and whatever's in the pot.' He jerked his head towards a cluster of men up beyond the high-water mark. 'I'm Jailan.'

'I'm obliged to you.' As they walked along the beach, Dev watched warily for anyone wearing weapons and armour. If hints of unknown dangers were coming up from the south, it was a safe bet there'd be chary eyes all around the beach and Taer Badul's swordsmen had an intolerant attitude to visitors at the best of times. Dev didn't want to do anything to draw suspicion his way, not with the temptations secreted in the *Amigal*'s hold. A faint frisson of danger stiffened his spine and he welcomed the rush of blood in his veins.

Men from the galley had pulled weathered logs into a rough circle around a long-established fire pit lined with cracked and blackened stones. Wary faces looked up to see who was approaching, judgement grudgingly reserved when they realised Dev was following in Jailan's wake. Dev kept his face neutral but in no sense humble. Cowering hounds had their throats ripped out at least as often as they saved themselves by grovelling.

'There's Master Uten,' Jailan nodded.

The shipmaster squatted on a solid round of nut palm wood weathered to much the same colour and texture as his own face. A burly man with a close-trimmed beard, his long wiry hair was braided with colourful cord trimmed with small gold and silver tokens: animals and leaves, fanciful depictions of the constellations and a few mainland coins. He was deep in conversation with a man whose uncut, uncombed beard, ragged clothes and faintly distracted air made it immediately apparent he was a soothsayer.

'Take a seat.' Jailan gestured to the logs around the fire. Dev did as he was bid, trying not to make it obvious he was curious to hear the soothsayer's low words. The seer was pouring small amounts from various bottles into a gourd resting between his crossed legs. He re-stoppered each bottle carefully and replaced it in a scarred chest with much-repaired brass bindings. His clothes showed the same kind of wear; washed almost colourless, patched trousers and a mismatched tunic. One of those charlatans who felt a sham of honest poverty rather than a confident air of prosperity would win trust and more handouts from the gullible, Dev concluded.

More crewmen arrived, carrying fresh fruit and flat saller bread still warmly fragrant from some islander's charcoal oven. A thin-faced man slipped through them, to throw himself to his knees before the galley's master, scrawny arms reaching out. 'I beg you. If I could—'

'I told you no!' The shipmaster kicked sand into the supplicant's face with a roar of fury. 'Get rid of this crotch louse!'

Jailan hastened to oblige, dragging the man away by arms and hair, his scrabbling legs digging futile gouges in the beach. Other rowers grabbed a handhold wherever they could and flung the hapless petitioner back towards a woman cowering in the meagre shade of a stunted perfume tree, wide-eyed, hungry children clinging to her soiled skirts.

'Who's this?' His conversation with the soothsayer interrupted, the shipmaster turned a sour eye on Dev. 'We're not looking to take on any more crew.'

'That's lucky,' said Dev agreeably. 'I prefer to let the wind work for me, not haul on someone else's oar.'

'This is Dev, trader, sails a one-master called the *Amigal*. Gyllen said you'd run across him before.' Jailan bent over the battered cook pot hanging over the fire. 'What's for dinner?'

'Fish stew,' the shipmaster replied without enthusiasm, his attention still on Dev. 'What do you trade in?'

'This and that, information among other things.' Dev grinned affably. 'I might have some seasoning for your stew if you tell me what that was all about.' He jerked his head towards the wretched family still cowering by the perfume tree. 'Or why I keep hearing I shouldn't be going south.'

'Dev? Of the *Amigal*?' The shipmaster nodded slowly,

recollection kindling a spark in his eyes. He spared the soothsayer a perfunctory nod. 'What are you waiting for? Go on, do your best by us.'

The soothsayer handed the shipmaster the yellow gourd. 'Swirl it round and then pour it out.'

Master Uten cast the liquid out so vigorously that the closest rowers had their feet anointed.

'Do not move!' The soothsayer's commanding voice kept them rooted to the ground, even though the noxious reek of his concoction was making Dev's eyes water.

'What do you see?' the shipmaster demanded.

'I see a sea flower,' intoned the soothsayer solemnly. 'And a squid.'

Dev studied the sand along with everyone else but, try as he might, he could see nothing but random splatters of dark sludge with flies fastening thirstily on them.

'The sea flower drifts through the ocean, seemingly insignificant yet trailing poison tentacles in its wake,' continued the soothsayer. 'As for the squid, there are said to be beasts beyond the western reaches with bodies longer than the biggest galleys, which spin whirlpools in the deeps to draw ships down into their maw.' He looked up sharply. 'We are all at risk of being sucked into dangerous waters, into perilous times. Certainly anyone sailing south risks meeting great peril, coming upon them all unseen, unexpected.' Then, startling everyone, he leaned forward to sweep away the stained sand, scattering the image. 'The rains will bring new luck, to wash away this stain on our futures.'

'If they ever arrive,' grunted the shipmaster. 'The Greater Moon's waxing and we've had no more than a couple of wettings. Bring me weather guidance in the morning and that might be worth something to put in your bowl.'

'I believe I've already earned some consideration,' said

the soothsayer, affronted. His gaze slid towards the bubbling cook pot.

'I don't think so,' the shipmaster glowered.

Dev watched with open amusement as the seer gathered up his trappings and his injured dignity and stalked away. These last days before the rains were always good for a few entertaining fights, with every temper so frayed by the incessant heat.

'Well now.' The shipmaster's tone warmed as he glanced around his oarsmen. 'I do remember Dev, now I think on it. And I reckon we've all earned a little relaxation after the pull we made to get here. Dev's the man to supply it, if anyone's got news that he might find of interest.' The unspoken command in his words was plain.

'I've just shipped in from the western reaches,' one man began diffidently. 'There was word of sea serpents beaching themselves in the Sier domain.'

'You never said,' remarked one of his shipmates with surprise.

The man shrugged. 'Didn't know what to make of it, nor yet if it might be true.'

'I don't see anyone making up such a tale.' Shipmaster Uten shot a challenging look at Dev.

'It would be a curious thing,' nodded Dev in apparent agreement. 'Anyone else heard of such oddities?'

'They're saying there's magic loose in the southern reaches.' A younger man volunteered this, half laughing, half looking for reassurance. 'You can ask what you like for a good talisman, I heard.'

'I heard it was warfare.' An older man beside him wasn't amused. 'Nearly as bad.'

'Which do you suppose it is?' Dev looked at the shipmaster. 'Certainty's worth more than guesses.'

The shipmaster turned to pick out a sombre face in the circle. 'Ruil, you joined us from a ship coming from

the Tule domain. What was the word on the wind thereabouts?'

'I don't know about words on the wind.' The man licked
cautious lips, sweat on his forehead gleaming in the low
sun. 'But there was certainly smoke.'

'How so?' Dev didn't have to feign interest at that.

At his shipmaster's nod, Ruil continued thoughtfully.
'It looked like cloud at first but too high up and with no
hint of rain. You could taste the char in the back of your
throat. Some days it was thicker than others, like fog, only
not. Some days, it was all but gone but then it came back.
Three babies died around the anchorage in the same night,
them and an old woman, and the spokesman's grandsire.
There wasn't a mark of illness on them but they were
dead all the same. Tule Reth decreed it an ill omen and
that no ships from the southerly reaches were allowed to
land. That's when I decided to come north.'

'That sounds more like pestilence than warfare or
magic.' Dev looked sceptical.

'Tule Reth wouldn't let ships coming out of the southern
reaches land but he let them pass.' Ruil shook his head
obstinately. 'If he thought they could be carrying some
disease, he'd have set his triremes sinking any that reached
his sea lanes. It was wickedness in the wind, not sickness.'

'There's no end of people looking for passage north.'
The shipmaster gestured around the shallow curve of the
bay now vanishing into a soft dusk. 'None are falling sick,
so whatever they're fleeing, it's not disease. Whatever it
is, it's bad enough to risk travelling through the rains to
get away from it. There's more than one of us heard
rumour that it's magic.'

'Warfare or magic.' Dev nodded slowly, still holding
the shipmaster's gaze. He'd be cursed if he was going to
look away first. 'Either way though, that's news worth
something to lighten your cares.'

The shipmaster grinned and snapped his fingers at a crewman with a bucket of wooden bowls. 'Give our friend something to line his belly.'

'Thanks.' Dev accepted a steaming bowl pungent with herbs and full of chunks of fish. The rowers crowded round to collect their share and Dev grabbed a torn slab of flatbread to soak up the broth well thickened with crab-meat. Tossing the empty bowl back into the bucket, he grinned at the shipmaster. 'That's the best meal I've eaten in a while. I'll go and see what I might have to liven up your evening by way of return.'

'Jailan, go and give him a hand.' The shipmaster jerked his head at the oarsman.

Back by the water, Dev climbed briskly aboard the *Amigal*. Once down in the cramped stern cabin where his few possessions were stowed in his hammock or shut away in the battered chest bolted to the floor, Dev fished beneath his tunic for keys hung on a chain around his waist. Kicking aside a couple of discarded scarves and an empty pot of face paint that one of the girls had left, he unlocked the door to the little ship's main hold and went in.

Dev closed the door, shutting himself into pitch-blackness. A moment later, a small white flame appeared, dancing on his palm, illuminating his grinning face. Taer Badul could issue his petulant edicts against magic, just like every other petty Aldabreshin tyrant. They wouldn't catch him. He didn't even need his magic to evade them, superior intelligence more than sufficed.

The flame brightened to throw light on all the various necessities for keeping the *Amigal* seaworthy and Dev fed that were stowed in chests and casks secured along one side of a hold barely tall enough for Dev to stand in, even with his less than common height. He turned to the row of barrels opposite. Beyond stood baskets well stuffed with tandra fluff, a motley collection of bottles poking out of the white fibres like bulbous green seeds. Dev made a quick accounting and scowled. This was the problem with coming so far south. Plenty of people wanted his wares but there were no opportunities to replenish his stocks.

Still, he would be the last one to go short. Dev pulled a horn cup from a half-empty basket and a dark bottle with a crusted wax seal declaring its distant barbarian origins. Tossing his cold little flame into the air where it hung, fluttering like a guttering candle, he levered the bottle's cork out with his Barbak dagger. He took a sip and rolled it thoughtfully around his mouth. The shining surface of the white brandy reflected the dancing flame and Dev's creased brow.

Should he bespeak Planir? Could he bespeak the Archmage at such a distance? Of course he could, working with the fire he'd been born to command. The Archmage would certainly be interested to learn these new rumours running with the tides and winds of the Archipelago. Would Planir have anything to tell him? Could there be northern wizards causing trouble in the far south? Surely not. No one from Hadrumal could have made such a voyage without Dev hearing about it.

Dev's smile turned contemptuous. No one from Hadrumal would have the stones to do something so bold, not once they learned any mage caught in the Archipelago would be skinned alive for his pains. In any case, why would they want to? Apprentices soon learned all their elders' prejudices against the world beyond northern wizardry's hidden island. The masters in the manipulation of air, earth, fire and water passed on their conviction that all wizardly knowledge was secure in their libraries and lofty halls. In their way, the great mages of Hadrumal were as spineless and ignorant as the dullards of the midden of a village where he'd been raised.

Not for the first time, Dev promised himself that one

of these days, in his own good time, he'd go back to that sprawl of hovels, let those bastards know he was the trusted confidant of the Archmage of Hadrumal, acknowledged equal with all the princes and powers of the mainland.

Though Planir wasn't going to be any too impressed if Dev couldn't pin down the truth behind these rumours of magic in the Archipelago. There had to be something behind it, especially now the news had slipped through the grasp of the warlords and their ciphered messages to become common currency along the trading beaches.

Dev scowled as he drank the fiery brandy. If it wasn't northern magic, what could be happening in the south? The magelight hanging in the air by his head brightened to an unnatural reddish tint. Where could magic come from to ravage the southernmost islands? Could there actually be some unknown land beyond those final domains, beyond the endless expanse of the southern ocean? There were wizards in Hadrumal who insisted there must be, citing their tedious study of oceans' currents and the swirling storms bearing rain to the Archipelago. Dev's eyes narrowed. What manner of unknown magic might unknown wizards bring with them? What elemental insights might he learn from them, to take back to Hadrumal and toss into the complacent circle of the Council, or better yet, to use to his own advantage around the busy ports of the mainland?

Dev drained his cup with sudden decision. He wasn't going to find out anything unless he sailed south and he wasn't about to do that without all the information he could possibly gather. Time to see if the man he was hunting was looking for his usual pickings among the human jetsam washed up on this shore. He hefted a little cask from the rack and set it on the deck. Master Uten's rowers could have that; nothing special but these Aldabreshi never tasted enough wine to know the difference between piss-poor and some more valuable vintage. Unlocking the door to the cramped space in the very prow of the *Amigal* he snapped his fingers to summon the mage-light and examined the small store of coffers and close-tied bags stowed safely within. Dev tucked a wash-leather pouch inside the breast of his sleeveless tunic.

Securing the little forehold, he swung the wine cask up on to his shoulder and passed rapidly back through the ship to the stern ladder, climbing it carefully with the awkward weight of the little barrel. Up on deck, he walked the cask to the *Amigal*'s rail and whistled to Jailan and one of the *Spotted Loal*'s other rowers who'd drifted over.

'Take this to Master Uten, with Dev's compliments.' Bracing a foot against the side of the boat, he lowered the barrel down to the oarsmen's eager hands, jumping down to join them a moment later.

'Are you joining us?' Jailan invited.

Dev shook his head. 'I want to take a turn along the sand before it gets too late.'

'Bring your quilts to share our fire, if you've a mind to sleep ashore,' Jailan suggested.

'Oh I'm looking for something softer than a quilt and I don't reckon to do too much sleeping.'

As the two men laughed, Dev walked away down the beach. Barely beyond the spill of light from the galley's fire, a man emerged from the shadows of the tree line.

'I see you've your own boat, master.' His smile was both desperate and ingratiating. 'But working it single-handed, I see. That must be wearying.'

If he wasn't the one who'd appealed to the galley ship-master earlier, he was similar enough to make no differ-ence. Dev shrugged. 'I'm used to it.'

'I can offer a strong back and willing arms to ease your labours,' the man persisted. 'If you're well rested when you make landfall, you'll be all the more ready to make the best trades.'

Dev allowed himself an appreciative grin. 'You've got a glib enough tongue to be trading yourself.'

'No, I'm a fisherman.' The man brushed unkempt hair out of his eyes. 'So I know boats and ropes. You need have no worries about that.' He had been wearing his beard in the jawline style of the Tule domain, Dev noted, but patchy stubble darkened his cheeks now.

Dev tilted his head on one side. 'Fishermen generally come with families.'

The man's air of confidence wilted a little. 'I have a wife and two children.' He summoned up a new smile. 'My wife can sew for you and cook, help with mending nets.'

'When she isn't running around to stop your brats falling over the side.' Dev pursed his lips with disfavour.

'They can be kept below,' the man pleaded.

Dev nodded, contemplative, waiting just long enough for hope to dawn in the fisherman's eyes. 'Good enough. I'll be sailing in the morning.'

Relief almost choked the man. 'You won't regret it.'

'We'll be aiming for Tule Reth's domain,' Dev began cheerfully.

The fisherman actually took a pace backwards. 'You're heading south?'

'Is that a problem?' Dev looked puzzled.

'It is for me and mine.' The fisherman's anxious politeness had vanished. 'Magical fires are burning everything in the south to black ash.'

'There are always fires this late in the dry season,' scoffed Dev. 'I don't pay heed to heat-addled foolishness about magic.'

'I'll believe what I've heard,' retorted the fisherman. 'You can sail south and find out for yourself.' He turned abruptly and vanished into the gloom.

Chuckling, Dev continued his slow meander along the shore. There was certainly something warranting investigation in the southern reaches. Dev wondered idly what it would have taken to put the fisherman off, if he had been willing to sail south. Telling the wife to lift her skirts for him and anyone else he offered her to; that would have probably sufficed. He wandered along, glancing at the fires and the people gathered around them in the deepening dusk, searching for any familiar faces. Men and women looked up as he passed, looking down again when they realised he was no one they knew.

Then a thin-faced man took a second look and scrambled to his feet. 'Dev, you cheating lizard! What are you doing here?'

'Warning honest folk against the likes of you, you thieving shark.' Dev stopped and grinned broadly. 'I heard you were sailing these islands.'

The skinny man took a stick to stir the flames of his fire; perfume leaves smouldering to keep off the evening bloodsuckers. 'Unless you're on your way to take your pleasure with Taer Badul's wives, you can spare a moment to say hello.' Beyond him, a gaggle of boys with the unmistakable stamp of his siring sweated over packing away an awning, and bundling up a miscellany of bags, netted fruit and freshly killed fowl. The remains of one such bird swung lazily on a spit above the embers. 'Help yourself.'

'I must have crossed your wake ten times between here and Mahaf waters.' Dev dropped to the sand beside him. 'What are you trading that's keeping you so busy?'

'Talismans, and I can recommend it as good business.' Majun leaned forward to pick a few shreds of succulent meat from the bird's carcass.

'Powerful ones?' asked Dev with a hint of amusement.

'Most potent,' Majun assured him solemnly. 'Links from bracelets that the most successful warlords of record wore into battle against the northern barbarians.'

'And presumably returned, victorious, untouched by enchantment?' asked Dev innocently.

'I also have rings that protected shipmasters on countless voyages into the profane waters of the unbroken lands.' Majun grinned. 'Rustlenuts? They're coated in honey and tarit seeds.'

'I've been hearing these rumours of magic to the south all the way through the Nor waters and plaguing Yava landings besides.' Dev shook his head. 'What's going on, Majun?'

'People are running so scared of enchantments on the breezes, they'd believe me if I said rubbing themselves with birdshit would avert it.' A sudden grin split Majun's face with a gleam of white teeth.

'I know that.' Dev sucked off the honeyed sweetness and the sharpness of the tarit seed before crunching the pungent rustlenut. 'What I want to know is why. Where's this rumour started from?'

Majun checked none of his sons were in earshot. 'What might you be trading for that information, that might ease a man's gripes?' His eyes shone meaningfully in the firelight.

Dev leaned forward to pull a length of crisp skin from the spitted fowl, deftly reaching into his tunic as he did so. Sitting back, he tucked something into Majun's hand.

Majun cast a cautious eye around the beach before fumbling a dark leathery leaf into his mouth. 'You don't want to be trading too much further south, my friend. There's trouble brewing and no warlord will stand for his people trifling with liquor when enemies might be landing any day.'

'But what kind of trouble?' Dev clicked his tongue with apparent exasperation. 'All I'm hearing is vague rumours of magic. It has to be nonsense. One duck mistakes a fallen branch for a lurking jungle cat and the whole flock joins in the panic.'

'That's what I thought till I got the measure of it.' Majun shuffled closer to Dev, eyes bright in the firelight, pupils paradoxically wide and dark. 'I can tell you something worth a goodly supply of leaf, my friend.'

'News that'll win me proper gratitude in the north, that'll interest the barbarians who keep me in leaf for the likes of you?' Dev queried sceptically.

'I had Jacan Taer's head maidservant down here yesterday.' Majun licked his lips with a stained tongue. 'She was looking for talismans for the children, specifically against treachery and deception as well as magic. She stayed for a goodly while.'

'You've given her a fair deal over the years, haven't you?' Dev let slip a suggestion of envy in his crude laugh.

'There's always a woman with a taste for some foreign seasoning to her meat,' chuckled Majun. 'And not only maidservants. Did I tell you about the time Siella Nor came looking for something to brighten up her day?'

'You certainly did,' said Dev with a lascivious smile. 'But what did this Taer maid have to say for herself?'

Majun frowned until he recovered the thread of his thoughts. 'Taer Badul's been getting special dispatches from Tule Lek. They're full of news from the Ulla domain.'

In double cipher and sealed with a special ring and brittle wax, thought Dev with well-concealed amusement. Strapped to messenger birds trained from the chick to avoid predators or any deliberate hawk flown at them. None of which was proof against Jacan Taer's incessant chattering and her maidservant's inexplicable taste for Majun's rough-hewn charms. 'What news?'

'Mostly, that Ulla Safar is planning on taking everything between Derasulla and the southern ocean for himself.' Majun shrugged, lazily savouring his leaf.

'So that explains the smoke coming up on the winds.' Dev scowled. This had a nasty ring of plausibility about it. 'Ulla Safar's just burning everything before him.'

'And starting rumours of magic to keep anyone else from interfering.' Majun paused to chew some more. 'But Tule Lek is saying—'

Commotion further along the beach interrupted him. All along the shore, people rose to their feet, a ripple of voices raised in question.

'What's going on?' Dev called to one of Majun's sons who was down by the water's edge with an unobstructed view.

'Taer Badul's swordsmen.' The lad's bewilderment was tempered by relief someone else was in trouble.

'Doing what?' demanded Majun with as much exasperation as the chewing leaf allowed.

'Breaking up a fire circle.' The boy dragged reluctant eyes from the spectacle to jerk his head at Dev. 'Smashing up a barrel by the looks of it.'

Dev sprang to his feet and hurried to stand by the boy. Yes, curse it; that was the *Spotted Loal*'s crew being rousted from their relaxation. The crack of splintering wood echoed along the beach, snapping through the confused protests of the men. Brutal rebuke answered them, firelight gleaming on chainmail and the flats of menacing swords.

'This is a bit much.' Majun joined them, stumbling slightly in the soft sand. 'Even for Taer Badul. That's not one of his ships. What's it to him if they addle themselves with liquor or smoke? A galley with no allegiance, they've no call on his triremes, not if they sink in a storm or wreck themselves on a reef.'

'That's looking ugly.' Dev scowled. 'Time for me to leave.'

'We can hide you in our hold,' offered Majun. 'If you want to make yourself scarce for the night.'

'I'm not leaving the *Amigal* unguarded.' Dev shook his head, still watching the commotion along the shore. 'This could all just be a ploy by Taer Badul, out to seize my cargo for himself. I never trust a man who protests quite so long and loud that he's never so much as sniffed distilled liquor.' As he watched, he saw the first punch thrown. 'I'll catch up with you some time soon.'

Not waiting to hear Majun's protests, Dev ran lightly along the sand, feet splashing through the slowly sliding waves. More chance of being seen down here at the water's edge, but he'd move a cursed sight faster than he could among the shadows of the trees, tripping over bemused traders and miserable beggars. Just as long as the fight was raging hot enough to hold everyone's attention, he could slip past and get back to the *Amigal* unnoticed. Yes, there'd be just enough water to carry him over the coral-choked channel. Could he get clear of the outer islets before a fast trireme could be signalled? He laced a little darkness around himself as he drew near to the heart of the upheaval, drawing his magic tight into himself to quell any hint of magelight.

'We'll have no drunkenness within our domain.' A tall man, commander of the swordsmen to judge by the brass sheen of his helm, was laying down the warlord's edict to Master Uten. Two armoured men held the mariner fast between them and the commander punctuated his declaration with backhanded slaps. 'No trade, no agreement, no bargain is valid here, unless all parties are sober. This is the Taer decree!'

Taer Badul's men had arrived in overwhelming strength, trampling the remnants of the cask along with food bowls, bread and fruit into a sodden mess around the wine-quenched fire pit. Even the cook pot had been stamped flat and split. Those oarsmen who'd protested had already been pounded into bloodied submission. Clustered around five deep, onlookers gaped.

Dev wrapped shadows still thicker around himself as he slipped past and dragged the *Amigal*'s anchor out of the sand. The boat swayed, just a little water beneath her stern. Dev climbed aboard as quietly as he could and hauled up the awkward weight of the anchor hand over hand, throwing a dense blanket of air over it to muffle any sound. He looked back to the shore. Taer swordsmen were challenging any men in the crowd whose expressions they hadn't liked. Gaps were appearing as other men hastened away, doubtless to dump whatever illicit pleasures they might be enjoying.

'Where do you think you're going?' The warrior in command tired of beating up Uten and pointed an accusing finger at another shipmaster who'd been drinking with him.

Dev crept along the deck to raise the *Amigal*'s sail, keeping the silence he'd woven wrapped tight around the mast. There was barely enough breeze coming off the land to stir the canvas. Scowling, Dev slackened his magic just enough to call up a stealthy gust. A wave took the little boat and the *Amigal* wallowed, afloat, if only by a hand's breadth. Dev ran forward to pull up the fore anchor, tense as he listened for any challenge from the shore. As he did so, two things struck him. Firstly, the *Spotted Loal* and the galley next to her were blocking his way out into open water. Secondly, there was someone in the little forehold beneath his feet. There was nothing in there that could have made the knocking sound he'd just heard.

He looked back at the beach. Satisfied that the galley's crew were thoroughly cowed, the swordsmen were spreading along the sand, new light blazing bright as anything they didn't like the look of was tossed to rekindle campfires that had all but died out for the night.

Dev wrenched the anchor free of the sea bed, and kicked a coil of rope on top of the fore hatch. Wrapping the weighty metal in yet more silence as he pulled it out of the water, he placed the twin-fluked anchor on top of the coil of hemp. Then he ran the length of the *Amigal*, feet slapping on the deck planking, dragging the long stern sweep noisily from its place beneath the side rail. Digging the heavy oar into the water, he drove the *Amigal* into the concealing shadow between the *Loal* and the other galley. Then he silently secured the heavy sweep against the rudder pintle with a cunning knot he'd learned from the man he'd tricked the boat out of.

Lifting the stern hatch with exquisite care, Dev slid silently down the ladder. He had to do this with natural stealth, not magic that might prompt unwelcome curiosity, even from a thief. Moving slowly, he found his keys and unlocked the door with barely a click. He sharpened his ears with a hint of enchantment, to hear any breath, no matter how shallow. There was no one there. Feel and familiarity guiding him, Dev walked slowly through the hold, anger held in check. All was as it should be, wine barrels secure, the tally of liquor bottles beneath his questioning fingers correct.

So this thief was after his other goods, chewing leaf, the powdered herbs blended for dreamsmoke and the expensive extracts that could spice a meal with myriad temptations. Dev reached unerring up into the cross beams barely a finger's breadth above his head and pulled down a long, curved knife with more than twice the reach of any of the daggers Aldabreshin warlords permitted in their domains. He walked towards the fore hold door on silent feet, feeling through his keys until he found the one he wanted. Unlock the door and be through it before the thief had a chance to think. The scum would go for the fore hatch and find it weighted. Dev would cut out the bastard's kidneys before he could make his escape.

He flung open the door and thrust with the knife in the same movement. His arm brushed past cotton loose over skinny ribs as some last-minute twist saved the thief from a gutting. Dev reached unerringly into the darkness and his merciless hand closed on a scrawny arm, the skin slick with sweat. He drew back his blade for a second thrust.

'Please don't hurt me!'

Dev's killing stroke halted halfway. That terrified shriek wasn't some shifty-eyed galley lad, nor yet some friendless fisherman driven to desperate straits. He'd caught some addle-brained slut of a girl.

'You come with me!' He hauled his squealing captive bodily out of the fore hold. 'Thought you'd try stowing away on my ship? More fool you, my lass. No matter, you can go naked into the shallows like the thief you are and take your chances with Taer Badul's men. They're so roused already they probably won't even bother asking your name, let alone your business.'

Dev dragged the wailing girl through the ship, not letting her find her footing, shoving her into the stern cabin and throwing her into a corner. She hit the wooden wall with a thud that set the whole ship rocking.

'Please don't hurt me,' she begged. 'Please don't hurt me.'

Ignoring her trembling sobs, Dev found his spark maker and reached for the lamp that hung from the beams. It was an awkward task one-handed but he wasn't about to put down his knife, not that she looked much of a threat. With the lamp lit, he saw a light-skinned girl about his own height, with hacked-off black hair no better than a rat's nest, her sleeveless tunic and knee-length trews rags over bruised and filthy limbs.

'Who are you?' He stood over the girl, voice cold. 'And I'll hurt you properly if you don't answer my questions.' He looked around for a piece of cord, a rope end, anything he might use for a lash.

As soon as he took his eyes off the girl, she moved. Not trying to reach the ladder; he was between her and that. She seized his knife hand, clawing it and biting. Taken off guard, Dev's fingers loosened and before he could regain his grip, the girl had the blade. She twisted away from him, one hand reaching for the ladder now behind her, the other holding the curved steel out.

'I want your word that you will not harm me.' Her voice was still shaking but the hand holding the knife grew steadier with every passing breath.

'You steal from me and you expect to get away without so much as an arse-kicking?' Dev laughed, mocking. He drew his Barbak dagger from his belt. 'Now what are you going to do, fight me?'

The girl quaked but the long curved knife stayed pointed at Dev. 'I know how to use this,' she warned. 'In under your breastbone, up into your chest to cut through lungs and liver.'

'And read your future in them?' He didn't take another pace forward. 'I can tell you a thief's future, lass, and it's full of pain, I promise you.'

'I am not here to steal,' she said hotly. 'I haven't touched a thing of yours. All I want is passage out of here.'

'You and half the stinking scum on the tide line,' Dev scoffed. Without taking his eyes off the girl, he stooped and caught up one of the discarded scarves from the floor. 'All right, explain yourself.' He sheathed his Barbak dagger and made as if to bind his scratched hand with the dirty silk.

'I didn't think you'd agree if I just came and asked.' She raised a defiant chin and Dev saw she had blue eyes that spoke of thoroughly mixed blood. They lent an exotic note to her narrow, undistinguished face. 'I thought I'd wait till you were out at sea and then show myself.'

'Then I'd have to put up with you?' Dev shook his head with insulting pity. 'You didn't think I'd just throw you to the sharks or the sea serpents? What do you take me for? Zamorin? Too lacking to stand up for myself?' He leered, his gaze lingering on her chest. 'Your reasoning's as lacking as your tits. I've just as many stones as the hairiest man on that shore. Want me to show you?' He gestured towards his groin.

'I don't care what you keep in your trousers,' she said stoutly, knife still firmly held. 'What I want is passage south. I'll do my share of the work. '

That surprised Dev more than her assault on his knife hand. 'South? When every man and his wife is scrambling to get a berth going north?'

'That's their business.' The girl's voice grew more confident. 'You're going south. I heard you on the beach.'

'What's your business there?' challenged Dev.

'I'm a poet.' Her fierce expression dared him to doubt her.

He laughed anyway. 'You?'

The knife didn't falter.

'Prove it!' he jeered.

'My bag, where I was hiding.' She jerked her head towards the prow. 'Fetch it and I'll show you.'

'That would be in the fore hold,' said Dev sarcastically. 'Much use you'd be, when you don't even know your way around a ship. Are you any use on your back?'

'I don't spread my legs and I can learn about ships.' she sneered back at him, uncowed. 'I know barrels of wine when I see them and bottles of barbarian liquor.' She nodded upwards, her eyes not leaving Dev's face. There was still an appreciable uproar to be heard ashore. 'What do you suppose Taer Badul's men would say if I told them what you're carrying?' She paused for a moment. 'Never mind the chewing leaves and dreamsmoke powders in the prow.'

'You think you can get ashore to tell them before I kill you?' Dev tightened the scarf between his hands with slow deliberation. 'I won't even need to dirty my dagger. Ever seen someone who's been strangled?'

'I'll wager I can get on deck and give one good scream. That'll bring them running, all hot-blooded, like you said.' She cocked her head on one side. 'Do you want to try explaining a dead body still warm in your hands as well as your cargo?'

'You've thought this all through.' Dev feigned admiration.

The girl's skin was pale enough for a blush to darken it. 'No poet can afford to be a fool.'

'And there's proof of that in your bag.' Dev pursed his lips. 'Let me see. I go looking for that and you grab whatever you can steal and make a dash for the shore where you betray me to Taer Badul's swordsmen.'

'I don't see much worth stealing here.' Her mockery answered his own, but this time, her eyes strayed towards his hammock.

Dev was on her in an instant, knocking the curved knife out of her hands, the silk round her neck, his fists crossing behind her head. Before she could summon more than a stifled whine, her knees buckled and she went limp beneath him. Smiling with vicious satisfaction, Dev rolled her over, tying wrists and ankles with the scarves, binding hands and feet together behind her arched back. When she stirred, scant breaths later, her puzzlement cleared to furious realisation. She tried to spit at Dev but her mouth was too dry.

'You just rest there,' he soothed as he unhooked the lamp from the beam. 'You've got me wondering, so I'll have a look at this proof of yours.' Stroking her matted hair tenderly, he shoved the last of the rags from the floor in her mouth and gagged her. Making sure she could hear him laughing, he sauntered through the main hold.

The first thing he did in the prow space was assure himself that the boxes and bags of leaf and intoxicants were untouched. Satisfied that the scrawny little bitch hadn't been lying about that at least, he caught up a tasselled shoulder sack of heavy woven cotton, yellow trumpet flowers embroidered on the dark blue cloth.

Swinging it thoughtfully from one hand, he went back to the stern cabin. 'Feels like you've been stealing from more than me. Let's see what your loot is worth.'

The girl's glare was as fierce as a netted jungle cat's.

Dev untied the drawstring and upended the bag, sending a cascade of oddments to the floor. Squatting down, he tossed aside a tunic even more ragged than the one the girl wore, then a faded silk dress. He shook his head disdainfully. 'A fine poet you must be, if this is your performing gown.' Ignoring smeary cosmetic jars and tawdry ornaments, he reached for a solid black cylinder. 'Now, what might this be?'

It was a scroll case, leather sewn tight over ironwood, painted with dark tarit tree resin. Dev twisted the cap off and tilting the case, he slid out a thick bundle of reed papers and uncurled them. '*The Ringed Dove*, *The Owls and the Crows*, *The Loal and the Turtle*.' He nodded with approval at the quality of the pictures. 'You stole this from a poet with a good repertoire of moral tales for children.'

The girl looked back at him for a moment before deliberately closing her eyes and turning her face to the planks beneath her.

'You'll pay attention when I'm talking to you.' Dev replaced the pictures in their case with some care, recapping the cylinder and tossing it up into his hammock.

Sitting cross-legged beside the girl he grabbed a handful of her hair and turned her face towards him. 'Try and bite me,' he continued conversationally, 'and I'll knock every tooth out of your head. Are we clear on that?'

The girl nodded but her eyes were still scornful rather than intimidated.

Dev chuckled as he ungagged her. 'You show plenty of spirit, I'll give you that.'

She licked her lips, working her dry mouth to moisten her tongue. 'You can give me my belongings and let me go.'

'But I thought you wanted passage south?' Dev looked quizzically at her. 'Changed your mind?'

She looked at him with contempt. 'Just untie me and let me go.'

'I'll give you passage south,' Dev said obligingly. 'If you are truly a poet. Though I must say,' he added with frank surprise, 'I've no notion why a poet would want to go in the opposite direction to all the potential audience.'

'I am a poet,' the girl said stoutly. 'I was apprenticed to Haytar the Blind.'

'Haytar the Blind is dead,' Dev pointed out with a grin. 'I heard that news in the Mahaf domain, not ten days since.'

She ignored him. 'Haytar was the greatest interpreter of *The Book of Animals*. Even a lout like you must know that.'

'I'd heard that said. Though I prefer poems about lecherous slave boys and round-arsed dancing girls myself.' Dev nodded, with an insolent glance at the girl's rump. 'So you looted his corpse and fled, did you?'

'I was his apprentice,' she repeated, tight-lipped. 'His last apprentice. He gave me that picture scroll on his deathbed and bade me use his poems to live by, until I should find a theme of my own, something to inspire a new cycle of poems that everyone would know by my name.' For the first time, tears shone in her eyes.

Dev raised sceptical eyebrows. 'And how exactly is making a voyage to the south going to lead you to one of those?'

The girl squirmed in her bonds. 'There's magic abroad in the southern reaches, truly.'

'Is there?' Dev hid his interest in disdain. 'What would a doggerel merchant like you know about that?'

'More than a vice peddler like you,' she shot back. 'There's warlords fighting wizards in domains clear across from Aedis to Ritsem. Take me as far south as you dare and when you run scared, I'll make my own way onward. There'll be tales of valour and tragedy in battles like that and I'll make an epic out of them.'

'To make your name,' Dev mocked. 'What would your name be, so I know your epic when I hear it?'

'Risala,' she said grudgingly.

'I always thought poets were mad.' Dev got to his feet, grinning. 'Now I'm sure of it. Very well, I'm tired of working this boat single-handed. I'll carry you south as long as you do whatever work I give you, and as long as you split whatever you take on shore for telling your little animal stories.' He paused by the foot of the ladder. 'Play me false and I'll cut your throat and throw you overboard for the robber eels.'

'Lizard eater,' Risala said with feeling. 'Aren't you going to untie me?'

'When we're good and clear of the beach,' Dev assured her. 'Far enough out for no one to hear you scream, if you've a mind to try tricking me from the outset. Now, you keep a civil tongue in your head, or I'll take the lamp away from you for a start.'

Risala opened her mouth again and then shut it, lips pursed.

Dev winked at her. 'Not so hard, is it?' He climbed up

the ladder, his amusement fading. How much time had that nonsense cost him? How far had the *Amigal* drifted?

Once on deck he was relieved to see the little ship was still lolling in the dead water between the two great galleys. Better yet, the fat-bellied ships had drifted apart to leave him a way out. There was still a fair amount of commotion on shore but Taer Badul's swordsmen appeared to have left the beach. Time to go before they came back. Loosing the stern sweep from its knot, Dev drove the broad blade through the water, manoeuvring the *Amigal* out into open water, wondering how best to turn this unexpected turn of events to his advantage.

So Majun said that Ulla Safar was starting a war? That could be true, then again, maybe not. The girl sounded certain magic was abroad in the domains just south of Ulla waters. The first thing to do when he had her well away from shore, with nowhere to swim for, was to find out just what that certainty was based on. She could tell him or bleed for it.

What then? A more important question: was this Risala any good? If she wanted to stay aboard, she'd better give him a little recital. If she was any good, she could be an excuse for him sailing south. Everyone knew poets were mad. A trireme's shipmaster might still look askance at him, but Dev could let slip he was pandering to the girl's whims by day in exchange for the favours she was doing him by night. Besides, sailing single-handed was attracting more attention than he liked. A girl aboard would put an end to that.

He leant hard into the oar, to ease the *Amigal* out through the narrow space between the great galleys. Risala had just been an apprentice, had she? A likely story. He'd wager old Haytar'd had at least one eye not yet blind and most poets' dancing girls were little better than the whores of the mainland docksides. The girl could drop on her back to satisfy any trireme shipmaster with a deaf ear for verse.

Looking up, Dev saw clouds that must surely herald the overdue rains obscuring the moons, greater still several days from full and lesser waning past its last quarter. He changed his mind about trying the channel in the uncertain light. Anchor on the sand bar in the middle of the bay, he decided, and sleep on deck. The light would wake him and he could cross the reefs while there was still enough water.

CHAPTER ELEVEN

Kheda stirred. Then he felt a distinct sensation of being watched. He opened his eyes to find he'd rolled over in his sleep, doubtless to escape the inexorable light of dawn. All he could see was the nut palm fronds he'd gathered to build a low shelter the previous evening.

Not that you need have bothered. When are the rains going to come? The nights are as hot as the days now. Is this delay some evil stirred up by the magic to the south, driving away the storm winds? What is that noise? There's definitely someone behind you. Who could it be? You hid yourself more than adequately.

He'd found a gully lined with thick cane brakes and well away from any game trails or the wider track running to some distant village. He'd lit no fire to risk attracting curious attention, even though his ankles throbbed with bites from the bloodsuckers hereabouts that weren't deterred by crushed perfume-tree leaves.

Besides, you had nothing to cook. Daish Reik wouldn't be too impressed, to see your efforts at fending for yourself in the forest. What excuse would you offer him, for your hunger and thirst and weariness? That you're waiting for Telouet to bring you breakfast?

Kheda rolled slowly over, doing his best to look like a man still asleep. The dry lilla branches he'd piled for a bed crackled softly beneath him. Slowly, he opened his eyes just enough to see through the lattice of his lashes. He was indeed being watched. A loal was looking warily at the sloping shelter of palm fronds Kheda had constructed, wide cat-like ears pricking towards him. It sat on its rump, long feathery tail curled casually to one side, a stick in its disconcertingly man-like hands for digging through the leaf litter. If it were to stand on feet more like hands than paws, it might be chest high to a man. It would be easily as strong as a man, its densely furred arms and legs quite as sturdy as Kheda's own. Its face had nothing that was human about it: a black muzzle sniffed the air, pink tongue startling as it licked the last fragments of some hapless lizard from long, white teeth. Any hound would have been proud to boast such fangs. It blinked slowly, eyes perfect circles, as dark as its woolly black-brown pelt. Concluding Kheda was either no threat or of no interest, the creature returned to digging, hunching shoulders bearing a broad white swathe of fur.

Which is why they call you a caped loal. I had no notion you grew so big though. The Daish domain's striped loals are half your size.

Something in the dirt caught the loal's eye and it snatched up a wriggling millipede, cramming it into its mouth and chewing with crunches audible across the clearing. Kheda cautiously propped himself on one elbow and found his belly was crying out for something to add to the shrunken hearts of a few succulent tarit stems that were all he'd been able to find before darkness had fallen. Kheda allowed himself a grin.

Poets tell of children benighted in the forest being offered ripe fruit or tasty nuts by loals. Do you have anything you'd care to share, something without quite so many legs?

In the nut palms and thick stands of red cane, Kheda heard glory birds rousing themselves to full song. As the sun rose to flood the gully with light, a deeper, more resonant note echoed beneath their trills. Looking up, Kheda saw more loals, smaller pied ones, like those he'd seen on hunting trips with Daish Reik. Sitting upright, they were facing the sun, arms raised and basking in the promise of warmth, crooning with pleasure.

'There are many reasons to despise the northern barbarians, my son, not least the way they turn the sun and the moons into meaningless gods, no better than singing loals.'

I wonder, do these southern invaders worship false gods of their own, my father?

The ceaseless urgency of his quest drove Kheda to a sitting position. A chittering in a nut palm made Kheda and the caped loal both look up. It was a smaller beast, a female clutching a delicate infant to its chest. It sounded most indignant.

This would be your lady wife, I take it, and none too pleased that you've not brought home her breakfast.

Abruptly the female stopped her cries, turning her face uphill. Her tail curled up sharply, a long fringe of fur falling across her shoulder. She barked something at the male, who abandoned his stick to climb hand over hand up the nut palm, long tail lashing behind him. With startling speed, the two beasts leapt across the void to a tall ironwood tree, propelled by the spring of their powerful legs, strong hands clasping the trunk. In the next instant they were gone, lost in the dense green canopy of leaves. The pied loals had fled too, ringing silence telling its own tale. A blue-backed crookbeak raised raucous calls of alarm in a cane brake further up the slope and a brief echo relayed the unmistakable sound of a man's cough.

Kheda reached for Telouet's sword and thrust it through his belt before crawling towards the sparse cover of a thicket of dusty sardberry bushes. He kept a wary eye on the ground, no wish to put his hand on some millipede or scorpion stirred up by the digging loal. The cough came again, cut short. Faint but deliberate, Kheda heard a crack of dry twigs and the rustle of the tightly packed red cane stems. Some hunting party was coming stealthily down the gully.

Even if they're not hunting you, you don't want to be explaining yourself to anyone who might carry word back to Derasulla, not when you're so close to the shore, not after crossing the whole width of this cursed island.

Wishing he had ears he could twist like a loal, Kheda skirted slowly around to put the berry bushes between himself and the sounds, searching the forest for any sign of waving greenery, any flutter of disturbed birds. The sounds of men coming nearer grew suddenly louder. Kheda rose to a crouch, turning to slip away down the gully as fast as he could, still bent to stay below a pursuer's natural eye line.

A cry went up, then another, higher in the gully. Kheda straightened up and ran. He reached the stream, no more than a chain of puddles around green-stained rocks. The dark soggy ground sucked at his feet. He sank to his ankles, thrown off balance, reaching out for a sapling only to find its roots so shallow, he pulled it bodily from the pungent soil.

'Want a hand?' A hunter appeared, grinning broadly. A net slung over one shoulder, he carried a sturdy spear that he levelled at Kheda. 'Come and see what I've caught,' he shouted to his companions.

Kheda studied the mire around his feet until he saw a firm place to brace the sapling and haul himself out. By the time he'd managed, six men surrounded him. Kheda kept his face neutral, eyes downcast.

Two of them on the wrong side of the stream and only armed with daggers; that's in your favour. You'll only have four to deal with in the first instance but two of them have spears, so better pick the right moment. What would Telouet say? 'Never start a fight until you can do it on your own terms.'

'What have you got to say for yourself?' Swinging a heavy, square-ended hacking blade, the leader of this hunting party walked slowly down the slope to stand face to face with Kheda.

'I have nothing to say to you,' Kheda replied curtly. 'I am just a traveller.'

The hunter's fist drove hard into Kheda's belly, just beneath his breastbone. 'You'll keep a civil tongue in your head, beggar.'

Kheda dropped to his knees, struggling to regain his breath, unable to stop the hunter as he bent and pulled at Telouet's sword, ripping it out of Kheda's belt and scoring a gouge across his naked ribs with the end of the scabbard

'Beggar or thief? Nothing to your name but the clothes you stand up in and the weapons at your belt. Honest traveller would have a wrap against the night, some goods to trade or the tools of his craft.' The man whistled with approval as he tossed his own hacking blade to a companion, the better to study the sword. 'Scum like you shouldn't be carrying a blade like this neither.'

Kheda managed to regain his feet, his side burning and his gut aching, and strove for a conciliatory tone. 'That is my sword, you have my word on it.'

'Your master's sword, slave,' the lead hunter chided as he lifted it for a closer look. 'Gilt and silver and sapphires in the hilt besides.' He slid the scabbard a little way clear. 'And a watered steel blade. No one carries something like this outside a warlord's retinue, nor wears silks.'

All the other hunters were dressed in coarse cottons, once dyed green, now faded from countless washings and marked with stains from innumerable hunts.

'Silk's no good for the journey you've been making.' One of the others smirked at the rips and filth ruining Kheda's trousers.

*No, it isn't. So why didn't you find something else to wear,
you fool? It's not as if you haven't seen enough clothes left
out to dry on the perfume bushes around those far-flung hill
settlements. Don't you think you're going to pay for those scruples now, all those worries about some innocent getting the
blame, some friendship soured by suspicion?*

'We've been tracking you for a day now.' Irritated by
Kheda's silence, the lead hunter shoved his shoulder to
get his attention. 'Since you crossed the ridge. Lost you
for a while but picked up your trail this morning.'

Kheda glanced involuntarily up towards the jagged
heights still lost in the morning mist. 'Then you'll know
I've done no harm, taken nothing but what the forest
offers.'

'You're still a fleeing slave,' sneered one of the men,
leaning on his spear.

'Daish slave, I see now.' The leader nodded at Kheda's
curved dagger.

Kheda couldn't help himself. His spine stiffened,
shoulders squaring defiantly.

'See him jump like a startled fowl,' another hunter
commented with warm satisfaction.

'That dagger's a fine piece.' The leader swung Telouet's
sword idly. 'That'll tell us whose household you've fled,
once we show it to someone in the know. Then I think
it'll make a fine price for bringing you back, don't you,
lads?'

*And as soon as Ulla Safar gets wind of this, he'll send an
army through the island to find the man Daish Kheda's dagger
has been taken from, dead or alive.*

'I am no runaway,' Kheda said quietly.

'They're saying Daish Kheda is dead, drowned no less.'
The leader leant forward, breath stale, hair and beard long
unwashed. 'You've made a break for it, haven't you, out
to get well clear before any new warlord is proclaimed?'

Kheda shook his head but his heart sank.

Of course. Ulla Safar will be spreading the news as widely as possible, thrilled to see anyone trying to take advantage of a Daish interregnum, all the while shaking his head with dismay. And slaves always go missing whenever a warlord dies, sometimes in droves. Sirket has no legal title to anything until he's proclaimed himself ruler and decreed inventory of the domain be taken. Ulla Safar will be more than happy for Daish losses to pile up in the interim. You didn't think to consider such possibilities, while you were crossing the highlands, admiring the scenery?

'Nothing to say?' the leader mocked, still swinging Telouet's sword. 'Run out of lies?'

'Do we take him back to Derasulla?' asked the hunter who'd taken the hacking blade.

'That's a hard route overland,' one of the others said doubtfully. 'Eight, nine days at best.'

'Body slave, swordsman, whoever he is, he'll be worth his weight in silk or sandalwood,' the leader rebuked him. 'But who will deal more honestly with us, Ulla Safar or Ulla Orhan?' He looked round for opinions.

If they think taking me back is going to be so simple, these men plainly have no idea how a body slave is trained to fight. Nor yet how a warlord's son is taught to escape assassins.

Kheda punched the lead hunter full in the throat with a sweeping uppercut. The man staggered backwards, pulled up short as Kheda dropped into a crouch, snatching Telouet's sword from his numb hands. The warlord drew it in the same fluid movement, the glittering arc of steel sending the second hunter recoiling in fear. A deft side-step took Kheda out of the path of the man's clumsy swing with the hacking blade and a full-blooded kick in his belly shoved the choking leader full into the second hunter. Both fell heavily with a crack of bone that left the man beneath yelping in sudden agony.

The hunter with the closest spear swung his net at Kheda, weights around its edge whistling through the air. Kheda stepped forward to catch the clinging cords full around his midriff, stiffening his belly to save himself from being winded. The net bruised the raw score on his ribs but ignoring the pain, he used the whole weight of his body to pull the hunter forward on to the point of Telouet's sword, ripping into his shoulder. He knocked the man's spear aside with the scabbard in his other hand, before punching upwards, fist weighted with that same scabbard, to smash the hunter's nose to bloody pulp.

As the man fell to his knees, clutching at his face, Kheda whirled around to catch the second spearman's biting blade between sword hilt and scabbard, shoving the weapon backwards to throw the startled man off balance.

As the spearman recovered himself, Kheda raised Telouet's sword menacingly. 'I am just a traveller and you have no call to hinder me.' He shot a threatening glance at the men on the far side of the stream. Both were gaping, one with a hand on the dagger at his belt but his face making it plain he didn't fancy his chances against this unexpected warrior. The other already had both hands raised in abject surrender.

'Then I'll be on my way.' Kheda kept Telouet's sword levelled as he tore away the clinging net. No one made a move towards him. The leader of the hunting party was still sprawled on the ground, struggling to draw breath, clawing at his injured throat. The second man cowered beside him; face wretched with fear and pain as he cradled a foot twisted at an excruciating angle.

'Go and may your journey be cursed,' the second spearman snarled, on his knees beside his companion. He wadded a filthy rag frantically into the wound gaping in the man's shoulder, blood already soaking the cloth slippery beneath his fingers. The injured man whimpered, tears and slime running through his fingers as he clutched at his broken nose.

'Follow me again and I'll kill you,' Kheda said with all the menace he could muster. 'All of you.'

He backed away through a spindly thicket of sardberry bushes, barely glancing over his shoulder to see what lay in his path. An impenetrable stand of wrist-thick red cane finally halted him. Pausing, he listened to the hunters' urgent shouts of argument and lamentation ringing loudly through the forest. There was no obvious sound of pursuit. Turning, Kheda ran, twisting between nut palm saplings tangled with logen vine, his immediate concern to put as much distance between himself and the hunters as he could.

Not down the gully; if they try tracking you, revenge in mind, that's where they'll look first. What will you do then? Kill them in all truth? You've probably killed their leader as it is, crushing his windpipe like that. That shoulder wound will likely fester and it's too high up to save the hapless bastard by taking off his arm, if the black rot gets into it. What did they do to deserve that, only seeking to do their duty by their lord and Daish Sirket, returning a runaway slave?

Sour bile rising from his empty stomach like acid remorse, Kheda pushed on through the lightest patches of underbrush, trying not to slide too far down the hill. He slashed furiously at tendrils of firecreeper, at frail tandra saplings, with Telouet's bloodied sword. Finally, he broke through to a narrow, overgrown track. Sweat stinging the countless scratches he'd collected in his flight, Kheda stopped, heart pounding. With all the birds and animals fled from the noise he'd made or crouching in silent hiding, the forest was tense with stillness. He counted ten deliberate breaths. There was still no sound of pursuit.

And you'd have been easy enough to follow, noisy as a raging fire. So much for all Daish Reik's lessons in stealth

*and forest craftiness. Now then, get yourself in hand. Where
are you in relation to the shore, to the trading beach you've
been making for? Getting clear of this domain is more essential than ever now, preferably before half that hunting party's
village come looking to nail your hide to a tree.*

Kheda walked slowly down the tortuous path, berating
himself. The forest stretched out ahead of him, all around,
ever changing, always the same. The morning wore away
beneath his feet. Only thirst finally put paid to his recrim-
inations, its stranglehold tightening around his throat.
Belatedly recalling one of Daish Reik's lessons, he left the
path to find a bristled creeper snaking up an ironwood
tree. Mindful of Agas's laughter when he'd got this trick
wrong as a youth, he made his first cut as high as he could,
slicing an arm's length of the dun creeper free with a
second lower slash of Telouet's blade. The plant's jealously hoarded water gushed free and splashed over his
face as he caught all he could in his gaping mouth, stale
and woody tasting as it was.

*And I wouldn't trade it for the promise of a dozen flagons
of the finest golden wine.*

He threw the length of cut creeper aside and such idle
thoughts evaporated as he glimpsed a yellowing square of
old palm fronds bright through the muted green of the
living trees, some little way down the slope. Moving
cautiously forward, as quietly as he could, Kheda saw it
was indeed what he'd guessed; the roof of a hut,
ramshackle and in need of considerable repair if the imminent rains weren't to soak anyone within as they lay in
their beds. The ground all around showed more recent
care though, newly dug with black earth piled high along
trenches waiting impatiently to capture all the precious
water that the tardy rains would bring. Kheda left the path
and circled round the edge of the dusty barrenness where
the underbrush had long since been taken for firewood.

*Long since, but none too recently. Those sardberry bushes
have a good few seasons' growth on them. There's no fowl
house either, ducks or geese ready to raise a commotion if
strangers come too close to a hut outside the more usual protec-
tions of a village.*

Behind the sparse cover of a withered perfume bush,
he hunkered down to see inside the decrepit hut's splintered shutters, hanging crooked on sagging hinges. From
his vantage point, Kheda could clearly see a heap of quilts
were tossed all anyhow on a narrow bed. A tumble of
clothes lay on the floor, together with a single lidded
cooking pot and a half-unrolled length of sturdy cotton,
such as any Daish islander might use to gather up a few
belongings for a short journey.

*Who's making a stay here? Someone not wanting to live
in such an isolated hut for the present but still making use of
the fertile garden until the forest reclaims it. But where might
this diligent farmer be now? Out foraging or squatting over a
privy scrape?*

Kheda crept closer, the skin between his shoulder blades
crawling with apprehension lest the unknown gardener
return. He sheathed Telouet's sword with sudden decision, driving the hilt home with a snap. Swinging himself
over the low sill of the window, he grabbed the topmost
quilt and a leather thong left curling across the floor.
Seeing a sweat-stained tunic, he pulled it over his head,
grimacing with distaste as he fought his arms through the
sleeves. Cut for a taller and fatter man, it would at least
help hide his own ragged trousers from a casual glance.

*Going bare-chested on to a trading beach will attract
entirely too much attention and I think we've had more than
enough of that this morning. So what else is there, to make
you look more convincing as a traveller? You can't afford
scruples, not now.*

Kheda knelt and made a rapid roll of the quilt, lashing

it tight. His stomach rumbled, startlingly loud in the quiet gloom. He lifted the lid off the cooking pot to find a cold smear of saller pottage, the grain long since cooked and mixed with crushed tandra seeds, some pepper pods and salt to keep it from spoiling. Lilla fruit rinds had been dumped on top of it. After a moment's hesitation, Kheda fished out the rinds and scraped the greasy remnants out of the bottom of the pot, spitting out fragments of lilla pulp and choking the humble food down over his first instinctive revulsion.

So it's come to this, eating a lowliest islander's leavings. Is this plan sense or insanity? I don't know. All I do know is, just now, food's more use to me than pride.

Then he saw the knife that had been used to cut the fruit. It wasn't much of a knife, a short length of clumsily sharpened steel stained with juice and pitted by rust. The wooden handle was cracked where it had once got wet and been left to dry without care or oil. Kheda sat back on his heels, one hand on the hilt of Telouet's sword, the other on his own dagger. Both blades marked him out, as a man belonging to some significant household. This knife would brand its owner as the lowest of the low. Everyone scorned a man who'd reached an age of discretion without a decent dagger to call his own, born to a father who'd never managed to trade sufficient goods, skills or service to be able to give his son such a gift.

Better the lowest of the low than an escaped slave, just at the moment.

Kheda sprang on to the bed. It raised him just high enough to reach up into the crudely hewn rafters. He threaded Telouet's sword carefully into the tight-packed palm fronds, twisting it sideways so it lay flat, hidden in the roof. Shoving his dagger up to join it, he jumped off the bed, caught up the quilt, shoved the paltry knife into the sheath at his belt and ran out through the open door.

Let this be a test of my judgement here, if I get clear without being called to account for this theft. That can be an omen to show me if I'm following the right course.

Tense with expectation of outraged shouts behind him at any moment, Kheda hurried down the winding path. The ramshackle hut was soon left far behind, along with any possibility of recrimination. Some way further, he stumbled upon a wider track and, following that, found it took him out along the top of a long reach of low, broken cliffs, waves lapping dark at their base. With no option but to go on, he finally rounded a corner to stand on a shallow bluff. It took Kheda a moment to realise he was looking down on the dappled stretch of sand he'd been seeking ever since he'd seen it from a vantage point high in the uplands.

Any satisfaction at this turn of events was short lived. Kheda scowled. There were only four galleys anchored in the sheltered strait between the beach and a sprawling palm-crowned reef and only a couple of smaller sailing vessels drawn up in the shallows. A few awnings fluttered bright on the beach, hiding whatever wares were on offer but there was no one passing along the sand to look or haggle. Kheda walked on a little further to see the broad space between two hospitable stands of spinefruit trees only boasted two cook fires. A warlord's retinue for a full progress could have set up camp between them without anyone feeling unduly cramped.

How delighted you would have been, not ten days ago, to learn Ulla Safar's most notable trading beaches are being scorned by merchants and the domain's people alike. What pleasure it would have been, to commiserate with fat Safar, in terms carefully calculated to let him see your satisfaction.

'It's entirely permitted to take pleasure in your enemy's misfortunes.' Daish Reik had always been open about such matters. 'Mind you, it's rarely wise to let them see you doing *so, unless you have their triremes sunk below hope of rescue and your swordsmen at the gates of their final stronghold.'*

But now Safar's ill luck is yours as well. What would Daish Reik have to say about that? *'You can wait for your fortunes to change, or you can make a lot of your own luck by taking any opportunity that offers itself.'*

Kheda watched a rowboat from one of the galleys approaching the shore, oarsmen hampered by water casks lined up between them. Sliding down the loose earth of the cliff face, he managed to reach the beach just as the rowboat grounded on the coarse sand.

'Can I be of any help to you?' Kheda stepped forward into the lazy surf.

The rowing master threw him a rope. 'Haul us in.'

Kheda gripped and pulled, the rowing master jumping over the side to join him. The boat rocked once with protest and then grounded solidly.

'I want those casks scoured and refilled and no one goes seeing what they can see until it's done.' The rowing master scowled mock ferocious at his crew.

'Doesn't look like there's much to see here on this shore anyway,' called out one of the oarsmen as the men began lifting the empty casks over the side of the boat.

'Let me help you with your barrels,' Kheda suggested a little stiffly. 'And I could take an oar with you, when you leave here.'

'An oar?' Surprised, the rowing master reached out to take his hand, turning it palm upwards to trace the red line where the rope had pulled across it with a finger callused and hard as old leather. 'Soft hands, my friend. You may be willing but you're no oarsman and we're heading for the northern reaches as fast as we can. There's no room on our benches for anyone who can't pull all day and all the next.'

Kheda forced himself to duck his head in acceptance. 'Of course.'

The last barrel splashed into the shallows as an oarsman heaved it over the boat's side. The rowing master hesitated. 'Help us fill the water casks and that should be worth some bread.'

There's a good question for a lordly discussion of ethics with your fellow rulers, over a full belly with sweetmeats to hand as you relax on silken cushions. Is it worse to be forced to steal from an islander who has nothing worth having in the first place, or to accept the charity of some good-hearted mariner, who pities your friendless and destitute state?

The realisation of how completely he was alone went down Kheda's spine like runnels of cold water. He took a deep breath. 'Thank you.'

'Here.' Someone tossed him a scrap of sacking. 'It gets scoured with plenty of sand or we're drinking green slime inside a couple of days.'

Kheda leaned to reach down inside one of the wide barrels, inadvertently clashing heads with another rower. 'Sorry.'

'Scrub as hard as you can.' The oarsman grunted with effort as he scooped a handful of gritty sand into the barrel.

Kheda did his best to do the same. It was horribly uncomfortable work, bent double yet still working at full stretch, the rim of the cask digging into his midriff. His breath echoed harsh in the confines of the wood and the man working with him didn't smell any too fresh.

He probably thinks you stink bad enough to scare fish. And you won't be finding Telouet ready with hot water, perfumed soaps and softly scented towels. The best you can hope for is a wetting in the sea and scouring yourself with sand. Ah, so be it. If I'm reduced to beggary, I can still be clean.

'That should do it!' The rower stood up with an explosive gasp. 'Let's get it rinsed and refilled.'

'Right.' Kheda toppled the barrel over and gave it a

shove towards the feeble spring staining the crumbling cliff face.

'Get them refilled before they dry out too much,' called the rowing master. 'Spring one of the staves and I'll thrash you with it.'

There was precious little water in the pool at the base of the bluff so rinsing the barrels free of sand was an awkward and laborious process. The cool of the water didn't come amiss though, not with the sun sailing high overhead. Kheda was startled to realise it was nearly noon.

'That's the last, is it?' The rowing master reappeared as the last cask had its top hammered securely back on. He handed Kheda a misshapen loaf of flat saller bread, split and filled with smoked fingerfish. 'Right, lads, let's get this lot aboard and we can be on our way.' The rowers left Kheda by the meagre pool without comment, no one sparing him so much as a backward glance.

No one wants your help getting the barrels back, even if they are heavier and more unwieldy now. No one wants to raise your hopes that you might be allowed aboard their galley. That's their choice and they've made it. What are your choices? To start with, not to stand here forlorn like some abandoned hound. You're entitled to that much pride.

Chewing on the bread and pungent fish, Kheda strolled along the sand towards the camping ground between the shade trees. Those men lounging around the ashes of the burnt-out fires spared him a glance, not hostile, not welcoming, barely curious.

They've all seen beggars before, after all, scavenging around the trading beaches, no domain to claim their allegiance, no island to call home, no village to shelter and feed them.

Uncomfortable at seeing himself through such people's eyes, Kheda kept walking until he passed the far stand of shade trees and found a broken line of grey-stained rocks running across the beach, like stumps of broken teeth in a weathered jawbone washed clean by the seas. He walked down to the water and on into it, washing himself clean as best he could. Coming back on to the beach, he enjoyed a moment's blissful cool before the unwelcome hot wind that would blow unceasing till sunset dried him. The fickle tides had cast up a curious array of debris among the rocks: dull urchin shells and knobbled rusty fragments of reef crab legs, rags of seaweed dried to papery twists.

Then a hard white glint caught Kheda's eye. Crouching, he swept aside the detritus to uncover a piece of ivory. It was the broken tip of a horned fish's twisted rapier, not long enough in the water for sand and sea to dull its sheen. It was barely scuffed. Kheda closed his fist around the white spiral. It felt warm and vital in his grasp.

Ivory. Incorruptibility in its whiteness, an emblem of rank in its scarcity and its durability. Sea ivory no less; a yet more potent symbol, coming from a beast of the waters that carries a horn like some animal of the land. Learned warlords have long written treatises, debating what such a thing can denote. Every theory differs but for one thing: there must be nameless evils in the deeps, to prompt such a mighty sea beast to wield such a weapon. Sea ivory washing up on a beach must always be an urgent call to arms.

'Any portent that comes unsought and unheralded is likely to be of the greatest significance.' That's what Daish Reik told you time and again. Can you trust this sign? Are you far enough away from the taint of magic to trust your intuition for the unseen currents of present and future? How can you tell?

Kheda stowed the ivory deep into his paltry quilt bundle before turning back towards the twin stands of shade trees. As he walked, he searched the sands, bending down, picking up shells, keeping some and discarding others.

'What are you looking for?' A merchant with no customers to reward his diligence strolled over, open ochre robe flapping over brightly embroidered trousers, a thick gold chain around his neck.

Kheda nodded an acknowledgement but continued looking. 'Storm eyes, well-matched ones, ten of them.'

'Here's one.' The merchant was happy to join in the search to alleviate his own boredom. 'Oh, no, it's broken.' He tossed the creamy shard away.

'I'm looking for the ones with the darker inside.' Kheda held up a white oval, its edges curling over towards each other, serrated edges not quite meeting. A rich brown sheen spread up grooves leading down to the hidden inner face, like lashes fringing a nearly closed eye.

'How about this one?' The merchant reached for another shell; a line marking sun-darkened skin from paler flesh showed as the sleeve of his robe slid up his arm. 'What are we doing, anyway, making a necklace?'

Kheda took the shell and compared it to his current haul. 'This one's a bit too pink inside.' A pace later an unbidden thought made him grin.

'What's the joke?' the merchant asked genially, stirring the sand with a darkly tanned foot.

Kheda cleared his throat. 'Nothing, just recalling something my father once told me.'

'The darker ones are storm eyes, plain enough. The pinker ones, well, let's just say they can remind a man at an age of discretion of something else entirely. You can gather a double handful of those if you're looking for particular divinations concerning a woman's fertility or the consequences of child-birth.'

'Either of these any good?' The merchant stooped and stood up with shells in each hand.

'That one, certainly.' Kheda took it. 'The other's a bit too yellow.'

The merchant looked at him, amused. 'Why so particular?'

Kheda shot the man a challenging look. 'I will be casting them for a portent.'

'You're a soothsayer?' Rapid understanding replaced the merchant's incredulity. 'Of course.'

'What else could you be, so ragged and filthy?' At least you've the good manners to leave that much unsaid, my friend. And it's true, isn't it, after a fashion? Why lie, especially when you're looking to test your skills? Daish Reik told you often enough, 'Speak the truth as far as possible, certainly when taking any augury. If you cannot govern the truth in your own words, how will you recognise the truths spoken by omens?'

'My father was a seer of sorts,' Kheda replied with an attempt at carelessness. 'I have something of his skill.'

'I've not seen you in these reaches before,' the merchant commented.

'I've not travelled much hereabouts. I had to leave my wife—' The break of anguish in his own voice surprised Kheda as his situation struck him with a brutality he'd not had to face on his resolute journey across the vast island, focused only on the path ahead, finding something, anything to eat, some shelter for the night. 'My children—' The words stuck in his throat.

Rekha and Sain, Sirket and Dau, Efi, Vida and Noi, little Mie and the unknown son or daughter that Sain is to bear. Will you ever see them again?

'I didn't mean to pry,' the merchant apologised, distressed.

'You weren't to know.' Kheda managed a wry smile as dark amusement lanced his hurt.

Let that pain bleed into your words when anyone asks and you surely won't be expected to explain yourself.

A gust of wind fluttered the nearby awning. The merchant seized on the chance to change the subject. 'I don't know where you come from but in my home reaches, we call this wind the dragon's breath. Foul, isn't it? Why don't you come and share my shade?'

'I will and gladly.' Kheda followed the man to the brightly striped canvas efficiently erected over a wide array of bells and chimes that he had displayed on a sturdy length of green cotton. Some of the bells were large enough for a village's talisman pole and the chimes went all the way down to straw-fine cylinders small enough to sew on a dancing gown's hem, for a gleaming fringe of silvery sound.

'Will those shells tell you when the rains will finally get here, before we all drop dead of the heat?' The merchant sat down on a travel-beaten chest, half covered by an assortment of drapery. He wiped sweat from his forehead with an exaggerated grimace.

'I can read the weather for you, if you want.' Kheda sat cross-legged, leaning forward to draw a perfect circle in the sand. He glanced up at the sun and then deftly notched the rim to mark the quarters and the three aspects within each quarter. 'This is looking for something else.' He felt his hand trembling so cast the shells before his apprehension could make a nonsense of any divination.

The merchant was intrigued. 'What do you see?'

Kheda looked up at the sky to make absolutely sure he had the earthly compass correctly aligned before allowing himself a look at the sand. 'Travel.'

The merchant chuckled. 'That's no surprise hereabouts.'

'And a successful journey.' Kheda felt a release going far beyond his own laugh as he studied the circle. No fewer than five shells had fallen within the arc denoting travel and all had their open sides uppermost. A most favourable omen.

'Anything else?' The merchant looked hopefully at the sand.

'Friends.' That was where four of the shells had fallen, the next most significant indicator.

'Old friends or new?' wondered the merchant, intrigued.

'New friends.' Kheda nodded with growing satisfaction. 'The shells are close to the edge of the circle. Old friends would be marked in the middle.'

'What about that one?' The merchant pointed at the last shell.

Kheda saw it had fallen on the cusp between friendship and enmity, closed side turned towards him in warning. 'I'd say that's just a reminder not to be too trusting.'

You haven't left every foe behind in Derasulla and don't forget it.

'That's not a divination that I've seen before but your face says it's offering sound advice,' approved the merchant. 'Would you cast for me?'

Kheda looked at the merchant, studying his dress properly for the first time. His embroidered trousers were striped with lines of little animals and trees, upside down from Kheda's perspective but entirely the right way for the merchant when he was sitting down. That style was a peculiarity of the furthest eastern reaches, he recalled. 'You're a long way from home.'

'Indeed.' The merchant waved a rueful arm at the all but empty beach. 'And picked a dire time to come voyaging, with all these upsets in the south.'

'You shan't make it back to the eastern reaches before the rains.' Kheda checked the horizon from ingrained habit. 'Do you have a safe anchorage to head for?'

'We're going to cut across to Endit waters,' nodded the merchant. 'And carrying a boatload of unsold goods with us,' he added apologetically, 'so we've no room to take a tame songbird on board, never mind a passenger.'

'That's all right; I'm going north, not east.' Kheda scooped up the shells and poured them carefully from one hand to the other. 'You spoke of trouble in the south. I'll trade you a reading of these for whatever you know.' He hoped the merchant wouldn't see the tension stiffening his spine into a rod of iron.

'There's magic abroad south of here, friend,' said the merchant bluntly. 'I've heard it from too many people for it to be falsehood.'

'In Redigal waters?' Kheda wondered with studied casualness.

'Nowhere so close.' The merchant shook his head with unfeigned relief. 'Chazen is all I've heard, magical fires setting the islands alight and everyone fleeing to Daish waters. Oh, have you heard the rumour that Daish Kheda is likely dead? Some people are wondering if that's just coincidence or malice working ahead of the magic.'

'I heard something about that.' Kheda didn't dare look up and meet the man's eyes. 'What do you reckon to Daish Sirket's chances, if he is to be warlord?'

'If he's as much his father's son as Daish Kheda was son to Daish Reik, he should be strong enough to stand up against anything short of outright wizardry,' said the merchant stoutly. 'I shall hold to that thought next time I sharpen my blade, to sharpen the lad's luck.'

Any portent that comes unsought and unheralded is likely to be of the greatest significance.' And how often did Daish Reik tell you truth often speaks through chance-heard words?

'Is there any word of this magic coming north?' Kheda asked, tension knotting in the pit of his stomach.

'No.' The merchant shook his head with welcome certainty. 'Not with the rains due any day.'

Kheda smiled warmly at the man. 'Let's see what the shells have to say about your voyage to Endit waters.'

He threw the shells and looked up with a smile. 'I'd

say you'll have fair winds to take you there and good fortune when you make landfall.'

'What are you at, friend?'

Kheda looked up to see three other men walking up the beach towards them, their attention caught by the only activity on the beach. Like his new acquaintance, they were evidently merchants who sailed as their own shipmasters.

'Having my fortune told. Our friend here's a sooth-sayer.' The merchant narrowed his eyes against the bright sun. 'I reckon I'll be under way before the day's end. There's no trade to be had here.'

'I'll probably follow you,' shrugged one of the ship-masters, wearing an Endit dagger with its sharply back-bent blade. 'We only had each other to deal with yesterday and it doesn't look as if we'll do any better today.' Wiry rather than muscular, his beard and hair were freshly plaited and he wore white cotton robes immaculate despite the inadequacies of the campground.

'If we all stay, we may yet tempt some of the Ulla people down from the hills,' protested a second, thickset man with grizzled hair and beard, his voice gravelly with years of shouting over wind and wave. Kheda noted a Taer blade with its deer-hoof handle at his belt. 'All we'll be sure of if we leave is sailing back home with a full half of the cargo we set out with. Where's the profit in that?'

'Endit Nai may not be thrilled to see me report such paltry trade but at least I'll be able to promise him a voyage as soon as the weather clears, with plenty of goods all ready to ship.' The dapper merchant had plainly made up his mind. 'And maybe this uproar in the south will be past,' he added with a meaningful look at the Taer ship-master. 'I imagine that's one of the things keeping the Ulla people close to their huts.'

'There's no word of that kind of trouble anywhere north of Chazen,' protested the Taer man.

'What does the soothsayer say?' The third galley master stood, weight on his back foot, arms folded as he watched the other two argue. All three wore the same style of clothes, sleeveless tunic and trousers like any other sailor, but his were of better cloth, better cut and embroidered sea serpents coiled around his shoulders. He was also as much of a barbarian as Sain's slave Hanyad, though younger, barely Kheda's age. The sun had burnished his skin to a coppery sheen and lightened his hair to a dull gold, as unexpected among the dark heads all around as a Mirror Bird suddenly alighting in their midst.

'Can you tell us when the first rains will arrive?' demanded the Endit shipmaster.

'Can you tell us if we'll prosper for a longer stay here?' interrupted the Taer merchant.

'I can read the auguries for you,' Kheda answered calmly. 'Whether I will or not depends what you can do for me in return.'

That silenced the Endit shipmaster and the Taer merchant both.

'What do you want?' asked the barbarian, amused.

Time to test your luck, Daish Kheda.

'Passage north.' Kheda was momentarily disconcerted to see the man had green eyes, not unlike his own. 'I am no rower, you can see that from my hands, but you have my promise that I'll do my best. I can carry water to your oarsmen, take a turn for a tired man, tell you everything I see of the weather and seas ahead.' He poured the shells from one hand to the other again.

'I don't think my rowing master would thank me for you.'

Kheda wondered if the Endit shipmaster had some reason to look so suspicious or whether it was just a habit.

'I can take you to Tule waters,' offered the Taer shipmaster grudgingly.

'How far north do you want to go?' asked the barbarian. 'We're an Ikadi ship and bound for home.'

The other merchants looked at him, surprised.

'He's the closest thing we're going to find to an augur on this shore,' the Ikadi captain pointed out. 'You can go looking in the villages if you like, but even if you find someone who can read you the portents, it'll cost you dear, you know that.'

Kheda was searching his memory for any mention of the Ikadi domain.

How far north is that? Nearly all the way to the unbroken lands? This has to be an omen in my favour. You were right, my father. Seize an opportunity and you can make your own good luck.

'I'll travel as far as you are going.' He smiled at the barbarian. 'And read the weather and the auguries for you all the way.'

'You've certainly got a good trade out of that.' The Taer shipmaster looked at Kheda with disfavour. 'What will it cost me for your insights, now I can't offer you passage?'

'A pair of trousers,' Kheda said boldly. 'A tunic, not new if you can't spare them but clean, if you please.'

'We should have had our pick of four or five sooth-sayers on this beach,' grumbled the Endit merchant. 'Last time there was that one with the chest of crystals and a silken star map to cast them on.'

'This time, there's just me.' Kheda smiled at the man. 'And if you want any warning of foul weather or anything worse coming up from the south, it'll cost you a bowl and a spoon and a water skin.'

'If your father was a soothsayer, was your mother a trader?' chuckled the eastern merchant who'd first befriended him.

Kheda winked at the man. 'Of sorts.'

'Oh very well,' said the Endit merchant with consider-able ill grace. 'It's a deal for my part.'

'If there wasn't this uproar in the south—' The Taer shipmaster broke off. 'All right.'

'Did you all share the same fire?' Kheda stood up and hitched his bundle up on to his shoulder.

'We did.' The Endit merchant looked dubious all the same.

Kheda led the three galley masters and the friendly eastern merchant towards the camping ground, stopping at the first blackened circle. 'This one?'

'And all our crews gathered firewood,' the Ikadi barbarian confirmed.

'Then we can take the augury here.' Kheda bent to pull a half-burnt stick from the ring of rocks and used the charcoaled end to score a circle on the ground. He went on to mark every quarter and arc in full, carefully drawing the signs for each constellation around the outside. When he glanced up, he saw the Ikadi shipmaster consulting a small compass.

He nodded approval at Kheda. 'You have north exactly.'

Kheda grinned. 'My father taught me well.'

'What now?' asked the Endit merchant impatiently.

'Tell us the prospects if we stay on this beach in hopes of more trade,' said the Taer shipmaster quickly.

Kheda was about to cast the shells on to the circle, when a sudden thought held his hand

You could give them any reading you wanted. You're not Daish Kheda, whose every pronouncement will be talked over, compared with previous utterances, your words scrupulously examined in the light of whatever events might later confirm or contradict them. No one will ever see a resemblance to the Daish warlord, once glimpsed on a distant trireme's deck or in some splendid procession aglitter with silks and jewels. You're nobody, a soothsayer they'll likely never see again.

Nobody but still a man with power. Not Daish Kheda's power but power all the same. You could foretell the direst consequences if they stay here, and not only for now, but if they ever return. You could predict disaster for any ship venturing into Ulla waters between now and the return of the dragon star to signal the new year. These mariners would pass the word to their fellows; they wouldn't dare not. You could do untold harm to the Ulla domain, with just a few well-chosen words. Beggarly oracle you may be but what reason would such a man have to lie?

'Well?' The Ikadi shipmaster looked intently at him with those green eyes so like his own.

No. I won't forswear myself, even for the sake of revenge on Ulla Safar.

Kheda lifted his face to the blazing bowl of the heavens as he cast the shells and then looked down.

'There's certainly no wealth in your futures here,' he said with some surprise. That arc of the earthly compass was entirely devoid of shells.

'How so?' The Taer shipmaster stared at the ground as if he expected to see words writing themselves in the dirt.

'What will the future bring?' demanded the Endit merchant.

'Travel, for all three of you. Honour, for two.' Kheda pursed his lips. 'Friendship, for the third.'

'Which of us would that be?' enquired the Ikadi barbarian.

Kheda glanced at him. 'I cannot tell, not without making individual readings.'

'What else do you see?' The Endit merchant was still gazing at the shell-strewn circle.

Kheda considered the rest of the shells. One lay within the arc that signified health, open side up, another close by within the arc of children. Without knowing more about these men, it was impossible to say whose family they might signify. Closed face up, the last had fallen into the arc for siblings. All three were at the midpoint between the centre of the circle and its outer edge.

'Your families will be glad to have you home again,' he said firmly. 'The sooner the better.'

'I hardly need a soothsayer to tell me that,' scowled the Taer shipmaster. 'Not that they'll be pleased to welcome me without my lord's favour to see us fed through the rains.'

'Better safe at home if a little hungry than drowned with a belly full of salt water. That's plain enough for me.' The Endit merchant sighed heavily.

'I suppose that earns you some cast-offs from my rowing master,' grunted the Taer shipmaster grudgingly. 'I'll wait for a better choice of soothsayer before I ask anything more.'

'Your word's good enough for me.' The Endit merchant smiled with better humour. 'I'll send your recompense to the *Springing Fish*, shall I?'

'If that's the galley I'm shipping on,' replied Kheda with a glance at the Ikadi barbarian, who nodded his confirmation.

'As you say, it's plain enough we'll not prosper here.' The Ikadi captain bent to gather up Kheda's shells, handing them to him with a smile. 'Bec!' His sudden shout turned heads by the shade trees. 'Let's make ready to get underway while we still have the tide in our favour!'

The crewmen from the other galleys didn't wait for their shipmasters' orders but immediately started collecting themselves and their gear, piling things on the sand by the water, a plain signal to the ships to send rowing boats ashore.

The eastern merchant nodded a friendly farewell to Kheda. 'My thanks for your reading of my path. I hope your journey prospers, and here's my payment for your augury, with my hopes that you find what you've lost.' He handed Kheda a small gold chime, the kind Janne liked to have hanging in her windows for the breezes to stir.

Startled, Kheda couldn't find a reply before the merchant moved away, calling out to his boat for his second in command to come help pack away their merchandise. All the lesser merchants were taking down their awnings now, wares packed back into their coffers and waiting to be hauled back on to their little ships.

Kheda turned the little gold bell over and over in his hands, spirits rising.

You did Ulla Safar a bad turn after all, and no need to dishonour yourself to do it either. You've passage further north than you could possibly have hoped for and a gift to give Janne on your return. What more proof do you need that you're on the right path, that your quest will prosper?

'What can you tell me of the rains, friend, if we're sailing today?' The Ikadi shipmaster looked quizzically at him.

Kheda tucked the bell securely inside his quilt bundle along with the twist of sea ivory and studied the skies. A tracery of white was spun out over the islands hiding the southern horizon but there was no hint of anything more substantial, no hint of the fine milky veil that would turn the sky the colour of mother of pearl, before the rising storms turned it the dour hue of an oyster's shell. Walking towards the shore, he looked for the run of the surf past the reef, the colour of the water out in the open seas. Turning to the land, he picked out the telltale perfume trees in the tangled scrub above the beach. Their leaves were curled, silvery undersides showing. The liquid song of a glory bird floated out over the trees, its mate joining in with a charming harmony.

'There'll be the afternoon hot wind and the evening showers but there's at least three more days before the first true storms arrive,' he said confidently.

The Ikadi shipmaster's forehead wrinkled in thought. 'Which will see us well into the main strait through Seik waters. That's sheltered enough for us to row through all but the worst weather. So, friend,' he added. 'If you're crewing on my ship, I'll know your name.'

'Cadirn.' His mother, Zari Daish, had had a body slave called that when he'd been little. The name had been close enough to Kheda's own to catch his attention most times she'd called.

'I'm Godine.' The Ikadi shipmaster walked towards one of his galley's boats, drawn up on the shoreline to load up their goods. 'We don't go much south of here,' he continued casually. 'But I wouldn't care to get on bad terms with any of the warlords. On the other hand, there are some warlords I wouldn't care to deal with, not given the way they treat their people.' He gave Kheda a meaningful look. 'Their people who don't have the choice to pack up their pots and pans and take a ship to the next island if they don't like the rule they're living under. If there's a domain where you'd better stay aboard whenever we make landfall, I'd appreciate knowing. You need not tell me any more than that.'

'My—' Kheda bit his lip, thinking fast. 'I have enemies; I will not lie to you. They think I am dead, but perhaps it would be as well for me to stay out of view until we are clear of Ulla or Endit waters, Tule too.'

'I was a slave,' Godine smiled with apparent inconsequentiality. 'You can see that much by my eyes and hair. Ikadi Nass bought me and my mother from Mahaf Coru's father. I was too young to remember much about that life, and my mother won't ever talk about it, but she has always told me we were lucky to be sold as we were. She'll carry lash marks to her grave, that much I do know.' He shot a sideways look at Kheda.

'And you rose to become master of that ship, the *Springing Fish*, is it?' Kheda looked at the galley to avoid meeting Godine's eyes.

'My mother bore Ikadi Nass a daughter, so we were both made free.' The mariner smiled, proud. 'My lord found me a place on his galleys and I haven't looked back.'

'Unless there's a storm coming up astern,' commented Kheda with a smile.

Godine looked at him, face serious. 'I'm hoping you'll be warning me about any storms coming up from the south, of any nature.'

Kheda looked at him. 'I will do all that I can.' That much was no lie.

'Good.' Godine gestured towards the galley's waiting rowboat. 'The first thing you can do is learn how to use an oar.'

CHAPTER TWELVE

Has any other warlord ever learned the art of rowing, three men to an oar on a merchant galley?

Kheda leaned over the thick wooden shaft, ducking his head to try and see out of the leather-shrouded oar port.

'So this is Beloc domain? What's it like?' They had reached waters Kheda barely knew by reputation, never mind accurate accounts. 'Whereabouts are we? Is this a central isle or somewhere on a border strait?'

His companion on the narrow seat on the *Springing Fish*'s rowing deck wasn't listening. 'Why does Rast have to pick now to change ships?' he grumbled, broad mouth downturned. 'We'll get some fuzz-faced youngling who'll be grizzling for his mother before we've gone a day's pull.'

How many warlords realise just how many men travel the Archipelago like this, taking ship for a few days, slipping ashore to find another heading in the right direction?

Kheda studied his own hands, palms now as hard as any galley master could wish. He ran a cautious finger over the shiny round scar of what had been a vicious blister.

Well, almost. Better get some salve on that crease or it'll crack again.

'If we don't get someone to take Rast's seat, you'll be bellyaching about doing two men's work, I suppose,' the man across the aisle commented.

I really did expect the rains to lift Ialo's mood; everyone else was a new man once the heat broke and we got cool winds

to help us north instead of that dragon's breath scorching us
from noon to dusk.

'I should be taking a prow oar by now, working with
the experienced men.' Ialo glowered at the backs of the
men idly chatting on the foremost benches. 'I shouldn't
be wasted back here with you island-hopping rabble.'

'I've been rowing merchant galleys since Asyl Nian
first gave me leave to quit his domain.' The man across
the aisle was indignant. 'Anyway, you came aboard three
days after me. I'll be moving forward before you do,
pal.'

'Reading your own fortune in your hands, soothsayer?'
queried the oar port rower from the bench behind Kheda.

He smiled. 'I think we can all see our futures, until
dusk at least.'

As he spoke, a whistle shrilled at the far end of the
long, dark deck. With resigned sighs and discreet groans,
the foremost rowers slid along their benches and began
filing along the gangway between them.

'Shift yourself, Ialo.' Kheda's oar mate was still
slumped on the seat.

The heavily muscled man looked up, sulky. 'I might
change ship here. Rast was all right and you're willing to
learn but why should I be landed with some kid who'll
just want the splinters picking out of his arse?'

The inboard rower from the bench behind gave Ialo's
shoulder a shove. 'Shift your own arse before it gets my
toe up it.'

Ialo got to his feet, still complaining. 'I used to row
great galleys, every man with an oar of his own. That takes
skill, let me tell you.'

'You have already, plenty of times,' muttered someone
across the aisle.

'Three men on the same oar, this isn't skill.' Ialo
continued talking, undeterred as Kheda edged him into

the gangway. 'It's just heave and shove and the laziest takes it easy.'

'I don't reckon Rast was trying to get a passage to the west, soothsayer,' observed the inboard rower across the aisle. 'He wanted to get away from Ialo's moaning. Not even the rains mend your mood, do they, you miserable tick!'

Kheda moved to join the line of men moving slowly along the rowing deck. 'You don't think it's the stink you've been raising drove him off, Paire?'

Paire shook his head at a general laugh, smile good-humoured through his sparse beard. 'I don't know what Godine was thinking, taking on beans for our rations.'

'Maybe he was reckoning on you raising a wind all by yourself,' chuckled the middle man from the same bench. 'Stand you on deck with your face to the stern, rig a sail, he could get home in half the time.'

Paire was unconcerned. 'Say what you like, it's keeping the vermin away.'

'That's another thing. The food's a cursed sight better on a great galley.' Ialo looked back over his shoulder. 'Warlords demand the best for their crews, not whatever some other merchant turns up, desperate to trade before it spoils.'

'You think you can do better elsewhere, you go ahead and try,' Paire told him scornfully. 'We've eaten better on this ship than the last two we've crewed on, haven't we, Tagir?'

'My oath on it,' agreed the barrel-chested middle rower with feeling. 'Do you remember that bread we had to pick the weevils out of?' He shuddered, the wooden beads plaited in his beard rattling.

'Come on, soothsayer.' Paire urged Kheda on with a hand between his shoulder blades. 'Let's get to some fresh air before those beans make themselves felt again.'

You never knew what your rowers were eating. It didn't ever occur to you to wonder, did it?

Kheda climbed the steep ladder that led up to the *Springing Fish*'s accommodation deck. This merchant galley was nowhere near as finely finished as the *Rainbow Moth*, though these cabins with their painted panels promised more comfort than the rowers enjoyed slung in their hammocks on the draughty rowing deck or down in the darkness of the windowless bottom holds.

No, you didn't know what your men were eating, because such concerns are a shipmaster's job and a wise warlord doesn't irritate competent men by constantly checking up on them. Daish Reik taught you that much.

'Warlords' rowers rest when a great galley's at anchor.' Ialo was still complaining as they climbed the wider stair out onto the broad deck. 'There's none of this hauling bales and boxes.'

'It's not raining yet, anyway,' Paire pointed out cheerfully. 'It'll be an easy enough job.'

'Foul enough, though.' Ialo would not be placated. 'Stinking Tule dyestuffs.'

'Look to the future for a change. Once it's done, the hold won't reek of agali root.' Kheda looked at the wide shallow bay where they were anchored, squinting in the brighter light even though the sky above was a rainy-season cloud of sullen grey. 'Reckon we'll get a chance to go ashore?'

Will you find what you're looking for here? How long are you going to go on looking, until you give up? Was starting this search just dry-season madness?

Godine's distinctive whistle pierced the bustle. Kheda looked to the stern platform and saw he was being summoned.

Ialo scowled. 'There's always some manage to do less work than others.'

'I'll teach you some divination if you like, Ialo, if you

fancy an easy life,' Kheda offered obligingly. 'Who knows? In five or ten years, you might be able to tell night from day.'

Laughter from the other men followed him up the steps to the helmsman's platform.

'We're stopping overnight here.' Godine spoke without preamble, not looking up as he made an entry in his records. 'I've this dyestuff to trade for sharpnuts and we may as well take on water and food while we've the chance.' He blew on ink to dry it and shut his leather-bound book with a snap. 'Bec's going ashore to see who he can pick up to replace Rast. Go with him and run a weather eye over the choices.'

'Do you want me to let you know what I see?' This wasn't the first time the shipmaster had asked Kheda to read the auguries concerning a new crewman.

'Only if it's something out of the ordinary.' Godine smoothed a spotless white tunic and pulled on a sleeveless blue silk mantle with a dramatic pattern of silver clouds woven into it. His hair and beard shone with scented oil and he wore a chain of snowy agates around one wrist. 'Any sign one's carrying disease, leave him on the beach, obviously. Come on, let's get ashore before it rains.' The shipmaster left the stern platform and Kheda followed, joining the rowing master Bec on the ladder reaching down to the water as the galley's rowboat was lowered over the side. Godine climbed aboard and settled himself in the stern. Bec and Kheda each took an oar. They pulled for the shore, the boat silent with all three men absorbed in their own thoughts.

Kheda took in the view out to sea as he rowed. The *Springing Fish* was anchored halfway between the gently sloping shore and two small islands in the broad bay that offered deep-water anchorage even when, as now, the tide left the sands a vast ribbed expanse of glistening white.

Both islands were crowded with cook fires and awnings rigged against the drenching rains that were barely starting to abate, even a full cycle of the Lesser Moon after their start. Beloc fishermen were doing a brisk trade ferrying goods and people to the pale beach in shallow boats that they sculled over the stern.

What must life be like, in these domains of the central compass, that any warlord who can keeps visitors off his shores as far as possible, only allowing them to land and trade by day? What was it Daish Reik told you about these unknown isles, half a lifetime ago?

'The central domains have astounding riches, governing access to the heart of the compass as they do. Do not envy them too much. The fighting over such wealth is ceaseless, vicious and bloody.'

Kheda looked over his shoulder to the shore. Beneath a long continuous line of awnings rigged to make a covered market place, the islanders of the Beloc domain were waiting to test their bargaining skills against the newcomers. Some sat alone, others in tight-knit groups; all with samples of the goods they had to offer set around them. Then the rowboat grounded on the sand.

'Right, let's see what we can do to make Ikadi Nass proud.' Godine settled his mantle on his shoulders rather in the manner of a warrior settling his armour before battle. 'I'll see you later.' Stepping out into the shallow water, he cut a straight line towards a single, substantial wooden pavilion set at the edge of the beach. It was surrounded by a flutter of attendants, familiar urgent activity visible even at this distance. An immaculate garden on all sides was vibrant with new greens and the vivid flowers that the rains had brought forth.

'He'll be there a good while; the ladies of the Beloc domain supervise their trade directly,' Bec commented as they dragged the rowboat clear of the sea's inquisitive ripples. 'And they're generally well disposed to a good-looking man with a nice line in flattery. That should give me plenty of time to find a rower.'

How would you turn that to their disadvantage, Rekha? What would you make of such women, Janne? How will you ever get the chance, if I don't return with the lore I promised you?

'I want to try and find some fresh herbs,' he told the rowing master. 'In case that watery flux recurs in the prow crew, and I need more of the makings for that skin salve for Munil. He'll get rot in that rash in this damp, otherwise.'

'It was a good day when we took you on board, sooth-sayer,' nodded Bec with approval. 'I'll come and find you when I've got a likely oarsman and you can see if there's white seas or black clouds in his future, agreed?'

'Sorry?' Kheda was puzzled.

'I keep forgetting you're not really a rower.' Bec shook his head. 'New men on a galley, they either bring white seas, that's good tides, enough wind to raise a sail and save everyone's shoulders for a while. Black clouds, that's storms and foul weather.' He shot a more serious glance at Kheda. 'I've been on boats where men have been dumped on reefs, because we couldn't shake bad weather with them on board.'

'If we hit a run of storms, Ialo will be first choice for dumping on some rocks, if the rowing deck gets a say in it,' said Kheda with feeling. 'Not that I've seen any portent, you understand,' he added hastily.

Lightning interrupted Bec's laughter and a few drops of rain landed heavy on Kheda's head. He looked up to see the hue of the sky had darkened from the soft grey of a messenger bird's wing to the opaque blue-black of a pearl oyster shell. A massive roll of thunder rumbled along the shore.

'Let's get under cover,' Bec yelled.

Kheda ran with him towards the covered market place. Even that short distance left them both soaked to the skin as the rain came down in torrents, splashes bouncing up around their knees as the beach was instantly awash.

'Saves on laundry,' laughed Bec as he wiped rain from his face.

The awning rattled above their heads as Kheda squeezed water from his unkempt hair and untrimmed beard. The skin beneath and his scalp both itched.

You'd suffer a good deal less from the rain and sweat both if you cut your hair and beard like a true rower. But you're not a rower; you're a soothsayer now and that only until you can reclaim your rights as warlord.

Bec was looking around at the other people sheltering from the rain, laughing and smiling as they watched the spectacular lightning out over the seas. A few scampering children squealed with delight as they dodged in and out of the gouts of water pouring over the edges of the awnings, black hair plastered to their heads, brown bodies wet and shining with water. Bec's eye fixed on a group of burly men in sleeveless cotton tunics. 'Those look like oarsman.'

'I'm going to have a look over there.' Kheda raised his voice to be heard above the drumming of the rains on the cloth overhead. 'For those herbs.'

As they went their separate ways, Kheda drew in grateful breaths of the cool, moist air. Beneath the awnings, myriad mingled scents assailed him: spices, herbs, freshly killed meat and saller cooked into the squat cakes these domains favoured. The gusts of wind from without carried just enough scent of the island's burgeoning growth to remind him of the luxuriant perfumes that refreshed the Daish domain once the rains had come. Recollection drew his eyes irresistibly south. The rain raked the scene, drawing a misty veil across the bay to hide the anchorage islands.

That rain brings life, one of the first things every child learns, throughout the Archipelago. That it puts an end to fighting and brings cooler weather for cooler counsels to put an end to the quarrels that make men take up arms; one of the first lessons a warlord's son learns. Well, there can be no reasoning with wild men speaking an unknown tongue who fight with magic, so you'd better be home before the dry season prompts those savages to consider their next conquests.

Now, find out what you can here, before Bec reappears; he never takes as long ashore as he promises. Of course, it would be so much easier for Daish Kheda to find out what knowledge floats along these sands, everyone's comings and goings waiting on his convenience.

Kheda smiled at a woman much his own age who sat on a chequered yellow blanket with carefully tied bundles of fresh-cut plants piled high in front of her. Her hands were stained with green and she had plainly been caught in the rain, her simple orange cotton dress clinging to outline a fine-looking figure.

Kheda reminded himself of what he had come looking for. 'Do you have any grey spear, or you might know it as deer leaf?'

'I have,' she replied obligingly, finding a handful of the pointed leaves with their downy grey pelt of hairs. 'What will you give me for it?'

Kheda reached into a pocket and produced a rustlenut shell packed with speckled salve. 'This is good against burns, from fire or rope.'

Curious, the woman took the shell and sniffed. 'Fowl grease?' She sniffed again as Kheda nodded. 'Quince glaze? What else?'

Kheda smiled. 'I'll tell you if you've any aidour to trade for it.'

'Fair enough.' The woman produced a sprig of tiny green leaves dotted with vivid red flowers. 'Well?' She held it tantalisingly out of reach, her smile teasing him.

'Penala,' Kheda told her. 'Dried is as good as fresh.'

She pursed her lips. 'That's an interesting mix. Where are you from, friend?' There was growing interest in her pale barbarian eyes.

'The far south.' Kheda hesitated and then sat down.

The herb woman's smile was inviting as she drew up her knees and laced her hands around them. She wore malachite beads around both the elegant ankles showing beneath the canthira-patterned hem of her dress. 'What brings you so far from home?'

'An omen.' Kheda smiled to mitigate any offence in his brief reply.

At least a soothsayer's infuriating beard means no one will ask anything else, when you tell them you're travelling thanks to some augury. Would that mean no questions in that intimacy after loving? It's been a long and wearisome voyage with no tenderness to ease my path.

The herb woman looked at him, concern wrinkling her forehead. 'There's bad trouble down there, from all I hear. Magic abroad.'

'You need not fear such things hereabouts, surely?' Kheda tried to keep his voice casual. 'Don't you have lore to ward away wizards in the northern reaches?'

'No.' The herb woman looked puzzled. 'Where did you ever hear tell of such things?'

'Down to the south.' Kheda shrugged, swallowing hard to contain his frustration.

Down to the south but never here, not in all the domains I've visited, all the beaches I've wandered and people I've talked to. They all shrug with the same bemusement and wonder how I could come up with such a notion as they add my herb lore to their own and I go on empty-handed. Maybe

I should take some other payments. Haven't I earned a taste of sweetness by now, out of all the women who've offered me one?

'Cadirn!'

Kheda looked up to see Bec approaching, an unremarkable man at his shoulder, black hair and beard cropped short like most rowers, neck and shoulders carrying enough muscle to suggest a fair amount of experience with an oar.

How am I to learn even that there is nothing to learn, if my time ashore is so often cut short like this? Or should I take this frustration as a timely reminder of my distant wives?

'That was quick.' Kheda coughed to hide his ill-temper.

'Quicker than I imagined,' Bec agreed. 'There's barely a ship looking to set rowers ashore or pick them up, bar ourselves and a couple heading over to Galcan waters. This is Fenal.'

'Used to rowing a shared oar?' Kheda glanced at the man's dagger but didn't recognise the style. He was finding that more and more, the further north they rowed

'Several seasons now.' Fenal looked warily at him. 'You're a soothsayer?'

'I have a little healing knowledge and some skills at reading portents.' Kheda shrugged. 'I'm taking an oar to the northern reaches.'

The herb woman looked at Kheda with new interest and Bec grinned at Fenal. 'You'll be sharing his oar, as long as he says you're healthy and not ill-omened.'

Kheda stood up. 'Let's have a look at your eyes, over here where the light's better.'

'Every ship needs a healer.' Fenal turned his face obligingly. 'A death on board is a foul omen.'

'You sound certain of that.' Kheda was pleased to see no sign of any yellow in the whites of Fenal's dark eyes.

'That's why I'm looking for a new berth. Don't worry,

it wasn't disease.' Fenal stiffened as Kheda pulled down his lower eyelid to see the colour there. 'A man went overboard and sharks got him.'

Bec grimaced. 'There aren't many worse omens than that.'

Kheda took Fenal's hands in his own, pressing hard on the man's fingertips. The blood flowed back quickly, pink beneath the pale nails. 'Let me smell your breath.' He grinned. 'Your last meal had sharpnuts in it.'

But there's no sickly sweetness to hint at honey hunger devouring your blood, no acrid acidity to betray any stomach malady.

'Hard to avoid them round here,' shrugged Fenal with a rueful grin.

'Any old injuries that might give you grief?' He watched Fenal in case the man let a hand drift to a weakened knee or a sore elbow. He didn't. 'Your piss runs clear? No pain?'

'As long as I'm on a boat where we get a decent water ration,' Fenal answered with unexpected sourness.

'We can promise you that,' Bec assured him.

'You've more than a little healing in you, southerner,' approved the herb woman. 'You'll find a welcome in the northernmost domains.'

'Cadirn, I've had a notion,' interrupted Bec. 'Now the worst of this storm's gone over. Master Godine will be dining with the Beloc ladies, so why don't we go back and eat on the ship? Any portents for Fenal's joining us will be clearer aboard, won't they?'

And you won't have to part with any of your precious trinkets for the sake of a meal ashore.

'Indeed.' Despite the disappointment he saw in the herb woman's eyes, Kheda yielded to the inevitable. They walked through the slackening rain back to the galley's rowboat. 'Which side do you want to row, Fenal?'

'Whichever suits you.' Fenal rubbed idly at one

shoulder. 'You do swap sides aboard ship, don't you?'

'Every couple of days,' promised Bec as he took the seat in the stern.

'Last overseer I had wasn't inclined to let us move from the oar he gave us.' Fenal settled his oar against the pintle and checked the rope grommet securing it out of evident habit.

'Godine sees no benefit in an oar deck full of hunchbacks.' Kheda nodded to Fenal and set the stroke. Water pattered down on their backs, cooling and welcome, settling into the steady rain that would last until sunset or beyond now, bringing a freshness and good humour to the air. As they rowed, Kheda watched the shore retreating.

Can I find an excuse to go ashore again tomorrow, before we leave? Is there any point, besides taking that herb woman's interest to a conclusion? Is there anything to be learned here? How long am I going to go on looking? How long before I forget Daish Kheda and truly become Cadirn, useful rower, healer and augur? Wouldn't that be a better fate than returning empty-handed to my domain?

Hauling on his oar with mounting frustration, he broke the rhythm of rowing with Fenal and the boat lurched awkwardly.

'Sorry,' frowned Fenal.

'No, my fault,' said Kheda shortly.

They rowed on in silence, without further mishap, until they reached the galley.

'There,' said Bec happily. 'I knew we could eat on ship.'

'Got a bowl?' Kheda reached up to tie the rowboat securely to the end of the galley's stern ladder as Bec climbed aboard

'And a spoon,' Fenal grinned, patting a leather shoulder sack that had travelled a good few domains.

'Let's find you something to fill them both.' Kheda

waved him up to the galley's main decks. 'You can earn a meal working the rowboat today, whether or not you join us.'

And I can earn my keep playing soothsayer for Godine. I may as well repay him with some guidance, even if I can find none for myself.

'There'd better be some meat today, not more cursed leaves.' Ialo was already in the line by the cookhouse on the deck. 'We can't row on slops.'

'You won't row at all if I knock you senseless.' The cook made a perfunctory threat with his heavy wooden ladle. 'And leaves stop your gums rotting.'

'Any saller cakes?' asked Kheda as he and Fenal reached the steaming cauldron.

'Help yourself.' The cook jerked his head at a heaped basket before dumping a ladleful of leaves, roots and roughly chopped fish into the next man's bowl.

'Take one,' Kheda instructed Fenal. 'Follow me.'

'He's a practical sort, our soothsayer.' Paire came over to join them by the side rail, shovelling food into his mouth with a stained horn spoon. 'Reads his omens in anything.'

Fenal looked at Kheda. 'What do I do?'

'Break the cake over the rail, with both hands.' Kheda watched the pieces fall.

A clean break into two pieces, that's a good omen in itself. Plenty of little fish coming up to nibble around that half, something larger lurking beneath. Not so good if it eats the fingerfish. Will the sea birds join the fishes? One or both will shun food from a man's hands if there's overt misfortune in his future. Jatta taught you that and he's yet to be proved wrong.

He waited but no dark shadow rose up to swallow the darting silver flashes and a pair of raucous pied sea birds appeared to squabble over the pieces of saller cake floating away, stabbing at them with their scarlet beaks.

'I see no reason why you shouldn't join the *Springing Fish*,' he announced.

'Glad to hear it.' There was distinct relief in Fenal's broad smile.

Paire jerked his head towards the cookhouse as he scooped up the last wilted greenery with his spoon. 'Better get fed, Cadirn, or you'll go hungry again, soothsayer or no.'

Are you still waiting for Telouet to appear at your elbow with whatever you need? That's past hoping for. All you can hope for is he lived, even if rumour trailing in merchant ships' wakes is never going to tell you if he died.

By the time Kheda had retrieved his bowl from the shoulder sack slung beside his hammock on the rowing deck, he was the last to claim his share of the stew. The rain was coming heavier again, so he retreated down to the rowing benches to find Fenal and Paire deep in conversation. Most of the stern contingent were down there, relaxing on their benches as the rain drummed on the planks overhead. A couple played an idle game of stones in the circle carved in the midpoint of the gangway.

'Mind where you're putting your feet,' one said to Kheda, not looking up.

'This is Gaska ware, isn't it?' The slighter man was studying Fenal's spoon. 'You've shipped down from the northeast.'

'I've been all over these reaches.' Fenal paused, looking around 'You've come up from the south, Bec says. All kinds of rumours from there are blowing along the beach.'

'Savages have invaded the southernmost domain, Chazen, sinking ships and burning islands with enchantments.' The tense note in Tagir's voice betrayed his fear.

At least that's the same tale as every man who's come aboard in the last four domains; always Chazen, never Daish. They've no reason to lie, so that has to be worth something.

Kheda sat down a few benches away and reached inside his carry sack for the piece of sea ivory. He pulled the sharp narrow knife that one of the prow rowers had given him in return for treating a persistent abscess on one foot out of the split and battered sheath where he wedged the crude stolen blade.

'That's old news,' retorted Paire.

'Is there word of any other domains under threat? Beyond Chazen?' Kheda carved a careful scale into the twisted ivory.

'You've heard the latest from the Daish islands?' Fenal looked grim. 'These savages who took Chazen before the rains have killed Daish Kheda somehow.'

That prompted a sharp intake of breath from Tagir. 'We'd not heard that.'

Is that Janne spreading such a tale to spur other domains into coming to Sirket's aid, lest he be lost and their islands face the murderous savages next? Or is Ulla Safar encouraging the misapprehension, to save himself from suspicion of killing me? Or is Daish invaded?

Kheda marked out another notched and pointed scale. 'But the fighting's still come no further north than the Daish islands?'

If you can keep your hands steady, your voice won't betray you.

'Not that anyone was saying,' shrugged Fenal.

'And bad news flies faster than a honey bird with its tail on fire.' Paire looked to the others for reassuring nods of agreement.

I wonder how many other warlords know just how much news travels outside their message birds, ciphers and coded beacons.

'We can row fast enough to keep ahead of trouble,' said Tagir determinedly.

Kheda blew a frail curl of ivory away from his blade.

'We don't want to run from magic in the south just to fall foul of some barbarian wizard harrying the northern reaches.' He studied his carving, holding it up close to his face, not wanting anyone to see his eyes.

Can I face asking the same questions, time and again? Hearing the same useless answers? Just where are all these wizards that everyone in the south says plague the north like sandflies round a rotting fish?

'Our soothsayer'll be over the side if we see so much as a hint of magic,' joked Paire. 'The very notion terrifies him.'

'I've heard nothing about magic in the north,' Fenal reassured him.

'Take that for an omen, will you, soothsayer.' Tagir wasn't looking amused. 'Stop stirring us all up with your fears.'

'What are you talking about?' Ialo appeared, taking a bench uninvited.

'How there's no magic in these reaches, no matter what disaster's befallen the south,' Tagir said doggedly. 'And I'm not going as far north as Ikadi, just to be sure.'

'You don't have to go to the northern reaches to fall foul of magic,' sneered Ialo.

'You'd know all about that of course,' Paire scoffed.

Kheda froze, head bent, narrow blade dug into the ivory.

I knew you weren't listening, you foul-tempered windbag, when I tried to learn what you knew. You were too busy making sure everyone heard your poor opinion of my clumsy oar stroke.

'I need some of that burn salve, soothsayer,' Ialo demanded.

'How about you trade me some news for it?' Kheda withdrew his knife, careful not to mar his carving. 'What do you know about magic in these reaches?'

'Shek Kul's domain, due east from here.' Ialo waved a spade-like hand vaguely. 'There were sorcerers running wild in his very compound, not three years since. Look, it's this hand. Stupid fool of a fisherman—'

'Shark shit.' Paire shook his head emphatically. 'No magic comes this far down from the unbroken lands.'

'There was something going on,' said Fenal apologetically. 'I was rowing in these waters around then. Kaeska that was Shek Kul's first wife, she was executed for suborning sorcery.'

His words left everybody silenced, not just Kheda, halting in mid-search for another husk full of his salve in his bag.

Paire licked nervous lips. 'Why did she do that?'

'People said it was something to do with her being barren.' Ialo smiled, pleased to be the centre of attention.

'That much was certainly true,' nodded Fenal. 'She was known as such, all through these domains.'

'There are ways around that without resorting to magic,' exclaimed Paire.

'What did she do?' Kheda rubbed a fingerful of salve into a nasty rope burn raw across the back of Ialo's knuckles.

'I never did hear the full story.' The big man looked chagrined

Everyone immediately looked at Fenal who rubbed a thoughtful hand over his close-cropped beard. 'I'm among friends, aren't I?' At their emphatic nods, he leaned forward. 'Shek Kul indulged the woman's quest for a child as long as he needed her ties with the Danak domain to keep Shek waters secure. Then her brother, Danak Mir, was killed, so Shek Kul and his second wife busied themselves with getting an heir for the domain at long last. Kaeska that was Shek summoned some wizard, to kill Mahli Shek and her newborn child with her.'

'She must have been mad.' Tagir shuddered with revulsion.

'Shek Kul did kill her, didn't he, her and the wizard as well?' demanded Paire urgently.

'Oh yes,' said Fenal with conviction. 'Kaeska was pressed to death, every hand in the domain turned against her.'

'A fitting death for someone who'd use magic for their own ends,' Tagir declared.

'What about the wizard?' Hope and fear tightened abruptly in Kheda's chest like a physical pain.

Is this what the condemned Kaeska felt, stone upon stone piled on her pinioned body, crushing the life out of her as she laboured for breath?

'He was killed in a sword fight.' Fenal frowned. 'Or some such.'

But how? Who can tell me that?

Kheda returned intent to his carving.

'Skinned alive, that's the right ritual,' objected Ialo. 'Isn't it, soothsayer?'

'Flayed, certainly, so that the skin can be turned inside out, to turn any evil that has been touching the domain back on itself. And the blood falls as purification, obviously.' Looking up he saw the others staring at him with appalled fascination. 'That's what my father told me, anyway.' He smiled awkwardly. 'I imagine there are other rituals.'

The wizard would have to be alive, for the blood to flow. How would you go about skinning a man who was still alive? You'd have to drug him, surely?

'Whatever Shek Kul did, it must have worked,' Paire commented. 'The Shek domain's not suffered.'

'Most powerful in these reaches,' Tagir agreed.

'No mean feat,' concurred Fenal. 'Not hereabouts.'

Kheda looked for Ialo to argue the point but the big man nodded reluctant agreement. 'His ships are always well spoken of, though you'd be lucky to get an oar aboard any of them,' he complained. 'Once a man gets one, he rarely sees reason to give it up.'

'Who are the biggest lords hereabouts?' Kheda asked casually, smoothing the white ivory with the back of his narrow blade.

'After Shek Kul?' Fenal jerked his head northwards. 'Kaasik Rai's nearly as powerful, holds a domain centred on the biggest isle in these reaches. They're closely tied. Mahli Shek that is first wife now, she was born Kaasik.'

'Danak domain covers more seaways than Kaasik,' Ialo interrupted. 'And their isles are better placed for trade.

'We're not going that way, are we, soothsayer?' Tagir looked at Kheda, concern creasing his brow. 'I hear too many galley losses are blamed on storms thereabouts.'

'Storms no one else catches sight of,' agreed Paire, serious. 'And Danak's main trade is zamorin.'

'That rumour sloshes round the bilges of every ship I've ever rowed.' Ialo laughed derisively. 'No one's ever actually met anyone it really happened to.'

'Because Danak triremes carry them off, cut them off and trade the ones who don't die of the shock out into the windward reaches,' retorted Tagir.

'Cadirn!' Bec appeared at the foot of the ladder down to the rowing deck and waved.

'There you go, Ialo, you get to take your ease while I'm set to work.' Kheda put away his carving in his bag, slung it on his hammock hook over his bench, and walked briskly to climb the ladder to the open air above.

Godine waved to him from the stern platform. 'The rain's passed,' he said somewhat unnecessarily as Kheda climbed the steps. 'But I didn't think we'd see clear sky again today. Is that some portent? Cadirn? You look very serious. Is it some omen?'

Up on deck, Kheda saw the sun shining in an unclouded

reach of the sky, turning the clouds directly above the *Springing Fish* a curious yellowy grey. Away from the sun, the clouds darkened and, as Kheda looked, a single sheet of lightning flashed across the sky.

Undoubtedly an omen but what does it mean, and for whom? What does it mean for you, now you've just heard the first hint of magic in your search, the first suggestion of a domain where you might find the lore you are looking for.

'It would indicate a new course for someone,' Kheda said slowly. 'It'll take some time to discern for whom, and heading where. I'll need to see the birds fly to their roosts. Peace among them will mean it's a favourable omen; quarrelling's more problematic, depending on which birds are involved. The winds will signify different things, if they're veering and backing, depending on how they move the trees, and which trees and whether they carry any sweetness or taint of fire or decay. The sequence of scents might be important as well. The cloudscapes will have a bearing on how everything fits together, especially the colour of the sky around the sinking sun.'

'I had no notion it was all so complex.' At something of a loss, Godine rose and gestured to his seat. 'Take all the time you need. Let me know when you can see it all clearly.'

Kheda sat and stared out across the sea towards the sun riding unexpectedly bright in a tumbled mass of cloud and imparting a curious yellow quality to the light. 'Are you thinking of sailing east, Master Godine?'

Since there's no chance of me finding another ship going that way, not given what Bec said on the beach.

'No,' Godine replied slowly. 'North to Bir waters and then home to Ikadi. Why, do you see reason for me to sail east? It's out of our way and there are risks aplenty even skirting the Danak domain. It's not as if I deal in zamorin.' Distaste thickened his voice.

Did you come close to losing your manhood? Was it something you were threatened with? Most zamorin are cut as little boys and by far the greatest number are barbarian born. Can I overcome your reluctance with lies about what I read in the heavens, just so you can carry me closer to the answers I am seeking? Shall I put everyone aboard this ship in danger of losing their stones, just to suit my convenience?

That he could even consider such a thing left Kheda almost choking on self-loathing. He coughed. 'I see no reason why you shouldn't take the course you're planning.'

'Are you sure?' Faint apprehension clouded the shipmaster's barbarian eyes. 'You don't sound entirely certain.'

Kheda took a deep breath. 'Leave me to consider it a while longer.'

'Very well,' said Godine. He looked as if he'd have said more but, changing his mind, he took the steps to the main deck in two quick jumps, waving to summon Bec. 'I need to talk to you about those sharpnuts!'

Kheda sat alone on the deserted stern platform, staring unseeing over the water.

What is there to consider? You have finally got some hint of the lore you've been seeking. If you're to be true to everyone you've left behind, if you're not going to forswear yourself and deceive Godine with lies and false portents, you have to leave this ship, this life behind.

Can you do that? Can you face any greater test these days than sharing an oar with Ialo, tending the scrapes and bruises of the rowing deck, winning pathetic trinkets off Paire and Tagir with wagers over how far the galley will travel in a long day's pull? Can you do that? You've left Daish Kheda and his certainty so very far behind. Do you want to do that? Wouldn't it be so much easier to wait and see if Ikadi waters might have some lore you could use, if not just staying aboard till the next landfall, and the next?

If you do leave this ship, what possible resources can you call on to carry you over to the Shek domain, when you don't even know the main seaways, let alone the lie of the islands between them? Apart from a single golden bell, you've nothing worth trading for more than a cup of water from someone who pities you.

Kheda got abruptly to his feet and went below decks to collect his bag from the hook where his hammock hung. Paire, Tagir and the others looked curiously at him but no one asked him any question. He returned to the stern platform and spread out his paltry belongings: the seashells brought all the way from Ulla sands, wooden bowl with a crack in the rim, the spare horn spoon he'd won off Paire, a string of polished ironwood beads that Tagir had given him in return for assurances about the health of his distant family. He fingered the edge of the quilt, where he'd torn strips of the cotton binding to wrap red and swollen hands in those first endless, aching days at the oar. The bedding was even more stained than when he'd stolen it.

You're a thief regardless, aren't you? The Lesser Moon, the Pearl, is at dark now. All that you were as Daish is gone, hidden. And now you have the choice of a new course. What is it to be? How are you to reach Shek waters? Is this the choice before you: concoct a false augury or steal the means to buy your passage across to the Shek domain? Another nice question of ethics for debate between warlords who've never known what it is to lack anything that they might need or desire.

Kheda wrapped everything up and shoved it back in the carry sack. Everything except the spiral of sea ivory, gilded by the strange light. Taking up the fine blade, he studied it for a moment and then began carving. The scales were nearly done. If he kept at it, he should be able to finish the grooved and fluted tip by the time darkness fell.

Is that an omen in itself? Does it matter? Let's see what

the dusk brings by way of guidance. After that, one way or another, you're done reading the omens aboard this ship.

He began to work carefully, steadily, and the day slid away unnoticed.

'All right there, soothsayer?' Bec came to light the lantern hung high on the sternpost and Kheda realised his head was aching from the strain of concentration and the knowledge of what he must do now plain before him.

'I'm fine, thanks.' He paused to rub his eyes and ease his cramping shoulders and worked on. Music floated up from the bottom deck; Munil could put his flute to more uses than just keeping the rowers pulling in time with each other. Some while later, the cook called out to offer anyone still hungry a last bite before he raked out his stoves for the night and threw the embers over the side.

Kheda ignored the answering bustle. If he tried to eat, he would choke. That would reveal him to everyone as faithless; everyone knew how to read that portent. Showers came and went, none too heavy, their coolness still refreshing with everyone's memories of the baking dry season slow to fade. Full dark came and cloaked the water in a muffling blanket. Voices echoed across from the islands in the bay, bright like the light from the fires flickering on the rocks, shadows and shapes fleeting across the flames. Lamps glowing like polished amber hung around the Beloc pavilion ashore, music flowing liquid and graceful from strings caressed by the hands of musicians as skilled as any the Daish warlord had ever heard. From time to time, laughter threatened to go a little beyond what was decorous but any such excess was soon curbed.

Kheda moved to take advantage of the stern lantern and continued carving as the various galleys at anchor grew still and quiet, oarsmen retreating to their hammocks, the more favoured crew to their cabins. The night closed in around every boat, only held at bay by the lights making soft golden islands of each stern platform. All sound ashore ceased.

'You should get some sleep, soothsayer. We'll be heading north with the dawn.'

Kheda looked up to find Godine looking at him with veiled concern. The lad who fetched and carried for the cook stood beyond him, ready to earn his sleep when the galley was underway by pacing her upper deck to keep the night watch.

'Very true.' Kheda stood and brushed shavings of ivory from his soft, worn trousers. His fingers ached but the carving was finished. He smoothed the edges of the hole he had painstakingly bored one last, unnecessary time. He cut a length from the leather thong he'd stolen along with the quilt and threaded it through the ivory, knotting the leather securely before slipping it over his head.

'What is it?' asked Godine, puzzled.

'A reminder,' Kheda said shortly. 'Good night.'

'I'll see you in the morning,' yawned Godine, disappearing down the wider stair to the accommodation deck.

Kheda followed and made as if to go down to the rowing deck. He didn't, stopping instead to sit on the narrow ladder, listening. The boy's soft footsteps brushed on the planks above his head before disappearing towards the prow. A few rustles and snores came up from the rowing deck but no sound to suggest anyone was wakeful down there. He couldn't hear anything from the lowest hold where the rest of the oarsmen must surely be sleeping soundly. He sat in the darkness and counted off all the constellations he could recall, in order, as they would be set around the unseen compass of the heavens above.

Finally, he moved, climbing noiselessly back up to the accommodation deck. He walked with agonised stealth past light doors fitted with louvred panels to let a little cooling air flow through the niggardly rooms. Not that

Godine, Munil or Bec would complain. Lack of living space was a trade they were happy to make, in exchange for the solidly walled storerooms beyond, a share set aside for their own use, their own assets hopefully increasing with every landfall.

Who are you going to steal from this time? It has to be the shipmaster or one of the overseers. If you steal from Ikadi Nass, at best they'll be flogged, at worst hanged from their own mast. No warlord could let such a thing pass, and they'd still be under suspicion even after they'd been lashed till their ribs showed. You owe Godine more than that and you had better make sure you reclaim your rights at the end of all this, so you can make recompense for his losses.

Kheda passed the storerooms close to the cabins where the men slept, where Godine guarded the valuables he carried in trust for his lord. The space they were granted for their own use lay beyond what little light came down the ladder from the stern lantern. Kheda took the heavy stained knife out from beneath his tunic; a dishonourable tool for a dishonourable job. Then he realised he didn't know which store had been granted to which man.

Let this serve as an augury, then, a test. If I am truly doing right by my domain, following a true path, I should find something that will buy me a passage to Shek Kul's domain. If I'm caught and killed, well, that disaster's already overtaken the Daish domain, as far as anyone else is concerned.

With that realisation, the slight tremor in his hands stilled. Feeling his way as much as seeing, Kheda moved cautiously to the first door. He eased the tip of the crude knife into the crack between the lock and the jamb. Leaning all his weight, he forced it in further, at the cost of muted splintering noises. He wrenched the knife towards himself and the wood gave way with a loud crack. Kheda stood, motionless, distantly wondering why the heart hammering in his chest wasn't breaking his ribs.

No one stirred behind the cabin doors. The boy on watch didn't come running on curious feet. No prying face appeared at the top of the ladder down to the rowing deck. Kheda pushed the door and slid inside the store. It was windowless, the better to foil any of the two-footed rats that skulked around some insalubrious anchorages. A small candle lantern hung on a nail beside the door with a spark maker on a little shelf below it. Kheda lit the lantern and put the spark maker back.

Fool. You're a thief now. Steal things that you might need, and think how best to avoid being caught while you're at it.

He pocketed the spark maker and used his bag both to wedge the door shut as best he could and muffle any tell-tale light slipping beneath it. In the dim candlelight, he considered his options. There were several bolts of fine muslin in pale colours and one of a red-shot golden silk as well as hanks of goat hair for shawls. Kheda ignored them, too big, too heavy, too bulky. He sniffed at a row of middling-sized casks. Sharpnuts, lemon spice and more of that cursed agali root. He stifled a sneeze. All valuable enough but worthless to him at present. An open-topped crate had smaller boxes made of roughly split cane stacked inside it. Kheda untied the cords securing the topmost.

Packed carefully in a nest of grubby tandra fluff, he found a trio of white crystal cups carved like coiled shells. Relief made him almost light-headed. He hastily reknotted the cord, reaching for the next. That held more Ikadi domain quartz, this time a nested set of bowls shaped like vizail blossoms. One more and that would surely be enough. His hand hesitated before snatching up a third box. He opened it to reveal a rock crystal goblet, its rim ornamented with canthira leaves.

Enough. It cannot be that far to Shek Kul's domain and any one of these should buy you passage clear across the Archipelago.

Kheda grabbed his bag and stowed his loot inside. Then he halted, motionless for a moment, before taking the cord from one of the boxes in the crate, knotting it around the leather thong holding the ivory spiral beneath his tunic.

The leather is for the man you stole the quilt from. The spark maker will remind you of the debt to Godine and the ship. This cord can be token of your debt to whomever you're robbing here.

Unbuckling his belt, he slid the end through the strap of the carry sack before securing it around his waist once more. He snuffed the candle with licked fingers and the darkness pressed all around him. His ears reassured him there was no one wakeful in any of the cabins, the only sounds the slow night-time creaks and shifts of the ship's timbers and the waters gently lapping around her.

Where is the cook's boy? If he sees or hears you going overboard, he'll raise a cry for rescue. That must most assuredly not happen, even if the unexplained loss of a man will be taken as a dire portent. Well, until Godine finds this store broken into, his choicest trade goods plundered. Then no one will wonder why you fled. All they'll wonder is how you concealed your perfidious nature for so long.

A sour taste in his mouth, Kheda moved slowly up the corridor, one hand trailing lightly along the wall, the other keeping the bag at his hip from hampering him. The faint light of the stern lantern outlined the stair to the deck above and he blinked as his vision strengthened. He climbed slowly, crouching as his head reached the upper deck, his eyes on a level with the planking. The cook's boy sat crouched on the stern platform beneath the lantern, intent on something in his cupped hands. As Kheda watched, the prize flew away. It was a moth drawn to the light. The boy pressed himself against the stern-post, face turned upwards, waiting for the next inquisitive insect to appear.

Kheda eased himself out of the hatch, keeping low to the deck, on knees and one hand, the other taking care his precious bundle didn't bump along the planks. He hurried into the shadow of the galley's deck rails, edging backwards towards the waist of the ship. He'd have to go over the side somewhere around here to fall clear of the steering oars. Rolling over the rail, he lowered himself to the full extent of his arms, feeling with his toes for the telltale upper edge of the oar ports. He braced his feet against the wood of the galley's side, to push himself away as he jumped. A splash might betray him but falling among the oars would definitely make enough noise to guarantee discovery.

He glanced down to see the night sea sliding mysterious beneath the galley, shimmers of curious light here and there beneath muted wreaths of foam. The pain in his shoulders was agonising, burning, tearing. His grip was slipping. Kheda barely managed to kick against the side of the ship before his hand pulled free of the rail and he was falling.

The sea came up to meet him before he realised, still trying to straighten himself for a smooth dive. The impact battered him with a cold shock that made him gasp. The waters closed over his head, filling his mouth and stinging his eyes. He shook his head, kicking and striking out, the bag at his waist trying to drag him down and down. As he reached the surface, it was the night air that felt cold on his skin now. Wet hair blinded him, clinging to his face like seaweed. He tried to tread water, to wipe his eyes clear, but the weight tied to him made that impossible. He began swimming; rolling on to his side as best he could to get a sight of the galley. Was any alarm being raised?

As his frantic breathing slowed and Kheda managed to raise his head above the water, he could make sense of the sounds around him. There were no shouts, no voices raised in panic or confusion. He looked to see where the closest ships lay and began swimming for the darkness between the glow cast by their stern lamps, lapping waves suddenly noisy where they were trapped between the anchored hulls. Beyond he saw the faint lines of the islets in the bay black against the star-filled sky.

Anchor ropes, eels or sharks nosing around the rocks; all manner of hazards could drown him if he got swept among those boats. Kheda kicked out, legs and feet suddenly feeling horribly vulnerable in the endless emptiness of the waters. The thought of dagger-sharp teeth fastening in his leg chilled him more than the sea.

Is it true sea serpents don't even kill their prey outright, dragging it beneath the water instead to the slow agony of death by drowning? What of it? Your people face death by magic if you don't succeed. You can wager your life against the certainty that you're doing right. That should be trial enough to set against the way you've forsworn yourself.

Turning away from the lights, he struck out through the rippling swell for the blackness of the wider strait beyond the bay. This was nothing like carefree afternoons in the lagoon at home, playing in the pretence of making sure all the children could save themselves from drowning. The night and the sea closed around him. He forced his arms and legs in endless repetitive actions, pushing against the water, the bag at his waist a ceaseless counterweight, sodden bulk bumping his thigh with every kick. His limbs grew heavy, hands and feet numb, but he could not stop.

It's very simple. Stop and you drown. You have to go on. Can you go on? Will there be some land before you have to give up?

Some measureless age later, a current took him. He didn't realise it at first, not until the rising pace of the seas buoyed him up, carrying him onwards. He wondered briefly if he should try to escape it then realised he didn't have the strength. All that remained for him was staying afloat, moving forward, snatching a breath with every sweep of his arms.

When the end came, Kheda was too dazed with fatigue to realise what was happening. Something caught at his hands, the unexpected blow rolling him over, breaking the mindless pace of kick and thrust that was all he had thought of through this endless swim. A flurry of foam swept over his head and he felt himself sinking, helpless, wits too slow to cudgel his exhausted limbs into a last effort.

Something caught at his hands: rope, knotted into a net. He grabbed at it, twisting his fingers painfully into the coarse mesh, rolling over in the rushing water, suddenly desperate to get his other hand to the resin-coated strands, panicking lest he let this hope of rescue slip. The net moved, pulling him up. He clung on; feeling himself lifted half out of the water. The net wrapped itself around his legs and he struggled to find some footing for his nerveless toes. Strong hands hauled him aboard, grabbing at his tunic, his belt, anything they could reach. Voices sounded around his head but he couldn't make sense of the unfamiliar dialect until he hit the deck. He lay there, gasping, hands still tangled in the netting, trembling uncontrollably.

'Some catch we've made tonight, lads.' Concern shaded a man's good-humoured rumble.

'Best get him dry, Da.' Brisk hands hauled Kheda up to a sitting position. Someone else tugged at the belt around his waist. He managed some inarticulate protest and pushed whoever it was away.

A slap stung his cheek. He blinked and saw a young man's face scowling in front of him. 'You let us get you dry and warm or we'll throw you back over the side to feed the eels.'

That futile struggle had been the last effort he could

summon up. Kheda nodded dumbly and closed his eyes in dazed confusion.

May as well cooperate. What is this boat? Fisherman? Is that fish I can smell?

Someone stripped off his sodden clothing and wrapped a length of coarse cotton around him. Remorseless hands rubbed at his back and arms, pounding the feeling back into his insensate body.

'Here, drink this.' The first voice, the older man, closed his hands carefully around a wooden beaker and guided it to his mouth. The rising steam told him it was steeping thassin leaves.

Good for shock and exposure.

Kheda gulped at the hot liquid, feeling its course down his gullet and into his stomach burn like fire. After a few moments, he began to feel some connection between that warm core and his outer skin now slowly reviving under the merciless assault of his rescuers.

'Thank you,' he croaked.

'What happened to you?' A lamp swung nearer and Kheda saw four inquisitive faces looking down at him. The eldest was plainly father to the other three, whose eyes were wide with curiosity. The youngest member of the family was kneeling before him, a girl whose face was creased with concern.

Kheda managed a smile, cheeks stiff and lips cracked.

'What was it? Shipwreck? Fallen overboard?' persisted the father.

Kheda took another swallow of the warming drink. 'I must get to the Shek domain,' he managed to say, voice hoarse.

'Must you indeed,' retorted the fisherman.

'I must—' Kheda cleared his throat and took another drink. He was too exhausted for subterfuge. 'It is a matter of life and death.'

Wagering your life against the certainty that you're doing right; that's supposed to be trial enough.

'Is it now?' One of the sons sounded a sceptical echo of his father.

'I don't suppose he was swimming in the open seas for fun,' the girl countered.

'We could swing over that way.' The eldest boy looked at his father. 'We could look for coral crabs.'

That's what that rank smell is: crab baskets. I remember it from the harbour at the rainy-season residence.

Kheda finished the drink and gave the cup to the girl. 'Thank you,' he said sincerely.

'You should get some rest,' she told him sternly, before pointing at a heap of nets and sailcloth. 'You'll be out of everyone's way over there.'

Kheda briefly considered trying to get to his feet. Then he opted for half crawling, half shuffling on his knees before collapsing on to the comparative softness of rope and canvas. The girl fluttered around him, pulling at the damp cotton swaddling him. With an exasperated hiss, she gave up and draped a fold of sailcloth over his legs.

'What do we do with him come morning?' The fisherman and his sons had returned to the more immediate business of sailing their boat.

'Set him ashore or find someone else to take him on his way, wherever that may be,' the father replied. 'I won't risk the ill-luck that comes with hindering him, if whatever drives him is truly life or death.

Or you can hand me over to some Danak trader, to be made zamorin and sold for a slave. Who knows?

Kheda really couldn't bring himself to care, so let sleep claim him with an oblivion as final as drowning.

CHAPTER THIRTEEN

Such a narrow strait, and it might as well be a thousand leagues wide.

Kheda sat cross-legged on the steeply shelving sand and burned with frustration. The dark, shingle-strewn bay opposite was twin to the one where he sat, the shallow waters between greenly opaque in the aftermath of the morning's violent storm. There were a few differences, crucial for anyone hoping to make that short crossing. An ominous grey-stone building stood foursquare at the water's far edge, its roof walk patrolled by armoured men, windows no more than arrow slits. The double gates were locked in a forbidding barrier of black wood and iron studs in contrast to the open doors and shutters of the simple houses clustered some way beyond. More of the single-roomed dwellings stretched up a curving track and spread out along the shore on either side. Swiping away insistent sandflies, Kheda watched children scampering to play in the lull between the rains, men and women idling after the noon meal that had brought them respite from their mundane tasks. Kheda's belly had been empty and griping since dawn and hunger distracted him yet again.

I don't recall ever being so famished. I wonder what they've been eating. Well fed and well defended, there's no reason for these people to have a care in the world. Not with that fortress protecting Shek Kul's residence. No ship's going to land on that side of the strait without permission, without falling to a hail of arrows from the watchful rampart.

The galleys and countless smaller boats jostling for anchorage in these waters knew better than to try, clustered instead on this side of the narrow seaway. There were intimidating guardians of the warlord's peace here too. Kheda looked dourly at the heavy triremes drawn up at either end of the beach where he sat. Beyond, fast triremes patrolled the more open waters, on the lookout for any opportunist vessel taking a course it shouldn't.

'You look very serious, friend. Get caught without shelter in this morning's downpour?' As unkempt as Kheda, another of the pathetic human flotsam washed up on the shore dropped down to sit beside him. 'Me too,' he said ruefully, gesturing at the sodden, tattered tunic draped across his bony arm.

Kheda hadn't bothered to try drying his clothing. The humid air hung around like a damp blanket in any case. He nodded at the heavy trireme closest to hand. 'I was wondering if anyone had ever managed to hide themselves aboard one of those.' It was the only vessel he'd seen making the infuriatingly short crossing in the day and a half he'd kept his vigil.

His companion laughed out loud. 'Not that I ever heard.' He shrugged pale brown shoulders. Like so many in these reaches he was light-skinned enough to pass for a sun-darkened mainlander. 'Some say there are domains whose trireme captains will take a bribe to carry a passenger unbeknown to their lords but I wouldn't risk it myself.' He shook his head with a shiver. 'Not and get thrown over the side at the first hint of trouble. Anyway, there's no chance any of Shek Kul's shipmasters would do such a thing.'

'I don't doubt that,' Kheda admitted ruefully.

Not with the power and competence of Shek Kul's rule so indisputably apparent in every move his people make, every word they speak. His all-pervasive authority makes any

*claims of the Daish domain look no better than Chazen Saril's
ramshackle governance. You've nothing left to bribe your way
aboard with either.*

The fisher family that had saved him had more than
earned their set of crystal cups. Set ashore on an islet
ringed by busy fishing vessels, Kheda had been forced to
give up the canthira goblet for a frustratingly short passage
to a trading beach. Each of the vizail bowls had carried
him a little further east and finally, the single gold bell
that he'd hoped to give Janne had been the price of passage
here. Now he'd arrived in Shek Kul's domain, he had
nothing. Kheda fingered the ivory hung around his neck.

Nothing I'm prepared to give up.

'I'm here for another few days at least.' The newcomer
jerked his head at a handful of galleys anchored close to
the shore. 'None of this morning's arrivals will be going
my way. How about yourself?'

'Nothing for me so far. Any news to share from the
ships you've spoken with?' Kheda asked with studied
casualness. 'Anything from the south? I heard rumour Ulla
Safar was getting above himself.'

'There's word of warfare.' His unsought companion
looked puzzled. 'But that the Redigal and Ritsem domains
are joining with Daish to divide the Chazen isles between
them. Does that sound right to you?'

'I've heard stranger things.' Kheda sounded suitably
dubious but a faint warmth kindled beneath his breastbone.

*Surely that must mean Sirket is backed by the allies I
hoped my apparent death would win him. The three domains
must be proving strong enough to hold their own against the
invaders, otherwise the news would have travelled north
faster than the breaking rains. I'll take that as proof that I
read the omens aright, to follow the course that brought me
here. But how long can they hold out, once the rains retreat*

and withdraw the protection of the smothering storms.

Kheda looked beyond the scatter of little houses on the far side of the strait. A dark stone wall cut a line through the green of the trees. Shek Kul's compound: ringed around with high walls ceaselessly patrolled, a lofty watchtower raised above the main gate vigilant day and night. Just beyond the tower Kheda could see a corner of a central palace doubtless built with defence at least as much in mind as luxury.

Somewhere inside that impregnable wall, someone knows how Shek Kul defeated magic and drove it from his domain. I have to know, if I'm to take back any hope of Daish holding off these savages whenever they choose to come north.

'What I was wondering,' continued his new companion in a wheedling tone of voice, 'is whether you'd hook up with me for the afternoon.' He twisted to look up the steep slope of the shore towards houses tucked in among lilla trees now moist with new green. The morning's rains had made pools of the saller grain plots firmly edged with sharp earthen banks and ducks were foraging happily in the liquid mud. Hens looked on aloof from the shelter of fowl houses with fans of saller straw making frivolous crests in their thatch.

'Someone up there should be happy to let two strong men hoe their garden while they sit in the dry and cook a dinner big enough to share round,' he urged Kheda.

Or one strong man and a narrow-shouldered runt with ribs plainly visible beneath his tight-drawn skin. No, that was unfair.

Kheda could see his companion was entirely willing to work. It was just that his narrow frame wouldn't exactly inspire confidence.

'That woman there.' The newcomer nodded towards one of the closer houses, where a brindled hound with heavy jowls lounged in the shelter of an arched gate set in a substantial clawthorn hedge. 'She gave me some meat for cleaning out her hen run a few days since.' The ugly beast pricked suspicious ears at the pair of them.

'I haven't seen any of the Shek so much gather their own wood since I got here.' Kheda surprised himself by speaking that sour thought aloud. 'Travellers do almost all their labours.'

Being aboard that galley loosened your tongue more than you expected, certainly more than is prudent.

'What of it?' The newcomer was growing impatient. 'Do you want to eat today or not?

Kheda noted his companion wasn't the only vagabond looking enviously at the shelter and food the islanders enjoyed, doubtless why spiked palisades or hedges surrounded each house and most boasted hounds bigger than any Kheda had ever seen in the southern reaches.

The spokesman of a large village would think himself lucky to win the least of these hounds as a reward from his lord. A warlord would think himself generous to make such a gift to a most favoured warrior. Here, they guard chicken houses.

'If you're not interested—' The newcomer rose, dusting with ineffectual hands at wet sand sticking to his scrawny rump.

'I'm interested. I have to eat.' Kheda spared one last look for Shek Kul's distant compound.

If I can't get inside those walls to find out how Shek Kul defeated insidious magic brought down by his erstwhile wife, perhaps someone outside might know something of use.

'I'm Shap by the way.' His companion led the way up the slope towards the house he'd pointed to before. The hound in the gateway rose slowly to its massive feet, russet hackles bristling and loose black lips curling back to reveal formidable yellowed teeth.

'Cadirn.' Kheda halted, folded his arms and stared the dog down.

Authority rather than challenge, just as Daish Reik taught you.

It held its ground but didn't start barking, plainly reserving judgement.

'Good day to the house,' Shap called out, watching the burly dog with considerable nervousness.

A woman appeared on the wide porch, wary of drips sliding down the nutpalm thatch over her head. 'What do you want?'

'We wondered if we could be of use to you today, in return for whatever food you might spare us,' Shap said humbly, taking a hurried pace back as the dog took an inquisitive step towards him.

'Wait there.' After some consultation inside the house, the woman reappeared. 'You can weed the reckal plot.' She jerked her head towards a row of neat furrows where pale-leaved seedlings were already showing themselves. 'As long as you know reckal from everything else?' Her question was severe.

'We do,' Shap assured her with ingratiating cheerfulness.

'Come in and be welcome.' The woman came down the steps of her house and opened the gate, nudging the dog aside with her thigh. Like most of the Shek islanders, she was taller and longer-legged than the women of the southern reaches. Shap made sure he kept Kheda between himself and the dog, to the woman's evident amusement. Once they were inside, the woman caught up the beast's chain and brought it inside the fence, fastening the gate securely. 'Leave your things with the dog. He'll keep them safe.'

'Thank you.' Shap handed Kheda an anonymous roll of closely woven cloth tied tight with dark, much-knotted cord. Kheda set down both their bundles by the gatepost.

'Good lad,' he soothed the dog as it cocked inquisitive

ears at him. Realising the woman was looking none too patiently at him he followed Shap.

Reckal. Toothed leaves and dark green, reddish veins on the underside. Janne's cook only ever serves the roots and then only when he feels their orange colour will enhance the look of a dish, given they taste so bland.

'You start at that end and I'll start here.' Shap was already on his knees in the stone-bordered vegetable plot, teasing errant sprigs of green out of the moist earth with his fingers.

Kheda crouched at the far end of the seedbed, studying the two- and three-leaved seedlings with interest. He separated them with a careful forefinger.

Firecreeper, inevitably. Redlance, good for the blood and especially women's concerns. Aspi, leaves good against worms and yes, the root oil makes an excellent wound wash.

Shap looked up from his furrow, annoyed. 'The reckal's the only thing with toothed leaves.'

'There are some useful healing plants here.' Kheda looked at him. 'They could be planted somewhere else.'

'She said nothing about that.' Shap already clutched a handful of green and white tendrils. 'Leave the reckal and get everything else out, roots and all, mind.'

'Very well,' Kheda conceded stiffly.

'If we don't make a good job of this, we don't eat,' Shap warned sourly.

'Throw the weeds into the hen run.' Kheda glanced around to see that the woman had brought an embroidery frame out of the house together with a stool and a basket of brightly coloured silks. He watched her needle dart in and out of the white cotton until she looked over to see what he was doing and scowled at his lack of progress.

Of course, the Shek domain is celebrated for its embroideries.

Kheda bent hastily over the narrow furrow and dug his

fingers into the soft, damp earth as the woman exchanged a few disparaging remarks with someone unseen inside the house. His back was soon aching and his eyes rapidly tired of searching out the minute differences between one dagged-edged seedling and the others clustered round it. His thighs cramped as he hunched and shuffled along the row, trying not to crush the frail leaves he had left behind. Standing to add to his paltry handfuls to the pile of wilting weeds was scant relief, hunger twisting his innards every time. His tunic hung clammy about him, damp trousers chafing, and fresh sweat making him unpleasantly aware of his own rank odour.

All things being equal, I'd rather earn my food as an oarsman than a gardener.

Shap interrupted his thoughts with an unimpressed sniff. 'If you want half the food, you'll need to do half the work, friend.'

Seeing the skinny man was a full furrow and a half further across the reckal patch than he was, Kheda bit down on any reply and crushed an errant seedling between finger and thumb, a smear of green adding to the soil stains on his hands. Then he tried to pick up his pace but Shap was a full two furrows further across the vegetable patch than he was when they finally met.

'You take that lot to the hen run.' Shap stood up and groaned, digging a hand into the small of his arched back, shoulder blades sharply pointed, every bone in his spine clearly visible. 'I'll see what the lady thinks we've earned. Get the bowls.'

Kheda scooped up the heap of discarded weeds. The hens plainly knew what was coming; setting up a shrill clucking that brought the dog to its feet, alert for any suggestion that the fowl were being stolen.

'Empty hands, see?' Kheda spread them out for the dog and then offered one, palm down, to the brindled beast. It gave a perfunctory sniff and then sat on its haunches, allowing him to retrieve their gear, ears still pricked as it watched Kheda rejoin Shap by the house.

'You've got bowls of your own?' The woman of the house was waiting with a burnished copper cook pot, ladle poised impatiently. From the way she carried the pot, it wasn't hot. Kheda and Shap both rummaged hastily to find their bowls.

The broth left from last night's stewed duck eked out with a few left-over vegetables and thickened with the dust from the bottom of the saller crock. Janne Daish wouldn't serve this to visiting slaves to insult their lord or lady.

Kheda spooned it up hungrily all the same, savouring the few shreds of meat. He cleared his throat and smiled. 'That's a fine piece you're sewing there.' He nodded toward the embroidery frame.

The woman nodded a perfunctory acknowledgement, scraping round the bottom of her cook pot. 'There's a little more. Do you want it?'

'Famous for its embroideries, the Shek domain, even in the southern reaches.' Kheda tipped his bowl to drain the dregs of broth.

And what are you going to say now? 'Trade good, is it? No one put off by the possible taint of magic clinging to the cloth?'

Shap thrust his own bowl forward as soon as the woman raised her ladle. She gave him a second substantial portion, leaving Kheda with only a few thin spoonfuls of gruel. 'You eat what you've earned.' Her sharp black eyes dared him to challenge her.

'You've our thanks and our hopes that your journeys prosper.' A bare-chested man appeared in the doorway, tall and copper-skinned with shoulders as broad as any Kheda had seen on Godine's galley. He thrust his thumbs into the broad sash that served him as a belt, the bone

handle of his serpentine-bladed Shek dagger white against
the indigo cloth. The hilt was carved in the likeness of a
heron.

Why not ask him? 'Tell me, friend, just how did Shek Kul
put paid to his erstwhile wife suborning sorcery? Your warlord
will naturally confide such things to you, and why wouldn't
you debate such sensitive matters with a ragged, servile trav-
eller?'

'If I don't get a passage out today, may I call on you
tomorrow?' Shap squared his narrow shoulders, plainly
disassociating himself from Kheda.

'You can, not that I'm promising anything,' the woman
said grudgingly. She didn't include Kheda in this.

'Good day to you, then.' Back straight, Shap turned
on his heel and headed for the gate. The dog barred his
way, advancing to the full length of its chain.

'Get back,' Kheda snapped at the animal, daring it to
disobey with a ferocious scowl. He unlatched the gate
while the confused dog was looking towards the house for
guidance and strode down to the sea, not caring where
Shap had got to. Sorely tempted to hurl his cracked bowl
out into the water, he crouched down and, instead, began
scouring it clean with sand and water.

That was certainly a humiliating waste of time spent
finding out nothing in the least bit useful. What now?

'Are you the palm reader?' A timid voice at his shoulder
startled him from his frustration. A girl was looking down
at him, barely more than a child and painfully thin, dark
skin muddy with hunger, crusted eyes a watery blue. 'That
man, back there, he said you'd read his journey in his hands.'

'I have some such talent.' Kheda stood, shaking water
from his bowl and spoon. 'Sharing it with you depends
on what you can do for me.'

The girl dropped her gaze and dug a toe into grey sand
pocked from the morning's rains and churned by busy

feet. 'I found driftwood this morning.' She was indeed clutching a scanty bundle of warped and splintered sticks scarcely thinner than her own arms.

'Then trade it for food and bring me half of whatever you get.' Kheda kept his voice hard as the girl raised wide, woebegone eyes to him, forcing him to explain. 'I can't promise you'll like what I read. Those men from the galley that sailed this morning, they promised me a share in their fish but when I saw ill-luck for their rowing master, I went hungry.' Anger at that unforeseen injustice soured his tone.

The girl's face turned sympathetic. 'I'll bring whatever food I can find.' Swinging her bundle of wood up on one shoulder with unexpected deftness, she trotted away through the shabby encampment ranged along the high-water mark.

Why did you tell her that? Why did you agree to read her future? A lost waif like that, she'll doubtless fasten on anyone who offers her kindness and if you see some hazard in her path, can you turn your back on her? The last thing you need is some vulnerable child dependent on you.

Kheda watched her thread her way through the ramshackle huts of branches and half-rotted lengths of sailcloth. The inadequate shelters changed hands with other every tide as far as Kheda could tell, as men and women came ashore or left with some departing ship, trading whatever necessities or trinkets they might have for protection from the daily rains. Some of the travellers held together in twos or threes, others didn't even bother bidding temporary companions a perfunctory farewell before taking a solitary berth on some galley heading in the right direction.

Give these people enough hints of favourable fortune and you could claim a decent share in food and shelter, not break your back grubbing in the dirt to get it. You've forsworn your

honour already, thieving from Godine. How many nights will
you suffer an empty belly before you compromise with a few
invented omens for the sake of some saller bread?

A welcome rush of splashes distracted him from such
treacherous notions. Ladders were being thrown over the
stern of the heavy trireme stationed down the beach.
Troops slid down them, barely bothering with the rungs
as they splashed into knee-deep surf. The men came
ashore in two rapid files, rhythmic chinking from their
mail coats, hands on their sword hilts.

Kheda looked around for any sign of disturbance.
Travellers were scattering like a villager's ducks but only
out of fear of the Shek swordsmen. Some cowered by their
inadequate huts, others hesitated, tattered bundles
clutched tight. The most terrified found themselves up
to their chests in the waters of the strait before they could
stop. Some ran inland to find villagers with brooms and
hounds on ready chains barring their way. The dogs reared
up, baying with excitement.

The swordsmen ignored them all, faces unyielding,
pace unvarying. Behind, the trireme was wheeling round,
blades poised before cutting deep into the water as the
unseen rowers drove the ship along the shoreline after the
troops. Commotion travelled up the beach like a storm
squall. Men who'd long since traded away their pride
cowered on their knees. Women begged with futile tears
for protection from the Shek islanders. The column
pounded inexorably along the beach.

Insidious, contagious fear pulled Kheda to his feet. He
found his horrified gaze locking with the gaze of the
leading swordsman, the man's eyes dark and determined
beneath the gleaming bronze brow band of his helm.

They're coming for you. What have you done? Does it
matter? You're just as vulnerable as any other beggar on this
beach. You're unarmed. Resist and they'll kill you. Unarmoured

is unburdened. You'll be faster on your feet. But there's nowhere to run. Try dodging past them? They'll be expecting that. The men at the end will just spread out to catch you.

He looked, all the same, for any chance of evading capture and saw instead the scrawny girl who'd asked him to read her palm. The girl clutched a bowl to her flat chest, scooping something up with her fingers, sticky orange smears all around her mouth.

You're betrayed? Who wants you so badly? Godine?

The thought that he might have been tracked, might be called to account for the stolen treasures he'd traded made Kheda feel so sick that he thought for one appalling moment he might truly vomit. He swallowed hard and gritted his teeth.

Vomit, and that morning's backbreaking work will all have been for nothing.

The distraction cost him any chance of flight. The troops were on him. Merciless and impersonal, the leading swordsman threw him down on to the sand. Kheda raised his hands to ward off further blows but all that did was offer up his wrists for deftly locked manacles. Arms wrenched, he was rolled on to his stomach, agonising pain in his back telling him someone was kneeling there in plated leggings. Mailed hands seized his flailing legs, weighing them down with shackles. A foot came down on his neck, forcing his face into the cloying, smothering sand.

The sea couldn't drown you but the land just might.

As Kheda's outrage yielded to this terror, cloth ripped; his tunic, his trousers, he had no idea. On his back again, he spat sand and earned a stinging slap across the face. Opening his mouth in angry protest, a wad of cotton stifled his words. Cloth tied tight, gag and blindfold both, reduced him to furious mewling. Sand trapped beneath the cloth rubbed his cheekbone raw and hair caught in the knot pulled painfully at his scalp.

'Take him up.' At their leader's curt command, unseen hands lifted him by shoulders, feet. Belly up like a beast trussed for slaughter, Kheda writhed and twisted, chains rattling. A fist drove deep in his stomach.

'Give it up,' a voice growled near his ear.

With a strangled groan, Kheda struggled to catch his breath through the choking gag. The duck broth rose in his gorge along with a new fear.

Vomit now and you'll likely smother in it before they can get this gag off. Let them think you've given in. Struggle much more and they could kill you by accident.

He went limp. To his chagrin, his uncooperative dead weight didn't inconvenience his captors in the least, their jogging run jolting him into anguished breathlessness. Then Kheda felt the salt breath of sea water beneath him, a few splashes cold on his skin.

'Drop us a rope!' someone yelled. Someone else pulled Kheda's hands up over his head and he felt thick hemp pushed between his forearms. Just as he realised the rope had been looped through his manacles, he was hauled upwards with a yank that threatened to pull his arms out of his shoulders.

You lizard-eating, star-crossed sons of cursed fathers.

He banged hard against the side of the ship on his way up, once, twice, each impact shocking what little breath he'd managed to recover out of him. As he hit the deck with a thud, it was all he could do to drag some air into his aching lungs.

'Don't let him roll off the edge.' The shipmaster evidently had little interest in Kheda beyond that.

'He's not going anywhere.' A firm foot was planted in the small of his back. 'Not beyond my lord's cells.' That jest prompted hearty laughter all around. A strident flute signalled to the oarsmen and Kheda felt the wood vibrating beneath his cheek.

You've spent the last three days wishing for a way to get across the strait, haven't you? How many times did your father tell you? 'Be careful what you wish for, you may just get it.' Very well then, what do we wish for now? A rapid end to this perilous voyage or some improbable delay before you're taken before Shek Kul? Or will you even be taken before Shek Kul? Perhaps you'll just lose your head on the guard commander's word, once Godine's identified your thieving, deceitful face.

Though they could have killed you for that back on the beach, all the better to warn any other beggarly travellers against pilfering and treachery. You're to be put in a cell. If the warlord's swordsmen hold you, could you draw one of them into conversation, find some clue as to how this domain defeated magic, without bringing suspicion on your-self? At the very least you might learn some truth of events in the south, brought by message bird or courier, uncorrupted by passing through countless mouths.

Frail hope raised Kheda's blind head when he felt the grating of shingle beneath the trireme's hull.

'Over the side with him.' The shipmaster sounded bored.

'What, like this?' Hands grabbed his feet and arms, swinging him back and then out, as if to toss him bodily into the sea. Kheda's instinctive, futile struggles prompted laughter all around until the frantic heartbeat drumming in his ears drowned it out.

'Let's have him.' Even when they'd had their fun with him, Kheda's fear was slow to fade. He was passed from hand to hand like a bale of cloth, fleeting moments between one grip and the next when all he could feel was the empty air between himself and the sea below.

'Get those chains off,' someone ordered with cheerful confidence. 'We're not carrying him.'

Hauled upright, Kheda reeled, dizzy. As the shackles

around his feet fell away, he stumbled to steady himself.

'Walk forward.' the confident voice commanded, a directing hand firm on his shoulder.

Very well, since you insist. So far, so good. They haven't killed you out of hand.

Kheda felt for the ground with hesitant toes, as slowly as he could without prompting retribution. The shingly sand of the beach soon gave way to the hard damp earth of a well-worn path and Kheda felt the land rising under his feet.

Are they taking you to Shek Kul's compound?

'This way.' The hand turned him abruptly. The screech of a pebble caught beneath a door and grating on a stone threshold send an involuntary shiver down Kheda's spine. Then the heavy slam of the gate behind him crushed hope like a flower beneath a heedless foot. Inside the hollow square of the fortress on the beach, big stones had been brought up from the shore to cobble the ground and Kheda stumbled, stubbing his toe and ripping the edge of a nail. He bit down on the cloth inside his mouth, against this pain and worse, his bitter disappointment.

'Where do we want him?' someone new asked.

'Lower level, over towards the sea.' With these words the confident voice that had brought him went away towards the gate. The outer door opened to admit unexpected laughter just as abruptly cut off by its closing.

'Let's have no nonsense from you.' Kheda's new captor untied the cloth blinding him. Kheda gasped for air, wincing partly from the light and partly from the feeling he'd lost half the hair on his head.

His captor studied him with frank curiosity and Kheda instinctively assessed the man in turn. Copper-skinned with a close-trimmed beard peppered with grey, he wore a mossy leather coat of nails rather than chainmail and boasted a brass-trimmed round helm and ornate, burnished vambraces as fine as any Kheda had ever seen.

So lengthy service has earned you lighter duties than running up beaches to beat beggarly travellers into submission, twenty men against one. Which authority probably means you could kick me to death without anyone raising so much as a murmur.

Kheda hastily dropped his gaze.

The jailer made a non-committal noise. 'Follow me.' He turned and walked away without waiting to be sure that he was obeyed. Kheda stood stubbornly still, looking briefly upwards and around. Above the fortress's two rows of shuttered and blind inner windows, archers on the roof walk watched him, bows ready, quivers hung at their belts. Someone unseen laughed derisively.

How long would you give me, before you shoot?

Deciding not to find out, Kheda hurried after his jailer, pulling the rags from his mouth with savage hands. His captor had already reached a door, sorting through keys on a chain around his waist. Opening the door on to steps sinking into darkness, he disappeared. Kheda followed, blinking, twisting his bound hands awkwardly to feel for the wall in the gloom.

'This way.' The jailer was lighting a tallow-caked candle lantern. He led Kheda down a windowless passage past a succession of iron-barred doors. The only sound was the smack of the jailer's sandals on the stone floor and the softer scuff of Kheda's bare feet. A chill settled on Kheda that had nothing to do with the dark cool of the under-ground passage.

If there are other prisoners here, they're either past making a noise or these cells are solid enough to keep any cries locked inside.

The jailer halted, raising keys to his candle lantern to see them more clearly. He grunted that same non-committal noise and unlocked a door with nothing to distinguish it from the others he'd led Kheda past. 'In you go.'

There's nothing else I can do, friend.

Kheda complied. At least the cell proved to be clean and dry, with close-fitted stone walls and bare floor. Some light filtered through a grille set high in one wall and Kheda realised it gave on to the inner courtyard.

'Let's have your hands.' The jailer reached for Kheda's manacles with another key ready. Taking the heavy steel cuff off, he swung them thoughtfully by their linking chain. Kheda braced himself for a blow but the man merely made that same non-committal grunt and left the cell. The solid clunk of the heavy wood against the rebated jamb was as demoralising as the well-oiled snick of the key locking it tight.

Kheda rubbed at the bruises the manacles had left around his wrists. His mouth was dry and not only from the cloth he still clutched tight.

Are you awaiting my lord Shek Kul's pleasure? Does he want his palms read? Or are you dumped down here to see if fear or thirst kills you fastest? This isn't going to be a comfortable stay regardless, on a bare stone floor with nothing to soften it. Some beach scavenger will have claimed your bag by now, maybe even that mangy little bitch who betrayed you. She'll doubtless think herself well rewarded, the poor little fool.

'What can't be mended must be endured.' *Daish Reik told you that often enough. Forget what you've lost and consider what you still have to call on: clothes, torn but still serviceable. That disgrace of a knife gone, fallen from the sheath or taken by one of Shek Kul's soldiers, no great loss either way. You'll hardly be fighting your way out of here with a blade that barely cuts cloud bread. Spark maker still in your pocket, remarkably enough, not that there's anything to kindle in here. Ah, but there is, once it's dried, anyway.*

Kheda knelt to spread the cotton that had gagged him out on the floor. That done, his movements slowed. He rubbed a shaking hand over his beard. Then his fingers closed around the ivory spiral still hung around his neck. At least he still had that.

He couldn't bring himself to sit and ponder what the next twist of unforeseen fate might bring him so he paced the length and breadth of the cell. Ten paces by eight. He measured each wall in the other direction to confirm the measurements. Standing beneath the grille, he tried to reach the lower edge. He couldn't. He took a pace back and did his best to estimate the height of the grille, how far short his reach was, how high that made the ceiling above.

Once he'd calculated every dimension and even the volume of water it would take to fill the cell, Kheda sighed and sat down beneath the grille, face upturned. He could just see a clouded fragment of sky high above the hollow square of the fortress. He studied the scrap of grey intently. A figure passed the grille. Kheda tensed but nothing came of the occurrence. He came to ignore the fleeting shadows, even growing irritated at the momentary obstruction of his view.

Late in the afternoon, the sky darkened and rain began to fall, pattering softly at first then pouring down on to the cobbled court. Kheda stood beneath the grille, tormented by the scent, by the dampness softening the air. His throat ached with thirst but Shek Kul's fortress had been built with excellent drainage. All those countless measures of water flowed away into hidden cisterns, barely a drop falling on to Kheda's sweat-smeared face. Dispirited, he sat down, ignoring the steel-hued sky and the voices he heard passing across the courtyard.

Two of the cloud breads popular in these northern reaches tumbling through the grille took him entirely by surprise. One of the puffy, hollow rounds bounced off his head. He managed to catch the other before realising fruit of some kind was following, hitting the floor with soft splotches. Kheda's hands searched the floor, pulling apart the husks, cramming the softness into his mouth, licking at juice running down his fingers, the sweetness inexpressibly welcome in his parched mouth even with its hint of decay. He was so hungry, so thirsty, he'd eaten three before he realised they were lilla fruit.

Overripe and so bruised a penned hog would turn its snout up at them. With all the wonderful variety brought by the rains, they couldn't offer me better than this? Why should they? Or then again, perhaps they know exactly what they're doing? Overripe lilla fruit on a totally empty stomach?

Kheda grimaced. Exploration of the cell had proved there was not so much as a drain hole. He set the two remaining lilla fruit aside and forced himself to eat the bread, chewing slowly, hoping it would give his stomach some belated defence. Then he found he had to eat the last of the fruit, desperate to quench his agonising thirst. Setting aside the pungent, empty rind, Kheda took a deep breath.

Now what? Back to the fruitless circle of apprehension and denial your wits have been endlessly scurrying round? Fruitless? Not lilla-fruitless, not any more.

The food putting new heart in him, Kheda grinned at the feeble joke in the gathering dusk. Reaching for the scrap of cotton cloth, he scoured the stickiness out of his beard as best he could. One of the lilla seeds pattered to the floor.

A seed. A new beginning. What was it Daish Reik always said about unbidden omens? Stuck in here, you might as well look for all the forewarning you can gather. It's not as if there are any other calls on your time, great lord.

Feeling around in the darkness, Kheda collected the

other seeds he'd spat heedlessly away, placing them carefully in a fold of cotton. Settling himself beneath the grille again, he looked up at the sky and waited for nightfall. As he did so, he pictured the lower room of the Daish observatory tower, turning his mind's eye to the top shelf of books turning east from the door.

It was an age ago when Daish Jarai started that first journal of omen and interpretation, every augury faithfully recorded and analysed in the light of later events, that later readers might be guided in their own interpretations. It takes a full year for the heavenly Topaz to move from one arc of the heavens to the next and it has made full circuit of the heavenly compass no less than fifty-six times since Daish Jarai's day. There must be something, in one of the books so carefully protected from damp and decay, that's relevant to your current predicament.

By the time full dark had fallen, Kheda had run through his recollections of every tome on every shelf of that first bookcase and moved on to the clumsy volumes bound in age-old, cracking leather stacked beneath the window. Only a cool breath of night air falling through the grille diverted him from trying to remember exactly what it was that Daish Pai had read into an unusually high tide just at the start of the rainy season. Kheda looked up. The sky was clear and even with his restricted view, he could see the third of the sky that held both moons.

That must be an omen in itself. How often do you see the stars so clear this deep into the rainy season?

Kheda took a deep breath and closed his eyes the better to picture the unseen night skies more clearly. Opening his eyes, he reached for a pulpy scrap of lilla rind, good enough to draw a circle on the smooth flagstones, moisture gleaming faintly in the dim light falling through the grille. Making sure he was orienting himself properly, Kheda deftly marked off the arcs of the earthly compass.

Sitting back, he calculated the positions of the stars, once, twice, counting on his fingers like Mesil at his lessons, determined to get it right. Heart quickening, he looked back up at the sky. Yes, he had tallied the days correctly. The Sailfish was clearly visible behind the Greater Moon. Higher in the sky, the Yora Hawk backed the Lesser Moon set out afresh on its voyage through the heavens only the day before.

Another new beginning for the Pearl that is Daish's most potent talisman.

Kheda grabbed the cache of lilla seeds and set them around his circle. Humble as they were, they would suffice to mark the positions of the heavenly jewels. He studied the pattern revealed and a shiver ran down his spine.

The Ruby, stone of strength and energy, of courage and blood, was in the arc of enmity. With the turns of the stars over the days since he'd left Janne, the Yora Hawk had also moved into that reach of the sky. The mighty bird was a predator, a warning of adversaries, a call to watchfulness, even before the invaders had mocked the constellation with counterfeits wrought from the hapless cinnamon cranes of Chazen.

You have strong enemies, ready to take advantage of any weakness you show. Be fearful and know your limitations. Though the Ruby will pass out of this arc tomorrow, so bide your time.

The Lesser Moon joined the Ruby in that same arc and the Greater Moon stood to one side in the arc of self. It was waning and the Sailfish was swimming in that same sweep of the heavens, so often a sign of good fortune and advantage. Not here, with those stars below the unseen horizon. The Opal, symbolic gem for the Greater Moon and signifier of truth, reinforced the message.

Your power is declining, your liberty restricted, your luck not to be trusted. Seek conciliation.

But what of the Lesser Moon, heavenly counterpart to the Pearl, source of all the Daish domain's wealth, even if it was in the arc of enmity? The Lesser Moon was waxing. Didn't that mean intimate strength returning to the Daish islands, just as the Ruby indicated a decline? Kheda placed another lilla seed in the arc of Friendship, of help and alliance, for the heavenly Topaz. Marking the turn of the years as it did, the Topaz was the most potent of guides, promoting new friendships and inspiration. At present, it was backed by the Spear, commanding sign of male vigour, and strength in battle. With the Greater Moon, it bracketed the Ruby, confining it within the arc of enmity.

Your power may be slight at present but stay strong and others will come to your aid. Stay alert and look for new ideas.

What of the heavenly Amethyst and Diamond? Kheda shivered again. Amethyst, jewel of calm and humility would ride below the horizon in the arc of death where the stars of the Net were spread, sign of capture and restraint. Did that mean he was destined to die in this prison? What else could the Amethyst mean? It was a talisman against intoxication in all its forms, from simple liquor to the arrogance of power. He frowned at faint recollection of an intense conversation with Daish Reik.

'The Net is a sign that can mean good and bad at one and the same time. Capture is an ill fate for the fish but a full net gives the fisherman's children full bellies. Make sure you always see all facets of an omen. The Net is one of those signs that a warlord must always take special heed of. A hunter's net subdues a wild beast, be it jungle cat or rampaging water ox. The Net is a guide if ever you are faced with a great commotion in your domain, some disaster bringing chaos in its wake.'

Kheda swallowed hard. Nothing could bring more chaos than magic. Though death had many facets, that much was certain. It could stem from unfulfilled wants or could be the only means of satisfying a need, bringing an inheritance, material or otherwise.

Is this a warning that your death might be the price of saving your people? But you are dead, as far as anyone but Janne knows. Is this in fact a favourable portent, showing that feigned death will indeed lead you to the means of subduing the invader's magic?

As he caught his breath on this new idea, he realised the Amethyst was set in a straight line across the heavenly compass from the Topaz. The Diamond hung directly beneath, in the arc of sky significant for children. The starry curve of the Bowl was there as well, symbol of nour-ishment, of love and security. The Diamond was the strongest of all talismans against corruption, against evil, key gem for rulers, promoting clarity of purpose and faith-fulness to a cause.

That must be a sign for Sirket, that my son is meeting the demands laid upon him by my feigned death.

With these jewels forming three corners of a square, there had to be some significance in the last quartile. Kheda found his hand shaking as he set down one last lilla seed. The Sapphire was in the last corner. Slowest, most mysterious of all the heavenly jewels, moving from arc to arc only in every seventh year. Emblem of the future, of wisdom and of truth. It was in the arc of wealth at present and that encompassed so much more than mere possessions. A domain's wealth was its people just as a man's true wealth was his family. The Hoe would be the stars in that arc, even though they would be hidden beneath the horizon at this season. The Hoe was another symbol of male strength but of building and the benefits of working in unity rather than attainment through battle.

These four jewels link your past, present and future without a doubt. There's a promise of rebuilding here, of regaining what you have lost. That could be your future, if you can somehow see your path until those stars are brought above the horizon.

Kheda squared his shoulders. As he did so, the rain-stiffened leather thong caught at the back of his neck. He lifted the twist of ivory over his head. It was warm in his hands, firm yet still somehow soft, a paradox just like the horned fish that had borne it, a creature of the sea yet warm-blooded, red blood in its veins, a beast that bore live young and suckled them. His fingers traced the scales he had shaped into the creamy ivory, fading into a sharp terminal spike.

A dragon's tail, favourite device of augurs, symbolising the hidden and unforeseen. That's what it looked like to me, so that's what I carved, just like Daish Reik had always taught me. It seemed a minor omen, prompting me to play the sooth-sayer. How many itinerant fortune-tellers know the full complexity of the lore underpinning that belief? Not many, and those that do will keep silent about it, if they value their hides.

He set the ivory down on his fading circle, the spiral luminous in the dim light. It was each moon that marked a dragon's head, in this ancient and seldom looked-for reading of the heavens. The Greater Moon first, that was how it was done, according to the faded parchment stored in the recesses of the Daish observatory library, smeared and stained, crabbed writing blurred where mould had been scraped from the kid skin. Kheda recalled his incredulity when Daish Reik had first guided him through the words.

'*The Opal is talisman against the dragons of earth and fire. As the Greater Moon holds the foul beast's attention, it looks away from that which is behind it. Just so, the Pearl is talisman against the dragons of air and water, the Lesser Moon drawing the monster's eye and leaving it oblivious to what might approach from the rear. Therein may lie your opportunity, in times of trial.'*

Dragons. Beasts of magic, embodiment of the chaos wrought by all sorceries and enchantment. Could this archaic reading show him something with a bearing on his quest to defeat the magic afflicting his people?

Opposite the arc of self, where the Greater Moon rode, was that reach of the heavens where portents spoke of a person's dealings, for good or ill, with other individuals, marriage above all else. Kheda shook his head in silent bafflement. The Sea Serpent would be the stars in that part of the sky, emblem of the mysterious, of darkness and unseen forces.

What of the other dragon? He moved the ivory twist to mark the arc of the compass devoted to daily duty and physical health where the Vizail Blossom bloomed opposite the Lesser Moon. But that was a constellation almost exclusively tied to feminine concerns. Wouldn't this just mean Janne and Rekha were fulfilling their usual obligations, despite the threats surrounding them? He'd never doubted that. Inspiration failed him and another recollection brought his father's words out of the darkness.

'It's a warlord's duty to watch the skies, to watch the birds of the air, wild beasts and tamed, to seek out every omen and portent that might have a bearing on his people's future. You must read and learn all you can from the records all our forefathers have kept and trade your choicest and most potent talisman gems for copies of such records from other domains. Never grow so arrogant that you dismiss anyone else's learning but rather seek out all such lore with a humble, open mind.'

Then Daish Reik had laughed and clapped Kheda on the shoulder, brushing into oblivion the pattern of both earthly and heavenly compasses that he had so painstakingly drawn in the sand to illustrate some earlier point.

'On the other hand, if you spend too much of your time

*with your head in a book or your face turned to the skies,
you'll miss what's going on around you. If you've done either
long enough to get a crick in your neck, you've been at it too
long. Chasing meanings and interpretations can just leave you
as giddy and useless as a hound that's been chasing its tail.
Learn when to stop looking. The significance of past and future
is only to serve the present and it is your people in the here
and now that are your main responsibility.'*

*The only person whose life you can influence at the moment
is yourself. What can you do? Try getting a good night's sleep,
so you're as fresh as possible for whatever trials arrive with
the dawn.*

Kheda swept the seeds away into the darkness, picked
up the ivory dragon's tail and hung it around his neck
once more. He moved away from the grille with its
persistent draught and wondered how best to settle
himself on the unyielding stone. Finding his way to the
corner closest to the door, he sat with his back in the angle
of the two walls. He drew up his knees, feet flat to the
floor and folded his hands in his lap. Leaning a little, he
could rest his head against the wall and he resolutely closed
his eyes.

*It's not going to be easy to sleep in here, so what will
make for a distraction from these discomforts? Calculating
the paths of the heavenly jewels, that's worth trying. Where
will the others be, when the Ruby is next in conjunction
with the Yora Hawk?*

CHAPTER FOURTEEN

There's nothing to be done about it. Admit it, you're awake. Still, scant sleep's better than nothing.

Kheda opened his eyes, got to his feet and began pacing back and forth from cell door to window, stretching the stiffness out of his legs and back. That scrap of sky paling above him, he listened to the distant sounds of the rousing fortress. A handful of shadows passed the grille, sentries' feet slowing towards a brief meal and then the sleep they'd been warding off all night. Others went in the opposite direction, pace quickening, low voices bright with greeting. Kheda could hear speculation about something in their tone.

I doubt they're discussing the weather.

A voice replied to an unheard question. 'He'll get what's coming to him and never you mind. You check the roster of ships due and departed.'

Any further discussion was lost beneath the sound of sandalled footsteps. The rattle of keys heralded whoever had been sent to fetch him out of this hole. Kheda stood below the grille as the lock snicked and the door swung open. The same jailer as before stood on the threshold, lantern raised to see where the prisoner might be before risking the cell.

His nose wrinkled with distaste as he took in the early-morning consequences of the overripe lilla fruit. Careful to avoid that corner of the cell, he tossed a plain cotton tunic and trousers on to the floor. The draught scattered the dry lilla seeds in all directions. 'Clean and dress your-self.' He stepped back to allow a younger man to enter with a bowl and ewer of water.

'Thank you.' Kheda couldn't quite hide his surprise. Stripping off his foul rags, he tore the cleanest patch from the tunic to use as a washcloth. More surprises followed. The water in the ewer was warm and a small vial of liquid soap sat in the bottom of the bowl. Even without the chance to wash his hair and beard, this was still a vast improvement on sluicing himself in the sea. Seeing the jailer raise a quizzical brow at him, he concluded his ablu-tions. Deciding against trying to dry himself with the foetid remnants of his tunic Kheda dragged the clean clothes over his damp body and walked through the door, head held high.

'No nonsense now,' said the jailer perfunctorily as they climbed the steps to the inner courtyard.

We both know there won't be. I don't suppose you're unhandy with those gem-studded swords you're wearing today and even if you were, you should be able to hold your own against a defenceless beggar.

Then his step faltered as the old familiarity of an armed man walking one pace behind tripped him with a treach-erous memory.

Are you recovered, Telouet, and guarding my son?

'Open up.' The jailer called ahead to a younger man guarding the gate. 'On you go.' He sounded a little impa-tient, pushing Kheda from behind.

I don't suppose one question can worsen my predicament.

He turned to his captor. 'Where are we going?'

The man's smile showed gapped teeth in the grey of his beard. 'My lord wishes to see you.' He spoke with all the courtesy of a respectful retainer greeting a privileged guest.

Kheda looked again at the man's swords. Braided with silken cord to ensure a solid grip, the end of the matched hilts were golden hawks' heads with emeralds for eyes; not talisman gems but still imbued with the same virtues of heroism and fidelity.

'I am mindful of the honour he does me,' Kheda replied with a deliberate suggestion of the authority he'd thought left dead behind him.

What do you say to that?

'Then let's do my lord the honour of not keeping him waiting.' His jailer's mouth quirked with a sardonic grin though there wasn't so much as a twitch in his shoulders to suggest the bow that any privileged guest would expect.

I don't think I have anything prudent to say to that.

Kheda obediently walked up the slow curve of the path leading towards the upper compound. He lifted his chin, ignoring the mildly curious glances of those Shek islanders already up and about their dawn chores. At first the path seemed endless; the ominous black gates staying as far away as ever with every step. Then all too soon, the forbidding grey wall of stone loomed over him, barely a shade darker than the cloud-filled sky above. Beneath the shadow of the fortress, the morning cool was enough to make him shiver.

'Open in the name of Shek Kul!' His captor looked up at the mighty watchtower, hands braced on his sword hilts.

Kheda clenched every muscle in his body to quell a bone-deep tremor that threatened to shake his resolve to pieces. A distant rumble of thunder did nothing to help.

A warning. For good or ill? What arc of the compass did that come from? What other omens might be rising in whatever quarter of the sky I should be looking at?

A thin-faced man with circumspect eyes opened the smaller door set into the implacable iron-bound wood. 'Be welcome in the house of Shek Kul.'

Kheda acknowledged him with a nod somewhere between a warlord's condescension and a suppliant's gratitude before stepping through the gate.

You're no common guard either, not wearing that finery. Whose body slave are you?

The swordsman standing watchful in the shadow of the tower wore finely wrought chainmail polished to a high sheen and belted with a wide leather strap all but invisible beneath its silver-mounted gems and the four daggers sheathed across his belly. Each had the serpentine blade that was so prevalent in these domains and a pommel of opaque green stone evidently carved by the same hand into a different animal's head: jungle cat, water ox, hook-toothed hog and loal. Swords of equal magnificence hung on either hip.

The man stood, waiting for Kheda to finish his candid examination, expression faintly bored. 'This way.'

Silent and any curiosity well hidden, the lesser guards around the gate and along the inner walk of the wall watched them go. Kheda followed the impressively weaponed body slave and his jailer fell into place behind, matching his every step. They passed the single-storeyed dwellings that lined the compound's walls, for Shek Kul's slaves and his household servants. Strange yet familiar scents and sounds all around him, a curious calm came over Kheda.

Quarters more extensive and more luxurious than anything Daish retainers can boast, though the bustle over breakfast and murmur over the day's prospects seem much the same. Are they wondering what Shek Kul wants with you; non-descript palm reader brought before such a mighty lord? Presumably he's not to hang you out of hand; he could have done that any time since you were seized. That good fortune will suffice for the moment. Though I wonder how far this courteous jailer's patience will stretch.

Kheda slowed slightly, taking his time to look around Shek Kul's extensive gardens, lavishly planted with carefully nurtured bushes and trees. Kheda recognised

redlance, firefew and all three varieties of penala. None of
the shrubs had so much as a twig out of place, not a leaf
marring the smoothly raked perfection of the rich black
earth beneath them. The paths between the beds were pale
in contrast, lined with creamy pebbles brought from some
distant beach. They reached a fork and the turn the well-
armoured slave took led past an airy aviary of gilded lilla
wood. Tiny brown vira finches scuffed and squabbled in
the dust and Kheda slowed still more, watching for as long
as he could though none of the birds were doing anything
that might conceivably indicate an omen.

Ahead, the slave preceding him had slowed too, never
looking back but plainly attuned to the pace of whoever
was following him.

A very well-trained body slave.

The man behind him coughed meaningfully and
Kheda's smile faded. They took another path past the
wide white bowl of a fountain with a marble canthira tree
glistening at its heart. The central keep of the compound
lay ahead, each floor marked by serried rows of shuttered
windows.

*The heart of Shek Kul's power, the fortress where his might
is supported by the guile and subtlety of his wives, where their
children grow in understanding of their inheritance and all
that comes with it.*

Kheda braced himself and was promptly wrong-footed
when the slave ahead took an abrupt turn to skirt the solid
square. Beyond, the gardens stretched out in artless curves
and delightful arbours refreshed by the kiss of the rain
and blooming in a riot of grateful colours. The scene had
been masterfully designed to soothe and enchant, though
the slave seemed oblivious to its charms, heading for a
long and lofty building set in a sea of white pebbles.
Kheda's throat tightened, blood racing in his veins.

The well-armoured slave opened the door and stood

aside to let Kheda precede him. With his erstwhile jailer
at his heels, he went inside. The slave pulled the door closed
and stood in front of it, hands thrust through his belt.

*You won't be leaving unless that man's own lord gives him
the word.*

The older slave, his jailer, swept past Kheda without a
backward glance. He strode down the central aisle of the
great, empty hall, measured tread on the polished black
marble echoing back from the walls. Swirls of green stone
marked his path, ending in a complex, interlaced circle
below a dais of three broad steps. The slave climbed the
steps to stand beside a throne of black wood inlaid with
silver and patterned with a criss-crossing lattice of green
stones and diamonds.

*Jade and malachite, neither very common in the southern
isles. Jade can be pale as mother's milk or dark as a rainy-
season sea but any shade is a talisman to link you to all the
wisdom of past lives in your domain. Malachite is a stone for
truth and self-knowledge and of course the silver will promote
cool and balanced judgement.*

Kheda's jumbled thoughts stilled to wariness as the
man seated on the throne beckoned him forward with one
slowly crooked gold-ringed finger. Shek Kul, warlord of
this sizeable and strategically significant domain was a
burly man dressed in a long tunic of black silk and green
trousers tied at the ankle in the northern style. The loose
cut of his clothes did nothing to disguise the powerful
muscles of his arms and thighs, just as their informality
did nothing to lessen the authority of his stern face. Dark
eyes looked down a hooked nose, heavy brows just hinting
at a frown. His skin was darker than many Kheda had
seen so far in this domain though still appreciably lighter
than his own. Shek Kul wore his coarse black hair long
and swept back from his face with oil that glistened as
well in his long, meticulously trimmed beard. Grey was

spreading through both hair and beard, at his temples and beneath his full-lipped mouth.

Daish Reik would have been much this age, had he lived.

'Who are you?' Shek Kul's words echoed through the empty hall, voice as imposing as his face, deep and resonant from his barrel chest.

Kheda halted in the middle of the green-stone circle. 'A traveller.'

Shek Kul sat, elbows on his knees, staring down at Kheda. 'I hear the southern reaches in your voice.'

'I have come from the south,' Kheda agreed cautiously.

'Far from home,' observed Shek Kul sharply. 'Where would that be?'

Kheda took another careful breath. 'I have no home.'

'None that you may return to, perhaps.' Shek Kul's thick black brows knitted into an unmistakable scowl. 'Answer my question. What domain nourished your ungrateful, unworthy youth?'

'I was neither ungrateful nor unworthy.' Kheda paused and moderated his tone. 'But my youth is past and may not be revisited.'

'You chop your answers finer than my cook chops pepper pods. Very well,' Shek Kul continued with surprising silkiness, 'I will play this game until I tire of it. You may not revisit your past yet we are each and every one the sum of all we have experienced. Everything we have done forms a link in the unseen chains that tie past to future. Where are your chains?'

'Back in the fortress on your shore,' Kheda said boldly. 'Your men did not think them necessary this morning.'

'I trust their judgement in many things.' Shek Kul smiled but it was not an expression to inspire reassurance. 'Though they'll load you with enough chains to force you to your knees if I wish it.'

'As is only right and proper, for men in service of so

great a lord.' Kheda tried to sound suitably humble.

Unexpectedly, Shek Kul laughed. 'Don't seek to flatter or grovel, traveller. It doesn't become you.'

Kheda ducked his head submissively.

'A traveller from the south,' Shek Kul continued thoughtfully. 'That's something in your favour, at least.'

Kheda couldn't help himself. He looked up.

Shek Kul was no longer smiling. 'You arrive on my shores, alone. No one knows where you've come from and you certainly don't care to share that information with anyone. You say you're looking for passage onwards but no one sees you talking to newly arrived shipmasters. No one knows which domain you're trying to reach. All I hear is that you read palms to fill your belly, which I find sufficiently curious to want to know more. You make safe enough predictions, I hear, nothing too outrageous, no promises of startling good fortune just beyond the turn of the stars. Any inadequate preying on men who prefer to work their way through life can do as much.' The warlord paused, eyes keen. 'Yet such parasites are far keener than you to spread word of their talents, hoping to bleed more victims dry with promises and blandishments. They don't, as a rule, insist on sufficiently unfavourable readings to be left abused and hungry. How will you win the reputation to keep you in idle luxury?'

Kheda kept his face impassive and his mouth shut.

'Still, you've avoided gloomy prognostications of general doom,' Shek Kul continued. 'As far as I've been able to ascertain, you haven't predicted death by disease or starvation or even drowning for anyone, though by all the stars, those travelling between the domains can fear that fate. My thanks for not casting such shadows over my domain with your skills.' The warlord's sarcasm cut like a lash.

'You might care to be grateful in return. If you were sharing your skills with an eastern accent, had your insights promised ill fortune for those drifting through my waters, you'd have vanished from my beach before the tide had washed away your footsteps. I'll not have my enemies sending false augurs to spread ill feeling in my domain, stirring up dissatisfaction and dissension where they may. I find even the cleverest, most treacherous tongue can be stilled by decapitation.'

Shek Kul paused to let the threat hang menacing in the empty hall. 'I have to ask myself though, are you merely biding your time before setting rumblings of disquiet along my beaches, rumours casting doubts over my future and that of all who stay loyal to me?' He leaned back, face hard. 'I'll have your answer to that, traveller, or my men will beat it out of you.'

'I am no soothsayer to speak ill of your domain.' Kheda shook his head vehemently. 'I only read palms and those can show no more than the life of one person.'

'So say all the sages,' agreed Shek Kul, voice cold. 'And those books that none outside a domain's inner circles generally ever see. There's another puzzle for me.

'You're a man of many puzzles, traveller. You deny you're a soothsayer yet you wear a dragon's tail around your neck. Granted, a galley rat might wear such a trinket, if he had won it in trade, but he'd just as readily trade it for a full belly and a night out of the rain. You won't give it up, preferring to chance the mercy of the skies and grubbing up weeds in a reckal patch for the sake of a meal.'

Shek Kul leant back in his throne, folding his formidable arms. 'More puzzles. You'll scrabble in the earth willingly enough but you show more interest in healing plants than those that'll fill a hungry belly. You're also a slow and clumsy worker. Do you realise what a poor bargain you offer? Is that why you can't accept what you earn with dignity?'

Kheda was stung into replying. 'I offer the best bargain I can.'

Shek Kul nodded as if the younger man had confirmed something. 'Ah, but you are just not accustomed to trading your labour. You're not in the habit of fleeing a domain's swordsmen either. Sezarre tells me you plainly had no expectation that they might be coming for you, until they were all but on you.' Shek Kul nodded beyond Kheda to the slave guarding the door and smiled.

'Everyone else on that beach ran, either from knowledge of their own guilt or, to be fair, from simple prudence. There are lords in these reaches who'll beat everyone friendless on a trading beach, for the supposed sins of one or two. Indai Forl tells me it helps keep the innocent honest as well as rebuking the guilty.' He raised a hand. 'But I am straying from the question. Other puzzles hang around you, traveller. Your workmate yesterday might be more used to trading his labour but he's not in the least accustomed to dogs. Few travellers are. Why else do you think I keep those particular islanders so well provided with the largest and most intimidating hounds I can breed? Though you didn't find them in the least unnerving. I ask myself this: where would you have learned such familiarity with dogs other than inside a warlord's compound? So I ask you once more; where is your home domain?'

Kheda swallowed. 'I have no home.'

'You've your own jewels safe between your legs, I'll say that much for you.' Shek Kul sounded more curious than approving. 'Do you realise what you risk by defying me like this? Do you want me to turn you over to Sezarre, to Delai, to have them wring the truth from you?' The warlord nodded again towards the door and then jerked his head towards his own bodyguard, Kheda's erstwhile jailer. 'Of course you don't. Then why are you prepared to run that risk?'

This was plainly no rhetorical question. Kheda chose

his words with exquisite care. 'For the present, I have no home. I have no domain. I did once, obviously. There are those I left behind. I would not see them suffer for my sake.' As soon as those words left his mouth, he regretted them.

Shek Kul bent forward in one swift movement. 'You've done something that warrants punishment?' Delai clapped a hand to a sword hilt before he could restrain himself and a shiver of chainmail from the door suggested Sezarre had done the same.

A guilty quiver ran down Kheda's spine. 'I have nothing to answer for in your domain,' he managed to say.

Not as long as Godine sailed north as he said he would.

'You seem to speak the truth and yet not all of the truth, if I am any judge.' Shek Kul relaxed in his throne again. 'You have remarkable eyes, do you realise that?'

Kheda was startled by the abrupt change of subject. 'I'm sorry?'

'There's no question over your southern origin,' mused Shek Kul. 'Your skin makes that plain, as does your speech. You're recently come north too, no local dialect's coloured your words. But those eyes show mixed blood, there's no question of that.' He waved a ring-laden hand in an airy gesture. 'Hereabouts, that much closer to the barbarians, we see all shades of skin, hair and eye, thanks to slaves traded down from the unbroken lands. Plenty get traded further on south. Are you some slave's get? Are you some slave? That would explain your familiarity with the ways of a warlord's compound. Should I be sending word south to enquire if any of my brother rulers seek a runaway of your description? Such a runaway must have committed a grave crime, to be fleeing so far north. I am not inclined to shelter such a guilty man, even if he has done nothing to warrant punishment in my domain.' His words were chilling.

'I am no slave.' Kheda lifted his chin and stared defiantly at Shek Kul.

Read the truth in my eyes if you can.

'No, you'd have had that arrogance beaten out of you, if you were.' A slow smile curved Shek Kul's generous lips. 'So where did you get those curious green eyes? Hereabouts, our wives heed their duty to bring new blood into the domain and many choose their own body slaves to do the honours. Is that the way of the southern reaches? Let's consider that notion. If you'd been born into a warlord's household, that would solve a great many puzzles. It might even answer the greatest mystery of all. Just how is it that you know how to draw the entire compass of the heavens from the barest squint at the skies? Come now, you don't imagine I would imprison you and not have someone keep a watch on you? Delai was quite fascinated, especially when you set your dragon's tail in the circle. He knows enough to recognise such things, though he would never presume to try them himself. That does incline me to believe your assurance that you are no slave.'

Kheda felt as cold as the marble beneath his feet. A tremor began in his legs and he couldn't stop it shaking the rest of him. He stared at the green swirls in the black floor and tried to think what to say. He came up with nothing.

'Mixed blood from the south, where it's comparatively rare among the free islanders, yet most assuredly no slave and as well versed in star gazing as any man I know.' Shek Kul heaved a sigh. 'What else could you be? You're not some zamorin set adrift to safeguard an elder brother's rights. A second son acknowledged lest some disaster befall the heir apparent perhaps? Are you a son raised to support an elder sister born to rule by right of age and suddenly superfluous now that she has married a man to rule her swordsmen for her? No, I cannot bring to mind any domain where any such circumstance applies.' The warlord fell silent.

Noises floated through the high windows set just beneath the eaves of the imposing hall. Someone ran up a gravel path, followed by laughter. A single fluting call prompted a liquid torrent of bird song. Breezes stirred the banners hung high in the ceiling and the silk pennants made soft snapping noises. The bird song took on a wary note. Another distant rumble of thunder sounded. Within the great hall, all was hushed expectation. Kheda looked up to find Shek Kul studying him intently.

'Daish Kheda is dead,' Shek Kul said in measured tones.

'I have heard that said.' Kheda found he was no longer shaking. 'Though his body has not been found.'

'No man of such stature could return from the dead.' There was warning in the Shek warlord's words. 'An islander, a fisherman or hunter given up for lost in a storm or an earth tremor, they might return and such good fortune would be celebrated. For a ruler declared dead to return and challenge the right of his son's succession, that would be a calamity to blight a domain for a full cycle of stars.'

'That would depend on the circumstances, surely, and such portents as were observed,' said Kheda forcefully.

'The Daish year thus far has been all disaster,' Shek Kul observed bluntly. 'The loss of their lord in such ill-omened circumstance would have been calamity enough, yet they're assailed with magic as well, if all I hear is true.'

'The Chazen domain was all but lost to savages with wizards' magic backing their attacks,' said Kheda grimly. 'The Daish domain still held out when I came north. I don't know how long they can last. The most powerful lords of those reaches couldn't see beyond their own squabbles to the necessity of joining forces against a menace that could destroy them all.'

'Such bickering played a part in Daish Kheda's

untimely demise?' Shek Kul looked thoughtful.

'I have heard that said,' Kheda replied evasively.

'Dawn will always follow the darkest night.' Shek Kul looked him straight in the eye. 'My sources tell me Ritsem Caid, Redigal Coron, Sarem Vel and Aedis Harl have all massed substantial numbers of heavy triremes at their southernmost outposts. At the first signal from Daish Sirket that these invaders are coming north, they will sail in his support.'

'That is indeed good news, for that domain.' Kheda didn't mind letting Shek Kul see his relief, not, in truth, that he could have concealed it.

Shek Kul watched him closely, discreet amusement deepening the crow's feet around his eyes. 'I hear there is some rift between Ulla Safar and Viselis Ils, though I've yet to hear what's caused it.'

The warlord spoke as one equal to another and Kheda replied in kind. 'I imagine Ulla Safar would turn greedy eyes to the northern isles of Sarem if Vel was sending his forces south. Aedis and Sarem have been allies since – since their warlords' great-grandsires' day. Safar would doubtless suggest Viselis Ils move against the Aedis islands at the same time.'

'Viselis Ils would not be interested in such conquest?' enquired Shek Kul.

'Without the threat of magic in the south, he would be tempted.' Kheda pursed thoughtful lips. 'It must have been Redigal negotiation that persuaded the Aedis and Sarem lords to ready their forces. Viselis Ils will not want to fall out with Redigal Coron.'

Shek Kul nodded. He looked down and rubbed some smudge from a sparkling diamond ring. 'You're plainly well versed in the intricacies of southern diplomacy. More than that, you appreciate the wider interests of those reaches, rather than the narrow pursuit of a single domain's advantage. I am surprised that such a man would turn tail and flee north, when danger threatened his people.' If Shek Kul wasn't looking at Kheda, the faithful Delai was watching him closely.

'Triremes, warriors, every defence that the Daish domain can muster is drawn up against the savages and those that wield their magic. One sword, my sword could add little to that strength.' Kheda folded his arms, challenge in his stance. 'There are other weapons and one of the most important is knowledge of your enemy. We in the southern reaches know little of wizardry, still less of how it may be defeated if force of arms proves inadequate in the face of magic. You in the north live constantly on your guard against barbarian wizards. One man could carry such lore to the south and bring more help than an entire domain's invasion fleet.'

Shek Kul slowly raised his face. 'How does that search bring you to my domain?'

'I have heard that your wisdom and resolve rescued your people from the peril of magic some years since.' Now Kheda looked Shek Kul in the eye.

'That's what they're saying on the beaches and across the galley decks?' The warlord's question was harsh.

'It is. Any soothsayer hinting otherwise would find scant belief filling his bowl,' Kheda added boldly.

'I wonder that my neighbours fail to read such wisdom in the skies,' Shek Kul muttered sourly. 'You seek lore to counter magic? There are those who'd beat you bloody merely for that curiosity. Others would drive you into the sea, just on suspicion that the magic plaguing the south might have touched you. Has it?' he snapped.

'No.' Kheda hesitated. 'I have seen the foulness wrought by magic. I have seen those it has burned alive and done my best to tend their hurts. I— That is, I was with those who went to discover Chazen Saril's fate. We found sorcerous monsters made from the very beasts of the domain and we killed them. We burned the isle their tread had contaminated to black ashes,' he emphasised.

Shek Kul said nothing. The silence lengthened. All at once, the Shek warlord rose from his throne. 'I must think on this.' He swept past Kheda, striding for the far door. Delai kept one pace behind him, the warrior's hand on his sword hilts. 'Sezarre. See him fed and kept secluded. He is to speak to no one.' Shek Kul left the great hall, the slam of the door echoing through the empty vastness.

Kheda turned slowly to look at the swordsman Sezarre and ventured a reassuring smile. 'I give you my word I will not go against your lord's wishes.'

Sezarre looked back, still aloof. 'Come with me.' He opened the door and stood waiting for Kheda to go through. After the cool of the great audience hall, the gardens outside were warm and humid. Sezarre nodded towards a distant bower. 'That way.'

Kheda walked where he was bidden, Sezarre close behind him. The bower was an arch of fretwork laced with nerial vines whose dull green buds were just splitting to reveal white and purple petals furled within. Kheda was disappointed to note the quality of the woodcarving was nothing compared to the finesse of the Ulla domain's wares.

'Wait here.' Sezarre gave Kheda a stern look.

He sat obediently in the middle of the marble bench, itself a green and white stone that mimicked the vine's leaves. 'I gave you my word,' he reminded the slave with some asperity.

I'm hardly likely to break it with Shek Kul's fist ready to close around me and crush me to oblivion.

Sezarre didn't respond, turning to take the white gravelled path towards the central keep. As Kheda watched him go, he saw three women in bright dresses appear around a tall stand of swaying afital grasses.

'Sezarre!' The tallest of the women called out to the slave and he hurried to bow low before her. She asked him something and he replied with gestures that clearly indicated Kheda's presence. All three women looked down the path towards him, all dressed in the lightest of velvets, intricate patterns scored through the richness of the nap to give the fabrics a lacy sensuousness.

The tallest was a big-boned woman with darker skin than most in these reaches set off by the whiteness of her gown. The fine, close curls of hair dotting her scalp denoted blood from the most distant western domains. She had a broad face with a wide smile now turned to the baby she carried wrapped in a shawl bright with silken flowers. Looking up again, she spoke with Sezarre and a little boy appeared from behind her ivory skirts, taking a few steps down the path to stare at this newcomer with undisguised curiosity.

'Nai,' the woman warned, with easy authority in her tone. The child scampered back, raising one little hand to the reassuring grasp of his mother's body slave. That man made his mistress look positively diminutive, heavily muscled and stern-faced as he gazed at Kheda.

Don't worry, my friend. I would truly have to have a death wish to even offer an insult to Mahli Shek, first wife of this domain.

The woman's rebuke didn't dissuade a second, younger child from wriggling between the adults to see what her brother was looking at. The little girl's head was a luxurious riot of loose black curls and her skin was markedly paler than her mother's, who skirted past the first wife to scoop her daughter up. She settled the little girl on her hip, quelling her squirms with a brisk admonishment before turning to look at Kheda herself.

If Shek Kul had looked for abiding intelligence rather than superficial beauty in his first wife, his second or whoever she might be boasted a luscious prettiness that would grace any warlord's audience chamber. Rounded of hip and bosom, she wore her close-fitted dress of azure velvet with a conscious seductiveness even secluded thus within the Shek compound's walls.

No wonder that tall dark body slave hovering at your shoulder has such an expression of fatuous adoration, my lady. Not that I would feel inclined to fight him for your affections, when he stands with such an expert swordsman's balance. Shek Kul's wives' body slaves are plainly acquired for more than warming their lady's bed when her husband is otherwise engaged.

Sezarre concluded his explanations to the woman and bowed low. Mahli Shek nodded before turning her head to say something to the second wife. The two women took another path, their attendant slaves close behind them, the little boy and girl scampering ahead, giggling.

As they disappeared beyond a stand of dark-leaved berry bushes, the third woman hung back by the feathery afital grass. Slightly built with coppery skin, her long black hair was simply tied back and her dress was a plain orange shift, unbelted given her advanced pregnancy. Sezarre caught her hands with an impulsiveness that startled Kheda and bent to kiss them. The woman pulled away and Kheda saw her brushing away a tear. He also noted that where the other women had boasted rings, necklaces, anklets and bracelets of intricate twisted silver, this woman wore only a single gold chain of lozenge links around her neck.

'Gar, we are waiting.' Unseen, the second wife called out with a hint of impatience.

'Coming, Laio.' The pregnant woman hurried away down the path, leaving Sezarre looking after her. A moment later he left down the other fork.

So, Sezarre, I'd say it looks very much as if you are,

formally speaking, that wife's body slave. Now, Janne or Rekha would blister my ears with their scolding if I ever tried to usurp their authority over Birut or Andit. Even Sain would be roused to protest, albeit with her endless excruciating apologies, if I started giving Hanyad orders. Not that I would dare to, and certainly not while she was so close to childbed. What have you done, my lady, which prompts Shek Kul to deprive you of your body slave's support at such a time?

Well, that's a curiosity that I had best let go unsatisfied. I doubt such questions would be welcome.

The little girl's giggles rang through the gardens with that unique quality indicating a child doing something it knows full well it should not. Outraged chirping burst from an unseen aviary, the disapproval of the heavily built body slave rumbling beneath it. The children's voices rose; the girl offering some hasty excuse while the boy self-righteously proclaimed his own innocence.

A pain that Kheda had thought safely locked away deep in his heart pierced him like a knife.

Would Shek Kul's excellent sources have told him whether the baby born to a minor wife like Sain Daish is boy or girl? Will he know how any other children of such a distant domain fare, those below the ages of reason or discretion that make them pieces to be played in the games between warlords and their wives? There's no reason to suppose he interests himself in such irrelevancies for the Shek domain. Even if he does know, how could you ask about such things without confirming his suspicions of your true past? As long as he can say he does not know who you are, you may be safe. Once he cannot deny the truth, all wagers are off the table.

But he was threatened with magic, wasn't he? He found a path through the danger and if his first wife's brush with magic did him no credit among his neighbours, his domain prospers. He may have lived long without an heir because of her but he's wasted no time filling his quiver with a sheaf of children to safeguard the Shek domain's future. That's what you must discover, how he did it, and then you can return to enjoy your own wives and children and look to the stars for a better future for all of Daish.

Between determination to find out just what secrets Shek Kul hid sitting in his stomach like cold dread and painful longing for his own family hot behind Kheda's eyes, he found he had little appetite when Sezarre reappeared some while later carrying a tray of covered bowls.

'My master bids you eat.' Sezarre set the tray down on the marble bench, his gaze not on Kheda but irresistibly drawn to the sounds of the women playing in the garden with the children. Kheda saw both sympathy and resignation behind the slave's carefully maintained mask of indifference.

Does that mean your mistress has merited the snubs her fellow wives and her husband seemed intent on dealing her?

To distract himself from inadvertently betraying such curiosity, Kheda lifted the lids off the bowls. The selection of food, as fine as anything Janne Daish's cook would deign to set before an unexpected breakfast guest, did in fact remind him of just how hungry he had been lately. Pale curds of fresh cheese nestled in dark honey and were dusted with crushed afital seeds. Purple berries glistened atop a bowl of pink-tinged saller grain moistened with a sweet, aromatic wine. Cloud bread, still warm from the oven, was wrapped in a snowy cloth beside a gold-rimmed pot of quince preserve. A goblet of many-coloured glass matched a ewer of clear spring water.

'Will you eat with me?' He looked up at Sezarre. The slave hesitated.

Of course. He heard what I told Shek Kul.

'Forgive me, I know I've been too close to magic for comfort.' Kheda hid his chagrin by busying himself with the ewer. 'You should not risk sharing my food.'

Sezarre surprised him by sitting on the other end of the bench and tearing himself a piece of cloud bread. 'We had a slave here once—' He paused, as he scooped up some cheese and honey. 'A good man, even if he had been born a barbarian. He denounced her that was killed for suborning magic. He knew her enchanter for what he was, because he'd encountered wizards in his earlier life. He was still a good man, even if he had been touched by such things.'

A good man but one firmly in the past tense.

'What happened to him?' Kheda reached for a spoon and began eating saller and the unknown berries, which proved to be refreshingly tart.

Sezarre shook his head. 'That's for Shek Kul to tell you.'

The slave took the other spoon and joined Kheda in eating the moist saller grain. They had nearly reached the bottom of the bowl when Delai crunched down the pebble path towards them.

'My lord Shek Kul would speak with you again.'

Kheda rose and Sezarre gathered up the dishes and tray. As the slave vanished, Kheda felt oddly bereft.

'This way.' Delai did not take the path to the audience hall but instead led Kheda towards the central keep. They skirted the vast edifice again and Kheda saw he was being taken to the watchtower above the gate.

'Up the steps,' Delai grunted. 'To the top.'

Kheda complied and found himself in a room that took up the whole width of the tower's upper level, wide windows on every side with slatted wooden shutters fastened back. Shek Kul was waiting, looking out over the strait.

'Thank you for the breakfast,' said Kheda politely.

'Delai, guard the stairs. I want no one within earshot.' As the slave closed the door behind him, Shek Kul moved to sit on one of the benches that ringed the room below the windows.

'Events that I do not propose to discuss taught me not to condemn a man merely for the misfortune of meeting with magic.' He smiled without humour. 'If that were so, I would have to condemn my wives, my firstborn and myself. But I know the depth and extent of enchantment's malice and I have watched ever since for any omen that suggests that hateful episode has blighted our futures. My neighbours may not agree but I have seen no such sign, so my concern lessens with each turn of the heavens.'

He looked at Kheda thoughtfully. 'I understand your concerns for the Daish domain. I don't know if I'd have had the courage to follow the path that I suspect has brought you here. Nor do I see any clue as to where your future path may lie, and that concerns me. You do realise that setting yourself against these wizards may well see you shunned by other domains, for even daring to risk the taint of magic, even if you save the southern reaches as a result?'

'Unwelcome as such a destiny would be, it would be a worthwhile trade,' Kheda said quietly.

Shek Kul's non-committal noise was an echo of his slave's. He twisted a thick silver ring around his thumb. It was set with an uncut polished emerald that could only be a talisman gem.

'I cannot tell you how to defeat magic that openly stalks the land and sows destruction in its path,' he said abruptly. 'Good fortune as much as good counsel saved this domain from the disaster that ill-starred woman would have brought down on us all. I can set you on a course that may lead you to the lore you seek, though I make no promise of that. I will tell you what I can, if I have your word, your oath to the death, that you will never make it known to another living being that I set you on this path.'

'I swear it,' Kheda answered fervently. 'By the skies that greeted my birth.'

Shek Kul frowned at some memory, not at Kheda. 'The

magic threatening this domain and other malice besides
was unmasked by a barbarian slave, newly come from the
unbroken lands. He was being used somehow, in some
plot of the enchanter who had beguiled Kaeska that was
my wife with promises of the child she longed for. I don't
know quite how this slave was involved and I made it my
business not to enquire. That much alone would have
warranted his death if there had not been omens in his
favour. He was alone on the shore when a sea serpent
showed itself in the strait. Any such appearance is a most
powerful portent for my domain.' Shek Kul's scowl deep-
ened. 'If it had eaten him, we'd all have known where we
stood. As it turned out, the sea serpent passed him by.
Just to complicate any interpretation, that was the day of
Shek Nai's birth.'

Complication hardly seems an adequate description.

Kheda stayed silent, waiting for Shek Kul to resume.

'As the accuser, this slave was set to trial by combat
against the foreigner Kaeska had brought here, the man
accused of actually working the magic. She was irrevocably
condemned when the wizard used his evil first to try
ensnaring the slave and when that failed, to flee unseen.'
Anger undimmed by the passage of time thickened Shek
Kul's voice. 'So as well as the portent of the sea serpent,
I saw this barbarian slave was somehow proof against
wizardry, and in denouncing it had done my people and
me great service. That should have won him his freedom
and my order that some village of the domain provide for
him for the rest of his life.' The warlord paused again.

'I gave him his freedom but wasn't about to see him
enjoy it within my islands. I took his oath that he would
never return and I judged him a man of honour, for all
that he was a barbarian. Even so, I made sure I had word
of his travels, until he departed the entire Archipelago,'
Shek Kul added grimly.

'He did so in the company of a man whom I have long suspected of ill-dealings. He's a vice peddler, trades in intoxicants and pleasures of the flesh, sometimes with willing girls, sometimes not.' Shek Kul shrugged.

'There are always such parasites to batten on the strong. This man is different though and not just because he's barbarian born. He trades dreamsmokes and liquor for information and shares information in turn for goods and services, as he needs them. He's not alone in that but from what I've learned, his ledgers never quite balance and, believe me, I have made it my business to learn all I can about this man since my slave took up with him so readily. What this vice peddler does do is disappear to the north from time to time and not just to replenish his stocks of barbarian vices. He trades information to someone beyond our seas but not in any of those mainlander ports that our galleys deal with, that much is certain.'

Shek Kul twisted the talisman ring around his thumb.

'Vice traders generally only enjoy their rewards until some fellow degenerate sticks a dagger in their back or their offences warrant sinking by a warlord's trireme. Several rivals have tried to kill this man and failed. One died in his sleep of no cause that any healer could determine. Another was knocked from his own deck by a spar that was as sound as any other yet suddenly broke for no reason. This particular man often traded his skills in diving and swimming to repair ship's hulls yet he drowned without lifting a hand to save himself. After that, his enemies went after this vice peddler in several boats together, only to all wreck themselves in an unseasonable fog.'

Kheda saw Shek Kul looking expectantly at him. 'You suspect this vice peddler of working magic himself?'

'I don't know what to think. I wouldn't have spared him more than passing contempt had his path not crossed this barbarian slave's in a meeting that looked suspiciously contrived.' Shek Kul shrugged. 'Now I learn that as soon as rumours of this magic loose in the southern reaches drifted north, this vice peddler pursued them like a shark scenting blood in the water. He sailed south into the teeth of the rains and the fiercest storms of the season, so plainly has no fear of magic but rather some all-consuming interest. If I were you,' Shek Kul loaded his words with meaning, 'I would want to talk to this man.'

You're not telling me all you know. You have some definite reason to suspect this man of ties to barbarian wizardry. You cannot pursue him yourself though, not without doubling and redoubling the whispers that plague you.

'How would I find him?' Kheda wondered aloud.

'I make it my business to know where this man is.' Shek Kul's smile was predatory. 'I don't ever want him entering my waters unseen if I can help it. He stopped to take on water and food at the southernmost trading beach of the Jahal domain some days ago.'

Kheda's heart sank. 'That is a long way. He'll be long gone before I can travel so far.'

'Take passage as an itinerant galley rower.' Shek Kul narrowed his eyes at Kheda. 'A fast trireme could do it in half the time.'

'Wouldn't your neighbour domains question you sending such a ship so far south?' Kheda tried to restrain his hope.

'I can find reason enough to satisfy the curious,' said Shek Kul with grim finality. 'As for my true purpose, my travelling friend, you're not the only one keen to protect the domain of his birth from the ravages of magic. Repay me by sharing whatever you learn of the man and his true nature. His name is Dev and his ship is the *Amigal*.' He startled Kheda by pulling the ring from his thumb and tossing it over. 'If you're the man I think you are, you'll find the cipher key in that. Someone with a similar ring will make themselves known to you. That'll be the person keeping track of this Dev for me. That's the person to trust with your letters to me.'

'You honour me with your confidence,' Kheda said soberly. The ring was too big for his own thumb so he pulled the leather thong over his head and began picking at the knot.

'Do not betray my trust,' warned Shek Kul quietly. 'Do so and I will be avenged, even if it takes me or mine a full course of the Topaz through the heavens to find you.' He stood up. 'Delai will fetch you when the ship is ready to leave.'

'I cannot thank you enough,' Kheda said impulsively. 'I only hope I may one day repay you fittingly.'

'I'm glad to hear it, traveller.' Shek Kul's laugh surprised Kheda. 'There's a little more to tip the scales in my favour. I made it my business to find out about these barbarians tied to the magic that led Kaeska to her death. I looked for other lore besides, in case such a disaster should ever threaten us again. It turns out various warlords over the ages have wondered how to frustrate the malice of magic. Walk with me in the gardens and we can discuss their theories while we wait for Delai. I don't know if they'll be of use to you...' He shrugged and let the sentence hang unfinished in the air.

But it won't harm you, for any spies who've insinuated themselves through your gates to hear your commitment to defending your domain against magic, even as you send a ship to the south where it's abroad.

'I will be honoured to walk with you.' Kheda bowed low and followed the warlord out of the lofty tower room.

CHAPTER FIFTEEN

'Why are we anchoring here?' Risala looked anxiously around.

'Why not?' Dev had forced the *Amigal* into the narrow inlet as far as possible. The ship's stern was wedged against the muddy bank and stubby knot trees cloaked the foredeck with their short fat leaves. Dev tossed the lees of his cup of wine into the brackish river, where the red stain slowly dissolved.

'Refill that and I'll break every bottle you've got aboard,' Risala snapped. 'If there are wizards and savages around here, I don't want you drunk!'

'What makes you think you've any say in what I do?' Dev grinned, unrepentant. 'Besides, drunk's probably no bad way to be, if you're going to be tortured by howling wild men.'

Risala chewed her lip. 'Don't think you can scare me off. I'm coming.' Her eyes were determined.

'I'm certainly not leaving you here to go wandering off,' agreed Dev. 'To get caught and betray me to their knives to save your own skin. Besides, if we're taken, you might just be the price of my freedom, sweetness.'

'How do we hide the ship?' Risala turned her back on him and studied the *Amigal*'s mast, sails furled close. 'So we can get away, once we've seen all there is to see?'

'I'll cut some greenery.' Dev was lacing thick-soled leather sandals with sides that pulled up over the top of his foot. 'We cover as much of the deck with it as we can.'

Picking up a heavy-bladed jungle knife, he climbed carefully over the ship's stern. 'Pass me the anchor.'

'Don't make too much noise,' warned Risala, struggling with the heavy weight.

'Keep your own mouth shut in case someone hears you.' Dev calculated how much slack to leave for the tide before wedging the anchor among the knot tree roots. 'Letting your tongue run loose all the time isn't what makes a poet.'

His sneering rebuke silenced her, so he turned to cutting the new shoots sprouting from the swollen bases of the gnarled grey knot trees. Dev was soon sweating freely, forced to summon a whisper of magic to keep the insidious blackflies at bay. He worked rapidly and soon had an armful of the fleshy yellowy-green twigs to dump on the deck.

'We'll want plenty on the bow.' Risala looked apprehensively towards the open end of the inlet. 'In case someone passes by there.'

'As you wish, my lady.' Dev bowed, mocking. 'And get a rope fast there while you're at it.' He went back to hacking at the trees. He kept an eye on Risala though and as soon as she was busy securing the fore anchor, her back turned, he brought his hands sharply together. A faint glimmer of dark blue light escaped his interlaced fingers as he jerked his hands apart.

Risala's head snapped round. 'What is it? Why have you stopped?' Her voice was tight with fear.

'Just catching my breath,' replied Dev. 'After doing all the hard work.'

Not rising to his antagonistic tone, Risala knelt to fix the stubborn branches more securely to the *Amigal*'s rails.

Dev closed his eyes the better to concentrate on the magic he was rapidly running around the ship's hull. Invisibility wasn't that hard to work, whatever the whining apprentices at Hadrumal might think, just bringing together the antithetical elements of air and water. That would shield the *Amigal* from enemy eyes.

'Are you going to sleep?'

'No.' Dev opened his eyes to see Risala looking at him, scratched and dirty hands on her hips. 'See those sandals by the hatch? Put them on and be careful where you walk around here. I'll leave you for the savages if you stick a knot root through your foot or tread on a spinefruit husk.'

'Which way are we going?' Risala didn't argue, dropping to the deck to wriggle her feet into the sandals.

'That way.' Dev pointed west where the ground rose clear of the knot tree thickets and nut palms swayed in the breeze. Jumping back aboard, he fetched a bulging leather water skin from the stern cabin and dumped it by Risala. 'Don't snag it on any branches.'

'This is the right island?' She looked up for reassurance. 'You've been here before?'

'I have,' Dev lied easily. He'd never so much as set foot in this remote reach of Chazen territory but that didn't bother him. He'd been scrying out a safe route in every cup of wine he'd drunk since they'd left Daish waters. 'Get ashore.'

Slinging a leather sack over one shoulder by its braided cord, he watched the thin cotton of Risala's trousers tighten over her rump as she climbed over the stern rail. He'd only use her to buy his way out of trouble if there was nothing else for it, he decided idly. The flasks of liquor and the potent leaves for chewing or burning in the sack would probably be enough. Then he'd be entitled to take her gratitude any way he wanted, if he'd saved her life.

Following Risala, he glanced covertly at the ship from the edge of the knot trees. The magic dappled the water beneath her hull but to the unfriendly eye, the *Amigal* would just be a random pattern of shadows on the water. Dev grinned. If he irritated Risala enough, wound her dislike of him to a high enough pitch, would she suddenly be unable to see the ship? Then he wondered what one of these savage mages might make of his working. What would he make of theirs? He turned his back on the ship, expression one of anticipation.

'Here's a game trail.' Risala pointed to narrow hoof slots patterning a bare stretch of earth.

'Going in the right direction. Let's take it.' Dev pushed past the girl to follow the damp score through the burgeoning undergrowth. As he pushed aside a creeper-choked branch, it whipped back to catch Risala's face.

'I don't see why I can't have a knife,' she muttered resentfully, swatting leaves from her hair.

'If we run into these savages, a blade makes you a foe to be killed.' Dev sliced away an encroaching lilla frond. 'Unarmed, even a scrawny piece like you is a prize for a commander to enjoy.'

Risala shuddered. 'I'd rather die than be taken by a wizard.'

'Keep talking and you can find out if that's an option,' suggested Dev sarcastically.

He pushed on through the branches and clinging vines, the girl following silent close behind. The humid air hung still and hot beneath the trees, broken only by the chirr of insects and the peaceable cries of loals and birds. There was no sign of other blades on the underbrush, so Dev allowed himself to believe this game trail was as little used as it had looked to his scrying spell.

'Watch where you're putting your feet,' he warned Risala curtly. 'Step on a sickle serpent and you'll be dead before you hit the ground.'

The inlet was long lost behind them when Dev, sweat coating his face, turned to Risala and snapped his fingers at the water skin slung over her shoulder. She proffered it and he eased the dryness at the back of his throat with a long drink. 'Drink all you can,' he ordered her. 'Then look for a stream to refill it.'

Despite the lushness of the forest all around, it was a good while later before Risala prodded Dev's shoulder and nodded silently to a rill. He kept watch while she knelt to replenish the water skin, moving off before she had got it settled on her back once again.

After the next stop to quench their thirsts, Dev began to move more cautiously. The trees were bigger now, mostly ironwoods reaching up to form a broad canopy whose shade denied the lesser brush of the forest floor. Logen vines and strangler figs swarmed up the tall trees to reach the distant sunlight. Dev and Risala made their way stealthily from one creeper-hung thicket to the next. As rotted figs squelched beneath his sandals, Dev looked up to see a flock of scarlet and yellow crookbeaks amiably bickering in the treetops. He caught Risala's arm, pointing upwards before pressing his forefinger to his lips. The last thing they needed was those birds scattering like a burst of flying flame, screeching out their alarm.

With the crookbeaks well behind them, Dev stopped and dropped to his hands and knees. The forest ahead looked lighter after the dense shade of the uncut depths and tandra trees were silhouetted against empty sky beyond. Wood rang as it was hammered and voices called out orders. Gasps and cries answered the crack of whips.

Dev crawled slowly forward to lie between two immature spinefruit trees struggling to rise above a robust cluster of sardberry bushes. Risala wriggled into the discreet hollow after him.

'What are they doing?' she wondered in a whisper no louder than a breath.

'Making defences.' Dev kept his voice low, even though

a shout would probably have gone unheard in the commotion they saw before them.

They looked out on a village standing at the top of a long fan-shaped bay. The low houses straggled along the line where sand gave way to soil, a scatter of vegetable plots and fowl houses further inland. Crops were trampled, fences broken, only a few damp drifts of feathers to mark the fate of ducks and hens. On the beach, the waters of the bay rippled over an unobstructed, shelving anchorage where fishing boats drifted on long tethers tied to heavy piles driven into the sand. The crude log boats of the invaders were piled haphazard along the high-water mark.

'I wouldn't mind getting a closer look at those logs, to see if I can recognise the wood,' Dev said thoughtfully to Risala. 'If we knew where their trees grew, we might know where these curs came from.'

'They just came right in and attacked.' Risala was gazing at the village where most of the houses had burned to stark charcoal skeletons, now sodden and weeping black stains into the ground. A couple of the storehouses and granaries had been broken down, left looted and empty. The others were packed with plunder, barrels and coffers stacked around them. 'The islanders couldn't have known what was happening to them.'

'These savages don't reckon on being caught like that.' Dev squirmed to bring his leather sack round, rummaging inside for a spyglass. 'Not so stupid as they look, eh?'

A new ditch sliced through the open expanse of beach. What looked like most of the men of the village were being forced to dig it deeper. The invaders, easily identifiable with their dark, painted bodies and their brief leather loincloths, were using spears and whips to drive women and children hauling heavy logs out of the forest beyond the village. Even with their crude stone tools, other wild men were making a competent job of sharpening wooden stakes to line the ditch's inner faces. Only a few narrow stretches were left untouched to give paths through the defences and more savage warriors guarded those with wooden spears at the ready.

'The savages are enslaving the Chazen people?' As Risala spoke, whips cracked to terrify a handful of girls struggling to tie ropes to a heavy log. 'And seizing their lands? Is this what they want from the Archipelago?'

'No way to say. They're destroying more than they're keeping, for one thing.' Dev counted the invaders beneath his breath. 'This ditch could just be temporary, to keep themselves safe from any Chazen islanders they've not rounded up. They might still be planning to sail north as soon as the rains are over.'

'These savages must be fools.' Baffled, Risala looked at Dev. 'Everyone knows you can't enslave a whole population. They always fight back sooner or later. Look what happened in the Fial domain when Lemad Sarkis tried to conquer it. What about Draha Akil's death, when all the barbarian slaves he'd brought for his oil tree plantations rebelled? You never keep too many slaves together, not if you've any sense.'

'I thought you were a poet, not a historian,' Dev murmured absently. 'You and I may know better but I don't suppose those hairy-arsed savages are too worried.' He handed Risala the spyglass. 'Watch those men, those Chazen islanders over by that stack of barrels.'

Risala peered through the bronze eyepiece. 'Do you think they're going to attack him, that wild man?'

'No.' Dev silently worked a brief spell to enhance his own sight and watched the knot of struggling islanders. The nearest savage had his back towards them and the barrels screened the arguing men from any other guards.

As Dev spoke, one of the Chazen men broke free from those trying to restrain him. He ran, feet skidding on ground still wet from the previous night's rains. He didn't attack the nearby invader but ran straight for the ditch, head down, arms pumping at his sides.

'He can't think he can jump it,' gasped Risala.

'That's not what he's trying to do,' said Dev grimly.

The Chazen man launched himself at the murderous spikes lining the ditch, arms spread, head flinching backwards. Risala clapped a hand over her mouth to muffle her gasp of horror. The island women filled the air with full-throated screams. There was a flash, like lightning, and their cries of dismay turned to piercing wails of despair. The man did not fall to his death but hung, impossibly suspended in the empty air by azure bonds of light. He kicked and struggled, arms flailing, captured by the magic.

'You're not the only one would rather die than live under a wizard's rule.' Dev hid a reluctant grin with one hand. No Chazen islander could have seen it but the wizardry coiling through the air after the would-be suicide had been plain enough to him. Invisible enchantment had boiled up around the man after his first few steps. The savage mage, whoever he was, could have caught the islander before anyone even noticed his futile defiance. Of course, mused Dev, letting the man run and then letting everyone see him twisting in the air, frustrated and humiliated, was certainly a valuable lesson for anyone else with thoughts of rebellion. 'Look, there.' He pointed eagerly. 'The one with the lizard-skin cloak.'

An invader stalked out from one of the few remaining houses of the village. The retinue fawning after him looked no different from the other wild men, crudely dressed and splashed with paint. The leader alone wore a long cloak made from the entire skin of a whip lizard. It trailed down his back, clawed feet flapping at his side, the tail scoring a line on the sandy ground behind him. The lower jaw had been cut from the blunt head and he wore the skull like a helmet, the vicious upper fangs curving white against his dark face. His own smile was as white as the whip lizard's teeth and his laughter rang out as the last glimmer of sapphire magelight faded from his hands.

The savages guarding those toiling in the ditch turned to acknowledge the newcomer, falling to their knees in abject obeisance. Seeing their distraction, one islander hurled a baulk of wood at the man in the lizard skin.

The invader raised a casual hand and the heavy timber hung motionless in the air before bursting into flames. Inside an eyeblink, the solid wood was no more than a shadow of ash, blown away on the next gust of wind.

'Is that the wizard?' Risala could only manage a strangled whisper.

'Hush.' Dev was watching intently.

As the savages' mage advanced, his followers joined in his loud amusement, nodding and laughing. The Chazen men cowered in the bottom of the ditch. The women and children slowed to a reluctant shuffle, averting their faces from the man still struggling in the empty air above the murderous stakes.

'What's he going to do?' Risala hissed.

'Leave him there,' Dev shrugged.

'What are we going to do?' There was a quaver in Risala's question.

'See what happens next,' grinned Dev. 'Should make a good few stanzas for this epic of yours.'

Risala gazed balefully at the scene before them, chin resting on her hands. Dev watched the man in the lizard cloak.

Ignoring the islander still imprisoned by magic, the savage mage was moving between the groups of wild men, nodding and gesturing. The invaders bowed low, some dropping to one knee or prostrate before him.

Mages have real power among these people, Dev thought silently. There's none of the scraping and apologising Hadrumal teaches, all restraint and self-denial lest mageborn offend the incapable mundane. Perhaps these savage mageborn banded together and dictated their terms to those that lacked their talents, instead of living on sufferance or being driven out as freaks and menaces.

'What's that?' Risala whispered urgently. She pointed at a vessel that had just rounded the far headland of the long bay, sliding over the water indifferent to wind and wave.

Dev abandoned his speculations. 'Offhand, I'd say it was a boat,' he replied sarcastically. Though it was an uncommon enough craft to warrant a closer look. Four of the invaders' narrow tree trunk hulls had been lashed together and roughly boarded over, a pair of scullers standing at the stern while everyone else sat crowded on the unrailed deck. There was a sizeable contingent of wild men aboard.

'Our friend the Lizard is keen to be first in line,' murmured Dev.

The savage mage was hurrying down from the village, his cloak lashing behind him. His spearmen all turned towards the water and bowed low, those closest to the newly arrived boat prostrating themselves on the sand.

Risala sank low to the ground as the strange vessel grounded in the shallows.

A man sitting cross-legged in the prow stood up. The bright colours of his own long cloak swirled around as he stepped off the crude decking. His feet didn't touch the water. Opening his arms so the cloak flapped like the wings of some enormous bird, he walked through the air on a path woven of magic drawn from both sea and air. The lattice of light veered from green to blue, bright beneath his feet, reaching out ahead of him. He arrived, perfectly composed, on the dry sand just below the newly dug ditch and the bridge of magic faded to a turquoise memory. His retinue splashed hastily through the shallows to gather in an obsequious half circle behind him.

'Is that a magic cloak?' Risala's eyes were huge.

'No, just glory bird feathers.' Dev considered the newcomer in his mantle of gaudy plumage. That spell to get ashore dry-footed was a simple enough trick but Lizardskin was bowing low, his whole body cringing. Feathercloak was capable of far more than that, it would seem.

Feathercloak was nodding, seemingly in approval, and Lizardskin stood upright, clapping his hands together. Brawny savages appeared from one of the larger storehouses carrying chests and a tightly tied sack. Lizardskin's ingratiating gestures plainly invited Feathercloak to help himself from the loot. Feathercloak stood aloof, raising one hand to beckon someone else forward.

'Now who do you suppose this is?' Dev wriggled forward a little on his elbows. A tall savage stalked forward from Feathercloak's followers. He bowed low to his master before looking down on Lizardskin with a supercilious sneer. He wore no cloak but boasted a breastplate of closely tied white bones and more ivory shards were woven into his thick hair.

'What sort of bones are those?' Risala swallowed hard. 'Do you suppose they eat—'

'Who cares?' Dev dismissed the question as the bone-decorated savage knelt down to open a coffer. He held something up to Feathercloak, who shrugged and shook his head. The Bone Wearer tossed it away. The warm colours of turtleshell showed dark against the sand, rimmed with gold bright even under the dull skies. Whatever the Bone Wearer found next satisfied Feathercloak, who summoned another underling to take

it, a man distinguished by a necklace of shark teeth. As
the Bone Wearer opened the sack, he offered up a handful
of something to Feathercloak. At the shake of his master's
head, he tossed the pearls aside, the gleaming drops hitting
the sand like priceless rain.

Risala watched baffled as more beautifully crafted
pieces in turtleshell and nacre were tossed aside like so
much rubbish. 'If they scorn such wealth, what do they
want?'

'They're finding something worth stealing,' Dev
disagreed. Whatever the Bone Wearer was showing
Feathercloak now plainly won his approval, and was
handed over to the underling.

By the time Feathercloak had examined all the booty,
he'd taken no more than a chest full. The underling carried
it down the beach while Lizardskin clapped his hands
sharply together. More of his own retinue appeared from
the trees, dragging a weeping column of men and women.
Most were grey-haired, all were stumbling with shock and
weariness, clothes creased and dirty. Their hands were
tied and a heavy leather rope had been plaited around
their necks to link them together. The only younger man
was a youth with a twisted foot, struggling to use his
crutch, dark weals on his naked back showing the price
he'd paid for failure to keep up. Savages walked on either
side of the shambling line, whips trailing negligently in
the sand.

'No warlord would treat a domain's elders like this.'
Risala was appalled.

'Can't see them having much value as slaves.' Dev
thought for a moment. 'Hostages, do you suppose? If this
lot don't do as they're bid, grandma gets a club to the
back of the head?'

Feathercloak and Lizardskin looked to be saying their
farewells. Dev burned with frustration. 'If we're going to

learn anything of value about these people, we have to know who their leaders are,' he commented to Risala. 'I'd say Feathercloak's higher up the pecking order than Lizardskin. We have to find a way to follow him.'

'That one's seen that man over the ditch.' She pointed with a shaking finger.

Dev watched the Bone Wearer stride arrogantly across the beach to look up at the hapless islander still hanging, despairingly, over the sharpened stakes. The Bone Wearer raised a hand, blue light streamed from it and the man fell with a scream of pure terror.

He still didn't find his longed-for death on the vicious splintered wood. A blast of azure power from Lizardskin shoved the islander sideways through the air, to leave him sprawled, motionless, on the sand. The Bone Wearer's head snapped round and he shouted at Lizardskin before going over to the islander and kicking him. The Chazen man didn't react and the Bone Wearer examined him more closely. He stood up, one hand knotted in the islander's hair, shaking the body to display a plainly broken neck, laughing derisively at Lizardskin.

Lizardskin shut his mouth with a slap of blue mage-light across the face. The Bone Wearer was knocked clean off his feet, breastplate clattering, and several white shards falling from his hair. Scrambling on to his knees, he swept a hand towards Lizardskin and ochre light surged through the sand. Lizardskin disappeared in a whirling cloud of dust shot through with amber flashes. The Bone Wearer got to his feet and laughed.

'What are they doing?' quavered Risala.

'Duelling,' Dev said with slow fascination.

The Bone Wearer stopped laughing, looking down, face twisted with fury and rapid thought. The sand around his feet was glowing with a dark, mossy light and he was sinking into it. Knee deep inside a few breaths, he thrust his hands downward and the greenish radiance fled. As it did, the storm of sand around Lizardskin exploded to reveal the panting mage within scored with countless gashes. He flung a handful of raw blue light at the Bone Wearer, which bowled across the sand scooping up razor-edged shell fragments. Some rattled against the other mage's breastplate, more cut deep into his naked arms and legs. The Bone Wearer swept his hands around like a man brushing away flies and the blue light vanished. He brushed sweat from his forehead, glaring at Lizardskin.

'Is it over?' Risala asked hopefully.

'They don't think so.' Dev nodded at the savages all prudently retreating, some to the shelter of the ditch along with the captive islanders or back towards the boat in the shallows. The only person unperturbed was Feathercloak. He stood, arms folded inside his bright mantle, head slightly inclined with a nimbus of protective magic shimmering around him.

Lizardskin walked around the Bone Wearer in a slow circle, one hand raised, palm outwards and fingers spread. The Bone Wearer pivoted where he stood, always keeping Lizardskin in view. He held his hands in front of his breastplate, palms pressed together. Greenish light dripped from Lizardskin's hand and vanished into the ground. Mist began gathering around the Bone Wearer's feet, dense and white. The Bone Wearer laughed and swept the nascent fog away with gusts of sapphire-tinted breeze.

The mist cleared but the sand beneath the Bone Wearer's feet wasn't mossy with magic summoned from water but suffused with an amber light that suddenly glowed bronze. The Bone Wearer screamed as he found himself up to his ankles in furnace heat. He lashed at the ground with his azure magic, sending gouts of molten sand glittering through the air, trailing spider's-web tendrils of glass. The searing missiles skittered across the sand, some scoring deep wounds in Lizardskin's legs, but the wild mage didn't falter, hate-filled eyes fixed on the Bone Wearer.

A column of flame erupted from the sand encircling the Bone Wearer. The fire roared, choking off his agonised scream, brightening to a white heat inside a few breaths. Abruptly as it had arisen, the blaze disappeared, leaving only a slowly twisting pillar of pale grey ash sinking to the sand. The mage in the lizard-skin cloak fell to his hands and knees, his eyes turned apprehensively to Feathercloak.

The savage wizard in the bright feathers walked slowly over to the pitiful heap of ash. Crouching, he took up a handful, letting it sift through his fingers. There wasn't so much as a splinter of bone left. He laughed, the ringing sound shocking in the frozen silence. Walking over towards Lizardskin, he offered the younger mage his hand. Lizardskin took it, rising stiffly to his feet, pride struggling through the pain of his burns.

Feathercloak summoned the underling who'd been entrusted with the coffer of acceptable loot. After a brief exchange, Lizardskin clapped a hand on the underling's shoulder and turned him around to face the people on the beach, his gesture eloquent. The invaders' bows to their new leader were immediate and fervent, followed by cheering and clapping, some drumming on the hard ground with their spears. Those who'd come with Feathercloak joined in the celebration, welcoming Lizardskin with laughter and smiles.

'You'd think he'd treated them all to a feast instead of burned a man to death with magic,' muttered Risala, revolted.

Lizardskin basked in the applause for a few moments before prostrating himself before Feathercloak in abject obeisance. Feathercloak nodded, content, and threw a shimmer of light across Lizardskin's prone body. The lesser wizard scrambled to his feet, the raw, sand-encrusted burns that had disfigured his legs entirely vanished.

'That's a good trick if you can do it,' murmured Dev, forgetting himself.

Fortunately, Risala was still transfixed by the scene before her. She jumped as a whip cracked. Spurred into action, the savages punished the bound column of aged islanders for sinking to their knees with brutal kicks and harsh blows. Feathercloak ignored all this, returning to his boat. He didn't bother with his bridge of patterned light, simply sweeping his mantle around himself and taking one long step to travel through the air and arrive dry-footed on the rough deck. Lizardskin splashed through the sea to join him, clutching the precious coffer of care-fully selected plunder to his chest.

'Come on.' Dev retreated rapidly on his hands and knees.

'Where to?' Risala's voice shook as she wriggled back-wards.

'They're walking that column of captives along the beach.' Dev kept a careful eye out through the veil of leaves as he began walking towards the shoreline. 'I want to see where they're heading.'

'Why do we want to do that?' Risala stopped, stubborn-faced.

Dev raised his eyebrows. 'Your epic wants a middle and an end as well as a beginning. Folk'll be throwing rotten fruit at you if you can't tell them where the invaders took those prisoners.' He jerked his head towards the beach where the captives were struggling to give as wide a berth as possible to the twisted pavement of glass where the bone-decorated mage had died. 'Where are they taking that loot? I deal in information, girlie, I've told you that. I'll get all the answers I can before sailing north again.'

'We'll neither of us be going north if we're dead and burned to ashes,' protested Risala.

'Go back to the *Amigal* then.' Dev shrugged. 'I might even come back for you, if I don't just steal another boat.'

'You would too, wouldn't you?' Risala took a reluctant step forward.

'You don't want to bet that I won't.' Dev's smile didn't reach his eyes. 'Come on.'

He led her through the brush at the edge of the forest that cloaked the headland reaching out into the sea. The finger of land narrowed to a tangle of knot trees and Dev began pushing his way through the fleshy leaves towards the water.

'What are you doing?' Risala was shrill with apprehension.

'Stealing a boat.' Dev unsheathed his broad jungle knife. 'Hold this. Get it wet and I'll trade you to a flesh peddler first chance I get.' He handed her the sack of liquor and dream smokes before wading cautiously into the shallows. Ducking down so only his head and knife were visible, he half waded, half swam towards a handful of the little boats Chazen islanders used to tend their floating net frames bobbing at the furthest end of a long rope tethered to the distant shore. Breathing easier once he was in amongst the concealing hulls, sawing through the plaited leather was the work of a moment. A breath of magic gave Dev a boost out of the water and he lay inside the shallow boat, straining to hear any shout of alarm from the shore.

None came. Dev grabbed a paddle, backing the little vessel towards Risala. 'Get in. Careful!' He glowered at her as she almost tipped the boat over.

'Sorry.' She clutched the sides with white knuckles.

Dev threw a paddle at her. 'Set to work.'

Risala knelt, and dug the paddle into the water. She

kept glancing towards the distant shore, her strokes going awry.

'Keep your eyes to the front.' Dev wrenched at his own paddle to correct their course.

'But what if they see us?' Risala looked from the beach where the savages were resuming the work on the ditch with shouts and whips to the far side of the bay where the feather-cloaked mage's double-hulled vessel was lazily keeping pace with the captives being driven along the shore.

'We keep well back and they'll just think we're one of their own boats out on some errand,' Dev said scornfully. 'They won't see a difference at this distance.'

Risala opened her mouth to object, then closed it again, resuming her erratic paddling.

Dev made a few sweeping strokes, just enough to maintain the water magic he was using to drive the frail little boat along. He decided on burnishing the air with fire to turn aside any invader's gaze straying in their direction, not the easiest of tasks with the water ceaselessly swirling beneath him and disrupting the elemental heat.

As they cautiously pursued the savages, he considered what he had seen on the beach. The Bone Wearer had been caught unawares with his hands full of enchanted air, too slow to throw it aside for the water that might have saved him when he found himself unexpectedly assaulted with fire. No loss that the fool was dead; there was nothing he could have taught Dev by the looks of it.

Nothing like that duel could ever happen in Hadrumal though. Master mages were always alert for any apprentice tempted to try his newly governed powers in some trial of strength. Such contests were stopped before they could start wherever possible and the consequences of discovery left everyone involved regretting they'd ever entertained the idea.

Cooperation is the only salvation for wizardry. Dev recalled the precept endlessly dinned into every prentice mage's head. The mundane world does not understand wizardry and what it does not understand, it fears. The solitary mage who does not restrain his powers will always fall eventually to the violence of a frightened mob. Dev's lip curled. The wizards of Hadrumal should try living his life for a season. Aldabreshin hatred of magic went far beyond anything felt by the princes and peoples of the mainland.

These wild men didn't seem scared of magic. Their wizards were revered and quite plainly in command. They weren't frightened of using their magic either, not even on each other. Dev gazed into the distance where the many-hulled boat was rounding a spur of sandy beach; the mage's cloak of feathers a bright splash of colour. What could such unrestrained, unashamed magic do for him, back on the mainland, back in Hadrumal?

'It's starting to rain.' Risala shivered as dark spots pattered down on her threadbare tunic.

'You're not made of sand,' said Dev absently. 'You won't get washed away.'

A glitter of unearthly blue ahead caught his eye and he abandoned the spell sweeping beneath their hull in order to sharpen his vision. The clouds over the invaders' vessel were pouring a deluge down on Feathercloak and his minions. Not so much as a wisp of the wizard's borrowed plumage was getting wet. The water veered away, streaming into the sea and leaving the boat untouched. Those plodding along the shore were getting soaked, tunics and wraps clinging to the elderly prisoners, sodden dresses and trews hampering their stumbling steps. Their captors strode on unbothered, rain running down their naked skins, smearing their body paint.

'We're in a current or a tide race or something.' Risala

hauled on her paddle in alarm but the boat continued to slow.

'Pull to the other side.' Dev suited his actions to his words. As soon as Risala turned her back, he hastily summoned up some magic to send them gliding smoothly through the water once more. In the meantime, the mage in his cloak of feathers had disappeared, his many-hulled boat rounding a rocky point as the column of captives disappeared into the forest.

Dev took a deep breath. Working so many spells was starting to get tiring. That was the other way magic could kill a wizard according to the precepts of Hadrumal. Any mage with ambitions to rule the world would die of exhaustion before he came anywhere close. So they said. Feathercloak didn't look at all wearied to Dev. He gritted his teeth and concentrated on driving the shallow boat past the stony hummocks of the point ahead.

'Oh, Dev.' Risala's paddle trailed uselessly in the water.

The rockier coast here embraced a deeper bay fringed with blue-green corals. A small village had dwelt happily among the nut palms swaying above the white sandy beach where scrubby berry bushes and tandra trees had been cut back for a neat array of vegetable gardens and saller plots.

This contented order was barely visible behind the massive encampment now sprawling over the beach. Saplings still green with stubs of branches and leaves were driven into the sandy ground and lashed together with plaited vines to form wide corrals. Between these crude prisons, sacks and barrels were piled higher than a man's head, haphazardly roofed with palm fronds against the rains.

'That's enough cargo to fill a fleet of galleys,' Dev concluded with interest. 'Even when our pal in the feathers is being so picky.'

'Dev, there are hundreds of them.' Risala gripped her paddle in consternation.

Countless savages took advantage of such shelter as the piles of loot afforded, most in idle relaxation, a few tending reluctant fires. A roar of welcome echoed around the bay as Feathercloak's boat was spotted. It glided serenely into shore, the rainbow haze around it sparkling with arrogant contempt for the persistent rain.

'What now?' Risala demanded. 'If they see us, we're dead or worse.'

'Back behind the headland.' Dev began backing furiously with his paddle. 'We can watch from there.'

Risala needed no urging. They wheeled the shallow little boat around and put the rocky rise between themselves and the horde of invaders. Half lifting, half dragging, they got the boat clear of the lapping seas. Crawling cautiously up the slope on hand and knees, they edged between the jumble of weathered rocks.

Risala looked along the shore to the point where the column of captives had disappeared into the trees. 'This must be where they're taking those poor prisoners. Do you know where we are, exactly, if we're to tell Chazen Saril where to come to rescue them?'

Dev nodded. 'Keep your head down.'

'What can you see?' Risala cowered beneath a rounded overhang where wind-blown lilla leaves and tandra fluff mingled with the sand.

'Give me the spyglass.' Crouched behind a flat table of rock, Dev stretched out a demanding hand. Risala hesitated then handed it over.

'You're right; those prisoners are arriving.' Dev paused to wipe wind-driven raindrops from the glass. 'They're being put into one of those stockades. There are people already there, lots of them,' he added with some surprise. 'All elders and incapables.'

Risala was perplexed. 'Slaves should be young and healthy, if they're to be worth their food and shelter.'

'These people don't seem concerned to keep their captives fit for anything much.' Dev watched the men releasing the newly arrived prisoners. Not a few fell, helpless to avoid merciless kicks. He saw one beaten to stillness before being tossed inside the crude corral.

Risala swallowed audibly. 'You don't suppose they're going to eat them, do you?'

Dev opened his mouth to scorn the notion but shut it again. 'They'd make for cursed tough eating, after a lifetime hoeing saller plots and hauling fishing nets.'

'What else can you see?' demanded Risala hurriedly. 'How soon can we leave?'

'Feathercloak's taking his chest ashore.' Dev twisted the ring of the spyglass to get a clearer view. 'Young Lizardskin's along to carry it. Now who do you suppose they're going to give it to?'

'Their leader?' Risala suggested, tense. 'The man Chazen Saril will need to kill?'

'For a poet you seem very interested in strategy.' Dev didn't take his eye away from the spyglass 'Well now, who's this?'

'Who?' Frustration brought Risala on to her knees before caution forced her back again.

'Feathercloak and Lizardskin are on their faces before him, so he must be important. He looks much the same as the rest, tall, skinny, hair all stuck together with coloured paint. But he's wearing an incredible cloak.' Dev leaned forward in an unconscious effort to see more clearly.

'How so?' Risala tried in vain to see what he meant but they were too far away.

'It's scales, like our friend in the lizard skin but there's just no comparison,' Dev breathed. 'It's red and polished or lacquered or something, it must be, to shine like that.'

Risala looked at the unbroken blanket of cloud up above. 'How can it be shining with no sun?'

Dev realised the ruby sheen on the rippling hide was magelight. The cloak was a full half circle cut from the belly skin of some massive beast, soft carnelian scales a finger's length or so. Dev swallowed the lump of disbelief in his throat. 'I think it's dragon hide.'

The new mage walked slowly towards Feathercloak and Lizardskin, who were still prostrate, hands outstretched. Rain falling anywhere near vanished into steam suffused with raw elemental fire.

'It can't be,' Risala objected. 'You only find dragons in poems.'

'And the frozen mountains of the unbroken lands,' countered Dev. 'I still say it's dragon hide. Hush, he's looking in the chest.'

'Can you see what they brought him?' Risala edged closer.

'No.' Dev shook his head in disgust and thrust the spyglass at her. 'You try, if you're so keen to see.'

A little confused, Risala nevertheless took the spyglass and turned it eagerly on the encampment on the shore. Dev looked for a puddle. All this rain had to be good for something. A hollow in a rock shone with moisture and Dev shuffled unobtrusively over for a clear view of the water's surface.

'See anything?' he demanded of Risala.

'No, not yet,' she said slowly.

'Try harder,' he told her curtly. He concentrated all his elemental affinity on the water, suppressing every hint of magelight in the scrying. An image floated on the surface like an instant of reflection caught in a sloshing cup and vanished. Dev took a deep breath.

'Fire!' Risala started so violently that she knocked Dev's arm. 'A flash like flames anyway. Some magic, or something.' She cowered as low behind the rock as she could without losing sight of the distant beach.

Ready to mock Risala for panicking at a newly lit cook fire, Dev's sarcasm died on his tongue with a taste like old ashes. In the mirror of the watery hollow, he saw the mage in the dragon hide raise his arms, the ruby iridescence of the cloak growing ever brighter. Magelight flickered in scarlet flames around his upturned hands. Even at this distance, the untamed power buffeted Dev's wizard senses. He gasped as he felt that power sent questing out over land and sea.

'Run!' He sprang to his feet and raced for the little boat. He didn't wait to answer Risala's incoherent questions, barely slowing as a stone sliding away beneath his feet wrenched at his ankle and he barked his shin on a vicious outcrop.

The boulder Dev had rested his elbows on exploded. Gobbets of molten rock shot overhead to fall hissing into the sea or splinter the stones as they landed. The ground shifted and buckled and Dev looked back to see a burning crack gaping where they had crouched on the headland. As he watched, a bright arrowhead of blazing magelight cut rapidly through the ground towards him, a fiery fissure widening behind it.

Risala whimpered frantically as she hauled at the little boat. Dev seized the nearest handhold. Between them they threw the shallow craft into the water, setting it rocking perilously as they leaped inside.

'Put your back into it,' rasped Dev. He thrust them off from a rock with his own paddle.

The magical rift pursuing them reached the water's edge and halted in a cloud of steam. Dev caught his breath on an instant of relief before the sea all around their boat began to seethe and bubble.

Risala snatched her paddle out of the water. 'We're

going to be boiled alive,' she wailed.

Dev threw his paddle away and thrust his hands forward, emerald magelight swirling around them. Ignoring Risala's horror-struck face, he gripped the sides of the boat. The green radiance crawled outwards to form a lattice over the surface of the wood. As his magic touched the water, Dev realised there wasn't any fire magic beneath their hull. The water wasn't boiling; something was stirring it up. A roiling confusion of earth and water enchantments was rising beneath them.

Risala screamed as a glaucous grey tentacle slapped across the boat in front of her. Another came up on her other side and the two began twining together. She hammered at the writhing knot with her paddle blade but more tendrils came to join it. 'Dev!' Her panic rose to a tearing shriek as more tentacles poured over the side of the boat and began curling around her legs. Thick slime glistened on her feet, pooling in the bottom of the boat. She wrenched at a slippery grey feeler trying to coil around her wrist, freeing herself with an audible ripping sound. Livid sucker marks marred her skin.

Dev sat motionless, feeling this enchantment, whatever it was, leeching the magic from his own working, sucking at the elemental power he had summoned from the water. This unknown sorcery wasn't only leaving him powerless, it was using the stolen magic to feed the abomination attacking them. He looked over the side of the boat into the foaming sea where countless pallid, boneless limbs were emerging from the depths. Wherever the blind greedy fingers touched his magic, the green light faded to nothingness. Thrusting his hands to the air he summoned the fire that had always been the foundation of his power, flames dancing on his palms. A moment later, the scarlet light vanished, mercilessly snuffed.

A cracking sound silenced Risala's frantic screams. The

little boat shuddered as the soft tentacles suddenly stuck fast to the solid wood. They pulled and cracks appeared between Dev's feet. Sea water flooded the narrow hull, trails of slime floating free.

'Give me your hand!' As Dev reached for Risala, the tentacles quivered and ripped the boat to splinters with a mighty convulsion. He fell into the water, struggling to keep his head out of the spume and slime, lashing out at the loathsome touch of the grey tendrils on his arms and legs. Risala's despairing sob ended in a gurgle as something pulled her below the waves.

Dev kicked out madly at the smooth slipperiness curling around his feet, pushing in all directions to keep from being entangled. Taking a breath as best he could, he dived down, fighting his way through the water. The treacherous tendrils slid away before curling back to try winding around his arms. His fist hit something solid. He grabbed for it. Not wood, nor sea monster, it was firm yet flesh. It had to be Risala. Inheld breath burning in his chest, Dev looked upwards and turned every inborn instinct of magic within him to the sky.

They hit the deck of the *Amigal* with a thud that left him gasping. Risala sprawled beside him, her face invisible beneath the clinging mass of her sodden hair. Dev dragged himself to his knees and rolled the girl over on to her front, scraping the hair away.

'Breathe, curse you,' he rasped. Seizing her around the waist, he raised her hips. A spasm of coughing racked her and she began vomiting water and slime. Dev used one of the mast ropes to haul himself upright. This was no time for subtlety. He scattered the branches that had hidden the little ship with sweeps of sapphire magic, all the while hurrying to rig the sail.

'Help me,' he snarled at Risala. 'Otherwise we're both dead. Get the anchors aboard.'

Dragging herself to her feet, she half climbed, half fell over the rail, ashen-faced and her wide eyes bloodshot. She stumbled along the muddy bank, dragging the anchors with the last of her strength. Dev set the sail flapping loosely around the mast. The wind that had brought them to this inlet blew steadily onshore.

'Take the tiller,' Dev ordered, scooping up the anchors with a flurry of azure light.

Risala shied away from it with a fearful inarticulate cry.

'Get aboard and steer the cursed boat.' He glared at her.

Risala stood, frozen for an endless moment before scrambling over the rail, whimpering with terror as she gripped the tiller as if that alone could save her.

Dev turned his attention to filling the sail with a breeze strong enough to drive the *Amigal* out of its hiding place. He reached for the water beneath the hull but it slipped away from him, cold and unresponsive. Water magic was entirely beyond him, antithetical to the elemental fire where his inborn affinity lay.

The *Amigal* lurched and shuddered her way out into open water. Risala hauled this way and that on the tiller, staring panic-stricken in all directions.

Dev sank to the deck, back against the mast, legs outstretched in front of him, face to the prow. He realised with distant surprise that his feet and ankles were ringed with sucker marks. 'I'll get us as far as I can,' he said, not looking back. 'Then it'll be up to you. Try and get us to the Daish domain at very least. I'll have to sleep.' Exhaustion so deep his very bones ached threatened to overwhelm him. He fought it, looking up into the billows of the sail, concentrating on summoning the wind to carry them forward against the natural currents of the air.

'What did you do?' choked Risala from the stern.

'Translocation,' he answered hoarsely. A particularly

draining spell, granted, but even allowing for the other magic he'd been working, it shouldn't have left him this enfeebled.

'You're a wizard as well.' Risala's voice shook with loathing.

'You want me to throw you back to wrestle that monster?' snarled Dev.

'I won't sail with a wizard.' The girl's voice was harsh with fright.

'Suit yourself.' Dev knotted his fingers tight together, welcoming the pain as it quelled the trembling in his hands. 'Don't think of betraying me to anyone though. Any warlord looking to skin me will want me to talk first. I'll happily oblige if it means your death along with mine. Enough people have seen you with me this last run of the moons. I'll say you're my apprentice, that you sought me out to learn all the magic you could. You'll be hunted from one end of the Archipelago to the other.' Speaking was such an effort he abandoned it, turning what little vigour remained to him to the enchanted breeze, to carrying them away from that murderous wizard in his dragon-hide cloak.

'It was all lies, wasn't it? I asked you and you lied to me. The way you claimed to know all the currents, all the wind patterns, all your boasts about the secrets of sailing south into the face of the rains? It was just magic, wasn't it? What else have you done?' Risala's questions came in ragged gasps. 'What other magic have you worked to taint innocent people and places? What are you seeking in these reaches? Are you working for some barbarian king or has some warlord betrayed his birthright to turn your evil to his advantage?'

Dev ignored her. As the *Amigal* escaped the windward shore, Risala steered desperately to catch the natural breezes. The full-bellied sail pushed the little ship faster through the water. Dev realised belatedly it had stopped raining.

'I suppose I should thank you for saving me.' Risala forced the words out eventually.

'That wasn't about saving you.' There was an edge of hysteria in Dev's mockery. 'That was not letting him win.'

When he woke, he was lying in darkness on the floor of the aft cabin, the canvas of his hammock loosely draped over him. After a moment of stiff shock, he relaxed, propping himself up one elbow. The ship rocked with the gentle motion of a sheltered anchorage and he realised he could feel the sea streaming slowly along the hull with his usual wizard senses. He had recovered that much magic.

'Risala?' There was no reply. Reaching out with his inborn talent for fire, he lit the lamp hanging from the beam above him. Tossing the canvas aside, Dev got slowly and painfully to his feet. They were still sore where the obscene tentacles had fastened around them, the marks livid and puffy.

'Risala?' He realised her pathetic belongings were gone. Taking the lantern from its hook, he hobbled into the main hold and along the fore cabin. Everything was as it should be. At least the bitch hadn't robbed him, though the loss of the sack he'd taken ashore was a heavy blow to bear, he thought sourly.

Climbing the ladder and throwing open the hatch took more effort than Dev liked, but once on deck he breathed more easily. The *Amigal* was securely anchored by one of the Daish domain's lesser trading islets, deserted now as it had been on their voyage south.

Dev nodded with grudging admiration. He wouldn't have thought Risala had it in her to find the way back to the place. He looked at the empty white sand, gilded with the last gleam of sunset, and wondered where the girl had gone.

CHAPTER SIXTEEN

'Suis, at last, what news?' Kheda looked up as the ship-master entered the cramped cabin the trireme's carpenter had grudgingly surrendered to him. The only reason Kheda was sitting on his roll of bedding was there was no room to pace. Two strides from his neat leather bag of modest possessions by the sternposts would have brought his nose up against the door.

'The Daish domain prospers, from all I hear and all I can see.' The tall man's head nearly brushed the boards of the deck above. 'Everyone seems well fed and well clothed, busy about the usual wet-season occupations. The trading beach is deserted but people are staying close to home, to stay out of the rains as much as from fear of savages.'

'You don't think they'll find our presence here unusual?' asked Kheda bluntly. 'So far from your own waters?'

'Unusual, yes.' Suis chose his words carefully. 'Still, with such strange tidings on the winds, it's not so remarkable that Shek Kul might send a trusted ship south, a trusted shipmaster to see with his own eyes and carry the truth back to the north.'

'So the Daish domain prospers. Do the people expect that to last?' Kheda stared at the solid wall of wood as if he could look through it to the seashore beyond. 'Don't they fear assault from the south? What news of the invaders?'

'Chazen holds the line of the Serpents' Teeth against the savages,' the mariner said in neutral tones. 'Chazen islanders continue to flee whenever they can. From what they say, these villains are making no preparations to come north. Redigal Coron's ships patrol the waters to the west nevertheless while Ritsem and Sarem forces wait in readiness.'

'To sail south as soon as the rains are over,' concluded Kheda grimly.

At anchor in Daish waters. I cannot so much as see my people and they most certainly cannot be allowed to see me, but Daish waters all the same. Do you realise I'm so frustrated by all this that I could cheerfully punch a hole through the hull of your ship?

The shipmaster stood, hands behind his back, wide shoulders hiding the door behind him, easily balanced as the trireme rode contentedly at anchor. 'It may be hoped other domains would send forces to help Chazen Saril whenever he sought to reclaim his rightful domain.'

'Isn't there word of firm alliances, commitments given and rewards pledged?' Kheda asked sharply. 'Are you telling me people don't read Chazen Saril's intentions thus?'

'His men are fortifying their positions on the islets of the Serpents' Teeth.' Suis fixed his gaze on a knothole somewhere behind Kheda's head. 'Building defences that face in all directions, in case the invaders might somehow outflank them, so Chazen Saril claims. Redigal Coron is said to have rebuked him for lack of faith in the Daish domain's ships but Chazen Saril says he fears magical treachery carrying enemy forces into their midst.' The shipmaster paused. 'He is said to argue this possibility makes launching a strike south foolhardy at best.'

Kheda frowned. 'What does he mean by that?'

Suis's reply was precise and neutral. 'Some of those

Chazen men holding the Serpents' Teeth against the invaders have been given leave to visit families sheltered in the Daish domain. It is said that they are doing their best to beget children.'

Kheda looked suspiciously at the mariner. 'Men in fear of their lives commonly feel an urgency to plant their seed for a new generation.'

'It is commonly believed hereabouts that Chazen Saril is encouraging his men to give their wives a stake in the Daish domain, by virtue of a child nourished and born within its bounds.'

There was a definite edge to Suis's words that grated on Kheda's ear.

You don't like that, do you? Shek Kul assured me you'd ask no questions and offer no opinions and you've been as unreadable as a blank page, just as he promised, but you don't like that. There's something more, isn't there, if I can ask the right question, to get you to tell me. What wouldn't I give for Atoun at my side, or Telouet, giving me straightforward reports and offering blunt advice?

'The Daish islanders don't believe Chazen Saril will sail south to reclaim his own lands, do they?'

The movement of Suis's broad shoulders might have been the suggestion of a shrug. 'Few here have a favourable opinion of his courage or battle hardiness. He is certainly not spending any great deal of time with his own people and there are few signs that he is making ready to sail south. '

Kheda held his temper in check with some effort.

It's not fair to blame Suis for the time it took to make the voyage. The days at sea might have seemed endless to you but this trireme made this passage faster than you had any right to expect. These oarsmen don't know who you are or what your concerns may be and have never so much as hinted at a question but they've rowed ceaselessly against the full force

*of the worst of the rainy season weather without complaint.
The sail master and his crew haven't so much as uncoiled their
ropes, the winds have been so contrary.*

Suis stood, patient, expressionless. Silence echoed
loudly in the confined cabin.

'Where is Chazen Saril spending his time and what is
he doing with it?' Kheda asked brusquely.

'He is presently a guest in the Daish household.' Suis's
gaze flickered to Kheda's face before fixing on the stern
planks again. 'In the dry-season residence, that is.'

'At whose invitation?' snapped Kheda.

'It is said he is spending a great deal of time with Sain
Daish, consoling her over her widowhood and soothing
her fears for the fate of her new son,' said Suis carefully.
'She has not travelled with the other wives to their rainy-
season residence to the north.'

'Why not?' Kheda was taken aback.

'She gave the domain a son on the very night the rains
broke.' Suis looked steadfastly over Kheda's head.
'Apparently the child is too young to make the journey.'

'Such concerns outweigh the possibility of attack from
the south?' Kheda shook his head suspiciously. Inwardly,
he exulted.

*A son for Sain and such a favourable omen, for the waters
of birth to coincide with the rains.*

'Daish Sirket has also stayed at the dry-season residence,' volunteered Suis unexpectedly. 'In case any invasion should appear on the horizon and doubtless for other
reasons, so the word runs along the shore.

'To protect Sain Daish?' Kheda wondered.

Or to keep an eye on Chazen Saril?

'The word on the wind says Chazen Saril now neglects
Itrac Chazen in Sain Daish's favour.' Suis let slip a speculative glance at Kheda. 'Though Itrac Chazen is not said
to mind since she is much admired by Daish Sirket.

Wagers are being made over Itrac Chazen quickening with Daish blood.'

Not if Janne and Rekha have anything to say about it. But what can they say about it, if they're not there?

It took considerable effort for Kheda not to say this out loud.

'Is there any word at all of this visitor we're expecting?' he snapped abruptly.

'Not as yet.' Suis looked properly at Kheda for the first time. 'It can't be much longer. May I return to my duties?'

Would you stay, if I said you couldn't return to your deck? No, of course you wouldn't. I have no rank aboard this vessel, not even a name.

'Naturally.' Kheda inclined his head stiffly.

Suis left the tiny cabin without so much as a bow, leaving Kheda to the endless questions that had tormented him throughout this interminable voyage south.

Just what did Shek Kul tell you, trusted shipmaster? Not that you'll tell me even if I ask. There are so many questions I can't ask.

What is Sain thinking of naming her baby, our baby, my new son? Is she recovered from the delivery? Is the child healthy, unblemished? What omens were read at his birth? Did Sirket remember to do all that was needful?

What is Sain thinking of, entertaining Chazen Saril? Is Hanyad warning him off with those dour looks and obstructive excuses he's so good at? What is Sirket thinking of, dallying with Itrac Chazen?

What were Janne and Rekha thinking of, leaving Sain and Sirket alone in the dry-season residence with Chazen Saril's insinuating charms? I suppose they wanted to take the other children as far from danger as possible. They'll be well placed to flee to Ritsem waters, if the worst happens. Haven't they heard these rumours, if they're common currency along the shoreline? Why aren't they discouraging Sirket from this folly with Itrac? Perhaps they've tried. Is Sirket showing them who's warlord now, asserting his independence? Are they allowing him his pleasures, as respite from the demands upon him?

What is Chazen Saril thinking? If Sirket begets a child on Itrac, she's still married to Chazen. Her first child will be the new heir to the Chazen domain. Is this what Saril wants? If he sires that child, there could well be whispers about a taint of magic clinging to him. Sirket is demonstrably untouched by any enchantment.

Would Saril be thinking so far ahead? He's never shown that kind of prescience before. He's not even looking ahead to the dry season, to sailing south to reclaim his domain.

Or is he thinking ahead? Is he thinking of something else entirely? Could he be looking to take over the southernmost Daish islands? Surely not. Sirket would fight him, with the backing of Redigal and Ritsem both.

But what if Sirket died, at a wild man's hand or from some pestilence? What if Sain, in her grief, her new Daish son fatherless, turned to wed Chazen Saril, whose remaining wife was also carrying a child of Daish blood? He would have a claim to rule, as defender of children of the last two warlords so tragically slain, in such ominous circumstances.

Janne and Rekha would have something to say about that, and all their children with them. Though entire families can perish in the same calamity, a fire, sudden illness. Such catastrophe would raise suspicions within the private counsels of Ritsem and Redigal but who could gainsay Chazen if all the signs pointed to sorcerous malice encompassing such deaths? He need be nowhere near, cosily ensconced with Sain in the southern residence.

What are you thinking of? You're weaving frustrated fantasies out of unfounded suspicion because you've been shut up in this cursed cabin ever since we reached Endit waters.

You're imagining convoluted conspiracies because you've nothing better to do.

'Then find something to do!' Daish Reik had never shown any patience with children complaining of boredom. 'Think what may be asked of you later, tomorrow, the day after. Make ready, study, plan ahead while you have leisure, so you don't come running to me weeping because you've failed at something.'

Kheda unbuckled the nondescript bag that Shek Kul's body slave had brought him before his departure. He fished out a small lacquered box holding reed paper, pens and an inkpot stuffed with tandra fluff to save spills. Pen hovering over the pristine paper as he wondered what to write, his eyes strayed to another small box that Shek Kul had given him, lid secured all around with wax and stamped with the warlord's personal seal on all four sides.

You've some news for Janne but there's still this messenger Suis has been promising for the last two days. If the messenger can take you to this Dev character, you may well have far more to tell her. How soon can you meet her? This will have to go by whatever courier Suis can find for you. Best to send it to the thousand-oyster isle; that's closer than the rainy-season residence. Either Janne will be there herself or some trusted slave who can send her a messenger bird. Better allow the time for her to get the message and travel to meet you. In the meantime hopefully you'll have talked to this messenger. You can't afford to waste any more time. What can you write? Nothing that might be understood by unfriendly eyes but all Daish Kheda's ciphers died with him.

Kheda drew a swift half circle and below it, larger, a full roundel.

As long as Janne has the wit to read that for the Lesser Moon's half and the Greater's full, that gives her fifteen days. That can be a wager against the future, that I'll have something to tell her. Her journey will doubtless catch Chazen

Saril's eye. Maybe he'll look away from Sain and Sirket for a while.

Rolling the reed paper tight, he found a small stick of wax in the box of writing materials and held it in the flame of the candle lantern Suis had grudgingly granted him to light this confinement. He sealed the tiny roll of paper with a thick wax drop and opened the door to the trireme's oar deck.

'Sail master Falce.' Kheda cleared his throat politely. 'Could you take this message to Shipmaster Suis, please. I need it taken to an outer reef known as the thousand-oyster isle. There's a tower of silence there.' He proffered the paper. 'There will be someone there to take it.'

'Very well.' Falce hadn't quite perfected Suis's immobility of face. His thick brows rose before he accepted the sealed roll with a shrug declaring louder than any words this was none of his business and he intended keeping it that way.

As the sail master took the ladder to the stern platform, Kheda found himself rebelling at the thought of going back into hiding. He took a deep breath of the fresher air and welcomed the light falling between the side decks to illuminate the gangway between the banks of oars, even if the sky overhead was the inevitable rainy-season grey.

He approached a couple of the rowers who were methodically checking the thole pins and oar ports. 'Is there anything I can do to help?'

One of the men looked at him, curious. 'Do you know how to check an oar lashing?'

'I do.' Kheda slid into one of the bottom seats, where the lowest of the three ranks of rowers toiled. There was a powerful stench of sweat, legacy of the rowers' unquestioning obedience to Shek Kul's command for a fast passage south. Kheda found the rope holding the oar to the thole pin had indeed worked slack. He tightened it as Ialo had taught him, bending hopefully to peer out through the oar port. The leather sleeve rigged against foul weather blocked his view.

'You've done that before.' A rower on the topmost seat above surprised him. 'And got an oarsman's calluses,' the man added as Kheda looked up.

'Tai!' Back on the gangway, Falce rebuked him with a sharp look. 'Less chat, more work.'

Kheda bent to checking the next convoluted knot and the next, and then the one after that. Working in companionable silence, he and his new shipmates were well on their way through checking the topmost rank of oars when Suis appeared down the ladder from the stern platform and nodded with slow significance.

'Yes?' Kheda moved out into the gangway as Suis came down the ladder.

'Your message is sent.' The shipmaster stood to one side. 'And the message you've been expecting has arrived.'

Kheda slowly rubbed leather oil from his hands as a slender girl descended from the stern platform. Undernourished, with stains of exhaustion beneath blue eyes that were almost as black as her hair, her much worn clothes were heavily travel-stained. She held up a tightly sealed packet of oiled paper, looking expectantly at Kheda.

'In the cabin.' Kheda followed this unlikely courier through the door with a nod of thanks to Suis. He relit his candle lantern, shaking fingers fumbling with his spark maker, and shut the cabin door tight. There was no seal on the wax sticking the oiled paper together. Kheda cracked it open to find a few lines of nonsensical writing. He tugged the leather thong over his head. The girl sat on the floor, tousled head hanging wearily.

'If you're the man I think you are, you'll find the cipher key in that.'

Kheda twisted Shek Kul's heavy silver ring until he could see the inscription inside, a meaningless circle of letters and symbols, unless you had the wit to lay it on your hand with the talisman gem aligned with the north and then to start reading from the arc where the heavenly Emerald would be riding high come nightfall. Kheda looked at the first letter of the message and found the same symbol within the circle of the ring. It was the ninth from the arc of health and daily duty. Mentally running through the usual alphabet, Kheda identified the letter 'I'. That was a promising beginning. He reached for his writing box before recalling Daish Reik's rebukes.

'Why bother with a cipher if you're going to write the words out clearly for any spy, thief or nosy servant to happen across it?'

He worked his way through the message in the safety of his own head and looked at the girl. 'Who gave you this? Where can I meet him?'

'No one gave it to me.' The girl looked up, her eyes bright and challenging. 'I wrote it myself. Read it back to me, to prove you're the man my master bids me help.'

'It says, "I like duck stewed with water pepper and served with saller dusted with tarit seed."' Kheda leaned against the wooden wall. 'Water pepper grows wild just about everywhere here but what have you got to trade for a fat duck? And that's a dish that wants long, slow cooking. I don't think we've got time for that. I prefer my saller plain or dressed with a little scalid oil.'

'Can't abide the taste.' The girl grinned at him.

Kheda stayed stony-faced. 'Where is he?'

'Close enough.' The girl shrugged. 'Or if he's moved, he'll be easy enough to trace.'

'Have you got a boat?' At her nod, Kheda caught up his belongings. 'Let's go.'

'My master's message told me finding this man was

life or death to you.' She rose but held the door shut. 'If you come with me now, there's no going back, you do understand?' Her low voice was peculiarly intense.

Kheda leaned forward to stare into her vivid blue eyes. 'Not when I've come this far.'

Motionless for a moment, the girl nodded abruptly. 'Come on then. We don't want to spend the rest of the rains chasing him.' She slid through the door, running lithely up the ladder to the open deck.

Kheda followed more slowly. Suis was on the stern platform, looking all around, broad shoulders tense.

'There's no one to see you, if you're quick.'

'I imagine this is goodbye.' Kheda held out his hand. 'Thank you.'

'I merely do as my master bids me.' All the same Suis smiled, if only for a moment. 'His word holds good, if you ever find yourself in the same anchorage as us, needing a passage.'

'Come on!' The girl was already disappearing down a ladder slung over the trireme's stern.

Kheda looked down to see her boat was a little skiff; single-masted, triangular-sailed, such as coastal fishers used. He looked uncertainly up at the clouds, darkening as the afternoon turned towards evening. Then he dropped his bag and bedroll down and slid down the rope ladder, smiling despite himself at the touch of fresh air after the stuffy lower deck of the trireme.

'Give me those.' The girl thrust his belongings under the stern thwart where she sat. She checked the breeze, one hand on the tiller, the other on the rope that governed the sail. 'Give us a push off and then get the oars out.'

'Yes, shipmaster,' Kheda said meekly.

The girl grinned at him. 'You want passage in my boat, friend, you pay for it by making yourself useful.'

Kheda dutifully pushed them away from the lofty side

of the trireme and took the oars. A few hard pulls took them out of the big ship's shadow and the sail bellied in the wind. Shipping the oars, Kheda moved to the prow, away from the danger of the sail's boom. He allowed himself a look at the islet they were leaving. High seas lashed by the rainy season's vicious winds had strewn detritus along the white sand beach but the few houses among the palms looked in good repair, storm shutters mounted solid against the weather.

These people are secure enough, as long as the invaders come no further north. Until these invaders come north. Unless a way can be found to stop them coming north.

'Where do we find this Dev?'

The girl kept her attention on the sail. 'What do you know of him?'

Kheda curbed his impatience. 'I know that he's a barbarian, with some kind of ties to their wizards, some knowledge of their magics.'

The girl's face remained impassive. 'That doesn't worry you?' She caught the breeze deftly and the skiff surged through the water.

'It worries me,' said Kheda frankly. 'But foul enchantments devastating the Chazen domain worry me more. I want to know how to fight them. I've travelled up and down the Archipelago in search of any such lore. Your master told me Dev might know something I can use.' Their course was leading them south and east, he noted. 'Are you looking to pick up the current to take us out around the windward side of the domain?'

'I'm surprised you know these waters well enough to tell.' The girl looked curiously at him. 'You're setting yourself against these wild magics? Who are you to be taking such a burden on yourself?'

'That's not important.' Kheda smiled to take the sting out of his words. 'For the present.'

The girl shrugged as far as was possible with both hands fully occupied 'Whoever you are, you're taking more on you than you can know, if I take you to Dev.' The warning in her voice was unmistakable.

'The man's a vice peddler, Shek Kul told me that,' said Kheda slowly. 'As well as a dealer in information. Shek Kul believes he takes word of Aldabreshin affairs to some northern barbarian lord who supplies him with his liquors and dreamsmokes. It seems he has some dealings with barbarian wizards as well. '

'Dev's a wizard himself, without a doubt.' A shudder ripped through the girl that set the sail sheet rattling and the little boat's course jerked abruptly. 'That's what I meant about no going back. I've been wholly caught up in one of his enchantments. Stay with me and you'll be touched with the same stain. I can still put you ashore and you can give up this foolish quest of yours.'

'He's a wizard?' Kheda stared at her. 'What is he doing in these waters? Allying himself with these invaders?'

'Spying on them for his own purposes.' The girl shivered again. 'He's fascinated by their magic.'

'He understands it?' asked Kheda.

'Enough to save us both from being ripped to pieces by it with magic of his own.' The girl looked helplessly at him. 'Do you believe someone caught up in magic innocent of intent can shed its taint?'

Mouth open, Kheda found he was lost for words.

'Do I put you ashore or not?' she snapped irritably. 'I don't want to lose him. I have to tell Shek Kul what he is and knowing where he sails is even more important than ever now.'

'Take me to see him,' Kheda said slowly. 'I have spent too long searching for some understanding of these wild men and their magic to turn back now, even if it does mean dealing with a wizard. My intent is honourable; that should surely protect me from stain, and simply asking some questions shouldn't imperil me.'

And you've already been caught up in the miasma of the savages' magic, in any case.

'Who are you,' the girl wondered, baffled, 'to run such a risk?'

'I'm Daish Kheda.' He looked round at the empty sea, not even a red-beaked seabird to hear such a dramatic declaration. 'Defending these waters, these people, it's the duty I was born to.'

'Daish Kheda is dead.' The girl steered the skiff carefully away from a foam-crested reef. 'Daish Sirket was proclaimed warlord.'

'We had no choice, if I was to search for such lore unhindered.' Kheda challenged her with a thrust of his jaw. 'I will not return to answer for the deception until I have some means of challenging these invaders' wizards to set against it. Betray me for who I am and I will denounce you as touched by magic.'

'Naturally,' the girl said without rancour. 'Much good it would do you. With everyone running scared of magic, you'd likely be stoned for your pains.'

'True enough,' Kheda acknowledged with an unexpected lifting of his spirits. 'We're entangled in each other's secrets now, so can we trust each other?'

'I think so.' She looked steadily at him as the little skiff rocked over rising seas now they were further from the shore. 'We most assuredly cannot trust Dev.'

'How so?' Kheda asked. 'Apart from his being a wizard?'

The girl steered the bucking boat through a maze of white-crested troughs. 'He's entirely without scruple,' she said finally. 'He'll get a man drunk enough to wake up blind, to learn some trifle he's seeking. When he can get a girl to sail with him, he'll offer her up willing or not, if that's the price of a juicy morsel of gossip from some panting brute. He boasts of addling freeborn islanders into stupidity and trading them into slavery just to make friends with a pirate shipmaster.'

'To learn some secret?' Kheda was uncertain of her meaning.

'Just because he can, sometimes,' the girl replied dourly. 'To see if he can get away with such wickedness.'

'The corruption of magic is said to stain bone deep,' commented Kheda with distaste. 'Why doesn't Shek Kul just have him killed and be done?'

'That was his intention, when he'd found out just who Dev sells his information to and what that person might want with the inner dealings of the Archipelago. I imagine he'll see him dead regardless, now it's definite the man is a wizard.' The girl looked thoughtful. 'If he can be killed before he realises his peril.'

Kheda shivered as a spray of foam spattered across his back. 'Tell me about the magic, and about the savages. If the Daish domain is to find any means of fighting them, we have to know more about them.'

'You'll have to trust that I'm telling the truth.' The girl took a deep breath. 'I wouldn't have believed it, if I hadn't seen it myself.'

By the time she had finished her incredible tale, she was having to shout above the clamour of a rising storm. The clouds had darkened to a pitch hue and rain was coming down in torrents. An awkward clash of waves sent a wall of green water crashing over their prow, leaving the little skiff knee deep. Kheda was already bailing out with a battered tin pot that came floating out from beneath the foremost thwart and redoubled his efforts. He was soaked to the skin, clothes clinging to his body, so chilled that he ached from head to toe.

The girl was just as drenched, ragged hair flattened, plastered across her honey-coloured face in black streaks, lips pale with cold. She clung to the tiller and to the rope governing the close-reefed sail, arms brutally wrenched by the wind's callous changes of direction.

When he'd got the water in the skiff's bottom down to a manageable level, Kheda worked his way awkwardly to the stern, every lurch threatening to throw him over the side. There was little point trying to make himself heard over the crash of the seas and the gale that was thrashing ropes and canvas into frenzy. He pointed wordlessly to the tiller. The girl let him take it, wrestling grim-faced with the vicious wind for mastery of the scrap of sail that was all they dared risk. Kheda sat beside her, the tiller gripped in both hands. The boat rocked and danced. Rain and sea alike battered them relentlessly in a tumult reflecting the turmoil of Kheda's own thoughts.

The stakes get higher with every turn of this game. Dealing with a barbarian claiming knowledge of northern wizardry is one thing; how do I deal with a proven user of magic? But what do I do, if I don't? Where else am I going to find any hope for my domain? If we live through this storm, it must surely be an omen. It must surely be a sign that we're following a path for the ultimate good of the Daish people, even if it does take me to a self-confessed wizard.

The girl's painful pinch on his cold arm startled him.

'We have to round that headland,' she yelled. 'I must lower the sail or we'll be driven on to the rocks.'

'Do it.' The boat rocked alarmingly as she crawled forward and brought the circumscribed sail crashing down, dragging the spars hastily out of his way. Kheda held out his hand, pulling her back to take over the tiller as he moved to the middle thwart and retrieved the oars. Rowing was agony, his chilled and strained muscles protesting with every stroke. Several times the rocking of the skiff left him pulling against empty air instead of sea with a sudden jerk that tore at his shoulders. Unable to see where they were headed, he fixed his trust in the girl clinging to the tiller, grim-faced as she looked beyond the little boat's prow. Kheda heard the crash of sea over rocks, the growl of surf on a stony shore. He ducked his head and pulled harder.

'Dev's ship!' The girl's cry, half relief, half apprehension, made Kheda look up.

He realised they had fought past the headland to win the relative calm of the leeward side. The seas were still running fast and furious but the oars no longer fought him so frantically. Twisting to look over his shoulder, he saw a small trading ship riding at anchor in the most sheltered part of the bay, sails furled and hatches tight barred

Kheda shouted to the girl. 'If he's aboard, we ask for shelter. If he's not, we sit out this storm in the ship and think what to do next in the morning.'

She nodded fervent agreement and Kheda bent over the oars for one last effort. They reached the *Amigal* with a bump that set the ship rocking but the girl managed to reach up and grab the rail. Before Kheda could stop or help her, she swung herself aboard.

'Throw me a rope,' she yelled.

Kheda hastily tossed the oars into the bottom of the skiff and scrambled to the prow. He threw her the bow rope with numb, awkward hands and she caught it with a clumsy grab. As she wrapped it around the bigger ship's rail, Kheda retrieved their sodden belongings, hurling everything he could find up to the *Amigal*'s deck. Bags landed with dull thuds and Kheda belatedly remembered Shek Kul's sealed box.

That'll be another sign, if that's survived intact.

'Come on.' The girl leaned over the rail, her hand outstretched.

Once aboard, Kheda looked uncertainly at the close-fitted stern hatch. 'Do you think he's here?'

The girl bit her lip. 'Only one way to find out.' She bent to pull the brass ring sunk into the hatch. As she did so, the wood rose up and smacked into her fingers.

'Risala, you ungrateful little bitch, what a surprise to see you here.' It was a genial enough greeting, apart from the actual words. 'You've brought company? Who said you could do that?'

'We're dying of wet and cold out here,' the girl said indistinctly, sucking on her stinging hand. 'Give us some shelter for pity's sake.'

'Plenty of shelter ashore.' But the man climbed up the ladder to open the hatch wider. 'All right, get in before we all drown.'

Kheda took the hatch and the man disappeared. The girl, Risala, gathered up their belongings and half slid, half fell down the ladder. Kheda followed as quickly as he could, pulling the hatch closed behind him. Dev was already back in his hammock, one leg dangling over the side, a horn cup resting on his belly cradled in both hands.

Kheda twisted the ring on the inner face of the hatch, turning a sturdy brass bar to secure it. He turned to Dev, composing his face to suitable gratitude. 'Thank you for taking us aboard.'

'Don't thank me yet,' Dev said cheerfully. 'I'll cut your throat and throw you overboard if you get on my nerves, won't I, Risala?'

'Doubtless,' she said shortly. She wrapped her arms around herself, shivering uncontrollably. 'Just let us get warm and dry first.'

'Best get out of those wet things.' He leered at her.

'I'll change through there, thanks.' She jerked her head towards the main hold.

'Let you loose with my stock?' Dev raised his eyebrows. 'I think not.'

'Why don't you and I go through, Master Dev?'

suggested Kheda tentatively. 'Risala,' he stumbled over the name and hoped he'd heard it right. 'You can change in here.'

'I don't know why my lady thinks her modesty is worth protecting. All right then, it'll give me a chance to see what you're made of.' The curiosity in Dev's face was undisguised. He swung himself out of his hammock and took the lantern from its hook. 'You can work by feel, girl. I want a better look at your friend here.' He unlocked the door and gestured Kheda through.

'Look all you want.' Kheda pulled his saturated tunic over his head with some difficulty, the cloth clinging to his skin. 'There's not much to see.' He tugged at the drawstring of his trousers, the knot swollen and tight.

'I don't imagine that's what the ladies say,' Dev said slyly, raising the lantern.

Kheda registered the man's hairless chin for the first time. 'If you're a man's man, I'm sorry to disappoint you,' he said curtly.

He turned his back on Dev, shed the trousers and dug in his bag for other clothes.

'If there's anything dry in there, I'll eat it,' the other man mocked.

Kheda didn't turn round, wiping water from his body as best he could with his wrung-out tunic. 'If you've anything dry for us to wear, we'd be in your debt,' he said with carefully calculated mildness.

'Why should that interest me?' Dev's words were an unpleasant blend of scorn and amusement.

'I thought you were a trader.' Kheda shook out the pair of non-descript trousers Shek Kul's slave had given him for a change of clothes. They didn't actually drip but that was their only advantage over the garment oozing a puddle on the boards by his feet. 'Don't you trade in obligation?'

'When it suits me,' Dev allowed. 'It doesn't happen to

suit me just now,' he added maliciously.

Kheda stepped into trousers that clung unpleasantly to his legs. 'Risala, are you dressed?'

'Yes.' She pushed open the door and the lamplight showed her in a thin dress clinging damply to her skinny body.

'Very fetching,' Dev admired before turning his attention back to Kheda. 'Has she told you what I am?'

'A vice peddler, selling liquor and leaf, dreamsmokes and the like.' Kheda leaned against the barrels he'd dumped his bag on, hands behind his back. 'And a wizard.'

'You came to see if it was true, did you?' challenged Dev. 'Another halfwit of a poet?'

'I'm a soothsayer,' replied Kheda.

'I asked him if he could purify me after being touched by your magic,' Risala said instantly.

'Is that so?' Dev raised a hand and a red haze enveloped Kheda. Enveloped in warmth, he nevertheless froze with shock, his spine a column of ice and dread. Dev snapped his fingers and the mist vanished. 'How will you do that when you're just as tainted?'

Kheda licked his lips and found them dry. In fact, he was entirely dry, clothes, skin, hair and beard, and the bone-deep chill was receding fast. He cleared his throat. 'There's a school of thought that argues an innocent victim of magic is not so deeply mired in it as someone who deliberately seeks out or effects its use.'

'Effects its use?' Dev echoed unpleasantly. 'Do any of these great Archipelagan thinkers know anything about effecting magic's use?'

'I really couldn't say,' Kheda shrugged.

'I really wouldn't think so,' retorted Dev. 'You know nothing, you Aldabreshi with your soothsayers and your stargazers and your books full of lore on what's to be read in a deer's innards.'

'I know I'm chilled half to death.' Risala could barely get the words out, her teeth were chattering so much. 'You can spare some wine to warm me, you bastard.'

'I'll do better than that.' With a negligent wave of Dev's hand, the same red glow swirled around her 'A cup of wine isn't a bad notion, mind. Then you can tell me what brings you back to me.' He shot a sideways smirk at Kheda. 'Other than my prowess as a lover.'

Kheda caught the speculative glint in the wizard's eye and kept his face impassive.

I've had better men than you, and worse, try to rile me into indiscretion, you tedious little barbarian.

He smiled at Risala who was shaking out the stiff and crumpled folds of her dry dress. 'I don't suppose this makes your contamination too much worse.'

'Ah, you wouldn't have touched her, not while she was so dirty with magic.' Dev turned to choose a bottle from an all but empty basket. 'That's why you're so keen to purify her, so she'll open her thighs out of gratitude? Sorry, friend, she's not worth the bother.'

'Still so keen on the sound of your own voice, Dev.' Risala wasn't rising to the bait either. 'Any chance you'll start speaking sense any time soon?'

'Make yourself useful and find the cups.' Bottle in one hand, lantern in the other, Dev jerked his head towards the miscellaneous storage boxes. 'You, soothsayer, back in there.'

Kheda dutifully returned to the stern cabin, followed by Risala. Dev hung the lantern on its hook and turned to lock the door to the hold. Kheda and Risala shared a glance and he saw his own determination mirrored in her face.

'If you're stained by my magic, I don't suppose the crime of tasting my wine will worry you too much.' Dev grinned genially as he twisted the wax-sealed cork out of the bottle. 'Let's have a drink, girl.' As Risala held out two horn cups, he sloshed dark red wine into them. 'There you go, soothsayer'

Kheda wordlessly accepted a cup.

'Be careful,' Dev warned, sarcastic. 'You can't go back to drinking that goat's piss you people call wine, once you get a taste for this.' With remarkable deftness, he got onto the hammock, found his cup and refilled it, feet swinging.

'Wizard or not, I'd take you for Aldabreshi.' Kheda sat down on the battered chest on the opposite side of the cabin. 'From some northern domain and with barbarian blood, but certainly born in the Archipelago.' He sipped cautiously, blinking rapidly as the powerful perfume of the wine momentarily overwhelmed him. 'Are you one of us?'

'Did you find some way to escape execution once the magic warping you became apparent?' Risala's blue eyes were speculative over the rim of her cup. She sat on the chest beside Kheda, her thigh pressing against his.

'Not me.' Dev took a swig of wine. 'I'm a barbarian, born and bred. None of your soothsayers ever saw that, friend.' He grinned cheerfully.

Kheda studied him. 'What could a barbarian wizard seek in the Archipelago, at the risk of his own hide?'

'That's my business, pal.' Dev scowled as he emptied his cup. 'I'm more interested in yours. This is my ship, so I'll ask the questions. What brings you hunting for a mage? And don't give me any tripe about helping the poor little soiled poet girl. I might believe it if you were looking to lift her skirts but I don't see that.'

'You're an astute man,' observed Kheda.

'I'd be long dead if I wasn't.' Dev saluted him with his cup. 'What really brings you to me? Apart from a glossy trireme all the way from northern waters.' He shook his head at Risala. 'You didn't think I'd let you go, did you, girlie? I've been keeping a wizard's eye on you, just in case you went selling my secret to some bastard who'd come looking to nail my skin to a fortress door.' He refilled his cup as he spoke. 'I was thinking it was a shame I had no one to make a wager with, against you two making it here alive, when I saw you fighting that storm.'

'Would you have done anything about it, if we'd foundered?' Risala stood up and took the bottle from Dev.

'And pollute you further with my filthy magic?' Dev pretended concern.

'There are worse magics than yours abroad in these reaches,' said Kheda curtly. He reached out and took the wine bottle from Risala.

'That interests you, does it?' Dev swung his feet idly but his eyes were alert.

Wizards cloak themselves in lies and twist anything they touch out of true. Can you read my words? Let's see how much truth I can tell you without you seeing the whole.

'Let's get down to business.' Kheda set his empty cup on the floor. 'I've offered counsel to the Daish domain before now and, for reasons I don't propose to share with you, I'm under a great obligation to the lady Janne Daish. I want to repay that debt by finding some means to frustrate this magic that's brought such destruction to the Chazen domain, before it can come north to devastate the Daish islands.' He raised an emphatic finger. 'Not that Janne Daish has any knowledge of my intent. You can't use that against her.'

'You think you can fight back against those savages and their magic? You're an idiot. All you Archipelagans, you're ignorant, magicless fools.' Dev gestured for the wine bottle. 'You cannot fight those with wizardry bred in their very bone.' For the first time, he sounded entirely serious, even without malice.

'You could.' Kheda jerked his head towards Risala beside him. 'She told me as much.'

'I could, true enough.' Dev swung up his feet and lay back in his hammock, tipping the last of the wine into his cup. 'I did, very effectively, I might add. What's that to you, soothsayer? Suborning magic will see you skinned along with me and her head on a spike, just for good measure,' he concluded with happy malice.

Kheda picked up his cup and drank the heady wine slowly before putting into words the furious debate he'd waged with himself, even as he and Risala had fought their way through the storm.

You've come too far, at the cost of too much pain, for you and all those you love to give up now.

'The malice of magic is what stains whatever it touches. These savages, they've proved themselves vicious beyond belief. Would dealing with a wizard to find some way to fight them, if that's the only way to fight them, would that be so very evil?' He looked at Risala, desperate to see some agreement in her eyes.

She looked at him, biting her lip, before shivering suddenly. 'I wouldn't like to stand before any warlord and plead that case for his mercy.'

'I once read an argument where magic was likened to a crystal prism,' Kheda said to her, beseeching. 'Splitting the pure light into broken colours. A second prism can restore the light. Might using a wizard's knowledge to quell magic not be the lesser of the two evils?'

'Pardon me for interrupting your philosophical debate—' Dev tossed the empty wine bottle into the air. 'Your assumption—'

A blue light sparked inside the dark green glass and died at once. The bottle crashed to the floor and shattered.

'Arseholes!' Dev sat up straight, mouth open. He waved

a hand at the lamp, which burned on steadily, golden glow unaffected. He half jumped, half fell from his hammock. 'What have you done, you bastards?'

'Mind the glass!' Risala warned, drawing her feet up to the top of the chest, hugging her knees.

Dev ignored the dull green shards scattered across the boards, glaring at Kheda. 'What have you done?'

'Tamed your magic, for the moment.' Kheda hoped he'd dusted the last of the powder he'd taken from Shek Kul's box from his fingers. 'I'd rather have your cooperation willingly but I'll force you if needs be.'

And thank you for that ancient concoction, great lord of Shek, even if you had no idea if it would work, as you were scrupulously honest in explaining.

'You think you can force me to work magic for you?' spat Dev. 'By taking it from me? What is this, one of your useless talismans actually working for a change?'

'I can't force you to help me,' Kheda said tightly. 'But I can keep you helpless and deliver you up to the rulers of the Daish domain. We can both swear to your wizardry and throw ourselves on their mercy and see you skinned alive to purify us both and ward the evil of the invader's magic from the domain.'

'Daish Sirket would owe us a tremendous debt, if we could offer him the protection of such a rite, to strengthen his men and those of Chazen, when they sail south at the end of the rains,' Risala said boldly.

Kheda could feel her trembling, as she pressed close against him. 'I imagine Daish Sirket and Chazen Saril would share in the ritual. There would surely be omens to be read in the mirror of your liver, in the coils of your entrails. If you will not tell us willingly how we might defeat these invaders, perhaps your death will serve our purpose despite you.'

Read the truth in that, you bastard, because if that's all the good I can wring from your twisted carcass to help my domain, then I swear I will do it. Even if I die for it myself.

'You just try it, pal.' Dev launched himself at Kheda, heedless of the glass on the floor.

Risala darted away to one side and Kheda ducked the other. Sharp pain in his feet slowed him and Dev bore him down to the floor, reaching for his neck with strangling hands. Bucking his hips to try and throw the lighter man off, Kheda thrust a fist upwards between the wizard's forearms. He couldn't manage a hard punch to Dev's throat but it was enough to loosen his grip. Kheda forced his other arm up and knocked the mage's hands aside. Dev's forehead came down to butt him and Kheda rolled his head aside to take the blow on his cheekbone. The pain of that was enough to make him gasp but it was Dev who yelled.

Kheda blinked away tears to see Risala's sharp fingernails drawing blood in the wide neck of Dev's tunic. Rising to his knees with a roar of anger the wizard swung round an arm but he couldn't reach her. A wrench of his shoulders instead pulled Risala around to trip over Kheda's legs. She went sprawling across the splinter-strewn floor but, clinging to Dev, she dragged him with her. Kheda scrambled up and flung himself at Dev, his greater weight knocking the mage flat. Glass crunched beneath them.

Ignoring the needle-sharp pains in his knees and shins, Kheda straddled Dev's hips, pinning the mage to the boards. Warding off Dev's blows with one forearm, he landed a jarring punch on the wizard. Dev's head jolted as his lip split.

'He's got a knife!' Risala had seen him scrabbling for something beneath his tunic and seized his hand. Leaning on it with all her weight, she bore it down to the floor. Kheda held it down with one knee and caught Dev's other hand in a vice-like grip, muscles built by half a season's rowing bunching beneath his tunic sleeve as he fought the wizard's wiry strength. With his free hand, he grabbed Dev's jaw and thumped the mage's bald head hard against the floor.

'Don't think you can get me to kill you, just to save you from the augur's knife,' he hissed.

Twisting his head free, Dev managed to bite Kheda between thumb and forefinger. Kheda punched him again, under the jaw, snapping his teeth shut.

'He doesn't have to be unmarked, does he, not like a sacrificial animal?' Risala panted with triumph as she held up the knife Dev had tried to use on Kheda. Steel caught the lamplight. 'Can't you hamstring him, to keep him from escaping? Cut the tendons in his arms as well. They all seem to wave their hands around to work their magic.'

'All he has to be is a wizard.' Kheda let his full weight press down on Dev.

'Working magic has nothing to do with using your hands, you stupid bitch.' The mage writhed beneath him.

Kheda took the knife from Risala and shoved the point between Dev's snarling teeth. The mage's instinctive recoil left him with a sharp cut in the corner of his mouth.

Kheda lent forward to look Dev in the eye. 'The last time a wizard was caught and killed in the Safar domain, they cut his tongue out ahead of time, so he couldn't curse anyone.'

Dev froze, tense but still, and Kheda slowly withdrew the knife.

'I shouldn't have waited to see if you drowned. I should've summoned the waves to sink you myself.' Dev winced and rolled his head to spit blood away. 'If I'd known you were going to be this much trouble. I could have done with consulting a soothsayer, couldn't I?' he added with vicious wit.

Kheda matched his sour humour. 'You're the one in

charge here.' Laying the knife alongside Dev's throat gave the lie to his words. 'It's your choice. Help us against these invaders and their magic or see your blood shed in hopes that it will protect the Daish domain. What would you rather do?'

'Suppose I do help you?' Dev's jaw jutted belligerently. 'What do I get out of it?'

'Besides a whole hide?' Kheda didn't have to pretend surprise. Cramp threatened in his thighs and he shifted a little. Needles of glass pricked his shins, a stickiness of blood warm on his skin.

'I thought you weren't a man's man.' Dev tested Kheda's weight with a suggestive twist of his own hips.

'You won't distract me with your nonsense.' Kheda pressed the knife harder into the leathery skin of Dev's throat.

'Don't you want revenge on the invaders?' Risala's taunt turned both men's heads. She shook her head at Dev. 'Don't you want to make that mage in the dragon-hide cloak pay for sending those tentacles to slap your sorry arse and try ripping you limb from limb?'

'Revenge isn't worth so much,' said Dev tightly. 'I'll want something I can trade for real value.'

'Pearls? Turtle shell?' Kheda shrugged. 'What's so funny about that?'

Dev licked at the corner of his mouth, the knife cut painfully pulled by his unexpected chuckle. 'Those wizards down south don't reckon much to pearls or turtle shell. They want gems, the bigger the better, talisman stones for preference.'

'That's what was in the coffer?' Risala asked.

'You're not the only one I've been keeping an eye on.' Dev slid a sly glance towards her.

'Why do they want talisman gemstones?' demanded Kheda.

'So many questions.' Still pinioned, Dev nevertheless tried to shrug. 'Every answer has its price, you must know that much, soothsayer.'

Kheda looked down at the wizard with undisguised contempt. 'If you're paid, well paid, with pearls and jewels as well as your worthless life, will you help us?'

'What does a penniless soothsayer with a slut of a poet in tow have to pay me with?' scorned Dev.

Tell him who you are and you give yourself over to his mercy. Is there any other way to win his assistance? Isn't this a wager that'll prove your cause, one way or the other?

Blood pulsing in his throat, Kheda kept his voice as calm as he could. 'I can reward you with more riches than you can imagine, fool of a barbarian. I am Daish Kheda, warlord of that domain.'

'And I'm the Emperor of Tormalin,' scoffed Dev breathlessly.

'You don't have some magic to know he's telling the truth?' Risala was genuinely surprised.

'You people do have some foolish notions about what magic can do.' Dev shook his head as far as he was able. 'Prove it.'

'Who else but a warlord would have the secret of disarming a wizard?' Kheda smiled with confident pride to mask his inner incredulity at what he was doing. 'Who else but the Daish warlord would risk himself in dealings with a mage in order to fight the magic that threatens his people? Why else would I hand you the valuable gift of knowledge of my true identity, if I wasn't trying to buy your cooperation.'

'Why does everyone else think the Daish warlord is dead?' retorted Dev, now trying in vain to find some purchase for his feet on the slippery deck.

Kheda pressed his weight down harder. 'Do you imagine I could have gone on such a quest with every eye on me, every tongue speculating as to what I might be planning?'

Dev's eyes narrowed. 'I don't imagine many other warlords would be too pleased to know what you're doing.'

'Then you can imagine what I'll be paying you, to keep your mouth shut about exactly how we drive these wizards out of the southern reaches,' countered Kheda coldly.

'Will you help us?' Risala demanded.

'I'll think about it.' Dev closed his eyes for a moment. 'If you haven't crushed the life out of me.'

'I'll let you free if you give your word not to fight again.' Kheda's own legs begged him to stand up.

'My word?' mocked Dev, his spirit returning. 'The word of a foul, deceitful, perverse wizard?'

'A wizard with no powers at present.' Kheda looked down at him, unblinking. 'A wizard I can hand over to any number of warlords who'll be only too happy to flay him alive.'

'You've already made a start on that, you bastard.' Dev's breath hissed between his teeth. 'I'll be no cursed use to you if I'm dead of blood poisoning.'

'Give me your word.' Kheda let his full weight press down again. 'If you keep it, that'll be worth some payment in its own right.'

'Show us we're wrong about wizards, we stupid Aldabreshi,' added Risala, her scepticism plain.

'I swear, by all that's holy—' Dev caught himself. 'By the fire that burns within my very bones, that I will help you fight the invaders and their wizards, just so long as you pay me all that you can. Betray me—' He paused and glared up at Kheda. 'And I will melt the flesh from your bones with sorcerous fire that will leave a stain on these islands for a full cycle of the heavens.'

Kheda got up, trying to disguise the shudder that racked him at those words. 'Good enough.' He paused, held Dev down with one knee and cut the key cord from around the bald man's waist. 'I'll hold these for the present, just to help keep you honest.'

Groaning, Dev rolled over. The back of his tunic was stained with blood and bright with broken glass. 'What have you done, drugged me? I don't feel doped but I can't feel the slightest touch of the elements.'

'That's my secret,' said Kheda shortly. He sat on the chest and grimaced as he picked glass out of his shin. 'Risala, can you get some wine to wash out everyone's wounds? And something to sweep up this glass?'

'Get the white brandy,' snapped Dev. 'In the basket with the blue withy rim.'

When Risala returned, stubby black bottle and a threadbare besom in her bloodied hands, Dev sat up and pulled off his tunic. 'See if you can clear up your new lover's mess.'

She didn't bother replying, simply handing the bottle to Kheda, before sitting to begin picking the fragments out of Dev's skin.

'Shit, that's sore!' Dev grabbed the brandy from Kheda and took a long drink.

Risala took the bottle from him and sluiced his wounds with the spirit.

'You're a lousy nurse, girlie,' Dev gasped.

'Find another,' she said unsympathetic, tearing a strip from his ruined tunic to wipe away the welling blood.

'I'll go ashore in the morning.' Kheda finished sweeping the broken glass into a pile and began gingerly tending his own wounds with a liquor-soaked scrap of cloth. 'Find the makings of a poultice for us all.'

'This is all the medicine I need.' Dev snatched back the bottle and glared at Kheda. 'Get lost and let me get some sleep.'

Kheda walked stiffly over to unlock the door to the

hold. 'You sleep in here.' He went into the gloom to retrieve his soggy belongings.

'You can take your hammock,' Risala said sweetly.

'I'll thank you to remember I'm the owner of this ship, girlie.' Dev unhooked his hammock from the beams nevertheless, carrying the bundle of sailcloth and blankets through into the darkness. He slammed the door emphatically behind him. Kheda locked it.

'Keys, please.'

Kheda threw the bunch. Risala caught the cord and unlocked the big chest, pulling out hammocks and blankets.

Kheda reached up to hook one end of a canvas length to the beam. 'Do you think he can see in the dark?'

'Who cares?' Risala shrugged as she secured the other end. 'Do you think he can hear us?'

'Depends how much of that white liquor he's drunk.' Kheda helped her with the other hammock.

'When will he get his powers back?' asked Risala in a low voice as she shook out a blanket.

Kheda took it, pleasantly surprised to find it herb-scented and free from damp. 'I'm not entirely sure,' he said softly.

'What did you do?' Risala moved closer, voice dropping to a whisper.

'Shek Kul gave me a powder,' mouthed Kheda, unable to restrain a grin. 'He found the concoction in some ancient book of lore. I had no idea if it would work but I put it in his wine. A warlord's son is raised to be wary of poisons. That teaches you all the moves to spice someone else's drink.'

Risala raised herself on her toes to speak close to his ear. 'Could you do the same to the invaders' mages?' She smelled of warm dry cotton and clean hair. Her black locks had dried to a feathery tousle.

'Perhaps.' Kheda allowed himself to feel a little hope. 'Do you suppose they're all sots like Dev? Could we get them to drink it in one of his barrels of wine?'

Risala surprised both of them with a slightly hysterical giggle. 'Do you think it could be that easy?'

Kheda sighed ruefully. 'I very much doubt it.'

Risala swung herself into her hammock with a flash of honey-coloured legs. 'Do you want to put the lamp out?'

You sound like Efi not wanting to be left in the dark.

'No, not for the moment.' Kheda got into his own hammock and tucked the blanket around himself.

'Do you suppose Dev will still be there in the morning?' Risala wondered wearily.

'Let's worry about that then, shall we?' Kheda's cuts were stinging and he couldn't quite decide if his bruises or his much-abused muscles ached more. 'Thanks for your help. He might have had me if you hadn't caught his knife hand.' A new thought struck him. 'He called you a poet. Are you one?'

'I'm a lot of things, when I have to be.'

I recognise that note in a woman's voice as well. If you were Janne or Rekha talking, a determined roll over would leave me next to a silent back.

Risala couldn't roll over in a hammock but she pulled her blanket up over her chin all the same, hiding her eyes.

'Good night.' He reached out and snuffed the lamp.

I'll settle for being warm and dry, not dead with a wizard's blade in my guts and, finally, after all these endless leagues, not so very much alone. We can pursue all these other puzzles in the morning. We've got this far; that must be a sign in our favour.

CHAPTER SEVENTEEN

'I thought you said one of these savage mages was camped on this shore.' From his vantage point in the *Amigal*'s prow, Kheda turned to look suspiciously at Dev.

'Last time I scryed.' Dev yanked on the tiller to turn the ship closer to the rocky shore. 'Somewhere hereabouts. There's a village he was taking for his own.' Above a wall of broken boulders, a stretch of grass dotted with palms separated white surf from the denser green of tangled brush rising up a steep slope.

'Then why risk sailing up in plain sight?' snapped Kheda. 'We should anchor and reconnoitre on foot.'

'Have you seen anyone to raise an alarm?' countered Dev. 'Any of those log boats? Not that they'll see us, not before we see them. I've woven an enchantment to be certain of that.'

'You take too much on yourself, wizard.' Kheda's skin crawled at the thought of unseen magic clouding the air all around him.

'Fretting about the taint on your future?' mocked Dev. 'I don't answer to you, not about magic. Does anyone answer to you, what with you being dead?' He smiled cheerfully.

'I can't see anyone ashore.' Just forward of the mast and knuckles white as she gripped the rail, Risala peered intently into the shadows beneath the trees.

'It's the same as everywhere else,' said Kheda bleakly. 'Everyone not captive has fled.'

Fled north to the Daish domain, and the longer they stay there, the less likely they are to ever return home. The Daish domain just can't support that many people. That many Chazen people will give Chazen Saril substantial backing if he does decide to try deposing Sirket.

Risala turned to address Dev. 'Where's this village?'

'You mean that one?' the wizard enquired sarcastically.

As the *Amigal* turned an abrupt corner in the shore-line, Kheda saw a narrow landing where the rocks gave way to a meagre length of coarse, many-hued sand. There was little left of the village that had flourished there. Some of the houses looked to have collapsed, all four walls falling outwards at once, palm thatch scattered in every direction. Others seemed to have been crushed inwards; walls toppling one on top of the other, roofs left intact and aslant on unsteady heaps of splintered wood. Saller granaries, up on stilts, were piles of debris pierced by posts. The fowl houses mostly looked as if a giant foot had stamped on them and great gouges scarred the unkempt vegetable plots where weeds were revelling in the moist untended soil.

'Could it have been a whirlwind?' wondered Risala uncertainly. 'Or a water spout?'

Kheda shaded his eyes with a hand. The rain clouds were holding off for the moment and the sun sparkled bright on the sea. 'There's no damage to the tree line. A whirlwind would have cut a path inland or along the shore, not just demolished the houses.' He turned on Dev. 'Is this some wizard's work? Could they have seen us coming? Are you sure they can't spy on us, as you're spying on them?'

'The correct term is scrying,' said Dev coldly. 'I've seen no sign that they know how to work any magic of that kind. They don't even realise when I'm scrying on them, I'll bet my stones on it.'

'It's all our necks you're wagering.' Risala glanced over her shoulder.

'Where has this wizard gone, the one that did this?' Kheda persisted.

'I don't know.' Dev saw something he didn't like in Kheda's expression and his tone soured. 'I've been looking the length and breadth of these isles to find out what wizard is where. I haven't been watching each one to see how often he takes a squat or a piss. Trust me on this or the deal's off. I gave my oath I'd help you but I don't have to keep it, not if you're going to disbelieve me. Where shall I take you? The Daish dry-season residence? What about you, girlie? Ready to tell me who you're spying for yet?'

Trust. Oh, I trust your magic, most assuredly, after seeing you draw pictures out of nothing into a bowl of water, proving beyond doubt that a wizard's insidious spying can reach anywhere. It's trusting you at my back, believing you won't somehow betray me, that's what I'm finding the real test.

Risala spoke up before Kheda could decide on a response. 'Let's go ashore and see just what happened.'

Kheda stared into the thick brush beyond the village where undergrowth flourished anew in the rain. 'Do you suppose there'll be any Chazen islanders able to tell us what went on here?'

'I can't even see a house fowl come back looking for grain,' Risala said sadly.

Dev deftly steered the *Amigal* round so the stern drifted into the grudging beach. 'Get the skiff, girlie. You, make sure we're secure.' He looked at Kheda and nodded towards the twin-fluked anchors. 'I don't fancy swimming for the ship if she drifts. There's sharks in these waters.'

Kheda hefted the heavy weight of the bow anchor and glanced at Risala. 'Do you want to stay aboard, keep watch out to sea?'

'I want to see what's gone on ashore.' She shook her head stubbornly.

Kheda threw the anchor over the *Amigal*'s prow and

hauled on the rope until he was confident it was dug deep into the rocky sand of the sea bed. Risala fetched the skiff round from its tether at the *Amigal*'s stern and smiled up at him as he dropped the second anchor. Kheda lowered himself lightly into the little vessel and took the oars. Dev joined them, gazing all the while at the beach. Reaching the shore in a few strokes of the oars, the three of them dragged the skiff up out of the reach of the sluggish waves.

'They were building defences,' Risala remarked. A ditch had been dug halfway across the grassy slope, though pointed stakes that had been stacked together were now scattered like straws in a wind.

'Much good it did this prentice sorcerer,' chuckled Dev with cruel amusement. 'I told you these people are more interested in fighting each other. I don't see them taking on any other domain at least until the end of the rains.'

'You said they were penning up prisoners like animals?' Kheda couldn't see anything like the stockades Dev and Risala had described.

'Looks like they were keeping them locked up in the huts.' Dev had already reached the splintered remains of what had been a substantial building.

Kheda joined him, kicking at a solid pole with floorboards still attached. 'Berale wood, seasoned, oiled against white ants, snapped like kindling.' The rough reddish inner grain of the splintered wood showed like a wound against the dark surface, polished with years of use.

'The saller's long gone.' Risala looked worried. 'I don't know what the Chazen people will be eating come the dry season, even if we do drive these wizards out.' She kicked at the end of a fallen roof truss. A litter of damp thatch slid away unexpectedly.

Her yelp startled them both. Dev was instantly four steps back towards the shore as Kheda reached for Risala, other hand drawing the dagger he'd taken from Dev. 'What is it?'

Risala shook herself like a hound coming out of the rain. Setting her jaw, she pointed at two corpses twisted in an ugly embrace, the shifting palm fronds releasing a foetid stench of death. Insects scurried away from the intrusive daylight.

'They may yet tell us something.' Kheda sank down to a crouch and looked closely at the two dead.

'Necromancy?' queried Dev, moving closer for a better look.

'You're not working any spells over them.' Kheda spread a hand protectively over the bodies.

'I thought you meant you were going to work some rite, for speaking to the dead.' Dev folded his arms and looked at Kheda, bright-eyed. 'That's long been the rumour in the north, what with all your people's insistence on past being linked to present and future. No? That's a shame. That would have been worth something to me.'

'I have no idea what you're talking about.' Kheda didn't know whether to be more appalled or bewildered by the notion.

'Can we discuss barbarian ignorance some other time?' Risala had turned away from the pathetic corpses. 'There's no saying when the savages might come back.'

'See what you can see; I'll see what I can find.' Dev wandered off.

Kheda looked down at the bodies. One was an old man with close-cropped hair and a grizzled beard and a paltry string of turtle shell beads around his neck. The other was a woman, her age-weathered skin sagging and wrinkled, dark eyes glazed in death. Neither showed much visible decay beyond the predation of carrion flies. Steeling himself, he lifted the man's clenched hand from the old woman's stomach. It moved limp and loose, a fisherman's calluses hard on the palm. 'They're not long dead, a day or so.'

'What killed them?' Risala asked softly.

'Hard to say.' Kheda examined the old fisherman's head with gentle hands. 'There's no wound that I can see.'

'There's blood on her neck,' Risala pointed out, swallowing hard.

Catching his lower lip between his teeth, Kheda moved the old woman's grey plait aside. Blood was clotted dark in a thin score around her neck. 'That didn't kill her. Something was ripped off her neck, a cord or necklace.' Kheda sighed, shaking his head as he stood to look down on the bodies with all the detachment he could muster. 'There's some bloating but they're so thin, I think they were starved by their captors. When this happened, whatever happened—' He gestured, baffled, at the wreckage of the prison and the wider destruction beyond. 'The shock, their weakness, I think they just died.'

'Why take prisoners and then treat them so badly?' Risala's puzzlement mirrored Kheda's own.

'Why take prisoners at all? What use is a domain with no one to work it?' Kheda scrubbed a handful of earth through his hands.

'Do you suppose they'll take the land for themselves?' Risala looked around uneasily.

'There's no sign of it, is there? If you're not interested in slaves, why not give them a clean death?' Kheda sighed. 'This is what threatens my own people, if we cannot find a way to stop it.'

'Or worse.' Risala's eyes were dark with apprehension. 'We still don't know what they want their prisoners for, if it's not to make them slaves.'

'Come, see what I've found.' Dev's shout rang with cruel satisfaction.

Kheda and Risala exchanged a glance before walking over to join the mage, who was crouching among the ruins of another hut.

'I told you there was a mage camped here.' Dev glanced up before looking back to something pinned beneath a fallen beam. 'Mind yourselves.'

Risala and Kheda stepped back hastily as the heavy beam, taller than Kheda and as thick as his thigh, flipped up and toppled away at Dev's negligent gesture.

'Was that him?' Risala gasped, appalled.

Dev chuckled. 'Not so pretty now, is he?'

Kheda stared at what had once been a man. 'Was he racked?'

'Not the way you mean.' Dev kicked at one of the corpse's mangled, contorted arms. Every joint had been pulled apart, knobbly ends of bones clearly separate beneath stretched yet unbroken skin. His legs had been similarly wrenched out of their sockets, thighs at an impossible angle beneath his hips. 'No signs of binding, no bruises.'

'Magic did this?' Kheda looked at the dead man's face, jaw hanging dislocated, teeth startlingly white in the clotted mess of blood choking his mouth. His head was misshapen, skull plates separated beneath the mud-caked bristly hair, eyes ruptured into oozing ruins surrounded by crude sweeps of reddish paint.

'I'd say so.' Dev nodded with satisfaction. 'You remember me saying he looked like the lowest in the pecking order?'

'I remember you saying you needed to see these wizards working their magic, to devise a means for us to work against them,' challenged Kheda. 'What does this tell you?'

'That this weakling has been picked off by one of his rivals. I saw him having some sort of parley with another of his kind a while ago. He ended up handing over loot and prisoners. Someone must have decided to take the rest. The wild men who'd been following him will all have gone along with the new top dog.' Dev kicked contemptuously at the body before glancing at Risala. 'I don't think that fight we saw between those two mages was anything out of the ordinary. I think you get to wear a fancy cloak by killing your way up the ladder.' He grinned at Kheda. 'More than one warlord's seized power that way.'

Kheda ignored the taunt. 'Can you tell what happened here?'

Faint blue light glittered momentarily over every ruined house and hut. Dev laughed as Kheda shivered and Risala recoiled from the tumble of splintered wood beside her.

'Someone knew how to work powerful magic with the air.' He kicked the body again. 'I don't know what element this fool had an affinity for but he didn't get a chance to use it. His enemy's magic ripped him apart, then did the same for his petty little holding. Whoever was responsible has another notch on his staff, or whatever these people use for a symbol of their power.'

'This is how it's done among your kind?' demanded Kheda.

Dev looked up angrily. 'My kind do nothing like this. This is crude, brutal magic, strongest wins and subtlety be cursed. We of the north, we prefer refinement in our enchantments, working to an understanding of the nature of magic, exploring every nuance of its potential.' He gestured at the dead mage with frustrated contempt. 'This is smashing an oyster with a building hammer and not caring if you crush the shell, the flesh and any pearl within it all into powder. My magic is sliding in a careful knife, winning yourself nacre, pearl and something to eat all at the same time.'

Kheda was unimpressed. 'Does this tell you how we may fight them?'

'No,' Dev said slowly. 'Though I think I know who'll be next on the list, if someone is rolling up the weaker mages hereabouts. I wouldn't mind seeing that fight. If I can see how these people use their magic, I can think of ways to work against them.'

'Do you mean you'll scry to see them fight?' Kheda looked dubiously at the wizard.

'Oh, no, I need to be there,' Dev assured him cheerfully. 'You can't tell who's winning a cockfight if you're standing outside the pit.'

Risala had been delving cautiously in the wreckage of a hut. 'They left the turtle shell and the pearls again.' She stood up, brushing her hands against her ragged trousers.

'If they scorn such wealth in favour of jewels, they're bound to go north sooner or later.' Kheda looked grim. 'That's where the Archipelago's gems are to be found.'

Dev nodded to Risala. 'Gather that lot up and get it aboard.'

'What gives you the right to rob these people?' Kheda challenged him immediately.

'Who's left to rob?' protested Dev. 'Anyway, you said I'd be well paid. We can call this something on account.'

'You go looting on your own,' Kheda said coldly. 'Once you've worked your spying magic to be sure no one's sneaking up on us. We'll bury the dead before we leave here.' He turned his back on the wizard and Risala dutifully followed him back to the lifeless couple.

'At least they died in their rightful place.' She looked around helplessly. 'Is there anything to dig with?'

'Go and look.' Kheda knelt to score a line in the damp turf with the dagger he'd taken from Dev and kept for himself, even if it was an undistinguished Viselis blade. He began levering the grass up. 'Otherwise it'll have to be our hands.'

'No sign of anyone around here at all.' Dev waved cheerfully, throwing aside a scoop of sea water in a broken pot.

'Keep looking. We don't want to be taken unawares.' Kheda concentrated on peeling back the stubborn turf.

'I don't want to be caught any more than you do.' The wizard waved a negligent hand. 'Though anyone with a pennyweight of sense will be sleeping out the heat of the day under a tree.'

Risala returned with two hoes, one with a charred handle, the other broken but still serviceable. 'This is the best I can do.'

Kheda took the broken tool. 'Then let's do our best for these two.'

The heat of the day seared their bent backs as they dug. Dev plundered the wreckage of the savage mage's hut, fetching sacks from the *Amigal*, and loading them with turtle shell and pearls, whistling insouciantly.

Is it the magic staining your bones that makes you so obnoxious? Or did you come to hide in the Archipelago because you'd made enemies of all your fellow wizards?

'Hitting him probably isn't the wisest thing to do.' Risala nodded at Kheda's tight grip on his hoe with a rueful grin. 'Though it might be worth it, to stop him whistling.'

'He's doubtless just trying to provoke us. I have a daughter, Efi, with a similar talent.'

'What do you make of this riddle?' Risala paused, leaning on her hoe to wipe the sweat from her forehead. 'Why are these people here? What do they want? They're not looking to settle, not from what we've seen. They're not planting any crops, not even husbanding their supplies. They're taking slaves or prisoners at least but that's all wrong as well. I don't know how things happen in the southern reaches, but when Danak Sarb killed Danak Mir for the domain, Danak Mir's people were given over to the troops for whatever use they cared to make of them; they were sold for slaves, kept for concubines, just raped and discarded. I haven't seen any sign that these savages have laid so much as a finger on the

Chazen women. What do they want? They're not even taking the pearls and turtle shell that bring this domain its wealth.'

'They want gemstones, we know that much.' Kheda shared her bemusement, jabbing his hoe into the earth in frustration. 'Why are those so valuable to them, to these wizards, that they'll risk deaths as foul as that?' He jerked his head back towards the dead and disjointed mage.

'I don't think it's about gems or land or women, willing or not,' said Dev unexpectedly, stopping to eavesdrop on their conversation. 'It's about whatever those wizards can give their followers. It must be something so tempting, so wonderful that they'll risk being ripped apart by someone else's wizardry, that these warriors will follow just for the chance of seeing their man win the prize.' The mage's eyes were dark and mysterious. 'I wonder what that prize might be.'

'What could be here that a wizard would want?' Risala protested. 'We don't have magic in the Archipelago.'

'You do at the moment and you want rid of it.' Dev went on his way, preoccupied by his speculations.

Kheda straightened up and considered the depth of the grave they had dug. 'This should do.'

Risala hurried to catch Dev as he came up from the shore. 'Give me one of those.' She took a cotton sack from his hands and ripped it along its seams, ignoring his protests. Returning, she handed Kheda a length of cloth, wrapping another tight around her mouth and nose. 'Let's get this done.'

The cloth muffled Kheda's sigh as he bent to take the old man's shoulders. Risala reached for his feet. The old man wasn't heavy. Beetles scattered as they lifted the corpse away, pale worms wriggling frantically over the damp, stained ground. There was no way to lower the body into the grave so they had to let it drop with a dull, unpleasant thud. The old woman was lighter still and landed with a muffled thump. The stench of disturbed death rose from the corpses and Kheda began hastily raking dirt into the hole while Risala scattered soil over the foulness where the bodies had lain.

'Do you suppose this will help their families, if they are still alive?' she wondered, words tight in her throat.

'It can't hurt.' Kheda looked across to the rising heart of the island. 'And their presence should do something to counter the past evil for anyone living here in the future.'

'What do we do about him?' Risala jerked her head towards the wrecked hut where the savage mage still lay.

Kheda scraped a last slew of soil across the grave and pulled the cotton rag from his face, using it to scrub away the sweat. 'We burn him. Fire purifies.'

Risala twisted the cloth between her soiled hands. 'Do you suppose we can ever be cleansed, after so much dealing with magic?'

Kheda heard a desolate note in her voice. 'I fully intend to free myself of all taint,' he said firmly. 'Just as soon as we see a way clear to freeing this domain of all these savage wizards. Let's make a start by burning this one and then we can see if Dev's any notion of making good his boasts about getting rid of the rest.'

'Thatch will get the fire started.' Risala caught up an armful of brittle fronds. 'We want hardwood after that, to burn hot.'

'The hotter the better,' agreed Kheda, pulling dry floorboards from the ruins of another building.

He was kneeling, trying to catch a spark in a tuft of fibres teased from the cotton rags, when Dev sauntered up.

'Why are we setting a smoke signal to draw every enemy eye?' wondered the wizard sarcastically.

Kheda didn't look up. 'You wanted to find out who killed him, didn't you?' The tow flared and Risala cupped her hands around the fledgling flame. Kheda fed it with torn pieces of palm frond.

'Find out, yes. Fight off his hordes, no.' The flame faltered and Dev laughed. 'I can do that for you.'

'No,' Kheda said curtly, carefully tending the smouldering tinder. 'We're trying to cleanse the magic here, not brand the very rocks with it.'

Dev snorted, annoyed. 'If you're not done when I'm ready to sail, you can paddle to the next island.'

Kheda didn't answer, though he kept a sideways eye on the *Amigal* as he and Risala built the fire ever higher over the dead mage.

'That should see him burned to ashes,' said Risala with satisfaction as she threw a final chunk of wood on the blaze.

Kheda nodded. His mouth was dry as dust.

The ashes will remain. We'll just have to hope for a good storm to wash the foulness away for the sea to dilute.

Once aboard the *Amigal*, Dev snapped brusque orders at them both. 'Get the anchors up. You, girl, help me raise the sail.'

Once he'd broken the anchors' determined grip on the sea bed, Kheda slung a bucket tied to a length of rope over the side. 'Fetch some of that white brandy, please,' he called out to Risala.

Dev was using the stern sweep to drive the little ship into deeper water. 'Got a taste for it now?'

Kheda knelt to scrub his hands in the bucket of water. 'Where are we going?'

'A couple of islands over yonder.' Dev nodded in an easterly direction. 'One mage with a sizeable mob was camped in a village split either side of a narrow strait. I've just had a look over there and now there are two of them staring each other down. I'd say one or other of them killed the one you've just toasted.'

'Two mages sounds like more trouble than we want to

meet head on.' Kheda scoured his hands red with the balled-up remnants of the cotton rag.

'Which is why we'll anchor some way off and approach them through the forest.' Dev's reply surprised Kheda.

'What do we do with this?' Risala reappeared holding a stubby black bottle.

'Wash your hands.' Kheda shoved the bucket towards Risala with one foot while pouring a generous measure of spirits over his own hands.

'How many ways have you people got for wasting good liquor?' shouted Dev with irritation.

'Account it against the pearls you just got.' Kheda fished his spark maker out. One snap of the metal wheels ignited the alcohol and he plunged his hands into the bucket. 'It doesn't hurt too much,' he assured Risala with a grin.

She held out her dripping hands mutely, eyes wide.

'When you're quite done messing around, trim that cursed sail,' growled Dev. 'Before we wreck on that reef.'

Once she had quenched her hands, Risala hurried to the mast's ropes. Kheda moved to throw the water from the bucket over the leeward rail.

Is there any point trying to read whatever signs there might be in the cast? Would there be anything to see in water already soiled with magic, in seas that must be running with the taint? Will even the heaviest rains and the fiercest storms ever be able to scour these isles clean of sorcery?

He flung the water away, without looking to see how it flew through the air. Risala appeared at his side and handed him a leather water bottle. 'Want to learn how to sail this ship?'

Once he'd quenched his considerable thirst, helping Risala with the ropes gave Kheda something to concentrate on for the short voyage to the next island, to drive out the recollections of those Chazen dead and to still the ongoing debate with himself about just what he was going to do, to see these wizards driven out of the Archipelago.

Dev steered the little ship deftly into a secluded cove, barely beaching the hull on the shelving sand. 'Get us secure.'

Kheda and Risala didn't argue, each deploying an anchor before splashing ashore through waist-deep water. Dev soon joined them, turning for a moment to gaze intently at the *Amigal*.

'Is that magic?' Kheda watched, bemused as the vessel shimmered like something seen through a heat haze.

'Quiet as you can through the brush. I don't want to use any more magic than absolutely necessary.' Hefting a broad hacking knife, Dev led the way through the tangle of shrubs and saplings with unerring confidence.

Kheda gestured to Risala to follow the mage and brought up the rear, one hand on his dagger hilt, glancing backwards every few paces to make sure they weren't being stalked in turn. The noontide jungle was still and silent, the heat pressing down like a palpable weight.

A dry clear day, just when we could have done with rain to keep all these savages close to their huts and give us noise to cover our steps. What kind of omen is that? Are you leading us into some disaster, wizard? Though Daish Reik would have thought you a fair enough hunter, you move stealthily enough. I wonder what places you have been sneaking around, to learn all our secrets for your unwholesome trade.

Then again, you move just as quietly, Risala, and you're still a puzzle to be solved. What places have you visited for Shek Kul? What news have you sent him, in return for what reward I can't guess at? How do you send him your news? At least I feel certain I can trust you.

Kheda abandoned such musings when Dev halted up ahead, raising one hand in warning. Risala crouched low on the scrape of a path. Kheda moved cautiously to one side for a better view. They were on a tree-cloaked rise above a scatter of storehouses and modest dwellings much like the ones they'd seen ripped apart by magic. A narrow strip of shallow water patterned with corals separated the two halves of the village. Across the water from their vantage point, a wider beach boasted racks of drying nets and a row of fishing skiffs much like the one Risala sailed.

Kheda saw invaders lounging on both sides of the strait. In twos and threes, they were taking their ease beneath the broad shady eaves of the huts they had claimed; roughly equal numbers on both sides of the narrow strait. Quilts had been plundered to soften the ground, bright embroidery now wet and dirty, though the Chazen islanders' clothes had been scorned; the savages still only wore their brief leather loincloths. Archipelagan food hadn't found much more favour. Gourds and jars of carefully hoarded foodstuffs had been opened, sampled and tossed aside. Flies clustered around preserved fruits discarded to rot and the darkness would see bigger vermin sneaking towards a side of smoked deer meat left half eaten over a fire, curling in the sun.

Every skiff had been holed, gently curving hulls splintered and gaping. The little vessels had been dragged aside, shoved askew, left at the mercy of tide and storm. Their sails had been stripped away, some entirely, some leaving rags drooping from remnants of cut and tangled ropes. Most of the nets had been slashed, others burned, blackened remains hanging from the racks of scorched wood. Up beyond the high-water mark, a neat row of the invaders' log boats was drawn up like black tally marks on the sand, each one tethered to a firmly rooted stake.

'No beach defences as yet,' Dev murmured, sinking low to the ground. 'There're your stockades.'

'One for each side of the water,' Kheda noted, joining him. He could see heads huddled inside the wooden walls of the crude prisons in a vain attempt to find some shade.

Bark still clung to the posts, leaves wilted and brown on half-snapped twigs, Trampled scars in the forest showed where trees had been hacked down, the trunks split, driven deep into the ground and lashed together with vines. Single vines, bristling with the rootlets ripped from the trees, not even plaited into anything like a rope. Kheda noted there was no sign of any gate in either tightly fitted circle.

Dev was looking at the crude log boats. 'Whoever these people are, they're certainly not carpenters.'

Risala was keeping watch at their backs. 'Or fishermen. Or farmers.'

'We know they're warriors. That's enough if you simply steal to meet your needs. ' There were plenty of weapons in plain sight, the same stone-studded clubs and spears of fire-hardened wood that he had seen before. Kheda glanced at Dev. 'Does being ruled by wizards give you the right to leech on the toil of others?'

'It gives you the power.' Dev laid a hand on Kheda's arm. 'Hush.'

The door of the biggest hut on their side of the water was opening. One of the savages lounging outside hurried in, head bowing like a river bird bobbing for fish. A stir ran through the other invaders, men rising to their elbows or sitting up, all their attention on the big hut.

That prompted curiosity on the far side of the water, the men gathering into fours and fives, some plucking spears from the sandy ground. A single runner hurried to hammer on the door of what had once been a saller granary. Some of the savages strolled down to the water's edge, insolence in every line of their bodies. One waved a rough-hewn club and shouted unintelligible taunts. Scathing response and counter-insult echoed between the beaches.

'We'll need to move quickly if they come this way,' Kheda said urgently to Dev.

'They won't follow us through a wall of fire.' Dev was offhand. 'I can keep one between us and them until we can get back to the boat. This is just the usual bluster. I've seen plenty of it, though I've no idea what they get so heated about.'

To Kheda's relief, the activity on the beach subsided, most of the savages returning to their indolence, only a few remaining to continue the posturing. 'Your magic can't tell you what they're saying?'

I've spent my life being warned of all the evil magic can do. Now I find myself with this wizard as my most unwelcome ally, all he tells me is everything he cannot do.

'Not my spells.' Dev was unbothered. 'Sometimes they give up after tossing a few insults around, the wild men that is. Other times they come to blows, until one or other wizard calls his dogs to heel. We're not going to learn much from that.' His gaze fixed on the sparkling edge of the strait below and a malicious grin slowly curved his thin lips. 'I think I'll stoke the fire a little.'

The water glittered in the sunlight and slowly, imperceptibly, began to shimmer with an uncanny green light owing nothing to the sun above. Lapping on the sand, falling back and lapping again, the sea began to reach higher, every ripple advancing further up the shore towards them. The green glowed brighter, colouring the foam cresting the little waves. The water began to surge forward around the invaders' log boats. The emerald radiance darkened around them, gouts of spray scattered on the breeze as the boats began rolling, floating free in the magic's embrace.

The desultory shouts of derision on this near side of the water turned to yells of anger as the wild men saw what was happening. Some of the savages waded thigh deep into the water, grabbing at the boats. A crash reverberated around the trees and startled crookbeaks fled shrieking as the door to the big hut flung back. An invader whose whole body was patterned with yellow handprints strode out into the sunshine. He flung one hand out in front of him and the green light in the water retreated into the depths. The painted wizard stood on the sand and looked across the water to the saller granary where the runner had taken his news. Amber light glowed and the ground began shifting beneath the posts holding it up. The timbers twisted and cracked as their foundations vanished.

A handful of savages emerged in a hurry, the first one stumbling as the sandy ground flowed away beneath his feet. Behind him, a man crowned with a fresh green wreath of leaves swept his hands around in a quelling gesture. The ground stilled and his laughter rang out over the increasing abuse the two bands of warriors were throwing across the water.

One wild man raced forward, brandishing a spear. Skidding to a halt on the water's edge, he sent it soaring across the water, straight at the wizard with the wreath of leaves.

'There's always someone too stupid to see sunset,' sighed Dev with scant sympathy.

The spear exploded into a shower of splinters and two blasts of magic, one from the wreath wearer and one from the painted mage, knocked the hapless savage off his feet. Wrapped in coils of green and golden light, the man screamed once before he collapsed in a heap.

'See, only wizards kill wizards,' Dev explained conversationally.

Risala sank down to kneel close to Kheda. He laid his hand over hers as grassy light crawled all over the split tree trunks making up the prison enclosures. 'Dev? What are you doing?' He winced at the feebleness of the despairing shrieks from the unseen captives.

'Not a thing, not any more.' Dev's face was rapt with

fascination. 'Shut up and let me see what they're about. Wizards only kill wizards but they can do a lot to discourage the spear-carriers. '

The vines tying the stockade together were glowing green and writhing as they uncoiled themselves from the wood. Wild warriors shouted with alarm as the tendrils curled speedily across the sand, catching at feet and ankles, tying up anyone they caught. Any man trying to free himself found his hands ensnared as well. Several fell heavily to the ground and one yelled with rising terror as a questing tendril looped around his neck.

The yellow-painted wizard made a sweeping gesture and the vines crackled into brittle fragments laced with crimson light. As his men tore the dry remnants away, their leader lifted his hand in a slow arc and the water in the strait quivered. A swollen wave ran up the beach on the far side of the strait, water bulging with amber radiance. The ripple left the water and continued up through the sand, the ground rising and falling like a shaken cloth. Most of the invaders were knocked clean off their feet. Even the men clustered around the wreath wearer staggered.

He alone stood upright, unaffected, and his retaliation was immediate. A storm of green light flashed around the village below them. Cries of pain outstripped the shouts of anger and men hugged themselves in agony, thrusting hands beneath their armpits. Some fell to the floor, clutching at their feet, others clapped hands to their faces.

'I don't suppose you people know what frost nip is.' Dev sounded more amused than concerned. 'This is getting nasty.'

The yellow-painted wizard spared no attention for his suffering followers. He swept both hands towards the far side of the strait and this time the ground turned to liquid mud beneath the wreath wearer's forces. Wild men sank up to their knees, the mud spreading in all directions as they tried to climb out. The painted wizard clapped his hands together with a golden flash that rivalled the sunlight and they found themselves struggling in solid earth once again.

'Predictable.' Dev was unmoved. 'Though effective. They're well and truly stuck,' he chuckled.

'What now?' The screams from the despairing prisoners tore at Kheda's nerves and Risala's hand tightened around his.

He might have said more but a brilliant green light swirled above the strait, aquamarine deepening to a dark ominous jade. The storm of magelight rushed ashore, a dense cloud obscuring everything, sounds of suffering sunk beneath its roaring. As suddenly as it had come, it was gone, leaving the beach strewn with men clutching gashes to their arms and legs or holding hands to bruised and bloodied heads. The sand was littered with pale, glittering shards and the breeze momentarily carried a chill breath brought down from the highest mountain's night.

'If you fancy a wager,' Dev remarked, 'my money goes on the lad with the leafy wreath. An ice storm like that is no easy trick in this heat—'

'Look, they're getting free of the ground.' Risala was watching the far side of the strait where the wreath wearer's men were freeing themselves, hard dry ground breaking up beneath the determined assault of clubs and spears.

The yellow-painted mage strode to the water's edge, still ignoring his wretched followers' sufferings. He flung out a hand directly towards the wreath wearer, who screamed and clutched at one leg, the lower bone snapping audibly, splintered ends ripping through his skin to bloody his frantic hands. The yellow-painted mage's men raised a ferocious cheer, drowning out the opposing force's insults. Risala quailed beside Kheda, pulling her hand free to muffle her ears. Kheda put an arm around her shoulders and held her close, but found himself unable to look away as, fallen to his knees, the wreath wearer punched at the painted mage, as if he could strike him where he stood.

The yellow-painted mage staggered backwards. Wounds appeared on his arms and legs, lengthening, his limbs swelling, skin splitting like overripe fruit to reveal a mossy light within soon lost beneath gouts of blood and corruption. Kheda coughed at the foul stench of gangrene floating up as the savage wizard fell to the sand, twisting and gasping in agony.

'That's interesting.' Dev leaned forward, keen curiosity in his dark eyes.

The yellow-painted mage rolled on to his belly, head whipping from side to side. He was entirely alone as his minions abandoned the beach. Twisting around and dragging himself to his knees, the yellow-painted mage raised one hand to throw vivid coils of amber magelight over the water. The enchantment scooped up stinging whips of sand, hurling rocks like slingshot. None of the magic came within a spear length of the wreath wearer. He looked as if he was laughing, his own followers bowing and congratulating him even as they too retreated with alacrity for the safety of the trees.

The wreath wearer sent a delicate tracery of emerald light floating across the water. A new sound rose above the strangled agony of the yellow-painted mage and the wretched whimpering of the unseen prisoners. Slowly at first, then gathering pace and volume, it was the unmistakable hum of swarming insects.

'We have to get out of here.' Memories of the foully distorted whip lizards that had killed Atoun choked Kheda. 'Whatever he's calling up, they could be as long as your arm.'

'We're in no danger.' Dev shook off his hand. 'Look.'

Seeing the insects were a normal size was scant comfort to Kheda. They were coming from all directions, abandoning the discarded food, winging in from the forest all around. They clustered around the injured wizard, covering his festering wounds, innumerable wings gleaming, rainbow colours jewel bright in the sunlight. Carrion beetle carapaces made a shimmering carpet on the ground as they appeared out of nowhere. The yellow-painted wizard's screams were choked as torrents of insects filled his eyes, ears and mouth.

The savage mage swept flies and beetles alike away in a sandstorm but only for a moment. The magic fell away into confusion as he clawed at his throat with frantic hands, his own blood coating his fingers. Falling backwards, he thrashed from side to side in convulsions, back arched so viciously only his head and his heels touched the ground.

Silence abrupt as a thunderclap fell as he died. The insects were stilled, the savages on both sides of the strait frozen, even the wounded stifling their torment. The wizard crowned with the wreath of leaves rose to his feet and limped slowly to the water's edge on the far side of the strait, his broken leg whole again. The painted mage's men immediately prostrated themselves, hands outstretched in supplication. All of the wreath wearer's own followers looked tensely at him, weapons in hand.

The savage wizard nodded and his own men began dragging their log boats down to the sea. Paddling across the narrow stretch of water, some headed for the big hut where the dead mage had dwelt, reappearing with coffers and sacks of loot. Others began ripping down the wall of the prison enclosure, taking the split logs down to the water and lashing together crude platforms to lie across pairs of log boats. The painted mage's erstwhile followers threw aside their weapons and cowered, abject, until the newcomers clapped them on the shoulder in welcome, returning their weapons with nods of approval. Once accepted, they eagerly joined in transferring all the painted mage had amassed to the wreath wearer's store of plunder.

Kheda tensed as the huddled misery of the Chazen islanders was laid bare. They weren't even trying to flee, hiding their faces from any hope of freedom.

Risala's words echoed his own thoughts. 'Isn't there anything we can do to rescue them?'

'And give ourselves up to that bastard?' Dev spoke almost absently, watching the wreath-crowned mage intently. 'No, I'm not going up against him or any of his kind until I've thought all this through.'

Risala looked at Kheda, face drawn. 'There's nothing we can do?'

'We can bear witness,' he said harshly.

To what all Daish fates will be, if I do not find some way to defeat these evil savages.

Having ransacked the huts, the wild men turned to breaking down the remnants of the stockade and dragging out their terrified captives. Cowering and wailing, Chazen islanders were forced on to the improvised rafts with blows and kicks, women dragged by their hair, men by their beards. Once across the strait, they were thrown to the ground in front of the wreath-crowned wizard. He nodded with perfunctory approval to the cringing savages now pledging their allegiance with fervent obeisance. His original followers were pulling apart the walls of their own prison enclosure, driving the new captives inside to join those already there.

'They're not going to have room to breathe,' Risala murmured with growing concern as another raft load were forced within the wooden walls.

'Much these savages care,' muttered Kheda wrathfully. 'Haven't we seen enough?'

'No.' Dev shook his head determinedly. 'I need to get down there, see what's been done to the ground, to that mage, if I'm to get any measure of their magic.'

Kheda looked at Risala, who shrugged helplessly. They sat beneath the bushes and waited. The wreath wearer got the pick of the plunder his men brought over from the dead mage's camp. His only interest was in small coffers that disappeared into his own hut. The savages lit fires with kindling bows and threw grain, fruit and meat all together in the biggest cook pots they could find. The smell of food made Kheda's belly rumble but the sight of the dead mage below being devoured by the insects the wreath wearer had summoned effectively killed his appetite.

Risala nudged him some while later and proffered a water skin. Kheda drank deeply, gratefully, and thanked her with a smile.

'Looks like they're on the move.' Dev hadn't taken his eyes off the scene below.

Kheda looked down to see the savages making more rafts from their log boats and crudely split planks. The loot from the wreath-crowned mage's hut was piled high on the biggest and the wizard stepped aboard to lounge idly on a heap of plundered quilts. The rest of his enlarged retinue made ready to leave, breaking open the stockade and dragging out the stumbling, sobbing captives. They were lashed into groups of five and six with vines tied around their necks and forced aboard the other rafts. A sizeable number were left behind, either moribund or dead. The savage warriors boarded those log boats that remained, standing upright and long paddles in hand. They surrounded the flotilla as it moved off.

'I don't know how they do that.' Kheda shook his head.

'A fair amount of it's magic.' Dev pointed to green-tinted water flowing against the run of the tide to carry the wreath-crowned mage's boat away down the strait. The rest followed, the savages barely having to make a stroke. Before long, they all disappeared around a jutting angle of the undulating shore.

'Dev, scry for him,' Kheda said urgently. 'We have to know where he's going.'

'I can find him again, any time I want to.' Dev gazed at the body of the dead mage with an avidity that raised the hairs on the back of Kheda's neck. 'I need to work out what he was doing with his magic before I try mine against him.'

Kheda gripped the wizard's arm with a firmly restraining hand. 'We wait till we're sure they're not coming back.'

They waited. The day began to cool and the scatter of clouds above merged and thickened. A spatter of rain fell and then drifted away. The birds of the jungle chattered softly in the trees as they gathered to feed. Sudden rustles in the underbrush turned Kheda's head, Dev's too. Kheda gripped the hacking blade; Dev raised a hand outlined in ruddy light. A rounded hump of brindled hide briefly broke through the dark glossy leaves of a berry bush.

'Just a hog.' As Kheda spoke, a couple of striped hoglets emerged from the underbrush, little noses rooting in the leaf litter.

'Good eating, if you can catch them,' observed Dev. The hoglets startled at his voice and darted back into cover.

Dev looked at Kheda. 'Our friend with the leaves isn't coming back and I want to see all I can before dark.'

'All right.' Kheda nodded reluctantly. 'Risala, stay here, keep watch for us, please.'

She didn't object. Dev was already heading down to the village and Kheda had to hurry to catch him.

'What are we looking for?' he asked, drawing level with the northern mage.

'Give me the blade.' Taking it, Dev dug the broad,

square tip into the soil. 'How much rain has this place had over the last run of the moons?'

Kheda rubbed earth dry as dust between his fingers. 'You'd think it was the end of the dry season.'

'One or other of them drew all the water out, as part of his spell casting. If you can call it spell casting,' Dev commented thoughtfully. 'Their magic is pure instinct.'

That meant nothing to Kheda so he moved to look more closely at the dead wizard, now a rotting sprawl of slack limbs beneath the crawling insects. The corpse looked as if it had lain unburied for days. 'How does magic do this?'

'Not sure. Effective, isn't it?' Hefting the blade, Dev cut deep into the meat of the corpse's thigh. The squelching sound and the stink made Kheda's gorge rise and he backed away.

Going pale enough to betray his barbarian blood, Dev nevertheless held his ground, prodding the dark slime oozing over the thirsty ground. 'There's no bone in here, just spongy fragments and bits of sinew.' Retreating, he studied the smears and nameless scraps sticking to the blade for a moment before stabbing it into the dusty soil to clean it as he stared across the water to the other beach. 'But that's not what he did to our friend in the wreath. His leg bones snapped, turned all brittle. How did he do that, I wonder? How did our friend in the leaves undo it?'

Kheda looked at the ground all around him, scattered with broken pots, discarded cloth, twisted lengths of wood. He frowned and bent to pick up a dagger. The blade was pitted and stained with rust, eaten clean through in places. 'Dev, what about this? This isn't just suffering from the rains.' He held the hilt in one hand and pressed on the tip of the blade with careful fingers. The metal twisted and crumbled.

'An Archipelagan would go bladeless before he'd carry

something like that.' Dev looked around and retrieved one of the invader's stone-bladed axes. 'Obsidian,' he remarked.

'Why?' demanded Kheda. 'They could have gathered all manner of blades from Chazen by now. Why still use fire-hardened wood and stone shards?'

'Magic,' grinned Dev. 'If fire and water rust the blade in your hand, you're dead meat. If cold shatters a piece of stone, chances are you'll still be left with enough sharp edges to cut someone's throat. A wooden spear or a club will still gut someone or bash out their brains even if it's warped or split.'

'Oh,' said Kheda.

So however many swords Daish, Redigal and Ritsem can raise against these savages, they'll most likely be useless unless we can rid the invaders of their wizards.

'Have you seen what you needed to see?' he demanded savagely of Dev. 'Can you tell me how to fight these people or not?'

Dev strolled back to the contorted corpse of the savage mage. 'This is a strange magic, my oath on it. As near as I can make out, it leeches the essential strength from the natural elements around the wizard.'

'What happened to him?' Kheda gestured towards the foul remnants of the invading wizard.

'Our friend in the leaves has a natural power over water.' Dev sounded fascinated. 'Once this fool lost his concentration, or whatever was protecting him from the other man's magic, his lungs, his brain, every tissue in his body filled with fluid.'

'Will knowing this help us defeat them?' Kheda asked. 'Can you tell us how to fight them?'

'You can't,' Dev said bluntly. 'I told you that before and I'm even more certain now. You need magic to fight magic and you people have none, thanks to your age-old folly and prejudice. Didn't see this coming, did you, with all your fancy predictions?'

Kheda barely managed to stop himself hitting the barbarian wizard. He wheeled away instead and stared out across the water.

'Besides, it's not enough to know how to beat these people. A wizard would have to know how they lose, how not to lose himself.' Dev took one last look at the fallen wizard and began walking back towards the rise where Risala waited. 'They all seem very closely tied to their inborn element. That could be a weakness. Most can only use one or two elements and really struggle with whatever's antithetical to their affinity. It's only the lads at the top of the pecking order who can use all four elements from what I've seen, the one wearing the lizard and that bastard in the dragon-hide cloak. That's not to say the others can't, of course, and I've no idea if they can manage blended magics, quintessential enchantment.'

Kheda let the wizard's meaningless words wash over him as he looked up at the sky, still cloudy but with no rain falling. 'We have to come up with something before the end of the rainy season.'

'Like I said, pal, you can't fight magic, not without magic.' Dev laughed unpleasantly.

Kheda halted and seized the barbarian mage by the shoulders. 'Can you do it? You talked of testing your magic against these mages. Could you defeat them?'

Dev knocked Kheda's hands aside. 'Give me one good reason why I should.'

'You wanted payment.' Kheda struggled to keep the distaste out of his mouth, for this foul, venal man and for the unforeseen impulse that had driven him to ask for Dev's help.

'Truth often speaks through chance-heard words.' I hope you were right, my father. I hope I'm right. We talked of

fighting fire with fire, back in Derasulla. I never thought it would come to this but now it has, can I step back, when I have seen the fate that waits for my people?

The libraries are full of dire warnings of wizards cutting down armies with their magic. These savages did as much. Are these wizards of the north stronger? Have I just wasted my efforts in seeking out this Dev, risking my future, even my life on a false omen?

'All the gems and pearls in the Archipelago won't do me much good if I'm not alive to trade them,' Dev was saying. 'Even if I live through a fight with these mages, if word gets out I'm as good as dead. I don't reckon much to my chances of fleeing the length of the Archipelago.'

'I could see you safely to the unbroken lands,' Kheda insisted tersely. 'I can send you on a fast trireme, with your bodyweight in pearls.'

And burn the ship to the waterline once you're off it.

'That's a handsome offer.' Dev laughed and waved an airy hand in the direction the leaf-crowned mage had taken. 'How do you hope to make good on it? Even supposing I come up with a means to fight these wizards –' he raised a warning hand to silence Kheda, '– besides provoking them into fighting each other, because I don't imagine that will work again, there are still hordes of these foot soldiers on every eyot and rock. Who's to say they won't spring another mage from somewhere, wherever they came from in the first place?'

'We will find some means of alerting Daish's allies to sail south as soon as the wizards are dead,' Kheda insisted stubbornly. 'Once they have no magic, we can kill the wild men and their blood on the tides can warn any they've left against sailing north.'

'That'll be a good trick if you can do it,' said Dev scornfully.

Kheda waited until they had rejoined Risala before

speaking. 'I have something to tell you.' He hesitated.

'He wants me to fight these wild mages for him,' said Dev with spiteful pleasure.

Risala nodded slowly. 'I thought he might.'

'You did?' Kheda looked at her astonished.

'You have no choice, I can see that.' He saw his own desperation mirrored in her pale eyes. 'What else can we do? How can we fight this magic without magic? If we can stop this madness before it destroys the Archipelago, even if our lives are forfeit for it...' She fell silent.

'I've no intention of forfeiting my life to anyone,' Dev said aggressively. 'And if you two reckon to sail to your doom, you can do it alone. If we're doing this, we do it with a plan that sees us all coming out of it with a whole hide and, as far as I'm concerned, as much payment as the *Amigal* can hold.'

'Can we do it?' Kheda demanded. 'Can you do it?'

'Can you beat that mage in the dragon-hide cloak?' Risala challenged him.

'That's what I want to do. I've a few notions that might set us along that path,' replied Dev with a secretive smile. 'But I can't cut down hordes of savages for you. You have to find some way of bringing the Daish and Chazen forces down on them as soon as the wizards are out of the balance.'

Kheda nodded slowly. 'I need to speak to Janne Daish and find out exactly what the southern warlords are thinking. There's a place in the Daish domain where we agreed to meet. I sent her a message when I arrived back in the south. If she's got it, she should be there for the full Greater Moon.'

'We should be able to make that.' Risala looked dubious. 'Can we afford such a delay though? What will these savages be doing in the meantime?'

'They'll be doing whatever they please, my girl,' said

Dev with amusement. 'And there'll be precious little you can do about it, or me, come to that, not for the moment. Don't get your braids in a tangle. There's still plenty of rain to come, so I don't suppose they'll be moving north any time soon. Besides, the longer we wait, the more of them will kill off their neighbours, if we're lucky. The more of their battles I can see, the better idea I'll have of their weak spots. I'm more concerned about what you do, Daish Kheda, if your lady Janne doesn't turn up. What are you going to do, come back from the dead and try rallying the domains on that account?'

'That would certainly get everyone's attention.' Kheda grimaced. 'The trick would be getting them to fight battles for the Chazen islands instead of clamouring for explanations and accusing me of bad faith and each other of sharing in some conspiracy. I'd rather have the savages safely killed before I have to get caught up in all that.'

'You are going to have an awful lot of explaining to do when this is all over,' commented Risala thoughtfully. 'Not least how you managed to find the means to defeat these sorcerers.'

Kheda heaved a shaky sigh. 'That will just have to be our secret, won't it? To save all our skins. Agreed?'

'Absolutely,' said Dev robustly.

'Risala?' Kheda looked at her, beseeching. 'Would you keep such a secret from your master?'

'To save my own skin?' She smiled at him but he could tell she was trembling. 'Don't worry. I saw what happened to Kaeska Shek. I've no wish to suffer her fate. I'll die on the day appointed to me but I've no wish to bring it forward.'

'Come on then!' Dev startled them both with a sudden clap of his hands. 'Let's get aboard the *Amigal* and find a safe and sheltered anchorage where we can come up with a decent, detailed plan that might have a hope of success.'

CHAPTER EIGHTEEN

'Do you think he'll be there when we get back?' Risala looked across the empty ocean towards the Chazen anchorage where they'd left Dev. 'Five days' sail, he could be anywhere by now.'

'What'll you wager on it?' Relishing the dry warmth in the stone wall at his back after the drenching they'd had overnight, Kheda hugged his knees. 'No, I'll scrub every barnacle off your skiff's hull if he isn't sat just where we left him, peering into his bowl of inky water.'

'You trust him?' Risala sounded wholly sceptical.

'I trust the way the puzzle of these savages intrigues him,' Kheda said candidly. 'What they're seeking and how their mages rule them.'

'I don't see a puzzle.' Risala shivered despite the sun nearly at its zenith. 'Fear and brutality keeps them all toeing the wizards' line.'

'Dev's adamant that's not the way of it in the unbroken lands.' Kheda stretched his legs out in front of him. 'He wants to know what these southern wizards have that his own people don't.'

'So he can set himself up as some tyrant backed by sorcery?' Risala scowled in the direction of the wizard, long since lost over the horizon.

'I'll make sure he can't try anything like that,' Kheda promised fervently.

I swear it by the tower of silence within this wall. I'll kill him before he can do anything of the kind.

'And if I can't, it's up to you to make sure Shek Kul sees him dead, one way or another.'

Kheda smiled reassurance at Risala. She didn't see it, studying the scraps of green-crested, white-rimmed land sparsely dotting the waters to the west, brilliant against the clean-washed sky and the darker blue of the peaceably undulating sea. 'Your people find these islands too far out, do they?'

'It's not so much the distance as lack of decent land for growing anything to eat. If you did manage it, some storm coming in off the ocean would probably blow it out of the ground. Supplies of fresh water are indifferent too, once you're more than halfway through the dry season. There's enough through the pearl harvest but once that's done, few people stay on.' All the same, Kheda scanned the horizon for any other vessels, great or small.

The last thing we want is some Daish pearl diver reconnoitring the reefs. I can't afford to be discovered, have to explain myself, and leave Dev to his own devices.

'Do you think she'll come today?' Risala turned to look at a chain of islets just visible on the horizon, leading away into the heart of the Daish domain.

'If she got my message,' Kheda said lightly.

And what if she didn't?

Risala opened her mouth doubtless to ask that very question so Kheda jumped in with one of his own. 'Did your picture scroll survive last night's wetting?'

'It did.' Risala's smile was relieved as she rested her head back against the white stone wall.

'I'd like to have a proper look at it,' continued Kheda casually. 'It looks a fine work.'

'One of the best Shek Kul's library could supply.' Risala grinned wickedly at him.

Kheda spread rueful hands. 'You can't blame me for finding you as much of a puzzle as Dev.'

'If you want to know something, you could just ask me.' Risala shifted to sit facing him, feet curled up beneath her.

'You'd tell me what I want to know?' challenged Kheda.

'That depends what you ask.' Risala was unperturbed by the prospect.

Kheda thought for a moment. 'Who taught you the poet's arts so well you could apprentice yourself to someone as notoriously choosy as Haytar the Blind?'

'You knew of him?' Now it was Risala's turn to be surprised.

Kheda nodded. 'I saw him perform once, when I was visiting the Tule domain. He was quite splendid.'

'He was, and a pleasure to travel with.' Risala smiled sadly. 'Did you ever hear of a poet called Gedut?' she continued briskly. 'His particular strength was satire.'

'The name means nothing to me.' Kheda shook his head. 'Satire's not the safest of styles to adopt.'

'Which is why he didn't travel over much,' Risala agreed. 'So I'm not surprised you've not heard of him. Anyway, twelve years ago, he composed a scathing attack on Danak Natin, which had the additional insult of being extremely funny. Danak Natin promised the weight of Gedut's head in amethysts to any man who brought it to him.'

Kheda saw a fondness in Risala's face. 'He was your teacher?'

She nodded. 'Shek Kul gave him shelter. Gedut repaid him by teaching some of us children to recite properly.'

'That's quite some insult for Shek Kul to offer Danak Natin,' Kheda said frankly. 'I thought Danak and Shek were none too friendly.'

'It's a relationship best described as "complex",' Risala said wryly. 'At the time, Shek Kul was looking to see how far he could push Danak Natin, to see if he could divorce Kaeska that was born Danak.'

'I don't think I've heard a quarter of that story,' said Kheda with open curiosity.

'That's more than complex.' Risala's eyes were shadowed. 'The heart of the tragedy was Kaeska was barren. She couldn't accept it, wouldn't trade for a nameless baby to raise as her own or provide Shek Kul with a chosen bed mate to beget one with her blessing.'

'Didn't she have sisters?' Kheda frowned. 'Most women would look to their family for a baby of common blood.'

'She was obsessed with raising a child of her own bearing.' Risala drew a shapeless squiggle in the dust with one long forefinger. 'Which led her, finally, to seek help from some enchanter from the north. Her brother Danak Mir, who inherited from Danak Natin, he'd been killed and his hold over the windward domains fell away.' She drew a spread of tiny islands in the dust before brushing them away.

'That hold was what made it so important for Shek Kul to protect Kaeska's position as first wife, even though she couldn't give the domain a child?' Kheda guessed.

'Danak Mir would have twisted any loss of her status into an excuse for attack.' Risala grimaced, turning to sit with her back to the stone wall once again. 'None of his allies would have dared ignore his summons. But with him and all his alliances dead with him, Shek Kul set about getting an heir with Mahli Shek. She'd been born Mahli Kaasik and that alliance, with the Kaasik domain, was enough to set other warlords wondering if there might not be an alternative to yielding to Danak might again.'

'How did he die, this Danak Mir?' Kheda was curious.

'Someone got close enough to cut his throat.' Risala shrugged. 'No one's sure if it was a hired assassin or some much-abused islander.'

'What happened then?' Kheda found he welcomed this distraction.

If I'm to ally myself with Shek Kul, it's as well to know such things. And it means I don't have to think about what I'm going to tell Janne.

'Melciar Kir was the first to move. He knew the other windward domains wouldn't stand for him annexing Danak territory directly so he proclaimed his second son Danak Nyl. The boy's mother had been born Erazi Danak, so the people of the Danak domain were only too happy to accept him, especially with every soothsayer seeing omens in his favour.'

'And to save themselves from being ground beneath armies fighting for domination over their islands.' Kheda could see only too easily how this had played out. 'I take it there was no love lost between Kaeska and Erazi?'

'Erazi Melciar was determined to see her son flourish and knew conciliation was their best course. Any hint that he had ambitions to be another Danak Mir would have seen his blood shed on the same sand.' Risala sighed. 'Kaeska knew she had no one to protect her status any more. Once Mahli's baby was born, she'd be reduced to fourth wife, not even left as second or third, and soon Laio and Gar would be with child. She was so desperate she resorted to magic. Discovered, that was the death of her.'

'I thought Shek Kul's children were very young, for a man of his years,' Kheda commented.

Risala shrugged, non-committal. 'He wasn't blind to the advantages of his situation. He could garner sympathy from other domains for his lack of an heir, the way his hands were tied. Lesser wives in several local domains were happy to let him give the lie to Kaeska's hints that he might be to blame for her barrenness, by bringing new Shek blood into their families. And while there were no children, he didn't have that vulnerability, the danger that they might be poisoned or abducted to force his hand over something.'

Kheda stared out over the sea. 'This time last year, if I'd heard Kaeska's story, I'd have said she must have been insane.'

But here I am, having made a pact with a wizard and waiting to explain myself to my wife.

'How did she die?'

'Shek Kul condemned her to be pressed to death. On the seashore. Everyone brought rocks to weigh her down, until she couldn't breathe,' said Risala sombrely. 'Then her body was burned, along with all her possessions, and the ashes left for the sea to take.'

Kheda shivered. 'But she was using magic against her domain. At least we're just seeking to use it against those who wield it themselves, without shame or restraint.'

Risala wasn't listening, her thoughts still in the Shek domain. 'Kaeska wasn't all bad. I don't think anyone can understand the hunger for a child that seizes some women. Anyway, the wizard, he was using her for his own purposes, so it was said.'

'After dealing with Dev, I can well believe that.' Kheda reached for the leather water bottle between them and took a long drink before wordlessly passing it to Risala. She drank deeply. It was hot and what little shade the tower and the wall cast at this time of day was falling on the inner side of the island.

'You're well informed,' observed Kheda after a few moments' silence.

'I was raised in the Shek compound.' Risala's face cleared a little.

Kheda raised an eyebrow. 'Slave or free? Your mother, I mean.'

'Free, one of the seamstresses.' Risala smiled fondly. 'She was no one special, except in my eyes.'

'Your father?' Kheda thought of the anonymous little children running around the Daish residences. Some were born to servants who dutifully approached one of his wives for permission to wed. Other girls simply shrugged and kept their own counsel when questioned about a swelling belly, unable to tell which of their swains was the father or unwilling to tie themselves to him in return for a claim on whatever he might offer the child.

I don't think I ever gave such brats a thought, beyond relying on Rekha to see them usefully trained and settled. Shek Kul evidently has a talent for using every resource within his reach.

'A gate guard.' Risala smiled fondly. 'Shek Kul granted him the tithes of a hill village a few years back. He and my mother live there now.'

'Reward for their faithful service or payment for your talents?' Kheda was intrigued.

I may as well keep on asking questions until she refuses to answer.

'A little of both.' There was a glint in Risala's eye as she ran the plaited cord of the water skin through her fingers. 'And, of course, there were the rumours.'

'Saying what?' prompted Kheda.

'When Kaeska did something to really exasperate Shek Kul, he would beget a child on one of her slaves. There was generally one happy to oblige him in making his point,' said Risala pertly.

'Because bearing the warlord's child saw them freed.' Kheda nodded his understanding. 'And Shek Kul deprived Kaeska of her valuable slaves at the same time.'

We of Daish may not have the Shek wealth but I'd say the peace in our household is more than a fair trade.

'My mother was Kaeska's seamstress,' Risala continued. 'When I was born, rumour whispered Shek Kul had begotten me.' She shrugged. 'The rumours came back with the tide when he picked me out for schooling and prenticing to a poet.'

'Do you think Shek Kul would approve of you telling me all this?' asked Kheda.

'He'll only know if you tell him I told you,' Risala replied with that same mischievous glint in her eye. 'Not that it matters who begot me. My father is the man who raised me.'

'He who tends the crop reaps the harvest.' Kheda quoted the old proverb. 'Whether or not he sowed the seed.'

Risala grinned. 'Anyway, Shek Kul picks out any child with a fair share of wits so he can use us as his eyes and ears.'

'Who looks twice at the slip of a girl carrying the poet's bags, when all they want to hear is Haytar's famous variations on *The Mirror Bird's Quest*?' Kheda smiled to show he meant no offence. 'You must have some tales to tell of your travels.'

'Not for anyone but Shek Kul.' Risala glanced over her shoulder to the rolling grass-crowned dunes that hid the far side of the isle. That was where the skiff had been stowed, mast unstepped, tucked between the battered vats used in the pearl harvest. 'I must let that case dry out properly. The leather's sodden and mould's a plague on the paper in the wet season. On the other hand, I don't want to risk the sun fading the pictures.'

'We keep little braziers alight in our observatory's book rooms.' Unexpected apprehension surprised Kheda. 'I hope Sirket's remembered to see to them.'

If he has, I hope he hasn't set the whole place alight. That would be a truly disastrous omen. Mould in the library wouldn't be much better. How soon will all this be over, so I can spend a peaceful day in there, reading about complete inconsequentialities?

'You can tell Janne Daish to remind him.' Risala took another drink from the water bottle.

'As long as she arrives sometime soon.' Desire to see Janne and apprehension over news she might bring tormented Kheda in equal measure. Unable to sit, he rose and fastened his gaze on the chain of isles that would guide Janne's vessel here. All he could see were indistinct blurs of sand and greenery and distant palms waving feathery tops in the wind.

Risala stood and brushed sand from her faded trousers before making another slow circuit of the wall enclosing the tower of weathered stone. Set away from the prevailing winds, the single door was sturdily built of wood bleached to a silver sheen by salt wind and rain. Within the wall, a spiral stair curled up around the solid core of the tower to the lofty platform rimmed by a low balustrade. The wind stirred something high above that rustled softly and then stilled.

'Nothing to see to the east or north,' Risala reported.

Kheda pointed. 'There's a light galley.'

They watched the sleek boat skirting the shoals fringing these distant islets.

'It must be her,' Kheda said with fervent hope.

'I'll make myself scarce.' Risala shifted uncertainly from foot to foot. 'You don't think they'll search the rest of the island?'

'She'll have told them she's here to contemplate my loss in the shadow of the tower.' Kheda shook his head abruptly. 'To see if dreams here show her what it might mean for the domain. No one else will dare set foot on the isle.'

The lithe galley soared over the sparkling waters towards them, its single white canvas wing of a sail catching an obliging wind, foam flying up beneath the prow.

'Until later then.' Risala disappeared around the curve of the wall.

Kheda walked round the tower enclosure and slid through the gate. It was appreciably warmer inside the wall, with no breeze to mitigate the force of the sun beating down and barely a veil of cloud drifting across the vivid blue sky.

Is there anything in here to guide me, any omen to be read?

A few scraps of cloth in the drifts of dust were faded to an indefinable grey, no way to tell their original colour. Kheda picked up a scrap and it crumbled to parched threads between his fingers. There had been no one left here for the winds and weather to carry their essence across the domain in Kheda's generation or Daish Reik's. Apart from the noise and upheaval of the pearl harvest, the sea birds had this vantage point to themselves year round. There were feathers everywhere, white mostly, some tipped with black, grey or gold, some dried by wind and sun to the fragility of straw, others newer. The white stone of the tower showed streaks where the birds nesting at the top had spattered the stone with their droppings. The rains hadn't yet washed all the muck away.

Pearl gulls, coral divers, even dawn wanderer feathers, of all sizes from down to wing pinions. A man could gather a fine spread of plumage to cast for a prediction. A man who wasn't afraid he was so deeply mired in magic any such reading would be meaningless.

Never mind. My ability to read omens may be compromised but everything I ever learned of reading the skies holds true. The Vizail Blossom is the rising sign, symbol of femininity and hope, of protection for the home, sweet scent in the darkness. It's in the arc of marriage and all such closest relationships. The Diamond's there, for clarity of purpose and talisman against evil, powerful gem for all who rule. It shares the sky with the Opal, for faithfulness and truth, talisman against magic, at its full, at its brightest.

This must be the right thing to do and I only have today

*to do it. Half the heavens will be changed by tomorrow. The
Amethyst, for inspiration, and guided by the Horned Fish,
that will move from the arc for honour and ambition to the
realm of friendship and alliance strengthened by the vigour
of the Winged Serpent. The Ruby moves from the realm of
the self, backed by the strength of the Yora Hawk, into the
arc of wealth and possessions. The Sailfish is there, for good
luck and happiness to come with the Pearl riding with it.
Talisman for my house, token of inspiration, talisman against
madness. This has to be the right thing to do.*

A rowboat grounded on the shore outside with a solid
crunch. Kheda heard low voices then the boat pushed off
in a slithering rush of water. Footsteps approached the
tower. Someone walked around the circle of the wall and
the latch rattled. 'Kheda?'

'Janne.' He walked around the tower, holding out his
arms. 'My love.'

'I was beginning to think I would never see you again.'
She closed the door in the wall behind her, dropping her
gaze as she put back the fine shawl covering her tightly
braided hair.

'There were times when I wondered if I'd ever return.'
Kheda's throat tightened.

Not that you look much of a returning hero.

Kheda was suddenly acutely aware of his mismatched,
faded, salt-stained clothes. His hair and beard were tousled
and untrimmed, his arms scored with old and new
scratches, outstretched palms marked with oar calluses.
'You look more beautiful than ever, my wife.'

Janne wore a sleeveless glossy blue gown vividly
brocaded with gold and belted with a thick gold chain with
hanging jewels of nacre and pearl. More pearls glistened
on fine clasps threaded through her braids. As she folded
her arms over the loose folds of her mantle of pale green
gauze, gold and silver bracelets thick on her wrists jingled:

She wore rings on every finger bright in the sunlight, silver and gold, their malachite bezels dull in contrast.

A stone to heal grief.

'What news have you brought back with you?' Janne's tone was all business. 'What plans for ridding Chazen of these savages?'

Kheda shook his head. 'You first. I've been hearing all kinds of rumours. Why have you and Rekha taken the other children north and left Sirket at the mercy of Saril and Itrac's blandishments? People are saying Chazen guile could undermine the Daish hold on the domain.'

'Naturally, gossip floating in the wake of merchant galleys along with the night soil and food scraps must be the truth.' Janne looked quizzically at him. 'We took the younger children north mostly for their safekeeping and also because that's our usual routine when the rains come.' She shot a hard glance at Kheda. 'They think you're dead, all of them. They're still grieving. We thought it best to keep as much of their life unchanged, to give them what reassurance might be possible.'

'Oh.' Chastened, Kheda wasn't sure what to say.

Janne absently twisted the edge of her mantle, gold thread in the soft sage catching the light. 'Sain had a difficult delivery and wasn't really fit for travel. The baby was healthy enough, a son—' She smiled fondly. 'We're calling him Yasi. But there was always the chance that one of them would die.' Her voice roughened with emotion. 'None of us wanted the children to be put through that, so soon after losing you.'

'I had to go,' Kheda protested.

Janne's unconscious movement might have been a shiver if there had been any breeze. 'Sirket has done his very best by the domain. He has stayed close to Chazen Saril in an attempt to put some backbone into the man,' she added with growing asperity. 'Just as Sain is doing her duty by our people. She encourages Chazen Saril to confide in her and discovers what he's learnt from his people fleeing north, much that he's not been sharing openly with us, I might add.'

'Such as?' Kheda demanded.

'These savages are indeed widespread across his domain but they're certainly not present in the overwhelming numbers that first reports suggested. Of course, they don't need superior numbers when they have magic to strengthen their evil.' Janne's expression challenged Kheda. 'Have you found an answer to that? Something to justify all the grief and uncertainty your so-called death has put your family through?'

'I wouldn't be here if I hadn't,' retorted Kheda, stung. 'What I need to know is will Chazen Saril lead his people south, to retake his domain, when my strike halts the savages' magic?'

'Chazen Saril is fit for nothing.' Janne's tone was scathing. 'According to Sain and Sirket's reports, he can barely decide between a dish of meat or one of fish. He spends his days lamenting for his dead wives and children and bemoaning the plight of his dispossessed people without actually doing anything to improve their lot. That was something else prompted me and Rekha to go north. Whenever some Chazen islander sought Saril's advice, he threw up his hands, claiming he feared to encroach on Daish suzerainty, and begged us to absolve him of all his responsibilities.'

'Isn't Sirket still in the southern residence?' asked Kheda. 'Doesn't Chazen just turn to him?'

'He's tried,' admitted Janne dourly. 'Sirket claims he's too burdened with the cares of the Daish domain, too preoccupied with taking all the omens, for guidance and warning of any new danger, too busy securing his alliances in case the savages come north. He has more than adequate justification.' Beneath Janne's pride in their son, Kheda heard weariness and frustration and saw lines of strain in her face that hadn't been there when he'd last stroked a loving hand over her hair. 'With you believed dead, every old alliance was broken. Sirket has been striving from dawn to dusk to keep our people from fear or despair, to maintain Daish standing with our neighbours in the face of these successive misfortunes. He's won everyone's admiration, their loyalty and more, their love, with his dedication and perseverance.'

'I'm sorry you've all had to suffer like this,' said Kheda, chastened.

'Better this than dying beneath some wizard's magical fire,' said Janne tartly. 'Do you truly have some means to quench their malice? Fear of magic torments our people and those of Chazen that we shelter. Redigal Coron and Ritsem Caid are equally frank in their apprehensions. They'll back Sirket in fighting men, however well armed, wherever they might have come from. They will not send their ships against wizards.'

'I give you my word I'll make sure they don't have to,' promised Kheda resolutely. 'But these wild men will remain, even when their wizards are dead. Can Sirket count on Redigal support, Ritsem ships, to back a Daish strike to the south, to kill the invaders? What about the men of Chazen?'

'Redigal and Ritsem will sail as soon as they are sent word,' Janne replied with conviction. 'Plenty of Chazen men will sail with their own ships or crewing on Daish boats, whether or not Saril risks wetting his toes. Itrac has been more than doing her duty by her domain, rousing their spirits and refusing to allow anyone to give up hope of return.'

'She's still loyal to Chazen?' Kheda broke in. 'Not looking to wed Sirket?'

'I told you I wouldn't countenance such a match, even if Chazen were dead.' Janne fixed Kheda with a stern look.

He waved away the subject. 'What news of Ulla Safar?'

Janne's smile surprised him. 'Ulla Safar is too preoccupied with his own domain to look beyond his borders. Ulla Orhan has taken it upon himself to ensure the domain is prepared for any attack from the south. He's made a close inspection of all their triremes and been considering how best to supply the domain's defences without stripping the islands of either crops to feed those left behind or men to till the land.' Janne's smile turned thoughtful. 'He's paying assiduous attention to all the domain's allies and working hard to repair any ties that might be fraying.'

'Fraying under the strain of Ulla Safar's brutal approach.' Kheda pondered this. 'Orhan's stressing his loyalty to his father at every opportunity, I take it?'

'With the greatest humility,' confirmed Janne. 'He's a wily youth and a clever one.'

'He'll have to be, to keep his head on his shoulders,' said Kheda candidly.

Janne studied her fingernails for a moment. 'He also makes no secret of wishing for closer ties with ourselves. He sent an emissary to Dau some days ago, to present some fine sun diamonds together with his sincerest admiration.'

Kheda was startled. 'What did she make of that?'

Janne paused before continuing. 'She accepted the gifts and sent a modest offering of dog tooth pearls along with polite thanks.'

'Was that wise?' Kheda couldn't help but scowl with mistrust.

'Offering anything that could be considered an insult would be less wise. Dau knows that without being told.' Janne shrugged. 'I don't think she'll seriously entertain any offer he might make.' Her voice hardened. 'Apart from anything else, as far as she's concerned, Ulla Safar encompassed her beloved father's death. She still weeps in the night. I hear her.'

'I will make reparation to all of you, however you want me to, when I come home.' Kheda strove to keep his voice calm.

'You've found a way to cleanse yourself of the stain of magic?' Janne's face was unreadable. 'As well as whatever it is you've discovered to use against these savages?'

Can you even begin to answer those questions in a way that will satisfy her?

'My path and all the omens that guided me led me to a northern wizard,' Kheda began carefully, 'who believes he can defeat these savage mages.'

'You're suborning sorcery?' Janne was horrified

'I am bringing to bear the only possible weapon I can find for defence of my domain,' said Kheda with quiet determination.

'Where is he?' Janne clutched at her mantle and the fine fabric tore beneath her fingers.

'Not here, not even in Daish waters,' Kheda assured her. 'He's watching the savages, planning how best to attack.'

'Oh, Kheda, what have you done?' Janne stared at him, utterly dismayed. 'How can you ever free yourself of such a taint?'

'My intent is wholly pure,' said Kheda with all the conviction he could muster. 'All I am doing, all that I will do, is in the best interests of my domain. The guidance of the stars and every omen and portent that's offered itself has confirmed me in this course of action.' He couldn't help it, his voice rose with anger at Janne's doubting him. 'Ask Sirket to read the heavens for you, as they stand now, today, here. Ask him if stars don't offer the hope of freedom for the Daish domain, from the fear of the savages and their magic, from the leeching burden of those fled from Chazen?'

'By finding a wizard to call down magic at your order?' Janne plainly found the notion revolting.

'Only against their wizards, and they started it,' snapped Kheda.

'That's a child's argument!' Janne pulled the fragile mantle tight around her bare shoulders and the tear worsened. 'What will Ritsem Caid think, or Redigal Coron? How can you prove you've avoided irreparable stain by associating directly with a wizard? How will you explain this sustained deceit to them now? I thought you'd return with something that would balance such wrongdoing, not compound it!'

'I am not required to explain myself to anyone.' Kheda restrained his temper with some difficulty. 'I will say I am oath-bound not to reveal the mystery of countering magic. Every domain has its secrets. This will become one of the Daish hidden skills. I'll swear I have undertaken every necessary purification. They will just have to trust me.' He managed a smile. 'They'll have to, if they want the assurance of Daish aid if these invaders and their sorcery ever return. For the present, all our allies need know is the magical threat is removed and we of Daish and Chazen need their help in killing the rest of the savages, at once, before they have any chance to summon new wizards. They must all sail south, launch a coordinated attack.'

'How will we know when to do this?' Janne sounded suddenly weary. 'You've no messenger birds. Even if you did, they take time to spread their word.'

'There will be a sign.' Kheda did his best to ignore the qualms knotting his belly.

You claim the purity of your intent shields you from the taint of magic. Will that clarity of purpose enable you to see the future past the perversion you are planning?

He took a dogged breath. 'You must tell Sirket this came to you, in your dreams here. There will be a red moon, or moons, I'm not entirely sure when. That's long been a sign of war. Sirket must tell the others to keep watch as well. As soon as they see it, everyone must sail south, to fight to the death.'

'You're certain this sign will be there?' Janne narrowed her eyes at him, mistrustful.

'I am,' said Kheda doggedly.

Because it will be no true sign, but one you'll be fabricating with Dev's collaboration. Will you ever admit such shame to anyone, that you suborned magic to raise a false omen? Will there be enough pearls in the next harvest to keep Dev's mouth shut or will he be leeching on your fear of exposure for the rest of your life?

Silence hung still within the circle of the wall but for a faint susurration from the tower above their heads.

'What then?' Janne was plainly suspicious. 'What happens after these battles, assuming you all live through it and no magic burns you to ashes where you stand, from north or south?'

'You and I will meet here,' Kheda said slowly. 'At the next full of the Greater Moon.'

'It'll all be over by then?' There was a desperate note of hope in Janne's question.

'One way or the other,' Kheda replied grimly. 'Then I'll take the omens and we'll consider how best to manage my return from the dead.'

He smiled at Janne but she did not smile back. 'Let's hope the omens are favourable.' She stirred a few of the feathers littering the ground with one gold-ringed, sandalled foot. 'If that's all we have to discuss, I had better look for guidance in whatever dreams might come to me here. Rekha and I have been visiting all the towers of the domain.'

'So no one would remark on your visit here.' Kheda nodded his understanding.

I hope these dreams bring reassurance that these are all steps on the right path, however distasteful.

'Among other reasons.' Janne's eyes were shadowed. 'Until I got that message, it was always possible you were truly dead. Even then, I could only hope it was from you.'

'It's nearly over, I promise you.' Kheda stepped forward to put his arms around her but Janne broke free of his embrace.

'You had better leave. I should be alone to dream true.'

'Until our next meeting, then.' Kheda bent to kiss Janne briefly on her lips. 'I'll be counting the days.'

'As will I.' Her wistful smile tore at Kheda's heart yet, perversely, encouraged him.

Stars above, she's plenty of reasons to be angry with you but she misses you all the same.

Kheda gave Janne one last smile and left. Careful to keep the tower between himself and any watchful eyes from Janne's galley, he headed for the line of dunes running down the spine of the island. Ducking to keep his head below the crests tufted with coarse new grasses, he followed the path he and Risala had scouted through the hollows and gullies. The beach on the sheltered side of the islet was thick with discarded oyster shells, crunching underfoot. Kheda hurried towards the ranks of vats made from discarded hulks of fishing boats. 'Risala?'

She appeared in the middle of the weathered, battered hulls drawn up well beyond the reach of the highest seas, tied to stakes hammered deep in the sand. 'Well?'

Kheda skirted the boats to reach the gap they had forced open to hide the skiff, sail stretched over the lowered mast and laced to the sides to give them some shelter. As he joined Risala the faint reek of rotting shell-fish rose all around him, summoned by the previous night's rains that had left the skiff ankle deep in rain-water.

Catching his grimace, Risala grinned. 'This place must stink to high heaven during the pearl harvest.'

'It does, believe me,' Kheda assured her. He looked at the vats waiting to be filled with the divers' haul from the sea bed, the precious pearls retrieved once the flesh had rotted away. 'I hope Dev's got his plan worked out by the time we get back. It's not that long till the harvest should start and we'll need its bounty more than ever, if we're to repay Ritsem and Redigal for their help.'

Risala returned to tending her brightly coloured scroll, carefully unrolled on the sand and weighted with oyster shells against the inquisitive wind. 'What did Janne say?'

'She's confident that the Chazen people are keen to go home as soon as they can,' Kheda said with relief. 'There doesn't seem to be anything to these rumours of Chazen Saril having designs on our domain. Redigal and Ritsem will fight with us too, as long as they're not facing magic. So let's be on our way.' Kheda began unlacing the sail and folding it as Risala had shown him.

Risala carefully rolled up her scroll, blowing stray grains of sand from the delicate reed paper. 'Are you all right?'

'Seeing Janne made me realise how much I miss my family,' Kheda said shortly. 'The sooner we get back to Dev, the sooner we can have this all done and over with. Then we can all go home.'

'It's low tide.' Risala nodded towards the sea as she capped the leather-bound scroll case. 'We'll have to carry the boat over the reefs.'

'Come on then.' Kheda reached for the rope at the skiff's prow and looped it around his wrists, laying the rope across his shoulder.

With him dragging and Risala pushing from the stern,

the skiff slid reluctantly over the furrowed sand. The sea was lapping lazily around the reefs, bright beneath the water but dull and dry where the tide had left them abandoned to sun and wind.

'We'll have to wade out a bit.' Kheda rolled his head from side to side to ease his shoulders. 'We'll just ground the boat if we get in here.'

'Fair enough.' Risala leant on the stern to catch her breath.

Striding into the shimmering water, Kheda shivered at the touch of the rain-cooled sea on his sun-warmed legs. The skiff was easier to pull with some water beneath its hull. Kheda looked down warily to the white sand beneath his feet, mindful of the hazards Daish Reik had warned him about.

'Watch where you're stepping. An urchin's spines festering in your feet can poison your blood for a slow death. The quickest way to die is frothing at the mouth because you've trodden on a sand lurker. Their venom fells in moments. It paralyses. Men have drowned in water no deeper than mid shin. Still, they're the lucky ones. That's a quick and painless death compared to the one sea snake poison brings you.'

End up dead through some stupid accident after all you've put everyone through and Janne will kill you, the mood she's in.

That amusement was short-lived. Kheda picked his way carefully between the rocks with their weeds and skein creatures. Kicking up sand as he waded, now waist deep, he saw small shapes dart away through the suddenly clouded water. Tension prickled between his shoulders as he found himself anticipating stabbing pain with every step. Splashes of salt water stung his dry and chapped lips and in all the scrapes and scratches he had collected.

What would happen now, if you were truly dead? These savages would tighten their grip on Chazen, unchallenged, at

leisure to move north and bring destruction to Daish when-
ever they wanted. Worse, you've brought a wizard here, whom
you cannot trust, who knows the worst of you and your plans
and could betray your memory any time he chose. Your death
would hand him your family's future. You didn't realise, did
you, on all that long voyage when your death would have
meant so little, that your return would be the most perilous
part of your journey, for everyone?

As it happened, the worst Kheda felt was the sharp
edge of a discarded shell scraping the side of his foot and
the brush of something unexpectedly solid against his
thigh as the sand fell away beyond the outlying line of
rocks. Startled and, at the same time, finding himself
forced to swim, Kheda looked down. There was nothing
to be seen in the darkening depths.

'In you get.' Risala climbed in over the skiff's stern
and addressed herself to raising the sail.

Kheda hauled himself around to the stern and climbed
aboard, dripping. He reached for the oars and deftly
mounted them on the thole pins.

It's nearly done. It's nearly over. As soon as it's done, you
can go home. You'll make it up to your wives and children,
if it takes you all the wealth of the domain and the rest of
your life to do it.

He hauled on the oars with grim determination, driving
the skiff through the waters until Risala captured an
obliging wind in the triangular sail and set them on the
wide, curving course that would take them out into the
ocean, beyond the reach of Janne's galley and swinging
round towards the anchorage where Dev would be waiting.

He will be waiting. He will have made his plans. We will
see an end to these savages and their magic.

CHAPTER NINETEEN

'Do I scrape the barnacles off the skiff or is there something else you want to claim for winning that wager?' Cross-legged on the *Amigal*'s deck, Risala grinned wryly at Kheda.

Leaning on the skiff, now upturned and stowed safe onboard, Kheda spared her a brief smile and noted the apprehension in her eyes. 'Dev, do you have a plan?'

Sitting beneath an oilcloth rigged from the mast to shelter him from sun and rain alike, the wizard was shuffling through a sheaf of creased paper, pen held between his teeth, heedless of a drip of ink on to his chest. His silver bowl was set to one side, the water within dark and oily.

He doesn't look to have shaved or bathed since we left him. Whatever else he may be, he's plainly not zamorin, not with that beard shadow and that receding hairline. Zamorin never go bald.

'Dev, for the last time, do you have a plan yet?' Kheda could see Dev's notes were half obliterated by copious amendments. 'I told Janne to tell Sirket and all the others to watch for a sign in the moons. At least one will have to be more than half to stir them to action, otherwise anything they'll see will be an ill omen and they'll just stay put. The greater's already at dark and the lesser's on the wane. If we don't act tonight, it'll be at least eight nights before we can do anything with hope of support.'

And the Ruby, the Amethyst and the Diamond are in triune. Red talisman against fire, carried by the Sailfish for good luck, for those as close as brothers. The purple gem for inspiration and new ideas, riding in the arc of friendship and alliance, led by the Horned Fish, guide and friend of all who sail the seas. Bright Diamond, potent talisman for rulers and defence against corruption, it's in the arc of marriage, with the Bowl as rising sign, symbol of refreshment and sharing. If that wasn't portent enough, it dances hand in hand with the Pearl, for the Daish domain and its warlord.

The mage looked up at the tense silence, smiling with satisfaction. 'I believe I have a plan.' He set down his bundle of papers and ran a hand over his bald pate. 'As long as at least one of you is good and handy with a bow.'

'My father had me trained in all such skills.' Kheda allowed himself a little scorn. 'A warlord cannot expect his men's respect if he cannot do himself what he asks of them.'

Dev looked at Risala. 'What about you, girlie?'

She smiled sweetly, though her eyes stayed hard. 'I carried my father's quiver when he went hunting for jungle fowl. As soon as I could string a bow, he set me practising on feathers tied to posts in the compound.'

'Ever hit any of them?' Dev didn't wait for an answer. 'We'll assume you did. Now—'

'We can't just expect to kill these wizards with arrows,' interrupted Kheda. 'They burn any missiles out of the air. Itrac Chazen told me—'

'And we've seen them do it ourselves,' nodded Dev, unperturbed. 'But they need their magic to do it.'

'I don't understand.' Risala was puzzled.

'I told you their wizardry draws its power from the elements around them.' Dev's smile was cruel. 'Given the sniff of a chance, they steal magic from each other as well. I'm fairly sure that's what happened to our friend who drowned in his own body fluids. Greenleaves cut his feet out from under him, magically speaking.'

'Fairly sure?' Kheda queried.

'Sure enough.' Dev sounded entirely confident. 'What we want to do is get all these mages together and then I'll start a fight with Dragonhide—'

'Why him?' demanded Kheda.

'Because he's top dog in that pack,' Dev replied promptly. 'I've been watching him and the other mages while you two were off on your pleasure jaunt. Each wizard has a sizeable cohort of their mud-headed troops, most holding a good few islands. The wizards spend their time doing the rounds of their followers, picking up any new loot that's offered. Then the minions go looking for loot to offer up the next time. They're quite happy to take it from some rival camp, if there's no wizard around to put a stop to their nonsense.'

'No honour or obligation between them then,' noted Kheda with distaste.

Dev shrugged, unconcerned. 'The wizards with any sense visit Dragonhide as well, banging their heads on the sand and handing over anything up to half of their spoils, coffers and prisoners. That way they get to keep what's left. Dragonhide goes looking for anyone trying to hide his loot up some out-of-the-way creek.' Dev looked around at the tree-choked inlet where the *Amigal* was hidden with some amusement. 'The ones who realise that game's up grovel and scrape and let Dragonhide take what he wants. Anyone too slow to roll over—' He shook his head. 'These wizards have some inventive ways of killing each other. You haven't seen the half of it.'

Nor do I want to.

Kheda shuddered. 'Dragonhide adds their plunder to his?'

'Captives and food and whatever jewellery they've gathered. He shares some of it with his favourites,' added Dev. 'There are three wizards sniffing round his arse now, and seven left who haven't decided which way to jump yet.'

'Is that all?' Risala was astounded. 'The Chazen people who fled were talking of hundreds of mages.'

'Hundreds of them would have rampaged the length of the Archipelago by now. Given the damage even one wizard can do when he puts his mind to it, I think you'll find eleven's plenty,' Dev assured her sarcastically. He looked at Kheda. 'There were probably more when they invaded but the weaker ones are smudges on the sand or beetle food by now. It's the stronger ones who've survived and they've all been on the move over the last few days, drawing closer together and closer to Dragonhide. They've got something planned.'

'Going north?' Kheda felt cold despite the warm sun.

'No idea.' Dev shrugged. 'I've listened on the wind but I can't make anything of their tongue, and I speak a handful of mainland languages besides just about every Archipelagan dialect.'

'Your spells won't have betrayed you?' asked Risala with alarm. 'That dragon-hide wearer, he found you before.'

'He didn't feel the spell looking at him.' Dev shot her an irritated look. 'He sensed someone new drawing on the elements close by him.'

Risala was unconvinced. 'What does that mean?'

'Nothing I can explain to anyone not mageborn,' retorted Dev with unpleasant superiority.

'I imagine if they were able to find you through your magic, we'd have come back to find you with a spear through your head,' Kheda said, placatory. 'So, tell us your plan.'

'The key is the way their magic's all instinct and raw power. Dragonhide's people seem to be the only ones who can handle more than one element at a time. I imagine that's what gives him his clout. Well, that wouldn't count for much in Hadrumal. Drawing on all four elements is the first thing we teach the apprentices and I studied with some of the finest wizards of the northern lands. Like I said, I challenge Dragonhide to a fight.'

Dev cracked his knuckles and grinned. 'That's the way these savages do things and he won't be able to back down, not without all the rest of them turning on him to rip him to shreds. We make sure they're all present and correct to see it. Then, as well as throwing my own magic at him, I'll raise a few wards around the wind and the sea, so he thinks I'm looking to cut him off from the elements around him. What I won't do is touch the other mages, so obviously, he'll draw in their powers.'

'Obviously?' Kheda couldn't help himself.

'He'll need to seize the easiest elemental source to cope with the demands I'll be making of him,' Dev assured him with brash confidence. 'Once the other wizards are caught up in his sorcery, their own defences will fail. As long as you two can each use a bow fast and accurate, you can stick an arrow in each one and they'll be down before they realise what's happening.'

'That's asking a lot,' objected Risala.

'You don't have to kill them outright.' Dev looked at Kheda. 'Just get an arrow in them that's tipped with whatever poison you used to stifle my magic. That should slow them down long enough for one of you to get a second arrow through their head.'

'That's not so tall an order.' Kheda rubbed a thoughtful hand over his chin.

'As long as we can get a clear shot at them all.' Risala was still dubious.

'Will the loss of their magic help you defeat the dragonhide wearer?' Kheda asked Dev.

'No idea.' The mage shrugged. 'That would just be a windfall, anyway. I've my own notions for killing him.'

And you're anticipating this a little too keenly for my peace of mind. 'Never trust a man too eager for a fight.' That's what Daish Reik always said.

'Which are?' Kheda fixed him with a stern eye.

'Meaningless, to anyone who isn't a wizard,' Dev said with more than a suggestion of smugness.

Kheda swallowed his irritation with difficulty. 'What about the wild men? What if they come after us, after you?'

'I really don't think that'll happen; minions fight minions, wizards fight wizards and minions get out of the way sharpish. Anyway, once I've dealt with Dragonhide, I'll be scaring them out of their painted skins,' Dev promised with a vicious grin. 'Just till your allies can come and skewer them.'

Risala was thinking about something else. 'You said we had to get all these wizards together. How do we do that without being caught and killed?'

'I show them something so disturbing that they all go running to Dragonhide.' Dev sorted through his papers, pulled out a leaf and thrust it towards Kheda. 'If we sail this course, we'll pass close by each of their current camps. Once we've stirred them all up, we have to get to Dragonhide's island ahead of them. Can you and the girl manage the *Amigal* between you?'

'I think so.' Kheda looked up from the precisely delineated map. 'What will you be doing?'

'Gathering my strength,' Dev said frankly. 'Working magic tires a wizard more than anything else in the world. If I'm going to defeat Dragonhide, I need to be fully rested.'

'What if you don't defeat him?' Risala asked sharply.

'He'll be your problem, because if he's not dead, I will be, torn to bloody rags all over the deck most likely.' Dev smiled sweetly at her.

And you can't wait to test yourself against him, to see if you can win the ultimate wager.

Kheda shivered involuntarily. 'Is there anything to be gained by waiting?'

'No,' said Dev with abrupt seriousness. 'We have one day to do this or it won't work.'

'We had better get going, if we're to have light enough for shooting these mages.' Kheda tucked the map into the breast of his tunic for safekeeping. He found his hands were clumsy.

Then Dev won't be the only one tested. We'll see if I've been reading the omens aright or following delusion to lead us all to disaster.

Dev raised an elbow and sniffed at his armpit. 'I need to bathe and shave now you two can keep an eye out for random savages stumbling across us. Find me some food as well, girlie. My belly's been thinking my throat's been cut regardless.'

'Where are we supposed to find bows?' Risala demanded.

'Behind the wine barrels,' answered Dev with a sly smile. 'You didn't think all I peddle is vices?'

'We'd better make sure they're still usable,' Kheda said with a qualm of uncertainty.

When he and Risala returned to the deck with long oilskin-wrapped bundles that they found in the straw-packed chests in the hold, Dev was stripping off his rancid clothes. As Kheda untied the thongs around the bundles, the wizard disappeared over the *Amigal's* side with a splash.

The oilskin protected fine, supple leather, which in turn covered thickly woven, soft cotton cloth. Kheda studied the weapons within carefully. 'The bows are sound enough. They're just straight staves, not so easy for the damp to damage as a composite bow. Some of the arrows want attention though. Did your father teach you how to fletch?'

Risala shook her head. 'That was a job for Shek Kul's armoury.'

'Don't worry; my father insisted I learn, thankfully.' Kheda rapidly assessed which arrows needed work and which were beyond salvage.

'Throw me a rope!' Dev yelled.

Risala moved to comply, stepping back as the naked, dripping wizard clambered back on deck. 'Those aren't hunting arrows,' she accused him.

'No, indeed.' Kheda held up an arrow with a broad-shouldered flat head with vicious barbs. 'For cutting flesh and ripping sinew. And here, for penetrating armour, mail or plate.' He picked up an arrow with a long, square-hammered, chisel-ended head. 'I can't think of a warlord who wouldn't have your head, just for carrying these, never mind trading them to his islanders.'

'He'd have to know I was carrying them first. You keep my secrets, Daish Kheda, and I'll keep yours.' Dev's glance took in both of them. 'What are you complaining about? You've a sight more chance of killing a wizard outright with those than using some game arrow.' Dev grabbed his discarded clothes and swiped at the water running down his muscular torso. 'Get me something clean to wear, girlie.'

'Get it yourself,' she retorted without heat.

Kheda looked up, a couple of arrows shedding feathers in his hand. 'The sooner he's dressed, the sooner we get under way.'

Risala sighed as she lifted the trap door to the stern cabin. 'Don't think I'm waiting on you hand and foot, Dev, whether or not you need to coddle your magical strength.'

Rapidly reappearing, she threw a bundle of well-worn cotton at Dev and then started rigging the *Amigal*'s sails. Kheda laid the weapons carefully aside and went to help. As soon as the sails were raised, Risala took the tiller and Kheda used the heavy stern sweep to shove at the banks

on either side, to stir the little ship. The onshore breeze
held them back regardless.

'Just a little magic,' murmured Dev, dragging trousers
and tunic over his damp limbs. 'Just to get us moving.'

The sails billowed obediently and the *Amigal* slid out
into a wider channel where a natural breeze pushed the
ship through the water.

'Think you can handle the tiller, girl?' Dev challenged
Risala.

'Of course.' She didn't rise to his bait.

'Make sure you keep a watch out while you're at that.'
Dev gathered up his discarded clothes and disappeared
into the stern cabin. He reappeared with the bowl he'd
used for scrying now holding a tightly stoppered jar of
liquid soap, a battered razor and a highly polished metal
mirror.

Kheda looked up from sorting through the arrows. 'Do
you have any glue?'

'Down in the main hold, third box back from the prow.'
Dev dipped a little fresh water from the cask fixed by the
mast and sat down. Rubbing soap into his stubble, where
it lathered reluctantly, he fixed Kheda with one speculative brown eye. 'So what exactly will you be putting on
those arrowheads to slow Dragonhide's pals down?'

'It's what I'll be showing to Redigal Coron and Ritsem
Caid, to explain how I managed to defeat these wizards.'
Kheda wound salvaged silk thread carefully round an arrow
shaft. 'So no one comes hunting you, to contain the taint
of magic by turning your freshly flayed skin inside out.'

Dev chuckled, unabashed, before taking his razor carefully to his cheek. 'That's all I need to know, is it?'

'For the present.' Kheda concentrated on smoothing a
ragged quill.

'Where did you get the hateful stuff?' Dev asked idly,
nose in the air as he scraped beneath his chin.

'In the north.' Kheda stood up and went to find the glue.

If I can put all our success down to the powder, and Shek Kul can vouch for that, if needs must, then that should answer the most immediate questions. We can turn any others aside as intruding on Daish secrets. I'll still have to find some purification and a powerful one at that, for Janne and Sirket's sake, never mind my own, but we can keep that between ourselves.

Kheda's spirits rose as he repaired the arrows and he found himself whistling under his breath. Clean-shaven and having decided to feed himself rather than tease Risala any further, Dev fetched a blanket from below and laid himself down on the deck. He was soon snoring softly. The sun climbed higher and higher in the sky.

They had travelled a good distance when Risala broke the silence hanging over the ship. 'I'm hungry. Can you take the tiller while I find us something to eat?'

'Of course.' Kheda took a moment to ease his cramped shoulders and then moved to the stern. Ignoring the sleeping wizard, Risala fetched smoked meat and saller pottage from the stores below.

'Thanks.' Kheda ate rapidly and returned to his work. By the time the light was perceptibly yellowing, he had the bows and arrows ready for use. He looked at the weapons and pondered a new set of questions.

How best to load these arrowheads with Shek Kul's powder? I'll have to make a paste of some kind. It'll have to be made of something with no potency of its own, so the powder's still fully effective. I wonder just what's in that mix? If Sirket and I can tease it out, that will truly be a valuable secret for the Daish domain. How much should I keep back, to study and to show Caid and Coron, to still their curiosity? How much should I use on each arrow? It'll need to be enough to be effective but I don't want to be relying on one shot for each wizard. We need enough arrows tipped and ready for several

attempts at each one. Hitting a bird on the wing's going to be
easy compared to this, whatever Dev says. And I'd better keep
back enough to deal with him, if he turns treacherous on us.

The thought of the struggle to come, lethal magic and
howling invaders all around and him with no more than
a bow in his hands, dried Kheda's mouth.

'Can I have a look at that map?' Risala was scanning a
maze of islands, thick with knot trees, ahead.

Kheda joined Risala by the stern, both studying the
crackling paper. 'We must be there.' He stabbed a finger
down on an irregular lump of land.

'You'd better wake him.' Risala looked apprehensively
ahead. 'We'll be coming up on the first of them soon.'

Kheda went to shake Dev's shoulder. The mage was
awake in an instant. 'Are we there yet?'

'Soon.' Kheda looked uncertainly at the wizard. 'Do
you want anything? Your white brandy, some chewing
leaf?'

'What?' Dev squinted up at him. 'No, of course not.
Liquor and magic's a dangerous combination, pal. I'd no
more be drunk to work serious wizardry than you would
be to read a beast's entrails.'

For some reason he didn't care to examine too closely,
Kheda found that reassuring. He turned to Risala. 'How
long till the headland?'

'Just coming up.' She deftly corrected their course.

Dev rubbed his hands together and blue light crackling between his fingers startled Kheda. The mage set
both palms flat on the deck and azure tendrils crawled
away to slip between the tightly fitted planks and disappear.

'What's that?' Kheda demanded.

'A little misdirection, to keep them looking the wrong
way. Right, my girl.' Dev stood up and gestured to Risala.
'Hold a nice steady course parallel with the shore.'

'What should I do?' asked Kheda.

'Help with the sails if she needs you.' Dev rubbed his hands together and moved to the rail for a clear view of the bay coming into sight. 'Otherwise, stay out of my way.'

Kheda saw the depressingly familiar pattern of a ransacked village with a rough prison of crudely felled timbers, a deep ditch to foil assault from the sea and the dark lines of the invaders' log boats haphazard as a child's game of picksticks above the high-water mark. A few figures were visible, idling between the huts and the shore defences.

This is what I'm wagering my life against, in dealing with this wizard, to save my people from such vile destruction.

Determination driving out his apprehension, Kheda glanced at Dev. The wizard was peering intently at the village, hands cupped as though he cradled something unseen, lips barely moving in some silent litany. Kheda braced himself for some explosion of magic, fire or lightning or nameless horror even worse than the abominations the two duelling wizards had wrought on each other.

Nothing happened. Dev stayed rapt in concentration, eyes unblinking, his whole body leaning towards the shore. Kheda was wondering how long until he might ask the mage what was happening, or, more crucially, failing to happen, when movement ashore caught his attention. Savages came swarming out of the various huts and storehouses like ants from a nest stirred with a stick. Some took up a belligerent stance by the shore ditch, spears visible, bristling above their heads. Others ran for the log boats, a few launched before some authority summoned them back to the village.

You can't have been more than Efi's age, no, more like Mie's. Daish Reik caught you up under one arm, grabbing a couple of your brothers with the other hand. Everyone was out in the gardens, servants, slaves, mothers and children. One of the kitchen girls was hit on the head by a falling roof tile.

While the biggest cone mountains that regularly spewed fire were no closer than the Ulla domain, tremors still shook the Daish islands from time to time. Whenever people felt the ground shaking beneath their feet, they made for the open air. It was one of Kheda's earliest memories and the scene ashore was just as chaotic. Then the frantic activity stilled, everyone gathering around a central hut.

'What's going on?' Risala wondered, anxious. 'They can't see us, can they?'

'I don't think so.' Kheda kept his eyes fixed on the shore. 'I hope not,' he added with some alarm as the savages scattered, this time with purpose that became all too familiar. Some carried panels ripped from the houses to the boats, lashing them together with crude vine ropes. Others hauled sacks and bundles out to pile them on the shore. The rest began breaking down the crude stockade and driving their captives down to the water.

'They can barely walk.' Kheda winced as the grievously mistreated Chazen islanders stumbled and crawled across the sands, their captors forcing them on with blows and kicks.

Dev let out an explosive breath and cackled with delight. 'That's got them on the move!'

'What has?' asked Kheda, exasperated.

Dev ignored him. 'Risala, hang on to that tiller. We need to get on our way before any of that lot get close.' The sails swelled with unnatural wind as he spoke and the *Amigal* dipped and shivered.

'What did you do?' Kheda persisted.

'Later.' Dev held out an insistent hand. 'The map.'

Kheda handed it over, doing his best to contain his frustration.

Dev studied it for a moment before flicking at a

carefully inked cross with a newly pared fingernail. 'That one.' Giving the paper back to Kheda, he sat and turned his back on them both as he lay and rolled himself in his blanket, pulling a fold over his head.

Risala looked at Kheda, uncomprehending. 'Is that it?'

'So it would seem, until we reach this encampment.' Kheda showed her the map. 'Which won't be long. They have all moved close together, Dev was right.'

'The wind's in our favour and it's building.' Risala looked up at skies now dappled with thickening cloud.

Kheda grimaced. 'There'll be rain tonight. Let's hope we can get all this done before it arrives.'

'I think it'll be over one way or the other,' Risala said grimly. 'All those log boats and rafts are following us.' Turning her back on them, she gripped the tiller tight, as if her urgency would somehow force the *Amigal* on.

'I'll get those arrows tipped.' Kheda lifted the hatch to the cabin below. 'We'll want something to hand, if any savage mage catches us while Dev's still snoring.'

In the dimness of the lamplight in the main hold, he worked rapidly to blend half of Shek Kul's powder with a little saller pottage and some of the fish-scale glue. He counted out the arrows. Thirty for him. Thirty for Risala. Half the ripping arrow heads, half the piercing missiles. He carefully tipped them with the paste, resolutely turning his thoughts away from the odds against them as he set them to dry.

That done, a new thought struck him. He went to look again in the chests where he'd found the bows. In the bottom of one, Kheda found a selection of daggers, old and new, plain and ornamented, some in styles he recognised and others entirely unknown to him. In among the sinuous shapes of the central domains, there was one with the curved blade and cross-braided handle of Daish. It was old, the silk braid dark with grime and sweat, the leather of the scabbard cracked and peeling away from the wood beneath.

Let this be an omen then, that I am right in coming back to fight for my own with whatever weapons come to hand.

Kheda tested the edge with a careful finger. It was as blunt as the crude knife he'd stolen from the Ulla domain farmer. Rummaging in the chest he found a whetstone and set about remedying that. He had just about restored the dagger to a state Telouet would have grudgingly approved when he felt the *Amigal* change course. Returning swiftly to the deck, Kheda saw Dev throwing aside his blanket and striding to the rail, expression one of intense concentration. As before, Kheda could see absolutely nothing happening ashore until the savages all roused as one man, thrown into utter confusion.

When they reached the next island, the pattern repeated itself, as it did on the following island and the one after that. By the time they had left all eight of the savage mages surrounded by encampments in chaos, Kheda's frustration was all but choking him and he had honed the Daish dagger he had claimed and the Viselis blade to an edge sharper than any razor. He watched the final island on the course Dev had plotted grow closer and closer. Finally he couldn't stand it any more. He strode down the deck to Dev.

'Just what are you doing?'

Dev was leaning on the *Amigal*'s rail, breathing heavily. He hadn't moved since they had fled the uproar wreaking havoc on the last savage wizard's encampment. 'Now would be a good time for that white brandy.' There was a dangerous light in his dark eyes.

Kheda fetched a bottle without comment. The stopper came out with a shrill squeak. Dev took a long swallow of the aromatic liquor and jerked his head towards the stern. 'The girl will want to see this, I daresay.'

Kheda followed him and stood beside Risala. She was

looking back along their wake. Kheda looked too. More than one of the invaders' log boats was visible in the distance, single-hulled vessels speeding ahead of the bigger raft-like ships. All were hurrying along the same course, hastening towards the mage with the dragon-hide cloak.

'Don't forget to look ahead as well,' Dev warned with a taunting grin. 'Don't run my ship on to any rocks.'

'In a channel this wide?' Risala retorted. 'Even you could steer it falling down drunk.'

'I could thread the *Amigal* in and out of the Serpents' Teeth dead drunk.' Taking another pull from the bottle of brandy, Dev smiled cheerily at her. Then his face turned serious. 'Just so you know, this is what I was showing each of those wizards.'

Dev concentrated on the empty air between the three of them and a faint golden glow began to build. A disc formed, coalescing into a perfect image of a beach. The radiance took on a greenish hue and diminutive trees and bushes flourished around the edges. An encampment appeared, larger than any they had just visited, with three corrals for captives and towering piles of booty heaped between them, crudely covered with palm thatch ripped from the ravaged huts of the village.

Kheda took an involuntary pace backwards and Risala's sudden clutch at the tiller put a visible kink in the *Amigal*'s wake.

Where are the people? There are no people.

A snap of Dev's fingers put paid to Kheda's unspoken bemusement. Two figures appeared, disproportionately large for the floating scene but all the more identifiable for that. One was the savage wizard with the dragon-hide cloak. The other was Dev, or at least Kheda guessed it was, from the bald head and arrogant stride. If it was Dev, he was dressed in more finery than Kheda would have guessed the wizard could boast.

The mage chuckled as the two little figures squared off against each other. Risala and Kheda both jumped as flames erupted around the dragon-hide wizard. The illusory blaze died away and a miniature sandstorm enveloped the Dev image. In the next breath, it exploded outwards in a ring of fire that broke, curled back on itself and wrapped around the dragon-hide mage. This time the flames didn't yield, rising every higher and shrinking inwards to a tight pillar of fire. The tiny Dev waved a hand and the blaze died away. There was nothing left of the dragon-hide mage but a twisted heap of scorched scales. The real Dev snapped his fingers and the illusion vanished.

'That's what you've shown the other invading mages?' Kheda stared at the empty air, the brilliance of the magic still seared on his vision.

'It is,' Dev confirmed. 'Which is why they're all scurrying along to see if it's true. If it is, they're doubtless eager to grab as much of Dragonhide's loot as they can.'

'And when they find out it isn't true?' Kheda asked with a frown.

'They'll have to explain themselves to Dragonhide.' Dev was unbothered. 'He'll want to know why they've all turned up, full of concern and clutching empty sacks. That should keep them arguing for a while.'

'Is that what you're going to do to him?' Risala's voice shook slightly.

'I don't know.' Dev shrugged. 'I'll give it a cursed good try, though. It depends what he throws at me.' Kheda saw that dangerous glint was back in his eye as the wizard took the helm from Risala, who yielded it without argument. 'We're going to make landfall just this side of that headland. Dragonhide's camp's in the bay beyond, so we'll cut across to a vantage point I've scryed out.'

Kheda watched the green, impenetrable shore gliding

past. 'Won't they have patrols out, watchmen posted?'

'They don't bother with things like that.' It wasn't entirely clear who was the target for Dev's scorn; Kheda or the savages.

'They're so confident.' Kheda shook his head. 'So arrogant.'

'Nothing's happened so far to make them think you Archipelagans are much of a threat.' Dev shrugged. 'The Chazen islanders all fled like rats from a burning granary. No one's come south from Daish, or any other domain, to make so much as a recce, not since you and Chazen Saril were sent running back north like whipped curs. Besides, I imagine they know just how fearful you people are of any magic. That's probably what encouraged them to attack in the first place. And with Dragonhide on your side, would you be bothering to send out patrols?'

Kheda couldn't contest that, much to his annoyance.

'Get yourselves armed and ready to go.' Dev hauled on the tiller and turned the *Amigal* towards the shore. He looked up at the sails, one hand raised to guide the wind.

Retrieving bows and arrows from the hold, Kheda handed Risala a full quiver. He brushed the flights of a bundle of arrows loosely tied with twine. 'Those are the ones for the wizards.'

'I wouldn't have minded a chance for a little practice, to acquaint myself with this bow.' She looked up at him, eyes huge with apprehension. 'I can hit a chequered fowl on the run, or at least, I used to be able to.'

'A savage is bigger than that, mage or no.' Kheda smiled reassurance as he handed Risala a belt carrying a broad jungle blade, pair to the one that hung heavy and clumsy at his hip. 'Here. If they see us shooting and come for us, we run as far and as fast as we can.'

She drew the newly honed Viselis dagger from the second sheath on the belt. 'What's this for?'

'In case we can't run fast enough. In case you need some alternative to being thrown into a stockade.' Kheda tried to recall something Daish Reik might have said that would be encouraging in their current situation. Nothing came to mind.

'Thank you, I think.' Risala glanced at Dev, who was still intent on guiding the *Amigal* to his chosen spot. 'What about him?'

Kheda hesitated. 'We have to trust he's as good as he claims to be.'

'It's not at all how I imagined it, the reality of magic.' Risala shook her head slowly. 'Even when Shek Kul told me it was my turn to shadow Dev, and I knew he suspected him of being a wizard, it never seemed quite real, not until I saw him wreaking havoc with a flick of his wrist and a handful of light.'

Kheda looked at Dev. 'Not so bad as you imagined, or worse?'

'Both.' Risala shrugged. 'How does it seem to you?'

'It's the only means to drive out these savages who are threatening my people.' Kheda set his jaw. 'That's all that matters.'

'I don't care if it taints me; I hope whatever magic's hiding us doesn't fail.' Risala was looking at the flotilla of log boats and rafts behind them, closing rapidly now that the *Amigal* had turned aside from her original course.

Kheda tensed with her as the savages grew closer and closer, before cutting straight across the curve in the *Amigal*'s wake. They swept past, unswerving in their determination to reach the wizard with the dragon-hide cloak and find out just what might be afoot. Standing in their narrow boats, the savages dug their long, thin paddles deep into the sea, the clumsy rafts scudding along on foam tainted with the lurid green of wizardry. Kheda breathed a sigh of relief to see every dark, scowling, vicious face turned forwards, intent on rounding the headland.

The *Amigal* lurched as Dev brought her alongside a deeply undercut bank where a fast-flowing stream coursed down a steep hillside to join the sea. The ship bobbed in a pool of momentary calm.

'Get us moored good and fast!' Dev barked.

Kheda and Risala didn't argue, hurrying ashore to force the *Amigal*'s anchors down into the clinging earth. Finally satisfied the flukes were as deep as he could drive them, Kheda looked up. 'Where's Dev?' As he spoke, the mage emerged from the stern cabin. Kheda stared.

Risala stood upright and whistled under her breath. 'Just what else have you got hidden in that hold?'

'I thought I should dress for the occasion.' Dev grinned, brushing a negligent hand down the shimmering white silk of his lavish gold-embroidered tunic. 'Since they seem so keen on gemstones—' He rattled a heavy gold bracelet loaded with rubies red as gouts of blood. There was another on his other wrist. 'Let's see if they can get these off me.'

'Where did you get those?' Kheda couldn't decide if the sizeable stones in the gold collar Dev wore were garnets or rubies but those were definitely diamonds striking fire from the sun in his many rings and in the anklets clasping his trousers tight.

The dangerous light in Dev's eyes was bright. 'The vice trade has its rewards.'

'You're not going to look so pretty once we've hacked our way through that.' Risala looked up at the steep, tree-choked slope of the headland.

'Want to wager on that?' Dev's smile broadened wickedly. 'A little shiny jewel of your own you'd care to share with me?'

Risala hesitated. 'Since you mention it, no.'

'Come on. The light's beginning to fade.' Kheda

headed for the only suggestion of a break that he could see in the closely tangled berry bushes. Pulling the broad, heavy blade free of his belt, he began cutting a path. By the time they were halfway up the slope, he was all but exhausted, having to force himself on through the clinging vines and the cloying, humid heat. Looking up between the sprawling canopies of the lilla trees, he saw the sunlight was turning distinctly yellow. The day was drawing towards a close.

If we don't hurry, it'll be too dark for either of us to worry about our lack of archery practice.

By the time they reached the top, Kheda was dripping with sweat. He could hear Risala panting behind him and turned to see her wiping her forehead with a shaking hand, seed burrs clinging thickly to her sleeve. Bloodsuckers hovered all around them. 'Dev?'

'Right here.' The wizard appeared behind Risala. His gleaming tunic was unspotted by sweat and there wasn't so much as a smudge of grime on him nor a fly within arm's reach.

'Get down.' Kheda was too tense to be impressed. 'They might see you.'

'That's the whole idea,' murmured Dev but he ducked down to join Kheda behind a tangle of striol vine. 'Come on. We've got to get closer. I've scried out the best spot.'

Stooping, he led them through the clinging greenery to an irregular fold in the land that offered a clear view of the beach, looking straight down the line of the wide ditch with its bristling spikes. Risala hung back, stringing her bow, face taut with determination. Kheda crouched low, his own arrows ready to hand.

If they look up, they'll see us. They'll be on us like hounds on a nest of jungle kits. We won't stand a chance of getting away, not this close. We'll just have to hope they don't look up, then, won't we? Daish Reik always said men rarely look

*above their eyeline unless they have good reason. We'd better
not give them reason till we have to.*

The scene below was almost the same as the miniature
Dev had drawn in his spell, with the three stockades and
the ragged heaps of booty piled among the plundered
houses of the village. Not quite the same though. Now the
beach below the wide spiked ditch was crowded with log
boats and rafts hauled up out of the water. Knots of
cowering, beaten prisoners were being driven ashore by
gangs of spear-waving savages. Some of those newly arrived
on the beach were defending the loot they had brought
with them. Others looked on the verge of attacking each
other. The dragon-hide mage's followers were blocking any
passage through to the village itself, five and ten deep and
loudly free with their scorn for whatever the newcomers
were claiming. Belligerent shouts rose high into the air,
pierced by the occasional scream of pain.

Kheda shivered. 'Are they all here, the wizards?'

'Most of them.' Dev scanned the shore. 'See him in
the spotted-cat skin, he's probably the most powerful still
holding out against Dragonhide. He's on good terms with
that one.' Dev pointed to a savage boasting what looked
like a shimmering blue breastplate.

'What is he wearing?' Kheda wondered.

'Butterfly wings, hundreds of them all threaded
together.' Dev shrugged. 'His people bring them to him.
I've seen him in a stand-off with that one over there, so
I'd say they're about as powerful as each other. You definitely want to drop those three first.'

Kheda peered down to the sand. 'Who else are we to
kill?'

'Our friend with the green wreath.' Dev took a moment
or two to find him. 'And that lad in the palm crown. I
saw him working with Yellow Paint.'

'Look!' Risala interrupted with an urgent whisper. She

pointed to a prodigious fleet of log boats rounding the headland on the far side of the bay.

Dev narrowed his eyes and then smiled. 'Now we can start the fun.' He handed Kheda his spyglass. 'See him in the biggest raft. Him and Catskin have had a few trials of strength but I've seen them both back down before forcing an end to it.'

Kheda lowered the spyglass, nauseated. 'He's wearing a necklace of hands.'

'He gets them off loals his men catch.' Dev was dismissive. 'Now, see those two on the beach; the one with the logen garland around his waist and that one all crosshatched in red mud, they've both paid visits to our many-fingered friend, separately mind you, not together. They haven't given him tribute as such, probably because that would win them a visit from Dragonhide but they've both sent him hands from the loals that their hunters bring in.'

Kheda turned the spyglass to the village side of the defensive ditch. 'Where is the dragon-hide wizard?'

'He won't show himself until I call him out,' said Dev slowly. 'There, by that middle stockade, the man with the sharks' teeth necklace. He's been running errands for the other two who've tied their ships to Dragonhide's stern rail.' He glanced at Risala. 'That's our friend in the feather cloak and the chancer in the lizard skin, remember them? They're best of friends now.'

'We should aim to kill them as early as possible, I take it?' Kheda did his best to commit the muster of wizards to memory.

'You're getting the idea.' Dev clapped him on the shoulder.

'When—' Kheda looked up to find Dev gone. Startled, he looked at Risala. 'Where is he?'

She pointed down to the beach. 'There.'

CHAPTER TWENTY

In the blink of an eye, Dev had stepped from their perch on the headland down to the empty dust between the defensive ditch and the first of the village huts. His white garb shone luminous among the sun-burnished savages as he stood motionless, hands loosely tucked through the golden chain of his belt. Some of the closest invaders were already gaping at him, a few raising wooden spears and stone-studded clubs. The commotion beyond the spike-studded ditch continued unabated, newcomers still intent on getting through the barrier.

Risala nocked a paste-tipped arrow. 'When do we start shooting the wizards?'

'That's what I was about to ask Dev.' Kheda ground his teeth. 'As soon as he gets his head stove in would probably be a good time.'

A circle of savages was slowly closing on Dev, weapons raised, ugly intent in their every advancing step.

Pillars of red light erupted from the dry ground, coalescing in the radiance. A giant bird appeared, towering over the closest savage, walking on legs as thick as a man's waist. It bent a sharply crested head to snap at his eyes with a viciously hooked beak. He screamed and recoiled, stumbling into those behind him. The apparition batted stubby, flightless wings and threw back its head to crow in harsh triumph. One wild man had the presence of mind to thrust his dark wooden spear at the apparition. It passed straight through the brilliant bird's fiery plumage and the man pulled it free without resistance. He turned to brandish the weapon in triumph and Kheda saw his mouth open in exhortation.

The magic-wrought Yora Hawk pecked at his head. The man's bristling, mud-caked hair burst into flames. He screamed, the shrill sound glancing off the stunned silence that had now fallen along the entire shoreline. His head was ablaze with scarlet fire, crimson drops falling all around, not of blood but of magical flame. It took hold on the empty ground, flowing together to ring him in an all-consuming conflagration. The wild men closest fled.

Those who'd been trying to attack Dev from behind weren't sure where to run. Four of them faced a serpent easily as tall as the Yora Hawk, rearing up on trailing wings of flame to stare at them with unblinking ruby eyes. A tongue of piercing red light flickered in and out of the lipless mouth as it swayed slowly from side to side. One man broke and the serpent struck, not biting but darting forward to loop itself around the man and drag him, shrieking, back across the sand. His flesh was already smouldering from the touch of its iridescent scales before the Winged Snake bit him in the neck with a flash of flame. The wound glowed as lines of fire beneath his skin showed the unearthly venom coursing through his veins. The hapless savage burned from the inside out, his skin finally cracking and crumbling into blackened embers. The other three ran but the snake swept past them on its burning wings, cutting off any hope of escape. It hovered, waiting for another victim to try fleeing, long tail lazily looping and coiling in the dust.

'For a barbarian, Dev certainly knows his constellations,' Kheda managed to say, mouth dry.

A massive Mirror Bird was standing guard on Dev's seaward side, another creation of shimmering flame, stalking back and forth, rattling the great fan of its tail as its long crested head quested forward. Those savages now retreating hastily towards the spike-studded ditch were doing their best to evade the speckles of light struck from the apparition by the sun riding low in the sky behind them. Every time one of the glints of red touched bare flesh, a man cried out. Leather loincloths and wooden weapons were already scarred with sparks. The bird opened its mouth and hissed and the invaders fled, throwing away weapons now burning in their hands. The recent arrivals on the beach had set aside their tussles and were now lining the other side of the defensive ditch.

I wouldn't be relying on that to protect me.

'I don't think I could make an epic poem of this.' Risala's voice was hoarse. 'Not without being stoned for it.'

'Look, there!' Kheda caught his breath as three men emerged from the biggest hut left standing in the village. The first was cloaked in the barbaric splendour of pale grey lizard skin; the second in multi-hued feathers; and the third wore a red cloak dark as dried blood yet somehow glowing in the sinking sunlight.

'That's the dragon-hide mage,' Risala confirmed shakily. 'Those two with him, they're the ones we have to kill as soon as we can.'

'Only when Dev has got everyone caught up in his magic,' warned Kheda, infuriated.

Risala tensed as the mage with his lizard-skull helm walked slowly towards the Yora Hawk. The great bird's head wove from side to side, as if assessing this new threat. The savages now forming in a dense, impenetrable ring at a prudent distance from this unknown sorcerer all took a pace backwards. The others still hesitating between the spiked ditch and the Mirror Bird seized their opportunity to flee. Those still trapped by the Winged Snake weren't so lucky. The monster's glittering head darted forward, mouth agape. One man fell to the sand, blood burning within his veins, then the next and the last. A murmur of apprehension swept through the invaders and the circle retreated a few paces more. Lizardskin was still studying Dev's proudly strutting hawk

'How will we know when?' Risala looked at him. 'What if he can't do it, what if Lizardskin kills him?'

'We'll just have to try shooting the most dangerous wizards.' Kheda shrugged helplessly. 'Perhaps they won't be expecting arrows. We might get a few of them.' He risked a quick survey of the seaward side of the ditch and found the savage with the grotesque necklace of loal hands. He was watching intently, his followers levelling their spears to claim a half circle of empty sand for their master.

'There's Catskin.' Risala pointed a discreet finger. 'And Palm Crown.'

The savages' deference was making both men comparatively easy targets. Kheda nodded slowly, still searching for the one with the butterfly breastplate. 'Can you make that kind of shot?'

'I can try for either,' Risala responded wryly.

'We've got more than one arrow for each of them.' Kheda assessed the steepness of the brush-choked slope beneath them and the utter confusion now swirling around the beach below the ditch.

Seeing us is one thing; they've got to reach us and that's no easy climb. We might get half our arrows off and still have a chance to run before they reach us. It had better be the arrows with the paste on. But where have the other mages gone? How are we supposed to pick them out of that horde? And it's not just spears we have to fear. If a wizard can see us, surely he can kill us. What hope then?

A flash of golden light wrenched his eyes back to Dev. A surge of dust was flowing across the ground. It rose like mist, sparkling and swirling. The Yora Hawk looked as if it were wading in mud, the Winged Snake's lashing coils were slowly being stilled and the Mirror Bird was struggling like a sea bird caught in a slick of filth.

Risala gasped as the fiery apparitions disintegrated, her cry as one with the rush of fearful triumph spreading through the massed savages. Kheda watched, breath held, as Dev's scattered magic drew itself back into a wall of flame that held back the rising, stifling dust. The flames rose higher, unnatural crimson painfully bright, hiding Dev from sight. The dust subsided and its colour faded from a sunlit gold to a darker, amber hue. The radiance slowly sank into the ground. Dev's wall of fire remained impenetrable.

'If he doesn't get on with this, there's going to be no light for shooting,' Kheda muttered apprehensively, glancing towards the west.

'Look!' Risala urged in shocked wonder.

The solid ground around Dev was turning to powder. The savages encircling the northern mage were scrambling backwards, the slower among them already stumbling, knee deep in sand. The landward edge of the ditch crumbled, stakes falling this way and that, earth flowing to fill the trench. The bottom of Dev's ring of fire hung in the air, unsupported.

The flames subsided, shrinking to waist level then to knee height, then disappearing altogether to reveal the wizard standing on a solid circle of untouched ground. Dev's hands were on his hips, his whole stance one of challenge and mockery.

Kheda tensed.

Lizardskin raised his hands and the dust surged upwards all around Dev. Dev gave a careless wave and a surge of blue light drove the choking cloud sideways straight across the ditch to send the savages there stumbling backwards, coughing and pawing at their eyes. Even as Lizardskin raised his hands intending some new attack, Dev snapped his fingers and sent a ball of scarlet fire straight as an arrow for the savage mage's head. Lizardskin batted it away with a shaft of blue light but another was already on its way, and another. As fast as the savage mage waved one ball of flame away, Dev sent two or three more arcing towards him. Lizardskin began ducking and weaving, successive fiery missiles getting closer and closer before they were abruptly quenched.

Kheda heard the feather-cloaked mage's shout at the same time as everyone else. A paralysed hush seized the entire shore. The feather-cloaked mage strode down the beach, waving his arms, his heavy mantle of iridescent plumes sweeping around him. A full-throated roar burst from the savages and raising their weapons, they charged as one man at Dev.

Dev raised his hands and every thrusting spear burst into flames. The hafts of stone-studded clubs split into smoking splinters and the stones themselves exploded into vicious shards. The savages fell back in confusion to cower among the huts of the village and hide behind the piles of plunder. Some clutched bloodied heads, others stumbled and crawled, hands groping, eyes blinded. Kheda saw the vicious wounds to their arms and chests were seared black or swollen with weeping blisters

The wild warriors weren't the only ones confused. Even as every weapon was turned against its wielder, Dev flung a final handful of fire at Lizardskin. This time the savage wizard was an instant too slow and the ball of scarlet flame dodged past the skein of blue light that Lizardskin cast out to catch it. The sorcerous fire caught him full in the chest. He staggered backwards, shrieking, clawing at the clinging magic. Fire ringed his torso with a brilliance painful to behold. Lizardskin threw back his head and screamed, falling to his knees. He toppled backwards, dead before he hit the ground. The flames vanished. Beneath the lizard's skull, his face was unmarked, frozen in a rictus of agony. His legs and feet were similarly untouched Between his shoulders and his waist, there was nothing left but a few dark knots of charred bone and a stench of burning carried on the breeze.

Feathercloak's howl of fury rose above the stifled pain of the injured savages and the fearful commotion among those on the seaward side of the stake-filled ditch. A spear of lightning arced down from the cloudless sky. The ground where Dev was standing exploded with an ear-splitting crack.

Kheda and Risala both jumped, startled beyond words. 'Is he dead?' quaked Risala.

'No.' Kheda pointed. 'There.'

Incredibly, Dev was now standing well clear of the seared sand.

Feathercloak gestured and more lightning seared through the air. Dev raised an out-turned palm and knocked the blast aside with a blue-white streak of his own magic.

This can't be lightning. We couldn't see it if it was. It would be too fast.

Feathercloak was sending spear after spear of the unnatural lightning at Dev. The northern wizard knocked each one awry with a shattering shaft of his own. Shards of azure light showered down on the huts and heaps of booty. Palm thatch started to smoulder damply.

A wind arose from nowhere, swirling with sapphire radiance. Gathering into a narrow spiral, a whirlwind danced along the shore towards Dev. The northern mage continued trading magic with Feathercloak, ignoring the swaying, bending spiral of destruction sweeping his way. The magical whirlwind darkened as it sucked up debris from the ground, now the smoky blue of a storm sky. Smouldering leaves on a nearby roof burst into open flame, fanned by the breezes drawn into the vortex. Pouncing like a jungle cat, the whirlwind doubled over and enveloped Dev in a funnel of livid, clouded light.

'Where did he go now?' wondered Kheda aloud. This time the wizard was nowhere to be seen when the whirlwind halted on the broken lip of the ditch. It slowed, magical radiance fading, debris falling from it. Feathercloak shouted harsh rebuke at his terrified minions hiding among the huts and piles of plunder. He gestured and a few reluctantly edged towards the spot where Dev had been standing.

Risala clutched Kheda's arm. 'Dragonhide!'

The mage in the blood-red cloak had emerged from the shadow of the doorway where he'd stood to watch the contest. A wail like the cry of a pack of whipped dogs went up as the wild men fell away before him, bowing low, arms outstretched in supplication. Dragonhide called out to Feathercloak with an impatient jerk of his head. Feathercloak turned to reply, hands spread in bemusement.

Disregarded, the whirlwind's speed slowly increased, a pale blue light threading through the spiral. The vortex widened and reached down into the ditch. Those who'd been clustered along the seaward side fled as the revitalised whirlwind uprooted the stakes, flinging them in all directions.

Whatever Dragonhide was saying to Feathercloak, his gestures eloquent of fury, was lost in the new commotion. Feathercloak faced the errant whirlwind, hands upraised in command, expression one of outrage. Sapphire light shot through the spiral like the crackled glaze of a lustre vase. The whirlwind was wrenched this way and that, ripped and distorted. It struggled in the bottom of the ditch then slowly, inexorably, advanced up the beach towards Feathercloak. The magic within it shone ever brighter. Kheda felt the hairs on his arms and the back of his neck bristle as if a thunderstorm to drown the world were about to break. The whirlwind slowed, a sight against all nature, but still it crawled up the shore, edging ever closer to Feathercloak.

He didn't take his eyes off the rebellious vortex but he did spare one hand for some frantic signal to Dragonhide. In the next instant, the whirlwind had claimed him. It spiralled upwards, taller than the highest trees on the slope behind the beach, narrowing, darkening to a dull lapis. Then, shocking the savages' appalled cries to silence, the whirlwind vanished. Feathercloak's body fell from the skies to land with a thud on the sands.

'He must be dead,' gasped Risala.

Kheda simply nodded. The savage mage's corpse was pierced time and again with splintered stakes from the ditch. Pieces as thick as a man's hand and as long as an arm or leg were driven clean through his chest, his belly, his thighs, one run through his head from just below his jaw to emerge above one ear. Blood oozed slowly over the raw pallor of the newly broken wood. Brightly coloured feathers slowly floated down from the empty air, drifting aimlessly in all directions. The wild men shied away from their fragile touch, swatting them away hysterically.

Dragonhide strode to the centre of the beach, cloak swinging as he looked this way and that. He ignored the swelling chaos around him, eyes intent on something only he could see.

Kheda reached slowly for a paste-tipped arrow. 'We had better be ready.'

'Not so many to shoot now,' said Risala with a humourless smile.

She might have said more but Dragonhide flung out a

hand and Dev appeared, falling and rolling across the beach, lashed by brilliant white light. There was a crack like thunder, the light vanished and Dev scrambled to his feet. Kheda saw red glistening on the white silk of his tunic.

That's not rubies.

Dev's head was hanging, his shoulders heaving. Dragonhide advanced towards him, still half crouched, like a hunting dog. He brought one arm around to his front, palm turned out. A shimmer of magic gathered around his hand. It rose and floated towards Dev, who lifted his head to gaze at it, mouth hanging open. He half lifted a hand but it fell back to his side, limp and defeated. The living magic swirled and grew, threaded through with sapphire, ruby, emerald and amber light. Dragonhide took another step, then another, every line of his body tense. The glittering sphere of intertwined magic floated closer and closer. Dev stood frozen, helpless.

Or just waiting for his moment.

As Kheda wondered with desperate hope, Dev suddenly reached out and caught the sorcerous radiance in both hands. Dragonhide fell back on to the sand as if he'd been punched in the face. The white silk of Dev's tunic glowed and then the northern mage disappeared once again. In his place stood a beast like nothing Kheda had ever heard tell of.

The body might have belonged to a loal, if there had ever been such a beast twice as tall as a Yora hawk. It was all colours and none, rainbow hues sliding over it and surrounding it in a haze of magical light. It had a tail but this was a lashing flail of jagged scales thick enough to cut a man in two. Furred, its head nevertheless had hooked beak rather than muzzle, white fire dripping from its down-curved end. The apparition gave a blood-curdling shriek that silenced the entire beach.

Dragonhide scrambled to his feet and disappeared in a blaze of emerald fire. As Kheda scrubbed at his watering eyes, he saw a new monster down on the sands. It had the blunt head of a sea serpent, crested with a glaucous fin, flowing neckless into a low, stubby-legged body vaguely reminiscent of a whip lizard. Its tail curved up and over its back, tipped with a spear-like sting. It shimmered with all the rainbow vividness of a butterfly's wing.

If Dev can deal with that wizard, it's down to you to deal with the others.

With a lurch, Kheda remembered why he was perched above this incredible scene. Tearing his eyes away, he searched the lower beach for the other savage mages. There was the man with the butterfly breastplate. He was standing alone; all his followers retreated some distance behind him. Loal Hands and Catskin were standing together now, closer to the water, their minions mingled in a belligerent circle around them. The lesser mages with their more paltry adornments were strung across the beach, each with a few terrified invaders in attendance, frantic glances betraying their consternation.

Kheda shook Risala's shoulder. 'We have to be ready.'

She was still gazing at the monsters the mages had become, mouth open.

The serpent-headed monster lunged at the loal-bodied one. It snapped heavy jaws laden with needle-sharp teeth and the loal-bodied one sprang aside, twisting to lash at the serpent-headed beast with its saw-scaled tail. The serpent beast jabbed and thrust with its monstrous scorpion-like sting but the loal-bodied one dodged it time and again.

The serpent beast's head broadened and grew wide, thick horns, its shoulders swelling, rising on lengthening forelegs. More ox than serpent now, it ducked its head and charged at the loal-bodied beast. Wings sprang from the loal monster's shoulders with a spread that knocked blazing thatch off huts on either side. Half flying, half springing, it leaped clean over the horn-headed monster. Its feet twisted into a new shape in mid-air, growing talons like a cliff eagle's, raking at the horn-headed monster's eyes. Wounded, the horn-headed monster did not bleed. Instead the gashes on its face were rimmed with many-hued magical light.

The horn-headed monster reared up on its hind legs, tail flowing into its spine, hips altering, legs lengthening to support it. It reached out long arms now tipped with claws as long as daggers and seized the loal-bodied one, dragging it out of the air, stabbing again and again, ripping rainbow gashes in the other monster's hide.

That hide turned to a hard carapace. Spiny shell like a coral crab's sheathed the loal beast's limbs. Its wings disappeared and the creature that had been the dragon-hide mage found itself overburdened with the weight of the monster that Dev had now become. It toppled backwards, the armoured beast landing on top of it, the spiral spear of a horned fish lengthening on its forehead even as Kheda watched.

It was Risala's turn to shake him. 'Look!'

Down on the shore, the savage mage painted in cross-wise stripes of red ochre was writhing in convulsions. Kheda looked for the other wizards. The wreath wearer was on his knees, one desperate hand raised to his followers, who were backing away in alarm. The palm-crowned mage and the one wearing the garland of logen blooms were luckier in their minions, both supported as they staggered away down the beach.

'They're heading for their boats,' Kheda realised with alarm.

'Catskin, Loal Hands and Butterfly Wings are still by the ditch.' Risala squinted as she picked them out. 'I'm not sure if they're caught up in this magic or not.'

Kheda let slip an exasperated hiss. 'We can't let those two get away.' He stood and drew down a careful aim on the more distant figure. 'I'll take Palm Crown.'

Risala rose beside him and the two arrows flew at almost the same instant. Both missed; Kheda's sailing high and unnoticed over Palm Crown's head while Risala's fell short to lose itself in the confusion milling around the sand.

Kheda lowered his bow and took a long, measured breath. His eyes met Risala's but there were no words to express such a potent blend of chagrin, apprehension and plain rage. They each carefully removed a second tipped arrow from their quivers.

This time they both shot true. The mage belted with logen blooms doubled over as a broad-bladed arrow caught him full in the belly. He writhed on the ground, maddened with the agony of the barbed blade driven deep into his innards, blood dark around his hands as he clutched at the wound.

Palm Crown stumbled as a chisel-tipped shaft went clean through his shoulder, only slowed by the fletching catching in the wound. He fell to his knees, vainly trying to stem the blood from a gash as wide as his hand and as deep. His followers whirled around in consternation, looking this way and that. To Kheda's overwhelming relief, no one looked in the direction of their vantage point. Better still, their cries of alarm went entirely unheard in the general commotion.

The chirrup of Risala's bowstring startled Kheda. He followed her gaze to see the red-painted wizard who'd been racked by convulsions now pinned to the sand by an arrow running through his chest. The wizard struggled feebly then lay still, blood trickling from his mouth.

Taking a careful breath, Kheda assessed their next

targets as he reached for another tipped arrow. 'If you can take the one with the butterfly wings, I'll try for our friend with the green wreath.' A quick glance showed him that the dragon-hide mage was now some nightmare sea beast with a plethora of strangling arms while Dev's monster had grown vicious pincers to tear them away.

Kheda's first shot at the wreath-crowned mage went wide and his second skewered a panicking savage who rushed forward at precisely the wrong moment. Ignoring a torrent of muttered curses from Risala, Kheda lowered his bow and closed his eyes before trying again. This time the broad-bladed arrow struck Green Wreath a glancing blow on one thigh, ripping flesh but not biting deep.

No more than a flesh wound. Will that be enough?

'I got Butterfly Wings.' Risala's voice was tight with anguish. 'I can't get any kind of shot at Catskin.'

'Nor me,' Kheda said through gritted teeth. 'Nor Loal Hands.'

Both savage wizards were surrounded by their followers, the men drawing in close, spears at the ready, driving off those scattered by the deaths of the other mages who came desperately offering themselves, pleading for protection.

Kheda looked back to the struggle engulfing Dev and Dragonhide. The shelled beast had grown spines all over its back and curled into an impenetrable ball. The many-armed monster had turned into a thickly plated serpent with crushing coils writhing over and around its foe.

Kheda reached for the untipped arrows in his quiver. 'I'll try to scatter the men around Loal Hands. See if you can get him.'

He loosed arrow after arrow. The knot around Loal Hands slackened, men knocked off their feet by arrows to the belly and chest. At Kheda's side, Risala shot once, twice, finally hitting the mage with her third chisel-tipped arrow. It hit the mage in the face, his cheekbone exploding in a gout of blood. Passing clean through his skull, the vicious arrowhead bit deep into the minion behind him. Loal Hands disappeared as his retinue clustered round.

'They're looking our way,' Risala said grimly.

'I can't see how we can get Catskin,' raged Kheda.

Risala gasped with fear. 'What's happened to Dev?'

Kheda looked to see the armoured serpent's coils collapsing inwards, unresisted. The spiny beast had vanished. 'There!' He saw Dev a few paces down the beach, half kneeling, half falling, covered in blood. The great serpent glowed, all the colours of the rainbow blurred around it.

Dev raised his hand, fingers twisted and broken. The armoured serpent writhed and its tail split into a fan of lesser snakes, each with gaping, questing fangs. Many-hued radiance crackled along the edges of every scale. Dev rose to his knees, both hands raised in denial, forearms clawed and bleeding. The light suffusing the snake monster grew brighter, merging into a blinding white. The beast began to split, scales separating, raw flesh beneath shining with a turmoil of magelight. It thrashed from side to side, scattering dust and bloody magic, carving a great gouge in the ground.

Kheda tore his gaze away. 'How many arrows do we have for Catskin?'

'About half of them.' Risala rubbed at her face.

'This is nearly over, one way or the other,' Kheda scowled. 'Let's use them.'

'On who?' Risala pointed down the slope to a knot of savages ripping aside the tangled vegetation as they started climbing towards the vantage point.

'Catskin,' Kheda said vehemently. He reached for the arrows, not caring which were tipped with Shek Kul's powder and which were not. Risala shot with the same abandon. Catskin was at the very edge of their range, hurrying down to the water, the heavy folds of his brindled cloak flapping. Arrows fell short, useless in the sand or wounding some frantic savage.

We're not going to manage this.

Then, startled, Catskin whirled round. He ran back up the beach, cloak flying out behind him. With a shot more instinct than calculation, Kheda let one of his final arrows fly. Risala's bowstring sang in his ear. Catskin fell, two broad-headed shafts hitting the same thigh, severing muscle and sinew, splintering bone. The screaming mage collapsed, leg nigh on cut off, and died in a welter of unstaunchable bleeding.

'Kheda!' Risala cried out in alarm.

Kheda looked down to see determined savages more than halfway up the slope. On the far side of the broken ditch, Dev struggled to his feet, painfully, slowly, blood smeared across his bald head. The nimbus of white surrounding the frantically writhing serpent monster began to contract. The light within darkened; ruby, sapphire, emerald and amber darkened, the snake disappeared and the dragon-hide mage stood there, blood trickling down his legs, his own hands upraised with the jewel colours of his magic swirling around him.

The circle of white light shrank further. The jewel colours within hammered at the inexorable barrier. It made no difference. With blood-curdling shrieks several savages hurled themselves at Dev, spears raised. With a single gesture, Dev sent them tumbling backwards, seared with scarlet flame. The sphere of white light around the dragon-hide mage took fire, flashed like rainy-season lightning before hissing with steam and cracking for an instant like crazed glass. Dev's wizardry held and then with a blast that struck Kheda like a physical blow, the magic collapsed on itself. In the next instant, the burning radiance burst outward in a shower of many-hued light. Rags of blood-soaked dragon hide and gobbets of torn flesh scattered all across the beach. Shaking his head in a vain attempt to regain his hearing, Kheda dug the heels of his hands into his eyes to clear the blinding after-image from his sight.

'Where's Dev?' Risala searched the far side of the ditch for their wizard.

'I can't see any sign.' What Kheda did see made his blood run cold. 'That man, that's the mage with the sharks' teeth necklace.'

The final, disregarded mage had gathered a gang of savages who were tossing aside the piles of loot, digging out caskets, dodging in and out of the burning huts to claim choice coffers. With Sharkteeth gesturing, the small contingent formed into a line, other savages grabbing salvaged weapons and simple lengths of wood to join them.

'He's getting away,' gasped Risala.

Shouts from below drowned out her cry as the savages climbing the slope below them drew ever closer.

'Not if I can help it.' Kheda threw aside his bow and gripped his heavy jungle blade. 'Come on.'

The dusk was really gathering beneath the lilla trees now, the warm air dense beneath the leaves. Kheda hacked at the clinging logen vines and the burgeoning berry seedlings hampering his every stride. He could hear twigs snapping in a commotion that was Risala or pursuing savages drawing nearer. He sliced at the thick vegetation, tearing at leathery green leaves and frail new fronds with his free hand. The fiery slice of cuts to his fingers brought him to his senses and he pulled his dagger free of his belt. The braided cord grip soaked up the blood slick on his palm. Plunging on, his breath rasped in his throat. As the dew rose to meet the approaching night, the rich scent of the dark forest surrounded them.

Risala bumped into his back. 'Where are we going?'

'Sharkteeth looks to be bearing this way. If we can move fast enough, we can cut him off.' Kheda slashed at the underbrush with renewed determination as shouts and trampling feet behind told him their pursuers were getting closer.

With Risala treading on his heels, whimpering in her frantic breaths, Kheda ran as fast as he could, heart pounding, chest burning. Stumbling on a faint trail, he nearly fell, recovering himself in the nick of time. He ran on and heard noises ahead. Curt orders in an unknown tongue punctuated the sound of urgent hands beating back underbrush with sticks. A new cry rose from behind, in triumph and cruel anticipation, as the savages chasing them found the path. Bare feet pounded on the bare earth.

'They're going to catch us!'

Stifling Risala's panic with a brutal hand, his dagger's hilt crushing her lips, Kheda dragged her off the path. Throwing himself beneath a berry bush choked with striol vines, he rolled on top of Risala, stilling her struggles with his weight. Her eyes, white-rimmed, stared uncomprehendingly into his as the savages who'd been pursuing them came howling down the path. Sharkteeth's men met this unexpected attack with brutal cries and vicious blows. The pursuers were ensnared in retaliation before they had time to realise what was happening.

Kheda slid his hand down to Risala's chin. Bloodied fingerprints showed dark on her skin. 'Any arrows?' he mouthed.

She twisted under him to pull her quiver out from beneath her back. Kheda gathered all the remaining shafts into a single bundle. 'Make for the *Amigal*,' he told her soundlessly.

Risala nodded, face frozen with fear. He left her crouching beneath the paltry shield of the bush, fumbling to draw her heavy jungle blade. Sheathing his own and crawling on hands and knees, Kheda headed towards the fiercest sound of fighting. The arrows he held caught themselves in the tangled ground plants. He sliced them away with his dagger. Sharp stubs bit at his knees and unexpected puddles of muck soaked his trousers. An invader, falling backwards through the bushes, fell over him, crashing to the ground, an attacker leaping on top of him. Kheda felt a spray of blood warm on his face as he sprang forward to dive beneath a straggling lilla sapling, unnoticed as the two wild men fought to the death.

Yells and abuse echoed around the trees. Kheda strained ears still ringing from the disaster that had befallen the wizards on the beach. He caught a note of command in a guttural shout and slowly rose to his feet, ready to attack any savage who might turn on him, alert for any hint of magelight. There was the wizard with the sharks' teeth necklaces, shouting furiously at the men laden with coffers of loot. Some had let caskets slip from their shoulders as they jostled and shoved in a panicked attempt to flee down the track.

In the same instant that Kheda took in the scene and realised Sharkteeth's unprotected back was towards him, one of the burdened savages saw this unexpected newcomer, raising a pointing hand, mouth opening to shout.

I've no idea if there's any of Shek Kul's powder on these arrows. I have to kill the invader's wizard some way or another. Skewering his kidneys should do it, regardless of his magic. If I die for it, so be it. If I live, all well and good. Let's worry about that later.

All these thoughts ran through Kheda's mind in the time it took the savage's hand to rise to shoulder height. Kheda threw himself forward, stabbing the bundle of arrows deep into the hollow of the shark-tooth mage's back just above his leather loincloth. Reaching round with his other hand, he reversed his grip and thrust his dagger into the base of the mage's throat, hilt deep, feeling the blade grate on bone. He pulled the man close, their bodies matched like lovers, the warmth of the wizard's back pressing the cold muddied cloth of his tunic to him. His nostrils filled with the savage's rank, animal scent. Kheda twisted and wrenched at the dagger. The mage's necklaces broke, sharks' teeth cascading in all directions, hard as little stones. Blood poured over Kheda's hands, down the mage's chest, soaking the moist ground, warm on Kheda's feet. The mage struggled feebly in his embrace, breath bubbling in his throat and his gasps spraying a fine mist of blood into the air.

The ferocious fight raged on, uncomprehending, all around. Those few who had seen the sudden attack stood transfixed with horror at the death of their leader. Kheda forced his way backwards through the undergrowth behind him, the limp mage a dead weight in his arms, a stinking burden as the man's bowels voided, but too valuable a shield to discard.

With cries of anguish, several savages hurled themselves towards him. Kheda threw the wizard's corpse at them and turned to dive through a tangled mess of striol creeper. The thorns pierced him from head to toe but he didn't slow for a moment. Throwing himself to the ground, he fled, wriggling beneath the impenetrable vegetation on belly and elbows, face in the leaf litter, expecting the agony of a spear in the back with every twist and turn.

None came. Kheda rolled on to his side and looked warily around at the blank, unhelpful leaves surrounding him. The sound of fighting subsided as the savages' cries turned to lamentation and audible indecision.

How long before they decide to beat the undergrowth for you, flushing you out like a hook-toothed hog and met with spears just the same? Not long, and they'll get Risala too, if she's still anywhere around. Time to run. But which way?

The ground rose sharply ahead of him. Kheda scrambled to his feet. Uphill was a start. They had come over the rise of the headland so the *Amigal* must lie somewhere beyond the top of the hill. He struggled up the slope as fast as he could, using hands and feet like a loal. Discovering he'd lost his heavy blade somehow, he skirted around berry thickets, shying away from the thorny tangles of striol.

Which at least means you're leaving no trail and moving more quietly.

Taken unawares by the crest of the rise, he slipped and fell down the far side, a tandra sapling breaking his fall and stabbing him painfully with snapped-off twigs. Panting, Kheda waited. The hue and cry that the savages were raising on the other side of the headland rose into the evening sky. Kheda's breath slowed and the hammering blood in his throat abated a little. The sound of pursuit was scattering, heading away from him, disintegrating into confusion. Kheda took a deep breath and the stench of death that coated him made him retch uncontrollably.

When he was finally done vomiting, he hauled himself upright on a handy lilla tree. Down below, he could see the untroubled sea fading imperceptibly into the distant blue dusk of the evening sky. Over to the west, the afterglow was fading on the horizon. He couldn't see the *Amigal* but now cold calculation replaced the trepidation of his flight. Calmly, he traced the lie of the land and worked out which clump of trees must be hiding the ship from view. Slowly, picking his path with care, he went down the slope towards it.

'Kheda!' Risala was on deck, jungle blade in her hands, ready to hack the hands off anyone trying to come aboard.

Unable to think what to say, Kheda dived into the water, ducking his head under the cool sea, rubbing his fouled hands over and around each other, scrubbing at his head and body. Rolling and twisting, he struggled out of his tunic, letting it float away, his trousers too. Broaching the surface with a gasp when he could stay submerged no longer, he found the salt freshness had driven away the stink hanging around him.

'Dev's here!' Risala hung over the *Amigal*'s rail.

Kheda wiped water out of his eyes, seeing Risala as no more than an outline against the first shimmer of the rising moon.

The Lesser Moon, just at half, distant and aloof, on the cusp of decline, so soon to be lost in the return of the greater jewel, but biding its time, knowing the next cycle of the heavens will see its full riding unchallenged in an empty sky.

Kheda swam for the rope Risala had thrown down for him. 'Where is he?'

'I can't get any sense out of him.' Risala was bloodied with scratches, dishevelled and exhausted, but there was a light of terrified triumph in her eyes. 'What's happened to him?'

Dev was huddled at the base of the *Amigal*'s mast. Kheda knelt and pushed him upright against the wood. The wizard's head lolled as he grinned crazily at Kheda, dark eyes rolling. The fine silk of his tunic was stained and scorched, his gaudy jewellery clotted with dried blood, the very metal broken and twisted. His arms were scored with deep scratches still oozing sluggishly. Even in the failing light, Kheda could see appalling bruises through the tears in Dev's trousers, one foot darkening and swelling with the hint of broken bones within.

'Didn't realise, did he? What was he was doing, drawing more and more elements into himself? I could do it, though, matching him turning himself wrongways out and upside down.' Dev waved a feeble, broken-fingered hand and Kheda saw all the nails were torn, thumbnail wholly missing. 'He didn't know what I could do. It's all very well, calling that kind of magic, as long as you've got somewhere to send it.' Dev licked ineffectively at the spittle coating his chin. His lip was split, there were bite marks on his chin and his bald head was scraped raw in places. 'You're as screwed as a tuppenny whore on market day if you've nowhere to go with such power. I slammed the door on him good and proper, didn't I? Bet Kalion couldn't have done it, nor yet Planir, not hardly, not likely. What say I challenge one of them to try it? That's how the savages do it, prove who's best. Who's still standing at the end, that's your man, not whoever can make the most friends in the halls and copyhouses.'

Kheda silenced the wizard's ramblings with a slap to the face that echoed across the deck. Dev looked at him, mouth open, shocked. Kheda could feel Risala's astonished eyes boring into his back but there was no time to explain.

'Get some of that brandy of his, quick!' He seized Dev by the shoulders and shook him. 'The moon, Dev, look at the moon. Remember, we have to send the sign, to bring the other ships down here. There are still hundreds of those savages. They're everywhere. They'll kill us if they find us. We need Daish men and Chazen to come and reclaim the domain. The moon, Dev, you have to raise a cloud to colour the moon!'

Loose and boneless in his grasp, the wizard blinked, bleary-eyed, trying to focus on the distant half circle of light in the darkening sky. 'The moon?'

Risala appeared at Kheda's shoulder. Kheda propped Dev up with one hand to his chest and took the stubby black bottle, pulling the stopper free with his teeth. He spat the cork aside, coughing as the reek of spirits bit at his throat. 'You said you could do it, remember? You said you could lift sand high enough into the air to colour the moon for anyone looking from Daish lands? You promised me you could do it!' He forced the neck of the bottle between Dev's flaccid lips and tipped white brandy into the wizard's mouth.

Dev choked and coughed on frenzied giggles. 'A cloud to colour the moon? I said I could do that?' He reached for the bottle with clumsy hands.

'You did. You swore it.' Kheda wrapped the wizard's fingers around the brandy. 'Don't tell me you can't, not after everything you've done today!'

Hands trembling, Dev took a long swallow of liquor, his body shaking like a man in the grip of fever. 'You saw it,' he said, husky with emotion. 'You saw it all. I did it, matched that Dragonhide and more. Didn't know if I could. Didn't tell you that.' His laugh was little more than a hysterical gasp.

'Can you colour the moon?' Kheda thrust his face close, forcing the wizard to meet his gaze. 'You told me you could do that! Was that the truth?'

Dev sat up a little straighter, grip on the bottle firmer, face turning ugly. 'No man calls me a liar,' he snarled breathlessly.

'I'm not calling you a liar.' Kheda sat back on his heels. 'I'm asking you to prove yourself.'

'That wasn't proof enough?' Dev gestured in the vague direction of the carnage beyond the headland.

White brandy sloshed from the bottle to land cold on Kheda's bare arm and sting his scratches viciously. He tasted it on the air, sharp and spicy. 'Can you do it or not?'

Furious, Dev hurled the bottle down the deck. The throw too feeble to break it, it rolled away leaving a glistening trail of brandy on the planks. 'Watch this, you ignorant pig of an Archipelagan!'

With a sweeping motion of one hand, Dev cast a swathe of faint red out towards the island. The magelight spread and faded and Kheda's heart sank as the last vestiges melted away into the ground. He turned away, sick at heart.

It's not going to be over then. There'll be no rest for you, no return home in triumph, not with these wild men still plaguing the Daish domain. How can we gather a force to fight them, before they summon some more of their iniquitous wizards?

'Look at that,' whispered Risala, awestruck.

Kheda opened his eyes to see red magelight rising from the shore; thicker now but dimmed, spreading like a mist but heavy with dust and debris from the ground. Dev thrust his other hand upwards and a shaft of searing blue light soared up to challenge the cold light of the first stars. It drew the haze of powdered earth inexorably upward, higher and higher, finally breaking like a fountain to be lost in the vastness of the sky. The dust kept on rising from the island, the magic darkening and deepening. The blue light carried it up, threads and flurries twisting and knotting.

Kheda waited, heart pounding in his chest. Slowly a shadow edged across the half circle of the distant moon, barely more than imagination at first but little by little thickening to a veil of red.

'That's your sign?' asked Risala.

Kheda nodded. 'It's a portent that everyone should be able to read. If Janne's done her work, it'll bring all the ships south. That should be swords and arrows enough to kill every last one of these accursed savages.' Hope twisted in his chest like the piercing blade of a dagger.

The magical radiance vanished like a snuffed candle. Dev fell to the deck with a heavy thud and Kheda and Risala dropped to their knees either side of him.

'He's barely breathing,' said Risala with consternation. 'What do we do?'

What does one do with a wizard? You were always taught magic was dangerous, destructive, corrupting. You've seen it for yourself and the slaughter that even a few mages can encompass. What does one do with a wizard? One kills it as one would a venomous snake.

He's helpless, unconscious. He's a mage who can scatter a beach full of armed men by turning their very weapons against them. He's a man who can burn men to char and ashes without so much as laying a finger on them. You've a dagger to hand, a Daish dagger no less. Cut his throat and who would ever blame you? Cut his throat and there's no one to tell Chazen Saril, Ritsem Caid or anyone else that you suborned sorcery as the only way of driving out these savages.

You don't think this barbarian, this traitor and vice peddler, you don't think he'll bleed you of every advantage he can, in return for his silence? Kill him now and there's no one to bear witness to you using his power to pervert the very skies in raising an omen that is pure falsehood. Kill him now and his blood might even cleanse you of the taint of magic that must surely stain you to the bone. You're no innocent victim, not any more; you've mired yourself neck deep in sorcery.

But there would be a witness. There'd be Risala. Are you going to kill her as well? She would truly be an innocent victim. Are you going to forswear yourself to Shek Kul, when he asks her fate? Don't you owe him better than that, for the secret of the powder and sending Risala to you? You'd never have found another way to drive out these invaders.

Don't you owe even Dev his life, vile though he may be, in return for doing what you could not, killing the mages who have given these invaders their overwhelming supremacy? Besides, there are hundreds of these savages still plaguing these islands, hundreds of islands to clear and reclaim. What if Dev hasn't seen all the mages? What if there are still some more to be found? Sharkteeth very nearly got away. What if more come from overseas, to find out what has happened to their fellows? It might happen, this season or next, there's no telling, not without Dev and his mirrors of water and sorcery. What will you do then, if you've no wizard to call on? Shek Kul's powder won't last for ever and there's no telling if you'll ever find out just what it is made of.

Kheda straightened Dev's contorted limbs. Cold sweat covered the mage, making the dried blood coating him shine like fresh wounds. 'We get him into his hammock. I don't know what ails him; I imagine it's something to do with the magecraft. He said it could exhaust him. All we can do is let him sleep and see if he wakes.'

If he doesn't, then I'll think through the significance of that omen when I've had some sleep myself.

Kheda looked across the prostrate wizard to Risala. 'I know it's nightfall but we should sail to a safer anchorage. Then we'll head for the thousand-oyster isle. I said I'd meet Janne there. She'll know what's going on across the domain. We can work out what to do next together.'

CHAPTER TWENTY ONE

'Have you seen any Chazen boats?' Kheda stood over Dev as the wizard peered into his scrying bowl held between his bandaged legs. The inky water tilted as the *Amigal* rode the broad swell of the open waters.

'No,' said Dev shortly. 'Pass me the chewing leaf.'

Kheda bent to pick the wash-leather bag from the deck where the roll of the ship had carried it. 'Look to the east. See if you can see any more triremes.'

'Give me that.' Dev looked up, cuts and grazes on his face liberally coated with salve. He held out his hand, the bruises on his arm now a myriad colours, mocking the magic that had armoured him in battle. 'Chewing leaf won't blunt my scrying abilities but the pain in my foot might. Or the spell could go awry. Do you want your friends seeing that?' He nodded towards the tall tower on the thousand-oyster isle now in plain sight.

Kheda hesitated then handed him the little leather pouch. Dev tugged out a dark, wrinkled leaf, wadding it up and shoving it in his mouth. Kheda did his best to contain his impatience as the mage's jaw worked and the lines of strain on his face lessened a little.

'So, Chazen ships over to the east. Let's see if we can find any there.' He bent over his bowl and little shapes danced in the light flickering over the surface.

Kheda turned away.

He'd be scrying whether I wanted it or not. He's no more wish to be sunk and killed by some hysterical Redigal trireme than me or Risala. He may as well tell me what I need to know while he's at it. But I need not look myself, not if I'm to leave all this magic behind me. Not now I'm finally to go home again.

'Kheda.' Risala's call from the tiller carried a warning note.

He looked at the rapidly approaching islet to see a faint thread of smoke rising into the clear sky. 'Can you see a boat?'

'It's way over there.' Kheda looked to see Dev gesturing towards the distant island at the head of the chain leading back into the Daish domain. 'It's a fast trireme, swordsmen all along both decks.'

'It must be Janne,' Kheda said slowly. 'She's here ahead of time.' He smoothed down his tunic, not a good fit since it had been cut for Dev but decent silk and better than anything else he might wear. At least the sleeves were long enough to cover the worst of the scratches scabbing his arms. The ivory twist of the dragon's tail made a fine enough ornament, if an unusual one, and he had Shek Kul's silver and emerald cipher ring to prove he had some claim to respect. 'Dev, I asked you to look for Chazen ships to the east.'

'I have and there aren't any to be found, not north, south or anywhere else,' replied the wizard with a robustness giving the lie to his manifold injuries. 'They haven't shifted from the Serpents' Teeth.'

There were no words to express Kheda's exasperation. He ran a hand over his neatly combed beard. The breeze was cool on the back of his neck, exposed where Risala had deftly trimmed his hair.

'Where do you want me to anchor?' Risala was scanning the shoreline.

'On the beach, in front of the tower.' Kheda made an abrupt decision. 'I've done with skulking and hiding.'

'Only once you've set Janne Daish spreading the word that we're not to be touched,' Dev said firmly. 'With a full description of the ship as well as me and the girl.'

Kheda nodded curtly. 'You'll be free to head north, as soon as you wish.'

'Don't want us spreading inconvenient stories?' There was a taunting glint in Dev's one eye that wasn't still swollen. 'Embarrassing you in front of your lady wife.'

'It would be the last thing you did and you know it,' Kheda retorted, unsmiling.

No one spoke as Risala guided the *Amigal* into the shore. Kheda slid over the rail into the tethered skiff, splashing as he rowed through the shallow water to the beach.

Janne was sitting alone on the sand, tending a small fire of driftwood and dried dune grass.

She looked up with a faint smile as he hauled the skiff beyond the waves. 'Kheda.' Janne was wearing a pale yellow tunic of modest cut and trousers of finely woven cotton gathered at the ankle with golden chains. Her hair was an unadorned braid hanging down her back, her single necklace a plaited rope of tiny pearls, while her rings and bracelets were plain gold bands.

'Janne.' Kheda found he wasn't at all sure what to do. All his much-rehearsed words of explanation seemed out of place now he found himself greeting his wife in modest dress and unassuming surroundings rather than justifying himself to the first wife of the Daish domain arrayed in all her splendour before the ominous height of a tower of silence.

Longing for the warmth of her arms around him, her perfumed softness within his embrace overwhelmed him but taking her in his arms wasn't really an option with her concentrating on poking her fire. He saw she had raked ashes and embers over serried rows of pale shells planted in the sand. 'White mussels?'

She nodded briefly. 'I thought we should eat together again.'

'How was your voyage here?' Kheda sat down beside her.

'Quite appalling.' Janne prodded the sand with the charred end of the stick in her hand. 'Have you seen what these savages did to the people they captured?'

'Something of it,' Kheda said cautiously.

Janne looked at him, eyes shining with unshed tears. 'Men and women dead of thirst when the rains have brought us rain to last all year. Children locked in pens like brute beasts and left to starve. Sirket sends me word of some new atrocity from every island that Daish forces reclaim. Even if they're alive when we find them, half are dead inside a day or so. We're burying them in pits, stacked like firewood, thin as sticks. What were they doing, Kheda, these savages? What were they doing all this for?'

'I don't know,' Kheda said helplessly. 'All I can tell you is they are dead, the men who planned this, who led these invaders.'

'The wizards?' Janne looked sharply at him.

Kheda nodded firmly. 'All dead.'

I certainly wasn't going to object to Dev making sure of that with his scrying.

Janne said nothing, concentrating on her cooking shell-fish.

Feeling increasingly unsure of himself, Kheda looked around the empty shore. 'How goes the campaign to retake the Chazen domain?'

'Well enough.' Janne set down her stick and shifted her position slightly. 'The hardest task is making sure every island is truly clear of these savages. Bands here and there still make night raids on villages that we had thought safe, though without their magic to back them, our swordsmen kill them quickly enough.'

'Our losses?' Kheda swallowed painful apprehension. 'And of our allies of Redigal and Ritsem?'

'Not insupportable,' Janne answered distantly.

'What of Chazen Saril?' Kheda tried to moderate his anger but his words rang harsh along the shore.

Janne rose to her feet and dusted sand from her rump. 'Ask him yourself.'

'What?' Kheda was entirely confused.

'Chazen Saril,' Janne called out commandingly. 'Come here.'

'Daish Kheda.' Chazen Saril sidled around the tower of silence with a nervous smile. 'I never thought I'd see you again.'

'I thought I'd see you and your ships in the vanguard of any assault to reclaim your domain.' Kheda saw no reason for restraint. 'Why are your ships still huddled around the Serpents' Teeth while others sail to shed their blood for your benefit? What are you thinking of?'

'My children, my Sekni, my Olkai.' Chazen Saril had lost considerable weight and his skin hung in loose jowls. Apprehensive, his eyes were dark in bruised hollows. 'That's who I think of. That's who I see when the dawn mocks my restlessness or when dreams tear apart whatever sleep exhaustion forces on me. I see them dying. I see the fire and lightning defiling them. I see savage wizards laughing over their dead bodies and planning the enslavement of my people. That's all I think of, Kheda.'

'You have much to grieve over, truly.' Kheda hardened his heart against the desperate appeal in the man's words. 'But you have to set that aside and look to your duty to your people!'

'How?' Saril asked in genuine bemusement. 'How can I look them in the eye and claim their fealty, when they've suffered so much, when I could do nothing to save them? I cannot face them—'

'Who will lead them if you don't?' Kheda interrupted, enraged.

'Ritsem ships are bringing their swords to clear out the savages, Redigal too, and Daish. All of you have more claim than me on these people's gratitude now.' Tears spilled helplessly from Chazen Saril's eyes. 'I've no way to repay any of you for coming to our aid. You may as well hold whatever you can salvage from the ruin of my islands.'

Kheda gaped at him. 'That's it? You're throwing up your hands and abandoning your people? Where do you intend to go?'

'We can stay in the islands around the Serpents' Teeth, can't we?' Saril took a pace forward, outstretched hands beseeching. 'We'd be no threat, not to you, not to anyone. We can be useful to you, join with your domain, share our skills with yours.'

'Share your skills? I see you're sharing our silks.' Kheda mocked Saril's embroidered blue tunic and trousers with a furious hand. 'Your grief isn't so crippling that you can't come here all dressed up with your beard neatly oiled and plaited, while your people die naked and alone. Get yourself some plain cottons, get your hands dirty with the earth of your domain. Lead your people in planting their crops, rebuilding their houses.'

'So the savages have something new to burn and despoil, when they come again?' Saril began shaking. 'I can't do it, Kheda, I can't. I can't go back to spend my life watching the southern seas for the first sign of magic coming to tear my life apart again.' He was sobbing now, nose running, cringing where he stood. 'I cannot face the skies, for fear of the judgement I might read there. I cannot look to the least omen or portent for fear of seeing some new disaster threatening us all. How am I to lead my people again?'

This is the man I feared was plotting to take over my domain.

Kheda stared at him helplessly.

'Chazen Saril, I need more dune grass.' Janne had been plaiting little mats from the coarse yellowy stems.

The two men looked wide-eyed at her for a moment, then Saril scrubbed at his face with a sleeve. 'Of course, my lady.' Stumbling, he hurried away towards the ridge behind the tower.

Kheda watched him go, incredulity warring with fury. 'What does he think his people will do, without him to guide them? What does he think the other domains will do if they see Chazen islands left for anyone to claim them? Fear of magic might have Saril pissing himself but Redigal and Ritsem will be thinking of the turtle shell and the pearls, now they've seen the wizards are gone. I don't imagine Ulla Safar will want to be left out and won't Aedis and Sarem have a claim on reparations for whatever ships and men they've sent against the savages? They have sent help, haven't they?'

As Kheda turned to demand Janne's confirmation, he saw Chazen Saril had returned clutching a handful of grass, shrunken and fearful, tears still rolling slowly down his face to lose themselves in his beard.

'We can at least eat together.' Janne deftly raked aside the embers from the white mussels and scooped up a couple on to a mat of grass. 'Careful, they'll be hot.' She handed the mat to Kheda. He took it and sat down, glowering at the wretched Chazen lord.

Janne handed Saril some of the shellfish. 'Let's see what counsel a full stomach can bring us.'

'Do you have some water?' asked Kheda curtly.

Janne handed him a finely wrought brass bottle. He drank and they ate in heavy, uncomfortable silence.

Saril was the first to speak. 'Janne Daish,' he began. He stopped and looked unsure.

'What?' Kheda demanded.

Saril grimaced, puzzled. He got awkwardly to his feet, one hand pressed to his belly. 'Forgive me,' he gasped, staggering away to vomit copiously.

Nauseated, Kheda threw away his remaining mussels. 'What—'

'Leave him,' Janne commanded instantly.

'What?' Kheda gaped at her before looking at Saril, who had fallen to his knees, racked with uncontrollable spasms.

'I said, leave him,' Janne repeated icily. She prised apart the last of her own mussels and ate the yellowy flesh within.

'He's ill,' retorted Kheda. 'Have you—'

'He's useless,' snapped Janne with startling viciousness. 'His cowardice forfeits his every claim on the Chazen people's loyalty and the domain's wealth. He's shirked every responsibility and proved himself entirely unfit to rule. There isn't a warlord in the southern reaches who would deny it.'

'He's choking!' Kheda got to his feet.

'Sit down!' Janne stood and barred his way, face implacable. 'His death will only be an omen to confirm what everyone has been thinking; that his blood is of no more use to the domain.'

'And what happens then?' Kheda gaped at her. 'We stand by while Redigal, Ulla and Ritsem start a war for the Chazen islands, along with whoever else feels inclined to join in? Or are you thinking we claim them for Daish and beggar ourselves rebuilding what the invaders destroyed? Janne, he can't breathe!'

'Daish will not take on so much as a finger length of Chazen territory.' Janne ignored Chazen Saril's weakening struggles behind her. 'The whole domain has been tainted with magic. We're not going to tolerate Chazen people in our islands and whatever corruption clings to them for a day longer than we have to either. They go home, rebuild or die, that's up to them.'

'We still don't want a war on our southern border.' Kheda raised a hand to push Janne aside, anger rising inside him. 'He may be a useless lord but he's the only one Chazen has got!'

'You must do it, rule Chazen, I mean.' Janne seized Kheda's arms, holding him back, digging her nails into him as he attempted to free himself.

'What?' He stared at her, disbelieving.

'You must rule Chazen.' She dragged him round, turning his back on Saril's desperate writhing.

'I am Daish Kheda,' he spat.

'Not any more,' Janne said with icy precision. 'Daish Sirket leads the domain and is doing so very effectively. He gathered the forces and allies to drive out the invaders and won the respect of all our neighbours in doing so.'

'Because I found the means to kill the wizards who brought these invaders on us.' Kheda couldn't decide if he was more astounded or angry. 'Is this my reward, to be dispossessed by my own son?'

'You stepped aside in his favour,' countered Janne dispassionately. 'He took nothing but the uncertainties and perils you left him.'

'You make it sound as if I abandoned him,' Kheda objected furiously. 'I went in search of the means to combat the invaders' magic, at risk of my own life, I may tell you, more than once. I brought it back and risked dangers you cannot imagine to rid the domain of those sorcerers. This is how you repay me?'

'The Chazen domain is modest but it has its wealth, its turtle shells and pearls. Those are untouched by the invaders' foul hands, from what I hear. You will have people to help you rebuild, on untouched land,' said Janne tightly. 'Children born to the domain will certainly be untainted and you may find some means of purification for the rest.'

Kheda shook his head, uncomprehending. 'You were the first woman I took to my bed, the woman I've shared myself, my life with for seventeen years. You're the mother of my children, my son and heir and the daughters that have blessed my days.'

'This must be so, for the sake of the children.' The first hint of emotion cracked Janne's voice. 'For all their sakes. Rekha and I are agreed on this, Sain too. I've told them what you've done – some of what you've done. We cannot have you back, not when the magic that stains you may bring disaster in its wake, to devastate us all.'

Kheda threw off her hands and then seized her forearms. 'What do you mean, some of what I have done?'

Now fear was plain in Janne's eyes. 'Not all the Chazen islanders died, the ones the savages took prisoner. They told us of the evil these wizards wrought, of the unknown wizard who defeated them with even more unspeakable sorceries. You told me you were allying yourself with this northern wizard, even if only to turn magic against these invaders. My mother told me how the seas in the central domains ran red with slaughter when she was a girl, for mere suspicion of a warlord contemplating such an alliance. That's what I told Rekha and Sain you've done. I haven't told them what else I believe, nor yet what I find myself suspecting now. You ask me about the campaign against the savages yet you seem to know more about it than I do. How do you know the Chazen ships haven't sailed south? You're dead. You've no couriers to bring you word, no messenger birds to carry reports. How do you know if you're not using these magics that let northern barbarians spy on us?'

'That has nothing—' Kheda began, all the more irate as his own guilt pricked him.

'What happened to the moon, Kheda?' Janne faced him, stiff yet trembling. 'How did the moon turn red?'

'It happens.' He hesitated, fatally. 'It's a portent recorded from time to time.'

'Recorded, yes,' hissed Janne. 'Foretold, no. I talked to Sirket about it, had him check and double-check the records, the observations back to the volumes from the earliest days. It's not an eclipse, to be predicted and precautions taken against its effects. No one knows when a red moon will be seen, not like that. Sirket says it only ever arises in a dry season too, when the hot winds come up from the south. Of course, that made it all the more potent as an omen, especially when I had told everyone to watch for a sign that the time had come to spill the wild men's blood.

'What did you do, Kheda, what deceit have you dragged me into? How could you know that a red moon would rise unless you had some hand in it? How could you do that without using this barbarian's magic? That's not keeping yourself at a remove from the taint of magic. That's using it yourself to distort the natural order, sinking yourself freely into depravity. Don't lie to me, Daish Kheda, I know you too well. I can see what you've done written in your eyes.

'Don't tell me what else you've done either. Don't tell me how you've forsworn yourself and everything we trust in. I don't want to know. All I know is the children must come first for me and Rekha and Sain. They are flesh of our flesh, borne in our bodies, nurtured at our breasts. Nothing can change that. The bond between us—' She snatched back her hands. 'We were only ever one flesh for fleeting moments. The bond between us is broken past mending.'

'You expect me to accept this?' Searing anguish twisted in Kheda's chest, worse than any pain since the death of his father. 'You expect the Daish people to accept this?'

'You would fight Sirket for the domain?' Janne challenged. 'You want to throw your children into the confusion of learning you are alive, when they have barely come to terms with your death? You want to bring them that poisoned joy and then have them see you try to kill their brother, your own son? You'd bring that disaster on the Daish domain, an internal war, when the people are still trying to recover from the depredations of those fled from Chazen? Barely half the crops that should have been planted by now are in the ground. It'll be a hungry end to the dry season, even if no other travails come upon us. You think any Daish people would rally to your side, after they learned you had abandoned them, when they heard you had been in the south, fighting magic with magic, no matter how noble your intentions?'

'There's a powder, it's not magic—' Kheda fell silent and looked at Janne for a long moment, the only sound the surf breaking on the reefs around the island and the mournful cries of some unseen seabird.

'It wouldn't matter what I said, would it? Any explanations I could offer, what justification, it wouldn't make any difference. You and Rekha, you'll make sure everyone sees it your way and I am condemned. What are you planning, if I refuse to cooperate? You won't poison me, not like poor Saril, that much I can promise you.' Seizing Janne by a shoulder, he forced her round to look at the twisted, soiled corpse.

'I didn't poison him.' Janne took a step forward as if to assure herself that Saril was indeed dead. 'We all ate from the same shellfish.'

'From your hands,' scoffed Kheda, incensed. 'Didn't you gather them? Didn't you know they were somehow spoiled?'

'A red tide had come and gone when I gathered them, that's true.' Janne folded her arms stubbornly. 'They could have killed us all or left us all untouched. His death is an omen that confirms me in my intentions. It tells me your destiny lies in the Chazen domain, not his. If I was in error, I would have been the one to die.'

'It's not your place to test the future with such follies,' Kheda snarled. 'Nor yet to read such omens.'

'No, it is Sirket's,' Janne said forcefully. 'He has studied the skies every night since he got word of your death and shared all he sees with me and Rekha. The Vizail Blossom, token for all wives and mothers, has left the realm of marriage and has ridden the arc of death. Now the Diamond joins it, stone for rulers, and the Opal for fidelity and harmony. There is an ending plainly told for us all. The Pearl rides with the Amethyst, jewel for new beginnings and inspirations, and both are in the arc of foes and fears where the Winged Snake twines around all people, promising new conjunctions to reward the brave. The Ruby floats in the arc for siblings and those as close as kin, offering protection against fire for the daring. The Sailfish carries it, promising good fortune and fertility. All the stars tell us the domain will prosper if Rekha and I can only bring ourselves to do this.'

'Sirket knows what you've been planning?' Kheda struggled with the notion. 'He approves?'

'No.' Janne shook her head vehemently. 'He knows nothing. He doesn't even know that you are still alive. He only told me what he read in the skies. Rekha and I saw how it bore on our situation.'

'What are you going to tell Sirket?' Now it was Kheda's turn to be cold as tears threatened Janne's composure.

'I will tell him that you have returned, that you did something, I don't know what, to defeat the sorcery that gave the invaders their strength.' She paused to swallow a sob. 'I'll tell him you see the impossibility of ever returning to rule the Daish domain, touched as you have been by magic. I'll tell him you're turning all your talent to rebuilding the Chazen domain, so that it might be a bulwark to defend Daish against any return of these savages. Are you going to make a liar out of me to our son?'

Her plea tore at his heart. Kheda rubbed a hand over his beard. 'I thought I knew you. I thought that sharing my bed and my heart and my fears and joys with you meant I knew you. I never did, did I? You kept yourself so very well hidden. All right, Janne, I won't bring all the grief you promise down on our children, or on my domain, my former domain,' he corrected himself sarcastically. Heart too full to say anything else, he threw up his hands and turned on his heel.

'Where are you going?' called Janne in consternation.

'What do you care?' Kheda threw back over his shoulder.

'Where do I send Itrac?'

Janne's unexpected query stopped Kheda in his tracks. He turned to look at her. 'What?'

'She's your responsibility now, Chazen Kheda,' Janne told him defiantly. 'The domain she was born to won't have her back, not with the taint of magic on her. I've pleaded her case but they won't yield. You can't let her loose, not till you're sure she doesn't carry Saril that was Chazen's child. If she bore such a babe, someone like Ulla Safar could marry her and try forcing a claim on the domain.'

'What will you do if I don't take her?' Kheda spat. 'Feed her some shellfish?'

Janne flinched as if he had struck her but she didn't relent. 'Where do I send her?'

Kheda gave up. 'The Chazen dry-season residence. Tell her I'll find her there.'

Who knows, by then, I might even have worked out what to tell her, how to explain what I have done and how it landed me in this mess. If it wasn't for the sand beneath my feet, the breeze in my face, I could almost imagine this was some horrible dream. But no, no dream. I couldn't dream such agony and not wake from it.

Kheda stormed down the beach to row back to the *Amigal*. As he swung himself up on deck, Dev and Risala were standing there, faces avid with curiosity. Kheda glared at them with challenge in every line of his body and both hastily adopted studiedly neutral expressions.

'Can't say that looked to be going well from here,' said Dev cautiously. 'Not that we could hear much, but isn't that Chazen Saril who's just died such a remarkably painful death?'

Finally, something to shake that bastard's composure. That might almost make this all worth it.

'He ate some bad shellfish,' said Kheda in as dispassionate a tone as he could manage. 'Which leaves the Chazen domain without a ruler. Janne Daish believes this is my destiny rather than returning to depose my own son. I am forced to agree with her.'

'Oh,' said Risala blankly.

'Forced?' Dev looked slyly at Kheda. 'There's a handful of ways that trireme could come to grief, before it ever comes to port.'

'I would hate to think of that happening,' Kheda said with cold threat.

'So where do we go now?' Risala tried to see past Kheda to the shore.

He didn't look back. 'I need to get to the dry-season 'dence of the Chazen warlords. I don't know what 'l be left of it but it's somewhere to start.' He glanced down at the little skiff bobbing at the *Amigal*'s side. 'Can I have this? You can take me as far as the main sea lane before you turn north, can't you?'

Dev's response surprised him. 'I'll take you all the way you want to go, never mind that.'

Kheda hesitated. 'You should go north, both of you. There'll be all manner of suspicions floating on the breezes round here.'

'Suspicions maybe, but none so many witnesses,' grinned Dev. 'No one understands that savage gabble.'

'Janne says there are Chazen islanders telling of the final battle between the invaders and some unknown mage,' Kheda said with difficulty.

'Crazed with fear and thirst and hunger, who can be sure what they saw?' Dismissing them with an airy wave, Dev limped painfully down the deck towards Kheda. 'You don't get rid of me that easily. You owe me and plenty, don't forget that. It's a good thing those savage mages weren't interested in turtle shell and pearls, otherwise you'd be hard pressed to pay me this side of the next new year stars.' He passed Kheda and went to sit by the tiller. 'You and the girl better raise the sail if we're to make Chazen waters by nightfall.'

Kheda looked at Risala. 'We can find you a ship going north, I'm sure of it.'

'Shek Kul will want a full report, not half a one,' she said, attempting to equal Dev's offhand manner. 'He'll want to know that you've got a firm grip on the Chazen domain.'

'Let's hope you can take that news north sooner rather than later.' Kheda looked down at the cipher ring pensively.

'The sooner we start, the sooner it'll be done,' Risala encouraged him.

Not trusting himself to reply, Kheda turned to use the

heavy sweeps to turn the little ship while Risala busied herself with the sails. Dev tended the tiller in unconcerned silence. Once they had the *Amigal* on her way across the open waters, Kheda went to stand in the prow, alone with his thoughts.

How can she be so cold-hearted, so ruthless? Her iron will's not so admirable now, is it, when it's turned on you instead of against the domain's foes? Rekha, of course she'd go along with Janne. I've always known there'd be no question for her if it came to a choice between me and her children. Sain, well, I've barely had time to lay claim to her loyalty.

How can I claim any loyalty from any of them, when in truth, I've done all that Janne accused me of? Did I misread the omens and the stars that led me to this? I don't believe so. But is it so unexpected that there be a price to pay for dealing with wizards, even if my intent has been pure? Have I brought this upon myself? If my intent had not been pure, perhaps I would be dead now, killed by the poison in the shellfish.

Could Sirket possibly have the right of it? He's not mired in magic the way I have undeniably been. There's certainly too much truth in what Janne had to say to ignore it. If no one claims the Chazen domain, we won't need invaders to bring disaster on the southern reaches; we'll bring it on ourselves.

What now? Do I dare take the omens from the stars tonight? Should I be studying the skies and all the signs of nature around me? How will I read them if I do, when I have absolutely no feeling for this Chazen domain, no claim upon its people and not the first notion what's going to happen now?